REN

&

DELLA

the Ribbon duet

NEW YORK TIMES BESTSELLING AUTHOR

PEPPER
WINTERS

Ren & Della

The Ribbon Duet

by

Pepper Winters

Published: Pepper Winters 2018: **pepperwinters@gmail.com**
Cover Design: Ari @ Cover it! Designs
Editing by: Editing 4 Indies (Jenny Sims)
Proofreading by: Landers Editorial Services (Tiffany Landers)

www.pepperwinters.com

OTHER BOOKS AVAILABLE FROM PEPPER WINTERS

Dollar Series
Pennies
Dollars
Hundreds
Thousands
Millions

Truth & Lies Duet
Crown of Lies
Throne of Truth

Pure Corruption Duet
Ruin & Rule
Sin & Suffer

Indebted Series
Debt Inheritance
First Debt
Second Debt
Third Debt
Fourth Debt
Final Debt
Indebted Epilogue

Monsters in the Dark Trilogy
Tears of Tess
Quintessentially Q
Twisted Together
Je Suis a Toi

Standalones
Destroyed
Unseen Messages
Can't Touch This

Book One

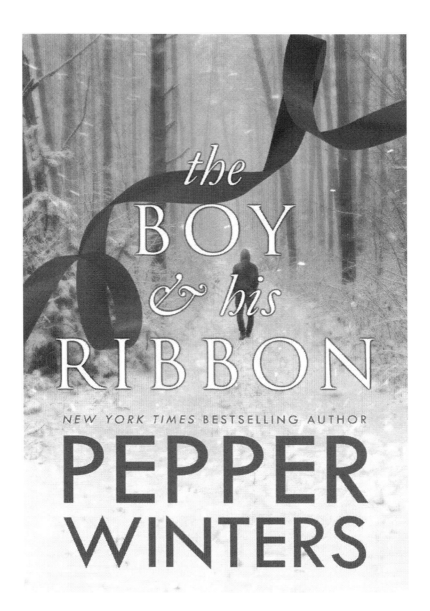

the
BOY
& his
RIBBON

NEW YORK TIMES BESTSELLING AUTHOR

PEPPER WINTERS

the
BOY
& his
RIBBON

NEW YORK TIMES BESTSELLING AUTHOR
PEPPER
WINTERS

Chapter One

REN

2000

"STOP! WILLEM, SHOOT him. Don't let him get away!"

Bolting from the farmhouse with its broken paint-chipped shutters and rotten veranda, I swung the large backpack straps higher on my shoulders and leapt the small distance from hell to earth.

The weight on my back wasn't balanced, sending me tripping forward.

I stumbled; my ankle threatened to roll. My useless ten-year-old legs already screamed it wasn't possible to outrun a bullet from the wife of a killer and slaver, especially with such a cumbersome burden.

Even if it wasn't possible, I had to try.

"Come back here, boy, and I won't cut off another finger!" Mr. Mclary's boom cut through the humidity of the night, chasing me with snapping teeth as I darted into the thicket of leaves and stalks, weaving like a worm around maize twice as tall as me.

My tiny fists clenched at the thought of living through that pain again.

His threat only gave me more incentive to escape—regardless if a bullet lodged in my spine and I died in the middle of their cornfield. At least this excruciating nightmare would be over.

"Kill him, Willem!" Mrs Mclary's voice screeched like the crows she liked to shoot with her dirty rifle from the kitchen window. "Who knows what he's got pilfered in that bag of his!"

A noise sounded behind me; a sudden cry jerked into silence.

An animal perhaps?

A cat?

I didn't care.

I ran faster, putting my head down and using every remaining drop of energy, pain, and hope in my wasted, skinny body. The bulky backpack dragged me down. The weight far heavier than I remembered when I'd slung it over my shoulders during a test attempt two nights ago.

I'd planned this for weeks. I'd scratched my escape route into the dusty floorboards beneath my cot and memorised the location of canned beans and farmhouse churned cheese so I could grab it in the dark.

I'd been so careful. I'd believed I could vanish from this rank place I'd been sold to.

But I wasn't careful enough, and I hadn't vanished.

Bang.

Corn stalks shivered in front of me, cracking in place where a bullet wedged at head height. The cry came again, short and sharp and close.

Gulping air, I leaned into the soupy skies and kicked my burning legs into a sprint. The backpack bounced and dug into my shoulders, whispering that I should just drop my supplies and *run*.

But unless I didn't want to survive past a day or two of freedom, I needed it.

I had nowhere to go. No one to help me. No money. No direction. I needed the food and scant water I'd stolen so I didn't perish a few measly miles away from the very farmhouse I'd flown from.

Bang.

An ear of corn exploded in front of my face. Mr. Mclary's voice warbled words with out-of-breath growls, giving chase in his precious field. My ears rang, blocking out another cry, amplifying my rapid heartbeat.

Just a little farther and I'd pop out on the road.

I'd find quicker escape on the sealed surface and hopefully flag down aid from some oblivious passer-by.

Perhaps one of the same people who drove past daily and smiled at the quaint rustic farmhouse and cooed at the diligent hardworking children would finally open their eyes to the rotten slave trade occurring in their very midst.

Bang!

I ducked and fell to my knees.

The backpack crushed me to the earth with sharp edges and sloshing belongings, yet another noise chasing me. I was strong for my age, so why did I find such a thing exhausting to carry?

Shoving away such delays, I sprang up again, wheezing as my stupid little lungs failed to grant enough oxygen. My limbs burned and seized. My hope quickly dwindled. But I'd become well acquainted with pain and threw myself head first into it.

This was my one chance.

It was life or death.

And I chose life.

* * * * *

Dawn crested on the horizon, its pink and gold daring to creep under the bush where I'd slid a few hours ago.

The gunshots had stopped. The shouts had ceased. The sounds of vehicles or people long since vanished.

I shouldn't have turned off the road and entered the forest. I knew that. I'd known it the minute I'd leapt off manmade pathways and traded it for dirt, but Mr. Mclary had chased longer than I'd expected, and I was starved, beaten, and not prepared to give up my life by running in full sight of his rifle scope.

Instead, I'd scrambled into the bushes of private, untended land and fought exhaustion until the hairs on the back of my neck no longer stood up in terror, and the thought of earning a bullet in the back of my head was no longer enough to keep me awake.

The bush had offered sanctuary, and I'd fallen asleep the moment I'd burrowed beneath it, but it wasn't the dawn that had awoken me.

It was my backpack.

A mewling, muffled cry came again, sounding alive and not at all like water and cheese.

The noise was familiar. I'd heard it as I'd run, but I'd been too focused on living to notice it came from the very thing I'd stolen.

The heavy rucksack was ex-army canvas with faded green stitching and buckets of room for bed rolls, ammunition, and anything else a soldier might need.

I'd barely used any of the available space with my meagre supplies, yet it sat squat and full in the dirt.

Another wail sent me scrambling into a squatting position, ready to bolt.

Leaning forward with shaking hands, I tore the zipper open and fell backward.

Two huge blue eyes stared up at me.

Familiar blue eyes.

Eyes I never wanted to see again.

The infant bit her lip, studying my face with a furious flicker of attention. She didn't cry louder. She didn't squawk or squirm; she merely sat in my backpack amongst canned beans and squished cheese and waited for…something.

How the hell did she get into my bag?

I hadn't put her there. I definitely wouldn't steal the natural born daughter of Mr. and Mrs Mclary. They had sixteen children working their farm and only the girl in front of me was theirs by blood. The rest of us had been bought like cattle, branded like a herd, and forced to work until we were begging for the abattoir.

The baby wriggled uncomfortably, sticking her thumb in her mouth and never taking her eyes off me.

"Why are you in my bag?" My voice was far too loud for my ears. Something small scurried off on tiny feet. Bending closer to her, she leaned back, wariness and fear clouding her inquisitive gaze. "What the hell am I supposed to do with you?"

A stream gurgled not far in the undergrowth. My thirst made my mouth water while merciless practicality made me think up other uses for the river.

I couldn't take her back, and I couldn't take her with me.

That gave me no option.

I could leave her unattended for a wild animal to make a meal of, or I could dispatch her humanely by drowning her just like her parents had drowned a boy three weeks ago for not latching the gate and letting three sheep escape.

She twirled a faded blue ribbon around her teeny fist as if going over the conclusions herself. Did she know I contemplated killing her to make my escape easier? Did she understand that I would treat her no better than her parents treated me?

Slouching in the bracken beneath my chosen bush, I sighed heavily.

Who was I kidding?

I couldn't kill her.

I couldn't even kill the rats who shared the barn with us.

Somehow, she'd crawled into my backpack, I'd stupidly ran with her even though I'd known something was wrong, and now my impossible task at staying alive just got even harder.

Chapter Two

REN

2000

I'D KNOWN I might face death if I ran.

If not from a bullet, then starvation or exposure.

That was why I'd waited far longer than I should have. Why I'd lost weight that I needed and strength I couldn't afford to lose. I'd been sold to the Mclarys two winters ago, and I should've been smarter.

I should've run the night they filled my mother's fist with cash, stuffed me in a urine-soaked car, then shoved me in the barn with the rest of their kiddie prisoners and introduced me to my education the very next day.

The night I was sold was hazy, thanks to a strong cuff to the head when I'd dared to cry, and these days, I couldn't remember my mother, which was fine because I never knew my father, either.

I only knew that we'd been made to call Mr. and Mrs Mclary Ma and Pop.

I'd obeyed out loud, but in my head, they were always the hated Mclarys. Just as hated as their blood relative currently foiling my escape plan.

I glowered at the baby girl, adding another level of intensity, doing my best to work up enough rage to kill her and be done with it.

Just like I didn't know my father, I didn't know how she'd ended up in my backpack. Had she crawled in by herself? Had another kid put her there? Had her mother even placed her inside for some reason?

The bag wasn't mine. The scuffed-up thing belonged to Mr. Mclary who filled it with booze and thick sandwiches when it was harvesting time. It sat bold and dusty by the door, hanging out with its friends the musty jackets, broken umbrellas, and well-worn boots.

I scratched my head for the hundredth time, trying to figure out the riddle of why my carefully plotted escape had somehow ended up with an unwanted passenger.

A passenger that couldn't walk or talk or even eat on her own.

Tears pricked at my scratchy eyes.

I should be miles away by now, but I still hadn't solved this problem. I still didn't know how I could run quietly and hide secretly with a baby who would, at any moment, start screaming.

Just because she'd been deathly quiet and serious since I'd found her didn't mean she wouldn't expose me and get me killed.

I cocked my head, studying her closer, hating her pink clean skin and glossy golden curls. Her cheeks were round and eyes bright. She was a mockery to every kid in the barn with sunken faces and withered bodies that looked like trees poisoned by petrol.

She was lucky. She'd been cared for. She'd slept in a bed with blankets and teddy bears and hugs.

My fists curled, reminding me all over again of my one missing finger on my left hand.

Would they miss her?

Would they search for her?

Would they even care?

I'd lived my life with one existence: where parents were cruel and beat their children, branded them with hot cattle irons, and fed them by trough and pail.

Up until a year ago, I'd believed that was how *all* kids were treated. That we were all *vermin only fit to toil*—Mrs Mclary's words every night as we crawled exhausted into our mismatch of cots and pallets.

It wasn't until the night Mr. Mclary cut off my pinkie for stealing some freshly baked apple pie that I saw a different story.

I'd tempted fate by sneaking back into the farmhouse—which was the very reason I had nine digits and not ten anymore. After passing out and coming to from the pain, I'd exhausted my search for a cleanish rag to replace the blood-soaked undershirt around my severed finger, and decided the farmhouse would have a tea towel I could borrow.

It was that or drip blood everywhere.

Mrs Mclary was screaming like a shot rabbit somewhere upstairs. She'd been as fat as a sow for months and I guessed her time to give birth had finally come. I'd seen enough animals and the grossness of new life to tune her out as I tiptoed toward the kitchen.

Only, in the raucous of babies arriving, someone had left the TV on and I became spellbound by its magic.

Moving pictures and colours and sounds. I'd seen the thing on before but had been chased out with a broom and starved with no dinner for sneaking a peek.

That night, though, I morphed into the shadows, holding my throbbing stump of a finger, and watched a show where the kids laughed and hugged their parents. Where healthy dinners were cooked with smiles and lovingly given to plump children at a table and not thrown in the dirt to be fought over before the pigs could eat our scraps.

Mr. Mclary constantly told us that we were the lucky ones. That the girls he dragged by their ponytails into the farmhouse after Mrs Mclary had gone to bed were the chosen angels bestowed an important job.

I never found out what that job was, but the girls all returned white as milk and shaking like baby lambs on a frosty morning.

In fact, having my finger cut off was my worst and best memory.

Having him grab my hand and snip off my pinkie with his fence cutters as if it was nothing more than a stray piece of wire had made me buckle and vomit in agony. The fever, thirst, and throb while watching that TV show had stolen my wits.

I was beyond stupid to stay inside the home where the devil lived.

But when he'd found me passed out from infection and blood loss in his sitting room the next morning, he'd taken me to the doctor.

On the ride over—in a truck filled with sloshing diesel for his tractor—he'd yelled at me not to die. That I still had a few years of use left and he'd paid too much to let me quit yet.

When we'd arrived at the hospital, he'd stuck his reeking face in mine and hissed at me not to say anything. My role was to be stupid—a mute. If I didn't, he'd kill me, the doctor, and anyone else who helped me.

I'd obeyed and learned what kindness was that day.

The tale spun to the medical team was my clumsy ass had severed it with a columbine blade while cutting hay. My dirty face and knobby knees were used as Mclary's evidence that I was a reckless, unruly child, and thanks to his reputation around town for being a good farmer, civil neighbour, and regular churchgoer, no one questioned him.

No one asked me how badly his lies stunk.

The infection was bad, according to the nurse, and after shivering on her table with teeth chattering and stomach heaving, she'd sewn me up, pricked me with an injection, and given me a look that made me want to spill everything.

I'd bit my lip, fear stronger than I'd ever felt welling in my chest.

I *wanted* to tell her.

I wanted so, *so* much to tell her.

But I kept my mouth shut and continued living Mclary's lie.

In return, she'd told me I was so brave, kissed my forehead, and gave me a bag of jelly beans, a sticker with a gold star, and a little teddy bear that said *Get Well Soon*.

I'd hugged that bear harder than I'd hugged anything as I reluctantly climbed into the fumy truck and buckled in to return to hell.

The moment we were away from view, Mclary snatched the bear and jelly beans from my hands and tossed them from the moving vehicle.

I knew better than to cry.

He could take my teddy and candy, but he couldn't take the kind smiles from the nurse or the gentle tutting of the doctor as they'd made my finger all better.

Not that I had a finger anymore, just a useless stump that itched sometimes and drove me mad.

I should've run that night.

I should've run a week later once I'd finished my antibiotics and no longer flashed with heat or sickness.

I should've run so many times.

The funny thing was that out of sixteen children at Mclary's farm, the sea of faces constantly changed. When a girl or boy grew old enough to harbour a certain look in their eye or gave up the fight after years of struggle, a man in a suit would come, speak pretty words, touch trembling children, then both would vanish, never to be seen again.

A few days later, a fresh recruit would arrive, just as terrified as we'd all been, just as hopeful that a mistake had been made, only to learn the brutal truth that this wasn't temporary.

This was our life, death, and never ending all in one.

My thoughts skittered over the past in spurts, never staying on one subject for long as the dawn crept to morning and morning slid to afternoon.

I didn't touch the baby.

She didn't cry or fuss as if she knew her fate was still fragile.

Halfway through our staring contest, she'd fallen asleep, curling up in my backpack with her tatty ribbon in a tiny fist and her head on my crumbling block of cheese.

My stomach rumbled. My mouth watered.

I hadn't eaten since yesterday morning, but I was well-versed in withholding food from angry bellies. I had to ration myself if I stood any chance of surviving.

I knew that at least.

Mrs Mclary called me stupid. And I supposed she was right. I couldn't read or write. I'd been hidden away in some dark and musty place with my mother until I was sold and brought here.

However, I knew how to talk and use big words, thanks to Mrs Mclary calling herself *a well-read and intelligent woman who liked to decorate her vocabulary because this town was full of simpletons.*

I got the gist of what she said some of the time, but most of the time, my brain soaked up the word, sank its baby teeth into it, and tore it apart until it made sense, then stored it away to be used later.

I forgot nothing.

Nothing.

I knew how many hammers Mr. Mclary hung in the tool shed and knew one had gone missing two weeks ago. I knew three of the four cows he had planned to slaughter were pregnant to his neighbour's bull, and I knew Mrs Mclary skimmed money from the pig profits before telling her husband their tally.

All stuff that was useless.

The only thing I knew of value was my age because according to Mr. Mclary, I was the same age as his prized mare that was born ten years ago during a mighty lightning storm that cleaved their oldest apple tree in two.

Ten years old was practically a man.

Double digits and ready to conquer a new existence.

I might not have traditional schooling and only been taught how to work the land, how to skin game, or drive a tractor using a stick to compensate for my short legs, but I had a memory that rivalled everyone's in the barn.

I might not know how to spell the months or seasons, but I knew the flavour of the sky when a storm was about to hit. I recognised the fragrance of summer compared to winter, and I remembered the passing of days so well that I could keep a mental tally even if I couldn't count.

I also remembered the night my stowaway arrived into the world.

Mrs Mclary's labour had been long and I'd been woken by a screech the evening after returning from the hospital, standing on my cot to peer out the barn's only window as the farmhouse lit up and a car spun into the driveway.

I didn't know why Mr. Mclary didn't take his wife to the doctors, but eventually, the screams stopped and a thin wail pierced the night, sounding so young, so small.

My finger throbbed with its stitches and phantom itch as I listened to the baby's arrival, my feverish mind tangling with pictures of sheep giving birth to lambs and sows giving birth to piglets until I collapsed back on my cot, convinced that the baby Mrs Mclary had delivered was part animal, part human.

I narrowed my eyes, inspecting the napping girl in front of me.

Her ears were cute like a human, not floppy like a cow. Her nose was tiny like a fairy, not shiny like a dog. Her skin was encased in a pink onesie, not downed with fur. She was as girly and as rosy as the well-cared for kids on that TV program, and it only fuelled my hate more.

* * * * *

Dusk stole the sharpness of the undergrowth, making shadows form and worries fester.

I'd been here too long.

And I still had no answer.

I'd left the baby an hour or so ago, slipping silently through the undergrowth to check out the river gurgling happily in the distance. I'd sat on its mossy banks for ages, staring at the ripples, imagining myself plucking her plump infant body from my backpack and shoving her beneath the surface.

Of the pressure I'd need to hold her under.

Of the ice I'd need to kill her and not falter.

And as try as I might, I reverted to the same conclusion I'd had this morning.

I couldn't kill her.

Even though I wanted to.

And I couldn't leave her to be eaten.

Even though I wanted to do that, too.

And I couldn't take her back because even though she was loved by the devils who hurt me, she could never be permitted to grow up to be like them. She couldn't be allowed to trade in lives or make money from unlucky kids like me.

I also couldn't take her back because by now the Mclarys would've given up looking on their own estate and headed three farms down for the deer hunter dogs that could sniff out prey for miles.

The river wouldn't be taking a life tonight, but it would be saving one.

A quiet scream cut through the trees and bracken, followed by a hushed cry. Unless I'd heard such a thing, I wouldn't believe a scream could be quiet or a cry hushed.

But Baby Mclary managed it.

She also managed to haul my ass up and send me rocketing back to her to slap my hand over her gaping little mouth to shut her up.

The hounds would be on our tail.

I hated that I'd left it this long to remember that would be the next step of Mclary's plan. We didn't need any more bad luck on our side by her calling out to them.

"Shut up," I hissed, my fingers gripping her pudgy cheeks.

Her blue eyes widened, glistening with tears and uncertain as a fawn's.

"We need to leave." I shook my head, cursing her for the thousandth time for making *me* a *we*.

I should be leaving. *I* should be running, swimming, hiding.

But because I couldn't solve this problem, she'd have to come with me until I could.

She hiccupped behind my palm, a tentative tongue licking the salt from my skin. She squirmed a little, her two miniature hands reaching up to latch around my wrist, holding me tighter, slurping wildly as if starved for any nutrition.

Which she was.

So was I.

I was past the point of hunger, but I was used to such a condition.

She was a spoilt breast fed baby who didn't understand the slicing pain in her chubby belly.

Tearing my hand away, I bared my teeth as her bottom lip wobbled and tears welled again.

Pointing sternly between her eyes, I snarled, "If you cry, I'm leaving you behind. You're hungry? Well, so are many other creatures who will gladly eat you for supper."

She blinked, wriggling deeper into the backpack and crushing my cheese.

"Oi!" My fingers dove into the bag, pushed her aside, and rescued the badly sat on cheese. "This is all we have; don't you understand?"

She licked her lips, eyes wide on the unappetizing curdled mess.

I hugged it to my chest, possession and unwillingness to share rising in me. Feeding time in the barn meant the tentative bonds we might have with the other slave children were non-existent. We might trade holey blankets or borrow fourth-hand shoes, but food? No way. You fight for a scrap or you die.

There were no hand-outs.

Her fingers clutched at her blue ribbon, over and over again as her belly gurgled almost as loudly as mine. Her ugly face scrunched up with the beginnings of another scream.

My shoulders tensed. Violence bubbled. I honestly didn't know what I'd do if she cried and didn't shut up.

But as her lips spread and lungs inflated for noise, she tilted her head and looked right into my soul. She paused as if giving me a choice, a threat—a conniving weasel just like her mother and father.

And once again, I had no choice.

Tension slipped from my spine as I sank into realization that from here on out, I would have to share everything. My shelter. My food. My energy. My *life*. She wouldn't thank me. She wouldn't appreciate it. She would expect it just like every filly, calf, kitten, or puppy expected their parent to ensure its survival.

"I hate you," I whispered as I looked through the trees for any sign of company. My ears twitched for any sound of baying hounds as my fingers tore open the plastic and pinched the warm, smelly cheese between them.

My mouth watered so much I almost drooled as I raised the morsel out of its bag. My legs shook to eat, knowing they had a long trek ahead of them.

But blue eyes never left my face, condemning me for even thinking about eating.

"I hate you," I reminded her. "I'll always hate you. So don't you ever forget it."

Ducking on my haunches, I shoved my hand in her face.

Instantly, a grimace twisted her lips in a strange sort of smile as her hands came up, latched once again around my wrist, and a tiny, wet mouth covered my fingertips.

She pulled back a second later, spitting and complaining, red fury painting her blotchy cheeks. She scowled at the cheese in my fingers then me, looking far older than her young age.

I scowled right back, fighting every instinct to eat what she'd refused. "This is all we have until we get somewhere safer." I pushed it toward her mouth again before I could steal it. "Eat it. I won't give you the chance again."

She took a moment. An endless moment while she cocked her head this way and that like a sparrow, then finally swayed forward and licked the cheese from my hold.

Her fingers never stopped twirling her ribbon, hypnotizing me as she quickly lapped at the miniscule offering and sat back in silence.

I didn't speak as I broke off another cube and placed it on my tongue. A moan of sheer delight escaped me as my body rushed to transform taste into energy and get me the hell away from here.

I wanted more.

I wanted the whole thing.

I wanted every can of beans and every bottle of water I'd been able to steal.

But even though it cost me, even though my hands shook with a brutal battle to seal the plastic and place it in the backpack with her, I managed.

Grabbing the sides of the canvas's zipper, I looked her dead in the eye. "We're going for a swim, so the dogs can't smell us. You're probably going to get wet and cold, and there's nothing I can do about it, so don't cry. You cry, and I'll leave you for the bears."

She blinked and stuck her thumb in her mouth with her ribbon dangling from her fist.

"Good." I nodded. "Don't...don't be afraid."

With a final look at her silky hair and innocent trust, I yanked up the zippers, drenched her in darkness, and swung her substantial weight onto my back.

She cried out as she thumped against my spine.

I stabbed her side with my elbow, striding fast toward the river. "Della Mclary, you make one more sound, and it will be your last."

She fell quiet.

And I ran...for both our lives.

Chapter Three

REN

2000

THE FIRST FEW nights of something strange and new were always the toughest.

I'd learned that the hard way, and the lesson came again as I crashed to my knees next to a falling down shed in the middle of an untended field.

Adaption.

That was what I'd done when I'd been sold to the Mclarys, and if I didn't remember the struggle it took to fall into routine, accept the inevitable, and find a new normal, then I probably would've curled into a ball, yelled at the vanishing moon, and suffocated the damn baby in my backpack.

Those first days at the farmhouse had been the worst because I kept expecting something *more*. Something kinder, better, warmer, safer. It wasn't the conditions I'd been thrust into or the back-breaking work I was assigned, but the hope that all of it would vanish as quickly as it had arrived.

But once that hope had been eaten away by my starvation, life had gotten easier. Acceptance had been smoother, and I'd saved up my tears for when they truly mattered.

Breathing fast, I peered into the dawn-smudged gloom for signs of a hunt.

My clothes were still wet from walking thigh-high in the stream for as long as I could physically stand it. My muscles had bellowed from the chilly water, my ankles threatening to snap every time I slipped off an unseen rock on the bottom.

It would've been far easier to sink below the surface and let the ripples take me. To lie on my back and rest.

But I couldn't do that because the baby zipped up tight would drown in the wet canvas, thrashing like the fish Mclary caught in his pond.

She'd cried a few times in our night-time journey. Once, she'd whined due to me slipping up to my waist and getting her wet. Twice, she'd mewled like a kitten, hungry and tired. And at some point, as the straps of the backpack cut into my shoulders and I leaned more and more into her weight, forcing myself to put one more step in front of the other, she'd squalled loud and angry as if in protest for her conditions.

I'd elbowed her again.

She'd fallen quiet.

And we'd continued on until I couldn't walk another step.

Rolling from my knees to my ass, I reached up with stiff arms and seized fingers to slip the backpack off my shoulders and scooted away to lean gratefully against the weathered boards of the shed.

The long grass kept us hidden. The light breeze kept us quiet. And the morning light revealed it was just us in the sea of rye that hadn't been cut or baled in years.

That meant the farmer didn't tend to his crops, and we were far enough away from the Mclary's holdings to be safe for a few hours of rest.

I barely managed to unzip the bag and let little blue eyes and blonde hair free before slipping to my side and dreaming.

* * * * *

Three days.

Three days of broken sleep, sore limbs, and the never-ending need to run as far as possible.

Three terrible days of learning what a baby ate reappeared ten times worse a few hours later. I'd had the gag-worthy task of figuring out how to remove a wriggling annoyance from clothing and clean up a mess that needed a hose rather than dry grass.

I didn't have a replacement diaper and didn't want her getting my backpack and food disgusting, so I ripped up my only spare t-shirt and Frankensteined a covering for her squashed little butt.

On the fourth day of hard-won freedom, Della Mclary crawled from the backpack and waited by my nose until I woke from exhaustion. I hadn't even thought of her wandering off while I slept, and her shadow hovered over me, creating horrors of farmers and enemies and guns.

My survival instincts, already on high-alert, lashed out, and I shoved her away from me.

She rolled away, silent with shock until she came to a roly poly mess covered with leaves.

And then she cried.

And cried.

And *cried.*

The code in the barn was to stick to yourself. No one got too close because no one wanted to risk getting hurt, either by Mclary punishing the friendship or because of the inevitable ticking clock that meant everyone left eventually.

Della had no such qualms.

She'd sat in her pink onesie, stinking like shit and chubby legs kicking in dirt, while her midget finger poked at my cheek; over and over until blurry sleep became blurry awake.

And now, I'd struck her.

I tore at my hair, not knowing what to do, itching to shut her up by any means necessary.

Crawling over to her, I cringed against the ripe smell and plucked her from the ground. Her weight felt heavier in my arms than on my back.

I twisted her closer, ready to slap my hand over her mouth, frantically looking at the horizon to see who or what had heard us, but the minute my fingers went near her tear-stained face, she clutched my index and sucked on it.

Her crying stopped.

Her sniffles and flowing tears didn't.

But at least she was silent, and there was no way I wanted to shatter that miracle, so I sat with her uncomfortably, letting her do what all baby creatures did when seeking comfort—nuzzling and suckling, creating another layer of frost on my hatred rather than thawing.

"Why did you mess this up for me?" I growled. "Why couldn't you have stayed with your awful parents?"

I would be so much better off without her.

I should've left her behind days ago.

We'd already gone through the food far faster than I'd planned. The cheese was gone and two cans of baked beans. I had one left.

I didn't even know if babies could eat beans, but I'd smashed it up and fed it as a paste, and she'd wisely never refused anything I offered. Not after my threat the first time.

Feeling trapped and useless and totally unprepared, I rocked my nemesis to sleep, both our empty tummies cawing as loud as the crows in the trees.

Chapter Four

REN

2000

EVERYTHING I HAD in the world now fit into two cargo pants pockets and an empty backpack.

I had no food or water.

I had no tent or blanket, no spare clothes, no medicine, no toothbrush or soap.

I'd done a terrible job at stashing away important things I'd need for this journey and regretted my stupidity on not planning better.

I'd done my best to keep us semi-clean by washing in the river we followed by day, and tried my hardest to keep us fed by hunting rats and rabbits and cooking them over the smallest fire I could by night.

Della screamed the first time I bashed in the head of a rabbit caught in my snare and skinned it in front of her. Unlike the previous times she'd cried, sucking on my finger didn't shut her up.

She'd cried and cried herself into a stupor until her gasps and hiccups trailed into sleep, and I'd woken her a few hours later with stringy overcooked meat.

Her golden curls had turned brassy with grease. Her pudgy pink cheeks white and sallow.

I wasn't used to seeing health slip so quickly from someone I saw every day. The kids in the barn all looked like filthy skeletons with wiry muscles and bleakness in their gaze.

No one changed inside that place once they'd given up hope and accepted their new fate. Della, on the other hand, switched from inquisitive infant to cranky monster, and my hate billowed bigger every day, swarming in size until I rubbed at my ribs, trying to dislodge the suffocating pressure whenever I looked at her.

If she cried, my hands curled to shut her up permanently. If she shat my t-shirt, my gag reflex begged to vomit all over her. If she crawled from the backpack while I was sleeping and burrowed into my side, my desire to shove her away was so strong I had to leap to my feet and back away to avoid hurting her the way I wanted.

I didn't want this.

I didn't want *her*.

I wanted my freedom, and she was just another form of imprisonment.

Sighing heavily, I once again rubbed at the ball of loathing wrapped around my throat and forced myself to relax. I was hungry enough without burning through more precious energy.

Ten days.

I'd made it ten days.

I could make it ten more—even with a no longer fat baby and an ever-increasing need to rest, eat something decent, and change into cleaner clothes.

Sitting in the shade of a massive oak tree, I scanned the horizon as I always did and split my attention three ways.

One, on Della as she lay on her back, twirling her dirty blue ribbon while wriggling in fallen acorns; two, on our surroundings and any sudden motions or noises, and three, on the measly tools in front of me.

I'd hoped by spreading out my worldly possessions, I would see an alternative for their use or have an epiphany on how to make life better. How to actually survive rather than continue what we were doing and slowly dying day by day.

My fingers stroked the nicked and tarnished blade that I'd stolen from the sheering shed last season. Mclary had whipped all of us for its disappearance, but no one knew I'd taken it, and I'd buried my guilt deep enough to justify everyone being punished on my behalf.

Along with a knife, I had a ball of baling twine, an oversize sewing needle meant for repairing sacking and tarp, a hay net that had come in handy making small animal snares, and a tin cup that had been assigned to me to drink from the well on the farm.

My one set of cargo pants, faded green t-shirt, and holey sneakers were days away from falling apart and covered in filth from living in the wilderness. And Della's pink onesie was now a disgusting shade of putrid brown from diaper mishaps, mud, and pathetic attempts to rinse in the river.

Like I said, utterly measly and totally lacking.

I should've grabbed a tarp at least for shelter, a blanket from my bed, cutlery, painkillers—not that I had access to those—and so many other handy things I missed.

The only thing we had on our side was the weather.

The temperature had stayed muggy and warm since leaving Mclary's and a small layering of leaves at night was enough to stay comfortable. With the river as our guide, we might be hungry, but we were never dehydrated, which I suppose was something to be thankful for.

* * * * *

I'd lost count of the days and nights.

I'd forgotten how long I'd lugged a baby through forest and farmland, putting as much distance between me and the Mclary's farm as I could.

All I knew was I needed something other than fish and rabbit to curb my ravenous appetite. I needed a brush to clean the fur from my teeth. I needed clothes that didn't reek. I needed a break from the girl making my life a living hell.

When I'd first run from Mclary, I shouldn't have entered the forest for fear of getting lost or dying, but thanks to my will to survive and basic education, I'd excelled better than I hoped. I didn't know what direction I travelled in most of the time, and I didn't know where I was going, but each day was a success if we ate, drank, and slept in safety.

Now, I was about to leave the sanctuary of the wilderness and do something else I probably shouldn't do. In fact, something I most *definitely* shouldn't do in my current stinky state with a listless baby who slept more often than cried these days.

If I'd survived better, I wouldn't need to do this.

If I didn't have an unwanted passenger, I wouldn't *have* to do this.

Cursing Della all over again, I gritted my teeth and took the first step from twigs and branches, trading it for paint and concrete.

Nothing happened. No one noticed. No bullet lodged in my skull.

I waited, twitching like a deer, sniffing the air, testing the waters.

When the night sky stayed silent and nothing suspicious moved, I gathered my bravery and slunk farther from the treeline.

Using the cover of darkness, I sneaked closer toward the small township in the distance.

Just like I didn't know where I was, I didn't know the exact time, but most houses were dark, no cars on the road, no people or noise or life.

The perfect time to steal the supplies I needed and then split.

Hoisting the backpack further up my shoulders, I stiffened, waiting for Della to make a sound. She'd been quiet all afternoon in her dirty carrier, and it was past time to eat.

Normally, by now, she'd grizzle and squirm enough to make me give up travel for the day and find somewhere to sleep.

Tonight, she didn't make a peep.

That ought to have relaxed tight muscles instead of digging my worry deeper.

I still hadn't forgiven her for making my escape so hard, but I'd lasted this long, and I'd fought too hard to ensure she lasted, too.

She owed me.

I didn't talk to her often, but when I did, I always earned a sunshine smile or serious stare. I supposed this would be a good moment to speak kindly, to reassure both her and myself that we wouldn't get caught and would be better equipped once this visit was over.

"Don't worry, Della Mclary. I'll get you something yummy to eat tonight." I patted where her butt would be and strode onward.

I didn't focus on how much lighter she was these days or how hard running had been on both our bodies.

Sticking to the shadows, I stalked through suburbia. Pretty, well-kept houses with tidy lawns and painted garden furniture—so unlike the paint-peeling unkemptness of the farmhouse—welcomed me in silver moonlight.

I kept going, heading deeper into family territory and totally unfamiliar concepts of slides and swings and paddling pools left unguarded on front lawns.

I didn't stop. I didn't dally.

I was hunting for a supermarket. Something I could smash my way into, stuff my backpack full of things, then vanish back into the forest unseen.

But the deeper I travelled through manicured verges and swept streets, the more my hope deflated. I wasn't in the heart of the town where such things as stores and restaurants existed.

I was in sleepyville where children from the TV show slept soundly in safe beds with kind-hearted parents to watch over them.

I continued down the road, no longer finding the houses pretty but mocking. Mocking me with everything I'd been denied and everything I ever wanted.

One particular house hurt my stupid ten-year-old heart as I stopped on its pavement and stared. Its blue and white paint, warm wood veranda, and large bay windows whispered of peace and somewhere to rest.

The large doorknob begged me to turn it and stroll right in, to claim a bed as my own, and forget all my worries forever.

Della's knee dug into my spine as she wriggled.

"Quit it." I growled over my shoulder.

A tabby cat shot from a pruned rose bush, darting past my feet and sending my pulse jumping. With the adrenaline shot came hunger so vicious and slicing, I stumbled and clutched my empty middle.

A small cry came from within the backpack. A cry that mimicked my craving. A cry she knew she shouldn't utter but couldn't help escaping.

I didn't even have the energy to elbow her into quietness again.

Who was I kidding?

There wasn't a supermarket or dumpster or any hope of a large area of food ready to be stolen. The only choice I had before I buckled on the sidewalk was to pick one of the dozing households surrounding me, and I'd already made my selection.

The house in front of me.

The one that welcomed me to take what was inside as if it'd been waiting for this very moment.

Once the idea popped into my head, I didn't think twice.

"Be quiet." I jiggled the straps on my shoulders. "You hear me?"

Silence was my answer.

"Good."

Looking left and right, I bypassed the blue fence and pebble pathway guiding to the entrance and slithered through the shadows toward the back door. Even the service side of the house was well tended with clean rubbish bins.

Slipping into the backyard, I saw a basket of toys neatly placed, and a large umbrella wrapped tight, guarding its family, the table and chairs.

Della hung heavily on my back as I stooped as low as I could to avoid the sensor light and made my way as carefully as I could to the back door.

I had my knife.

I could smash a window or jimmy a lock.

But as I climbed the deck to investigate, my eyes fell on an oversize cat flap. Ducking, I tested it with my hand, punching it quickly.

The plastic flopped open, letting me stick my head into the warm scents of cooking, clean linen, and happiness.

I practically drooled on their welcome mat.

For once, I was thankful for my small size and skinny frame. It would be a tight fit, but I could contort myself to gain entrance. Hell, I could do anything if it meant earning a full belly tonight.

Shrugging the backpack off my shoulders, I shoved it against the side of the house out of the way. Unzipping it a little, I placed my hand on Della's dirty blonde curls as she popped up like a jack-in-the-box. "No. You're staying here."

Her blue eyes searched mine, achingly hungry and begging for any scrap of attention, food, or whatever else kids like her were used to getting.

Her helplessness did not work on me, and my heart grew ever harder. "I'm going inside to fetch supplies. Do. Not. Move." Her head ducked beneath my hand as she slouched sadly back into the bag.

I didn't know if she understood what I was saying, but I didn't take my hand away. I squeezed her tiny skull with my fingers. "I'm warning you. If you run off, I won't search for you. You'll die and get eaten by a dog. Do you want to be eaten by a dog, Della Mclary?"

Her nose wrinkled and tears welled, making her eyes glow blue.

"No crying. I don't like cry-babies." Grabbing the zippers, I pushed my face almost to hers. "If you're good and sit here quietly, I'll bring you fruit and chocolate and even new clothes, okay?"

The tears teetered on her bottom lashes but didn't fall. Twirling that confounded ribbon around her tiny fist, she plonked down and ducked her head.

I took that as a yes.

"Remember, be quiet as a mouse, and no one will hurt you."

I zipped up the bag and crawled through the cat flap before I could change my mind.

Chapter Five

REN

2000

ONLY A FEW minutes I spent in that house, and I made the first mistake of my short life within thirty seconds of them.

The kitchen was freshly scrubbed from cooking, the dishwasher sloshing quietly in the corner, a gold fish bowl humming with a night light revealing lazy, glittery fish.

A cat sprang onto the granite countertop, its yellow eyes glowing in the darkness.

I waved a hand at it, not daring to speak just in case the heavy silence carried my voice to wherever the people slept in this place.

It ignored my command to leave, never blinking, its whiskers prickling at my invasion.

Giving it the finger, I slunk deeper into its home. The cat followed me, flicking its tail, silent paws hunting my every step.

Goosebumps trailed down my spine as I entered the dining room which spread out into a family room with comfy golden couches, large TV, and a shaggy rug full of toys. The mess on the rug was the only thing out of place with large artwork staring down from neatly painted walls and dust-free figurines judging me as I spun around and headed back toward the kitchen.

I didn't need to steal anything of value, just things of practicality.

Like food.

Delicious food.

And that was when I saw it.

The booster chair wedged up against the breakfast bar ready for someone of Della's size to hang out with their much larger family members.

This family had kids.

This family had a baby like Della.

Unlike my backpack baby who sucked my finger for lack of food and slept with a stained ribbon for comfort, their baby had a cat to squeeze and fish to coo at. Unlike Della who slept beneath trees while blanketed in moonlight, their baby had a comfy crib, soft sheets, and all the food it could ever want.

My fists curled to think of his luck and Della's misfortune. Whoever this baby was I hated him because he had something Della never would.

Consistency…familiarity…*home.*

My feet froze to the crumb-free floor.

The idea unravelled too fast to stop it.

Leave her here.

I'd been begging for a way to be rid of her ever since I'd found her squishing my cheese. It wasn't that I hated her because she was the blood of my enemies but because, day by day, she was robbing me of my only chance at making something of myself.

I couldn't run far. I couldn't travel fast. All my ideas of finding a new place to call my own had been scrapped because of her endless needs.

She would end up killing us both, and a solution had just landed squarely in my lap.

The cat meowed, weaving around my legs as I strode quickly toward the back door. Shoving the creature away, I ducked on all fours and wriggled my shoulders back through the tight rectangle.

I'd have bruises tomorrow, but I wasn't counting. I already had more than normal along with scars and bumps and missing fingers.

With my body half in the kitchen and half on the deck outside, I strained to reach the backpack and dragged it unceremoniously toward me.

Della grumbled as it tipped sideways.

"Hush up." I yanked her closer, so I could unzip the top. Ripping it down too fast, a blonde curl got caught in the zipper's teeth. Her face scrunched up with indignation, her mouth wide and ready to scream.

My heart jack-knifed as I clamped a hand over her tiny mouth. "Don't you dare," I hissed in her ear. "It's just a little pain. It's nothing."

She wriggled beneath my hold, little whimpers and struggles unmatched for my wiry strength from working the land and wrangling unhelpful livestock.

The cat swiped at my ass still lodged in its exit. I tried to kick it and lost my grip on Della's mouth.

I stiffened, already preparing to run the moment she cried.

Lights would flick on, feet would pummel stairs, and I'd be caught stuck in a cat flap like a failed, stupid thief.

Why didn't I use the door?

I could've unlocked it from the inside.

Hating and cursing my idiocy, I didn't breathe as the moment stretched so long my teeth ached. My body already vibrated with her scream. But slowly, her lips closed, anger faded from accusing eyes, and her teeny hand rubbed her scalp with her ribbon clutched tight.

I let out the breath I'd been holding.

"Good girl," I whispered. "You're very brave."

The transformation in her entire body blinded me. A smile spread. Cheeks pinked. Spine straightened. Any sign of sickness and starvation from living in the wild deleted, all because of one morsel of praise.

There was a key in that.

A message that all humans—tiny or ancient—needed nutrition in the form of love as well as everything else.

It made my recent decision even easier because I was not capable of feeding her everything she needed. I'd gotten her this far. My job was done.

"Get out of the backpack." I pushed the canvas sides to collapse on the deck.

Giving me a sideways look, she bit her lip uncertainly.

"Get. Now." Pulling her once chubby arm, I knocked her off balance and dragged her out. She didn't make a sound, not caring her filthy onesie got caught on a deck splinter or that the only place she'd found safety in was now tossed out of reach.

Keeping my fingers locked around her midget wrist, I backed through the cat flap, pulling her with me. "Come on."

It took a few attempts with the cat trying to squish past me and Della wriggling the wrong way, but somehow, I managed to get her inside without too many grizzles.

I really should've just unlocked the door, but we were inside. The cat shot outside. And the house slept on none the wiser.

The minute all limbs were inside the kitchen, I stood and stretched out sore muscles, ignored my growling stomach, then scooped her from the clean floor.

The novelty of not having to knock off leaves from her ass or check her for beetles and ants was nice as I carried her into the lounge and placed her on the rug with all the bright plastic toys.

Instantly, she latched sticky fingers around some sort of ring with rainbow disks slipping and sliding. Once again, she gave me a smile so blinding, so pure, so *grateful*, I buckled under a different type of hunger.

A hunger for the same thing I couldn't give her.

A hunger for something that offered safety even if everything around us was dangerous.

"Don't make a sound." I pointed at her, backing away to the kitchen. "I mean it."

She watched me go, blue eyes never leaving mine as I ducked around the breakfast bar and wrenched open the pantry.

She stayed quiet as a chipmunk as I grabbed packets of crisps and chocolate biscuits and brightly wrapped lollies. The foils and wrappers made a horrendous noise in the quiet, making my ears twitch for company and eyes flicker to the dark corridor beyond.

Abandoning them on the counter, I turned to quieter things.

Knowing I was on borrowed time, I yanked open the fridge and fought every instinct to dive straight into the cool crisp shelves full of deliciousness.

Grapes dangled with a cheese platter wrapped in cellophane. A chunky pink leg of ham smelled of smoke and honey. Beer clattered in the door along with apple juice packs and little glass jars with a picture of a baby on the front.

I couldn't read what flavours they were, but one was orange, another green, and one a greyish pink. Grabbing all three, I shoved them into my cargo pockets, grabbed the platter with cheese and grapes along with the ham, and somehow balanced my haul back to the living room.

Plonking them beside Della, I dashed back to the kitchen drawers to pilfer a spoon for her. I didn't need cutlery. I was too hungry to eat with manners.

"Sit still," I ordered as I landed next to her on the plush comfy rug. I wanted to take this rug. To sleep on it. Wrap myself up in it in the forest. I never wanted to leave its comfy-ness.

But it was too big, too heavy, and after tonight, I would be travelling light.

I'd no longer have a baby to haul across the country.

I could fly.

My stomach growled at the enticing smells, and I ripped off the cellophane, dug dirty nails into the ham, and ripped off a handful.

Della licked her lips as I tore it apart with my teeth, swallowing before properly chewing, forgetting I was human and becoming an animal instead.

Her smacking grew louder as she squashed herself against my leg, reaching for the ham. I didn't stop her as she copied me, powerless fingers clawing at the meat, little tongue licking air for a taste.

Even though part of me wanted to strike her for touching my food, I fought those instincts and tore her off a piece. She snatched it as if possessed by the same feral obsession, sucking and mouthing the smoky meat, frustrated tears filling her eyes as she failed to chew.

"Ugh, you're so useless." I grabbed another handful of ham, feeding the monster in my belly so I could at least find some compassion to be kind.

Content, if not annoyed with her lack of progress, Della sat quietly and let me eat. She never tore her eyes off my mouth and swallowed when I swallowed and smacked when I smacked, and when that crawling, tearing emptiness inside was sated, I shoved as many grapes into my mouth as I could then twisted off the lids from the baby food jars.

With ham-greasy fingers, I scooped up a bit of orange slop with the spoon and held it in front of her nose.

She gagged and fell backward.

I snickered. "That good, huh?"

I didn't help her up. She'd been the one to tumble; it was up to her to figure it out, but I did shove the spoon in my mouth to taste what she'd refused.

"Yuck." My lips puckered at the overly mushed paste that tasted vaguely like pumpkin. Nothing like the sun-ripened, freshly picked pumpkin that we'd grow at the farm, but a vegetable pretending to be a close cousin.

Tossing it to the side, I pulled a strip of ham off the bone and waited as Della figured out with her hopeless legs and arms how to sit up and wave her hands for something to eat.

I placed the ham on my tongue and chewed it. I chewed until the meat was juicy and tender, and then I passed it to her.

Instantly, the ham vanished from my hand to hers, then disappeared into her tiny mouth.

She bounced on the spot as she swallowed, eyes bright for more.

I didn't know if it was the familiarity of the routine from living in the forest together—eating rabbit and rat—or if I'd turned her into a carnivore with our previous measly choices; either way, I tried offering the pumpkin on the spoon again, only to have it splattered over my cargos with demands for more ham.

Seeing as this would be the last time I ever saw her, I obeyed. Stripping ham, chewing, and giving it to her until she'd had her fill.

When her eyes finally grew heavy and the sparkle of dinner and toys dimmed, I stood and returned to the kitchen.

Della did her best to watch me as I reached outside the cat flap for my backpack and stuffed it with as much food as I could. But by the time I'd finished squashing in apple juice cartons and filling up a few empty bottles I found in the recycling bin with water, she was curled up on the rug, snoring gently.

The cat slithered past me, giving me a cold glare before trotting over to the baby on his rug. He sniffed her, investigated every inch, then curled up beside her as if accepting this new human in his home.

She didn't need me.

Soon, when the sun rose, she'd have brothers and sisters and parents who would raise her as one of their own. For now, she had a cat to watch over her, fish to blow bubbles at her, and a kid who'd never meant to be in her life disappear.

She'd forget all about me.

She'd stay alive and bug free.

This was where she belonged.

"Goodbye, Della Mclary."

With a final look, I unlocked the back door and strode out of her life forever.

Chapter Six

DELLA

Present Day

INTRODUCTORY ASSIGNMENT FOR: Creative Writing Class
Professor: Diane Baxter
Brief: To write a non-fiction piece about our lives that reads like fiction

Dear Professor Baxter,

I know you asked us to write something true that reads as fake, but I have a problem.

I'm not trying to be difficult and refuse to do the assignment but…well, this problem of mine…it's a fairly big problem.

You see, I'm not allowed to tell the truth.

Ever.

Like literally, forbidden on pain of death.

Ever, ever, ever.

You want us to write a story based on reality, but my entire life I've lived a reality based on a story.

Every town I ever lived, every school I ever went to, every friend I made, and enemy I crossed, they all got told a tale.

That's probably why I'm so good at your class. Because creative writing wasn't just something I was interested in but a skill that ensured I stayed alive.

I know I'm not making any sense, but you'll understand by the end.

If I do this assignment, of course, which I'm still debating whether or not I can.

It's not that I'm afraid anymore. I know nothing can hurt me (now). And I know if I don't do it, it will affect my grade and possibly even my graduation.

What I'm worried about is what will happen if I tell the truth, and what will happen if I continue to live the lie I've been living since the day I was born.

Then again, if I don't write it, no one will ever know how unbelievable real life can be. But if I do write it, I'll probably never show you.

Round and round I go, Professor Baxter. Hopefully, I'll make my decision very soon, but whatever choice I make, whatever story I tell…my life?

You'll never believe me.

Even if I tell you the truth…

Even if I reveal every secret…

You'll never believe me.

No one ever does.

Chapter Seven

REN

2000

FOR FOUR DAYS, I hung around that town.

I didn't know its name.

I didn't know how many people made it their home or the names of those I stole from.

All I knew was I missed the trees and open spaces and the smells of dirt and rain and sun. Concrete, paint, and petrol covered the softness of nature, hinting that I might have been sold to a farm, but my soul had found sanctuary there. I missed fields and animals and even the toil of turning seed into crop.

I was too wild for a city and struggled with what that meant. I had no recollection of my life before I was sold, and now that I was free, all I wanted to do was return to what I'd run from, but on *my* terms, not Mclary's.

I wanted the caw of cockerels at dawn.

I wanted the bay of cattle at lunchtime milking.

I wanted to be free to make my own way, and unfortunately, the city was the opposite of freedom.

It had rules that came with punishment—just like the farmhouse.

It had expectations that came with penalties—just like the farmhouse.

Civilization was a foreign, scary place for someone like me who had no urge to become a clone, co-existing in the town's matchy-matchy houses.

All I wanted was to be left alone, and that was the heart of my problem.

I didn't want to be touched or talked to or cared for or told off. I didn't need company because company came with future complications.

All I wanted was *life*.

And it left me with only one solution.

Along with hurting my body, Mclary had hurt any chance I had at finding safety in normal society because how could a nine-fingered ten-year-old kid who'd seen things that he could never unsee, who couldn't read or write, who'd never been to school or learned how to make friends...how did that kid become one of these adults? These shallow adults who scowled at messy children and laughed in condescending tones?

The answer that I grudgingly came to was...I couldn't.

I was in a town surrounded by homes, yet I was homeless.

I was a kid, but I didn't want parents to feed me or give up the tiny shred of independence I'd claimed for myself.

I was free, but I breathed and twitched with claustrophobia to *run*.

And so, that was what I planned to do.

Even though my heart pounded to leave immediately, I forced myself to sit down and plan. I wouldn't make the same mistake twice, and I wouldn't leave this place until I had better supplies.

The one silver lining was life was infinitely easier not having a baby screaming at random times or having to carry her heavy ass through car parks and hedgerows.

For four nights, I'd slept beneath slumbering houses or even sprawled on a lounger if the yard didn't have a security light. I chowed through my stash of food and returned twice to different homes, slinking through cat flaps to restock my smelly backpack.

I'd washed in paddling pools left on front lawns. I'd stripped and scrubbed my filthy, scrawny body, diligently cleaning between every toe, every finger, and even my belly button. Crystal clear water was left a murky, muddy brown ready to be explained by confused parents and wailed over by angry kids.

I hoped they knew that even though I was a pest to them, their belongings were a godsend to me. Their food was appreciated. Their deck chairs highly rated. And the paddling pools wrenched utmost gratefulness from every bone.

I'd never had a bath at Mclary's—unless I sneaked a dip in the pond—but then I'd end up smelling of algae and duck shit and be beaten for it anyway.

Paddling pools were much better, and I despised the feeling of slipping back into rank, grubby clothes after scrubbing so clean. I hadn't gotten around to stealing a new wardrobe just yet, but soon. Very soon.

Clothes were yet more items on the long mental checklist I kept adding to. I was thankful for my good memory because without skills to write what I needed, I couldn't afford to forget anything vital.

During daylight hours, I rested out of sight or wandered streets unvisited by locals, going over my upcoming vanishing act back into the forest.

Occasionally, my thoughts tripped back to Della, and I'd stop short, wondering if she was safe. Was she fed, clean, warm? Had she forgotten all about me?

The hatred in my heart slowly faded, leaving behind an uncertainty that I'd done the right thing.

On the third night, I was tempted to return to the house with the bay windows and welcoming blue paint to see if she was happy. I let my thoughts convince me that I was responsible for her future even though that was an utter lie.

She was the daughter of my enemies, and I shouldn't care about someone who had such tainted blood running in their veins.

Besides, she *wasn't* my responsibility.

She was never supposed to get mixed up in my life.

She was better away from a kid who didn't have a plan apart from staying hidden, staying alive, and figuring out what he wanted to become.

Did I want to be Ren? The kid with no last name, no parents, no home? Or did I want to be someone else? Someone who had every right to walk down neat streets and sit at fancy restaurants?

Someone who was *someone* not *something*.

I did want that, but I also wanted *more*.

I couldn't explain it, but whenever I looked at the treeline on the outskirts of town, the itch inside built until I physically scratched with the desire to disappear inside it.

I wanted twigs cracking beneath my shoes and grass swaying around my legs. I wanted the reward of hard living because every day was sweeter for having survived with no one and nothing.

Perhaps I was punishing myself, or maybe I'd lost all trust in people.

Either way, on my fourth night, I found myself in front of a camping store in the middle of the shopping district of the sleepy little town.

My fingers smudged the glass as I pressed my nose up and stared past the streetlight reflections to the tempting merchandise beyond.

Tents and sleeping bags and everything I'd ever need to turn the wilderness into my home.

It didn't take me long to figure out how to break in, spying the back delivery door with a flimsy lock and no reinforcement. All it took was a twist of my dull blade and the mechanism gave up, swinging the door open with a whisper of invitation.

No alarm shattered the night.

No security guard grabbed me by the scruff of the neck.

I spent the rest of midnight wandering aisles, staring at pictures on packets and squinting at words I didn't understand.

I tested the weight of tents and camping stoves. I snatched sharp knives and Swiss army blades and stashed them deep in my pockets. I stole a foldable saw, small hammer, and a handy toolkit with screw drivers, pliers, and other miniature hardware I'd no doubt need.

Scooping up two first-aid kits complete with everything from needles to painkillers, I gathered a pile of water purifiers, strange dried food, bendable plates, cups, and cutlery, and finally, after much deliberation, I chose the smallest one person tent I could find that weighed less than Della.

Trading my dirty backpack, I upgraded to a cleaner one with waterproof flaps and hardwearing zippers. Khaki green with navy blue stitching, it fit my tent, sleeping bag, and everything else I needed with plenty of space left over for food.

Once I'd exhausted my checklist, I headed toward the clothing racks and helped myself to two of everything.

Two long sleeves. Two t-shirts. Two undershirts. Two trousers. Two belts. Two jumpers. Most were too big, but they were well-made and warm and would last me a lifetime if I took care of them.

For the heavier things, I deliberated far too long, doing my best to make the right choice. Eventually, I settled on a windbreak, waterproof duck-down jacket along with tramping boots a size too big, a four-pack of woollen socks, and some underwear.

At the last minute, I also shoved in a pair of flip-flops for reasons I wasn't entirely sure of, along with a beanie, scarf, gloves, and sunglasses.

Dawn slowly blinked fresh eyes and yawned away the night, giving me a heads-up that it was time to leave.

Hoisting up my new bag of possessions, smoothing my stolen wardrobe, I crept from the camping store, pulled the door closed behind me, then headed to the supermarket across the street.

* * * * *

I had everything I needed.

I was ready to trade closed-in civilization for wide open spaces.

For the first time in my life, I felt an unfurling of excitement.

No one had caught me raiding the supermarket. No one saw the small smashed window in the staff bathroom even though they'd opened an hour ago and customers came and went.

I strolled boldly down Main Street in my clean earth-coloured clothes and dared them to say I didn't belong.

My eyes latched onto the horizon where beckoning trees and twinkling sunlight promised a new beginning.

And then, I made the second biggest mistake of my life.

I glanced to my left, toward an appliance store selling computers, stereos, and TVs, and there, on the four giant screens in the window was Della.

Her scrunched up face, purple from crying, her fists flailing, her mouth wide in an ugly scream.

My legs shot across the street before I could stop myself, slamming to a stop with my heavy backpack bashing against my spine as I pressed a shaking hand against the window.

Della.

Why was she crying?

Why was she on TV?

And where the hell was her ribbon? Her little fists were empty of her favourite belonging.

Her blue eyes shot red with tears, her little legs kicking as some strange man held her with a heavy scowl.

I wanted to kill him for holding her with such disgust and inconvenience.

My fingernails clawed at the glass, trying to comfort her even though I'd been the one to throw her away.

Then screaming Della was replaced with a severe woman in a pink suit.

Her mouth moved but no sound came.

There was nothing more important to me. I *had* to hear what she said.

Shoving my way past a customer exiting the store, I stomped my way inside and latched onto the closest TV. The sound was turned down but loud enough to make out words I never wanted to hear.

A few nights ago, a baby girl was found in Mr. and Mrs Collins home. No sign of forced entry, no note explaining who she is, no hint where she came from or if whoever left her plans on coming back.

Mr. and Mrs Collins kept the child for a few days, hoping whoever had left her would see the error of their ways and return, but when no such visit occurred, they contacted local authorities and requested she be collected by Social Services until a foster family can be found.

If you or anyone you know is missing a baby girl, approximately one and a bit years old, blonde hair, blue eyes with a birth-mark similar to a sunburst on her left thigh, then please, ring the number below or call the police.

For now, the baby girl is having one last night in Prebbletown before facing an

Social Services.

Unwanted.

Unknown future.

My knees turned to water as images of Della being sold, same as me, to a fate worse than me crashed through my mind.

She'd end up being the girls with ponytails forcibly taken into the house by Mr. Mclary to do special tasks. She'd become broken and rageful and full of vicious hate at a world that'd failed her.

At a boy who had failed her.

My heart traded hate for something else.

Something that tasted like obligation, commitment, and a tiny thread of affection but most of all, like sour seething possession.

Della Mclary had become mine the moment she ended up in my backpack.

I was the only one who could hurt her.

Not that man holding her. Not Social Services. Not Mclary or false parents or men who might buy her for special tasks.

Only me.

I spun in place, the cutlery clanking loudly in my backpack.

"Hey, what are you doing in my shop? Where are your parents, buddy?" an elderly shopkeeper waddled from behind his desk, but he was too late.

I bolted from his store as the little bell jangled my departure.

I ran down the street.

I sprinted all the way to the pretty blue and white house where something of mine waited for me.

Chapter Eight

REN

2000

SCENARIOS RAN IN my head as I careened to a stop outside the house where Della Mclary waited for me to fix what I'd broken.

Midmorning meant people inside would be awake. Bright sunlight meant I wouldn't go unnoticed.

I could wait until darkness and steal her back, but then I ran the risk of stumbling into the wrong bedroom and being caught. I could wait until Social Services arrived tomorrow and grab her, but then I ran the risk of being grabbed myself.

Or—and this was really my only option—I could march up to the front door, knock, and demand Della be given back to me.

I looked over my shoulder at the forest in the distance, seeing my dream of living alone vanishing bit by bit.

I wasn't afraid of darkness or predators or being completely vulnerable with no one to rely on but myself. But I was afraid of taking Della to such a place.

She was useless.

She was a *baby*.

I already knew she didn't fare well in the wild thanks to the previous few weeks we'd survived. She'd inched closer toward death every day.

Only because you weren't prepared for her.

Only because you didn't take what you needed.

It wasn't because I didn't know how to live off the land, and it wasn't because I couldn't provide for us.

She'd been a surprise.

And this time...I had shelter, tools, and equipment that meant we'd flourish not perish.

She wouldn't be a death sentence anymore, merely a complication

I willingly chose.

I stepped back from the house.

Wait, did I willingly choose this, or was I doing it out of fear? Was living with me better or worse than living with another? Just because I'd been sold and the girls sharing the barn with me cried themselves to sleep every night, didn't mean that would happen to Della.

Perhaps the best thing for her *would* be to wait for a foster family to take her, love her, house her in a pretty little home and feed her with supermarket purchased food instead of being carried for miles by a boy then bedding down in a tent with a belly full of hunted rabbit.

After all, wasn't that what I tried to do by leaving her with a family who already had a baby? Why didn't they want her? They already had one. What was the difference in raising two?

Mclary had sixteen and managed.

The sun beat down on my head, making my back sweat against my pilfered gear. I had to make a decision. I had to leave town before I was noticed—before the owner of the camping store saw his merchandise walking down the streets unpaid for; before the supermarket manager noticed his broken window.

But…Della.

My eyes shot back to the house.

The front door swung open, revealing a woman with a lemon dress and a blue dish cloth in her hands. Her brown hair hung down her back while pink spots decorated her cheeks from chores.

I froze.

We stared at each other.

We stared some more.

Slowly, she lowered the dish towel and stepped off her porch then down the pebbled path to the front gate.

My knees jiggled to sprint. My thighs bunched to flee.

She smiled, cocked her head, and said, "Hello."

I swallowed.

I hadn't spoken in days. I'd almost forgotten how. Before I could be polite, she added, "I saw you in the window. Are you okay? Are you lost?" Her gaze landed on my backpack, questions scrolling over her face. "What's your name?"

Her questions were landmines, and I didn't want to get blown up.

Looping my fingers under the straps of my bag, I raised my chin, narrowed my gaze, and said coldly, "You have something of mine."

"Excuse me?"

"I made a mistake."

"What mistake?"

"I left something behind."

She frowned. "Left what—" Realization widened her eyes. "Wait, are you talking about—"

"Della Mclary." I nodded sternly. "She's mine. I want her back."

I noticed my stupid error too late.

I'd given her true name.

I'd revealed her family—the name connecting her to everything I was running from. Once again, I looked over my shoulder at the forest with its waving leafy arms and the message on the wind to hurry, hurry, hurry.

"Give her to me." I wiped my mouth with the back of my hand. "Now."

Her gaze slid over me from head to toe. "But...but you're a kid. What do you mean, she's yours?"

My heart sped up. I hadn't thought this through. How could I tell a stranger the truth of how Della and I ended up as a we?

The reality...I couldn't.

So, I told the first lie of many.

I boldly looked into a stranger's face and spun the beginnings of a tale that would last the rest of our lives.

"She's my sister. And I want her back."

* * * * *

It took what I assumed was fifteen minutes or thereabouts.

I couldn't tell the time, but the sun's shadow didn't move from the beginning where I stood on the street and demanded a baby, to the ending when I bolted from the house with her in my arms.

The woman was home alone with two of her own children, harried and split in all directions, so I was yet another mess to her already messy morning.

A boy about half my age drew on the walls with her pink lipstick—only for her to scream at him to stop. Another boy, a little older than Della, tossed his mug of milk from his booster seat, spraying the kitchen and his mother with white.

Two little devils, undeserving of love and protection and a life littered with possibilities.

They didn't know how lucky they were.

They didn't know how evil the outside world could be.

And then, there was Della.

Forgotten and alone on the very same rug where I'd placed her, her little shoulders sank almost to her tiny hips. She was a puddle of despair, and it tore me up inside.

Her hair was cleaner than I'd last seen but not sparkling like the two boys causing mayhem. Her cheeks were a little fuller, but her colour wasn't perky, just blue.

Blue eyes, blue heart, blue aching sadness.

Left behind and unwanted, she sat sadly, silently, staring at the rug with no toys in front of her, no cat to cuddle, no fish to coo at, no love or friendship or company.

And I'd done that to her.

My feet glued to the kitchen floor as an axe cracked through my ribcage. I wasn't much older than the boy running circles around his mother, yet in that moment, I felt like a man.

A man who'd made a terrible, heart-clenching mistake. A man who'd left behind a baby but had returned for a friend.

The woman said something, but I didn't hear her. All I could hear was the eternal emptiness, the sucking vacuum, the crippling need to fix all the pain I'd caused little Della.

My backpack crashed to the floor, clanking and clunking, uncared for as I took my first step toward a future that would mean a life of struggle, hardship, unpredictability, uncertainty, and an unbelievable consequences.

She looked up as my newly booted feet stomped onto the rug.

For a moment, she stared at me blankly. Her mouth pressed together, her blue eyes distrusting, wary, and hurt.

But then a change happened in her.

A change that stole the sun and radiated from her every golden strand and poured from every infant pore.

Something physical slammed into my chest.

Something unmentionable and powerful and so damn pure, I'd never felt anything like it before.

I thought I'd wanted to be on my own.

And I did.

But I wanted to be on my own.

With her.

And then, she cried.

Her arms swept up, her lips spread wide, her joy manifested into tears and gurgles and a crawl so fast and lurching, she looked like a drunken crab desperate to reach the ocean.

I ducked on my haunches and waited for her to scramble into my arms.

And when she did, I knew I would never let her down again. I would die for her. I would live for her. I would kill for her.

In my ten measly years on this unforgiving, cruel, terrible earth, right there I found home, and no matter where we ended up, I'd always be home because I would never let her go again.

"I'm sorry, Della Mclary." I hugged her tight, squishing her face into my chest, pressing a kiss to her strawberry smelling hair.

That would be the last time she'd ever smelled fake. The next time she'd have a bath, she'd smell like streams and grass and silver-scaled fish.

As much as I didn't want to upset her by moving too swiftly, I also knew we couldn't stay here. Behind me, the woman was on the phone, muttering to someone, whispering about me and Della, telling them to come quick and stop whatever I was about to do.

Because she knew what I was about to do.

Della knew too, and the biggest grin split her tiny lips, revealing equally tiny teeth that I'd only just noticed. At the supermarket, I'd grabbed a toothbrush and two tubes of paste. She'd have to share mine. She'd have to share everything of mine.

Yet there were some things she couldn't share.

I stood upright, and she squalled in fear, wrapping fierce arms around my legs.

Ducking down, I patted her head. "It's okay. I'm not leaving you. I won't do that again. You have my word."

As if she understood, her fear vanished, smothered by indignation and the glow of a pissed-off female. It was a look I'd seen multiple times on her mother as she'd swatted me with anything close by. It was surreal to have the same stare given in two completely different circumstances.

I chuckled.

I'd never chuckled before.

The mother hated me.

The daughter liked me.

I was stealing her for everything the Mclarys had stolen from me.

I would keep her, mould her, train her, turn her into the exact opposite of what they would have made her become, and I would change her name because she no longer belonged to them.

She belonged to me.

Yet something was missing…

I studied her, inspecting the brown trousers and grey long sleeve she'd been dressed in. I frowned at the micro-sized sneakers on her feet. She looked like a tomboy and was happy about it.

But still, something was missing.

Her hands.

They were empty.

No blue satin.

No ribbon.

Ripping her from the carpet with my fingers under her arms, I plonked her on my hip and turned to face the woman. "Her ribbon.

Where is it?"

Her two boys continued to reap anarchy as she slowly put down the phone.

"What ribbon?"

Della squirmed in my arms. I squeezed her tight in warning. "The blue ugly thing she loves."

The woman glanced over my shoulder toward the trash can in the corner.

My teeth clenched. "You threw it away?" Marching toward the can, I manhandled Della so I could hold her with one arm, ripped up the lid with the other, then dropped it before ploughing my hand straight through eggshells and bacon rind until I found the slipperiness of her disgusting ribbon. The moment I pulled it free with new stains and old, Della snatched it.

I wanted to snatch it right back. It needed a wash, but for now, I had other problems to take care of.

Turning back to the woman, we stared some more until she finally admitted, "I called the police. You can't take her."

I stepped toward her. "I'm leaving."

"Just because I let you into my home doesn't mean I'll let you take anything out of it." She slithered from my path, putting the bench in our way. "You can't take her. You can't just steal a person like you stole our food."

Ignoring her tirade on my theft, I said calmly, "I *can* take her, and I am." Placing Della by the sink, I tapped her nose. "Don't fall off. It will hurt."

She planted her hands—complete with threaded ribbon through her fingers—on the granite and pressed her little sneakered feet against the cabinets below. Trusting her not to be stupid, I wrenched my heavy backpack from the floor.

She would no longer be able to travel on my back.

The extra complication should've layered me with doubt, misgivings, and hate.

Not anymore.

Now, I only looked for solutions.

Glancing around the welcoming space, I fell upon a laundry rack drying a mismatch of baby clothes and sheets.

Giving the woman a sharp look, I strode toward the rack and ripped off a few t-shirts, shorts, and jumpers all in blues, blacks, and browns for little boys.

They would fit Della. They'd be too big right now, but she'd grow. We both would.

At the last second, I stole a sheet then stuffed the baby clothes into my backpack, wrapped the sheet around my neck and back and copied what I'd seen Mrs Mclary do when she'd carried Della out to the fields to see her husband.

A sort of pouch on my chest to support Della's butt with her legs on either side of my waist and arms poking out the sides. She would be a nuisance. I wouldn't be able to travel far with her weight and our supplies.

But for now, my time had run out, and we were leaving.

Della gurgled something happy as I marched toward her and ducked a little to put her legs in the wrapped sheet first. Once in position, I slipped her into the hammock on my belly and tested the knots around my waist and neck.

Claustrophobia drenched my blood being so burdened, but my mouth watered for the forest.

Sirens sounded on the breeze, far enough away not to be urgent but close enough to warn they were coming. And quickly.

Storming past the woman, I stopped and stared. "You didn't want her. I changed my mind, and I do."

Her mouth opened and closed as I unlocked the back door.

"You're a kid. Where are you going to go?"

"Home." I shrugged. "We're going home."

"And parents? Do you have someone to take care of you?"

Heat filled my limbs, a fiery sort of scorn that put her beneath me. "*I'll* take care of her."

The woman shook her head. "But you? Who will take care of *you?*"

The door swung wide as a gust of sweet-smelling air swirled in, leaves dancing over the welcome mat, tree branches bristling with speed.

I was being called just as surely as the sirens were running me out of town.

As the police wail grew louder, I stepped from her house and smiled. "I don't need anyone to take care of me. I have her. She has me. Family takes care of each other."

Not waiting for a reply, I half-ran, half-stumbled over her lawn, unbalanced with Della's weight.

I didn't look back as I raced through suburbia, chased the wind, and then vanished into the forest.

We were just figments of her imagination.

Ghosts she thought she saw.

Children she thought she'd met but would never remember.

Chapter Nine

REN

2000

THAT FIRST NIGHT, I travelled as far and as long as I could.

Della didn't grumble or squirm, no matter how many times I stumbled over tree roots that I couldn't see with her on my chest or ducked under low-lying branches.

Running on sealed roads was a lot easier than running through untamed wilderness, but no matter the strain on my back from carrying two different weights, and no matter the gradual aches and pains in my body the more miles I put behind us, I was happier than I'd been since...well, since I could remember.

And it didn't make sense.

Because I had nowhere to go, no guarantee of survival, and a baby reliant on me for every tiny thing.

I ought to feel terrified and trapped, not the exact opposite.

The same river we'd followed before welcomed us back, and I fell into step with the gurgle and ripple, occasionally tripping over slippery bracken but not wanting to travel too far from its banks.

I followed it for hours, silent and serious, delving deeper and deeper into the forest.

Digging my hand into my new cargo trouser pockets, I pulled out the last thing I'd grabbed on the way out from the camping store.

A compass.

I knew enough from farming that the sun was my biggest ally and greatest foe. The only letters Mr. Mclary thought to teach me were N, S, E, W for the four corners of the world where rain lived one day and drought lived the next.

Back at the farmhouse tacked to his wall in the kitchen, hung a large map with weird squiggly lines over hills and valleys. He'd caught me looking at it one day, and instead of cuffing me around the head and kicking me from the kitchen, he'd clasped my shoulder with dirty fingers and gloated. "That's mine, boy. Every boundary and treeline from here until as far north as Dead Goat Creek is all mine."

I'd done my best to study how to read such a magical piece of paper that showed every piece of property he owned, but the scale didn't make sense and the scratchings of words and numbers hadn't been taught to someone like me.

When I'd failed to respond in whatever way he expected me to, he'd twisted my ear, dragged me past his wife feeding Della in her booster chair, then threw me out, not caring I tumbled down the stairs to the dusty ground below. "The house isn't for the likes of you, boy. Boys stay in the barn." He slammed the door, making it rattle on its well-abused hinges.

I blinked aside old memories and focused on the compass. The needle pointed Northwest.

I didn't know what existed in that direction but it was the opposite of Southeast where Mclary's farm was.

Stopping in the middle of the forest with darkness descending rapidly and roosting birds all around us, I shoved the compass back into my pocket. "I'm tired. We'll sleep here."

Della's head raised from resting against my chest, her blue eyes bright and intelligent. Her little legs kicked and her hands raised, complete with filthy ribbon wafting in the air, as if to help me lift her out of the sheet sling.

"Wait." Stiffness already cramped my muscles now that I'd given my body permission to quit moving. It was always that way after a long day of labour. Keep pushing, keep moving, and the pain couldn't find you.

Stop…and it leapt on you like a herd of cattle.

I winced as I arched my back and let the backpack slip to the ground.

Hissing under my breath, I massaged the back of my neck where the sheet knot had dug into me for long hours. Fumbling with the tight bow, I gave up and bent myself enough to unhook it over my head.

Della slipped backward without the support.

I scowled. "Hold onto me. If you don't, you'll fall."

Her lips pursed as if trying to understand but didn't do what I asked.

"Ugh." Wrapping my tired arm around her, I held her tight as I undid the knot at my waist and the sheet tumbled down my front. Bending, I placed her on top of it, finally ridding my body of the weight it'd been carrying for so long.

It was sheer heaven.

All I wanted to do was leap into the river and fall asleep under the stars, but I had responsibilities now. And I had to do them before all my energy deserted me.

I was used to working on dregs. I was strong and stubborn and been taught by the land that to achieve anything you had to work and work hard.

This was no different.

For the next hour, I set aside the things we'd need from my backpack, fumbled around as I figured out how to erect the tent for the first time, and spread out the one sleeping bag inside it.

Once shelter was finished, I grabbed Della, stripped her of the boy clothes she'd been dressed in, stripped myself until we were both naked as furless animals, and carried her into the river. I couldn't let her go as the current was too swift, but I managed to at least rinse off the sweat from a long day.

Once we were semi-clean, I pinched her ribbon and used sand from the bottom to scrub it the best I could. She pouted the entire time I handled it as if not trusting me with her prized possession.

By the time we'd dried off, dressed in clean clothes, and eaten dinner of tuna fish on squashed, stolen bread rolls, my eyelids drooped and Della curled into a ball on the sheet by the small fire I'd made.

I curled up beside her.

The tent went unused that night.

* * * * *

We stayed there for three nights, getting used to the equipment I'd stolen, sunbaking in the dappling light through the leaves, eating squished bananas and apples, and growing fat on melted chocolate bars and deliciously salted pretzels.

I'd never eaten so well or had time off just to do nothing.

I didn't care we went through our rations crazy fast.

I didn't care we should probably keep moving.

This was every birthday that I'd never had, and I wanted it to last forever.

Della seemed to go through a growth spurt just like the lambs at Mclary's. One night, the baby sheep were all legs and skinny, the next they were fat and bouncy.

Della did the same thing.

The colour returned to her cheeks with regular food, and the sun browned the rest of her thanks to us barely wearing any clothes.

We learned to share the sleeping bag, clean our teeth with one brush, and scrub our clothes with the single bar of soap.

So many chores just to stay healthy and alive, but everything was so much more rewarding than fighting for scraps after a never-ending day raking, baling, feeding, milking, tending, mending…an eternal list of tasks.

In the evenings, we listened side by side to night crawlers and creatures and stayed dry and warm as a rain shower found us on the second night. The splatter of droplets on the tent lulled us to sleep instead of keeping us awake and shivering under a tree.

Life had never been so good.

And on the third night, when my mind was busy with plans of finding a new paradise, Della wriggled upright in the sleeping bag, pointed at my nose, and said, "Boy."

Chapter Ten

DELLA

Present Day

OKAY, I MADE *my decision, Professor Baxter.*

I'm going to do the assignment. I'm going write a non-fiction tale and make it read as fiction. However, I can't take all the credit as it already reads fake without any embellishment from me.

I suppose I should start this tale with the requisite address that's always used at the beginning of a story.

I don't know what sort of grades my biography will earn from you, and I'm still marginally terrified of the consequences of what he'll do for breaking my promises, but I'm actually excited to relive the past. To smile at the happy times. To flinch at the hard. To cry at the sad.

There are so many moments to sift through that it's like cracking open a jewellery box after decades of dust, pulling out gemstones and diamonds, and struggling to choose what to wear.

That was what he did to me, you see? He made my entire life a jewellery box of special, sad, hard, happy, incredible moments that I want to wear each and every day.

He always said the truth was ours, no one else's.

Well, now it's yours, so here it goes...

* * * * *

Once upon a time, there was a boy and a baby.

This boy didn't say much, he scowled often, worked too hard, cared too deeply, and nursed a deep distrust of people and society that nothing and no one could soothe. He had scars on his skinny body that clenched my heart the more stories he told. He had wisdom in his eyes that came from suffering, not age. And he had mannerisms born from a man who already knew his fate rather than a boy just beginning.

This boy and the baby were never meant to be together.

They were from different blood, different people, yet because of what the baby's father and mother had done, they were technically family in a strange, unexplainable way.

They say a child's earliest memories occur when they're as young as three years old, but those memories aren't there forever. There's a phenomenon called child amnesia that starts to delete those memories when they reach seven or so and continues to erase as you grow into adulthood. Only recollections of great importance are retained while the rest becomes a life-blur with no clarity.

I don't know about you, but I know that to be true.

When I was younger, I remembered more. I know I did. But now I'm eighteen, I struggle to recall exact days unless something happened so crisp and clear it's burned into my psyche.

I suppose you're thinking how then can I tell my life story starting as early as a baby? I don't know what happened, and my memory isn't a reliable witness.

Well...I can tell you because of him.

I can tell you every day from the day I came into this world because that very same night—or it might've been the night before—my father cut off his finger. I can retell every night we ran and every night we swam. I can tell you every moment until right now while I sit in my room typing this paper.

I know I'm not following the fiction-writing rules by breaking the fourth wall and talking to you as if you here beside me, but it helps this way. It helps trick me into thinking once I tell you the truth, it will be forgotten the same way I've forgotten so many precious things. It helps pretending I'm not writing this down, so there is no permanent scar on the secrets I promised to keep.

So with child amnesia and adulthood slowly stealing my past, how can I sit here confidently and tell you my tale?

I'll tell you again.

It's because of my favourite thing of all.

The thing I'd beg for, the thing I'd do anything he asked for, the cherished time of day that no one could steal.

A story.

A bedtime story meant to lull a frightened babe to sleep but turned into something so precious and coveted, I'd get goosebumps whenever he agreed.

You see, he was my only form of TV, book, radio, internet, or cartoon.

Without him, I would know nothing; I wouldn't have grown through the adventures he gave me. I'd still be a child born to monsters.

But I'm getting ahead of myself. Before I share his bedtime stories, I first need to introduce him.

The Boy.

That was my first word, you know.

He said it was because as a baby I would've heard my parents calling him Boy. They never used his name—probably never knew it. And because I was their little monster, unchanged yet by what he would make me become, I called him what they called him.

Boy.

A thing not a someone.

A possession.

I don't remember, but apparently the first night I called him that, he'd left me in a hurry. He'd stalked the forest on his own until his famous temper cooled, and he returned to me in the tent he'd stolen and the sleeping bag we shared.

I hadn't been sleeping, waiting for him to return with tears in my eyes and my ribbon wrapped around my fingers so tight they'd turned blue to match the satin.

He'd sat cross-legged in front of me, glowered with his endless dark eyes, and thudded his chest with his fist. "Ren," he'd told me. "Ren, not Boy."

It didn't occur to me until much later why he didn't have a last name. That night, he wouldn't let me sleep until I'd wrapped my infant tongue around those three little letters.

Apparently, once I'd mastered it, I never shut up.

I said it all the time, to the point he'd slap his hand over my mouth to stop me.

Even without his bedtime stories filling in the blanks and painting pictures I've forgotten, I can honestly say Ren is my favourite word.

I love every history attached to it.

I love every pain lashed to it.

I love the boy it belongs to.

I don't know if Ren looked the same when he was ten as he did when I started to remember him, but I can say his hair never changed from its tangled mess of sable and sun. Dark brown in winter and copper bronze in summer, his hair touched his shoulders one year then cut short the year after. But the tangled mess was always the same, shoved out of his coal-coloured eyes with nine fingers not ten, his nose slightly crooked from being broken, his cheekbones so sharp they were cruel.

Even as a boy, he was beautiful.

Too beautiful to carry the depth of suspicion and guardedness he never fully shed.

Too beautiful to be responsible for the wake of misdeeds left in his path.

Too beautiful to be normal.

Chapter Eleven

REN

2001

FOR FIVE MONTHS, we lived in that tent.

We walked to new campsites when we wanted a change or if I felt we'd overstayed. We never settled too close to civilization, and I always ensured we had enough supplies to last two weeks completely self-sufficient.

Della grew every day, to the point where she was too heavy to carry along with my backpack for long distances, and had to trot awkwardly beside me for short lengths.

The longer we chose trees to house us and stayed alive by hunting and foraging, the less fit for society I became.

I adored the open air, freedom, and ability to do whatever I wanted whenever I pleased.

I loved jumping in the river naked. I loved napping under a bush with the sun kissing my skin. I loved being quiet and not having to fight to survive.

Life away from people was the easiest path I'd ever chosen, and I wouldn't give that up.

For anyone.

But that was before winter hit.

For five months, the weather stayed consistently warm before gradually growing colder and colder. Our tent no longer kept the icy chill from our bones, and the sleeping bag wasn't warm enough to exist without other forms of weather protection.

My shorts and sunglasses were traded for jacket and beanie, and I ensured Della wore all her clothes, including a layer of mine, tied in places and pinned in others, to ensure she stayed as snug as possible.

One night, as ice started forming on the grass before we'd even crawled into the tent to sleep, I faced a decision I'd been putting off since my last hunt in a local town and a raid of their lacklustre supermarket.

I regularly visited towns to supplement our diet of meat and fish with things my body craved—sugar, salt, and carbohydrates. I had no qualms about stealing and did my best to break in as subtly as I could and only take things that would go unnoticed, so police would remain none the wiser.

We were a couple of days' walk from the last town and too far north according to the chilly air and the way Della shivered even hunched close to the fire.

Winter was fast approaching, and if I didn't change our circumstances, we wouldn't make it.

So I put aside my reservations of people and houses and began the long journey to the next congregation of matching homes and cloned society, doing my best to go south as much as possible to outrun the frosts determined to freeze us.

* * * * *

We found a township on the second day, and for a week, we hid in someone's garden shed where the rickety wooden walls and faded newspaper taped to the only window held the wintery blast at bay.

Our diet consisted of pre-packaged sandwiches and over-processed meats—thanks to a forage to a local store—and we chased the awful taste away with orange juice and soda.

Every hour spent in town, sneaking in shadows and staying hidden, drained me. I hated being surrounded by people. I hated watching my back and suspecting everyone.

I missed the simplicity of nature and the basic rules of win or lose.

Trees couldn't lie to you.

Bushes couldn't hurt you.

Humans were complicated creatures, and smiles were full of poison.

I didn't let Della come with me on any of my explorations, not because I worried she would prefer to trade our wilderness life for a family who didn't want her but because I feared she'd be stolen from me.

She was cute and smart and far too brave for her own good.

She'd make anyone an excellent daughter or special task giver like the girls Mr. Mclary invited into the house.

She had to be protected at all costs and kept hidden from everyone.

On my third scout for food, I ran past a bookstore with local newspapers displayed in the window. The black and white pictures stood out from squashed lines of unreadable text. Ever since seeing

Della on TV, I'd studied the images of children on magazines and stories in newspapers, searching to see if the Mclarys were still searching for us.

I didn't know what I'd do if they were hunting for my one and only friend.

Over the past few months, Della and I had fallen into a habit we were both content with. She learned so fast—intently watching me do chores around the camp, until one day, she'd try to copy me as if she'd been doing it her entire life.

Collecting firewood—or more like fire sticks—she'd scatter them around instead of pile for an easy blaze. She'd fist the slippery soap and smear it on clothing without rinsing—mainly because she didn't fully grasp what she was doing and also because she was banned from going near the river unless I was with her.

She even tried to steal my knife one night after watching me sharpen the end of a stick to grill a fish over an open flame.

I'd drawn the line at that.

I liked her with ten fingers. She didn't need to copy me in everything and end up with nine.

Out of the two of us, Della talked constantly while I said hardly anything at all. She'd point at things all around us: sparrow, rock, plate, mug, water…waiting for me to name it before storing away the sound to be used later.

It hinted at yet another future complication in our life.
Education.

She was a sponge, and I only had a limited amount of knowledge for her to soak up. I could teach her how to live on nothing and not only stay alive in the forest but flourish, but I couldn't teach her the things that people learned in schools.

I couldn't show her what a real family was or how parents made you feel. I didn't know those things myself, so how could I pass on such details?

Throughout the months when she grew from baby to toddler, I grew harder and older but also softened thanks to her sweet innocence toward everything. She wasn't dragged down by hate or grudges. She didn't judge anything before she'd tasted or tested it for herself.

She taught me not to be so narrow-minded, granting a fleeting chance to be a child again when such a novelty had been stolen from me.

I often found my heart swelling with warmth for my young, tiny friend and cracking in pain knowing this life we shared couldn't go on forever.

She would eventually need more.

She would eventually outgrow me.

But for now, at least, I'd upheld my side of the bargain and kept her safe.

As we hung out, hidden and miserable from the weather in some stranger's shed, I played the naming game with Della and answered her eager finger as it flew from mower to sickle to drill to axe to rake. Rusted tools rested unused and forgotten, draped with cobwebs and dusted in beetle carcasses.

She repeated the words quietly like an eager parrot, her eyes aglow with learning.

We couldn't light a fire, so we spent our evenings huddled together in the sleeping bag, looking for ways to entertain ourselves.

This place reminded me of the farmhouse, and for the first time in a while, the fear I'd constantly lived with returned, and I locked my attention on the only entrance as Della grew drowsy and crawled into the tent I'd haphazardly put up amongst discarded household junk.

She grumbled some made-up language of baby tongue and badly phrased things I'd taught her until I obeyed her commands to come to bed and grudgingly agreed to tell another bedtime story.

Somehow, she'd latched onto the stupid retellings and stared at me with dreamy eyes and utmost contentedness on her pretty face whenever I succumbed to her demands.

The first one I'd told out of desperation when she didn't settle after something large and most likely hungry sniffed around our tent a few months ago.

I'd squatted on my haunches with two knives in two fists, ready to slice any creature that found its way into our sanctuary.

But whatever it was gave up after a while.

It didn't mean Della calmed down, though.

She'd whimpered and sniffled, clutching that damn blue ribbon as if it was her only friend in the world.

That had hurt.

I'd grown used to her seeking comfort from me—of her crawling unwanted into my lap at the worst times or snuggling too close in the night.

I wasn't used to contact from another and definitely not used to contact given so readily and often, but to have her deny what I'd grown accustomed to that night, especially after I'd been prepared to slaughter whatever it was to keep her safe reached into my chest and twisted.

Perhaps it was the feral mind-set I'd been in, already bathing in blood of whatever beast I would kill, or maybe it was the way my fists turned white from clutching the knives—whatever it was, her tears cascaded faster once the threat of danger had passed than they had when it'd been snuffling and pawing at our door.

So I'd done the only thing that popped into my head.

I'd placed aside my blades, pulled her into my lap, and told her a horror story to take her mind off the one we'd just avoided.

I told her about the farmhouse and what it was like at dinner-time. I let the fact that some animals wanted to eat us colour my retelling of starvation and helplessness in the barn. I'd killed rats and eaten them raw before. I'd torn pumpkin from another starving kid's hands. I sympathized with the hungry—human and beast—and did my best to make Della see that it wasn't personal. It was just nature's balance, and it was our responsibility to stay at the top of the food chain because we'd encounter so many that wanted to steal that position for itself.

She'd fallen asleep clutching me as tight as she clutched her ribbon, and although it shouldn't, although I was stupid to be jealous of a tatty piece of blue, I slept with a smile on my face and my friend in my arms all night.

Tonight, though, she wasn't satisfied with just a normal story.

She wanted the truth, and I was too young to think of sheltering her from it.

A few weeks ago, she'd noticed what I tried to forget every time I washed. She'd gawked at the marked piece of flesh on the side of my hipbone.

We always bathed together out of necessity and safety. I didn't care about being naked around her because all the other kids in the barn dressed and undressed to the point it was normal seeing each other bare. But there were some things I wished she didn't see.

Scars I'd endured.

Punishments I'd deserved.

Mistakes I'd made.

And that.

The one thing I could never run from.

The brand Mclary used to mark all his property from his horses to his cows to his bought and paid for children.

Della poked my hip with a tenacious finger, her face scrunched up as a stuttering please fell from her lips.

Before, I had more willpower about denying her things; I could easily say no and mean it. These days, I struggled *especially* when she threw back the same temper I used on her to get my way. She'd learned too well, and I sighed heavily, knowing tonight I would tell her just to stop her bugging me about it.

Keeping one eye on the shed door barricaded with an old generator and fallen apart rocking chair, I snuggled deeper into the shared warmth of the sleeping bag and began:

"A farmer with lots of cattle has only one way of making sure he can keep track of his inventory. With other farmer's stock sometimes wandering into his fields and rustlers stealing his herd at night, it makes sense to have a way to identify what belongs to him and what doesn't."

Della blinked, wriggling closer to pull up my jumper and push down the top of my trousers.

Instead of shoving her away like I usually did, I let her run her fingertip over the raised scar tissue on my hip.

While she studied the embossed *Mc97* in a neat oval stamped into my flesh, I said, "Your parents have a brand. I don't know entirely what the numbers are for, but I guess the *Mc* is for their name. Every single animal on Mclary's farm has the same brand. Their sheep, their cows…me."

Della let my clothing go to stick her thumb in her mouth and stroke her ribbon.

"Don't do that." I yanked her thumb from her tiny lips. "You'll have crooked teeth."

She was a pretty kid, but that didn't mean she'd stay that way if she had teeth as bad as her father's thanks to chewing tobacco and bad hygiene.

Slipping straight back into the story, I pushed her tiny hand into her lap. "The brand is found on all animals on their rump to the left, unless it's a sheep and then it's on their ear because of the wool."

Della nodded as if she understood every word.

I shrugged. "There isn't much more to say. It was the first morning I arrived at the farm. I remember being pulled from bed after crying myself to sleep and being stripped with four other boys in the crushing stall where the stock are wormed and drenched. There, he had two other farmhands hold us down, and branded us with his stamp of ownership."

I did my best not to let my mind skip down that painful memory lane, keeping my voice level and emotions out of it. "The smell was almost identical to that when he did the calves a few hours later. The burn hurt more than my finger."

Della's face fell as her little hand found mine. She squeezed with all the wisdom of a girl twice her age, full of sympathy I didn't want.

Snatching my hand from hers, I shrugged again. "It was fine. I was just like his herd to him. I got why he had to mark us. He said it was so no one could steal us because we belonged to him and he'd come claim us, but I knew it was so he could find us if we ever tried to run."

I rubbed the scar, wishing I could erase it permanently. "It doesn't matter, though. He'll never find me, brand or no brand."

Della smiled a vicious little smile.

I returned it, laughing under my breath. "He'll never find you, either. Will he, Della Mclary?"

I was a possession, and she was his daughter.

Both valuable in our own ways.

Both vanished, never to be his again.

Chapter Twelve

REN

2001

THAT FIRST WINTER was spent scurrying from one garden shed to another.

Sometimes, we'd find an abandoned house for a night or so, until the neighbours reported two stray children lurking around. Sometimes, we'd crawl through broken basement windows and boldly sleep beneath families who had no clue we lived beneath their feet.

For the coldest months of the year, I relied more on the humans I despised to feed and shelter us than the wilderness that lived in my blood.

As more time went on and the days grew shorter and the nights longer, I craved the scent of new leaves and sun-warmed bark.

I struggled to keep my discomfort and itch to be out of the city from Della, even though she suffered her own annoyance at being trapped in a place where the wrong people cared and the right people didn't open their eyes to two kids living rough right amongst them.

I liked that I could walk down Main Street with Della's hand in mine and only get a courtesy glance by those who believed all children had a family to return to and a warm meal to fill them.

I held my head high with arrogance when people stared at me and saw a kid not yet a man—a boy who would surely die if left alone and never know how wrong they were.

I liked being underestimated and enjoyed having a secret they didn't know.

What I didn't like were the men whose eyes lit up when their gaze slid from me to Della waddling beside me on her tiny toddler legs. What I didn't like were the cold glowers from women who judged me and pitied Della and believed I was the very same vermin that Mrs

Mclary thought me to be.

The hairs on the back of my neck never relaxed from living close to people I didn't trust. My hackles stayed up, so when I crawled into bed at night, I was more exhausted than I'd ever been in the forest.

It all came to a head one night when lights flipped on and the door leading to family rooms above cracked open, and for the first time, we were at risk of being caught.

We had to make a choice.

Squatting in people's basements was just asking to be separated and sent to Social Services. So what if snow banks had gathered outside or snowflakes stuck together so heavy even the leafless trees bowed under their weight?

We couldn't keep doing this.

I couldn't keep doing this.

Luckily, I'd been smart and kept our gear tightly packed. Instead of setting up the tent and sleeping bag, I'd hidden us behind some cardboard boxes and used the musty smelling blankets found in the corner.

All we had to do was yank on our boots and bolt.

Whoever's house this belonged to clomped down the steps as I ripped the backpack off the floor and shoved it through the broken window. Scooping Della from the nest of blankets, I pushed her after it into the snow, then hauled myself up and out.

Instantly, the wind chewed through our jackets and gnawed on our naked hands and face. Della cried out as snow flurries danced in front of our eyes, obscuring our path, turning everything foggy and white.

A voice shouted behind us but we ignored it.

Working fast, I shrugged into the backpack and tore Della from the snow.

I wouldn't be able to run far but at least we hadn't been caught.

At least, we were still together.

＊ ＊ ＊ ＊ ＊

That night was one of the worst and best of our lives.

Worst because we trekked through one of the coldest storms that winter. Worst because by the time I stumbled onto our new temporary home, Della shivered and shook with a cold, and not just the temperature.

And the best because, although we'd had to flee our last hidey-hole, the one we found to replace it was so much better.

I hadn't realised how close to the outskirts of town we'd been and only a few miles down the road, an old farmhouse rose from snow and ice, beckoning us closer.

I avoided the house even though no lights burned and no chimney puffed smoke, and carried Della into the barn farther down the gravel driveway.

The smells of hay and manure had faded, hinting that this farm hadn't been worked in a while. It made me sad to think of untended fields and forgotten livestock but grateful that the chances of being caught were slim.

Sneaking deeper into the barn, I deposited a sneezing Della onto the straw-covered floor and set about making an igloo out of brittle hay bales. It didn't take long, and the moment I spread out the sleeping bag and placed a piece of tarp over the entrance to our hay cave, the temperature warmed and the howling wind muffled thanks to the thermal properties of the dried grass.

The next morning, Della was achy and shivery, and I knew we weren't going to be leaving anytime soon. The supplies and first-aid kits I'd stolen didn't have soft Kleenexes for her runny nose or stuff to stop her coughing.

The storm had passed, so I left her tucked up tight and explored the farm in search of food and better medicine.

I didn't want to approach the house, but I had no choice if I wanted to ensure Della fought the virus as fast as possible. With a knife in my hand, just in case another man like Mclary lived here, I crept up the veranda and peered into dirty windows.

Nothing.

No furniture, no people, no knickknacks or signs of inhabitants.

It was abandoned.

And ours for the taking.

The front door was unlocked as I strolled in with shoulders braced and knife at the ready. I explored the three bed, one bath wooden farmhouse, doing my best not to see similarities with the Mclary's home but struggling.

The lounge was big with a large stain on the hardwood floor, hinting a coffee table had once lived there and someone had spilled something. The bathroom was peeling yellow with soap scum embedded in the claw foot bath. And the bedrooms were sad with their drooping curtains and mouse skeletons.

But it was dry, mostly weather tight, and had one queen mattress leaning against a wall in the third bedroom.

My thoughts turned to Della and getting her comfortable enough to fight the fever and stuffiness in a cosy bed in a proper house.

There was nothing to steal, and my raid on the pantry yielded an ancient can of peaches, an out-of-date box of Cocoa Puffs, and a sachet of noodles with a chicken on the front.

Mostly worthless but I could source other food.

I couldn't find other shelter.

Not in the middle of winter.

Leaving the meagre food on the wooden countertop, I didn't take them back to Della.

Instead, I brought Della to them.

I took the risk of claiming the unwanted house, bunkering down for the season, and doing what I needed to make her better.

I became a homeowner…however temporarily…for her.

Chapter Thirteen

DELLA

Present Day

WOULD YOU BELIEVE the boy and the baby lived three winters in that house?

No one noticed that the farm went from untended to small patches of veggies growing here and there. No one knocked when the chimney was swept and a fire roared, keeping its two illegal inhabitants warm inside. And no one cared when the empty house slowly filled with furniture, salvaged from rubbish piles and back alleys.

You see, humans are funny creatures.

The farmhouse was far enough away from society not to be an immediate concern but close enough that it was a stain on their otherwise perfect existence.

It was forgotten, ignored. . .just like us.

When Ren would return from scoping out tourists or seeking weaknesses on shop security, he'd smile a secret smile and feed me town rumours about the Old Polcart Farm.

You have to understand, Ren was a ghost when he wanted to be. The older he got, the more invisible he became. To a child, I found it utterly fascinating how adults just flat out ignored him.

He'd see things, hear things, steal things without ever being noticed.

And a lot of what he'd steal was information.

He'd spill unsugarcoated tales about how the son had shot the father before running off with two hundred chickens, geese, and turkeys. The father had rotted on the living room floor of Polcart Farm for weeks until the sweet smell of decay reached the town's noses.

The local police department removed every shred of furniture, paid a professional cleaner to delete the evidence of death, then put it on the market in foreclosure.

Only problem was, no one wanted to live in a house where a corpse had lain for weeks.

But us?

Ren and me?

Well, we were funny creatures, too, and we didn't mind the lingering smell or the dark ominous stain in the living room. We covered it with an old grain sack from the barn and placed a crate on top for our coffee table. A few bales of hay covered in blankets was our couch for that first year, while a few pallets beneath the mattress raised us from the floor, and Ren even made a lampshade for the single bulb from bent fence wire and old sheep wool.

He even found out how to turn on the electricity thanks to weathered solar panels and a broken wind turbine meant to operate water lines for stock. Thanks to his problem solving and determination, he learned how to redirect the naturally generated power to service the house.

In the summer, we never ran out of electricity. In the winter, we struggled but we didn't need much. Ren taught me to be grateful and to enjoy each little thing no matter how awkward or fleeting.

To me, Ren was magical.

He might not have been able to read and write, but he was the smartest person I knew.

Now, I know you're probably thinking, "Well that isn't high praise, seeing as you were a baby whose only friend and family was a farmyard boy" but I'm here to clarify that, even now as I'm about to cross the threshold into adulthood, I still maintain Ren is the smartest person I've ever had the privilege of knowing.

Everything he touched became useful or full of purpose. My days were spent waddling after him (his words, not mine) watching him endlessly, soaking up everything he did, squeezing my ribbon in awe as he wielded axes, planted seedlings, fixed hinges, and constructed fences.

He never stopped working.

He scolded me, berated me, and rolled his eyes at my need to follow, watch, and mimic, but I could tell he liked having me around. He called me a chatterbox, but that was only because he didn't say much, so I talked for both of us. But when he did speak, wow…my ears would throb for more.

His voice, even as a boy, was husky and low and almost dangerous with things he didn't say.

He had a fury inside him that scared me sometimes.

A single-mindedness that glittered in his eyes with dark ferocity.

I often wondered if he'd ever outgrow his savage tenacity, but he never did.

His relentless need to work and tend and toil was a product of his past that was so ingrained even I couldn't fix him.

I wish I could paint a better picture of how much I looked up to him.

How much I worshipped him.

How much I loved him even then.

He was everything *to me, and his intelligence didn't come from book smarts but life itself. He listened to its lessons, he excelled at its exams, and he gave me every piece of himself by sharing all that he knew.*

He didn't shelter me from things like other parents might have done.

He made me kill my first rabbit when I was two. He made me sew up his arm when he cut himself when I was three.

He treated me as capable and brave and bright, and that's what I became because I never wanted to let him down because he would never let me down.

Simple as that.

Chapter Fourteen

REN

2004

WINTER CAME AND went.

The sun warmed frozen land and sprouted new growth.

The trees rustled in the warm breeze and beckoned me back into their depths, yet whenever I looked at Della, I didn't have the heart to grab our already packed backpack and leave.

She'd sprouted over the past few winters from curious baby to independent person, and I didn't want to deprive her of the chance to grow up in a place where a roof meant stability and walls offered solid sanctuary.

She had free roam of the house—safe from drowning in rivers or being mauled by wildlife. I didn't need to watch her endlessly and enjoyed the freedom that gave me in return.

The veggies I planted in spring gave us enough variety to our diet that with regular hunting and a little patience, we didn't need to risk ourselves by heading into towns and stealing.

Realistically, it would be stupid to leave.

For over three years, no one had bothered us. No one noticed or cared.

We were as invisible as we'd ever been, and I was determined to give Della a home...if only for a little while.

Our first summer at Polcart Farm, I'd focused on better equipping the house for the next winter. I'd repaired the leaks in the roof; I'd salvaged old drapes from a local dumpster and hauled things back that made a house a home.

A table and chairs.

China plates instead of plastic.

A few discarded toys with tangled-haired dolls and missing-piece puzzles.

And, one night, when I cut through the back streets of the town after sizing up how easy a local corner store would be to break into if we ever needed emergency supplies, I stumbled upon a TV.

The screen was cracked in one corner and the picture jiggled in the other, but when I first plugged it in, using sun and wind as our power source, and Della snuggled up next to me with joy spread all over her face, it was worth the back-breaking trek back home.

When winter hit the second time, we were more prepared with rations and warmth, but boredom was a problem neither of us knew how to face. I'd already spent the time creating flowing water thanks to redirecting well water with the aid of a stock pump. I'd plugged holes in walls and cleaned dirty appliances.

The house was well cared for and didn't require much more.

I wished it did—if only to keep my brain from going stir crazy.

I wanted the chores of staying alive, of travelling, of learning a new place and circumstance. And if I couldn't have that, I wanted farm animals to tend, upkeep to dally with, and general busyness that kept my mind from the past and firmly focused in the now.

As fields were slowly deleted with more and more snow, Della became naughty, exploring areas she shouldn't, disobeying me, arguing with me, generally being a brat I wished I could toss out onto the frozen deck and teach her a lesson.

When she screamed in frustration because my lack of teaching failed her communication skills, I screamed right back. When she threw a corn on the cob at my face when I ordered her to finish every bite, I made her eat every kernel off the floor.

There were many things I permitted and indulged because she was my everything. My best friend, my little sister, my penance in real life. But if she ever wasted food…that was when my temper wouldn't be mollified.

We might have it easy now. She might have had it easy in the farmhouse while I wasted away in the barn. But there was no separation between her and me now. We were stuck with each other, and soon, when the seasons thawed and Della was bigger, stronger, faster, we would leave this place.

This wasn't a permanent solution.

And she had to know the value of things.

A TV wasn't something to be protected because it was worthless away from electrical sockets and satellites. A mattress wasn't special because it could never come with us when we ran.

But food? That was infinitely precious.

Our tent? That was priceless.

She might be young, but she was never too young to learn those lessons, and I gave her no leeway when it came to learning them.

She could cry all she wanted. She could hate me for days. We could fight until I stalked from the house and slept in the barn, but she would never win with me.

I was older.

I was in charge.

But I was also aware I was everything she had and wouldn't jeopardize that for *anything*.

Once the fire in her baby blue eyes simmered and the rage in my blood cooled, we'd awkwardly sit on our hay bale couches and slowly trade stiffness for solidarity.

She'd inch closer toward me with her ribbon trailing after her, and I'd open my arm for her to wedge tightly against me.

And there we'd sit, our apologies silent but completely heart-felt and true. I knew it was wrong to find such comfort in the sharp relief and drowning affection that came after an ugly fight, but I'd never had the aftermath before.

I'd had the shouting, the screaming, the striking, the kicking, but I'd never been held afterward or kissed on the cheek by an adoring little girl.

Just like we could cause each other's grief, we had the power to raise the stars. When Della was happy, I was happy. Her smile was infectious. Her eagerness to learn an absolute gift when I was desperate to teach.

To teach the opposite of what I'd been taught.

But I was also keenly aware that what I had to teach was extremely limited.

One dark winter's night, Della flicked through the TV stations at warp speed. We didn't get many channels due to bad reception, but sometimes, the weather allowed a snippet of movies and cooking shows, and now, a kid's channel.

She squealed and bowled toward me where I sat on the couch carving a stick into a lynchpin to be used as a new hinge in the gate I'd repurposed to keep critters out of our veggie patch. My knife scraped and shavings littered the floor.

Quickly, I palmed the sharp blade so she wouldn't impale herself as she bounced into my lap. I laughed and looked up at the bright TV where fake puppets and badly drawn cartoons wriggled around like idiots.

"Ren, look!" She waggled her ribbon-clutching fist at the TV. "Toons!"

"Cartoons." I pushed her gently off my lap so she sat beside me on the couch. It wasn't that I didn't like being touched; I just became overwhelmed whenever she did. It'd gotten to the point where I was afraid that one day, I wouldn't be able to breathe unless she touched me all the time.

She was my one weakness, and I was determined to stay immune to her for her own protection.

The TV squawked some stupid song, parading out knives and forks and bowls and fruit, flashing letters on the screen and screaming the name along with it.

Della jiggled to the song, repeating household items.

I returned to my carving, keeping one eye on her and one eye on whittling.

Time ticked on, and we fell into a comfortable rhythm; that was until Della exploded from the couch and ran to skid to her butt in front of the TV. Her little eyes danced over the brightness, her fingers drawing in the air the letter on the screen.

"A is for apple. A is for ape. A is for a great big *albatross*. Can you say albatross?" The cartoon puppet blinked as if we were a bunch of morons who couldn't say A.

I rolled my eyes, then froze solid as Della yelled, "Albwatloss." Turning to face me, she pointed excitedly at the screen. "Ren! A. It's A for appwle." She stood and traced the letter on the screen, then twirled around with her blonde ringlets bouncing and her blue ribbon twirling.

My heart stopped with how perfect she was. How smart. How kind. How brave. I'd never look at the colour blue again without thinking of her. I'd never hold another ribbon again without wanting to hold her.

Up until that moment, I'd kept a hardness inside me.

I'd treated her dearly, but I'd kept a piece of myself tucked away. But there, as she repeated the alphabet and started to excel me in every way, she nicked the fortress around my stupid heart, and I had no choice but to give it to her.

She was my Della, my ribbon, and I couldn't stop myself as I placed the knife back into its holder in my boot, crawled across the floor, and sat beside her.

She beamed and pointed at the letter S on the screen.

The one of four I knew thanks to Mclary and his compass lesson.

I repeated along with her and the stupid cartoons. "S is for snake. S is for snow. S is for a bright yellow *sun*!"

We lost track of time as we soaked up the knowledge gifted by ugly puppets. I didn't cringe at the childish songs. I didn't roll my eyes at the baby talk. I put aside my ego and imprinted every letter into my brain.

I did it for me but mainly I did it for her.

Because eventually, I would need to be more than the illiterate boy who'd carried her away in a backpack. I'd have to be a role model, counsellor, and friend. And I was determined to be a friend who could read and write.

As the night wore on and my eyes scratched and head throbbed, I glanced at Della, who'd turned drowsy and soft.

Normally, she was the one who instigated affection.

But that night, I was the one who dragged her droopy, sleepy body close and kissed her cheek. I nuzzled her sweet-smelling hair and murmured, "You're the one teaching me now, Della Ribbon. Please don't ever stop."

Chapter Fifteen

DELLA

♡

Present Day

OOPS, I TOTALLY forgot to finish that last chapter.

It was a little off tangent I'm afraid, but at least, hopefully, it will help show you how special Ren was and how unique a man he became.

Now, before I lose my train of thought to such bittersweet memories again, I want to tell you three events that are so real to me.

I don't know if I recall them from my own experiences or if Ren was such a master storyteller, he manufactured the history to suit his own ends. Either way, they're some of my favourite, and this tale wouldn't be complete without them.

I suppose I'll begin with the very first one made at Polcart Farm where we lived for over three years. There were so many memories created there: antidotes Ren would tell me, jokes he'd spin from things I'd done, and lessons he'd remind me of from prior mistakes.

I knew Ren was happier in the forest away from society, but he put that need aside for me. He watched cartoons with me as we learned to read side by side. We cowered together when a hurricane threatened to tear the roof off, and celebrated when we cooked our first meal entirely self-sufficient.

So many things.

Too many things to mention in this assignment, so I'll only mention the three that totally stand out.

The first was when he finally called me something other than Della Mclary. I didn't have the words at the time to tell him how much I hated that name. That whenever he called me that, it was if he reminded himself that we weren't meant to be together and did his best to create distance.

But that night, when he finally called me Della Ribbon as we watched educational cartoons, he never once called me Mclary again. From then on, every time he called me Ribbon, my insides turned gooey, and I'd do anything he said— even if I didn't want to.

Amazing what love can make someone do, right?

In my toddler brain, I associated him calling me Ribbon with his admittance of loving me. He'd accepted me as his own. He no longer needed to remind himself that I wasn't born to be his.

The power of that nickname could stop my tears, cease my anger, soothe my fears, and to this day, he doesn't know how much it still affects me. How the gooeyness inside has morphed from child infatuation to adult intoxication. How gradually, over the years, my love has turned less pure, and I've kept that secret for years.

Anyway, moving on…

The second thing that meant the world to me was once we'd mastered the alphabet together, Ren left me at home one mid-spring afternoon and returned with his arms full of books.

Picture books.

Baby books.

Bibles.

Encyclopaedias.

And literary classics.

I'd spent the night curled around the musty delicious pages, stroking their pretty covers, gawking at the words I desperately wanted to know.

When he'd finally dragged me to bed, I'd clutched at a picture book about a lost little puppy trying to find his parents. Instead of a bedtime story made from truth and fact, I wanted Ren to read fiction to me.

I wanted the luxury of listening to his husky, throaty tone. Even before his voice dropped, I'd been addicted to it, and now that he sounded like a man and not a boy, I was obsessed.

Sometimes, and don't judge me for this, but sometimes, I would do something naughty just to have him yell at me. I know it was wrong, but when Ren yelled, he drenched it with passion.

He vibrated with the need to scold, and it thrilled and terrified me.

He'd bring that same passion to the tales he told while snuggled in bed. He'd regale how he'd helped birth baby lambs and how he'd once seen a foal being born. He was fluid and crisp and told a mean story that kept my attention for hours.

That wasn't the case when he cracked open the picture book and bit his bottom lip in panic. There was no husky voice. No story about a puppy finding his parents. Instead, there was a stutter and a pause and an attempt at sewing together the letters we'd learned into words we hadn't.

It'd been the first time I felt sorry for him. The first time my juvenile heart had the ability to think of him as hurting or helpless and not the invincible, magical Ren I adored.

It made me love him even more.

That night was the first night of many when we stayed up late and slowly learned how to read and not just parrot what the kid programs tried to teach.

And as we learned to read, we took turns stumbling over simple sentences *until one of us would smooth it out and repeat it again and again until it was as effortless as speaking.*

And finally, the third memory is a strange one. You'll think me mad for even mentioning it, but something about that night firmly fixed Ren as not just my father-figure and brother, but also my idol.

An invincible, immortal idol who I never ever wanted to be away from.

That first winter at Polcart Farm was bad. The icy freeze taught us that we might be able to live in the wild in summer but when the snow hit...unless we were able to grow fur and hibernate, we would die. That became even more apparent when I'd fallen sick with a simple cold the night we'd found the farm.

Due to the icy temperatures and my young age, it took weeks for me to come right, even with medicine Ren stole from the local pharmacy. He couldn't read the label so who knew if what he poured down my throat was the right dosage or the even correct drug, but he did his best, and I survived.

For days, he fed me stolen soup and cuddled me close so I could benefit from his body heat. Whenever I woke, he was ready with warm milk, medicine, and a story or two about life on a farm with sixteen children.

He didn't leave my side for longer than a few minutes, and when my fever finally broke and my chest no longer rattled with cough, he bundled me up in every clothing I had then carried me outside wrapped in the sleeping bag.

Snow covered everything, muffling sound and sight and senses. We could've been in a world completely uninhabited. We could've been the only two creatures alive, and I wouldn't have been happier because the boy who was my everything held me close and showed me the farm we'd borrowed.

He murmured how in spring he'd plant vegetables so we'd never have to risk getting caught stealing. He'd pointed out snow-softened bric-a-brac and said he'd transform rubbish into furniture and make us a home for as long as it took for me to grow strong enough so I was never sick again.

Like I said, that first winter was hard.

But the third winter at Polcart Farm was worse.

The fire never seemed to warm us, the mattress stayed damp from chill, the thrill of TV and learning—when we had electricity from meagre sunlight—was muted under the very real need to stay alive and not freeze to death.

One night, a blizzard blew so hard a window in one of the bedrooms shattered, spilling snow flurries all over the floor. I followed Ren upstairs, needing to be near him but trying to stay out of his way so he could fix it.

"I have to go to the barn to get wood and nails." He brushed past me, stomping in the boots that'd become too small for him and shrugging into his jacket.

"I'm coming too." I clattered down the stairs behind him, yanking on his beanie and wrapping his scarf around my tiny neck.

He grabbed me by the scruff as I went to dart past him into the swirling snow. "You're staying here, Della Ribbon."

"Nuh-uh. I'll help."

"You'll help by staying out of the cold."

"It's cold in here." I pouted. "No different."

"Della." He growled. "Don't argue. You know you won't win." The familiar angry light in his eyes pleased me. I enjoyed annoying him because it made him focus more on me than the many tasks and chores around the house.

Nodding once, I backed over the threshold and watched him vanish outside amongst eerie silver shadows and crunchy snow. My plan was to wait until he was too far away to throw me back into the house, then chase after him.

That was before a loud bellow echoed across the pristine white. My heart kicked and my little legs charged down the porch steps after him, tripping in the snow. "Ren!"

I fell splat on my face, scrambling out of freezing flakes to come face to face with a black and white monster. "Ren! Ren! Ren!"

The beast bellowed and nudged me with a shiny black nose.

"Ren!"

My scream tore through the night, bringing my saviour leaping over snow drifts and skidding to a stop in front of me. He shoved me behind his back, facing the monster on his own.

He'd be hurt.

Eaten.

Killed.

"No!" I scrabbled at his back, desperate to help but his dark laughter filled my ears.

His hand came up to land on the shiny nose as his voice lowered to a soothing murmur. "Hey, girl. Where did you come from?"

I couldn't stop shivering as Ren twisted to look at me over his shoulder. "It's a cow, silly Ribbon. It won't eat you."

A pink tongue lashed from its mouth, licking around Ren's palm.

"You hungry, girl?" Ren stood, reaching down to help me up while keeping his other hand extended to the cow. She didn't run off as I climbed to my feet and brushed away cold slush.

The black and white animal shivered same as me, her ears quaking in the blizzard.

"She doesn't have a brand," Ren said, searching her flanks with experienced fingertips.

My eyes fell to his hip where, beneath his many clothes, his own brand was a permanent link to my father.

Pointing at the house, he commanded, "Go inside before you freeze, Della. I'll be back soon." Not waiting to see if I'd obey, he nudged the cow with a soft hand and guided her through the storm to the barn.

Now, I know what you're thinking...I really should have obeyed and gone inside, but this was Ren—my idol. I couldn't let him out of my sight, not for a *moment.*

So I followed with soaking socked feet that quickly became numb as I trailed in the snow, falling over again and again until I entered the dark hay-smelling barn and watched Ren guide the skinny cow into a stall.

There she bellowed and shoved her face into past seasons bales, shaking off snowflakes and accepting Polcart Farm as her new home.

Ren closed the gate over her stall and jolted when he spotted me.

"Goddamn you, Della Ribbon, what did I say?"

I didn't care what he'd said because I was completely obsessed by the glossy-eyed black and white beast.

He scooped me from the shadows, tore off my ice-sodden socks, and kicked off his own boots to replace them. Once he'd jabbed my feet into his warm boots, he stood barefoot and glowered with the same black look he always gave me, and the look I always loved because it meant he cared for me fiercely even when I drove him mad.

"Do you want to die?" He waited for me to reply, and when I didn't, he huffed. "If you get sick again, I'm leaving you behind when it's time to leave. Don't say I didn't warn you."

I threw my arms around his neck and nuzzled him close.

He froze, permitting my hug but not returning it, his worry and anger keeping him stiff and unyielding.

But I didn't mind.

I never minded when he didn't return my affection because he loved me in other ways.

I was his, and he was mine, and through that bond, I felt things he never said aloud.

I mean, just the way he looked at me?

Wow, I wish I could draw instead of just write so you could see what I saw and feel what I felt.

The way Ren looked at you made you suffer beneath his expectation and glow beneath his praise. He touched you deeper than any hand could reach. He affected you harder than any spoken word ever could.

He cared with his entire soul and committed with entire being.

I might have been raised differently from so many kids. I might have missed out on things and probably lived through events that others would baulk at, but I was luckier than anyone because I had Ren.

I was never lacking for love.

I never felt unwanted or hurt or scared.

He was my entire universe, and he treated me like I was his in return.

Walking with bare ice-block feet toward a hay bale, he placed me down and commanded me not to move. I kicked my little legs and plucked prickly grass from beneath me and nodded with solemn promise to obey.

Muttering something under his breath, he left for a second but returned from another stall with a dinged up metal bucket. With a stern look, he entered the stall with the hay-chowing dairy cow and squatted down beside her.

"She's bruised from too much milk." His voice carried through the hushed barn. "She's wandered from her herd and hasn't been milked in days." His strong hands latched around her teats, and I hopped from my ordered spot to tiptoe closer.

Like I said, everything Ren did was magic.

Watching him milk a cow with strong sure pulls made my mouth fall open in awe. Hearing the slosh of fresh milk land in the pail made my tummy gurgle and thirst spring from nowhere. And bearing witness to that cow as Ren took away her uncomfortably full udder and left her empty and eating made me realise that Ren didn't just care for me with the fierce passion I recognised in his eyes.

Nope, he cared that way for every creature.

Every mammal, reptile, and beast.

He would bend over backward to protect, tend, and soothe.

But never humans.

Never people.

I was the one exception.

And that made me special...just like him.

Chapter Sixteen

REN

2005

I WANTED TO do something special for her.

I had no clue when her birthday was, or mine for that matter, but they fell sometime around summer. So far, we'd had a couple of weeks of perfect sunny weather, and I figured it was close enough to celebrate.

This time of year was the hardest for me.

Winter kept me grateful for the farmhouse we'd borrowed for the past few years, but summer made me *hate* it.

All I wanted to do was burn it to the ground and run away from its ashes.

The packed and ready-to-leave backpack mocked me for not having the guts to grab it and return to the life that lived and breathed in my soul.

If it was just me, I would have vanished the moment the nights turned shorter and the days became warmer, but it wasn't just me.

It hadn't just been me for four long years.

And although I felt trapped some days, although life would've been easier and simpler alone, I would never trade the little girl who trailed beside me as I guided her into town.

She blinked up at me, her blue ribbon tied in her hair today, keeping blonde curls from her eyes. Summer always made the blonde turn almost white, and her blue sparkling eyes seemed to grow in wisdom every day.

"Why we here, Ren?" she asked in her soft, childish voice. She glanced fugitively at the shoppers around us, some with supermarket bags and others with gift shop junk in their arms.

I hadn't taken her into town in almost a year.

We had no need to, and I preferred to stay as far away from these people as possible to avoid any disruption to our invisible world on their fringes.

But today was special.

And I wanted to *do* something special. If that meant something out of the ordinary and something we'd never done before, then I was prepared to do whatever it took to make this day stand out.

"It's our birthday." I squeezed her small hand in mine. "I think we deserve to eat something that we don't have to skin and scrub first, don't you?"

She slammed to a stop. "It's my birthday?"

Pulling her into the shadows of a bookstore—the same store where I'd stolen the books we'd studied and learned from—I nodded. "Yours and mine. Or at least...we'll pretend it is." I shrugged. "I don't know the exact dates but figured we should at least celebrate something."

A giant smile cracked her face. "We'll have cake like that TV show did when it was their birthday?"

"If you want."

"With candles and balloons?"

"Probably not."

Her face fell, then instantly brightened. "I don't care. This is the best day *ever.*" She danced on the spot, her hair and ribbon bouncing. "Oh, wait..." She studied me, deadly serious. "How old are we?"

I fought the urge to tug her golden curls and pulled her back into walking. "Not sure but I was ten when I ran, and you were about one or something, according to the news reporter in the town I left you."

She scowled a perfect imitation of my scowl. "Yeah, don't do that again."

I chuckled. "I promised I never would, didn't I?"

"Huh. You might if I annoy you too much."

I chuckled harder. "You annoy me all the time, and I'm still here."

Her eyes widened with worry. "I do? I annoy you?"

"Yep." I spread my arms to incorporate a huge amount. "This much. Constantly."

Her lower lip wobbled. "But...you won't leave me...right?"

The barb of her sadness caught me right in the heart, and my joke no longer seemed funny.

Crouching to her level, I pressed my palm against her rosy cheek. "Della Ribbon, don't you get upset over something silly like that. You know I'm joking. I'd never—"

She shot off, squealing in laughter. "I win. You lied. I don't annoy you. You loooove me!" She spun in the street before I grabbed her bicep and dragged her sharply back onto the pavement.

Wild little heathen.

I ought to have been stricter on the rules, but somehow, I'd failed at creating uncrossable boundaries. I did my best to yell and bluster, but for some reason, my temper seemed to amuse and soothe her rather than scare the living daylights out of her.

Keeping her glued to my side with tight fingers, I muttered, "When you act like this, I second-guess that promise."

She blew raspberries at me, and for a second, two images slid over one another.

An image of a little girl with blonde hair and distraught eyes limping painfully from Mclary's farmhouse and crying herself to sleep, and then Della with her vibrant soul and fearless confidence.

Mclary lived to tear children apart.

I lived purely to ensure Della became everything she ever wanted.

It wasn't until a couple of years ago that I'd figured out what Mclary was actually doing with his 'special tasks.' That form of education came from a tatty, well-read magazine I'd salvaged from a dumpster.

I'd never seen so much nakedness in one place before and never naked adults.

And the things they were doing?

It made me sick. At least...the first couple of times I sneaked a peek. The first time I'd cracked open the glossy sun-bleached pages, I'd slammed them shut again, disgusted.

The second time, I'd been curious and looked at every graphic image cover to cover.

The third...well, by the third time, my body felt different—tighter, harder, strange.

After that, the sickness turned into more of a sick fascination, and my body burned with heat and need, swelling uncomfortably between my legs.

Over the past few years, my voice had dropped, I had hair growing in places that embarrassed me, and now an undercurrent of hunger and searching for something I didn't understand lived deep in my belly.

It didn't happen overnight.

The familiarity of a boy's body slowly faded into foreign lands of a man.

Even though it took a few years to fully understand what the heavy ache in my groin was or why my heart beat faster when a pretty girl came on TV, it didn't mean I accepted it.

I *hated* not having control of my own body.

I hated having dreams of skin and touching and things that the magazine portrayed in explicit detail.

When I was younger, I'd woken to wet dreams with pleasure coursing through my body and not understood what happened. These days, I understood enough thanks to memories of helping Mclary breed his stock and watching bulls with cows and stallions with mares.

I'd come of age to reproduce, and I got the principal of why I hardened.

But I despised it.

I despised the complications it brought with it. I hated the random rage filling my blood and loathed the nasty demands, desperate for ways of releasing the pleasure lurking inside.

I didn't like lying frozen beside Della as she slept unaware. I didn't like having to hide my rapidly growing needs or lie to the one girl I promised never to lie to about why she wasn't allowed on my lap at certain times.

The body I once knew was now hijacked with desires I didn't.

For a couple of weeks, I'd watched Della to see if she felt different like me, but when I asked if parts of her were acting strange, she'd laughed and patted me on the head, saying if I was sick, she'd look after me.

But that was the thing…I wasn't sick. Unless, I was mentally sick because looking at that dirty magazine did things to my body that I kept hidden from Della at all costs.

I started bathing on my own because I couldn't control the hardness that sprang from nowhere. I started wearing underwear around her when before, we both didn't care—especially in summer if we went for a swim in the farm's pond or sun-baked on the porch.

That was another reason I wanted to do something different today.

I *felt* different, and it scared me. I didn't want to change because I knew my body. I knew its strengths and weaknesses. Now, I didn't trust it, and I was frustrated with the coursing newness and wants.

"Ren. Reeeeen. Ren!" Della planted hands on her narrow hips. She wore one of my sandstone coloured t-shirts as a dress with a piece of baling twine as a belt. She'd outgrown her clothes last year, and I'd yet to either make or steal new ones. "You're not listening."

"Sorry." Shaking my head free of the horrors of living in a sex-evolving body with no manual or anyone to ask if these urges were normal, I smiled at her tiny temper. "What? What am I not listening to?"

"Me. You're not listening to *me*." She stomped her foot.

I let her display of disrespect fly, finding it amusing rather than brattish. "And what were you saying?"

"Ugh." She blew a strand of hair from her eyes like an exasperated teenager—like me—and not like a five-year-old. "You didn't tell me. How old are we?"

Skipping back to our original topic as if my mind hadn't turned to less innocent subjects—like it did a lot these days—I said, "I'm going to say you're five, and I'm fifteen."

Thank God for the kid TV program; otherwise, I would still be a stupid farm boy unable to count his own age. Then again, who knew if my math was right. It probably wasn't and I'd just added or subtracted a year I shouldn't.

She wrinkled her nose. "Why can't I be fifteen, too?"

"Because you can't."

"That's not a reason."

"You haven't been alive for fifteen years."

"Neither have you."

"I'm closer than you are."

She studied me like someone studied livestock to purchase. "I don't think you look fifteen."

I returned her look of underwhelmed judgment. "And I don't think you look five."

"That's because I'm *not* five." She trotted off, heading toward one of the two diners in this sleepy town. "I'm fifteen, same as you."

If that was the case, she'd be going through the same crazy changes I was, and I'd have someone to share this minefield with.

But she wasn't.

She was still just a kid, and I was responsible for her happiness and well-being.

With her chin arched like a princess, she pranced right past the diner with its garish stickers of delicious looking food and loud jingling bell on the door.

I called, "Della Ribbon."

She spun instantly—like she always did when I called her that—her face happy, eyes glowing, body crackling with obedience and energy. "Yes, Ren Wild?"

I shook my head, chuckling—like I always did when she called me that. I didn't know where she'd come up with it.

For so long, I was used to her mimicking me and instantly recognising where she got certain mannerisms from and similarities in speech and tasks as it all stemmed from me.

But lately, she'd taken what she'd learned and adapted them to suit herself. She chose different words, spoke in different rhythms, and even attempted to do simple chores in her own way not mine.

Adding the word Wild to my first name had taken me by surprise.

I'd asked her why she called me that.

Her reply?

"Because you're wild like the bobcats we see lurking around our dairy cow sometimes. You're wild like the wind that blows in the trees. You're wild and don't have a last name so that will be your last name because it suits you and because you're wild."

Her child logic was simple and spot on and despite myself, my heart swelled every time she used it.

I was proud to be called Wild.

Proud that she recognised and understood me without having to spell out just how hard it was to live a domesticated life when I wanted to return to the untamed one we'd tasted for just a few short months.

"You went too far." I strode to the diner door and pushed it open, smiling as she gawked at the bell ringing our arrival. "This is the place."

She sidled close, tugging on my waistband for me to duck to her level. Whispering in my ear, she said, "But there are people in there. They'll see."

I stood and pushed her gently so she'd go ahead of me through the door and into the grease and sugar smelling diner. "I know. Don't worry. I have it under control."

I'd planned this for weeks. I'd ensured we both dressed smartly and didn't look like homeless ragamuffins who didn't eat or bathe. I'd dressed in a pair of shorts that were too short thanks to a growth spurt but still fit around my waist. My t-shirt was a little grubby with holes under the arms from scrubbing, but overall, it was presentable.

I'd even snuck out late one night while Della was asleep and broke into a house on the opposite side of town. I didn't stay long and didn't take anything apart from the cash in the wallet on the counter and coins from the handbag on the kitchen bench.

Thanks to a money section on the cartoon channel, I laboriously worked out I had forty-three dollars and twenty-seven cents to buy Della the best damn birthday lunch she'd ever had.

"Whoa." She slammed to a stop in the middle of the entrance, her blue eyes dancing over everything as fast as she could.

I knew how overwhelming this would be because it was just as overwhelming for me. We'd never been around this many people. Never been to a restaurant. Never had someone cook for us.

But thanks to television, we knew the principals of it, and as much as I wanted to stay off the grid and renounce my place in the human race and truly live up to the last name Della gave me, I couldn't.

For her.

One day, she would want to be normal.

She would want to have friends other than me.

A husband.

Children of her own.

She had to become used to people looking and talking and being cramped in a tiny space all eating together.

A woman in a purple and grey uniform with a stained apron spotted us lurking by the door. She waved with a pad and pencil, brown hair escaping her hairnet. "Grab a place anywhere you want, kids. I'll be right there." She returned to the people at the table before her, scribbling something down on her pad.

"Ren." Della tugged my hand, pressing her body against my leg. "I don't like it."

All around us bright lights flickered, plates clattered, people laughed and talked. The walls were painted the same purple as the waitresses' uniform, the booths wood and grey vinyl.

Not letting her fear override a new experience, I grabbed her hand and tugged her toward the closest booth by the door. I kept my own discomfort hidden, but I couldn't conceal the fact my hand trembled slightly in hers, matching her jumpy need to run.

"Get in." I pushed her onto the booth then sat beside her, gripping the table with my fingers. This was supposed to be fun.

It was terrifying.

Della scowled as if she was mad and hated me but cuddled close due to fear. "I don't like birthdays."

Sucking up my own issues with this outing, I kept my voice cool and commanding. "You're not a baby anymore. You have to deal with new things so you grow up."

My voice sounded hypocritical even to my ears.

My legs bunched and bounced beneath the table ready to bolt. My fists clenched to strike anyone who looked at Della wrong.

"I want to go home," she whined.

"And I want to go back to the forest," I snapped. "But we can't have everything we want."

Her eyes filled with liquid. "I want to go back to the forest, too."

"You don't remember it."

"Do too."

I rolled my eyes. "You were in diapers. Trust me. You don't remember it."

"Liar. I do. I do. I want to go now. I don't like it here." She scrambled at my arm, trying to raise it so she could climb into my lap.

I kept my elbow locked and remained unmoved by her terror of new things. "Della Ribbon, don't make me get angry."

She lowered her chin, her shoulders sagging even as her small body continued to quake with nerves.

"Now, kids. What can I getcha?" The waitress from before appeared, flipping her pad to a new page and looking at us expectantly.

I stiffened as her gaze slipped from my face to my chest then over to Della who'd turned into a tiny pouting mouse beside me.

I waited for her to recognise us.

For her to announce to the entire diner that we were the kids from Mclary's farm all those years ago.

But her eyes remained void of recognition, and no child snatchers appeared from the walls.

Della looked up with big blue distrusting eyes. Distrust that I'd put there from my own distrust. I'd failed her in that respect.

She shouldn't fear her own species, and I needed to fix that error on my part.

The waitress suddenly leaned on the table, planting her elbows in the middle and reaching for Della.

Della shrieked and practically crawled into the vinyl booth while I couldn't stop my natural instinct to protect.

My hand lashed out, locking around the woman's wrist, stopping her mid-touch of the only thing I loved, the only girl I ever needed, the only friend I ever wanted. *"Don't."* My voice smoked with ice. Possession snaked in my gut.

Della was mine, and I would kill anyone trying to hurt her.

The waitress froze, leaving her wrist in my iron-shackle grasp. "I wasn't gonna do anything. She looks sad poor poppet. Only gonna cheer her up."

I let her go, narrowing my eyes as she straightened and rubbed her wrist. She glanced over her shoulder to see if anyone else had witnessed the vicious teen grabbing her.

I glanced at the exit already planning how to run.

This was a bad, *bad* idea.

"Look, sweetie." The waitress waved kindly at Della. "I only wanted to touch your beautiful hair and tell you what a pretty little thing you are." She smiled.

Della bared her teeth like a feral kitten.

The woman carried on unfazed. "You know…I work at the school down the road on weekdays and never seen you guys there. Are you new in town?"

I crossed my arms. "Something like that."

"What school do you go to?"

"Mr. Sloshpants and friends," Della whispered. "It's the

program—"

I wrapped my arm around her tight shoulders, squeezing her in warning. "No school you will have heard of."

The woman pursed her lips. "Well, if you're new in town and don't have a school to go to, you should come to ours. We always have room for newbies."

Della perked up as the woman smiled bright as the sun. "We have finger-painting, playgroup, story time, maths and sciences and English—"

"Story time?" Della asked. "As good as the stories Ren tells?"

The waitress flicked me a look. "I dunno if they'll be as good as that, but they're pretty darn amazing." She winked. "You should come sometime. We'd love to have you. Show you around. You get a backpack full of crayons and colouring books and exercises. We even provide a uniform free of charge thanks to a grant from the government for small rural towns and our slipping education." She snapped her fingers. "Oh, and I almost forgot the best part!"

I didn't buy the sugary sweet delivery, but Della slurped it up like it was her new favourite food. "What?"

"You get homework and gold stars if you do well, and each class has their own pet. I believe there's a rabbit in one and a guinea pig or two and even a parrot. Pretty cool, huh?"

Della stopped shrinking into the booth, scooting to the end and beaming. "Whoa."

"I know." The waitress nodded solemnly. "It's awesome. Like I said, you should come along." Her eyes met mine. "You too, Ren. Brothers and sisters are all welcome."

Ignoring that she'd used my name thanks to Della giving it away, I opened the menu in front of me, unable to read most of the words but glancing at the pictures in record time. I wanted this woman gone. Now. "We'll have two burgers and anything else suitable for a birthday party."

"Oh, it's your birthday, sweetie?" She clapped her hands at Della. "How old are you turning?"

Della bounced on the vinyl. "It's me and Ren. We're fifteen."

The waitress laughed. "Wow, you look really good for fifteen. Bet when you're fifty you'll still look like an eighteen-year-old."

Della scowled. "I'm not fifty. I'm fifteen."

The woman laughed harder. "Okay, okay. Fifteen. Well, I better make sure the chef puts fifteen candles on your cake, huh?"

"Cake? There's cake?" Della's smile split her face. Her fear was gone. Her trepidation over new things vanished.

"Sweetie, there is *always* cake. Give me ten minutes and I'll have your bellies round as barrels."

I should thank this woman for making Della's first diner experience so easy on her.

I should smile at least for making *my* first diner experience more tolerable.

But all I could manage was a cool nod as she gave us one last grin and turned toward the kitchens with our order.

Chapter Seventeen

REN

2005

THE BIRTHDAY LUNCH cost me thirty-four dollars and ninety-one cents.

But it was worth a million, thanks to Della's happy squeals when the waitress brought out three iced-pink cupcakes all squished together with fifteen candles stabbed into them.

The cheery flames flickered all over Della's cute face as she stared, hypnotized.

Her sheer amazement made me forget we sat in public, and I grinned, loving her happiness.

It was the only time I dropped my guard. The entire meal, I'd watched, just like I did in the forest and at the farm, suspecting everything and everyone, making sure nothing could take me by surprise and hurt Della.

A little while ago, a family walked in with a girl about my age. She caught my eye and flipped her long black hair over her shoulder in a way that made my stomach clench. Not being around people meant I didn't have the worries of another version of my mother trying to sell me or another Mclary trying to buy me, but it also meant I didn't meet girls like her.

Like the dark-haired one who never took her gaze off me the entire time I sat steadfast beside Della.

She unnerved me—not because she stared and licked her lips full of invitation just like the dirty magazine showed, but because I didn't like my body's reaction to her.

I had no control over the hardening and tight discomfort in my shorts.

I hated that I had to push Della away with no explanation apart from a strict grunt not to come anywhere near my lap.

I missed simplicity when touching Della didn't make me feel dirty or wrong. When a hug was just a hug and not a moral struggle full of fear in case things happened outside of my control.

Glowering at the dark-haired girl, I did my best to ignore her. She made me feel as if I betrayed Della in some way, and nobody, under any circumstances, would make me break any promises I'd made to my blonde-haired best friend beside me.

I didn't know how long it took us to eat, but it had been longer than I wanted. Not through fault of the staff or food but because Della and I weren't used to being served. We flinched when our main course arrived. We jolted when Cokes and milkshakes appeared. And we froze in a mixture of disbelief and awe as the first mouthful delivered an explosion of different flavours instead of just one.

The waitress had been true to her word and went out of her way to make Della happy.

She brought placemats for her to colour in with bright rainbow crayons.

She laughed as Della tasted her first salty fry and promptly stuffed a fistful in her face.

And she kept her distance so I didn't feel trapped but remained attentive, never letting us run out of sauces or drinks.

This outing was for Della, but as I took my first bite of beef and cheese wrapped up in a buttery bun, I'd groaned with sheer pleasure.

Innocent pleasure.

Pleasure I was allowed to show and share with my tiny ribbon beside me.

And now, with bellies so full they hurt, Della crawled transfixed over the table to reach the glowing candles.

I grabbed her around the middle, holding her back from setting herself on fire.

The waitress beamed, waiting...for something.

When Della continued to gawk at the candles and I grew impatient with her squirming to get closer, the waitress said, "So have you made a wish? You need to make a wish, sweetie, and then blow out the candles."

Della scrunched up her face. "A wish? What's that?"

Even with the catalogue of words she asked me to give her on a daily basis and the TV, she still lacked so many. I hadn't thought to teach her what a wish was because to me, it was the constant urge to leave humans behind and hide in untouched wilderness.

And when I still belonged to Mclary, a wish was a desire for the long days, starving nights, and harsh punishments to stop.

A wish was hope, and hope killed you faster than anything. A wish was running away, and I didn't want Della to go anywhere.

The waitress gave me a strange look before answering. "A wish is asking for something you want so badly but don't know how you'll get it. It's a request for something you don't think will come true but believe in with all your heart anyway."

I gritted my teeth as Della nodded solemnly. "Oh." Her intelligent blue eyes met mine, studying me as if forming a wish full of complications and tough requests. "I wish for Ren to always be mine. To take me everywhere. And to give me more birthdays." Her white teeth flashed as she beamed at the waitress. "Do you make my wish come true now?"

"No, sweetie." The waitress giggled. "Now you blow out the candles, and it will come true by the power of pink icing and vanilla sponge!"

Della leaned closer and spat all over the cupcakes, blowing raspberries instead of air.

Not one stopped flickering with its mocking fire. I swallowed down my laughter as her joy deflated, and she looked at me forlorn. "Does that mean my wish won't come true, Ren?"

Ugh, this was what I didn't want.

Della lived in reality.

She knew the cost of hunting because she helped me kill what we ate. She knew the cost of shelter because she helped maintain the house we'd borrowed. But now she knew the cost of wishing for fantasies and the heartache when they didn't come true.

She didn't need a stupid wish to make her requests become real. I had no intention of ever leaving her again—I'd learned that lesson years ago. The next time we were apart, it would be because of her. She would leave me when she was ready. I would be the one heartbroken when she woke up one day and decided she needed more than what I could offer.

For now, though, she was still mine, and I wouldn't let her think for a moment she couldn't have everything she ever wanted.

Yanking her onto my lap—now that I was back in control of my thoughts and reactions—I dragged the cupcakes closer. "It only means the wish comes true faster and stronger." Giving her a smile, I said, "If we blow them out together, it will mean we're never apart. Want to do that?"

"Yes!" She bounced on my thighs. "Yes, please."

My chest ached that even in the middle of something as new as blowing out candles for the first time, she remembered her manners—the same manners I hadn't been raised with but learned were just as important as respect and discipline.

"Ready?" I puffed out my cheeks. "One, two, three…"

We blew out every candle.

We helped ourselves to our very first taste of sugar that didn't come from fruit and left the diner thirty-four dollars and ninety-one cents poorer.

Our crazy sugar high kept us chuckling and racing around the farm's fields, cannonballing in the pond, and playing with our dairy cow named Snowflake until the moon and stars appeared and we retreated into the house, exhausted.

* * * * *

Della watched me clean my teeth with a look in her eyes I hadn't seen before.

Scrubbing away the remnants of our overindulgence today, I spat mint into the sink and rinsed my mouth. She'd already cleaned hers thanks to the second brush I'd stolen her a few months ago.

Drying my hands on my shorts, I brushed past her to enter the corridor and head to our bedroom. She padded after me in my t-shirt without the baling twine belt—her version of pyjamas—still silent and staring at me with an intensity that made my skin crawl.

We shouldn't have had that nap on the couch before. She seemed just as wired now as she did when she'd stuffed a full-size cupcake in her tiny mouth.

"What?" I barked, climbing into bed and pulling the unzipped sleeping bag over me. She didn't crawl in beside me like usual. Instead, she stood by the foot of the mattress, crossed her twig-like arms, and announced, "I want to go to school."

I sat bolt upright, my heart racing. "School?"

She nodded, her button nose sniffing importantly. "Yes. I'm old now. I'm fifteen. I need to know what fifteen-year-olds know."

"I'm fifteen, and you know as much as I do."

"I want to know more than you do."

I fought the urge to crumple. I'd known this moment would come—I was thinking on it just a few hours ago at the diner—but to happen so fast?

Rubbing the sudden ache in my chest, I growled. "It's not safe. You know that."

"*You* keep me safe."

"I can't keep you safe in school."

"Why not?"

"Because I don't want to go, and even if I did, we'd be in different classes."

"Why?"

"Because we're different ages."

She stomped her foot. "We're the *same.*"

I rolled my eyes, dropping my hand as the fear of losing her was drowned out by the frustration of arguing with her.

Della had a mean temper—just like I did. We didn't often get into screaming matches, but when we did...I was grateful we didn't have neighbours because the police would've appeared on our doorstep.

"You're not going to school, Della. That's the end of it."

"No!" She raced from the bedroom, clattering down the wooden steps like a herd of sheep and not a barefoot five-year-old.

"Goddammit," I groaned under my breath. I didn't curse often because I hated the way Mclary had mastered the art of throwing words with such anger they had the power to make you flinch almost as much as a fist could.

I never wanted Della to be afraid of language or of me talking to her.

But when she acted like this...

Well...*fuck.*

Throwing off the sleeping bag, I charged after her in my boxers, racing down the stairs to find her cross-legged in front of the TV, flicking through the channels, desperately trying to find the educational kid's one.

She wouldn't find it.

The past few days' reception had been terrible, leaving us with hissing snow on most channels.

"Della," I warned. "Don't start a fight over something as stupid as going to school."

"It's not stupid! I want to go." She turned her back on me, crossing her arms. "I should've wished to go to school with the candles instead. Then I could go to school, and you couldn't stop me!"

Raking my fingers through my hair, I moved in front of her and ducked to her level. "You know why you can't go."

"No, I don't. We live in a house. We're normal! No one cares." Tears welled and spilled down her cheeks. "No one cared we were in town today. No one said anything."

I shook my head, hating that my stupid idea of doing something special had already backfired. "It was a mistake to go. I'm sorry if I made it seem like we can have that sort of life, but we can't." I reached out, my hand trembling a little like it always did when we fought.

Fighting with her stripped me of every reserve I had, draining me to the point of emotional and physical exhaustion because I hated denying her things, but at the same time, she needed boundaries.

She would have everything she needed, but she would never be spoiled.

She wrenched away, crawling out of reach. "No! I want school. I don't want you. I want colouring and stories and painting."

"Now you're just being hurtful." I sat on my ass with my knees bent and feet planted on the floor in front of me.

"You're being mean. You won't let me go to school!"

"It's for your own safety."

"No. It's because you're mean!"

"I can't deal with you when you're like this. You're acting like a child."

"I'm not a child. I'm fifteen!"

"How many times do I have to tell you? You are *not* fifteen. Goddammit, you are five years old, and it's my responsibility to keep you safe and I can only do that if you stop arguing and being a brat and *listen* to what I'm saying."

She glared at me across the lounge, her legs and arms tightly crossed, her body language shut off and hating me.

I didn't care.

She wanted to know the real reason she couldn't go to school?

Fine, I'd tell her.

Keeping my voice chilly and cruel, I said, "You can't go to school because of me, okay?"

Her forehead furrowed, eyes narrowed.

I continued, "You don't have any parents to take you or meet with the teachers or sign any forms. You don't have any money. You don't have anything that the other kids will have, and people will notice. They'll ask why your mum or dad don't drop you off. They'll pry into your home life. They'll grow suspicious of who I am. They'll—they'll take you away from me."

My anger faded as, once again, the heaviness of missing her even while she sat in front of me squashed my heart.

Della sniffed back tears and scooted closer toward me—still wary, still angry, but her face lost its pinched annoyance. "Why would they take me away? You're Ren."

I smiled sadly. "Because I'm not your father or brother. I'm not your family, and they'll figure that out. They'll know I stole you and put you with another family who won't love you like I do. You'll be trapped in a house in the middle of streets and people, and I'll never find you again because they'll chase after me for stealing you. They'll try to lock me up, and we'll never be together again."

I tried to stop there. I didn't want to layer her with guilt for asking for something she should have by right, but I couldn't stop myself from whispering, "Is that what you want, Della Ribbon? To never see me again?"

She burst into noisy tears, speed-crawling across the floor to barrel into my arms. She curled into a ball in my embrace as I rocked her and kissed the top of her head. Her little arms wrapped around me tight and strong, and we both shook at the thought of losing everything we knew and cared for.

"No! No. No. *No.*" Her tears wet the side of my neck as she burrowed her face into me, and even though I'd earned what I wanted and had Della obeying me and wanting what I wanted, I couldn't help the awful taste in my mouth for being so nasty.

For shattering her dreams.

For denying her a future.

I froze.

What have I done?

Just because I was terrified of what would happen didn't mean it wasn't what was best for Della. There was no denying she would be better off with a family with healthier food and warmer beds. I'd always known that, yet my selfishness had stopped me from giving her up.

Della's tears slowly dried as I stroked her blonde hair and battled a war deep inside me. This was the first thing she'd ever asked for. The first thing she was passionate about. And I'd twisted the truth to kill her dream before it'd even been fully realised.

My shoulders rolled in horror. "I'm sorry, Little Ribbon."

Her face appeared in front of mine, and I studied the beautiful blue eyes, button nose, rosy lips, pretty cheeks, and lovely little curls.

She was far too innocent, and because of that, I was far too protective.

If I didn't keep myself in check, I'd suffocate her.

"I'm sorry too, Ren." She wiped her tears with the back of her hand. "I don't want to go to school. I don't want to leave you."

Half-smiling, I held her close and stood. She weighed so much more than she had when I'd carried her in my backpack, but I still thought of her as a baby sometimes—completely helpless and tasty for anything to come along and eat.

But she wasn't.

She had claws even if they were short.

She had teeth even if they weren't sharp.

Carrying her up the stairs, I whispered, "I changed my mind. You can go."

Her entire body stiffened in my hold. "You mean it?"

No.

"Yes. I'll say I'm your brother and our parents are out of town. I'll lie and keep you safe."

She threw her arms around my neck. "Thank you, thank you, thank *you*!"

"You won't be able to go for long. Eventually, someone will ask questions, and then we'll have to leave."

"I'll go wherever you say."

I placed her on her feet in the corridor, needing her to hear how serious this was. "I don't mean leave school, Della. I mean we'll have to leave this place. This house. Once they know who we are, they won't stop. Do you understand?"

She backed away nervously. "But...I don't want to leave."

I shrugged. "We'd have to leave eventually. Someone will want to buy this place. We always knew this was temporary."

Fear filled her face then drained away as she straightened her spine. "Okay. I go to school, and we leave when you say."

I held out my hand. "Shake on it?"

She placed her small fingers in mine and squeezed with her tongue sticking between her lips in concentration. "Promise."

Letting her go, I padded toward the bedroom. "Let's go to bed. You and your temper have drained me."

She followed with yet another strange look in her eyes.

I groaned. "What now?"

"We don't have the same name."

I stopped, turning to face her. "Huh?"

She came as close as she could, grabbing my waistband above the brand embossed into my hip with urgency. "If you say you're my brother, we need the same name."

Goosebumps scattered over my arms at how smart she was; how effortlessly she saw the future and plotted potential problems at such a young age. "What do you suggest we do then?" I already knew what we would have to do, but I wanted to hear her theory first.

"Well..." She curled her nose, thinking hard. "You're Wild, and I'm Ribbon. One of us needs to change."

"Change?"

"Duh." She rolled her eyes, then her little lips widened in a brilliant smile, and she hugged my leg, her face going terribly close to the part of me I could no longer control. "I know!"

Tugging her away to put distance between us, I asked, "Know what?"

"You're my brother, so I need to be a Wild too. Can I? Can you share your last name with me?"

The amount of emotions this kid had put me through tonight was nothing compared to the crest of pride and love now.

"You want to share my name? The name you gave me?" I didn't know why that meant so much. Why I placed so much weight when really there was no weight at all. Why it felt so much more permanent and full of promises than a simple fix to an unfixable situation.

"Yes! I want to be Della Wild, and you're Ren Wild, and together, we're a Wild family."

I dropped to my knee and hugged her right there in the dingy corridor. "It would be a pleasure to share Wild with you and an honour to be yours."

It wasn't until Della snored softly beside me and dawn knocked on the horizon that I realised I'd deliberately not finished that sentence.

I'd meant to say it would be an honour to be your brother.

But I hadn't.

Because that wouldn't be enough.

Nothing would be enough because Della was more than just my sister and friend.

She was my world.

And I could already feel her slipping away.

Chapter Eighteen

REN

2005

FOR NINE WEEKS, Della went to school.

I accompanied her every day and waited for her every hour until she was back in my possession. The park across the road offered a convenient place to protect her without lurking outside and earning the wrong sort of attention.

That first day, I investigated every inch of the park and chose a tree high enough to look over the wall separating the school from the street and kept an eye on her. Trees and shade and shadows were my allies as I watched from afar, ready to run to her if she ever needed me.

It meant the chores at the farm went untended, that weeds grew in the veggie patch, and dinner was delayed due to later hunting, but the change in Della was one hundred percent worth it.

All weekend—as I freaked out how to handle her away from me for hours at a time—she'd talked about nothing but school, school, school. My ears rang with what she expected, and her dreams were full of happy thoughts as she tumbled into sleep with a smile on her face.

She'd laid out her clothes for her first day, and I'd swallowed my anxiety, knowing she couldn't go into public with what she'd chosen: a holey t-shirt and underwear far too small for her with the pair of flip-flops I'd stolen that I'd cut down to fit her.

No way.

That would be a sure way to announce we weren't a typical family and to invite deeper investigation.

So, as Della slept, I'd sneaked out and patrolled the town, looking for any laundry left on washing lines—hopefully a family with a little girl.

I hadn't found anything that easy, but I had found a house with a back door unlocked and a little boy's wardrobe folded neatly on the dining room table along with fresh sheets and towels.

I took two towels, some underwear, a pair of jeans, two t-shirts, and a jumper with a dinosaur on the front. They'd fit Della now that she'd outgrown her other stuff, and it wasn't like she'd grown up wearing pink princess stuff. She was used to navy, black, and brown.

At least she had clothes that weren't hand-me-downs and held together with plaited twine.

The morning of her first day, she'd been a vibrating bag of nerves, soaring with excitement to shivering with terror as we'd dressed, had breakfast of freshly gathered milk and eggs from the two hens I'd managed to steal from three farms away, and left the house.

I'd clutched her hand so hard, she'd complained about pins and needles as we strolled as casually as we could onto school property and told the receptionist we'd been invited to attend by the waitress at the diner.

Turned out, the waitress was also the deputy principal and came bouncing from the staff room, whisked Della from my hold, and promised to give her back at precisely three p.m.

And there I'd sat in my tree until three, glowering at every vehicle that entered and every person who exited, making sure no one ran away with my tiny responsibility.

When Della sprinted from the school as the bell rang, I was there to scoop her up and listen to her torrent of adventures from finger painting to a boy who said he had a dinosaur jumper like hers but it had mysteriously disappeared. He reckoned it was gremlins. Not that I had a clue what gremlins were.

I'd winced as she pitied him, all while hoping the kid wouldn't miss his jumper too much, and it was shop bought and common rather than grandma knitted and unique. What if I'd painted Della as a thief on her first day?

I made a mental note to destroy it and steal her something plain.

At home, she'd shown me everything she'd been given and true to her word, the waitress/deputy principal, had provided her with a red backpack full of crayons, exercise books, a drink bottle, lunch box, and a uniform that Della showcased for me with such joy, I'd struggled to remember why going to school was the most dangerous thing she could do.

Dangerous because as much as I lied to myself that we could run fast enough if we ever got caught, I knew the reality of that happening was slim.

When she was away from me, anything could happen, and I wouldn't be there to stop it.

I wanted to hate that cute red and white uniform with its dark grey pinafore, frilly socks, and black shiny buckle up shoes, but I couldn't.

I could only love it because it gave her access to a piece of life I'd been denied, and I wanted her to have it all.

From that day on, red was her favourite colour with only one exception.

Her ribbon.

Every morning, without fail, she'd have me plait or ponytail her hair and thread or bow her favourite blue ribbon. And every evening before bed, she'd have me free it and fall asleep with it wrapped around her fist.

I'd given her stolen teddy bears before. A stuffed unicorn. A talking hamster. But she wasn't interested in any of them—stuffed or plastic. Nothing, apart from that damn ribbon.

That first week, as we repeated the routine of the day before and I dropped her off to strangers while forcing myself not to threaten them not to touch her, was the hardest week of my life.

I lost weight because I stopped eating while wedged in my tree.

I grew cranky because I didn't sleep at night listening for noises of people sniffing around our house.

But as the days turned to weeks and Della returned time after time in her red and white uniform with pictures of smiling sunshines and squiggly writing as she learned more than I could teach her, I was forced to learn something, too.

I had to let go.

I had to allow life to take her the way she was meant to be taken and stop fighting the inevitable.

That was until everything changed.

Until the ninth week of school, when autumn arrived with bronze leaves and blustery chill and our time at Polcart Farm came to a sudden end.

Just like I knew it would.

Chapter Nineteen

DELLA

Present Day

THIS IS WHERE the assignment gets hard, Professor Baxter.

I can tell you right now that there are things in my life—sorry, my story—that won't be approved by some, won't be believed by others, and will be judged as downright idiotic by most.

You see, if you ask someone how many birthday parties they've had, they'd most likely list the number of years they've been alive. If you inquired how many pets they had, they could probably give you a definite answer.

I have definite answers, just not on those subjects.

My subjects are strange.

Such as I hear you asking…

Well, I can tell you that there were four times that Ren and I separated. Only four, but they were the worst times of my life.

The first was his fault.

The second was mine.

The third and fourth…well, I'll save those for another chapter.

Other topics that I have definite answers for are on trickier subjects than birthdays and pets. They are what you'd call confessions, I suppose.

Confessions of things I did because of hurt feelings and broken promises. Things he did because of loyalty and propriety and his unbreakable sense of honour. But again, I'm getting ahead of myself.

What I wanted to write today was the second time we separated, and how it was entirely my fault. He'd warned me what would happen if I went to school, but as a bold, invincible five-year-old, I didn't believe him.

I teased him for being such a worrier. I made jokes at his ever vigilant watching, and even went so far as to yell at him for never relaxing and trusting other people.

He was right.

I was wrong.

It all started on a Wednesday morning I believe.

Ren dropped me off and I went to class, I smiled at Jimmy who loved dinosaurs, I drank my carton of milk even though it tasted like paper and glue compared to the freshly milked stuff from Snowflake, and I enjoyed yet another day of education.

My teacher—I can't remember her name—made us copy a few math equations, and I think we did a science experiment…again, I can't remember, but what I do remember—and this isn't because Ren told me this story because he wasn't there—but after lunch we had Show and Tell.

I didn't know what that was to start with until other kids stood, talked about a toy or special possession, then sat down with praise from the teacher.

Sounds easy, right?

Yeah, I thought so too.

Seeing as I hadn't brought anything to school with me, I asked if I could borrow Frosty the rabbit, and beamed as the teacher carried the white rabbit's cage to the front of the class and smiled at me encouragingly.

I pulled Frosty from her hutch and held her tight just the way Ren taught me. And then I told them what he'd told me.

I explained as detailed as I could how to kill a rabbit quickly and painlessly. How to nick its fur around its neck and then rip off its jacket in one move. How to gut it fast so bodily fluids didn't contaminate the meat, and how to cook it properly so we didn't die of rabbit fever.

I was so proud.

So self-satisfied as I stood before my class of students and nodded matter-of-factly; so happy that they could now fend for themselves—just like I could. I fully believed in my naïve little heart that I'd just delivered a perfect lesson on things everyone should know.

I didn't see the horrified glances until it was too late.

I didn't hear the sniffles and crying as children squirmed in their seats.

I didn't understand the jerky movements of the teacher as she snatched Frosty from my arms and stuffed her back into her cage.

And I didn't know why I was grabbed by the arm and escorted to a room with a stern-faced man and the nice lady from the diner who gave me cupcakes.

I didn't know any of that until Ren arrived.

And then…it was too late.

Chapter Twenty

REN

2005

SHE NEVER APPEARED at three p.m.

By 3:01, I was hammering on the receptionist's desk demanding to know where she was.

Instead of a worried woman bending over backward to produce my tardy Della, she gave me a grave look and quick shake of her head, ordering me to follow her. She said in an appalled, judgy tone that there'd been an incident. That the principal wanted to talk to Della's parents.

Alarm bells clanged in my head, drowning out the squeals and giggles of kids as they spilled from classrooms and into caregiver's arms. My legs were stiff wooden posts as I trailed after the woman, fighting every urge to kick her to the floor and run down the halls screaming Della's name.

She couldn't be here anymore.

I couldn't be here.

And there was no way to fix it because we had no parents to call.

My fists curled hard as rocks as the woman opened a door and said, "Go in. They're expecting you."

This was what I'd been afraid of.

This was why I hated walls and doors and locks.

Because once I stepped inside, there was nowhere to run. No way to get free. No gullies to disappear into or bushes to hide beneath. I would be *seen*.

I stepped back from the threshold as images of rain droplets on trees and sun dappling bracken filled my mind. If I left now, I could have those things. I'd never have to be trapped in a house with people again.

My heart galloped as I fought the overwhelming urge to flee, but then my gaze met Della's terrified one where she sat on a chair too big for her with her little legs dangling and hair tangled around her face where she'd yanked her ribbon from her plait.

She clutched it tight—tighter than I'd ever seen with a plea in her eyes to fix this.

Swallowing my matching terror, I squared my shoulders and strode into the room with every shred of rage and anger I could materialize. "What the hell is going on?" I went straight to Della and planted my hand on her small shoulder.

Her body quaked beneath my touch, and I squeezed her gently, wordlessly telling her to trust me. That we'd get out of here together.

A self-important man behind a self-important desk with degrees and accolades plastered to his walls ignored me, scowling at his laptop as he spoke into the phone held to his ear. "Yes, okay. Will do. We'll keep them here until you arrive. Thanks so much."

I pinned my glare on him as he hung up. "Who was that?"

The man smoothed his plaid suit with a quick glance at the waitress from the diner who looked distraught over whatever was happening. "That was Social Services. Our school has a policy to reach out if anything disturbing occurs." He cleared his throat. "Where are your parents? Before we release Miss Wild here, we really need to speak to an adult in charge."

I prayed my tongue wouldn't fail me as I prepared to tell convincing enough lies to get us free. "They're out of town."

"Oh?" The man raised his eyebrow. "How long have they been out of town?"

"Does it matter? I'm old enough to take care of her without their supervision."

"That's true." The man nodded. "But Miss Lawson here tells me that she's never met your parents. That Della's been coming to our school for over two months and no forms have been filled in or emergency contacts given." He gave the waitress/deputy principal a heavy scowl. "As she's new to the position and excited about educating young minds to the detriment of following protocol, I will overlook the lack of information we have on you and your sister and permit her to stay *if* we meet your parents, and *if* we have a strict conversation on subjects that are suitable in a classroom."

Della shrank into the wooden chair, her fingers twirling and twisting her ribbon.

I squeezed her again as I growled at the principal. "If you tell me what happened, I can give you the answers you need. Our parents are busy. They'd prefer not to be dealing with nonsense."

The principal shifted behind his desk, his greying hair slicked with oil. "This is not nonsense, boy."

"Don't call him boy," Della piped up, her girlish voice cutting through the tension. She cowered as all eyes landed on her, mumbling, "It's not Boy. It's Ren."

I smiled softly, letting her know how much I appreciated her having my back. "It's fine, Della."

She bit her lip, tears welling. "I'm sorry..."

"Don't apologise."

"But—"

I shook my head sharply. "You did nothing wrong."

"I beg to differ," the principal said. "She told her fellow students how to kill, skin, and cook a rabbit while holding the class pet. She's traumatized most of them, and I already have parents demanding to know how this could've happened." His brown, beady eyes narrowed at Della then slid to me. "Do you mind telling me why a girl of her age knows such things?"

I gave him the same condescending look. "She knows because I told her."

"Why tell her such terrible—"

"Because she needs to know the cost of life and death. She knows if she wants meat, she has to kill. She knows if she wants vegetables, she has to plant. She knows if she wants to survive, then things must die to achieve that." I crossed my arms. "Isn't that what education is about?"

"That may be the case, Mr. Wild, but we still need to talk to your parents." The waitress-deputy teacher smiled sadly. "I'm sorry, but we really must insist."

The atmosphere in the room changed from inquisition to punishment. My arms uncrossed, and I reached down for Della's hand.

She grabbed it instantly, wedging her ribbon between our palms.

"When our parents are back in town, I'll have them call you," I said smooth as ice. "But now, I'm taking my sister and going home."

Della leapt from the chair as I tugged her toward the door.

The closed door.

"Let us out," I snarled at the principal.

"I'm afraid that's not possible. Not until Social Services have met Della, yourself, your parents, and investigated the type of home you are currently being raised in." He steepled his fingers importantly. "This is for your own protection, you understand. We're not here to be the bad guys; just making sure you and Della are in a healthy environment and are happy."

"We *are* happy," I snapped. "Now open the door."

The waitress stood from her chair beside the principal's desk. "You're free to leave, Ren. Go and call your parents and let them know how urgently we need to see them. But Della needs to stay here. I'll look after her. I promise."

Della blinked up at me, her eyes huge and hurting. "Ren...don't leave me."

My ribcage squeezed, making it hard to breathe. "Never."

A ghost of a smile twitched her lips, trusting me even though I had no idea how I'd keep such a promise.

My mind raced, charging ahead, doing its best with its limited knowledge and teenage capabilities to figure out a way to stop Della from being taken and to give us enough time to disappear.

A thought popped into my head.

A risky, terrible idea but literally the only one I had.

I wished I could tell Della.

I wished I could warn her.

But there were too many eyes and ears in the room. I just had to hope she forgave me once it was all over.

With gritted teeth and pounding heart, I pried her hand from mine and pushed her back toward the chair. "Sit down. Stay here. I have to go."

It took a moment for my voice to worm its way into her ears and drill a hole into her young understanding. "What?....*No!* No, you said you wouldn't leave me. No!" She launched herself at me, sobbing wet and loud. "Ren! I'm sorry. I didn't mean to. I'm sorry I told them about the rabbit. Please. I'm *sorry!* Ren, please!" She dissolved into tears, wrapping her shaking arms around the top of my thighs. "No. Please. *Please* don't go. Please, please, don't leave me." She looked up with blotchy cheeks and gut-wrenching sadness, and my heart literally cracked in two.

I bled a river inside, hot and red and painful.

I swallowed back the guilt and the all-powerful desire to stop her tears, and forced myself forward with the plan.

The *only* plan.

"Our parents arrive back today, remember?" I cupped her chin, willing her to understand. "The Social people will bring you to the farm, and they'll sit down with Mum and Dad, and this will all be fine, okay?"

Normally, Della would read between the lines—her whip fast intelligence picking up on my lie and realising, if not completely understanding, that this was a lie and lies were our weapons.

But today, her panic had overridden her ability to see, and she'd bear the brunt of believing I was about to abandon her for the second time.

Nothing could be further from the truth.

I just needed time.

Time to get things ready.

And even though it butchered me to press a sobbing Della into a cold wooden chair and leave her with people who didn't love her, I did.

I glowered at the principal, gave him the location of our farm, and promised that my parents would be there to meet him when he dropped off Della with the government officials.

He promised he'd be there at four p.m. sharp with my sister, and we'd get this nasty business sorted out.

I had forty-five minutes to pack up our life.

Forty-five minutes to figure out a way to steal Della, stop them, and vanish.

Chapter Twenty-One

REN

2005

IT TOOK ME twenty minutes to sprint home.

Ten minutes to zoom around the house, grabbing toothbrushes, clothes, towels, and food that would travel.

Five minutes to stuff the sleeping bag, tent, and every other belonging I could fit into my khaki and navy backpack, and another two to curse the zipper as it kept getting stuck on a sock shoved down the side.

My breathing was ragged and torn. My stomach knotted and coiled. My body covered in sweat from fear as well as exertion.

In the remaining eight minutes I had, I holstered every knife I owned down my boots, jeans, and back pockets, then jogged to the barn and opened the gate for Snowflake to leave her stall. She normally grazed in the field during the day, but now, I unlocked every fence and removed every obstacle, hoping she'd wander to a new home just like she'd done when she'd wandered into ours.

The chickens would survive without us. The house would still stand. The veggie patch would suffocate beneath weeds. And in a few short months, the farm would look just as abandoned as it had when we'd arrived.

I wished I'd had more time to steal thicker trousers and better jackets for us. I wished I'd thought up better travel arrangements and double checked the waterproofness of the tent.

I should've been more prepared for this.

I'd been stupid, and now, we were about to pay the price.

Gravel crunched as a car drove up the driveway for the first time in years. The house seemed to puff up in pride to accept visitors after so long of being cast out of society, hating me as I stood barring entry with my arms crossed on the front porch.

I forced my shallow breathing to become calm inhales. I clamped down on my jittery muscles and embraced ferocity instead of panic.

Panic that Della wouldn't be with them.

Panic that she'd been taken already, and I'd never see her again.

The headmaster climbed from the vehicle first, followed by the waitress who turned to open the back door and help Della out.

My heart kick-started again, revealing that it hadn't pumped properly since I'd left her forty-five minutes ago.

Such a short time but it had been a goddamn eternity.

Della wiped her running nose on the back of her hand, then spotted me and exploded into speed. She didn't get far. The waitress grabbed her gently, whispering something in her ear.

My fists curled.

I held my temper...barely.

Another car rolled up behind the minivan the teacher had driven. This one was black with an official looking logo and tinted windows.

The two front doors opened and out stepped a severe looking woman who resembled a stick insect in a burgundy suit and a man with a beard trimmed so perfectly it looked painted on.

I'd started shaving a year ago and barely managed not to gorge my face apart with cheap stolen razors let alone create facial perfection like he had.

"Mr. Wild?" The two Social Service agents prowled toward me like predators. "Ren Wild?"

I nodded, crossing my arms tighter to prevent throwing my knives at them or doing something equally as stupid. "I want my sister."

The man with his strange looking beard glanced at the waitress. "You can let her go. Thanks."

"Okay." She let Della go, and I held out my hand, begging her to come fast, come now, come quick.

Della saw my urgency, bolting up the steps and slamming against my leg. I wanted to bend down and tell her that she had to do everything exactly as I said, but we had an audience.

Instead, I smiled huge and fake. "Mum made you lemonade. It's on the counter. Take a glass and go out back to the pond, okay? I'll come play with you in a bit. The pond. Nowhere else, got it?"

Her face tilted to search mine, her eyes narrowed and uncertain.

Slowly, her confusion switched to enlightenment, and she nodded. "Okay, Ren. Pond. Got it." She took off, leaping into the house and vanishing into its darkness of living rooms and staircases.

The two agents climbed the steps, pausing in front of me. "Can we come in? Where are your parents?"

I cocked my head like I'd seen actors do on TV. The ones who pretended they were innocent but had just committed mass murder.

"I can't let you in without their permission. Stranger danger and all. We're raised with strict rules, you see." I smirked as they looked at each other with annoyance. "But you can go and see them."

"We were told they were at home," the woman agent snipped. "Are you saying they're—"

"I'm saying they're behind you. In the barn." I pointed at the A-frame, paint-peeling structure where until a few minutes ago Snowflake had called it home. "They're milking our cow."

"A cow?" the Beard asked.

I nodded. "We're home grown here. Nothing but organic foods and good ole'-fashioned labour. That's why Della knows so much about the circle of life and the food chain. Not because we have a bad upbringing, but because we're not hidden from the truth."

"Right." The man nodded. "That makes sense, I suppose."

I smiled just as fake as before. "I'm glad. Okay then, go talk to my parents. I'm going to play with my sister and pull some carrots up for dinner."

The syrupy crap falling from my lips sickened me, but I'd dress up in smart clothes and quote the Bible if it meant they fell for my story and gave me time to keep Della safe.

The principal scowled but had nothing to say as the Social Service agents descended the stairs, crossed the driveway, and gave me one last look before disappearing into the barn.

The principal and his deputy followed.

I waved, animated and idiotic, cursing them under my breath as all four adults traded sunshine for shadows and vanished into the barn.

And that was when I made my move.

I flew down the porch steps, slammed the single wooden door closed, wedged the piece of wood I'd made with the simple hinge to lock them inside, then sprinted as fast as I'd ever sprinted before.

To the pond.

To my backpack.

To Della.

* * * * *

"I'm sorry, Ren."

"How many times do I need to tell you? You don't need to apologise."

"But I ruined it."

"You ruined nothing."

"I did." She dragged the stick she'd been playing with through the dirt as I built a fire from gathered twigs and logs. Her red uniform, frilly socks, and shiny black shoes were now bedraggled and forest worn. "I shouldn't have said that about Frosty."

"I don't know who Frosty is, but you did nothing wrong."

"I told them how to eat a rabbit."

"And where is the harm in being honest?" I looked up, willing her guilt to stop beating her up. "Honesty is better than lying, Della. You know that."

"I know but...I don't think the kids liked being told how to gut a bunny."

"I'm sure they didn't. But that's the point." I broke more twigs into kindling. "It's because parents teach their kids that meat comes in packets and not alive like them that's the problem. Not you for pointing out the truth."

"Is it wrong to kill?" She looked up with nerves dancing in her eyes. "Are we bad because we eat meat?"

I stopped what I was doing, giving her my full attention. "People have forgotten so much, Della Ribbon. They've forgotten that behind their supermarkets and houses, beneath their fancy dresses and suits, they're still just animals. We're not bad for eating meat because we only eat what we need and don't waste. It's everyone else who doesn't appreciate the cost of things who are bad."

I dropped my gaze as I used one of my four lighters—ever the resourceful—to start the fire I'd built.

Della had been subdued all evening from the moment I'd skidded to a stop beside her by the pond, hauled on my backpack, then took her hand and jogged until she couldn't jog anymore, to now when all we could hear were crickets and insects, and our house had been replaced with a canopy of tree leaves.

I tried to hide my joy at being back where I belonged.

I tried not to smile or laugh in sheer pleasure at being away from cruel people and rotten societies.

I was happier than I'd been in a while, but Della was sad, and I didn't want to make her feel worse by treating this as a celebration rather than a serious escape from potential separation.

She poked a leaf with her stick. "I thought you left me."

"I promised I never would."

"But you *did* leave me."

"Only for forty-five minutes."

She stuck her bottom lip out, pouting dramatically. "You still left me."

I chuckled under my breath. "Okay, what can I do to make it up to you?"

She peered at me from beneath her brow. "I don't know yet."

"Well, while you're coming up with a suitable punishment, how about I put up the tent so we can go to bed?"

She nodded as if permitting me to do that one task but nothing else.

Despite our close call today, she was still the same opinionated five-year-old I cherished.

Traipsing through the soft undergrowth to where I'd propped my backpack against a huge tree, I unzipped it and began the process of yanking out almost every possession to get to the stuffed tent beneath. I also took out comfier clothes for Della. She'd no longer need her school uniform. Some animal could use it as a nest come winter.

As I shook out our shelter that hadn't been used since our last two-night camping trip a few months ago, I did my best to visualise where we were.

We'd cut over the farm, following well-known tracks and clusters of trees thanks to previous exploring during the summer heat.

Ideally, we should start to make our way south so we could avoid the cold for as long as possible. I had my compass. We could follow the autumn sun.

Wherever we ended up for winter would remain a mystery until we got there.

At least, we'd escaped this time. For hours, we hadn't stopped moving deeper and deeper into the treeline, and I'd pushed Della until she'd stumbled in exhaustion.

We weren't far enough away, but she was too heavy to carry for long distances, especially with an overstuffed backpack already killing my spine.

I gambled we'd be safe here for a night or two. No one had yelled or chased, and we'd successfully traded fields for forest.

We were just two unknown kids that adults would rather forget existed than file paperwork and begin a manhunt for.

We were alone.

And I wished I cared more about what we'd just left behind.

I wished I had some sort of homesickness for Della's sake, so I could understand how traumatic this sudden disappearance would be to her.

But I didn't.

I didn't dwell for a second on running from a house and saying goodbye to TVs and mattresses and couches.

All I felt was utmost relief and freedom to be back in a simple world where life grew all around me, creatures were safe to do their own thing, flowers and weeds grew side by side, and not one of them tried to trap or change us.

Once the tent was secured and our sleeping bag inside, I pulled out a few eggs that I'd wrapped carefully in our clothing and fried them on a rock warmed in the fire.

Della curled next to me as we ate, leaning against tree roots and watching grey smoke from our orange fire mingle with the black sky.

The taste was a thousand times better than anything cooked on a range. Smoky and earthy and seasoned by nature itself.

It wasn't just food that tasted different away from town.

The colours were brighter, bolder.

The night sounds deeper, wilder.

My heart beat softer, calmer.

Della nuzzled into my side as I leaned back and wrapped my arm around her. I couldn't give her language or history or math.

But I could give her perfect simplicity.

And a bedtime story or two.

Chapter Twenty-Two

REN

2005

FOR THREE MONTHS, we lived like feral royalty.

Washing in rivers, playing in forests, eating whatever we could hunt and gather.

It was just as perfect as the first few months I'd run from Mclary's—actually, it was better because Della had a personality now, voiced opinions regularly, and had an over inquisitive mind that learned fast and excelled at making fires, gutting game, and even cleaning a few rabbit skins to save for something useful later.

She said she remembered our life before Polcart Farm. She said she remembered the many nights we slept tentless and covered in stars and how much she'd hated roasted meat to begin with.

I didn't disillusion her and argue. I doubted she remembered any of it. Her daily awe and fascination of every little thing said this was her very first time.

But sometimes, she would surprise me and quip about hiding in that guy's shed with its piles of junk or hiding behind cardboard boxes in some family's basement.

I couldn't tell if she parroted the stories I'd told her or if she truly did remember. In which case, I made sure to teach her everything she wanted so if, heaven forbid, we were ever separated, she could fend for herself, light a fire, javelin a fish, and create a snare for smaller prey.

She even knew how to wield a knife without cutting off a finger and understood how to sharpen the point of a stick for cooking and other chores around the camp.

Overall, we excelled.

I'd always been strong thanks to the many hours of labour I'd been born into, but now, my muscles grew and height spurted and hair grew untamed or shorn.

Della often tugged on the slight patchy beard I couldn't trim without a mirror, calling me a hairy monkey. I'd try to bite her fingers until she'd squeal and run away, playing hide and seek in the trees.

The clothes I'd stolen before leaving grew tighter as yet another growth spurt found both of us and almost overnight Della lost the chubbiness of her baby cheeks, slimming, sharpening, showing glimpses of the young girl she'd become.

On those rare moments, when she sat like an adult or strung a complicated sentence together like any well-read philosopher, I'd freeze and stare.

I'd flash-forward to a future where she'd be a beautiful woman, strong and brave and based in reality, where hard work layered beneath her quaint fingernails and outdoor living whitened blonde hair and browned pink cheeks.

I was proud of her.

So damn proud.

And to be honest, proud of myself that I hadn't killed her yet through neglect or sheer incompetence.

Despite all odds, she'd flourished, and I only had myself to clap on the back and say good job.

Along with the many miles we travelled, we continued to supplement our rural lifestyle with quick forages where people massed and congregated.

Occasionally, we'd come across a small township where I'd leave Della on the outskirts while I slinked through oblivious city folk and help myself to toothpaste, packaged veggies, and canned fruit.

Della asked more than once if we could have lunch at a diner again.

It killed me to refuse, but I couldn't risk it.

We were still too close to our previous town, and I'd hate to put her at risk all over again.

I was older now.

Old enough to know I'd technically kidnapped her, and if Social Services ever found out her real name, my future would be worse than just living without her. I'd be living in *prison* without her.

At night, I battled with wondering if that was why I kept her hidden—for my own stupid sake. But when she bounced from the tent in the mornings, bright and happy and excelling at everything she did, I allowed myself to hope that my selfishness was really about her.

I loved that she loved the life I could give her.

I worried she'd hate the life someone else would force upon her.

So, even though I refused diner and city visits, I did my best to cave to her every other whim. I came up with crazy hair styles with her ribbon threaded as artfully as I could. I indulged her whenever she asked for stories, even if it was on a hike to our next camp and not just as a tool to make her drowsy. I let her wear my clothes and stuff one of my socks with soft moss to make an ugly toy snake.

Some days, when summer made a reappearance and chased off the autumn chill, we'd forget about travelling or hunting and spend the day sunbaking by the river and jumping into the cooling depths.

Those days were my favourite.

The ones when no responsibilities could find us and the world where men branded kids as property and women permitted their sons to be sold no longer existed.

At first, I'd worried about the new needs running in my blood and the pleasure my body insisted on finding sometimes in my sleep. I'd refused to skinny-dip and didn't let Della cuddle too close when we slept.

But gradually, the wariness I wore whenever we were around people fissured and shed, leaving me a boy once again.

A boy who might be turning into a man against his wishes, but out here…with nothing but trees for company and woodland creatures to judge, I could act stupid and make Della laugh. I could cannonball into the river butt naked and not feel as if I'd done something wrong.

I could be happy with my tiny stolen friend.

Nothing could make our life any better, or at least that was what I'd thought until Della rolled on her belly and poked my cheek as we lay side by side with our tent flap open and the sounds of night blanketing us.

"Hey, Ren?"

My eyes cracked open. "I thought you were asleep."

"I faked it."

"But I told you two stories, Della Ribbon. The deal is I talk, you sleep."

"I never sleep when you talk." She yawned. "I like your voice too much."

I narrowed my eyes. "You like my voice, huh?"

"Um-hum." She rubbed her chin where an indent of the sleeping bag zipper had pressed into her. "I like all of you."

The starburst of affection she caused made me choke. I cleared my throat, turning to stare at the tent ceiling and focus on the lining and seams. "I like all of you, too."

"No, you don't."

I scowled, risking another look at the blonde tussled kid who had every power to suffocate me beneath happiness and rip me to pieces in despair. "I don't?"

She giggled. "Nope. You love me." She blew kisses, then flopped onto her back and placed her forefingers and thumbs together to form a crude looking heart. "You heart me like this."

I chuckled at her impersonation of a cartoon skit she'd seen. I wasn't the best one to teach her what love meant. To be fair, I wasn't sure how to describe it apart from I felt for her the exact opposite of what I'd felt toward the Mclarys.

The cartoon explained love was when you wanted to do everything for the other person without needing anything in return. Love was simple with one rule: if you hurt the person you love, it would be as bad as hurting yourself.

I sighed heavily. "You're right. I do love you."

She wriggled under the unzipped sleeping bag, her little legs kicking mine. "Yay!"

A smile quirked my lips even while, for some inexplicable reason, I'd gone sad. Sad because I loved something? Sad that loving someone terrified me? Or sad because she was the first, and I'd missed out on loving the people who created me?

Either way, she didn't let me wallow, poking me in the cheek again. "I love you too, Ren Wild."

And that, right there, that made those few months back in the wilderness the best months of my life.

Nothing came close after that.

Nothing was ever that simple.

Nothing.

Chapter Twenty-Three

REN

2005

WINTER HELD OFF longer than I anticipated.

Some days, we didn't bathe as the thought of diving into icy water and walking back over frosty bracken wasn't exactly enticing. Some days, we went hungry due to animals snuggled up warm in burrows and towns too far away for a day's hike in the first snow fall.

Until the last week, it was liveable.

However, we'd stayed in the forest longer than we should. I knew that. I'd steadily grown more aware of how fragile we were as the weather became cooler.

If it was up to me, we would have found another abandoned building or some other alternative to survive the upcoming freeze.

But we were still here...alone.

No one knew we existed.

No one cared if we survived or died.

It was just me and Della, and Della had decided she didn't want to go back.

I'd rubbed off on her too much. I'd proven what a wondrous place simplicity could be, and she'd fallen in love with the life that had always lived and breathed in my heart.

But even I knew what we could overcome and what we couldn't. This was her fault we sat shivering in the tent, too lethargic and exhausted to do anything but try to stay warm.

Every time I mentioned we needed to find warmer, better shelter—that even though I agreed with her and didn't want to leave, we had to be smart and find a place to ride out the upcoming blizzards and heavy snow—Della would shake her head and pout.

She'd stomp her foot and snap her refusal, and that would be the end of it.

Until I brought it up again and again...and again.

For days, I tried to convince her. Until finally, I didn't pussy-foot around. I didn't tell her gently of my plan to head down the hill toward the small town we saw glittering through the trees at night. I didn't tell her to help me pack or to dress warmly for the journey.

What I did do was dismantle the tent with her still inside and wait until she crawled out in a huff before commanding her to move.

We were leaving.

This was stupid.

I wasn't about to let her freeze to death after keeping her alive this long.

Our dynamic was simple. I was older and in charge. Normally, she bowed to those points of authority, and our arguments were short and sharp, then gone.

But this time?

She threw a tantrum that gave wing to shocked crows, screams that ricocheted around the hillside and left her out of breath and hiccupping. She'd thrown a few tantrums as a two-year-old, but this was the first since then.

I'd done my best to refrain from yelling back, but after thirty minutes of her shout-sobbing that she never wanted to go back to a city, promising she'd hate me for eternity if I took her from this place, and vowing with snapping little teeth that she'd run far away and leave me, I lost my temper.

I shouted back louder. I stomped around harder. I cursed her with every swear word I deliberately refused to use. I dared her to run because if she ran in this, she would die without me to warm her at night and feed her by day.

She'd screeched that she hated me.

I'd roared that I hated her more.

She'd pummelled my belly with stinging little fists, and I'd held her hands until she'd torn away from me then threw her moss-stuffed sock snake in my face.

After that, I shut down.

I marched over to her, snatched her damn ribbon, and held it ransom until she calmed the hell down.

It took a while.

It took all day while I led the way from wilderness to civilization. Her disapproval stabbed me in the back as she followed, her newly returned ribbon clutched in frozen fingers and lips pressed tight together.

My anger faded with every mile we travelled, and by the time we reached the outskirts of town, my chest ached with regret.

I waited for her to catch up, her shoulders no longer stiff with temper but rolled with tiredness. She refused to make eye contact, and the ache in my chest wrapped tight around my heart and squeezed.

We'd never had a fight that lasted longer than a minute or two. This grudge was new, and I *hated* it.

I didn't know how to make things right, and it hurt. It hurt so damn much to have the one person I loved withhold the love I'd become so accustomed to.

She was my one constant, and this was unknown, scary territory.

Turning to face her, I dropped to one knee and balanced with the weight of my backpack with my fingers jabbed into the dirt below.

She tucked her chin down, avoiding my eyes, twisting her ribbon with tight jerks.

Blowing out a breath, I wondered how to fix this. Her body language screamed not to touch her, but everything inside me needed to. I needed to bridge this terrible gap and I risked having my hand bitten off by cupping her chin and forcing it to rise.

Her beautiful blue eyes narrowed as she finally looked at me.

I stared into her for a long moment, trying to study her, to understand what I'd done wrong, and how the hell I could make her happy again. "I'm sorry, Della."

She flinched, ripping her face from my hold and backing away from me. "I want to go back."

"You know why we can't."

"I don't. We've lived through rain and wind. It's just snow."

"Snow can kill."

Her forehead furrowed. "We won't die."

"We would. Eventually." I smiled sadly. "We aren't equipped like the other creatures. We don't have furry jackets or warm nests."

Her bottom lip wobbled. "But I don't want to leave. I like it there. I like just being us."

"It will still just be us. It always has been, hasn't it?"

She paused, digging her dirty sneaker into the earth. "I guess."

Sensing a slight thaw in her, I rushed, "Nothing will change, Della. It will still just be us—as it's always been. When spring hits, we can go back. We can find another farm perhaps, or a tiny cabin somewhere. It will be fun, you'll see."

Her eyes skated to mine. "Fun?"

"A holiday." I grinned bright.

"Promise it will just be the two of us."

I drew a cross over my heart. "Promise."

"Good." She nodded sharply. "Because I don't want to share you."

I chuckled. "You'll never have to share me."

"Good," she said again. "Let's go then."

This time, she held out her hand and smiled without any remnants of our fight. My heart beat easier; I breathed deeper; my world was righted once again.

Only thing was, I should never have promised it would just be us.

Because I lied.

Without even knowing it.

Chapter Twenty-Four

REN

2005

IT TOOK THREE weeks of hiding in rickety sheds, occasional kid tree-houses, and a basement or two before life threw us another curve ball.

I'd searched for something permanent, but this town kept itself too well tended.

The streets were salted and swept of snow every day, the houses painted and cared for. Even on the perimeter of the town, no dilapidated buildings waited to house two homeless kids, and no farm promised space away from people but close enough to ride out the winter by stealing from their supermarkets and larders.

On the third week of searching, I came down with the flu. It was my turn to be shivery and achy, struggling through my daily chores of petty theft and cooking to ensure Della had a full belly to stay warm.

The first couple of days in town, I'd been able to steal her a couple of warmer outfits complete with ski jacket and trousers from a rich family who'd left their kids snowboarding gear on the front porch overnight.

I made do with jeans that got constantly wet and boots that pinched my toes from being too small. I forgot what it was like to be warm and did my best to hide my rapidly fading strength from Della.

She couldn't suspect I needed a rest. She didn't need to worry because I carried the worry for both of us. Only thing was, the stuffiness in my nose and cotton wool in my head made my reactions sluggish and instincts falter.

And that was how we got caught.

We'd steadily crept our way toward the boundary of the town and found a farm too far to see the twinkling city lights of its far away neighbours.

It wasn't abandoned.

Smoke curled from the chimney, recent footsteps melted the snow in the driveway, and the sounds of family laughter trickled through the starless night.

But it was late, and I was done—utterly unable to travel another step with the heavy backpack.

Keeping Della close, I guided her around the back of the cheery looking homestead toward the barn lurking in the darkness. Cracking open the double doors, I coughed heavily and stumbled toward one of the stalls.

Unlike our previous borrowed farm, this one was immaculate with polished brass fixtures, cobweb-free beams, swept cobblestone floor, and freshly-stuffed hay nets currently being munched on by two happy horses, warm and cosy in bright red rugs.

Della's eyes widened as the creatures snorted at us, ears pricked and swivelling in curiosity. "Can I go pet them?" She drifted toward their stables.

I pinched her shoulder, keeping her by my side. "Maybe later."

My eyes danced around the space. The tack room smelled of leather and oats, the racks of folded towels and bottles of vitamins and grooming gear sat dust-free and tidy. All this care and neatness meant whoever lived here took pride and time in their home. Our presence wouldn't go unnoticed, and usually, I'd run.

I wouldn't take the chance.

But right now, I would most likely tumble into a snowdrift and suffocate before we found anything else. It was this or nothing. And I desperately needed to sleep. I needed a new nose, new brain, new throat, new bones.

I needed to be taken care of, but there was no one to do that, so I sucked up my aches and fevers and smiled at Della who stood in rapture as the horses nickered then continued to devour their hay.

I daren't crash here where we would be found if the farmer came to check on his beasts. Instead, I looked up to where a loft held sweet-smelling hay and sacks of feed for livestock.

It was as good as it was going to get.

"Come on, climb up," I barked around a cough, desperate to shed my snow-wet jeans, peel off my icy-damp socks, and crawl beneath our sleeping bag. I was too tired to eat. Too tired to attempt to feed Della.

Guilt drowned my heart along with sickness, but I had nothing left.

I just needed to rest.

Della looked at me worriedly before scooting up the well-made ladder to the loft above. I started to climb after her, but the weight of the rucksack was too much.

I fell back down, tripping over a cobblestone and landing on my ass. I groaned in pain as my ankle rolled and my head snapped forward from the bulk behind me.

Della peered down from above, panic whitening her face. "Ren!"

"Quiet!" I whisper-hissed, very aware that this was a temporary situation with owners extremely close by. "I'm fine." I needed us to go unnoticed, so I had a few hours to catch up on some sleep before pushing on before dawn. "We have to be quiet, so we don't get caught."

She bit her lip, nodding once, even though the desire to climb back down and help shouted all over her tiny face.

With another wet cough and no strength, I shrugged out of the backpack and left it at the bottom of the ladder. Ripping open the zipper, I coughed again and again, cursing the rattle and noise as I yanked out the sleeping bag then hoisted my flu-riddled body up the vertical ladder.

A rush of light-headedness made me trip at the top, and Della squealed as I landed on all fours with the sleeping bag trailing in hay dust.

"Ren." Her little hands did their best to pull me upright, and I thanked her with a weak smile.

My body was shutting down, forsaking me, leaving me weak and wobbly and useless.

"I can manage, Della Ribbon." With the promise of sleep within reaching distance, with the knowledge of a roof above our heads, and shared body heat from animals below, my endurance reached its end and threw me head first into exhaustion.

I somehow crawled toward the stacked and inviting looking bales and barely managed to shed my jeans and boots before a deep, flu-congested sleep slammed into me.

* * * * *

"Ren, wake up." Something shook me. "Ren...please wake up."

I groaned and swatted at the annoyance.

My teeth rattled as I shivered with a bone-deep chill. I wanted to stay asleep, so I didn't ache so much, so I didn't struggle to breathe, so I didn't know what it was like to freeze to death slowly.

"Ren!" The shout was barely louder than a whisper, but it was delivered straight into my ear, along with the tone of terror and crippling urgency.

My eyes flew open even as my vision remained foggy and gritty. "Wha—" I coughed, loud and wet. Clamping a hand over my mouth, so Della wouldn't catch this awful bug, I waited for the tickle to pass, but it never did.

The ache in my lungs kept going and going, wrenching out air I needed, tightening around ribs I'd already bruised.

"Ren!" Della curled into me, diving her head over my shoulder in a terrified embrace.

I tried to shove her away. She shouldn't be close with me this sick, but she glued herself against me, trembling in fear.

I opened my mouth to assure her I was okay, to say the coughs sounded worse than they were, but then I heard what'd spooked her.

What I should've heard minutes ago.

What I should've never heard because I should've been smarter never to stay in a place so well loved by owners that only lived a few steps away.

Footsteps on the cobbles.

A voice murmuring to horses.

Daylight trickled weakly into the space from skylights above.

No!

I shot upright, planting both hands tight over my mouth, willing the wheeze and urge to cough again to vanish.

Someone was below us.

Someone was about to find us.

Della shook harder as I froze in place. My jeans were across the loft where Della must've hung them over the ladder rail to dry. My boots were neatly placed out of reaching distance. My socks spread out and smelly on a sack of molasses-infused animal meal.

My bottom half was practically naked, and my top half could barely breathe.

A cough exploded through my fingers, uncaring that it had just condemned both of us to discovery.

"Who's there?" a female voice snapped.

A horse whinnied, followed by the sound of running footsteps then the creak of the ladder as weight shimmied up it.

"Ren." Della squirmed closer, seeking comfort and safety that in my stupidity and sickness I couldn't provide. *I'd* chosen this place. I'd been the one unable to wake at dawn. I'd been the one who didn't leave before we were noticed.

I was the one to blame for *all* of this.

Another cough spilled from my lips as my fever crested, and I blinked back teeth-aching chills.

All I could do was hold Della close and hope to hell I could talk my way out of whatever was about to happen.

A head appeared.

A head with long brown hair the colour of the bay horse below, green eyes, red lips—wariness and anger the perfect makeup on a very pretty face. About my age or slightly older, the girl's petite hands gripped the ladder as she locked eyes on me.

Three things happened.

One, my flu-riddled body threatened to pass out from added stress.

Two, my boxers tightened as my body reacted to stimuli it'd been denied for months.

And three, the strangest sensation of guilt and unease filled me, because even though she was my enemy, I wanted to *know* her.

The moment ended as suddenly as it'd begun.

She raised her chin, cocked her head, and snarled, "And just who the hell are you?"

Chapter Twenty-Five

DELLA

Present Day

SO...THIS IS where my story might turn a little odd, Professor.

I've told you pretty much everything you need to know up to this point.

I've introduced you to sweet little Della—the innocent child who looked up to her big brother, Ren. I've revealed the rapidly growing, ever inquisitive Della—the mischief maker and stubborn mule who idolized and sometimes despised her best friend, Ren. And now, I suppose the time has come to introduce you to complicated Della—the child who somehow became a girl with intricate complexities that even she didn't understand. The girl who suddenly knew Ren meant so much more but didn't know what.

And it all happened in a moment.

One second, I was secure in my world, protected and guarded by my love for Ren and his love for me. The next, I was full of things I didn't understand. Things that made sense for a woman to feel but not a child. Things I didn't fully accept or even have names for until many years later.

You see, that moment—that instant—when I heard the barn doors opening and Ren stayed catatonic beside me, I'd known our lives were about to change.

Horrors of being torn from his side like I'd been at school drowned me. Terrors at being clutched by teachers who spoke too close and asked prying questions about what Ren meant to me and if he ever touched me inappropriately made me want to leap from the hay loft and run.

I know our second separation wasn't a long time, but it affected me, it aged me, it changed me more, in a few short minutes, than a month living our normal happy life in the forest.

I'd already been kicked from childhood into the next part of growing up, so I suppose, it was only natural to be protective and guarded of Ren in return.

He was mine.

I didn't have much, but I had him, and I had no intention of ever losing him.

I know I'm rambling, but I'm trying to make you see that I felt different.

Back then, I had no name or maturity to grasp how I felt differently. Now, of course I do, and as I sit typing this, I wonder if a child could feel those things or if I'm just placing such well-worn and long-lived emotions onto her.

That's possible.

Because what I'm about to tell you probably won't make sense.

It's time for my first confession. And I say confession because, well, there is no other name for it. It's twisted and wrong and one I've never told anyone...not even him.

Do you feel lucky that you're the first?

You shouldn't.

Because I've come to the conclusion that I can never show you this. The more I write about my past, the more I'm aware that I'll have to erase every word and burn every edit because realistically, Ren was right.

No one can know that my real name is Mclary or that he took me when he was ten or that we lived so unconventionally for so many years. Who knows the sort of trouble I'd cause him and the nightmare that might come after me.

And so, because I'm now entirely convinced I'm going to delete this, I can be more open. I don't know what I'm going to do when I have no assignment to turn into you, but now that I've started...I can't stop.

I want to keep going because it hurts.

Funny, right?

Every word I write about him hurts. The heartache I live with. The deep-seated longing that I've grown to accept has magnified tenfold since you gave me that piece of paper with this assignment.

You were the one who gave me permission to pull out dusty desires and polish them until they're so bright and blinding, I can't stop it anymore.

I can't pretend.

I can't ignore.

I can't lie to myself, and I don't know where that leaves me.

You see, there was never a day in my life when I haven't loved Ren Wild.

Every memory, he's there. Every experience, he's with me. And for that...I almost hate him.

There is no me without him, and perhaps this complicated mess is all his fault, but the sweet agony I'm putting myself through by writing this—the unrequited ache that I feel every time I recall how perfectly he raised me and how dotingly he adored me is nothing *compared to the agony of growing up loving him in a way I knew was wrong.*

Are you ready, Professor, to never read my darkest secrets? To never see the dirtiest of confessions?

No? Well, good because I don't know if I'm ready to write them, but here I go...

In my eighteen years, I've been guilty of all seven deadly sins: lust, gluttony, greed, sloth, wrath, envy, and pride. I was never innocent, and I'm not afraid to be honest and share them with you.

But how about I start with my first one?

Wrath.

My first true sin.

And it all happened the moment I met her.

Let's just say, I hated her.

From the second she popped up on that ladder to the many years and memories later, I hated her.

But...and this is the kicker, I also loved her.

Her name was Cassie Wilson, and she was the daughter of Patricia and John Wilson, sister to Liam Wilson, friend to my girlish adolescence, and biggest enemy to my fledgling womanhood.

When she found us, I clung to Ren—partly trying to protect him from her and partly wishing he'd protect me. Even so young, I knew our lives were about to change, and I knew it was all because of her.

She'd vanished as quickly as she'd appeared, slipping down the ladder with skills of doing it a hundred times before, and bolting across the farm to grab her father.

In the few minutes we had alone, Ren barked for me to grab his jeans and boots and used the last of his remaining energy to hoist on sodden, cold things and helped me safely down the ladder.

He'd tripped going down and tripped again as he struggled to haul the backpack onto his shoulders.

In his flu-fugue state, he'd left our sleeping bag upstairs—our one valuable piece of equipment second only to our tent, and he'd left it behind.

At the time, that terrified me.

To have someone so strong and invincible suddenly become so sick and lost rocked my small world.

Not that it mattered.

Because we didn't get far.

John Wilson arrived, flanked by his curious handsome wife, devious pretty daughter, and cute little son.

And that was when Ren pushed me behind him, stood to his full height, and spoke with the gruff and rasp of sickness to let us go. His hand flexed around the hunting knife in his jean's waistband, his knuckles turning white, then pink, white, then pink as he flexed in preparation.

He was my protector, and he'd promised I wouldn't have to share him with anyone, yet here I was...sharing him.

I wanted to run in front and scream for these strangers to let us go, but Ren kept a solid grasp on my bicep, keeping me wedged safely against him.

With my limited interaction with humans, I expected them to grab us and maybe murder us there and then.

I'm pleased to report, they didn't.

Instead, they changed our lives.

They welcomed us into their home, fed us a home-cooked breakfast of bacon and eggs, and called a doctor for my brother and best friend.

And through it all, Cassie Wilson never took her eyes off my Ren.

And my hate grew wings and flew.

You see, I loved her for being so kind to me, for everything she became to me.

But I hated her for taking something from me, for claiming the only thing I had, for stealing the boy I loved in all the perfectly right and terribly wrong ways that a sister ever could.

Chapter Twenty-Six

REN

2005

I DIDN'T WANT to be here.

I didn't want to be under the scrutiny or charity of John Wilson and his family.

But I had nothing left.

I could only accept their assurances that they meant us no harm, bow my head in gratitude as a warm-cooked meal filled the icy emptiness in my belly, and cough my thanks as Patricia Wilson led me into their guest room complete with donkey figurines and crocheted blankets thrown over yellow bedding and left me alone with a doctor they'd called on my behalf.

In my fuzzy state, I permitted them to close the door without Della by my side. In a flash of lucidity and rage, I remembered why Della had to be with me, why I hated strangers, and how I could never trust anybody.

This might've been their plan all along—to lull us into a relaxed state, then steal her and kill me.

If my strength was at full capacity, I would've left right then.

Then again, if my strength was at full capacity, we would never have been in this situation in the first place. I wouldn't have slept too long, and under no circumstances would I have ever entered a house occupied by unknowns.

All I could do with my lacklustre brain power and my pathetic excuse for endurance was to immediately storm from the guest room and demand Della to stay with me.

She was only too happy to wrap her arms around my thighs and take my command literally, even as Patricia Wilson tried to argue that I should be examined on my own and for Della to keep her distance so she didn't get sick.

Their logic tried to undermine my confidence.

A thread of fear filled me that she might come down with what I had, but it was a risk I had to take because I wasn't risking her in any other way.

I wouldn't leave her alone to be hurt by them, taken by them, or touched in any way, shape, or form.

Just because they hadn't punished us for sleeping on their property, shared their food, and called their doctor didn't mean I trusted them.

The only family I trusted was ours.

And Della would stay with me at all times.

Back in the guest suite with the doctor who'd patiently waited, Della wedged herself in the rocking chair and cuddled a pillow with an embroidered donkey on the front.

With one eye on her and one on the exit, I submitted to the doctor's many questions. I steeled myself against allowing him to use something that was cold and hard called a stethoscope and gritted my teeth with discomfort as he poked and prodded my chest and belly then felt under my throat.

I let him touch me more than any other human had before, and it drained me of my final reserves. I was a model patient, up until the end when his forehead furrowed and a strange new light filled his gaze—made worse when he found the brand on my hip and missing finger on my left hand.

He didn't ask questions but did ask to perform a full examination with worry in his voice. He looked at me as if I was worse off than just an annoying cough.

He already knew more about me from reading my body than I'd ever tell him verbally, and I had no intention of letting him guess more of our story than the lie I'd told the Wilsons.

The lie that Della was my baby sister and we'd been travelling on a bus to visit our cousins in some state far from here. The bus had broken down. And we'd hitch-hiked ever since.

I knew the tale had holes—my backpack was well-used and our gear adapted for life in the wilderness. I knew Della wore clothes meant for boys and her hair, even now, had leaves stuck between the strands.

She looked scruffy.

She looked wild.

Just like me.

But the doctor didn't give up, murmuring how he'd keep our confidence, that he knew there was more to us than we'd said, and his only interest was to help. He went on and on how he only wanted to ensure our full health and that Della needed examining just as much as I did.

He'd lost all my cooperability at that point.

I'd crossed my arms, did my best to stifle my ever-worsening cough, and told him to leave.

To my surprise, he did, with only a final word that he was around if I changed my mind.

The moment he was gone, I plotted a way to leave this farmhouse and the strangely nice family before they devised another way to delay us.

Only, Patricia Wilson knocked on the guest room door, interrupted my plans, and held out medicine while relaying the news from the doctor that the flu had turned to mild pneumonia, and I needed to start a course of antibiotics immediately so I didn't get worse.

I argued it was just a cold, but Della cried when Patricia shook her head and listed my symptoms. Each one she got right from the bruised ribs, continuous sensation of being out of breath, painful chest, and the incessant cough.

All of that didn't scare me—it only made me mad to be so weak— but what *did* scare me was the knowledge I was no use to Della in my current state. I couldn't protect her the way I wanted. I couldn't defend her if I needed.

Despite my desire to be far away from these people, I had to swallow those needs and accept help, for Della's sake.

I sat heavily on the mattress and grudgingly accepted the first tablet. With my spare arm, I held out my hand for Della to join me.

She threw away the donkey cushion and soared into my embrace.

Clutching her close, I eyed up the glass of water Patricia Wilson pushed toward me, then drank deep, washing the medicine deep into my belly so it might start working faster.

Patricia Wilson smiled kindly at us; her motherly instincts, already pronounced from raising her own kids, latched on to caring for us.

I didn't get the feeling she was cruel like Mrs Mclary or saw me as dollar signs like my own mother. With her red hair, freckles, and purple frilly apron, the only threat she delivered was her fascination with Della. She couldn't take her eyes off her, and my hackles rose.

Placing the glass on the nightstand, I stood and said around a cough, "Thank you for breakfast and the medicine, but we really need to go."

"Yes!" Della popped off the mattress faster than I'd ever seen, flying to the door where she wrenched it open, then promptly slammed it shut again as the girl with brown hair called Cassie peered in, catching my eye.

"Tell her to go away. I want to leave." Della stomped her foot. "I'll take care of you, Ren. You'll get better."

Patricia Wilson moved toward her and squatted down with a sad shake of her head. "Sweetheart, your brother is sick. He's lucky he found a doctor. Otherwise, he might've gotten a lot worse." Throwing me a look, she added, "You're both welcome to stay. In fact, I insist on it until everyone is healthy and no more coughing, okay?"

I didn't do well with instruction even when it came with a promise of being beaten and starved. And I definitely didn't do well with it after years of freedom and being solely responsible for myself and Della.

"But I don't want to stay." Della pouted, beating my refusal.

Patricia Wilson laughed kindly. "Are you sure? When the weather clears, you can go for a ride with Cassie if you want. Or maybe play snakes and ladders with Liam while having a treat of milk and cookies. He's about your age and loves new friends. Don't you want another friend, Della?"

My fingers clenched into a fist, regretting, in my weakened state, that I'd told these people our real names. At least, I'd said our surname was Wild—we had that element of protection—but if they happened to research any news or contact Social Services or decide to call the police...

We can't stay here.

I stepped forward, cursing under my breath as the room spun. A loud, painful cough shredded my lungs, sending me crashing back down on the mattress.

The bedroom door opened, and the entire Wilson family poured in. Liam, a lanky kid with short brown hair and green eyes like his father and sister, clutched a plastic lizard and ran to his mother who still squatted in front of Della. He looked Della up and down, then promptly shoved his lizard in her face.

Della stumbled back, indignation all over her.

I wanted to go and act as a barrier between her and all these people, but the girl with red lips stepped toward the bed, her arms crossed and one green eye covered by bay coloured hair. We stared at each other, her gaze flittering all over me while mine stayed transfixed to her face with the occasional stray to her full chest. Through her tight t-shirt, the indents of a lace bra showed.

I jumped as she said in her crisp, haughty voice, "Dad said you're not going anywhere."

My legs bunched to prove her wrong by walking out of there. I barely managed to stand again, let alone shove her out of the way to leave. "We aren't your prisoners."

"No, you're our guests," she snarled. "So how about you start acting like it instead of damn hostages?"

I blinked.

"Ignore my daughter, Ren Wild." Her father, John Wilson, stepped around Della, his son, and his wife to stand squarely in front of me. His height towered over me, his thick bushy beard putting my scraggly teenage one to shame. "I have something to say but before I do, I want your word that you'll hear me out and not use that knife in your waistband or try to push your way out of here, got it?" He narrowed his green eyes, waiting for me to speak.

Locking my knees as the room rolled and my legs threatened to buckle from lack of oxygen, I peered around him to Della who'd retreated to the rocking chair, glowering at everyone as if they were our mortal enemies.

And who knew, perhaps they were, but unfortunately, I wasn't at my usual strength, and I had to be smart about leaving that wouldn't end up with us split apart or me being shot by a farmer.

Because a bullet in my brain was a real possibility.

All farmers had guns.

Just because he didn't carry one right now didn't mean I was safe.

Sticking out his hand, John Wilson grumbled, "Do we have a deal?"

It took another few moments for my fuzzy head to clear, but I finally concluded I didn't have a choice. I had to continue playing nice and hopefully whatever drugs I just took would work fast and we could be out of here by this afternoon.

I nodded, keeping my hands by my sides. "You have a deal, but I won't shake your hand. According to your doctor, I'm sick, and I don't want you to catch it."

John Wilson cracked a smile. "Courteous fellow. I like that." Striding from the bedroom, he threw over his shoulder. "Come on then. Let's talk in the kitchen."

It took a few minutes for everyone to shuffle from the guest bedroom, down the wood-panelled corridor to the peach and cream kitchen.

Another minute later, Patricia Wilson had ensured each of her children, husband, me, and Della had a mug of something hot placed in front of us at the dining room table.

Once settled, John Wilson sipped his drink, looked me up and down, then glanced at my dirty, tired backpack wedged against his kitchen cabinets. "Okay…first, I'm going to start with the obvious."

My heart rate picked up. I wrapped my fingers around the hot cup to stop myself from grabbing Della and running.

"Obviously, you lied to us about a bus trip and visiting relatives. I understand why you did and appreciate your need to protect yourself and your sister, but that's the last lie you're ever allowed to tell me, understand?"

My teeth clacked together. I didn't reply other than narrowing my eyes in warning.

He continued, "Correct me if I'm wrong, but you two don't seem to have a home. If I was to put money on it, I'd say you've been living rough for a while. It's winter. You're going to freeze out there. To be honest, I don't know how you've survived with the cold snaps we've been having."

"Honey, don't go off on a tangent," Patricia Wilson piped up, smoothing her son's hair who sat next to her.

My eyes strayed to her daughter who sat directly in front of me, her gaze burning me with an intensity that prickled my skin and not from fever.

I sat back in the chair, resting my hands on my lap before Della's tiny one crept across and slipped into mine, squeezing me. Scooting my chair closer to hers, I did my best to resist the urge to cough and squeezed back.

John Wilson carried on, "I pride myself on being a good judge of character, and I like you, boy."

"Not Boy," Della immediately snapped. "Ren. He told you his name. It's Ren."

Cassie Wilson tossed her hair over her shoulder. "Ren Wild. Yes, we know." She rested her elbow on the table and rested her chin on her palm, studying me. "What I want to know is *who* is Ren Wild? Why did I find you in our barn?"

Della squirmed, opening her mouth with some retort, but I squeezed her again and said, "I'm sorry we slept above your horses, but I wasn't feeling well."

Cassie cocked her head. "You weren't well, and you wanted to keep your sister from the cold. That's what you said before."

I nodded. "Yes."

"Where are your parents?" she asked, fast and sharp.

"Dead."

Her coldness suddenly thawed, her shoulders rounding and a sweetness she'd hidden filling her gaze when she looked at Della beside me. "I'm sorry."

"It's fine." I squeezed Della's fingers harder.

"Is my dad right? That you've been on the streets for a while?"

I shot her father a glance. He'd said I couldn't lie, but he didn't say

I could omit the truth. "We've never slept on the streets."

Technically, it wasn't a lie. We slept in forests with tents and sleeping bags, never on empty concrete in heartless cities.

"I don't believe you." Cassie Wilson crossed her arms. "You look like you've just crawled from the jungle."

My lips twitched, not from her joke, but from pride. I liked that I looked more feral than civilized. I enjoyed being different to her even though the longer I stared, the more I found to notice about her.

Her hair caught the kitchen lights with golden strands as well as brown. Her eyes had specks of hazel and not just green. She licked her lips when she was angry or nervous. And she vibrated with energy I desperately needed so I could get better and leave this place.

She made me nervous, and I daren't analyse why.

"I don't care what you think of me," I muttered. "We made a mistake sleeping in your father's barn."

She waved her hand. "Meh, I don't care that you slept there. You didn't hurt my ponies, so you're already better than some of our old farmhands, and you care for your sister like I care for my brother, so that makes you kind. Dad says to give you a chance, so I will." Her eyes slipped back into suspicion. "But don't make me regret it."

"That's enough, Cas." John Wilson cleared his throat, then pinned his eyes on me. "Before Cassie steals this entire conversation, I better come out with it. My wife and I have discussed options. Our first instinct was to call the police and have them tell your parents where you are. You haven't told us your ages, but I doubt you're legally able to live on your own with a minor. I didn't invade your privacy and go through your bag, but if I'm right about you guys being homeless…that leads to the question of why."

"That's none of your business," I said coldly, calmly. "Our life is our own. It's not your place to call the police or—"

"Ah, see that's where you're wrong." John Wilson held up his hand. "It *is* my place if I believe you're at risk, parents are missing you, or if you're up to no good. We've dealt with a few runaways while operating this farm, and most of them we send directly home to parents who are sick with worry and only have love and honourable intentions for their children. Other times, we…" He looked at his wife, trailing off.

"Other times, you what?" Adrenaline filled my veins, already hearing horror stories of eating children for lunch or selling them like I'd been sold.

Such filth shouted loudly in my head, so I wasn't ready for him to say, "We give them a safe place to rest and figure out what they want to do. We don't pressure them to go home and we don't call the police with the understanding that there are no secrets between us."

He leaned forward, planting his large hands on the table. "I've been around a while, Ren, so I know a kid that's been abused versus one that has been loved. Winter is a slow time of year for a farm, but I'm willing to offer you employment, if you want it, and a place to stay with the only proviso that you tell me the truth."

I froze. "You're offering me a job?" A cough punctuated the end of my question, bending me over with wracking convulsions.

John Wilson waited until I'd stopped coughing before chuckling. "When you're better, yes, I'm offering you a job. For now, your only task is to get better."

I shook my head. "I-I don't understand. Why are you doing this?" I searched his face for an ulterior motive. I begged my instincts to strip back any falsehoods and help me see the fine print of such a deal.

No one could be that generous…surely?

"I'm doing this because a while ago, my eldest boy ran away thanks to a fight we had. He was missing for three years. We all believed he was dead and mourned every day from lack of news and guilt for failing him. I should never have lost my temper. He was just a kid—your age or thereabouts. It was my fault."

Patricia Wilson reached out and patted her husband's hairy hand. "It wasn't just your fault, John. Adam was as much to blame."

He smiled at his wife and shrugged at me. "Anyway, the good news is one day, a few years ago, we received a phone call from a family two counties over. They said they'd found our son sleeping behind their local supermarket. He was pretty beaten up, but when they'd tried to call the police, he'd hobbled away on a broken leg to avoid the mess between us. Instead of tying him down and calling the authorities, they took him in, cared for him, and believed him when he said he'd run from an abusive home and didn't want the police to send him back."

Pain shadowed the old farmer's eyes, a wince smarting even now. "Obviously, he lied to them, but they gave him shelter and offered him no judgment or expectation. They helped him find a job, earn some money, and mature enough to see that our fight was stupid and idiotic and not worth the estrangement anymore. Finally, my son told them the truth; that he wasn't from an abusive family, bore the brunt of their disappointment that he'd lied, let them call us with the news, and came back home."

Cassie picked up where her father left off. "What my dad is trying to say is now he has a debt to repay the kindness of the family who took Adam in. Without them, he would probably be dead. Instead, he's at university and about to graduate as a lawyer."

John Wilson nodded. "I've always felt humbled that complete strangers gave me back my son. If you need a place to stay, money to earn, and time to do whatever you need to do, then I want to give you that." He held up his finger. "Under one condition."

My thoughts raced, trying to unravel the story he'd just told and doing my best to sniff out the truth, but his gaze was clear and honest, earnest and fair unlike the evil that lived in others.

"What condition?" I asked around another cough, even though I knew what it was. Honesty. Truth I didn't know if I could share.

Della scooted closer, resting her head on my arm in sympathy.

John Wilson smiled at Della's move to touch me, understanding what anyone who wasn't blind could see—that our bond was tight and true. That we looked out for each other. That she cared for me as much as I cared for her.

He said, "That you tell me the truth about who you are and why you're running. Whatever your answer is, I swear to you my offer will not change. I won't judge. I won't call the police. I won't interfere in any way. If you've run away from a family who misses and loves you, then my one stipulation would be to call them and say you're safe and give them my number so they can contact you while you're away from home. Do that and the only reason my offer will expire is if you hurt my loved ones, steal from me, or I find out you were lying." The kind-hearted giant was replaced by a gun-slinging lawmaker with a single harsh look, hinting he was the reason his daughter had inherited a sharp tongue.

"So..." He crossed his arms, looking me up and down. "What's it going to be?"

I swallowed past the razor blades in my throat and looked at Della.

She shook her head, a whine falling from her lips. "Forest...please, Ren?"

It killed me that I couldn't give her what she'd fallen so in love with, but I also refused to kill her by *giving* her what she'd fallen in love with.

I didn't want to stay either.

But winter was our nemesis.

The moment the snow melted, we'd leave.

For now...this was our best option.

Sitting straighter, I locked eyes with John Wilson and gave him a blended version of truth and lie. I lied because I didn't separate Della from my own tale. We'd already said we were blooded brother and sister and not just two kids who'd found solace in each other. I intended to keep that secret for however long we stayed here.

And I told the truth because her tale was now my tale, and I wouldn't hide behind false veneers. I wasn't afraid of showing the ugly truth that went on behind closed doors.

I coughed, swallowed, and said, "We ran from a farm that buys children for cheap labour. I have a brand just like their cattle. I lost a finger due to their strictness. I ran before they could do such things to my sister, before they could sell us for cheap, or before they put us in the offal pit where other livestock go once they've died. There is nothing for us in our past, and I won't allow anyone, *anyone*, to jeopardize our future."

It was my turn to switch my tone from respectful to threatening, fighting off yet more coughs. "I know hard work, and I'm not afraid of it. I'm strong. I'm skilled. I will obey and do what is required, but I won't do it for you. I'll do it for my sister, and as long as she is treated kindly, then I will be forever in your debt. But if there comes a moment when she's not, I won't hesitate to do what is necessary. Do *you* understand, Mr. Wilson? Don't see a kid who's sick. See a man who is prepared to do whatever it takes to protect what he loves."

John Wilson held my stare then slowly nodded. "I see a man who reminds me of myself. I understand."

Della pushed her forehead against my shoulder, knowing she'd lost the battle, and I'd condemned our next few months to be with strangers and not our chosen sanctuary of aloneness.

My gaze left John Wilson's and settled on his daughter, Cassie.

She gave me a look that wasn't full of suspicion or ridicule like usual. Instead, it was filled with fire that made my blood thicken and a feminine smile that made me feel strong for putting aside my mistrust and dislike of people and weak because despite myself...I liked one.

I liked her.

I liked her defending her family and home.

I liked her spirit and snap.

I liked her enough to know I should run far away from her, but I'd just promised to behave for the winter and work for her father.

It was a decision I would live to regret.

Chapter Twenty-Seven

REN

2005

WE STAYED AT Cherry River Farm all winter.

We made a temporary home in the single bedroom with its own bathroom off the barn. After that first afternoon when the Wilsons escorted us to the private quarters and showed us where we would stay, Della had shown a glimmer of acceptance at having our own place even though she still tugged on my hand to run.

I must admit, I'd sighed in heavy relief.

I hadn't considered where we would live, and if he'd given us rooms in the main house, we would've lasted a night before the loner inside me bundled Della into stolen jackets and vanished into the snowy night.

At least, even with our days filled with people, our evenings and nights were still ours...alone.

That first week took a lot of getting used to. I had no choice but to take it easy with my lungs sloshing with liquid, and Della paced like a caged tiger cub, desperate to run and leap while confined to a small cage.

I couldn't tell her stories to keep her mind off my commitment to be an employee because I coughed too much, and I couldn't ask for a TV to continue our unconventional education as I had no right to ask for more than what had already been given.

All I focused on was taking my medicine religiously until I no longer rattled with coughs, did my best to settle my jumpy nerves at being around people, and calm Della enough with promises and assurances that the moment we wouldn't freeze to death, we'd leave.

A few weeks passed where John Wilson gave me simple, easy jobs around the house, barn, and fields. He showed me his paddock boundaries, pointed out landmarks, and gave an overall rundown of what he expected.

His farm focused more on hay and produce rather than milk and meat and had more acreage but less livestock than Mclary.

This was a world I was familiar with, and my time in the forest had given me an even greater arsenal of skills so anything he tasked me with was easy.

I spoke politely, did what was asked quickly, and fought against the memories of doing similar chores for a much nastier boss.

It wasn't that I hated working—the exact opposite.

I adored working with my hands, twisting metal back into place on broken fences, chopping firewood, or hammering nails into posts. Despite the conditions back at Mclary's, I'd loved working the land, smelling the air full of animals and sweat, and waking up with the noisy cockerels every sunrise, knowing I was as connected to the land as I would ever be.

But there was something about working for someone else that itched and chewed, never allowing me to relax. I was still an asset to someone and not free. I didn't own anything. I didn't work my own stock or increase my own equity.

I was treading water, watching the frosts and judging when it would be time to run. I was fifteen, and although I had nothing and no way of knowing how, my dream was to have a place like the borrowed Polcart Farm with its boundaries in forest and bush.

I would have my own slice of wilderness one day where nothing and no one could touch me and Della without permission.

As the weeks went on, it wasn't just me who preferred evenings when the farmhouse turned quiet and I finished work for the day. Della found more and more excuses to hide in our one-bedroom home rather than accept the offer of hanging with the Wilsons around their warm fireplace.

She tolerated Liam, glowered at Cassie, and didn't let the adults get too close. She was a distrustful little thing, and I hated that I'd been the initial cause of such guardedness but also that her only experience with strangers had been good to begin with, then ended with teachers trying to rip us apart.

I didn't blame her for her wariness.

I shared it.

And despite Cassie's smiles as I worked around the farm and her offers of dinner with her family and the occasional gifted cookies as I repaired one of her horse jumps or helped stock hay nets, I never accepted an invitation.

Not because of the weird patter in my heart or tightening in my jeans whenever she was near, but because Della turned into a little monster whenever she saw us together.

I'd expected her to enjoy having another girl around. Instead, she took it as an offense whenever Cassie asked how she was or if she merely grinned her way.

I didn't say anything or ask why my sweet Della Ribbon turned into a nightmare whenever Cassie was around, but something niggled inside me to reassure her in some way. To prove she hadn't lost me. That we were still just me and her—an *us*.

On the third night at Cherry River, we'd pushed the two single beds together after being unable to sleep. We were too used to being within touching distance.

The bedroom was stark with its wooden walls and charcoal curtains but well insulated, protecting us much better than our tent.

We'd stayed sleeping with our beds together, hands occasionally touching, legs sometimes kicking, and I hadn't thought anything of it until Cassie poked her head in one morning at the end of the fourth week.

I looked up from tying a bow with Della's ribbon, securing a high ponytail she'd asked me to do. She might not like Cassie, but she copied her hairstyles often.

"Do you need something?" I turned from where Della sat on the bed to face the door, temper filling me that our sanctuary had been invaded. "I'm due to start work in ten minutes. I'm not late."

Cassie glanced around the room, her eyes narrowing on the rumbled sheets and pushed together beds. "You guys sleep together?"

Della jumped to the floor and grabbed my hand. "We do everything together."

"If I slept with my brother, I'd end up smothering him with a pillow." Cassie smirked, and I couldn't tell if she was being sweet or sarcastic when she rolled her eyes at Della. "Don't you find he snores?"

My shoulders stiffened as Della bared her teeth. "I like it."

"You like it even when he hogs the bed and kicks you?" Cassie's eyes met mine, revealing her teasing. I didn't know how I felt about her teasing Della when she'd never been tormented by anyone other than me. But I let her continue, holding tight to the tiny hand in mine, willing the ice to melt and Della to calm.

I knew what she felt because I felt it, too.

Cassie fascinated me in all the wrong ways, from her curves and skin and smell. But she also terrified me because she had a habit of popping up from nowhere or hanging around longer than comfortable.

For two kids who'd adopted the forest purely because it was away from humans, it took a lot of adjusting and acceptance. I'd always thought Della would be the more adaptable one in that respect, but it turned out, she was a master at holding grudges and staying aloof.

"He doesn't hog the bed." Her pretty little chin came up, blue eyes almost as dark as her ribbon with challenge. "Go away."

Cassie giggled. "Feisty wee thing, isn't she?" She glanced at me. "Aren't you afraid you're going to wake up one morning with your fingers and toes nibbled on thanks to her tiny teeth?"

Della stepped forward, dragging me with her. "I'd never bite him. But I'd bite you."

"I'd bite you back." Cassie leaned on the doorframe, completely unfussed. Brown hair slung over one shoulder, thick boots and tight jeans barely visible under the long puffer jacket zipped tight against the cold. "I've heard little girls are tasty treats." Her eyes flashed to mine with a lick of her lips.

For some reason, my ears twitched at the way her voice lowered, and I swore an invitation echoed behind her joke.

Della looked as if she'd happily murder her. "You can't eat me. Ren won't let you. He loves me." She looked up, her eyes wide and wild, her cheeks pink with worry. "You do still love me...right?"

And once again, she successfully cracked open my ribs and ripped out my heart. Cassie was no longer relevant as I dropped to one knee and clutched Della close. With my face buried in her sweet-smelling neck, I murmured, "I will always love you, Della Ribbon. Until the day I die and even past that."

She threw her arms around me, trembling in a way that hinted she acted brave and brattish, but really, her fear was deep-seated and hurting her. I needed to spend more time with her. She should accompany me while I worked. We were so used to being in each other's pockets that this new dynamic wasn't acceptable.

"I'm sorry," she whispered into my ear. "Can we leave now? I'm ready to go."

I stroked her back. "We can't leave. It's still too cold, and I like you alive and not covered in snow."

"I could be an ice princess." She pulled away, rubbing at the quick glisten of tears on her cheek. "I'd keep you warm, you'd see."

I chuckled, climbing back to my feet and tugging her ponytail. "With your temper, you would keep me warm from fighting with you."

A smile appeared, barely there and still unsure thanks to Cassie invading our privacy, but at least whatever terror had clutched her was gone.

"Can I say something?" Cassie asked, pushing off from the doorframe and entering our bedroom uninvited.

I arched an eyebrow as she came closer, doing my best to assess her threat while very aware she was my boss's daughter. "What?"

"Not to you." She pointed at Della. "To her."

Della squared her shoulders, her blonde hair rippling with resentment. "I don't want to talk to you."

"You sure about that?" Cassie closed the distance then sat on her haunches in front of her. "Do you know what day it is today?"

"The day we can leave?"

"No, not yet, I'm afraid." Cassie shook her head. "That will be a sad day to say goodbye, not a happy day. For me, anyway." She flashed me a look, and once again, her tone thickened and eyes shot a message I didn't understand. The moment was gone as fast as it'd happened as she turned back to Della. "Today is much better than that. Want to know why?"

Despite herself, Della asked, "Why?"

"Because today isn't a normal work day. Ren doesn't have chores, and you don't have to stay in here all day."

"Why not?" Her eyebrows scrunched together. "It's not a Sunday. Ren works every day but Sunday."

"Not today, he doesn't."

I shuffled on the spot, fighting two polarizing emotions. One, I couldn't stop the warmth spreading through my chest at Cassie treating Della so kindly. I still hadn't made up my mind about her as a person, but the fact she spoke to Della as intelligent and not an idiot layered her with more than just physical appeal. And two, I struggled with the possession in my gut. The snaking, hissing knowledge that with every word she spoke, she cracked Della's coldness and made her interact.

She was making me share her, and I both loved and loathed it.

"Why not today?" Della wedged the toe of her sneaker into the threadbare carpet. "Tell me."

Cassie grinned. "Because today is Christmas!" Clapping her hands, she lost the sensual way she normally moved and acted like Della did when I agreed to tell her a new story. Excitement glowed on her face, making her so damn pretty that I had to move away to hide the evidence of my interest.

I had no idea what she was so upbeat about, but if it made her this attractive, I would have to avoid it at all costs. Strange heat bubbled in my belly. My lips tingled for something. Those frustrating, hated desires whenever I looked at dirty magazines returned in full force.

"What's Christmas?" Della cocked her head, her ponytail swaying.

"Oh, my God, did you just ask what Christmas is?" Cassie's mouth fell open. "How the hell do you not know what Christmas is?"

"Is that like when the TV families have a big meal, open gifts wrapped in bright paper, and then moan about eating too much?" Della nodded importantly. "I forgot. I do know Christmas."

Cassie rose to her feet, shrugging helplessly, and pinning me with a disbelieving stare. "Please tell me you know what Christmas is."

"Like Della said. We know the principal of it."

"But you've never celebrated it yourself?"

This was one of those questions that asked so much more than a simple query. Her tone said she didn't believe us. Her face said she pitied us if it was true. Her body language said she'd run to her father and tell him regardless of my answer.

I mulled replies in my head. I couldn't exactly say that our lifestyle meant we didn't follow dates, only seasons. I couldn't reveal the full truth that Della had been too young to remember, and I'd never had one since I was sold.

But then again, I *could* tell her because John Wilson had insisted on the truth, and I'd already told him we'd escaped from a farm that bought children for labour.

I was so used to lying that the truth felt bitter on my tongue. "You know where we came from. Do you honestly think people who buy kids for work would give them Christmas?"

I hadn't meant my answer to be a bucket of water on the cheery blaze of her excitement, but Cassie's face fell, her eyes darkened, and she looked at me deeper, harder, wiser than she had before. "You were telling the truth about that. I didn't think you were."

I shrugged.

"Can I see?"

"See what?"

"The brand you said is like a cattle mark."

Della shot toward me, clamping her hand over my hip. "No. He doesn't show anyone. Only me."

Cassie held up her hands. "Okay, fair enough. I get it." Struggling to find her previous light-hearted happiness, she said, "I came here this morning with two messages from my parents. One, today is a day off, and you're not to work. And two, if you'd like, we'd be honoured to have you join us for Christmas lunch."

It was my turn for my mouth to fall open. "You want us to join you?"

"That's what I just said, isn't it?" She smiled away the sharpness. "But, yes. Do whatever you need, then come to the house. I want to be the first to introduce you to Christmas."

She left with a smile at Della, lingering glance at me, and the sense that today would mark yet another change, a new adventure, a first experience...for both of us.

* * * * *

"Ren, can I talk to you for a moment?" John Wilson entered the cosy country lounge with large caramel couches and woven rugs where I sat beside Della on the floor beside a giant pine decorated in garish flickering lights and round coloured balls.

Somehow, Della and I had traded our aversion to company and accepted the invitation to Christmas. We'd eaten things we'd never eaten before like buttery brussel sprouts, juicy cranberry turkey, and pecan spun-sugar pie.

My stomach was no longer flat and hard but bloated with too much food.

It was a luxury I could get used to.

Without thinking, my hand found Della's head, and my fingers slipped through her long blonde hair. She'd undone her ponytail when the Wilsons had given her a small wicker basket full of ribbons in every colour of the rainbow. She'd compared her blue satin to the purples and pinks and yellows, her face brighter and happier than I'd ever seen.

The fact that the Wilsons had taken notice of her and seen her most prized possession was a tatty, dirty ribbon made my reserved nature falter a little. This family was the exact opposite of the Mclarys, proving good balanced out evil and kindness deleted cruelty.

Patricia Wilson doted on Della, giving her anything she wanted. More lemonade. Another cookie. Teaching her to plait the ribbons together to form one pretty braid. Setting up puzzles and games for Liam and Della to squabble over together.

She'd adopted her, and I'd been in a state of confusion all day thanks to the generosity of these people. I struggled to believe and not try to see past the truth, expecting the same rotting greed like the people I'd run from.

This was the family Della should've been born into.

This was the family that taught me not all humans were creatures to run away from.

"Ren?" John cocked his head toward the corridor, hurrying me along.

With a wince, I climbed to my feet, making sure to take the new knife Cassie Wilson had given me from under the tree. I hadn't expected presents. I didn't even know people gave gifts without requiring anything in return unless they loved them like I loved Della, but when I'd opened the blade and stroked the goat hide handle, I'd been speechless.

I still hadn't said thank you, and it ate at me every time Cassie smiled from across the room.

I had a feeling she knew the depth of my gratitude, though.

Her cheeks carried a pinkness that flushed whenever our gazes met. Her smile held a weight that sped up my heart and thickened my blood.

All day, I'd been aware of her and her of me, almost as if we were having a silent conversation while surrounded by our loud-spoken loved ones.

"I'll be right back." I looked down at Della.

She beamed. "Okie dokie."

Chuckling under my breath at the change in her, I followed John Wilson from the comfy lounge full of family laughter and scents of sugar to the spare bedroom where I'd been checked by the doctor.

Once inside, John turned to close the door.

My hackles instantly rose. My hands fisted. The knife in my back pocket heavier and begging to be used. "What are you doing?"

Memories of Mclary taking girls into his house crashed over me. Fear that something similar would happen to me. Terror that all this time, he'd been the one lying, and I'd given him my truth to be used against me.

My breath came quick and fast; my heart exploding in my chest.

"Hey, son, calm down." John put up his hands, quickly opening the door again. "Easy, easy. Just wanted to have a quick chat in private."

I gulped back the sudden panic, rubbing my face with a shaking hand. "Sorry."

Where the hell had such things come from? I was a teenager now, not a boy. I'd lived on my own for years. Why the hell had a closed door made me react so stupidly?

My questions had no answers, and I shoved them to the side as John pulled out a crushed envelope from his back pocket and held it out to me.

I steadied myself before taking it, so he didn't see my weak tremble. "What's this?"

He nodded with his chin to open it. "Your first month's salary. I'll pay you fortnightly in the summer, but winter is always a little tight with more outgoing than incoming, I'm afraid."

"Salary?"

Would it reveal how much of an idiot I was if I admitted I didn't know that word?

Running my thumb under the glue of the envelope, my eyes shot to his when I saw what was inside. "This is money."

John scowled. "Eh, yes. I know it's not much, but I'll give you a few bonuses when we bale and sell the hay in summer."

I ignored that part and didn't bother reminding him I wouldn't be here in summer. All I could focus on was a wad of cash I didn't have to steal. A wad of cash that was given to me for services rendered.

Cash I'd *earned*.

My ability to count had drastically improved, but it still wasn't good enough to flick through the ten and twenty-dollar bills to find out what he'd valued my work at.

But it didn't matter.

Because I already had something in mind to spend it on.

Passing back the envelope, I said, "Thank you but keep it."

He refused to take it. "What? Why? You're my employee. You get how that works, right? You do what I ask, and I pay you for your time." He looked at me as if I was an imbecile. "I'm not taking it back, Ren."

"I want to spend it." I urged him to take it until he reluctantly held out his hand.

"On what?"

"On Della."

His face softened. "I see. What would you like me to buy her for you?"

I could've said trinkets and knickknacks, but we had no space for possessions. The only thing we had space for was education, and I knew how much it meant to her to learn. Every day she'd come home from school, she'd been a hive of energy and buzzing with new things.

I didn't want to keep that from her.

And the only way I could give it to her was while we had temporary permanency.

"It's complicated." I sighed, eyeing him, wondering if this man was as good as he seemed, or if I was about to get myself into a world of trouble.

"Give me complicated and I'll see if I can make it simple."

"Okay." I paced a little, needing to walk and think. "I want Della to go to school, but to do that, she needs people who will say they're her parents and an address for teachers to know she's taken care of. I-I can't give her that."

John crossed his arms, crinkling the envelope against his side. "So you want us to lie and say she's ours?"

"I want you to give her a chance, so she can become somebody better than me."

"Don't do that," he said sternly. "Don't put yourself down. She has a good role model in you, Ren, and if she turns out to be half as noble, then you've done well raising her."

I shrugged, uncomfortable with praise and ready to return to Della. "Will you do it?"

"School doesn't start back until next week. I can see if there's room to enrol her. I'll say we're her guardians, but her family is her brother, and all communication needs to go through you. Sound fair?"

"Yes."

"I'll do that for you, but you need to do something for me in return."

I froze. "What?"

"Take the damn money." He held it out. "School is expensive. Not to mention uniforms and books and excursions."

I backed away from the cash. "I know that. That's why I'm going to ask another favour."

"Go on."

"Keep everything I earn. Never give me a penny. But whatever you feel I'm worth, give it to her. Buy her new clothes. Give her books. Send her to the best school my skills can buy, and you have a deal."

John Wilson shook his head. "You're really something, you know that?"

"I know the responsibility I have to Della and mean to fulfil it."

"She's very lucky to have you."

I shrugged again. "And I'm lucky to have her."

"You know…" His eyes narrowed with thought. "Winter won't last forever. If she gets into school, she'll only be there a few weeks if you're intending to leave in spring."

My spine slouched.

I hadn't thought of that.

Here I was planning a future for Della that would end the moment the thaw came. She wanted to leave, but if we did…she'd never have what she deserved.

She'd never read and write properly. She'd never grow up with the skills to make her dreams come true.

I looked out the window at the silver moon on white snow and the silhouettes of trees beckoning me back into their depths.

The urge to run crippled me.

But my love for Della broke me.

She wouldn't like it.

I would hate it.

But this was about more than what we wanted. This was about what she needed, and any sacrifice was worth that.

Inhaling with steely resolve, I asked, "Do you need a farmhand for summer?"

A half-smile tilted his lips. "A kid with your skills and work ethic? I could use for multiple summers."

I looked once more out the window, toward the waving boughs of forests and promises of vacant untouched land, and then turned my back on it.

The rivers and forest would still be there.

For now, my role was to give Della everything I had to give.

Holding out my hand, I said, "You have a deal. Help me give Della things I can't on my own, and I'll stay for however long you need me."

Chapter Twenty-Eight

REN

2006

"YOU DIDN'T COME to the house last night."

My head shot up from where I was checking the blades on the hay cutter.

Cassie leaned over the tractor's front wheel, uncaring that dried mud and horse manure wedged in its big tread. "Where were you?"

I frowned. "Where was I?"

"Uh-huh." She nodded, licking her lower lip, dragging my attention to places it shouldn't go.

Clearing my throat, I grabbed the rag in my waistband and wiped away the grease on my hands. "In bed. Where I normally am once I've finished for the day."

"You do realise it was New Year's Eve, right? Dad said he invited you and Della to the house to watch the ball dropping in Times Square on TV."

"He did invite us."

"So why didn't you come?"

I glanced at the door leading toward the room I shared with Della. She'd been helping me all day—sweeping out the tack room, sorting out old bags of feed, and generally doing a tidy up. Poor thing was knackered. I'd found her having a nap face down on the bed when I went for a glass of water, and she hadn't emerged since.

Moving my attention back to Cassie, I brushed past her to grab another tube of piston grease resting on the tool chest. "Tired, I guess."

"You guess?" She followed me, crossing her arms and cocking her head in that annoying but somehow attractive way. "You don't talk much, do you?"

What did she want me to say? That I'd declined their invitation because, although Christmas had been amazing, it had drained me of all my reserves? That I'd reached my people quota and so had Della?

We'd spent the evening chatting about old campsites and wondering what the New Year would bring—both of us nostalgic for open air and cool streams.

When I didn't respond to her question, she tried another one. "Do you have any New Year resolutions?"

I shook my head, once again moving past her to return to the tractor and its hay cutter. "I didn't know I was supposed to."

"It's a thing."

"To make resolutions?"

"To have goals you want to do differently this year than last." She moved back to where she'd leaned against the huge wheel, watching my every move. "What did you guys do last year? Was my dad right when he said you'd been living rough for a while?"

I pursed my lips, pretending to be absorbed with using the squirting gun to apply grease.

"Silent treatment again, huh?" She rolled her eyes. "One of these days, I'll learn more about you, Ren Wild."

I flashed her half a smile. "Nothing to know."

"Oh, I don't believe that." Pushing off from the wheel, she pointed at the floor in front of her. "If you won't answer my questions, you better do something for me instead."

It was my turn to cock my eyebrow. "Do what exactly?"

"Come and stand here." She waggled her finger. "It will only take a second."

Doing my best to see a trap and unwilling to participate in whatever she wanted, I took my time to place the grease gun on the hood of the tractor and reluctantly moved to where she pointed. "What do you want?"

"I want what all girls want on New Year's Eve."

"And what's that?"

She waited until I stopped a few steps away from her. She licked her lips nervously, her cheeks pinking and feet fidgeting. "You honestly don't know?"

I jammed my hands into my jeans pockets, rocking backward on my heels. "Know what?"

"What happens at midnight on New Year's?"

"The clock switches to a new year. That's why it's called New Year." I frowned, wondering if I'd assessed her wrong, and her intelligence level was lacking instead of above par.

She sighed heavily as if I tried her patience. "No." She raked both hands through her hair, the brown strands cascading over her shoulders. "God, you're not making this easy." She laughed suddenly. "Normally, it's the boy making these moves."

My heart quickened. "What moves?"

A long pause, then an explosion of speed as she closed the distance between us, stood on her tiptoes, and breathed, "This."

Her lips landed on mine, freezing both of us to the spot.

I didn't know what the hell she was doing. All I knew was if her father caught us, I'd be fired and Della wouldn't be allowed to go to school anymore.

Tripping backward, I wiped my mouth from hers. "What the hell was that?"

"A kiss. But not a very good one." Her eyes locked on my lips. "Want to try again?"

I wanted to scold her like I'd scold Della for doing something I wasn't comfortable with. Instead, common-sense drowned beneath hot, hard need and my silence answered for me.

My brain emptied of reasons and rationality, and even the fear of ruining the bargain I'd made for Della's benefit didn't entice me to run.

Slowly, hesitantly, she stepped toward me again. Her hands fluttered by her sides, and my heart winged like a trapped bird. We didn't speak as she stopped with her shoes touching mine.

I wanted to stop her.

I wanted to grab her.

I stayed locked in stone as she once again balanced on her toes and pressed her lips to mine.

This time, I didn't stumble away, and she didn't disappear.

She smelled sweet and young and innocent. My eyes hooded, wanting to close, but I kept them open. I didn't know what I was supposed to do and didn't want to insult her by shutting her out.

With a soft breath, she moved closer, her chest brushing mine, twin roundness so different to my flat hardness. My arms twitched to encircle her, but I couldn't move.

My jeans hurt as my body swelled beyond normal. I wanted to readjust myself but daren't move in case she stopped whatever magic this was.

And then, the softest sweep of warm wetness and my eyes snapped shut on their own accord. Her tongue came again, and I gasped, opening my lips, letting her tentative quest go deeper.

My first kiss.

And hell, it was better than anything I'd experienced.

Cassie moaned as my tongue moved to meet hers—testing, learning, tasting. We stood there, hidden behind the tractor and kissed awkwardly, but somehow, that awkwardness only added to the blistering awareness and want.

My fingers curled to push her against the wall and kiss her harder.

My lungs gulped air to stop from going light-headed.

We slowly learned the other, and when it was over, Cassie smiled softer, happier than I'd seen. Her eyes were dewy. Her mouth wet from mine. Her steps floaty as she nodded once and whispered, "Thanks for my New Year's kiss, Ren."

With a lingering look, she left me to pick up my brain from the hay-dusted floor, wrangle the unbearable ache in my jeans, and somehow remember how to work.

* * * * *

That night, Della was subdued and not her usual self.

It took everything I had to lavish her with attention and be as supportive as I could when the only thing on my mind was a repeat of the kiss this afternoon.

When Della threw aside one of the few books we'd brought with us from Polcart Farm and curled into a tight ball, shutting me out and not responding to any of my suggestions to play, I lost my temper a little.

She wasn't sick. She didn't have a fever. She was just being a spoiled little brat, and I didn't have time to offer her stories or promises to do anything she wanted when all I earned was her skinny back and a savage little growl.

Leaving her to pout and deal with whatever mood she was in, I returned to the barn and found solace in Cassie's horses.

I didn't know their names, but they stuck their heads over the partition, nickering in the night for treats.

Stroking their velvet muzzles, I allowed the urge to spill my annoyance about Della's attitude to blend with the amazement of indulging in my first kiss.

The two extremes kept me standing there long into the night.

Confused.

Elated.

Frustrated.

And most of all, wary of what other surprises this New Year would bring.

Chapter Twenty-Nine

DELLA

Present Day

SO YEAH, I'VE been dreading writing this next part.

I've kind of been putting it off if I'm honest. Even knowing I'm never going to show you this assignment, it doesn't make typing it any easier.

I suppose there is no easy way to say this, so I'll ask a question instead.

How many times do you think a person can survive a broken heart?

Any ideas?

I would like to know because Ren has successfully broken mine, repaired it, shattered mine, fixed it, crushed mine, and somehow glued it back together again and again.

Then again, I don't need an answer to that question.

I'm living proof that a heart can be broken a thousand times and still function, still keep you alive—desperately hoping that it won't happen again, all the while knowing it will.

That cracking pain. That nicking, awful slicing has become horribly familiar to me now. I suppose my predicament could be seen as terribly romantic or horrendously stupid.

You'd think, after almost two decades of agony, I would've outgrown it by now…turns out, I'm stupid because I can't stop it.

Anyway, let's get on with the story…

The first time I caught him kissing her, I thought my chest would explode, and I'd plop dead right there where I hid in the barn shadows.

He didn't see me.

But, holy ouch, did I see him.

I saw his lips touch hers, his body tighten and breath catch, and I wanted to pelt toward them, scratch out her eyes, then kick him in the shins. I wanted them both to understand how much they'd wronged me.

But that was the thing…they didn't *do anything wrong.*

Ren was more man than boy, and I, as much as I despised it, was still a child.

I was trapped and hurting and ran back to our one bedroom with my heart gasping and insides smarting, curling around my agony with no clue how to stop it.

He got mad at me that night.

When he came to bed after kissing her, I couldn't bear to look at him. I couldn't let him see the depth of emptiness and loneliness he'd caused.

Instead, I ignored him.

He stormed off when I refused to uncurl and look at him. It took everything I had to hold in my aching tears, but once he'd vanished into the stables, I let loose the crushing agony and sobbed into my pillow.

I think back now and know my pain wasn't from seeing him kiss Cassie. It wasn't the fact I'd woken from my nap, bounced from our bedroom, and couldn't wait to help him with his chores again. It wasn't because, even though we lived across the driveway from the Wilsons, we were still separate, still us. And it wasn't because I knew that a kiss meant more was to come and as bodies grew closer so too do minds and hearts.

I was too young, you see.

I didn't know what kissing meant.

But the pain he injected into my heart? That was real and I felt betrayed, forgotten, and so terribly lost.

I was jealous that he was close to another when I was supposed to be the only one. I was angry that he turned to another for comfort and didn't come to me. But most of all, I was in shattered pieces because I wasn't enough anymore.

Crazy, right?

Such complex emotions for such a silly girl. I've read enough on the subject of unrequited love—especially when there are factors like age and experience separating two parties like they do with me and Ren—to understand my first broken heart wasn't about lust or sex or even understanding that a kiss like that eventually led to more.

All I knew was the one person who meant the world to me—the boy who kissed my cheeks and cuddled me close and kept all the monsters at bay—had betrayed me by liking another.

At least, I'm not unusual in my pain. Apparently, lots of children have issues with their parental figures when they start dating again after a failed marriage or other life situation. But that knowledge didn't help my fractured little heart, and it didn't help glue me back together again.

Funny enough…Cassie did that.

Remember how I said I both hated and loved her?

Well, I hated her for stealing Ren, but I loved her because she didn't just want his company.

She wanted mine, too.

I wish I could fill this assignment with slurs like she was a slut, a bitch, and a conniving little witch.

But…and this pains me to say…she wasn't.

She was reserved and protective of her family—just like Ren.

She was generous and attentive of her loved ones—just like Ren.

She was patient and kind, and little by little, she wore down my hate until I no longer hissed at her when she came into the barn to find Ren but ran out to meet her just as eager as him.

I can probably skip ahead a little because Cherry River Farm wasn't just a snippet of my life. It wasn't our home for just one winter like Ren had promised. It turned out to be my childhood playground until most of my earlier memories of tents and trees were overshadowed by barns, horses, and school.

Ah, school.

I almost forgot.

See, this is how Ren systematically broke and repaired my heart, time after time again. He broke it by kissing Cassie Wilson. He fixed it by sitting me down a few days later, while I still moped and sulked, and instead of scolding me for the fiftieth time about my unusual surly attitude, he held my hands, swept hair off my face, and told me I would be going to school.

Amazing how when you're a kid, you can switch from pain to elation so fast.

I didn't see it as bribery or search for an ulterior motive—not that there was one. I just threw my arms around his neck and squeezed as hard as I could. He still loved me. He still cared.

That first day of school, he helped me dress in a baby blue and navy striped uniform. John Wilson drove, and Ren sat in the back seat of the Land Rover with me as I bounced with barely contained energy. Instead of like the last school where my attendance was strictly temporary and based on people not asking questions, this time, it was legitimate.

Ren guided me down massive corridors and spoke proudly of me as we met the principal. And when it came time for Ren to leave me in my new classroom and return to work, I didn't mind in the slightest that he was going back to a girl called Cassie who I wouldn't be able to monitor or stalk whenever she spent time with Ren.

All I cared about was learning.

And I threw myself into it with a feverish addiction that comes from never knowing how long something good will last.

Every day, I woke up, tore around to get ready, and leapt on the school bus that stopped to pick me up. Every evening, I would do my homework and hang with Ren, and it was the happiest times of my life.

It wasn't until I finished an entire semester there and ice melted and snow turned to sun that the enjoyment faded a little thanks to the incessant urge to return to our camping way of life.

Ren had promised when the world thawed, we would be just us again.

But when the birds chirped at night and woodland creatures woke from hibernation and I asked when we would be leaving, Ren told me the second part of his bargain.

He'd agreed to stay working for John Wilson in return to sending me to *school.*

I'm embarrassed to say, I screamed at him for that. Here he was sacrificing everything for me, and all I could do was complain that the almost fairy-tale way of life before Cherry River was now forbidden to me for a regular one.

Even though I loved our regular one where he had a job and I had school and together we made friends with Cassie and Liam.

I'm making myself sound like an ungrateful cow, but I have to make you see the topsy-turvy world I lived in to understand how fragile my heart was.

How one moment I was queen of everything good and happy, and the next I was princess of everything bad and painful.

So much happened at that farm.

For me and for Ren.

And along the way, I lost count how many broken hearts I endured.

Chapter Thirty

REN

2006

SUMMER ALWAYS MADE everything better.

Longer days, warmer nights, happier animals, and a crap-load of work that needed doing.

When Della jumped on the school bus each morning, I'd throw on the cargo shorts and t-shirt that I'd stolen—that frankly needed to be replaced soon—and head to the back door of the main house.

There, John Wilson would meet me, try to convince me to share a cup of coffee with him and his wife—which I always refused—before listing what he'd like done for the day.

To start with, he came with me, not quite sure of my skills or abilities on using heavy machinery or trusting my methods on doing things.

Within a few days, I'd surprised him that I knew how to drive a tractor, how to attach different equipment like mowers and balers, and had the strength required to lift things even he couldn't lift.

Mclary had been good in that respect—he'd given me a crash course on how to build muscle that no ten-year-old kid should have, which only increased in strength now I was fifteen. He'd shoved me in his cantankerous tractor when my feet barely reached the pedals and expected me to figure out how to use it because if I didn't, I wouldn't be getting any scraps for dinner.

Thanks to that harsh education, I could make John's temperamental tractor purr like a sports car.

Occasionally, I'd catch him watching me with a mixture of awe and sadness.

I didn't like that look.

I didn't like him pitying my past while being astounded at my present.

It made me feel like a freak.

However, slowly, as more time passed, and he trusted me with more and more responsibility, the more I grew into my belief that I was worth something, even if I only had nine fingers and a rusty knowledge of reading and arithmetic.

I liked being busy because it gave me something to occupy my time with until the school bus would trundle down the road, screech to a halt at the top of the Wilson's driveway, and Della would bound down its steps and charge to wherever I was on the property.

It didn't matter if I was in the furthest field or on the highest roof, she found me, demanded a hug no matter how sweaty and gross I was, then promptly sat down, pulled out two juice boxes from her rucksack, and gave me one.

The first time she produced a bag-warm blackcurrant juice, I'd raised an eyebrow and asked where she'd gotten it from. Thanks to John Wilson keeping my salary, he had the cash to buy food for Della as well as his own children, and when Cassie left for high school and Liam left for an all-boy's primary, Della was always third in line to receive a lunch bag full of fresh sandwiches, yoghurt, water, and a cookie or two.

I stood beside her every morning to make sure she said thank you and didn't miss the bus, so I knew what she had to eat and drink and what she didn't.

Turned out, she'd watched me closer than I thought whenever I'd steal something. She'd become a perfect little thief, and when the school provided extra juices to ward of dehydration during recess, she'd grab three. One for then, and two for later.

I warned her she'd get caught and wouldn't be allowed to go to school anymore.

But every day, she returned home and smugly gave me her pilfered juice box, proud and happy. She said she thought about me even when I wasn't there and wanted to make sure I had enough liquid while working out in the heat.

The fact that she cared and thought about me when I was so sure she'd be enthralled by new friends and teachers and forget all about me made my heart burst.

I couldn't believe I'd ever thought I didn't want her.

I couldn't stand remembering how I'd left her behind, if only for a few days.

My life wouldn't be nearly as rewarding if she'd never stowed away in my backpack and become my most favourite thing in the world.

And just like Della was my one and only, she was loved by each Wilson just as much. Liam would often search her out after he came home from school, and they'd play tag or swim in the river that cut through the Wilson's back paddock. Cassie took her under her wing and taught her how to be around horses safely, how to brush them, feed them, and even, on a muggy summer night, helped her climb aboard and led her around the paddock where Cassie jumped and schooled her horses.

Della had fallen asleep that night with the biggest grin on her face, legs and arms star-fished under the blankets in utter bliss. I'd watched her sleep for a while before sneaking from the bedroom and going to thank Cassie.

Her bedroom window was above a goldfish pond with pretty lily pads and noisy frogs. I often wondered if the position of the quaint pond directly beneath Cassie's window was to prevent her from easily scaling the flat roof and shimming down the ivy growing on the brick.

The more I got to know her, the more I learned who she was, and she had a rebellious streak. She might love her parents and brother, but she didn't necessarily like rules. She'd already tried dope, drank with her friends when she said she was staying the night to do homework, and generally acted like an adult when really, she was still a girl.

In many ways, Della seemed older than her with her serious attitude, utmost concentration on learning new things, and almost magical way she retained everything.

Where Cassie favoured sarcasm for laughter, Della preferred wit and a dry sense of humour. Where Cassie protected Liam and got angry with him over the slightest thing, Della cared for me as deeply as I cared for her, and we never had stupid arguments.

When we had arguments, they were never stupid, but hell, they were loud and long and drained me until all I wanted to do was kneel before my tiny ribbon and beg her to forgive me, even if it wasn't my fault.

That night, as I stood by the pond and threw a small pebble at Cassie's window, I knew I was crossing the friendship boundary that we'd danced around ever since that first kiss a few months ago.

She hadn't tried to kiss me again, and I was too much of a wimp to try myself.

Yet here I was about to do something that made my legs quake and belly knot, and in a way, it was thanks to Della.

It was her happiness that made me want to make Cassie just as happy because I was so damn grateful she'd befriended her. The fact that she let Della ride her prized pony was one of the most selfless things I'd seen her do.

Her window slid up on the third pebble, her brown hair mused from her pillow and one cheek red from lying on her side. "What gives? What's happened?"

"Meet me at the kitchen door," I whispered, keeping a close eye on her parents' blackened bedroom three windows away.

Not waiting to see if she'd obey, I jogged around the farmhouse, avoiding the perfect flower beds that Patricia Wilson spent hours tending, and waited nervously as soft footsteps sounded on the flagstone floor then the rattle of a lock and opening of the door.

"It's past midnight. Why am I out of bed?" Cassie blinked with blurry eyes. "You do realise Dad asked you to get up at dawn to do the first cut of the season, right?"

I nodded. "I know."

"That's in…I dunno, four hours or so."

"I know that, too."

"Well, how about you tell me what you're doing here, so I know if you've gone insane or not."

I smiled, climbing the small stoop so we were eye level. She was shorter than me but not by much. Her arms weren't as strong. Her legs not as fast. Her smile not as pure as Della's.

Funny how I compared the two.

Strange that I found both perfect in their own way.

"You're staring," she murmured, her voice dropping into the husky undertones that never failed to make me hard.

Clearing my throat, I said softly, "Thank you for letting Della ride your horse today."

She tilted her head so thick hair rivered over her shoulder. "That's what you woke me up to say?"

I shrugged. "I needed to say it."

"Well, I needed to sleep." She smirked, her cheeks pinking with pleasure instead of annoyance as she pretended.

"I also…" I coughed, doing my best to get up the courage. "I also wanted to do something."

"What something?"

Why was this so hard? How had she kissed me that night in the barn? It took a hell of a lot of guts, and it made me respect her that much more for being the first to do it.

"I—" Gripping the back of my neck, I squeezed hard. Doing my best to suck up my fear, I leaned toward her. "I wanted to kiss you again."

She gasped just as I closed the distance and pressed my lips to hers.

We stood frozen and awkward, her in the kitchen, me on the stoop, and my heart roared in my ears. I didn't know what to do next. I'd done this all wrong.

Cursing myself, I pulled back only for her arms to shoot around my neck and her mouth to seek mine. She yanked me to her, making me stumble against the doorframe and brace myself on the wood.

Her lips weren't innocent like last time. They'd had practice and now had a brave assurance that mine lacked.

Her tongue didn't flutter shyly, it didn't dance or ask. It pierced my lips and entered my mouth with a flavour of mint and teenage need.

Her arms tightened, deepening the kiss and wedging her body against mine.

And that was all I could take.

I'd come to give a heartfelt thank you and deliver a courteous kiss, yet Cassie turned it into a clawing, drawing need for more.

My hands left the doorframe and wrapped around her waist, jerking her against me, groaning at the delicious friction of her against every hard ridge of me.

She moaned as I spun her out of the house and crashed her against the porch wall. Our mouths never separated as our breathing turned quick, and our hands roamed with no direction.

Her tongue fought mine, adding another element to the kiss, turning it sloppy and violent. I didn't care about technique or learning how to do it better. I let her guide me, following her lead, kissing her as savagely as she kissed me.

And when her leg cocked over my hip—the very same one with a cattle brand and so many memories attached to it—I snapped out of the stupor she'd put me in and fell backward, breathing hard.

Stumbling down the steps, I stared at her, almost buckling and returning for more.

She stood in cute cotton shorts and a nightshirt with bright pink flamingos, hair wild, lips red, chest panting, and eyes begging me to come back.

It was thanks to her blatant invitation and the fact I knew exactly what she was asking that gave me the power to walk away.

The night sky was my salvation from temptation as I put one foot in front of the other and dared let my hand wander and squeeze the excruciating ache between my legs.

Just before I reached the garden path, a sultry voice fell like starlight. "Della can ride my horses anytime she wants. I'll share everything with her...as long as you continue to kiss me like that, Ren Wild."

I didn't turn around as the kitchen door closed quietly.

* * * * *

The rest of summer was filled with late afternoon swims with

Della, Liam, and Cassie; cold lemonade and barbecues thanks to Patricia and John, and a sensation of rightness as Della excelled at school and I indulged in my calling to work the land.

My hands were never fully clean from dirt. My skin was always browned from the sun. My body lean and strong, no matter how much Patricia tried to feed me.

I never saw a penny for the many hours I worked. It didn't matter if I started at dawn and finished long past dusk, John never gave me a dollar.

But it didn't mean he wasn't keeping tally.

During the busiest time of the year, when we had countless equestrians and fellow farmers coming to buy lucerne and meadow hay, and my life was a never-ending loop of cutting, fluffing, raking, baling, loading, and sowing, strange new possessions started appearing.

Patricia often stole Della to go with her and Cassie on shopping trips into town, and Della would return with sugar still rimming her pretty lips and her hands full of bags. She'd force me to sit on the bed as she tried on outfit after outfit, giving me a fashion show of colourful summer dresses, practical winter jackets, and frankly far too revealing swimsuits.

It was odd that the one-piece daffodil coloured swimsuit she wore whenever we'd swim in the river annoyed me more than skinny-dipping ever did.

There was something about the way it made Della switch from uncaring natural child to fledgling young woman who copied Cassie's every move that made me look away as if I'd breached some sort of code by looking at her.

As Cassie prowled around in her black bikini with toned legs and perky breasts, Della would puff out her flat little chest and sunbake on flat rocks with her legs crossed in perfect imitation.

It made me uncomfortable but also indulgent.

I didn't like to think of her trading innocence for whatever Cassie dabbled in, but I also couldn't ignore that she was almost six years old—maybe already six years old, seeing as I didn't know her birthday—and time was speeding up.

Every morning, she seemed to look different with a wiser glint to her gaze and harsher pinch to her lips if I annoyed her. She kept me on my toes—almost as much as Cassie did.

I struggled most days around Cassie, and my body was in a total flux of pain whenever we'd swim together. She'd pin me with an inviting stare, her body lithe and tempting and I'd have to turn my back to avoid revealing just how much she affected me.

Little Liam was the easiest to hang out with because all he cared about was lizards and helping his mother in the garden. He wasn't growing up too fast or trying to lead me directly into sin.

Despite my growing awareness and steadily growing desire for what Cassie tempted, I loved working for the Wilsons. They were true to their word and among the many kindnesses they did for Della, they also ensured I had a treat now and again, too.

I did my best to ensure their farm ran as smoothly and productively as possible, and I guessed they appreciated it because one night, after a particularly gruelling day hauling hundreds of hay bales from the paddock and stacking them in the barn for winter feed, I lugged my tired, aching body to the one bedroom I shared with Della and heard music and voices coming from within.

A man's voice.

My heavy steps turned quick as I barrelled into the room only to find Della sprawled on her belly with her chin in her hands, watching a comedy on a brand new flat-screen TV.

"Where did that come from?" I plopped exhausted beside her on the end of the bed, laying my arm over her shoulders and playing, like I always did, with the blue ribbon trapped in her ponytail.

"Patty and John." She shuffled closer, uncaring that her clean skin pressed against my hay-covered sweat.

"Wow."

"I know." She nodded importantly. "I made sure to say thank you."

"I think they deserve multiple thank yous."

"Cassie let me ride her horse today after school, too." Her face split into the biggest grin. "I got a gold star in class, got to ride a pony, and we have a TV again! Best day *ever*!"

I kissed her head, inhaling the sweet milk and honey shampoo she favoured and ignored my skipping heart. "I'm going to get clean."

"Okay." She flashed me a smile then turned back to the TV. As her attention fixed on the ridiculous show, I dragged myself to the shower and stripped.

I stood under cold water, trying to wash away heatstroke and prickly grass while doing my best to inject energy into tired muscles because I wouldn't be crawling into bed to fall asleep beside Della.

Not yet, anyway.

Della had ridden Cassie's horse.

And that meant I owed someone a kiss.

Chapter Thirty-One

REN

2006

I COULDN'T REMEMBER when I'd taken Della to the diner for our shared birthday lunch, but today was my only day off, and I wanted to spend time with her just the two of us.

The exact date didn't matter because it wasn't the right one anyway. All that mattered was marking the calendar of her turning six and me turning sixteen.

Instead of stealing a wallet to pay for a single lunch, I politely asked Patricia if I could pack a wicker basket of fresh ham sandwiches and some of her banana and raspberries muffins freshly baked and steaming on the windowsill, and head to one of the boundary paddocks where willow trees dragged long fronds on the ground.

Once there, I laid out a plaid blanket, served Della our birthday picnic, and when our fingers were sticky with muffin crumbs, I pulled out the only thing I could give her.

I had no cash as everything I made went to making her life easier. I had no income because I trusted the Wilsons to spend it better than I ever could.

All I had were my hands and snippets of time while Della slept softly beside me.

"That's for me?"

I nodded. Guilt that it wasn't something better and uncertainty that she might not like it rolled my shoulders. "It's not much but—"

"It's awesome."

"You haven't even opened it yet."

"Right." She smirked, stroking the orange striped dishtowel and baling twine I'd used to wrap it. "Can I open it?"

"It's yours. Of course, you can."

With her lip stuck between her teeth, she undid the bow and let the material fall away.

Inside, the carved horse gleamed from the hours I'd spent polishing it with saddle conditioner. The tiny girl atop the horse could've been anyone if it wasn't for the long ribbon trailing behind from her long hair.

It'd taken me hours and multiple attempts after snapping the delicate ribbon so many times while carving.

No one knew I'd done it even though I'd borrowed John's tools to make it happen. It wasn't perfect, and I hated a lot of it with my clumsy cuts and annoying mistakes, but it showed how much I cared. It revealed just how proud I was of her learning to ride and how terrified I was of her getting hurt. She'd taken a tumble a couple of times, and my heart literally quit beating until I knew she was okay.

My fear of her falling off a horse was nothing compared to the sudden terror drenching me as Della switched from chatty live wire to quiet, subdued seriousness beside me.

Silence fell, interrupted only by the breeze whispering through the willow leaves. I waited for as long as I could, my skin prickling with unease, my heart racing with dread.

Her fingers trailed over and over, stroking the carved mane, touching slightly too long legs, and studying not quite perfect nostrils.

I couldn't wait any longer.

Pinching it from her hands, I shoved it behind my back. "Forget it. I knew I should've asked John to buy you that laptop the school requests everyone to have. I'll-I'll tell him tonight. You might have to wait a few months while he saves up my salary to buy it, but I'll make sure you have something of use instead of—"

She sprang into me, bowling me over, slamming both of us to the blanket below. "Give it back."

My elbows bent awkwardly, my spine jabbed by the carved willow-wooden horse in my hands. "Wha—"

"My horse. Now. Give it back, Ren."

I wriggled beneath her as she sat on my chest, her shorts riding up suntanned thighs and lavender t-shirt right in my face. The sun silhouetted her, showing a faceless girl with curling white-blonde hair with her hand straight out and reckless determination bristling all around her.

"Now, Ren." Her voice turned sharp in the way she'd mastered from listening to Cassie telling me off.

Untangling my arms from behind my back, I lay flat and gave it up as a peace offering.

She continued to straddle my chest, snatching the horse and rider, the long ribbon sticking out between her fingers. "You can't give it to me then take it away. That's not how gift giving works."

Propping my head up with my hands, I tried to tame the clenching in my belly and did my best to accept that she liked it. Liked it enough to attack me to take it back, anyway. "It's not very good—"

"Zip it." She grabbed my lips between tight fingers, forcing my mouth closed. "I love it. It's better than all the shopping trips and all the ribbons." She squished my lips harder. "If you say one more bad thing about it, I'll...I'll—" She pouted, looking over my head toward the forests and fields. "I'll leave you here for something to eat."

I shook my head, dislodging her hold. "And here I thought you loved me."

"Not when you're being a moron."

"Hey, I just gave you a birthday present."

"And then took it away again." She scowled. "Not cool, dude. Not cool."

"Dude?" I chuckled. "Where the hell did that come from?"

Her personality had evolved leaps and bounds ever since she started hanging out with Liam and whatever kids she'd befriended at school. I'd even heard her curse the other day and told her off for such language.

I was fairly sure she hadn't picked that up from me seeing as I was super careful with how and what I said around her.

"Some girl in class."

"A girl you like?"

"I guess." She shrugged. "Stop changing the subject. Don't touch my gift."

"Okay, okay. I won't take it again."

"You better not."

I licked my lips from where her touch had been, tasting raspberries and sugar. "Now that we've got that sorted and you've attacked me on my birthday, what do you want to do for the rest of the day?"

She rolled off me, flopping onto her back and holding her horse aloft with the sun sparkling on its glossy flanks. "Dunno. Something."

"Something isn't helpful."

"Something with you."

"Did you want Liam and Cassie to come?"

Her blue eyes locked on mine with fierce certainty. "No. Just us."

"In that case..." Climbing upright, I helped her stand. "Let's go home for the day."

Her face brightened as she spun to face the dense treeline on the edge of the Wilson's property. "Truly?"

"Truly."

Slipping her hand in mine, we stepped into tree-shadows just as she yelped, "Oh no! I forgot to get you a present. It's your birthday, too!"

I shook my head. "Just spending the day with you is enough."

"But Cassie said that sweet sixteen means you get lots of stuff."

I stilled. "What sort of stuff?"

"Dunno. Stuff."

"This 'dunno' business is getting old real fast, Della."

She clutched my hand harder as she rubbed the toe of her sandal into the grass. "She wanted me to tell you something, but I don't wanna."

I crouched down, pulling her closer. "Tell me what?"

Her face scrunched up as if she'd taken a bite of sour lime. "She asked where we were going on your day off."

"Okay…"

"I told her it's our birthday."

"And…"

"And she wished me happy birthday and promised she'd teach me how to jump on Domino tomorrow as my present."

"That's nice of her."

"No, it isn't. 'Cause I know what she gets each time she lets me—" She sighed as if she carried the weight of a thousand problems. "I mean…I guess so."

I stiffened. There was no way she could know the standing arrangement between Cassie and me, trading horse rides for kisses.

Pushing that stupid thought aside, I murmured, "Tell me what's eating you, Little Ribbon."

"Nothing." She sniffed, staring at the dirt.

"It's something."

I hated her being so glum but I also couldn't help if I didn't know what her problem was.

I reached out to touch her golden head but she jerked away at the last second, stabbing me as surely and as perfectly as only she could do. Della was the only one who could make sunshine live in my chest then suffocate it with perpetual night, depending on how she tolerated me.

I hated when she was mad because nothing felt right. My heart didn't beat right. My body didn't behave right. She made me sick and the only medicine was to earn her smiles and hugs again.

"What's wrong?" My patience thinned, batting away the ache at letting her down in some way. Even though I wanted to demand she spit it out, I forced myself not to push her. She had a habit of shutting down these days over things I didn't understand. She'd give me the cold shoulder if she caught me laughing with Cassie and hadn't been a part of the conversation. She'd glower if Cassie was there, handing me tools and giggling in her school uniform when Della leaped off the bus.

She'd always been an open book, so the silent treatment confused me.

It hurt too, but I didn't feel I had the right to be in pain when she was obviously hurting because of something she refused to discuss.

Dealing with a growing girl was exhausting.

"Della...it's okay. You don't have to tell me." I brought her tiny hand to my mouth and kissed her knuckles. "Let's just go for a walk—"

"She said she's going to give you a special birthday treat tonight because sixteen is a big deal and sixteen-year-old boys deserve special treats." Tears glassed her beautiful eyes as she yanked her hand from mine. "I don't want her to give you anything. You're mine. And I forgot to give you something, and now you're going to get all the things from her and forget all about me!" With an agonizing gasp, she tore off into the trees.

What the—

"Della!" I chased after her, following the crash and crunch of twigs, trying to catch up as she ducked under low branches and weaved around Della-sized bushes. "Come back here."

She didn't stop. She didn't slow.

"Della Ribbon, you get your butt back here this instant!" I leapt over bracken, grateful for years of hard labour and a body good at endurance. She was a speedy little thing, and I had no intention of letting her get away with shutting down this time. *"Della!"*

Goddammit.

Something crashed to a stop in front of me, sending me skidding on the brakes as I almost ran into her.

She looked up beneath a curtain of blonde curls, her eyes tight and lips thin but tears no longer glittered. I almost wished there were tears because the calm collectedness in her stare terrified me.

"I'm sorry that I didn't get you a gift." She let me grab her and wedge her into my stomach. Her thin arms wrapped loosely around my hips as she breathed hard into my lower belly. "I didn't mean to be a child."

"You weren't a child."

"I forgot. I'm not supposed to say anything about Cassie."

I peeled her away, staring into her face, but once again, that blank collectedness stared back. "What aren't you telling me, Della?"

"Nothing."

"There's something."

"Nuh-uh. I'm fine." She smiled bright and brittle. "See?"

I didn't buy it, but my brain didn't work fast enough to figure out what she was hiding.

I fumbled for something to say, some reassurance to utter, some way to bring back the happy kid I loved with all my heart, but I was too slow, and Della's truth slipped through my fingers.

"Wanna play tag?" she asked, already bouncing away as if the past few minutes never existed. "You won't catch me." The flavour of heartache vanished as she giggled and took off at a dead sprint, long hair trailing, ribbon twirling.

I stared after her, lost.

What had just happened?

Della laughed, already a fair distance away. "Ren! Come on, slow poke!"

Whatever it was wasn't over, but I didn't want to taint the rest of our day together.

For now, I let her fake normalcy and bought into her assurances that whatever worried her wasn't too overpowering that it stopped her from playing.

I'd protect her from everything, but until she told me what hurt her, I had to trust she was okay.

I took off, leaping forward into the trees I adored over any house or barn. "Oh, you're in so much trouble when I get you!"

Her happy squeal tried to delete the strange, painful moment from before.

But it never quite removed the shadow she'd painted on my heart.

No matter how long we ran like the wild creatures we were.

No matter how much time we spent in the forest that was our true home.

Something had happened between us.

And it would have to be dealt with…sooner or later.

Chapter Thirty-Two

REN

2006

THAT NIGHT, WHEN Della had fallen asleep and I lay staring at the ceiling beside her, a soft knock on our bedroom door told me Cassie had come to give me her present.

Glancing down at Della, part of me wanted to pretend I hadn't heard her while the other part desperately wanted to find out what she'd give me.

It took a minute of internal warfare before I slid out of bed in just my boxers and hauled on a pair of shorts that were my cleanest pair. I debated whether to stay shirtless.

Which would seem worse? Shirtless while hoping we were about to make out, or clothed while hoping we were about to make out?

I chose modesty and grabbed a black t-shirt from the floor.

Tiptoeing toward the door, I held my finger to my lips to keep Cassie quiet as I slipped through a crack, looking back once more at sleeping Della, her hair spread all over my pillow and tiny body tucked under cosy covers.

Cassie nodded, following me silently toward the stables until I stopped by the tack room.

I didn't know what to say because we both knew why she was here. I didn't want to be the idiot to ask what she wanted or pretend anything was wrong. Just staring at her told me everything I needed to know.

No words were uttered as she stepped into my personal space, stood on her toes, and kissed me softly. The familiarity of kissing her now didn't mean my heart stayed calm. Like always, it leaped and thudded as warm wetness and slippery intoxication turned my brain to mush and body to granite.

Wrapping my arms around her, I backed her into the tack room wall, pressing her tight and daring to wedge the length of my frame against hers.

She moaned into our kiss, her fingers slipping through my hair as she tugged me closer. Our heads tilted as we deepened the kiss, breathing hard, tasting, and licking—quickly losing propriety in favour of clutching hands and clawing need.

Her hands left my hair, slipping over my shoulders and running down my chest.

I gasped as her touch disappeared up the hem of my t-shirt and fingernails ran along my belly. She tugged the waistband of my shorts, murmuring, "Can I give you a birthday present?"

I could barely speak intelligently when I was of sound body and mind; asking me a question while blood pounded between my legs and my heart acted as if it was in a death metal band made me utterly unable to talk.

"I take your silence as a yes." Slowly, she dropped to her knees. Her eyes glistened, mouth gleamed, tongue flickered over her bottom lip.

The air prickled around us, full of forbidden danger and illicit taboo. I was playing with fire. I was touching the boss's daughter, yet really, she was the one touching me.

I trembled as she pulled my shorts and boxers down in one go, freeing me, sending a flush of embarrassment through my blood, and leaving the tight elastic of my underwear clinging to my upper thighs.

Her fingers traced the raised scar tissue from the Mclary brand that I'd never be able to remove. She looked up, eyes full of questions. Questions I would refuse to answer.

She bit her lip, deliberating.

I stopped breathing, waiting.

Then her touch moved away from the mark, slipping to cup around my length.

I jolted with mind-numbing awareness as her fingers pulsed, and her voice trickled into my ears, "Have you had a blowjob before, Ren?"

I gulped, shaking my head like an idiot. I'd always known Cassie was forward and far more worldlier than I was. I'd seen her kiss different boys if she got dropped off from school in muscle cars or dinged up 4WDs. I'd heard her father yell at her not to be so loose, and her mother to scold her on her friendship choices.

Although, nothing seemed to stop her from searching for something, trying new things, and sampling experiences she probably wasn't ready for.

She'd even told me that I kissed differently to an old boyfriend she'd dated for two weeks a year ago. She made me feel terribly young and stupidly inexperienced.

I didn't want to be taught these things. I wanted to be able to participate and blow her mind just like she blew mine. But despite her forwardness, she remained sweet and kind, making me worried that one day, she'd be taken advantage of.

She also worried me around Della.

Della was still too young to know what painful passion felt like, brewing constantly in your veins. She believed kisses on the mouth were for unconditional love between anyone—friend, parent, or anyone else who deserved it. She already had older views on body image thanks to Cassie in her bikinis, and I didn't want her growing up too fast that sleeping in the same bed suddenly went from comforting to downright unpermitted.

She was a kid.

My kid.

And I wanted to keep her that way for as long as possible.

Funny, when I pictured her kissing a boy like I was kissing Cassie, red anger hazed my vision. I'd kill any boy who touched her and didn't quite know how I'd deal with her when she entered her teenage years.

A flutter of hot breath on my upper thighs was the only warning I had.

My mind shot blank as a tongue met my hard flesh, and my knees threatened to buckle. I slammed one hand against the wall, my other landed in her hair. A grunt escaped me as her tongue came again. My head swam, and I felt nauseous and invincible and fragile and immortal all at the same time.

"I take it this is your first time?" she whispered around my length.

My fingernails dug into the wood and clenched around her hair, holding her tight, not knowing if I was allowed to pull her closer and stop her torture by making her do what she promised.

I managed some sort of non-cohesive reply before her head bent again and that intoxicating puff of air stroked my body.

"Happy Birthday, Ren Wild." Her voice licked around me just as her mouth sealed hot and tight *everywhere.*

My head flopped forward.

My oxygen rushed out.

And my body jerked in bliss.

I thought of nothing but the sensation of wet heat and the pulling deep in my belly.

I'd grown wiser than I'd been a few years ago when puberty first started making my life a living nightmare. I'd learned how to shave without bleeding and how to combat unwelcome erections—most of the time.

But I'd never been comfortable making myself orgasm.

Either I was working and didn't feel right while being paid, or I was in bed beside Della.

Animals didn't self-pleasure, even if those dirty magazines said men did. The thought of jerking off, touching myself, and searching for that ever-wanted release didn't seem ethical.

But right here, right now, with a girl sucking me and every single worry deleted, I didn't care.

I was entirely in her hands.

I was her student, and I would take whatever she taught me.

Her fingers wrapped tighter around me, squeezing as her mouth slid deeper.

The pulling in my belly evolved to an outright pain, travelling in quaking lightning bolts up my thighs into my spine and crackling between my legs.

I winced as her teeth caught the tip, adding a thread of agony to an otherwise mind-numbing experience, but instead of stopping the impending snarling release, it magnified it.

"Cas—" I groaned as she grasped me tighter with one hand and dug fingernails into my ass with the other. She yanked me into her mouth as she sucked with noisy pulls.

I honestly had no control.

I couldn't stop it even if I pulled away and ran as far from her as possible.

The release had already captured me, and as she sucked me hard, fast, and unrelenting, I came.

I jerked and bowed and blinked back stars as Cassie very generously gave me my sixteenth birthday present in the doorway of her tack room, in the very same barn where Della and I were found.

* * * * *

That first intimate moment set in motion regular meetings between Cassie and me.

Over the next year, she taught me that blowjobs could be used as a punishment as well as a reward, depending on if I'd pissed her off or pleased her.

Some weeks, we'd sneak to somewhere shadowy and private on a nightly basis. And some months, we'd return to just being friends as she entered a relationship with a new boy from school or some peacock masquerading as a cool almost-adult instead of a drop-out teenager working minimum wage at a local store.

We never went further than touching and kissing, and that was mainly because of me.

I supposed, with my unconventional childhood and learning everything by myself rather than having society or family teach what I should and shouldn't do, meant I had a wariness that took time to accept new things.

I was still a loner, and some weeks, I struggled with humans even as nice as the Wilsons. The only person I never grew sick of was Della, and that was probably because she felt the same way as me.

That kid adored school.

She came home with constant assignments and excelled in every exam. She put her hand up for extra activities and even joined a few sport-teams.

However, when school holidays rolled around, she'd spend the first few days in bed unable to stand being around people, claiming she was exhausted and needed space.

I understood her exactly.

And having a likeminded friend let me accept that part of myself and not change...for anyone.

My reserved nature drove Cassie crazy, but I didn't know how to stop it. Luckily, it didn't prevent her from teaching me how to touch her...all of her...and my first experience fingering a woman had almost made me come as fast as my first blowjob had.

It was unlike anything I'd ever touched, and I become an avid learner.

It hadn't taken long to switch Cassie's response from indulgent smile and soft instruction to heavy breathing and scratching nails as I made her come just like she made me.

The first time I'd successfully made her unravel, my wrist and forearm held lacerations from where she'd scratched me mid-orgasm.

The next day, Della had asked what happened.

I'd blushed and blamed the barn cat who fed on the mice eating horse feed and burrowing into hay. She'd tutted and shook her head, telling me in her best parental voice to be more careful and to treat Blackie with more respect next time I tried to catch her.

Cassie had tried to laugh about it the next time we met, but that was one thing I never tolerated. She could laugh at Liam's escapades and discuss her family, friends, and boyfriend drama with me, and I would forever listen politely.

But try to pry into my background, try to make me laugh at Della's expense, or try to make fun of things I loved, and I shut down.

I didn't permit her to even mention Della unless it was to regale me with stories of her quickly improving equestrian skills or ask questions that would benefit their relationship.

I didn't know why, but I couldn't let my guard down about Della or relax enough to give Cassie answers to the questions she constantly asked.

Questions about the place where I'd been sold.

Questions about my mother.

Questions about how I ran away with Della.

I either turned mute or changed the subject—not because I didn't have answers but because something inside refused to give up that part of myself...to anyone.

A year after Della and I were caught sleeping in their barn, Cassie blew up at me for being quiet and elusive. I didn't know why she called me elusive when I made sure to be friendly and polite to every single one of the Wilsons.

She'd tried to enlighten me, saying she didn't know me at all even after a year of fooling around and seeing each other every day, that my refusal to talk about my past, that my preference to stay at home rather than head to the movies or gatherings, and the fact I didn't give anything of myself was a drain and a bore, and frankly, she wanted someone more outgoing.

After our fight, she'd announced that we could only be friends as she was with some new Nathan or Ryan or Paul.

I didn't mind either way.

I wasn't jealous of her with other boys.

I wasn't annoyed that I was passed over for what she called better alternatives. In fact, I rather liked being ignored because it meant I returned to a simpler lifestyle where my only desire was looking after Della and making sure she was as happy as I could make her.

Chapter Thirty-Three

REN

2007

ANOTHER WINTER CAME.

My work around the farm went from crazy to part-time, and with idle hands came the itch to leave. Every night that Della slept beside me, taller, prettier, more girl than child, I wondered where our future would take us.

There was no question that if I left she'd come too, but I was trapped by both returning cold weather and Della's love for going to school.

On the last week of her term, before winter closed classes down for a while, she seemed off when we ate together in our room. I'd taken to keeping produce that I'd helped plant and tend in a mini fridge that John Wilson had delivered to us a few months ago.

I had a camping stove and preferred to cook on my own rather than accept the nightly invitation to eat with the Wilsons in their snug home. Not because things between Cassie and I were strained right now, or even that, as I grew older, I became more wanderer by heart and outsider by nature, but because I enjoyed keeping my skills sharp.

One day, I would live off the land again, and when that day came, I couldn't be soft and useless when it came to skinning rabbits or preparing meals for two. I'd already let my talent at thievery turn rusty thanks to earning an honest wage, but it was never far from my mind.

I didn't think that mentality would ever fully leave me. Even at seventeen, I still studied unprotected spots in house defences, body language of easy prey, and weaknesses that I could exploit if I wanted to.

That night, instead of a normal Wednesday evening when Della and I curled up in front of the TV with a simple meal of simmered carrots and honey glazed chicken, my life took a swerve into terror territory.

She accepted her dinner with her usual politeness and even gave me a weak smile.

But something was off.

My heart, that usually calmed down and found happiness whenever I was around her, skyrocketed with anxious nerves. "You okay?" I asked softly, brushing aside hair that'd stuck to her cheek.

The instant my fingers connected with her skin, I yanked them back faster than a whip. Immediately, I took the plate she held listlessly, climbed off the bed, and scooped her from the end.

She didn't mutter one annoyance or frustration which layered my already anxious heart with more fear.

"Della…"

With as much tenderness as I could, I placed her on top of the bedspread and gathered her hair away from her back and neck so it draped over the pillow out of the way.

She groaned softly as if lying on a comfortable mattress hurt.

"Tell me what's wrong." I kneeled by the bed, hoping I looked in charge and strong when really, I was dying inside. "What is it? Something you ate? A cold? Tummy bug?"

We weren't immune to everyday illnesses, especially now that Della spent the majority of her time around grubby children and unhygienic school classrooms. We'd had enough colds to know the symptoms.

But this was different.

She'd been listless yesterday too but still chirpy when I pushed her. Then again, she'd only eaten half her dinner and none of her dessert, when normally, she wolfed whatever I put in front of her.

I'd stayed up late, watching her sleep, and she'd been deep under all night.

I should've been more diligent. I should've known she was worse than she let on.

She had a habit of hiding things—keeping secrets close to her chest. Most of the time, I could handle her need for privacy and lived in constant hope that one day, she would trust me enough to share her secrets.

But today wasn't that day, and I should've known better than to accept her lies.

She'd fibbed right to my face about her health and put herself in harm's way.

Didn't she know that was the worst kind of punishment? I loved her unconditionally, and she'd hurt herself yet again by keeping things from me.

My hands curled.

I wanted to tell her off, but instead, my mind raced with questions and theories of what could be wrong as my fingers rested on her forehead again, wincing at the heat radiating from her.

Goddammit, how had I not noticed?

Why did I let her go to school this morning?

"You lied to me. You said you were feeling better." I cupped her cheek, willing her to open her eyes. "Little Ribbon…what have you done?"

She moaned, her lips parting just enough for a flinched breath. "I'm sorry."

"Don't apologise. I just wish you'd said something."

"I had to hand in my science project that you helped me with."

I scoffed. "I think two caterpillars turning into chrysalis and butterflies in a jam jar could've waited if you weren't feeling okay."

A lonely tear leaked from her left eye. "I'm sorry."

I bent and pressed my forehead against her cheek, curling my arm around her head. "Don't. It's me who should apologise."

"But I made you mad."

My heart cracked. "You didn't make me mad. You made me worried. Big difference." I couldn't take my eyes off her as she winced and wriggled in discomfort. "You have me so damn worried, Little Ribbon, and here I am scolding you when I should be making you better."

"I'm sorry." She snuggled into my embrace even though her body was a mini furnace.

"Stop saying that." I held her tight, willing the chaos in my brain to settle enough to talk without bite and ask questions gently. "I'm the one who's sorry, and now I'm going to do everything I can to make you better."

Kissing her softly on her nose, I asked, "Tell me what's wrong. List how you feel." I'd watched Patricia Wilson deal with Liam when he was regularly ill from kids at school. I'd lurked outside while Cassie recovered from a bad flu on the couch and she was doted on by concerned parents.

At the time, I thought them lucky to have such care—their only worry was to heal and be a demanding patient where all their wishes were met.

Now, I understood it from the panicked caregiver's point of view. The anxious hovering over their baby to ensure they were still breathing. The nervous voice when they asked how they were, dreading a reply of worse and begging for an answer of better.

Now, I was that parent, and I would do anything in the world to trade places with Della and suffer whatever she was going through.

She bit her bottom lip as she wriggled away from my embrace, sweat dotting her upper lip. "I'm hot."

"Tell me what else. Tell me how I can fix this." All I wanted to do was slaughter her pain and send it directly to hell.

"I'm thirsty." She blinked with wide eyes. "Um...I'm hot. My legs ache. I'm...tired." She yawned as if on cue, trying to roll onto her side.

I didn't permit it, holding her firm. "Anything else?"

Shaking her head, she moaned, "I dunno. Just...everything doesn't feel right, Ren." She tried to roll again, but I kept my hand clutched on her shoulder, dislodging her pink knitted jumper, revealing her back.

A red rash invaded the perfection of her porcelain skin.

Fuck.

Leaping clumsily onto the bed, I scooped her close and yanked off her jumper.

"No..." She protested weakly and not her usual spit fire attack. That alone made my belly knot and heart shut down.

All over her chest and back was a rash. An enemy infiltrating everything I loved in the world.

She batted me away with a feather-weak hand as I let her flop back down and undid the zipper on her jeans. Her head lolled on the pillow as I pulled them as gently as I could down her legs, my lips thinning and head pounding as I found yet more red rash.

Outside, snow had started to fall, and my mind regressed to when she was sick the first time, and we'd stumbled upon Polcart Farm. That place had saved her life. Perhaps Cherry River would save her this time.

Because as much as I would slay dragons for her, I was not a doctor.

I didn't have a clue what was wrong, and I couldn't stop my morbid thoughts from filling me with agony of her dying due to my incompetence.

Pulling her jeans back up, I hastily buttoned them, bundled her up in one of my jumpers, then clutched her tight.

Striding from the room, I carried her through swirling snowflakes and pounded on the Wilson's door.

* * * * *

Della was admitted to the hospital.

For three days, I paced those antiseptic corridors and slept curled up on a hard, cold couch at the foot of her single cot.

I hated that place.

I *despised* that place.

But I refused to leave even for a moment.

Della couldn't leave; therefore, I couldn't leave.

Turned out, thanks to scientific words I didn't understand and people I couldn't tolerate, Della had chicken pox. Normally, a kid contracted the virus and dealt with it no problem, but Della had a worse than normal reaction to Varicella, which according to some doctor I wanted to punch in the face, was the correct term for the red spots, obsessive itchiness, migraines, tiredness, and vomiting that Della endured.

She couldn't keep anything down, and her body looked more crimson than cream thanks to the invasion of spots and her tendency to scratch until she bled.

It ripped out my guts to see her in so much discomfort and not have any power to help.

This was the first time I'd been in a hospital since my finger had been cut off. Back then, I'd been given candy and a toy. Back then, I'd felt cared for and in good hands—until Mclary threw my gifts and their kindness out the window, of course.

But right now, I doubted everyone. No one had the power to stop Della's pain, and I hated them. I'd expected miracles, and Della had received subpar attention with lacklustre results.

Despite their un-miracle-working care, she slowly got better. I didn't give the tired looking doctors and harassed looking nurses any credit.

I gave it all to her.

Della was strong.

She fought hard.

And when she finally stopped vomiting and her symptoms abated to an annoying scratch with no fever, she was released, and John Wilson drove us back to Cherry River.

Cassie, Liam, and Patricia all wanted to crowd and cuddle my patient upon her arrival, but I forbade them.

My possessiveness only grew worse now the doctors had relinquished her back into my care. Not that they had technically. They'd put her into the Wilson's care as I was still a minor.

Before, when I was young and terrified of having someone's whole existence hinge entirely on me, I would've been grateful to the Wilsons for loving Della as much as I did. If they had been the ones I left her with, I would've made the right choice.

But that was years ago, and things had changed. Della no longer needed me to survive, but I sure as hell needed her, and even with her sick, I needed her close.

At least the Wilsons knew she was mine and backed off after their initial welcome.

Della was my responsibility, and I ensured her every beck and call was met: applying lotion to her spots, duct taping her hands into my thick baling gloves to stop her from scratching, and feeding her whatever she wanted.

No matter that I was left alone to do whatever Della needed, I still couldn't get over the desire to growl at anyone who came close or snarl at those who offered help.

I acted like a controlling, dominating bastard but that was what Della's fragility made me become. I patrolled around her like a wolf would his cub, ready to bite anything that dared damage what was his.

I'd do anything to make her well again; including destroying anyone who got too close.

The Wilsons provided us with healthy soups and drinks—when they braved my temper—and when Della blinked awake one afternoon from yet another nap and her familiar strength started to glow beneath her illness, I found my selfishness at keeping her to myself fading.

I 'borrowed' John Wilson's Land Rover—which was so much easier to drive than a tractor—and headed into town where I used a handful of change found in the middle console to purchase Della's request for a Filet o' Fish happy meal.

For so long, we'd never had processed food, and I didn't particularly like that she'd grown to enjoy it. Ever since she started having lunches and weekend play dates with friends from school, her palate had adapted to not only enjoy fresh produce but also greasy takeaway.

I preferred to keep burgers and fries as birthday treats but Cassie called me old fashioned whenever I'd grumble about Della's new favourite foods.

John saw me arriving with the cab of his truck reeking of takeout but didn't say a word as I parked on his driveway and climbed out with the brown paper bag.

We stared at each other.

I tipped my head in gratitude along with the acknowledgment that I'd been a grumpy bastard and taken something I shouldn't. He nodded back, forgiving me and understanding.

Giving him another nod, I jogged back to Della to give her what she craved.

If junk food was the recipe to getting my favourite person back, then I'd do it.

I'd do anything for her.

Just like I'd stayed here past winter for her.

Just like I'd sacrifice anything of mine so she could have everything.

Chapter Thirty-Four

DELLA

Present Day

THERE ARE SO *many things I remember about Cherry River, but one of my sharpest memories isn't the itch and horribleness of chicken pox—to be honest, I don't really want to remember it so I probably shoved that part aside.*

What I do remember is what happened afterward.

What was that, you ask?

Well, the boy who nursed me back to health hadn't factored in his own invincibility against diseases we hadn't been around or vaccinated against.

Ren gave me everything he had those few weeks while I was ill.

He barely slept. He delivered my cravings. He gave me anything I asked for.

And what did he get in return?

Chicken pox.

I noticed it one night when his usual tossing and turning was eerily catatonic. Ren didn't sleep well. He never had. I'd been selfish and never minded because if he was awake, it meant I was safe sleeping beside him.

But this time...Ren didn't move when I whispered his name in the darkness. He didn't move just like when he'd had the flu-turned-pneumonia which led us to being befriended by the Wilsons in the first place.

That catastrophe had a happy ending.

I didn't want to tempt fate by seeing what would happen if he got terribly sick again. But those spots on the back of his neck and even one on his cheek above his five o'clock shadow hinted that he was about to endure what I'd gone through.

The next few days, he grew worse.

Somehow, as he grew sicker, I grew stronger, and our roles reversed. I was the one dabbing his flesh with lotion to stop the itch. I was the one dishing out painkillers for his fever, and I was the one carrying soup across the driveway courtesy of Patricia's awesome cooking skills.

Well, I was the one...until Cassie took over.

She infiltrated our bedroom and sat beside Ren on our bed. She touched his brow and whispered secrets, and all I could do was return to school, hiding the hissing jealousy in my heart and not able to focus at all on what the teacher said.

Cassie had school too, but she always seemed to be in my spot beside Ren when I got dropped off by the bus and there until late when it should just be the two of us.

My frustration steadily grew.

I'd sit in the corner chair with my legs bunched up and my arms wrapped tight around them, glowering at Cassie touching my Ren.

Every time she leaned in and touched his cheek. Every time she laughed at something he mumbled.

Ugh, it was times like that that I hated her all over again.

She'd been so kind and generous to me—letting me ride her favourite pony, teaching me how to canter and jump, and even letting me tag along to a local show when she competed.

I struggled because she was a genuine person and didn't hang out with me to get to Ren—I would've been able to tell; believe me, I was suspicious for a very long time—which made my despising her worse because I felt like a horrible, terrible child, and all I wanted to do was grow up faster so I wouldn't be so silly and petty.

Funny how I'm older now but whenever I think about Cherry River, I still have both love and hate inside me. I think, if I had to relive that time, I would be just as jealous as I'd been as a seven-year-old, only this time, I'd probably be arrested for murder.

Instead of just hero worship and parental adoration, I now have forbidden cravings and achings and all the things I know I shouldn't feel.

I know you're probably thinking...eww, how could you fall in love with your brother who is technically your father and definitely your uncle or some other untouchable life figure?

In my defence, I'll ask you a similar question.

How could you not fall in love with a boy like Ren Wild?

How could you not fall in love with a boy who puts you first in everything, protects you at all costs, worships the ground you walk on, gives you things you didn't know you wanted, who can hear your thoughts and see your fears? A boy who sacrificed so much without even telling you, leaving you heartbroken when you're old enough to figure it out for yourself?

If you'd been taken and raised and cherished by a boy who was closer to your age; therefore, he understood your childish tantrums better, could get in touch with his imagination easier, and have a better ability at discipline because he wasn't afraid to growl if you got out of line with no grudges or pause between instruction and praise, I think you'd fall in love, too.

Ren was simple.

Ren spoiled me.

Ren kept me in line.

No one else came close.

But it wasn't his skills at raising me that made me fall in love with him.

Oh, no…

It was everything else that happened as I grew older, and he grew into a man.

I suppose you're wondering if I'm ever going to enlighten you on our third and fourth separation.

I haven't forgotten.

I'm just getting up the guts to tell you, because…the more you learn about me from here on out, the more you'll probably end up rolling your eyes, and thinking I didn't deserve all the sacrifices Ren made for me.

I had been his Ribbon—special, brave, and smart.

But then, through my own actions, I became argumentative, opinionated, and stupid.

I wish I could say I'd do things differently, but I honestly don't know if I would.

Crazy, right?

Crazy looking back at the heartache I caused both of us and still selfish enough not to change.

I was the reason we separated that third time.

I was the one who ruined everything.

For so long, I blamed Cassie.

I pinned all the guilt and regret onto her.

But it wasn't her fault.

As much as I wished I could type a lie and make you hate her just like I did.

I can't.

The fault was mine.

And I guess, eventually, I'm going to have to tell you.

But not right now.

Right now, I want you to continue liking me…for just a little longer.

Chapter Thirty-Five

DELLA

Present Day

ME AGAIN.

Strange, huh?

I closed my laptop a few hours ago, intending to put aside my past and the emotions that are tearing me up inside, but I can't sleep.

I can't stop thinking about Ren.

Always Ren.

I want to cry to relieve the aching pressure in my chest every time I think about him, but all I can do is laugh in the darkness and try to expand my ribs to contain the ever ballooning need that will never earn what it wants.

Melodramatic enough for you?

Too much for me, and I'm the one living this soap opera.

You know, until that last chapter, I've never actually said those words out loud…

Those terrible words that tear away the curtain and light up the truth in blinding stage lights with orchestras playing sad strings and empty amphitheatres pitying the poor wretched soul admitting such a tragedy.

Never really allowed myself to admit what I've known for so long.

I'm in love with Ren Wild.

It looks even worse in bold, doesn't it?

It looks like a life sentence I can never be free of…which, in a way, is exactly what it is.

I can't pinpoint the exact moment my childish affection turned to teenage crush turned to forever kind of addiction.

But what I do know is I will always love Ren.

I will always be in love with Ren.

And I also know I will never have him, and I'll end up marrying some other man who doesn't reach into my heart or has power over my every living breath like he does.

Anyway, enough of my present-day dramas.

You're not here to hear about that…not yet, anyway. There's still a fair piece of the story to go before I can share what I did yesterday or today or what I have planned for tomorrow.

Spoiler alert: I have no plans for tomorrow apart from ensuring my lies are hidden and my smiles are innocent, and my deep, dark desires are tucked far away.

Same as every day…nothing new, so I might as well give you something interesting.

Let's return to Cherry River.

I ended the previous chapter talking about Ren being ill with chicken pox and kind of went on another tangent about Cassie (grr) and my idiotic behaviour (ugh).

Cassie…

My favourite subject, and yes, I'm being sarcastic.

I know I keep flogging this subject, and this is the last time, I swear, but when it was just me and her…I loved her. I need you to see that.

I wholeheartedly adored that girl.

But when it was the three of us…well…what can I say that I haven't already?

Ren was mine.

Even as a kid, I'd known that. To a seven-year-old, my need for Ren stemmed from being the centre of his attention, the favourite in his heart, and confident in my place as first within his life.

Cassie threatened all of that.

And now, as an almost-adult, I can say she threatened my future too.

I didn't know it then, but over the years, she and Ren got close—even when they weren't sneaking behind barns or into stables to make out, they still had a fondness for each other.

Ren would often drop everything whenever she called on the emergency cell phone she'd make him have on the nights she'd sneak out with her troublemaker friends.

I'd tagged along with him for a few pickups.

Whenever that phone rang—way past midnight when John and Patricia believed their innocent daughter was safely tucked up in bed—Ren and I would 'borrow' the Land Rover and drive to wherever she was currently tipsy and partying.

She'd squeal my name, grab my hands as if I was her favourite person, then dash to the driver's side and plant a big, wet kiss on Ren's mouth.

I hated that, but I didn't mind her floppy and giggly in the back seat, regaling us with tales of bonfires and who hooked up with whom that night.

She was hard work, but she made it enjoyable by including us in her escapades.

Ren and I would share a look from where I sat up front with him. He'd roll his eyes and whisper things under his breath only I could hear—copying her or mocking her—our own little game.

In a way, Cassie made us become closer.

We had something in common, and we all shared a secret that the adults didn't know about. Even Liam didn't know what his sister got up to at night, and I enjoyed being in the big kids group even if I didn't understand what she meant when she used words like fucked and fingered.

During those conversations, Ren would turn on the radio and make me dance along with him. He'd drive one-handed while grabbing my arm with the other, distracting me with loud music from whatever naughty things Cassie was confessing.

Anywho, I did it again...I went on another Cassie tangent.

I'm not talking about her again for a while.

Ren.

I want to talk about Ren.

I better start by saying, he survived the chicken pox.

Obviously.

He healed faster than I did, bounced back to a boy full of health and was back on the tractor even before his skin was spot and scratch free.

Cassie returned to her popular world of friends and sometimes-boyfriends, and I was able to focus in school again, returning to the top of the class and hanging out with a girl called Celine who I swapped lunches with (she got chocolate while I got yoghurt...so naturally, I wanted what she had).

Life was good.

In fact, it was super good for the rest of the year.

During summer, I'd help Ren with his copious amount of chores around the farm, and in winter, we bunkered down just the two of us in our warm one bedroom.

I'm sure some days stood out where happiness was acute and misery was absent, but right now, I'm drawing a blank on anything super special to write about.

I don't mean to sound as if life wasn't amazing because it was.

Life on a farm was full of routine and new things every day.

Sunrise was our alarm clock, noon was our opportunity to stuff hungry bodies with delicious home-cooked meals, and evenings were spent with the Wilsons or ourselves.

The Wilsons gave me and Ren a safe place, and Ren gave his labour to ensure I lived a perfect childhood.

I couldn't have been luckier.

And that's why I'm going to start skipping forward to years I do remember clearly because, as much as this assignment is no longer for public reading, I don't want to bore myself. Especially, when I have some juicy memories just begging to be written.

Let's start with 2008.

The year started off awesome because it was just me and Ren camping in the hayloft in our old tent for New Years. It was smaller than I remembered and cramped, but we spent the evening eating candy, and Ren caved under pressure to tell me story after story.

He told me what he did during the days while I was at school. He painted pictures of himself saving a couple of sheep from a neighbour's farm who had tangled themselves in the boundary fence. He regaled secrets of getting too hot hauling hay on his own and jumping naked into the same river where we all swam.

He made me laugh.

He made me fall asleep knowing 2008 was going to be the best year ever.

And in many ways it was, but it was also full of embarrassing moments as I started to grow up faster than before.

For the past year or so, I'd been acutely aware that older kids and even adults kissed, touched, and did things that I was curious about.

I'd wanted to ask Ren why watching him kiss Cassie made my tummy go queasy, but a curiosity welled to know more, too.

But I never dared.

I never asked the questions burning inside me, swallowing things like: 'Why do you have different body parts than me? Why does Cassie rub against you like a moronic cat? Why does Liam have the same body as you but smaller? Do you rub against Cassie like a moronic cat, too?'

Silly things but things I desperately wanted to know.

Kids at school tried to educate each other thanks to overhearing parents talk, and so far, I'd gathered snippets about birds and bees and squirms infecting eggs and eggs being delivered by cranes which weren't really eggs like chickens laid but babies, and sometimes babies were caused by other magic when daddies touched mummies where pee comes out and then she got fat.

It made no sense to my unenlightened child brain, and I was too embarrassed to ask Ren.

I was even too embarrassed to ask Cassie.

So who did I ask?

Probably the one person I shouldn't as he was just as clueless as me.

I turned to Liam Wilson. Nine years old, boisterous but shy and still obsessed with lizards.

Including the lizard in his shorts.

And that was how Patricia Wilson found us one summer afternoon.

God, I'm blushing even now.

I can't believe I'm about to write this down, but here I go...

Liam and I hung out but not all that often.

I liked him, but I found him so young and silly compared to the calm, collected reservation of Ren. Liam squealed and charged. Ren spoke with rough serenity and moved with assurance.

Ren was mature with his rough-stubble cheeks and strong muscles. Liam was juvenile with his baby face and twig arms.

But Ren was too perfect to sully with gross things like what I wanted to know, so I figured Liam would be the perfect teacher.

Basically, I asked him to show me his if I showed him mine.

Obviously, I know now why he was only too happy to oblige. It seems all boys are happy to get naked for the right incentive.

We clutched hands, heat blooming on my face and scandalous danger welling in my chest as we left the house where Patricia was tending to her roses and walked quickly to the shaded grotto around the pond.

There, we stood awkwardly until Liam pointed at my summer dress with splashes of purple and pink and told me to pull it off.

I remember the rush of naughtiness even then, quickly swamped by shivers of fear.

Hiding my quaking hands, I grabbed the hem and jerked the dress over my head and stood bravely with just my white knickers on.

He nodded all business-like and the severest nine-year-old scowl I'd ever seen, then unbuckled his shorts, shoved them down his legs and ripped off his t-shirt.

I'd seen Ren naked many times—not so much recently, but I had memories of thick legs, hair-covered thighs, heavy flesh dangling between them, and a stomach and back rippling with light and shadow whenever he moved.

Liam was a sapling while Ren was the oak.

He shrugged in his white underpants, almost identical to mine. "Now what?"

"I dunno." I shrugged back. "Where are your squirms?"

His nose wrinkled. "Squirms?"

"You know, the things that make mummies fat, and then birds deliver babies."

"You're weird." Pointing at my knickers, he commanded, "Maybe you have squirms. Take them off and we'll see."

"You take yours off, too."

He nodded sharply, hooking his fingers into his underpants waistband. "Okay. One...two...three."

We both shoved down our underwear and kicked them away at the same time. I stood barefoot.

He stood in his socks.

We stared at the differences in our bodies, moving closer in fascination.

"It's so small." I reached out to touch the worm-like thing between his legs. "Ren is bigger. Did yours shrink?"

He batted away my hand, poking his finger in my nipple. "You have no tits like Cassie. Did yours shrink, too?"

I looked down at my flat chest, so much like Liam's and not at all like

Cassie's fullness. An awful pressure of inadequacy filled me, of fear that I was deformed, of terror that I needed what Cassie had to make boys like Ren notice me.

My shoulders slouched. "I don't know how to get tits."

Liam sighed. "I don't know how to get a bigger worm."

His melancholy matched mine, and I found a kindred soul. Wanting to cheer him up, I smiled. "It's a nice worm, though."

He returned my smile with a trace of self-consciousness. "Thanks."

We looked at the ground, exhausting our ability of conversation and not sure what to do next. Then I had an epiphany which well and truly got us into trouble.

"Liam?"

He looked up. "Yeah?"

"Do you know about kissing?"

His nose wrinkled again, but this time his whole face joined in, scrunching up like a prune. "Eww. Mummy and Daddy do it, but it's gross."

"Cassie and Ren do it," I confessed. "And I don't like it."

"I don't like it, either." He stuck out his tongue as if he'd tasted something nasty. "Yucky."

"Want to try?" I gulped, cursing the words but also eternally curious.

"What?" He backed up again, his worm bouncing. "Nuh-uh. No way."

"Just one. Don't you want to know?"

"I know already. It's gross."

"I know but how gross?" I followed him as he stepped deeper into the grotto; his socks soaking up the damp ground and my bare feet skating over slippery leaves. "Don't you want to know why they keep kissing if it's so gross? Don't you want to know why they seem so happy afterward?"

I rubbed at the fist wrapped around my heart.

Happiness was never something I'd begrudge Ren, but happiness from kissing Cassie drove me into a painful place that I couldn't untangle.

"I dunno." He finally stopped, not that he had anywhere else to go. His back pressed up against the weeping willow, its fronds all around us like a magical fairyland. "Why do you want to know?"

"'Cause I'm sick of not knowing. I want to know everything." Brushing aside a frond, I stood directly in front of him.

He eyed me warily. "I want to go back."

"We'll go back after a kiss, okay?" I hated that I was the younger one, but I was the teacher in this. I didn't like it. Here, I was seeking answers, and instead, I was giving them to him instead of the other way around.

"One kiss?" He looked at me sceptical. "Then I can go?"

"Yup."

"And you won't tell anyone my worm is small? 'Cause if you do, I'll say you have no tits."

"Deal." I stuck out my hand, glad he made us promise because I didn't want

that secret getting out. Tits were something older girls had, and I wanted so much to be an older girl.

I was sick of being in the dark and categorized as too young to know.

Liam placed his hand in mine, and we shook hard. Still touching, we brought our heads together while our naked bodies stayed put.

He puckered his lips.

I copied.

He sucked in a breath.

I copied.

Our lips met in a flurry of pressure.

It was over.

It'd been the same sort of kiss Ren had given me time and time again. There were no secrets, no answers, no wisdom to be found.

"Again?" I asked, tugging him forward, bitterly disappointed but determined not to stop until I understood why others seemed to enjoy it so much.

"Ugh, you said only one." Liam exhaled, yanking his hand back. "This sucks."

"One more and then you can go."

"Promise?"

"Cross my heart and hope to die." I drew an X on my flat chest.

"Fine." He leaned toward me, looking bored.

I leaned toward him, trembling eagerly.

And just as our mouths met a second time, our little experiment was shattered.

"Liam! Della! What on earth do you think you two are doing!?"

Liam squealed and took off.

And all I could do was turn around and stare at Patricia Wilson's sandal-covered feet, naked as the day I was born and still just as lost.

Chapter Thirty-Six

REN

2008

"DO YOU WANT me to talk to her?"

I hugged myself against what Patricia Wilson just told me. "No. I can deal with it."

How, I had no clue?

I had a mind to spank her. To pull her dress up like she'd done today and smack her bare backside until she understood that being naked around boys was never going to be an option for her.

I groaned under my breath, rubbing my face and trying to rid the images Patricia had put there.

Liam and Della.

Naked under the willow tree.

Kissing.

Goddammit, how the hell did I deal with this? She was eight, for God's sake, not eighteen. It had never crossed my mind that she would be like me and start seeking answers to her feelings inside. I'd been older than her when my first urges appeared, and I'd had the benefit of already knowing that two animals climbing on top of one another equalled a baby a few months later.

I knew that lesson so well, it was the main reason I hadn't let Cassie tempt me any further than fingers and tongues.

I did not want a baby.

I already had one.

And I'd ruined her by keeping information away from her.

Keeping my eyes downcast, I mumbled, "They didn't...have sex, did they?" I winced, already dreading her answer. The thought of someone touching Della, even if it was Liam, made things inside me hiss and howl.

Did that mean Della was pregnant just like the Mclary's ewes after one visit with his ram? And if she was, how the hell would we deal with this? How the hell would I get over the sick feeling inside?

"No, nothing like that. It was just kids being kids." Patricia shook her head, clutching a tea towel stained with berry juice from making jam. "They're curious, and it's my fault that I left the talk with Liam so long. I'll sit him down tonight and make sure he understands everything about sex and body parts and make sure it never happens again."

The minute I'd come in from the fields, Patricia had asked me to share a cup of coffee with urgent things to discuss.

I'd wanted to refuse.

It'd been a long day, and I suffered a little of heatstroke and wanted shade, cold water, and quiet in that order.

But now, Della had screwed up my plans by being as loose as Cassie was.

Perhaps, I better pack a bag right now and leave.

If Cassie's tendencies were rubbing off on Della, no way would we stay here. No way would I stand by and let her open her legs for the local boys and riff-raff in this town.

No *fucking* way.

My nostrils flared as my temper grew hotter.

The thought of it.

The images.

God—

Patricia noticed, standing up and moving into the sugary-smelling kitchen. "It's not the end of the world, Ren, and I'll gladly talk to Della as well as Liam. I've got a book with illustrations. I'm not embarrassed to answer any questions she might have."

My heart pounded.

A book?

I still couldn't read very well.

How the hell was I supposed to teach Della from a book?

As much as the thought of talking to her petrified me—worse than any farm incident or even a Social Services visit—I couldn't allow myself to pass the responsibility onto Patricia.

Della was my problem.

I'd deal with her.

"Like I said, I'll take care of it." Stalking toward the back door, my hand barely wrapped around the handle before Patricia said, "Be gentle on her, Ren. She's not being naughty. She's being a young girl transforming into a woman."

Great. All the things I'm not equipped to deal with.

Moving toward an overflowing bookcase by the fireplace, Patricia pulled a book free with a title in green and a man and woman smiling on the cover. "This is the book and has graphic pictures and explanations." She practically had to force it into my hand, patting my knuckles as she moved away. "She wants to know what her body is going through. She needs to be prepared for when her breasts start growing and pubic hair starts appearing and periods start hurting."

"Right." I wrenched open the door, desperate to get away from words like periods and pubic.

I'd only just recently found out about periods myself thanks to Cassie turning into a dragon at certain times of the month. At first, I had no clue why she was such a bitch, but she wasn't afraid to discuss what happened to her body or the by-product of not getting pregnant every month.

I knew animals came into season, but I'd never seen them bleed if they weren't mated.

Frankly, humans grossed me out, and I didn't want to know any more about it.

"Send her to me if it gets too much!" Patricia called after me as I jogged across the driveway to the barn and our one bedroom.

I waved once as I disappeared into the hay-scented building and prepared to do something I was woefully unprepared to do.

* * * * *

I found her curled up on the bed, her back against the headboard, her arms wrapped around her legs, her dress wrapped tight and tucked into her feet, and her face buried against her knees.

Her whole posture screamed 'leave me alone', and that was exactly what I wanted to do, but I had a job, and I couldn't rest until I'd done it.

She looked so young.

Far too young for what she'd done.

But she was the same age as the girls that Mclary would abuse.

The same age to know that her body was fragile when a man wanted it for his own pleasure.

The same age to be protected at all costs.

Images of her naked and kissing Liam exploded back into my head, and my temper that'd been steadily simmering overflowed.

Marching forward, I growled. "What the *hell* were you thinking, Della?"

She burrowed deeper into her dress-wrapped knees, not replying.

Tossing the book onto the covers beside her, I paced at the end of the bed. "Do you have *any* idea what you could've done? Do you know what happens when a man takes from a girl? Do you know how badly you could've been hurt? What are you trying to do? Give me a goddamn heart attack? You're a *kid*! You don't need to know about sex or babies or—"

Her head popped up, tears staining her face and matching anger red on her cheeks. "I'm *not* a kid. I'm eight years old. I *do* want to know about babies and kissing and—"

"You *know* what kissing is. We kiss all the time." I breathed hard, trying to get myself in check. "Kissing is a way to show love for each—"

"But you don't love Cassie, and you kiss her more than you kiss me. You kiss her with your tongue!"

My jaw dropped. "When have you seen me do that?"

I'd been so fucking careful.

I'd made sure Cassie never surprised me around Della. If Cassie kissed me in front of her, it was simple and innocent and exactly like what Della was used to from me and Patricia; hell, even Cassie kissed her.

"I'm not stupid. I know if I wake up sometimes and you're not here that you're off kissing her. I know where to find you. It's not hard. I've seen you touch her..." She gulped. "You know...down there. I've seen her kiss you...down there. I've seen so many things, and the kids at school tried to explain it to me but no one seems to know and it's making me so mad not to know and I'm sad that I'm stupid and I'm angry that you don't want to tell me and now I'm wondering if you actually love her more than you love me because you let her kiss you in more places and it hurts so much and I'm so confused—" Her rush with no punctuation or pauses ended as she burst into tears, wedging her face back into the wet patch already on her dress.

My temper switched from bubbling volcano to vast ocean full of condemnation and litres of painful guilt.

I exhaled slowly, letting the rage in the room seep through the door and cracks in the window until the only sounds were from my pounding heart and Della's soft crying.

Perching awkwardly on the edge of the bed, I picked up the book and stroked the smiling faces of the cover. "I'm sorry."

She hiccupped, her tears still loud.

I tried again. She deserved it.

Patricia was right.

I should've been gentler.

This wasn't her fault.

I'd done this by sneaking off whenever my libido got the best of me and not thinking she wouldn't notice.

"Little Ribbon..." I waited until she raised her head just enough for her red-rimmed eyes to meet mine. The moment she sniffed and stared at me, I let go of the aching fear I'd carried since hearing about her putting herself in harm's way. I let her see just how much I cared and just how angry I was that I wasn't prepared for her to grow up just yet.

I wanted to keep her for as long as I could, and now I'd been slapped in the face with the reality.

She wasn't a little girl anymore.

And I couldn't shelter her without serious consequences.

She had to know about sex, if only to protect her from men like her father.

"Can you forgive me?" I whispered. "And you're wrong about me loving Cassie more than I love you. No one will ever come close. You have my heart. You know that, and it kills me to hear you doubt it."

In a scramble of pink and purple splashes, she kicked away her dress and launched herself across the bed and into my arms.

Her weight was solid and warm and familiar, and it took everything inside not to give in to the wet ache to grieve over everything I was losing by saying goodbye to the kid I'd raised through impossibilities and miracles.

I kissed her hair, inhaling her scent; clutching her so tight, she squirmed for air but made no move to get away.

I wanted to smother her in hugs if it meant I could buy a few more innocent years, but when she finally sat up and her gaze fell on the book in my hands, I knew my time was up.

I felt the acres of distance that would slowly grow bigger and bigger between us as she read the title as easy as breathing and revealed that my sacrifices had been worth it.

"The Business of Babies and Everything in Between." Her voice cut me deep because I'd refused to hear it until now—underneath the childish tone hinted a rich depth that would rival any woman's.

Husky and melodic with just enough sweet and sour to drive boys insane.

And she could read.

Better than I could at half my age.

She could understand.

Better than me at any age.

She wasn't just my equal anymore, she was my shooting star, sending her far out of my reach.

Keeping my arm around her tiny waist, I cleared away the heartache in my voice and smiled with all the light-hearted lies I could manage. "You want answers. Let's get answers."

She looked up. "Truly?"

"Truly." Opening the cover, I schooled myself not to flinch against the first graphic image. A penis with muscles and tubes and scientific sketches but still a penis and something far too crude for her eyes. Clearing my throat again, I said carefully, "Well, this…is a penis. And…um, you already know that, eh, I have one and…um, you don't."

My head ached with pressure and embarrassment. "You have a, eh…vagina. And it will get hair on it one day like…um…my penis did…remember? You asked why I had hair between my legs and on my face?"

She soaked it in, her cheeks pink, but her eyes alive and desperate for more. "Okay." She turned the page, reading aloud, "Males have penises that grow hard with blood in order to have int—inter—" She looked up, meeting my tortured gaze. "What's that word, Ren?"

My entire body flushed with humiliation.

I couldn't tell her that if she couldn't read it, there was no way in hell I could. The word was nothing but jumbled up letters.

Instead, I flicked to the next page where the sketches of a woman's vagina gave way to a detailed drawing of a penis inside it.

"I think they mean sex."

"Sex…" She rolled the word slowly on her tongue. "Ssseeeeeexxxxx." She insisted on making me suffer by asking, "What exactly *is* sex?"

I looked at the ceiling, wishing something up there would swap places with me, and this terrible evening could be over with.

I wanted to stutter. I wanted to stall. But I gulped deep and said quickly, "Sex is when a male animal puts his penis in a female animal. His hips thrust a little and then he comes and the stuff he releases makes a baby in the female, and she gives birth a few months later."

I dreaded how uninformative that was and how many questions I was about to receive.

"Is there squirms in the stuff?" she asked, deadly serious.

"Squirms?"

"At school, a boy said his mum told him that squirms make eggs turn into babies that are delivered by birds."

I groaned under my breath. "Sex has nothing to do with birds."

"Bees?" Her eyebrows rose.

"Bees, either."

"So all it is, is a man putting his worm into a woman's pee place?"

I hunched into myself. Hell, this was my worst moment so far. "Something like that."

She bit her lip, chewing over my terrible answers, obviously finding me lacking in the professor position. It wasn't like I had personal experience yet. This was all theory and barnyard knowledge, and I was failing...drastically.

A few minutes passed while she read the book, flicking a few pages to more graphic images of a man on top of a woman and her hands on his ass.

My own body reacted, and I unwrapped my arm from around Della, putting some distance between us.

She didn't notice, far too absorbed in her new friend.

"Ah! It's not squirms, it's sperms!" She tapped a line of text that looked like gibberish. "See, here? Men have sperms, and they swim like tadpoles up a woman's something after he's been on top of her."

"Awesome." I strangled, standing up and pacing again, anything to stop the sudden shyness about discussing this sort of stuff with her.

"Ren?"

I stopped, daring to look at her. "Yeah...?"

"What is so great about kissing Cassie?"

I swiped a hand over my face. "I'm sure the book will cover that."

"I want to know from you." She bit her lip again, worry and unease painting her pretty face. "Please?"

"Ugh, okay." I could never refuse her anything when she said that word. "Kissing is...nice." I did my best to conjure how I felt when Cassie had her tongue in my mouth. "It's different to normal kissing. It looks gross, but it feels warm and...comforting. And sometimes, my eh..."

God, I couldn't say that.

I couldn't admit that kissing made me hard and her wet and was the perfect prelude to sex. That would be too much, and I literally choked on the words. "Yeah, it's...nice. That's all you need to know."

"Would you show me?"

"No!" I stumbled backward. "That wouldn't be appropriate, Della Ribbon."

"Why not?"

"Because...kissing that way isn't done with family. It's done with a mate...a lover."

"Oh." Her spine rolled then straightened as she said, "Think Liam could show me?"

My temper fired back into full heat. "If you *ever* go near Liam naked again, I'll tie you to a tree and never let you come down."

She giggled. "I like trees."

"Believe me, you wouldn't like this one. I'd make sure to find a wasp's nest and put it up there with you. They'd sting you every time you thought about kissing someone."

"You wouldn't."

I narrowed my eyes. "Just try me and you'll see how deadly serious I am about you never being naked with another boy again."

She pouted. "You're mean. Why are you allowed to get naked with Cassie, and I'm not allowed with Liam."

"Because I'm older."

"So when I'm older, I can?"

"No."

"But you said—"

"Never mind what I said." Prowling toward her, I tapped the pornographic educational book. "Read this. It has all the answers."

She eyed me before finally nodding and turning her inquisitive gaze back to the pages.

For the next few hours, I sat in the chair in the corner, clutching the handles with white knuckles, and instead of telling Della about sex and kissing and everything in between, she told me.

She read the words she knew and stumbled over those she didn't.

She dashed across the driveway to see Patricia and came back armed with terms like Fallopian tubes and ovaries and clitoris.

And it was to my utmost mortification that she became the teacher on a subject she'd begged to be a student in.

A student who must never know she'd far exceeded the capacities of the boy who said he'd teach her everything.

The boy who now knew absolutely nothing.

Chapter Thirty-Seven

REN

2009

ANOTHER YEAR, another autumn, winter, spring, and summer.

Della and I celebrated our joint birthday where she turned nine and I turned nineteen. The day was simple and sweet, and we exchanged gifts that cost no more than ten dollars thanks to John giving me some cash from my salary instead of pre-empting what Della would need and spending on my behalf.

For the past year, Cassie had been dating a twenty-four-year-old mechanic who'd attended family dinners and been grudgingly approved of by her parents. She still hung out with Della, and they'd even gone to a local show jumping competition with Della riding Domino and Cassie riding HeatWave, earning a bunch of ribbons in the process.

Our lives had settled into the routine of living across the driveway from each other, and things couldn't be better.

The itch to leave still came with the warmer weather and shorter nights, but now, instead of leaving to search for better things, I had things I'd miss by going.

I'd miss Patricia Wilson's amazing lasagne and raspberry torte.

I'd miss John's steady guidance and unjudging leniency.

I'd miss Cassie's secret smiles and ability to make me mad and happy in the same sentence.

And I'd even miss Liam, even though I'd never truly forgiven him for what happened between him and Della.

Life marched onward.

One more year and I'd leave my teenage years behind.

And I was still a virgin.

These days, it wasn't because of my unreadiness or fear that Della would catch me or even the fact that Cassie was in a long-term relationship—I'd met some of her friends when they'd come round for dinners and two of them blatantly said the offer was always open for a booty call—whatever the hell that was.

I was ready.

If I was honest, I was dying with readiness, but I still couldn't take the plunge because I knew the consequences of sex, and as much as I loved Della and was grateful for her in my life and besotted with everything she did, I refused to raise another.

Sex talks and naked days and the terrible circumstances of watching her body turn from washboard to budding with breasts had drained me. Her body was no longer a kid's and had to be covered in public, making her self-aware, and stealing the remaining days of her childhood.

I was tired.

Frankly, I was exhausted, and I just wanted to give in to the thick desire in my blood whenever I looked at a pretty woman and forget about rights and wrongs and pregnancies.

But I couldn't.

Because I did *not* want to be a father.

And once I'd had sex once, I had no doubt I'd want it again and again and just like the stallion or bull who serviced an entire herd, delivering each mare and cow with a foal and calf, I did not want to have multiple Rens running around, killing me slowly.

That was my view on the world.

And because I never talked about my concerns, my beliefs became fact until one night when Cassie drove home with a squeal of tires in her second-hand red Corolla and bolted into the house.

Yells and sobs flowed from the farmhouse for hours, making me wonder what the hell happened.

Whatever it was made her angry and sad, and later that night, past midnight and almost at witching hour, a pebble dinged against the window above my head and I shot awake.

Della had always been a heavier sleeper than me, and just because she was flirting with puberty didn't change that fact.

Shrugging into a t-shirt and pulling on some shorts, I stumbled from our room to find Cassie pacing like a caged ferret with her hair wild, white nightgown flowing, and lips pinched with an aura of hurt female bristling amongst the hay and horses.

"You okay?" I asked, clearing the scratchy sleep from my throat.

The moment she heard me, she barrelled toward me, snatched my hand and yanked me into a free stable. The moment the stall door closed, she shoved me against the wall, leapt into my arms, and planted her mouth on mine.

I stumbled beneath her weight, instinct causing my hands to cup her ass and my arms to bunch and hold her close.

Her legs wrapped around my waist as her tongue plunged deep, kissing me with a kind of passion I'd never tasted before.

It triggered something in me.

I went from courteous and willing to help to matching monster like she was.

Spinning around, I crushed her against the wall as hard as she'd slammed me.

Her moan only ignited me further, and our kiss turned savage.

We devoured each other with nips and thrusting tongues, struggling to breathe and spit slippery between us.

While our mouths attacked the other, our hands roamed.

Mine fisted her full breasts, kneading her with choking desire, being more aggressive than I'd ever been, unable to rein myself in.

I pinched her nipples, and she mewled.

I bit her neck, and she gasped.

I thrust the aching steel between my legs directly against her wetness, and she begged for more.

Her rapid fingers slipped down my front, cupping me, squeezing, fisting, jerking me off until I thought for sure I'd come.

As quickly as she'd grabbed me, her touch was gone, focusing on tugging down my shorts.

My brain was mush. My heart smoking. My blood black and thick with uncontrolled need.

I couldn't think or stop as she yanked out my pounding length and shoved aside the material of her nightgown.

The heat of her...*holy shit.*

The wet slick and tight promise pressed against my tip, and I groaned loud and long—a growl with every want I'd denied myself for so long.

I thrust upward, needing what she offered before my heart exploded and my life ended.

My aim wasn't right, and we slipped apart.

I stumbled to the side, crashing against a spade and sending it clattering to the cobblestone floor.

The noise reverberated around the stable, freezing us.

My heart kept thundering, obscuring my hearing as I did my best to look in the direction of my bedroom where Della hopefully continued to sleep none-the-wiser.

My chest squeezed as if I was doing something against her wishes. As if I was breaking her trust. Ever since our sex talk, we'd had an unspoken agreement that sex was an open topic. If she had something she wanted to ask, she asked it, and I swallowed down my chagrin to answer her.

She knew exactly what kissing meant, and what it led to, and what sex was between two parties.

She'd come with me to the neighbouring farm to watch ducks mate and pigs and dogs and even fish in the farmer's pond. She knew the mechanics now.

Therefore, she would understand what I was about to do with Cassie if she walked in.

Tripping backward, I unwrapped my arms from around Cassie's waist, dropping her to the floor.

My cock stuck out, glistening and angry beneath my t-shirt hem.

Cassie looked one last time toward the door leading to my room, then hissed with frustration. "She won't know."

"That's not the point."

She clamped her hands on her hips, looking girlish in her white nightgown with pink flowers and all woman with her puffy lips and tight nipples. "Then what *is* the point, Ren? Why do you keep stopping this?"

"Stopping what?"

She laughed with a trace of rage. "*This!* Every time we come close to fucking, you stop. You act all guilty and shy and shut down." She laughed again. "Do you know how many times I've returned to my bed, only to have to make myself come with wanting you? You're like the prized horse no one is allowed to ride." She smirked. "Get it? Not allowed to ride…" Her head lowered, brown hair cascading over one eye. "I want to ride you. I want to ride your dick so hard, Ren, and you shoot me down every time."

Her words and thick invitation sent more blood pumping to my cock.

Normally, I could ignore the punching, clawing desire, but this time, I almost buckled beneath it.

I struggled for a reason we couldn't do this. *Any* reason. I wouldn't tell her I'd jerked off to images of sex too, but she wasn't the one who starred in my daydreams. Some faceless female always did. Someone blonde and kind who didn't mind my inexperience.

And the fact that my ideal partner was blonde just ate more chunks away at my soul because how fucking disgusting was I to want an older version of Della.

Not that I wanted an older version of her.

But I liked blonde hair.

And I liked kindness.

And I wanted so fucking much to fuck something, but I didn't want to support more kids. I had no idea how Cassie had sex with so many men and never once got pregnant.

Maybe she was infertile.

And if she was, she was lucky she was human and not a sheep or cow; otherwise, her usefulness of reproducing would be replaced by the slaughterhouse and she'd end up on someone's plate.

"Are you going to say something?" She paced in front of me, her breasts high and tempting, her steps short and full of the same urgent wanting I suffered with.

I clenched my hands as the need to squeeze my tortured cock almost overrode my brain. "What about Kevin or Calvin or whatever his name was."

"Gavin and I broke up."

My eyebrows rose. "When?"

"Tonight. Bastard was cheating on me."

"I'm sorry."

"Yeah, well." She blew hair out of her eyes. "I wasn't interested in him anymore anyway."

"Oh."

Stagnant desire turned the stables full of festering appetite.

Knowing she was single again shouldn't add more fever to my already out of control yearning...but it did. I took a step toward her, only to take it back again as her eyes latched onto mine with a cat-like gleam and lick of her lips.

"There you go again," she moaned. "You want me. I know you do." Looking over her shoulder toward the door where Della slept, she did something she'd never done before.

I'd seen every part of her but only in glimpses and only with buttons undone or zippers half-mast. I'd never seen her fully naked.

But I saw her now as she tore off her nightgown and stood bare before me.

I swallowed hard, unsuccessfully silencing a desperate groan.

"See, you *do* want me." She walked toward me, her hips swaying, breasts bouncing, and wetness glinting on her inner thighs. "Help me forget him, Ren. Just for tonight. You never have to touch me again. Just...please...."

I scrambled backward as another flush of rebellious lust made me so damn hungry I almost forgot how to fight it. "Can't."

"Yes, you can."

I shook my head as fast as I could. "You'll get pregnant."

She froze. "Wait...what?"

Shit.

Her tone layered me with self-consciousness. I hadn't meant to say anything. I *shouldn't* have said anything.

But Cassie's face lit up and her edginess melted into the kindness I needed. "Is that why you've refused me all this time? Refused my friends? Never once tried to fuck me? Oh, wow, you think I'll get pregnant if we do?"

Her questions could've been condescending and cruel, but they weren't. Cassie was intricate and had two distinct sides. One side was all about her and she could be harsh without thought, yet the other was sweet and doting. And when it was activated, she could be an angel sent from above.

"Wait here." She scooped her nightgown off the floor, shook away the hay strands, and slipped it back over her head. "Don't go anywhere. I mean it." Slipping from the stable, she pointed a finger in my face. "I mean it, Ren. If you vanish, I'm going to tell everyone what a great lay you are and set up a revolving door of women. Won't that be torture for you?"

She vanished before I could admit that that would be my worst nightmare to have so many delectable beauties and not be allowed to touch a single one.

Not that she would do that... *would she?*

I had no idea why I stayed in that stable, standing deathly still in the dark and nursing an agonizing erection, but I did.

I didn't move to put my shorts on.

I didn't move to return to Della.

No way in hell could I climb into a bed beside her in this state anyway.

I either had to make myself come or think such gruesome thoughts that it went away.

Thanks to Mclary, I had more than enough gruesome thoughts to deflate myself—just a glance at my missing finger or many memories of our living conditions was enough, but before I'd been able to delete a tenth of my lust, soft footsteps sounded on cobbles and Cassie slipped back into the barn.

She didn't have anything.

She didn't look any different.

It didn't mean she was any less confident as she entered the stable with her chin high and nipples still pebbled.

"Come with me." Taking my hand, she gently led me toward a pile of horse blankets that had been dumped there last winter. Pushing me down, she held out her hand and revealed a tiny silver packet. "I can't believe you don't know about these things but...this is called a condom. It stops any sexually transmitted diseases and removes about ninety-five percent of risk of unwanted pregnancies."

She'd just talked witchcraft, but all I could focus on was the word disease. I didn't have a clue what sort of diseases you could catch through sex. Maybe it was another version of chicken pox, which I definitely didn't want.

I managed to keep my mouth shut about that, but I couldn't about the other fact. I stupidly asked, "Why only ninety-five percent?"

She sighed. "Not sure. I guess if you nick it with your teeth or fingernails or if it's not held down when you disengage. Who knows? My point is…you can fuck me. No more excuses. I'm actually on the pill, and you're clean, seeing as I'll be your first time, but you should learn how to use one of these for the future, and I want to teach you." She smiled softly. "I've enjoyed teaching you over the years."

I looked away, my mind racing.

Pill and clean and condoms…she spoke a different language. Pill for what? Clean from what? But my brain had relocated to my cock, and it'd just been given a free pass to proceed.

No more fear of pregnancy.

No Della spying in the shadows.

No reason to say no.

Grabbing the hem of her nightgown, Cassie once again switched clothing for nakedness, and I no longer had any arguments not to feast my eyes on her flesh or allow the quaking desire to gather between my legs.

"I want you, Ren," she murmured. "Do you want me?"

This time, there was no debate.

I nodded, licking my lips and reaching for her from where I sat on the blankets.

"Oh, thank God." Kneeling before me, not caring about her knees on cold stones, she tore the tiny packet and pulled out something slimy and small. "This is going to feel a little strange, and you can't come while I put it on because I only brought one, got it?"

I bit my lip as she came closer, doing my best to control my trembling and the bobbing of my overeager cock.

Shifting the condom in her hands, she fisted me and pressed it on my tip.

She was right.

It did feel weird.

Weird good.

Weird strange.

Weird *'holy crap I don't know how I'm going to be able to control myself.'*

It took her an eternity to roll the slippery thing down my length, and when she'd finally finished, my vision was half-cross-eyed, and I panted as if I'd run to the paddocks and back.

I reached out to touch the casing around me, but she swatted away my hand and placed both of hers on my shoulders. Climbing up my body, she kneeled over me as I spread my legs out in front and ceased breathing as the scent of her arousal and the illicitness of what I was about to do almost sent me into cardiac arrest.

"Ready?" she breathed, leaning down to kiss me.

I'd passed the point of conversation and half-gasped, half-grunted as she slowly sat on me.

My mouth went slack beneath hers.

The sensation of her tight heat blew my mind.

The tremble of her thighs as she eased down and the small hitches in her breath as she threw her head back and let me fill her, activated the same trigger as before.

I was no longer Ren, the considerate teen thrust into fatherhood and homeless runaway. I was Ren the nineteen-year-old who'd been hungry for something for years and had finally found it.

She sank the final distance, her body clenching around mine, and I grabbed a fistful of her hair. Cradling her, I shot upright, spun her so she was on the blankets and slid her down until she was on her back.

And then I did what stallions and bulls and every male animal did when he was given access to a female.

I fucked her.

No other words.

I fucked her.

I thrust as fast and as hard as I could.

I turned animal as I bit her neck, raged upward, held her down, and punished her for making me unravel so completely.

And when that tickling, tingling warning came and my balls tightened and my cock swelled, I locked my mouth on hers and rode her harder.

And I came.

I officially entered adulthood.

I was a boy no longer.

Chapter Thirty-Eight

REN

2010

TWENTY and TEN.

This shared birthday was one of the more important ones because Della reached double figures, and I reached the milestone of any kid.

I was no longer a teenager.

I was a man.

A man who'd had sex—quite regularly, in fact—a man who still felt like a kid most of the time but was also no longer at the mercy of laws of minors or the judgment and pity of adults.

I was my own person, but it didn't mean our life changed.

It didn't matter the wanderlust in my veins switched from suggestion to downright obsession. It didn't matter, as I sat in an echo-plagued school hall and watched Della play the role of a Sandy in a younger, less suggestive version of *Grease Lightning,* that I suffered both pride and bittersweet sacrifice. And it didn't matter that as I grew older, the more I burned for something I hadn't found yet. Something I didn't know but wanted more than I could stand.

Even though my heart begged me on a daily basis to run into the forest and never look back, I knew I could never be that selfish.

The Wilsons had been nothing but good to us.

They'd given me the ability to grant Della the best foundation I could with her education and personal development. The fact that she had a surrogate brother and sister in Liam and Cassie meant the world because no way should she grow up with only me as her companion.

Not only had the Wilsons ensured that the hours I put into running their farm, increasing their bottom line, and turning a hobby crop where Patricia had to work part-time at a local accountancy firm and John picked up odd jobs here and there into a thriving income where they could retire, but they also taught me the basics in life.

Things like regular doctor and dentist visits.

The first time I'd taken Della and myself to the dentist, I didn't know who hated it more. Luckily, I'd ensured she kept up with regular brushing, and I was a bit obsessive when it came to cleanliness, even while living rough, so we didn't have too much wrong. A filling or two and we were done for another year.

Another year older.

Another year wiser.

And another year where I fought my lone-wolf tendencies and forced myself to stay for her.

For my Little Ribbon.

And it was the right decision because as the spotlight shone on her glossy blonde hair and her cherub cheeks glowed and her blue eyes twinkled like stars, she wasn't just Sandy from *Grease Lightning*, singing a song about a boy and summer.

She was Della Wild, and she was perfect.

* * * * *

Two things happened a month later that proved to me just how far apart our worlds had become.

The first, Patricia and John believed it was time that our two pushed together single beds should be split back apart, now that Della was getting older.

I'd swallowed back the denial that always followed when someone remarked how tall she'd become, how willowy and pretty and strong. I'd also gulped back the sudden terror that I'd never be able to sleep again unless I could reach out in the night and touch her—to appease my fear that she might be hurt in the darkness just like those kids at Mclary's barn.

The day when the bed we'd slept on for years was suddenly broken back into two singles and shoved to opposite sides of the room, the dynamic between Della and I switched again.

We'd been so used to our routine.

We didn't think anything of it or stopped to think that it might be strange for others to see a 'brother and sister' sleep side by side.

Even though I'd raised Della, I never truly thought of her as my sister. Somehow, even all this time later, when I looked at her, I saw her as a Mclary...not mine.

She looked nothing like her mother or father—which was a blessing—but she also looked nothing like me.

I was dark and angles and broody desire to be left alone.

She was light and curves and infectious kindness toward everyone.

Ten years separated me and my slavery at the Mclary's, yet it had carved something deep inside me, covering me with wariness, cloaking me with suspicion, and never letting me relax in company no matter how old I became.

I never stopped to think that sleeping next to her would be seen as inappropriate and never viewed our relationship from an outsider's point of view.

Della would kiss me often. Smacking my lips with a strawberry-lip-glossed mouth before running off to class or to play with Liam or help Patricia in her garden or ride with Cassie.

Her quick-fire affection always melted my gruff heart, and she was the only one who could touch something inside me—slipping past my walls, infiltrating my fortresses to remind me that I might not like many humans but I loved one more than I could stand.

Needless to say, both Della and I didn't sleep that night, or the next, or the next. Our hands somehow found their way from their covers to dangle over the edge and reach for each other, never quite touching no matter how much we wished.

Her ribbon would wrap and drip over her fingers, kissing the dusty floor and reminding me all over again that she wasn't a baby anymore, but she still had childhood ties.

Eventually, we got used to sleeping apart, and neither of us ever said how much we preferred sleeping in one large bed. I kept my mouth shut as I didn't want to overstep important boundaries, and I guessed she didn't feel the same way because after that first week, she went shopping with Cassie and purchased a bedspread covered with leaping horses frolicking in ocean spray, leaving my drab black sheets looking like a black hole in the corner.

The second thing to show the growing distance between us was a mid-summer evening where John opened his paddocks to the public to purchase hay bales directly off the meadow the moment we'd finished baling.

With over two thousand bales to sell and already a barn full of supplies for our own livestock in winter, John put me in charge of choreographing the countless arriving Utes, trucks, and trailer-pulling cars, directing them to appropriate fields and keeping tally of how many bales they took so I could grab the cash as they left.

I'd had a minor panic attack when he waltzed back to the house to do whatever he needed to do. That minor attack turned full blown when the first customer finished loading ten bales and drove toward me manning the exit gate.

The guy with his sunburned nose and stalks of hay on his t-shirt asked, "What do I owe you?" He cocked his head at the back with his loaded hay. "Ten bales at what price?"

I looked at the farmhouse, cursing John and wishing someone, *anyone,* would come out and help, but no one did. I sucked up my disgrace that all this time I'd never let John know the extent of my illiteracy. I'd never counted in front of him, never read anything. I'd always gotten around doing the books and tabulations because Patricia was an accountant by trade and enjoyed crunching numbers.

"Hey? You hear me? How much?" the guy pushed.

Rubbing the back of my neck, I muttered, "It's eight dollars a bale so…" I did my best to force a brain that had never been taught arithmetic to perform a miracle.

"Eighty bucks." The guy grabbed some cash from his pocket and peeled off four twenties. "Here you go."

Our hands met as he shoved the bills into my palm and gave me a quick nod. He drove away before I could hope to work out if I'd just been ripped off or if that was the correct amount.

A red car started in the distance with a trailer piled high with hay.

I gulped as it turned toward me and the gate.

Shit.

Wedging the cash into my back pocket, my eyes trailed back to the farmhouse, begging for rescue.

And that was when I saw her.

Della.

She leapt out of Cassie's Corolla, laughing at something Cassie said as they made their way toward the kitchen door. At the last second, Della looked up as if she sensed me staring at her.

Our eyes locked across meadows and driveways, and she waved once.

I waved back, adding a come here motion at the end.

I held my breath. She could go with Cassie. After all, it was school holidays, and she'd been spending a lot of time riding and going to the mall as well as playing with friends her own age.

I still didn't trust Cassie's loose morals wouldn't rub off on her, but I'd been fierce with her on our second or third time sleeping together. I'd flat out warned her if she ever let Della kiss, fondle, or fuck a boy while she was with her, I'd murder her with my bare hands.

She'd laughed.

I hadn't.

The subject hadn't been broached since.

Instead of continuing into the house like Liam would've done, Della said something quick to Cassie then tore toward me.

Her bony knees flashed beneath her yellow skirt, the matching yellow and white daisy top flopping on her shoulders while her hair gleamed as bright as the sun above.

Sweat glistened on her forehead as she finally careened to a stop beside me, squinting in the brightness. "Hey."

"Hey." I smiled as she threw herself into me, wrapping her arms around my waist. Sometimes, I was taken aback to find her head reached my ribcage when only yesterday her face was the very inconvenient height of my groin. "Have a good day in town?"

"Meh, it was okay. Just hung at the mall. I'm getting bored of doing that. Would much rather be here with you."

"I'd rather you be here, too." I kissed her hair as she pulled away, looking at the unusual traffic on the paddock.

Her nose wrinkled as two incompetent city folk struggled to lift a bale and place it into their shiny new Ute. "What's happening?"

"Free for all."

"Uncle John is giving his hay away for *free*?" Her mouth fell open. "Whoa."

"Not free, free." I moved position and rested my elbows on the moss-covered gate. "I have to charge them as they leave."

She eyed me carefully. "Having fun?"

I snorted. "Does it sound like something I'd do for fun?"

"Nope." Her giggle made me so grateful that I had at least one person I could be honest with. Who knew me. The *real* me. Not the Ren Cassie flirted with, or the Ren John and Patricia nurtured. Ren, the runaway who'd never learned how to read and write.

She climbed the gate, her white sneakers blinding compared to my dirt-covered steel caps. "I can help...if you want?"

I ordered myself not to nod like a demented dog. Instead, I cocked my head and looked at her critically. "Think you can handle adding up hay bales and then multiplying by eight dollars?"

She frowned. "I think so? I dunno..."

"Well, how about you try one?" I suggested. "If someone had ten bales, how much would they owe?" I had to look away, hating that I was using her to double check I hadn't been screwed over. A kid helping an adult do his job. What sort of asshole was I?

Della looked at the sky, her little lips moving before she announced with a flourish, "Eighty dollars."

Great, he didn't screw me.

I gave her a high five. "Awesome work. Your brain is a flawless machine."

She beamed. "So...can I help?"

"I'd love your help." The urbanites and their new Ute rolled toward us, their windows down and the wife fanning herself with her hat. "In fact, here's your first client."

Thank God, I had Della beside me because my heart itched with panic as my eyes flew over the stack of bales they'd chosen.

No way could I count and add that many.

The driver with his thin beard said, "We have twenty. What's the damage?"

I should be able to snap out a figure. I *wanted* to. But unlike when it came to building something or surviving in the elements or seed management and crop rotation, my mind shut down and went numb.

Della's soft, pretty voice piped up beside me, "That will be one hundred and sixty dollars, please." She flashed me a look as the guy fisted out the bills and passed them to me.

I grunted a thanks and shoved it into my pocket with the rest.

As the car accelerated, giving room for a new customer to trundle across the paddock, I inched closer to Della and squeezed her shoulder.

She gave me a sad pout. "I forgot. I'm so mean."

"Forgot what?" I whispered under my breath.

She kicked the gate, her spine rolling. "That you can't calculate."

I stiffened. "It's not something I need to know in order to live my life." Forcing a grin, I added, "That's why I have you."

She gave me a weak smile, moving away from my touch and toward the customers pulling to a stop in their black SUV.

The elderly man beamed at her. "We have three bales."

She looked at the sky, counted, then said, "That is twenty-four dollars, please."

The guy passed over three tens and Della turned to me. "Do you have change?"

Aside from yanking out all the bills in my pocket and checking what I'd stuffed in there, I didn't know. Instead of embarrassing myself, I shook my head. "Sorry. We did specify correct change only."

Della stood frozen. "What do I do?"

The driver assured her, "Keep the change, honey. Buy yourself something nice for the holidays."

He took off before I could punch him for calling her honey.

For the rest of the day, Della was my calculator, business manager, and boss.

And each time she gave a customer a figure, I battled with the knowledge that I would never be her equal again as she was utterly brilliant, and I would forever remain adequately passable.

* * * * *

That night, I lay staring at the ceiling, doing my best to figure out how people took one number and multiplied it by another to form a different one.

I did what the TV show had mentioned, but try as I might, steps were missing that I didn't have.

As much as I loved working with my hands and running the farm, I really should teach myself basic things like math and English.

Somehow.

Della's voice threaded through the darkness from her single bed across the room. "Ren...?"

My head turned on the pillow to face her. The slightly less dark of her bedspread and lightness of her hair were the only things I could make out. "Yeah?"

"These school holidays...can I? Um, do you want me to.... I can show you what I learned if you want?" Her voice dwindled before coming back sharp with determination. "What I learned at school. I'll show you. I mean, only if you want."

My heart fisted hard.

I didn't answer, not because she'd unmanned me or made me feel like an idiot, but because her offer was so perfectly her. So kind. So sweet.

When silence became oppressive, and I still hadn't said yes because I was so in awe of her generous offer, she murmured, "Tomorrow, I'll show you a couple of things. You can decide after if you want to know more." She rolled over, giving me her back.

And I lay in the darkness, thanking her.

Chapter Thirty-Nine

DELLA

Present Day

A WHILE AGO, I mentioned I'd committed all seven deadly sins starting with wrath when I hated Cassie at first sight.

I was hoping I could skip over the others as I don't really want to reveal just how awful a person I became, but I don't think I have a choice. Not because I'm actually rather normal and felt nothing that someone else hasn't before me, but because I committed the rest of them all in a three-year period.

Clever, huh?

I went from innocent child to terrible human being all in the space of a few short years.

The first one I'll mention is pride.

And that one was Ren's fault.

I was taught at school that it was okay to be proud of achieving high marks if you'd studied hard and deserved it. It was okay to be proud of a drawing or accomplishment because that was the reward for striving to be better and succeeding. As long as you didn't brag or boast, a bit of self-praise was encouraged.

So, armed with that free pass, I already had a complex relationship with the meaning of pride seeing as I'd flirt with the feeling on a regular basis thanks to my love of learning and ability to recall most things that the teacher said.

I had a good circle of friends—only a few who I can remember names now—but I do remember a group bullying me and calling me a teacher's pet. Funny how I didn't mind. I was rather glad because if I was a teacher's pet that meant I was loved more because I did the right thing.

Or at least, that's what I figured it meant seeing as a pet was a family's pride and joy—not that Ren and I had one, and the barn cats that lived at the Wilsons were there as hunters to keep the grain nibble-free rather than to be cuddled and pampered.

Anyway, I'm digressing...these tangents I keep chasing are becoming worse the longer I write. If I wasn't just going to delete this entire thing, I'd have some serious editing to do.

Anywho…

Pride.

Ren.

That's right…get back to the story, Della.

Where can I start?

Ren was my superstar. He was my hero in all things and never more so than the day when my eyes were no longer blinded by self-obsession. The day I helped him count hay bales and tally payment was the moment I grew up a little.

I didn't judge him or ridicule him for his lack of knowledge. I didn't laugh like the kids at school did when someone couldn't give an answer or screwed up a teacher's question. I didn't pity him or scoff that a boy so much older than me couldn't do simple math.

It made me sad.

It hurt my heart.

Because, all this time, I'd never stopped to think about what he'd given up to grant me my dreams. He'd stayed in a place so I could learn. He'd worked in a job so I could play.

He'd never had a childhood.

Never had a week off.

Never been given the gifts that he'd given me so often and so generously.

My offer to teach him what he'd made possible for me to learn wasn't something pure or offered out of the goodness of my heart.

No.

It was because of guilt. It was because of a child epiphany that I was literate and book smart all because of what Ren had sacrificed to make it happen.

And it hurt.

Because I'd been so selfish and only now seen the reality of what it had cost him.

I owed him. Big. Huge. Massive. So, for the next three years, I paid off that debt by teaching him everything I knew.

Every night during the school holidays, we headed to the hay loft where we'd first slept and sat on hay bales while I pulled out the box full of old work-books and texts that Ren insisted we keep.

I sharpened a pencil for him, gave him my brand-new eraser, and stumbled over how to teach a twenty-year-old boy primary grade English and math.

It took a few nights to find our groove.

I flew too fast through equations, and Ren grew frustrated.

I went too slow, and Ren felt like I babied him.

We bickered and squabbled about right terminology, and we ended for the night with clenched teeth and stiff posture from doing our best to work with each other while struggling with yet a new dynamic.

By the end of the second week, we had a system where Ren would read the text he could, point to the ones he couldn't, and wait patiently while I gave him what he needed.

I didn't try to interfere or pre-empt, and our scuffles gave way to happy cohabitation, hunched over workbooks, quietly studying side by side.

For most of my life, I'd believed I was special—mainly thanks to Ren's perfection at raising me, ensuring I was solid in the knowledge that I walked upon the stars in his eyes. My teachers had further cultivated that mind-set by encouraging me and being awed at my easy progress through the grades.

However, sitting beside Ren as he memorized and problem-solved, I felt the first kernel of lacking.

I'd always known he was unique.

I'd loved him far too deeply and for far too long not to believe he was magical and immortal and every prince, knight, and saviour I could ever need.

But I'd always envisioned him as a boy in dirty clothes, sun-browned and field-worn rather than a neat gentleman with glasses, all library-kissed and book-learned.

Ren Wild was all those things, but now he was something more to be looked up to.

He had a quick-fire intelligence that made me proud and envious—two sins in one.

He might not have had the chance to learn such things, but it wasn't from lack of cleverness. Even at his age and being fairly stuck in his ways, he soaked up numbers and letters as if he'd been thirsty his entire life for such knowledge.

And that was where my second deadly sin started to manifest.

Instead of going to bed frustrated at being teacher to a student far surpassing her, I fell asleep with pride tinting my smile that I was the reason Ren went from counting on his fingers to effortlessly reciting the times tables.

Without me, he still wouldn't be able to spell or read the words he used on a regular basis such as tractor, paddock, and twine.

Now he could spell all manner of things, and I beamed like a proud parent as we held spelling bee standoffs in the hay loft, testing each other, blowing raspberries when we got it wrong and giving high fives when we got it right.

Pride.

Pity it felt so good because every time Ren nudged me with his shoulder in gratitude or read aloud a text that would've caused his cheeks to pink and anger to rise with the unknown, I suffered more and more pride.

I glowed with it whenever he chuckled over a simple word with a strange spelling. I beamed with it whenever he surprised himself by adding up two large numbers and getting the total correct.

For three solid years, our routine never changed.

Some nights, especially in high-summer when Ren pulled fourteen and sometimes sixteen-hour days to get all his work done, we fell exhausted into bed without a lesson, but most of the time, we both looked forward to hiding away, just the two of us, and trading information.

Because what I taught him, he taught me in return.

He taught me how to drive a tractor on my eleventh birthday and sat me on his knee for the first time in a very long time as my legs were too short to reach the rusty pedals.

He taught me how to drive the Land Rover on my twelfth birthday, and even accompanied me to the movies with Cassie and some of my friends when I said I'd love to go see something with him because he'd never come into town with me before.

It was like asking a bear to leave his comfortable den and enter a world full of chaos and calamity.

His eyes never stopped darting. His ears never stopped twitching. His body always on high alert and ready to maul an enemy or protect a friend.

But he did it.

For me.

He happily drove me there, took me out for a burger and fries just like our first official birthday together, and sat beside me while we watched some animated cartoon that I caught him rolling his eyes at but gushed about afterward for my benefit.

He even refused to hang out with Cassie's entourage even though she practically begged him to go clubbing with them once I'd been deposited back home. She claimed he needed a birthday night too; her voice syrupy sweet with that hateful twinkle in her eye that reeked of sex.

She had no right to look at Ren that way, especially as she'd been dating some guy called Chip for six months, and Ren was far too good to be sloppy seconds.

The familiar wrath suffocated me, and it didn't fully go away even as Ren shook his head, escorted me back to the Land Rover, and drove home with me.

I didn't sleep that night, constantly checking his single bed was lumpy with him beneath the covers and not smooth with his absence.

During the midst of winter, we hired movies that we both enjoyed and held book discussions over reading material I brought home from the school library.

For three years, life didn't change too much.

We focused on learning, farming, and family.

And all the while, my girlhood slowly slipped away beneath teenage hormones. I forgot how to be innocent Della Ribbon. I forgot how to be anything, if I'm honest. I didn't know if I wanted to be sweet or sour or kind or cruel. I didn't know if I wanted my handwriting to be cursive or block. I didn't know if I wanted to be a rebel like Cassie or stay true to Ren and his many morals.

The constant war inside stripped me of my childhood values, and that was when the true sins began.

After pride came envy and my complex relationship with Cassie was no longer just black and white. I no longer just liked or hated her. I was twisted with awe and wanting to be her and dirtied with spite with wanting to be what Ren sought.

    Over the years, Cassie finished high school and attended a local university. She was a middle-of-the-line student, but thanks to her background in horses and farming, she landed a full scholarship for Equine Science and Stable Management degree.

    Her dream job was to event and scoop up the mega prize pools. In the meantime, she was wise enough to know she needed pieces of paper to her name to ensure a paid gig while she schooled herself and her horses to greatness.

    Liam started high school in a county over being a year older than me, and I was left in the past, just waiting for my life to begin.

    It also didn't help that my choices in TV shows and movies switched from feel good Disney to romantic comedies and everything in-between. Soap operas with brooding men and hurting socialites. Dirty kisses and naughty groping...anything to do with sex and connection was my kryptonite, and Ren often caught me starry-eyed and obsessed with a terrible show, crushing on the hero, my mouth tingling for kisses like they indulged in and wondering what it would feel like to have a boy touch me in places like the girls on the screen permitted.

    The more I watched, the more envious I became and not just of Cassie.

    I became envious of anyone with a boyfriend.

    I tried to coax Liam into kissing me again, but he turned me down. I wasn't interested in him as anything more than a river-swimming, meadow-exploring friend, but it still hurt for him to wrinkle his nose and laugh about kissing me.

    I wanted to shout that I was sure his worm hadn't grown any, but I was still nice enough to hold my tongue on hurtful things. Just because my tits hadn't grown past tiny bee stings didn't mean I should tear into his self-consciousness like mine chewed me every day.

    My malice made me teeter on a knife-edge of tears whenever I caught Cassie flirting with Ren. Especially as he reshod her horse in the stable on a hot afternoon, bent over and shirtless, his torso glistening with sweat from hammering nails with harsh clangs into her latest warmblood cross.

    He was so damn beautiful.

    All muscle and masculinity, moving in that effortless way that used to make me feel safe but now just made me lick my lips and hide my gathering confusion.

    Watching him was torture. Not because he made me feel things I'd only felt for movie heroes but because my mouth dried up, my heart pounded, and I hurt so much because I wanted something.

    Something that made me itch and yearn. Something that made me snappy and hot-tempered whenever Ren gave me the smile reserved just for me and tried to gather me close to his sweaty bare chest in a joke.

    Instead of slotting into his side where I belonged, I pushed him away because something inside no longer wanted innocent, carefree hugs.

    It wanted what Cassie got.

    It wanted more.

But how could I want it from Ren?

He was Ren!

Why suddenly did my eyes see him differently, my nose smell him differently, and my heart act like a cracked out raccoon whenever he came close?

I was thirteen and more confused than I'd ever been in my life.

The pain and hunger were excruciating when Cassie dragged a fingertip along Ren's back and rubbed her pads together, smearing his sweat and smiling that secret adult smile, making me want to tear her pretty brown hair out.

I hated this new vibrant painful world my emotions had thrust me into. I missed the simple days of girlhood where happiness came from riding Domino, doing well on a test, then hitching a ride with Ren on the tractor while he baled.

These days, I could do something I adored and still find ways to feel wrath and pride and envy.

And if it wasn't those three terrible sins, it was the other four.

Greed I often felt, especially around kids who had things I wanted.

Girls with boyfriends.

Girls with horses.

Girls with short hair or dyed hair or the freedom to paint their nails or dress with low-cut tops and high-waisted shorts.

Those girls attracted the boys.

The ones who were edgy and cool and smoked cigarettes stolen from their parents' private stash.

I was still the cute little good girl, and no one wanted her.

So yes, greed was a regular companion just like slothfulness. On hot summer days after a long day at school and a complicated day of soaring and plummeting emotions, I found myself hiding more and more from chores and farmyard duty.

Before, I'd bolt off the bus to wherever Ren was, desperate to help him, eager to be of service and earn his wonderful treasured smile. These days, I slinked off the bus and found a shady spot and curled up beneath stencil patterns of leaves. I'd stare at the sunny sky and lament about all the ways my life wasn't perfect.

In other words, I transformed into the brat who no one likes, and I look back now and wish I had the ability to reach through time and slap myself.

I want to shake my thirteen-year-old self and scream, 'Get over it! Your life was perfect. You were perfect. You had everything you were envious of and greedy for right beneath your stupid little nose, but you ruined it. You made it all disappear, and it was all because of the last deadly sin.'

Lust.

Chapter Forty

REN

2013

2013 STARTED LIKE all the rest.

Cassie tried to tempt me out to a local party where sex was guaranteed and liquor was compulsory. Even though I was twenty-three and of legal age to drink, fuck, and do all the stupid shit adults do, I still had responsibilities. I still had a girl dependent on me. I still had a life I valued and secrets I needed to keep secret.

So, just like all the other times, I declined.

And just like all the other times, Cassie promised she'd be back later and would give me my New Year's Eve kiss. It didn't matter she was getting serious with Chip. She believed that because I'd been in her life for so many years, I wasn't classified as cheating.

However, I was done being the other man.

I was done sleeping with her period.

Frankly, I'd grown tired of her games and immaturity a few years ago, but because I had no desire to find another girl to sleep with, I allowed my cock to keep me in an arrangement that offered no other satisfaction apart from a cheap release. But even that couldn't compensate for the shame I felt afterward, knowing some poor schmuck was in love with her and this was how she treated him.

Instead of doing the usual soul-crushing hook-up, I stayed in my room with Della and stayed up far too late laughing at some stupid TV show and falling asleep amongst chip packets and lolly wrappers.

We hunkered down through winter, believing nothing would change and our content, happy lives had nothing to fear.

For months, we continued to study by night and go off to our separate lives by day, and Della continued to transform into a stunning young woman.

As much as I would like to, I couldn't call her a girl anymore. Sure, the softness in her eyes still said child rather than woman. Sure, the roundness of her cheeks when she smiled hadn't given way to the incredible sharpness of her cheekbones just waiting to sweep up and steal her forever from childhood.

Her body had hips with the fledgling hint of breasts. Her stare was full of both heartache and innocence, and sometimes, just sometimes, when she'd flick her hair and the rippling gold cascaded over her shoulders, I'd have to suck in a breath because I lost sight of the kid and only saw a beauty that I'd have to keep locked away so she wouldn't be devoured by hungry men.

She was far too beautiful, and it made me uncomfortable.

I cursed morning and night when she'd change in front of me.

Before, I didn't care if she'd strip off her top beside her single bed and slip into a nightgown. I didn't think anything of it when her jeans slid down her legs and she kicked them across the room with all the care of a teenager who didn't believe in housework.

For years, I'd refused to get undressed around her. I'd ensured I dressed in the bathroom after a shower and only swam in board shorts rather than skinny-dip.

She should follow those same rules.

But for some reason, I struggled to tell her to hide when it wasn't her with the problem but me.

Her innocence at strolling from the steaming bathroom with just a towel wrapped around her breakable, beautiful body made my eyes avert and heart stop because it wasn't right for me to look.

Not anymore.

Her growth from child to almost-woman should've been the first hint that things were about to change.

Drastic things.

Things we could never undo, and things that would ruin any future we might have had at Cherry River Farm.

Chapter Forty-One

DELLA

Present Day

OKAY, I'VE SLEPT on it, and I think I'm ready to tell you how I screwed up.

I'll tell you about our third separation.

My hands are shaking on my keyboard. My heart is rushing. My head's a mess with everything I did and everything I should've done differently.

Or better yet, never done at all.

I destroyed everything.

I was the idiot that took paradise and tore it to pieces.

How do I begin this?

I can't just jump in and say I ran away...because...well, you don't have context and will be wondering what the hell was there to run away from?

You'll shake your head and call me stupid, and I'd totally agree with you. Even knowing why I ran makes me shake my head and call myself stupid, so you're not alone.

If only I hadn't done what I did, I wouldn't have had to.

But I did, and I'll never forgive myself.

And he'll never forgive me, either.

Okay, assignment-that-will-never-be-turned-in-and-is-just-an-exercise-in-agony, let's do this.

Let's start two days before I ran away, shall we?

No wait, it was three days...no, you know what? I need to start at least four days before I ran.

Cassie.

Funny how it's always freaking Cassie.

I'm going to fast forward what happened until the important stuff.

I got up. I kissed Ren goodbye. I went to school. I learned stuff. I got back on the bus. I came home. I hung with Patricia in her kitchen. I had dinner with Ren. We studied a little. We went to bed.

A perfectly normal day. Innocent. Sweet. No incredibly idiotic screw-ups to deal with.

However, this perfectly normal day wasn't so normal. While I helped Patricia make rhubarb jam in her cosy kitchen, my lower belly started to ache. My head started to hurt, and by the time I'd finished my homework while Ren read my last terms textbooks, the ache had morphed into a terrible throb, radiating down my legs, my inner thighs, even up my back.

I did my best to sleep, but the discomfort never went away, and I woke up cranky and sore and with a zit the size of Antarctica on my forehead.

Ren kissed me goodbye as spring was a busy season with harrowing and replanting, and he started with the dawn.

I waved him away, doing my best to conceal the awful red spot destroying my confidence and was glad he disappeared because it meant I could curl up on my bed and nurse the terrible tummy ache I suffered.

Because I was normally a diligent student, no one suspected I didn't go to school that morning. No one came to check on me. And I spent the day alternating between great big wracking tears and hunching over in the bathroom as I endured a nightmare.

Blood.

Everywhere.

In my knickers, down my legs, on my sheets.

The pain intensified to the point where I grew light-headed with agony, moaning under my breath with every belly squeezing ache.

I knew what it was.

I'd read the books.

I'd devoured the articles online about what classified a girl from a woman and how they had to start menstruating to be called a proper adult.

My breasts ached and tingled.

My head crushed and pounded.

And my moods didn't know if they wanted to be angry with the mess, rage at the pain, or be grateful that I was no longer a kid.

It was one of the longest days of my life, and I didn't dare leave to get food because I couldn't risk running into Patricia or John.

I loved food, but the embarrassment at how disgusting my clothes and bedding had become meant I didn't move a muscle. I tortured myself with scenarios of Ren arriving home and seeing the bloodbath I lay in. Of him asking awful questions. Of him knowing that blood was coming out of me in places that I never wanted to discuss.

More tears came on the tailcoat of those thoughts, knowing I should get up, swallow some painkillers, and strip my bed and body of dirty things.

But the pain continued, and I just didn't have the energy.

I didn't know the time, but eventually the sound of Cassie's Corolla crunched on the driveway, and I hunched deeper into my pillow.

Normally, she came into the barn before going into the house, looking for Ren and sometimes me to say hi before the routine of dinner and homework.

Perhaps, she'd forgo her usual visit today, and my nightmare would go unseen.

I held my breath, hoping against hope that she'd stay away while also a huge part of me wanted to be cared for, for another girl to help me, and to be told I wasn't going to die with the amount of pain I was in.

Her footsteps sounded outside the bedroom door. Her gentle knock reverberating in my pounding my head. "Hello? Anyone home?"

I groaned under my breath, burrowing my head into my pillow, my face on fire and body in agony as she opened the door and found me.

"Oh, my God, Della." She dashed toward me, dropping her messenger bag and cupping my face with her cool hands. She'd grown from the rebellious teenager I looked up to, to a confident young woman who I envied, and here she was, being kind to me.

I burst into tears as she dragged me into her arms.

I could tell you in graphic detail how she helped wash me, dress me, strip and remake my bed, feed me comforting yummy food, and fill me with painkillers, but I won't bother. There's no point because you won't read this, and I don't feel like living that particular part of my life any more than necessary.

By the time she sat me on the couch in her room with music posters and trophies won at horse shows and dressage competitions, I felt somewhat normal and listened intently to the lesson she gave on pads versus tampons and what to expect during my new cycle.

A closeness blossomed between us, and I'd never felt so in-tune with her.

She was my angel, and I'd never forget what she did for me.

By the time Ren returned, smelling of earth with dirt under his nails, my secret was hidden, my newfound womanhood none of his business, and now, for the first time, Cassie and I shared a smile that spoke of our own special secrets.

She didn't tell anyone I hadn't gone to school, and the next day, instead of heading to her uni classes, she took the day off and grabbed me as I forced myself out of bed.

I was still sore but nowhere near as bad.

"Is Ren gone?" she asked, looking around the messy one bedroom.

I nodded, struggling to get up the energy to haul on my school uniform. "Yep."

"Good. Get dressed in your joddies and boots. You're not going to school today."

"I'm not?"

"Nope." She grinned with her hair plaited with a ribbon similar to the one I wore every day. "My mum let me have three days off school when I had my first period. She bought me flowers and cakes and told me turning into a woman was something to be celebrated even though I wanted to yank out my womb and never have another one."

I giggled softly, standing in my pyjamas with one of the pads she'd given me between my achy legs. "Me, too."

Her eyes warmed. "You don't want me to tell anyone, so it's come down to me. I know you don't really like the mall, so we're gonna go for an all-day ride. I have a hot water bottle for your tummy in my saddlebag and lots of painkillers. I'm sure you probably don't feel like it, but the doctors always say exercise and endorphins help the pain."

She was so full of life and friendship that I couldn't say no.

I didn't want to say no.

This was Cassie accepting me as a friend not just as a younger nuisance, and she wanted to spend all day with me.

Needless to say, I loved her for that too. She let me ride my favourite of her horses—black and white Domino—and she rode her newest warmblood cross called Mighty Mo.

Armed with salad sandwiches and a slice of strawberry sponge cake, we headed off and spent the day riding, chatting, and being two simple girls sharing each other's company.

It was one of my favourite days, despite the lingering ache in my belly.

As we rode, propriety fell away, and we giggled at crude things, gossiped about people at her uni, and generally didn't care about right or wrong.

As our bond deviated from polite conversation to openness, more complicated topics filled my head. There were so many things I wanted to ask her, but embarrassment kept me silent.

That was, until she asked if I wanted to gallop over a rolling meadow after our lunch by the forest edge, and we'd ended up racing each other. Hair streaming beneath helmets, hands clutching reins, and legs tight against saddles.

The adrenaline hit me, making me giddy and chatty. Nothing was better than a gallop. I felt free. Not trapped by age or expectation. I was just Della, and she was just Cassie, and for once, we were equals.

She laughed as we slowed to a walk, rubbing her large breasts with a grimace. "These girls have been handy in the romance department, but holy shit, they hurt when riding."

I blushed a little, looking at my flat chest. "I don't have that problem."

She smirked, eyeing me. "Don't worry. Now that your periods have started, your breasts will grow almost overnight."

"Really?"

"Yup." She nodded wisely. "I went from surfboard to D's. My dad was horrified when Mum took me shopping, and I came back with bras bigger than hers."

I laughed under my breath, picturing all the upcoming trials of my life. Bras and tampons and girly stuff that I didn't want Ren knowing about.

We rode a bit more before I had the courage to ask. "Do the boys mind your...eh. When you're on your period, um..."

She raised her eyebrow. "Spit it out. I won't tell anyone, and you can't shock me. You should know that by now."

"Okay." I sat taller in my saddle. "Do boys care about periods? Like when you kiss them and stuff?"

"You mean can you have sex while on your period?"

My face flared.

I didn't know if that was what I meant, but I nodded so I didn't look stupid.

"I guess. I mean, some do. It's not exactly fun. But some boys aren't squeamish. It's natural, after all. Not our fault we bleed once a month."

I pouted. "Once a month is too often."

"I agree." Cassie sighed. "It does get in the way of some things, but tampons are great if you want to go swimming and stuff. And to be fair, a boy will normally stay clear 'cause of your mood swings, not just the blood."

"Does Ren stay clear of your mood swings?"

She laughed. "He seems to stay clear of me a lot these days." The sad wisp in her voice made me wince, partly because I was glad he avoided her and partly because I pitied her, because once you'd been graced by Ren's affection, it was hard to have it taken away.

"I do miss him, but I'm with Chip, and things are going well, so I guess I can't be greedy."

Greed.

That sneaky little sin again.

Questions exploded in my mind. Questions like 'Am I greedy wanting things like what you have? What is it like? Is Ren a good kisser? How often did you do it?'

But each one of those questions was guaranteed to rip out my heart and leave it in the hoof prints of my horse.

I swallowed them down, only for Cassie to somehow sense them and blurt, "I have no one else to talk to about him. I've never told my friends that I've been with Ren because I didn't want them thinking he was available, and I didn't want the news getting back to my parents. But…" She flashed me a pained look. "I really like him. Like…I think I might be in love with him. Stupid, right?" She laughed and sighed at the same time. "When he's with me, he gives me his full attention, but getting him to that stage…it's hard work. It's like there's always something else on his mind, stealing his heart." She glowered at the reins in her hands. "Almost as if he's searching for something else, and I'm not it."

I sat deathly silent in my saddle.

Not even the sway of Domino's steady walk or the increasing ache between my legs now that the painkillers had worn off could distract me from the bitter sweetness of finally getting answers I'd begged for all while hoping I didn't get anymore.

"Have you kissed a boy, Della?"

I sucked in a gasp even as my head answered for me with a sharp shake, lying. She smiled. "I envy you. That first kiss is the best."

"I...I kissed Liam once."

"Did you?! Oh, my God!" She burst out laughing. "Oh, wait. Is that when Mum got super mad and made Liam recite every body part so he knew what each did?" She laughed harder. "That's too funny."

I hunched. "I didn't find it funny. It wasn't good, and his worm...I mean...anyway." I shrugged. "I want to kiss someone soon. I'm a woman now. I should know what it feels like."

She flicked her plait over her shoulder, her ribbon fluttering like mine in the breeze. "Well, my suggestion is to kiss someone you love with all your heart. Don't settle for a cheap thrill. Save it for the person who means the world to you."

That advice, right there...did you see it?

Did you understand what my young foolish heart heard?

If you didn't...you soon will.

Cassie continued, "Sex isn't something to be done with just anyone, you know? You have to trust them impeccably. Love them. Want them. Believe in them. Know that they will never hurt you and always have your back. Okay?"

I nodded, still obsessing over her previous advice on who to kiss.

There was only one person I loved that much.

One boy who meant the absolute universe to me.

Doing my best to stop runaway thoughts, I asked the stupidest question I could've asked, "What was it like...sleeping with Ren?"

Her eyes narrowed, her breath inhaled, and she studied me for an eternity before admitting, "The best I've ever had."

I should've stopped there.

I should've known that something wasn't quite right with me that I wanted explicit details on the man who'd raised me.

I should've known nothing good could come from taboo conversation and dealing with amplified emotions while on my period.

So many reasons to stop.

I wanted to stop.

But this was adult territory, and I was an adult now.

I could handle it.

I could handle the filthy feeling inside at asking about Ren.

I could handle the strange greed, envy, and unfurling lust, even though all three emotions should've been massive alarm bells that I was broken in many ways. That I was on the precipice of doing something forbidden and disgusting and wrong.

But...I had no willpower.

And I'd been waiting for honesty like this all my life.

"How was it the best?" My voice was small, afraid, already hurting.

Cassie tore her eyes from mine as her hand found its way into her horse's mane and twirled the black strands. "How?"

"Uh-huh..."

Tell me.

Don't tell me.

Ruin me.

Don't ruin me.

"Because Ren has never been a boy. Even when he was younger, he was braver, stronger, more attractive than any of the boys who think they're men but are still just silly little children. He carries this melancholy melody inside him that just makes me want to protect him and have him protect me at the same time. When he touches me, it's like fire. When he kisses me, it's like drowning. When he pushes me down and thrusts inside me, it's like falling into space, trusting him to never let you go, all the while hoping he will let you fall and then fall right along with you."

Her voice dwindled away with longing. "He's aggressive in all the right ways. He's dominating and generous and ruthless and..." She shrugged helplessly. "Sleeping with Ren is the best thing I've ever done because he doesn't just live to deliver pleasure but because he gives so much of himself when he does. He has his secrets. He has his moods. But when he's in your arms...that's when he lets himself be seen. His kisses are full of tragedy. His touches are full of sorrow. And when he comes...wow..." She looked at the sky full of sunset-pink clouds. "He breaks your heart every damn time because he's everything you could ever want and everything you'll never have because Ren is wild. He's untouchable. And the knowledge that he'll always be that way tears off a piece of your soul, letting him steal it. He pockets it like his secrets, and he carves a hole inside you until you ache for one tiny piece of his in return."

She sighed with all the pain she felt and all the matching misery I was about to cause. "I'm in love with him, and he doesn't even notice. He doesn't care because whatever he cares about isn't me, and I'm done trying to be what he wants when I doubt even he knows. It's just...it's the perfect combination of grief and bliss, I guess. And I stupidly became addicted to it...just like I became addicted to him."

Now, I'm sure I've embellished what she said to me that day.

I've added flair that creative writing has taught me and put phrases into Cassie's mouth that an Equine Science student probably would never say.

I also, maybe, probably, put in my own bittersweet knowledge, because I understand her now. I might not have slept with Ren, but I know her pain. I recognise her craving because such catastrophe lives within me.

Of course, I didn't know that then. But...that's how I heard it.

I listened to a tortured tale of unrequited love and fell for it.

I'd never heard something so beautiful as being told Ren was unclaimable while in another woman's arms, and it sent my stupid adolescent heart wondering if I would be different.

If I was what he was searching for.

If he was what I was searching for.

If all of this was for a reason, a purpose, an ending that would complete whatever journey we were on.

It cracked open the blinders I'd had on all my life and gave me a glimpse at the man behind the boy.

The man I'd caught myself staring at.

The man I'd dreamt about.

The man who was my everything and would now become the reason for every tortured day thereafter.

I've loved Ren Wild all my life.

But it wasn't until Cassie Wilson ripped back the curtain that I fell in love with him.

I fell into the idea of him.

I fell into the idea of being his.

And unfortunately, once that idea was formed...there was no going back.

As we rode into the farm as dusk fell and Ren appeared from the stable with his reserved smile, tanned skin, and perfect love, I tore my gaze from his dark soulful eyes. As he asked about our ride and helped untack our horses, I kept my thoughts buried and my body averted from his hugs.

And when night-time descended, I lay in bed mulling over Cassie's words.

Over and over again.

Ruining myself, condemning myself until I had no other path to take.

"Well, my suggestion is to kiss someone you love with all your heart. Don't settle for a cheap thrill. Save it for the person who means the world to you."

In bold, it looks just as bad as my last confession of being in love with Ren Wild.

Her advice wasn't meant to be taken the way I took it.

She didn't mean to kiss the only boy I'd ever known.

She didn't mean to set in action something that I'd regret for the rest of my life.

I knew that then, and I know that now.

But did it stop me?

Of course not.

Chapter Forty-Two

REN

2013

DELLA HAD BEEN out of sorts for the past few days.

I tried to ignore it and give her space. I trusted that if it was important, she'd tell me, and if it wasn't, then I didn't want to pry.

However, the day after she got back from her ride with Cassie, she was standoffish and strange. She refused to eat dinner with me. She gave me her back the moment she slipped into bed. She didn't want to watch TV or study or do anything that involved spending time with me.

I tried not to be hurt by her behaviour, but I lay awake most of the night missing my best friend and wondering how the hell I could fix what I'd most assuredly broken because her mood must be my fault.

Why else did she hate me?

By the time the next afternoon rolled around, I finished early, had a shower so I didn't smell of sweat and earth, and used the Wilson's barbecue to make Della's favourite: honey covered yams with brown sugar and soy sauce roasted chicken. I even threw on a few foil-wrapped bananas with maple syrup, indulging in her sweet tooth on all three elements of the meal.

When she returned from school, she gave me a weird smile, opened her mouth as if to say something, then darted into our bedroom.

She returned a little while later with blonde hair dark and damp down her back from a shower, and a turquoise summer dress with a heavy knit cream jumper to ward off the spring evening chill.

I cleared my throat. "I made us dinner."

The weirdness in her faded when she pulled up the barbecue lid and spied the deliciousness underneath. "Wow, everything I love."

Her eyes gleamed with what suspiciously looked like tears before she blinked them away and beamed just like normal. "Thanks so much. You're the best."

The Della I knew and loved was still hiding, but for now, I'd settle for the reserved little woman smiling at me. I couldn't stop my arms from grabbing her in a bone-crushing hug.

I held her so damn hard, wanting to delete the strangeness between us, wishing I could ask what she hid from me.

There were too many unsaid things these days and it made me nervous, as if I'd already lost her when she was still in my arms.

She returned my embrace but not as fierce as she usually would, and when I let her go, she sprang away quickly, when normally, she'd linger. We always lingered around each other. We liked each other's company. I liked to know she was in reaching distance if she needed help. And she liked to snuggle up and make me laugh.

Where had that ease gone?

Why did her smiles make my heart thud in familiarity and foreignness at the same time?

It seemed she no longer needed that closeness, and I did my best to ignore the pain as we sat down on the outdoor picnic set at the bottom of the garden to enjoy our meal.

With birds roosting in trees, Della regaled me of tales about school and teachers and how she was excited to start high school because she wanted to learn the hard stuff and was done with primary.

I nodded and grinned and fixated on the shiny blue ribbon that she'd tied around her throat in a choker.

She'd often used the ribbon as a bracelet or even tied it around her ankle once, but this was the first time she'd used it as a necklace, and I couldn't take my eyes off the way it showed off her stark collarbones.

She looked like she'd lost weight.

She looked older, wiser, moodier.

If she was losing weight, why wasn't she eating? Was it school? Was she being bullied? I made a mental note to ask Cassie if she knew anything while I piled another piece of chicken onto her plate.

I merely shrugged when she raised an eyebrow in question.

Even though the atmosphere between us was a little strained, we smiled and laughed and pretended everything was normal.

So many things lately had been pushing us apart. The knowledge that something festered beneath the surface that neither of us was addressing itched at me just as much as returning to the forest did.

Strange to think I'd only been a boy when I'd found my calling of living in the trees, yet as a man, I'd never accept anything else for my home.

Regardless that circumstances like these made me hunger for space more often than when things were good between us, I forced away such thoughts and focused on Della.

I hated to think of her growing away from me, but at the same time, I welcomed it because it meant she was becoming her own person. I despised the thought of her one day not sharing everything with me and having her own secrets and shadows, but that was a guarantee and yet another piece of growing up that I had to accept.

I didn't know how John and Patricia did it—watching their kids grow from entirely dependent to utterly independent.

It was heart-soaring and soul-crushing all at the same time.

We finished our meal in silence, sipping on fresh glasses of milk and staring at wildflowers dancing in the evening breeze. The chill turned icy as I took her plate and told her to get warm in our bedroom.

She shook her head and followed me to the kitchen instead, standing beside me as I washed the dishes. She dried away the bubbles, and together, we walked from the Wilson's home to ours in the barn and closed the door on the world.

Normally, the sense of contentedness overflowed the moment we were back just the two of us.

Tonight though, nervousness flowed instead, and I didn't swap my jeans for pyjama bottoms like I usually did. For some reason, my instincts were on high alert, and the element of danger wasn't coming from outside the room but within it.

From her.

From my Little Ribbon who perched on the edge of her bed alive and brittle and not paying any attention to the movie we'd chosen.

To be fair, I didn't have a clue what we watched, and by the time she yawned and the clock said it was time to sleep, my heart whirred with smoke and anxious anticipation.

Of what, I didn't know, but as we said goodnight and climbed into bed, I lay in the dark waiting for an attack...just not knowing where it would come from.

* * * * *

I had a dream.

A nonsense kind of dream of darkness and trees and winter.

I'd lost something in the dark, and no matter how fast I ran, no matter how hard I searched, I couldn't find it.

It wasn't a simple trinket I'd lost but something fundamental. Something that would kill me if I didn't find it.

I kept searching, kept hoping, only to run through vast sections of emptiness, finding nothing.

I didn't know how long I ran for or where the trees disappeared to the longer I sprinted in nothingness, but eventually, sunlight beckoned, and I chased harder, faster. My legs burned. My lungs tore.

But I kept running, kept gasping until the one thing I wanted more than anything found me.

A figure appeared from the darkness.

A woman with flowing blonde hair and white angelic dress.

I slammed into her, halting my chase, welcoming me home.

I moaned at the feel of rightness. The sense of belonging. The knowledge of finding the one person I was meant to find after all this time.

Then I stopped breathing as perfect lips pressed against mine.

Soft and hesitant.

Innocent and testing.

I couldn't see the face of my dream-kisser, but I knew, without a shadow of a doubt, she was the one I'd been searching for. She was the one born for me. She was the one I needed to find before I lost everything.

I closed my eyes and gave into the dream.

I didn't try to see her face or know who she was.

All I wanted in that moment was to live beneath her touch, to taste what she gave me, to bow to whatever gift I was worth.

Lips pressed harder, hesitation mixing with determination.

It was as awkward as my first and just as intense.

My heart thundered all around me in the dark forest where I stood.

The innocence of mouths touching but no tongue or deeper invitation wrecked me until my knees buckled, and I collapsed before my dream-kisser.

Lips vanished. Breath caught.

And I groaned for more, to not be abandoned by those I loved, to not fear the future where I might be alone, to not have to clutch something so hard only to lose it anyway.

She heard me.

Lips returned, pressing sweetly, worshiping kindly, and I fell in ways I'd never been able to fall before.

No other kiss compared.

No other intimate moment existed.

This simple faultless, guiltless, sinless kiss was *everything*.

My hands came up, seeking to touch, to stroke, to claim.

My fingers met long, soft hair.

I opened my mouth to deepen the virginal affection.

But then a noise interrupted the purity.

A sound that wrenched me from the dream world, yanked me off my knees, and hurled me into an existence that was no longer fantasy but pure fucking hell.

Della bent over me in the gloom of our bedroom. Her hair was tangled in my fist, lips wet from mine, eyes as wide as blue moons, and her face as gorgeous as untouched snow.

No.

"Stop!" I shoved her away, my fingers burning as if I'd touched acid, my mouth twisting as if I'd ingested poison.

She stumbled backward, landing on her ass between our two single beds. Her nightgown rose up her legs, flashing me white underwear and cream-colored thighs.

I almost retched.

What the *hell* happened?

My body trembled so bad, I scrambled twice for my sheets before I was able to tear them away and leap out of bed. Standing over her, I gripped my hair with terrified hands, and barked with horrified rage, "What the *fuck* do you think you were doing?"

How could I do this?

How could I sleep through something so sick and twisted and wrong?

How could *she* do this?

What the *hell* happened?

"Della! Speak to me!"

I was a trapped animal wanting to slaughter something for having the one person I loved more than anything be the entire reason I'd just lost everything.

Pacing before her, I had to get out of there before I did something I'd regret.

Wrenching open the door, I bolted into the stable and charged down the barn.

The scramble of feet and the flurry of mistake chased me. "Ren!"

I spun and swooped on her, grabbing her bicep, digging my fingernails in as hard as I could. She'd fucking *gutted* me. If I hurt her half as much, it still wouldn't be enough.

"*Why?*" I roared. "Why did you fucking have to do that?!"

Tears sprouted from her eyes. She tried to hold my gaze but couldn't match my fury. She stared at my bare chest as rivers spilled down her cheeks. "I'm sorry. I'm so sorry. I-I don't know what I was thinking."

I shook her. "You *weren't* thinking. That was the problem." I wanted an explanation. I needed it. Now. Before I went insane.

Was she sleep-walking? Was it involuntary? Perhaps a dare or something just as stupid but understandable thanks to teenage guts and idiotic attempts.

Shoving her away, I wiped my hands on my pants, desperate to get rid of the feel of her. The chilliness of her arms reminded me she'd stood over me, fucking *kissing* me, instead of snug and innocent in her bed. I rubbed my mouth, mad with the need to delete her golden taste.

I wanted to vomit.

I should stick my fingers down my throat and retch all over the cobblestones because that was the only way to get the devil out from inside me.

Della collapsed on the floor, her hands fisting her nightgown, her face bowed behind curtains of blonde.

She sobbed.

She begged.

And I couldn't do a damn thing.

I couldn't console her even though every tear cracked open my ribcage and took a pitchfork to my bleeding heart.

I couldn't hug her even though her quaking shoulders buckled my knees and ordered me to fall before her.

I couldn't do anything I would normally do because she'd just ruined everything normal.

Sudden tears filled my own eyes.

Shock and horror and the knowledge that we could never sleep in the same room.

That we could never return to age of innocence after this.

That it was over.

All of it.

"You ruined everything, Little Ribbon." My voice broke. *"Everything."*

She nodded furiously, gulping back tears, tripping over herself to explain. "I'm sorry. Cassie and I were talking about kissing, and I said I'd never been kissed, and I just thought about you and how much I love you and how nice it would be to share my first kiss with someone I love and how I know you'd never hurt me and I just wanted to *know*. I wanted to know, Ren. I'm *sorry!*" She crawled toward me, her white nightgown growing grey with dust and dirt. "I'm *so* sorry! It was wrong. I won't do it again. I promise. Please...please say you'll forgive me. *Please!*"

She reached for my ankles just as the barn door swung wide, and Cassie strode inside with her arms wrapped around her pink dressing gown and her hair mussed from sleep. "I heard noises. What happened?" Her gaze landed on Della collapsed before me, then to me with a rogue tear decorating my cheek and the aura of brokenness littered around us.

Della's sobs turned louder as she buried her face in her hands. "No! Go away! You ruined everything!"

Cassie's face, normally so trusting and up for anything, turned black with suspicion. "What did you do, Ren?"

"He didn't do anything. It was me!" Della yelled through clenched fingers. "Leave. Go away. You're only making it worse!"

Cassie ignored her wishes, running toward her and sliding to a stop beside her.

I backed away, unable to stop the sensation of waking up to kissing my little Della. Unable to stop the repeat of her taste and touch and the dream and the wondrous feeling of finding everything precious, only to lose it in a heartbeat.

The exquisite joy of my dream was now crushed beneath utter despair.

I couldn't breathe beneath the weight of it.

I couldn't exist beneath the horror of it.

How could she *do* this?

How could she break me so spectacularly after everything I'd sacrificed? After every year I'd given her. After every milestone and accomplishment I'd shared with her? I fucking loved her, and this was how she repaid me? By killing me with a simple kiss.

A kiss that could never be permitted.

A kiss that was as dirty and dangerous as everything monstrous and evil.

Cassie locked her fingers around Della's wrists, forcing her to remove her hands and stare into her distraught, blotchy face. "Tell me what happened."

Della cried harder.

Cassie's gaze met mine. "Or you tell me. Someone better. Otherwise, I'm calling my father."

Della squirmed, trying to get out of her hold. "No, don't call him. Please!"

"You better tell me what happened then. Right now."

Her scolding worked, and Della's bottom lip wobbled with confession. "I kissed him. I-I did what you said and only kissed the boy I loved with all my heart."

Cassie fell back, ripping her hands from Della the same way I had. Her own heartbreak shattered all over her face as she looked back at me.

I couldn't do a thing but stand there with my head shaking and my hands opening and closing in helplessness.

"Is that true?" she breathed. "Did you *kiss* your baby sister?" Loathsome disgust painted her features. She switched from happy-go-lucky Cassie to judge and executioner. "What sort of fucking *pervert* are you? You let her *kiss* you? Are you insane? What the fuck else do you do in that one bedroom, huh?" She climbed to her feet, stalking me, backing me into a stable. "Have you fucked her, Ren? Is that why you won't like me? I'm too old for you? All this time, you've been sleeping with someone half your age. Someone who shares your blood?!" She dry heaved as she slammed the stable door with me inside and slammed the lock home. "Don't fucking move, you sick, twisted asshole. I'm getting my father."

The fact that I stood there, locked in place even as Cassie flew from the stable was a testament to how wonderfully Della had crushed me.

I had no energy to fight for my own freedom.

I had no ability to argue my defence so John Wilson wouldn't call the police for suspected incest and child abuse.

I just stood there, staring at Della on the floor.

Begging her silently to fix this.

To rewind time and never do what she did.

"Ren…" she murmured between thick tears. "I'm so, *so* sorry." She stood and wobbled toward me, grabbing the locked partition between us for support.

I backed away, deeper into the stable until the hay net stopped my retreat. "Don't come near me."

The desolate brokenness on her face matched the caving, crumbling destruction inside me, and we stood staring, silently cursing, painfully accepting that this was it.

There was no turning back from this.

"I love you," she whispered. "I didn't mean for this to happen."

Somehow, her wounded voice snapped me from my stupor, and I charged forward. Reaching over, I unbolted the lock and stepped as far away from her as possible.

I might not have anything to say in my defence, but I had plenty to say on behalf of Della's. I should never have returned that kiss. I should never have given in. Dream excuse or not, I should've known better. I should never have let her believe such boundaries could be crossed. I should never have encouraged hugs and kisses and affection.

This was my fault, not hers.

And if anyone was going to be punished, it was me.

John had to know the truth, and he had to know it now before the police came to take me away. Before they found out I was the runaway who stole a baby named Della Mclary. Before they found out I was a criminal who'd kissed that stolen child. Before they found out my past as a slave and knitted my sad sorry tale together and the newspapers wrote fiction, lamenting that anyone who'd been sold and forced into labour before he was ten years old was bound to have issues. That it was only natural for his story to end with him in jail for molesting the very same kid he stole.

I was *understandable*.

I was a statistic.

Della was not.

She was so many things.

So many wonderful things.

But she was no longer mine.

We were no longer Ren and Della.

No longer fake brother and sister.

No longer the Wilds.

Backing away from her, I grunted around my fury and grief, "Go back to bed, Della. I need to fix this."

I left her in the stables, crying and beautiful and perfectly screwed up from my lack of skills as a parent. *I'd* been the one to break her. I was the one to muddle her mind and make her think kissing me was appropriate.

And as I knocked on the Wilson's door and prepared to face the symphony that I'd conducted, I didn't think she'd ever disobey me.

I believed I would fight for her right to stay with the Wilsons.

I thought I would shoulder all the blame, be taken away in hand cuffs, and leave Della in the capable control of a family I'd grown to love as my own.

But just like I'd trusted Della never to overstep our friendship, I ought to have known what would happen.

I ought to have seen that as I entered the Wilson's house and prepared to do battle, Della Mclary would pack my old backpack, dress in warm clothes, and sneak unseen through the starlight, leaving me, leaving us, leaving everything behind until the only thing that was left was her twisted kiss on my lips.

By the time I realised what she'd do, it was too late.

She was gone.

Chapter Forty-Three

REN

2013

DELLA.

Every single part of my life, she was there.

Every single memory, she was in.

Every single achievement and ability, she was responsible for.

And now, she was the reason my heart was broken as I stood in an empty bedroom without her.

She'd gone.

She'd left.

Where, I didn't know.

For how long, I couldn't be sure.

Would she come back?

Should I stay or hunt for her?

What was the *right* thing to do?

My hands balled as a crippling wash of loneliness, despair, and confusion threatened to drown me.

How could she do this?

How could she rip apart our world and then run the moment I'd put it back together again?

How could she turn her back on me when I'd stood before the Wilsons and done my best to repair everything?

For the past few years, Della had spent her evenings teaching me spelling and multiplication and science. She'd traded the knowledge I'd bought her and gave me hours upon hours of her time.

She was selfless.

She didn't care about hanging out with girls her own age. She ignored the cell phone John and Patricia insisted she had and preferred to check my answers on tests she'd already aced, rather than respond to teenage texts.

Every night, I'd been gruff with her. I'd been impatient to learn faster. I'd been frustrated at her mercy and taken her tutorage, not with utmost gratefulness, but with tense irritation that my inadequacy stole more of her childhood.

Even though I sat stiff and surly through most of the lessons, it didn't stop my eyes from settling on her bent head or my fingers from itching to sweep away her hair so I could see her face.

I was in utter awe of her—in absolute wonder that my best friend was so smart, so capable, so perfect.

And that was the only reason I'd been able to hide most of my frustration and smile when she graded my division skills and laugh when she critiqued my sentence structures.

I'd never been more thankful for that gift as I'd stood before John, Patricia, and Cassie Wilson. I'd held my head high, able to use words I knew how to spell and give explanations I knew how to deliver, ripping apart their trust.

They'd welcomed us into their home under one condition. One measly condition, and I'd shattered it.

My lips still seared from hers. My dream still tainted my reality. Thanks to Della, I'd just had my world snatched away, all the while, she was the reason I was no longer an illiterate farmhand.

Pushing her out of my mind, I'd focused on ensuring this mess didn't ruin her future.

I'd make sure she had a *better* future.

One with firmer boundaries.

One that I didn't screw up.

John stood with his arms crossed, his maroon plaid pyjamas severe as a prison sentence. His wife stood with furious dots on her cheeks, and Cassie stared at me as if I was a stranger, hugging herself with white-knuckled fists.

No one spoke, but the air was heavy with condemnation. The phone rested in Patricia's hand either used to call the police or still waiting. Either way, I'd run out of time, so I said the only thing that mattered.

"She isn't my sister."

Cassie's mouth fell open, followed by her mother's.

John cleared his throat as if he hadn't been expecting such a confession. "Pardon me?"

I stood straighter, shoving aside the lies we'd told. "I did run away from a farm that bought children for labour. I did raise Della since she was a baby. Those weren't lies. And I do love her, with all my heart, but our last name isn't Wild and we're not related."

John scowled. "I...don't understand."

"She was the daughter of the people who bought me. Their name was Mclary. I don't know where their farm is. I don't know how much they paid for me or what my surname was before I was just Ren. Della was theirs. She was born the night after my finger was cut off for stealing food, and somehow, when I finally got the guts to run away, she was in the backpack I'd prepared with meagre supplies. I didn't mean to steal her. In fact, I tried to leave her with a family because I knew I would be no good as a parental figure. But...I went back for her. I took her with me, and I've kept it a secret ever since."

I stepped back, withdrawing myself from their world. "I know what you must think of me, but I never meant for this to happen. I don't know why she kissed me, and I definitely didn't condone it. She'll be disciplined, and I'll ensure she has better rules because I think it's time I left. She needs parents, like you, not a kid who doesn't know what he's doing. I'm not telling you this to excuse what happened. I'm as disgusted as you are. But I *am* telling you the truth, so you know how real I am when I say I'm sorry. You have enough information to ruin my life. I'm sure I'm wanted by the police. Della's been missing for twelve years...if her parents even care she's gone. Who knows? They might've been arrested for buying kids for all I know. But what I *do* know is, I love Della. I've loved her since I stole her. But that's all it is. I've never touched her. I've never kissed her inappropriately. I've never thought of her in any way apart from family. She might not be my sister, but I love her as one. And under no circumstances will I allow her to forget that, ever again."

Silence fell, heavier but friendlier than before.

Cassie was the first one to speak. "The brand on your hip. The one you said they put there. It has MC before the number...for Mclary, right?"

I gritted my teeth, cursing that permanent reminder. "Yes."

"And you swear on your life you've never done anything else? Never been tempted? Never gone too far in that one bedroom in the barn?" Her eyes blazed with distrust. "That kiss was the first and the last?"

I thudded a fist over my heart. "I promise on my life."

A thick pause settled around us, cushioning the night.

"I believe you," Patricia finally murmured. "I hear the honesty in what you're saying."

I nodded gratefully. "I'm sorry."

She shook her head kindly. "Nothing to be sorry for. She's young. Just like the day I caught her and Liam naked, she's merely exploring her sexuality and confused on where desire fit in."

I swallowed hard, refusing to let the word desire anywhere near the thought of Della.

John stepped forward, his face weary and wrinkled. "I think you better go. It's late. We'll all get some rest and deal with this in the morning."

"I can't sleep in that bedroom, sir." My voice thickened with urgency. "I...I can't stay here. I need to leave. That's why I'm here. I need you to take care of Della. I'll find another job. I'll pay for her upkeep. But—" I glanced at Cassie's whose eyes glassed with tears. "I don't think it's fair for me to continue trying to be her role model when I'm obviously failing."

"You can't go," Cassie whispered. "That's just stupid."

"I...I don't think I have a choice," I whispered back, wishing I could offer sympathy but sensing that to touch her now would be the worst mistake of my life. I'd always known something deeper lurked beneath Cassie's sweet affection and fierce tumbles in the hay. She pretended it was just casual sex between us, but occasionally, I'd catch that look in her eyes. The one she was giving me now. The look that petrified me because Della gave me the same look, only innocent.

It was love.

And love had hurt me enough.

"I'm sorry." I rolled my shoulders. "To all of you."

Patricia joined John, taking a few steps closer. "Don't be silly, Ren. We love you and Della. We want both of you to stay. Move your things into the hay loft if it will make it easier. We'll arrange for one of the stables to be converted into an extra bedroom. Now that Della knows kissing you is not permitted, things will go back to normal...you'll see. No one needs to leave." Her voice softened. "And besides, who will help John in the fields? You've been the best help we could have ever asked for. You're family, not just an employee, and we won't hear of this nonsense about you leaving."

I was trapped.

Trapped between trying to do the right thing and being given permission to do the wrong one.

I didn't *want* to leave.

The thought of walking away from Della ripped out my guts and left me dying, but how could I ever relax around her again? How could I speak to her without second-guessing if it was too affectionate? How could I ever touch her without fearing I was giving her mixed messages?

The carefree innocence we shared was forever lost.

John came closer and clasped my shoulder with his large, hairy hand. "I don't like that you lied to us, but I know you're a good man, Ren Wild. It's late. Go to bed. I'll come see you in the morning." His eyes flashed with more, but he held his tongue.

With nothing else to do, I murmured goodnight and returned to the barn where I'd assumed Della would be curled up tight in bed. I should've just headed to the hay loft to sleep amongst the grain and grass, but something made me check. Something clawed inside to see...to make sure she was okay.

She'd been just as distraught as I was and had no one to console her.

Part of me was glad she suffered—if it taught her the valuable lesson never to do it again, then so be it. But most of me twisted with agony, knowing she was sad and I hadn't been there to dry her tears and hug away her heartache.

My thoughts were tangled as I snuck into the bedroom, my eyes locking onto Della's bed.

Then nothing else mattered.

Not the kiss.

Not the mess.

Nothing.

Because she wasn't there.

Her bed was empty.

The barn, too.

It took me two minutes to learn that the emptiness inside the place we called home was just the beginning of the emptiness inside me.

I tore apart every hiding place she'd ever used. I galloped over the fields and screamed at the top of my lungs for a reply.

But she wasn't there to answer.

She wasn't there at all.

And now, after pointless wastage of time, trying to decide what I should do, I made the only decision I could.

I couldn't let her be out in the world on her own.

I couldn't forget her and turn my back.

I would *never* forgive myself, just like I would never forgive her for every disastrous consequence she'd caused by kissing me.

What was the *right* thing to do?

The right thing was to chase after her, keep her safe, and bring her back here...to where she belonged. I was the one who should leave.

My hands shook as I hurried to our one piece of furniture and pulled out one of the lined workbooks she'd given me to practice with. The shared dresser beneath our TV held a jumble of hers and my belongings—blending together, just like us.

Her socks on my socks.

Her dresses beneath my shorts.

Even our goddamn clothes liked to be close, and I slammed the drawer with a nauseous roil.

Perching on the edge of my bed, I quickly—or as fast as I could with my chicken scratch—wrote my third apology for the night.

Della had run, and I was about to vanish after her.

There were no times for goodbyes.

Dear John and Patricia,
What can I say?
I have to go after her. It's the only thing I—

"Ren."

My head shot up, my pen skidding across the page.

John stood on the threshold, his face tight and a black dressing gown thrown over his plaid pyjamas. "Can I speak to you?"

I stood, tossing the unneeded letter onto the mattress. "I need to talk to you, too. I'm leaving. She's run away."

"Oh, shit." His eyes turned forlorn as he nodded. "Of course. You must go after her."

I didn't know why he was here, but I was grateful he'd come, if only so he knew why I was about to walk out of his life with no guarantee of coming back.

John stood awkwardly while I yanked up my sheets and ducked to yank my old backpack out from beneath the bed.

Only, it wasn't there. Just a dust-free patch where it used to be, along with a skid mark from where Della had pulled it free.

"Shit," I breathed. *"Shit."*

Clambering upright, I glanced around the room. There was nothing else I could use to carry the supplies we might need.

"Eh, here…this is for you." John cleared his throat. "Take it."

An eerie sense of déjà-vu hit me. Years ago, I'd stood in their guest bedroom as he offered my first salary, and I'd traded it in for Della's well-being.

Now, he held out an even larger envelope.

"What are you doing?" I asked.

"It's the rest of your income and bonuses."

"But I thought you were spending it on Della's education and things?"

"She's in public school, and she costs very little to run with most of our produce coming straight from the garden. If Cassie cost half what she did, I'd be a rich man." He smirked half-heartedly. "Never a day went by that I didn't ensure I was paying you what you were worth. Patricia ran the books. With the bonuses and business increase you helped create, you have more than enough saved to put a deposit on your own place or do whatever you need to do."

My feet locked to the ground. I narrowed my eyes. "Why do I get the feeling this is charity?" Anger tinged my voice. "I'm not some homeless kid anymore. I'm twenty-three. I don't need your—"

"I know you don't, and it's not. This is rightfully yours, and I wouldn't feel right keeping it." The air thickened as he crossed the distance between us and forced it into my hand.

I swallowed as the weight of money settled into my grip.

And then I knew why he'd given it to me.

Tonight would never have had a different ending—regardless if Della had run away or not.

My fingers tightened around the cash. "You're saying goodbye."

John shoved his hands into his dressing gown pockets, looking at the floor. "Patricia is right. We love you like family. You're not just an employee, and I don't want to see you go. I love having you and Della here, and I'm eternally grateful for all your help. But…this is a small town, Ren. I know you said you and Della aren't blood relatives…but that doesn't change facts."

I sighed heavily, feeling disgusted all over again. "I know."

"If people find out. If Della tries it again—"

"She won't," I snapped. "Believe me. When I find her, she'll never wish to kiss another person again."

"That might be." He nodded. "But here, people believe you're brother and sister. If Cassie talks or even if Della talks, you stand a high chance of arrest just from local gossip. You've done well by that girl. No matter what you think, you are a good role model for her. But right now, this place would only hurt you if you stay."

Clutching the wad of money, goosebumps scattered over my arms. "You don't want us to come back."

He smiled sadly. "It's not that I don't want you. Hopefully, one day you'll visit, and things will be back to normal. But for now, you need to be somewhere that hasn't watched you two grow up and already have their perceived realities."

"There *are* no perceived realities." I growled. "There's nothing going on. We *are* brother and sister. No more. No less."

John backed toward the door with a wise smile that irritated and angered me. "Realities can change. I'm not blind. I've seen what's gone on over the years with you and Cassie. I never spoke up because out of all the boyfriends she's had, you were a good influence on her. But I also know it'll break her heart when she wakes up to find you gone tomorrow."

I glanced toward the farmhouse as if I could see through walls and witness Cassie asleep in her bed. "I didn't mean—"

"I know you didn't." He held up his hand. "But that's just who you are, Ren. You care about others so much they feel incredibly special. You give them the clothes off your back. You donate every penny for their benefit. You have no other purpose in life but to support those you care about, and that sort of dedication can be hard not to fall for."

"You're wrong." Guilt squeezed. "I was never that kind to Cassie. And I'm only generous to Della because it's my fault she has no parents—"

"I don't believe that. It sounds as though Della is lucky you took her that night. Her parents are monsters. And you treated Cassie better than most. Don't let that weigh you down. You're a good kid, Ren." He crossed the threshold, shuffling with reluctant steps. "But if I can give you any word of advice for the next few years of raising Della, I would say let her trip up occasionally. Pull back. Let her make mistakes. Let her know you're there for her but don't be her everything. Do that, and this passing phase will be just that—a phase. But if you don't...you'll have trouble."

I stepped toward him, desperate for guidance, while at the same time, wanting to run from any future problems. I just wanted her normal. I wanted things to be normal between *us*. There was no doubt in my mind that I would find her; even now, the urge to chase built every second until I struggled to stay in one spot.

But this was one of those moments that made the hair on the back of my neck stand up with importance. I hadn't been guided in my role as a guardian, and so far, I'd managed to keep her alive but not enforce the rules she badly needed.

I looked up to John, and if he wanted to share a piece of wisdom, then I wanted to listen. "What sort of trouble?" I asked softly. "What am I doing wrong?"

"You're not doing anything wrong. You're doing everything right. Too right. So right, in fact, you're giving her an unrealistic view of the male sex, and when she starts dating, the only person she'll have to compare them to is you, and she'll find them lacking every time." He smiled kindly. "Show her you're human, that you have flaws and a temper just like everyone else. Otherwise..."

"Otherwise what?"

"She won't just use you as an experiment next time. She'll fall in love with you and everything you've built together will vanish because you won't permit her to want you and she won't be able to keep living with something she can't have. You'll break apart, and the surname that links you together as surely as mine does to my wife and children will mean nothing."

He pulled the door to behind him, granting final words that stopped my heart. "Figure out a way to keep her as your sister, Ren. Otherwise, you won't have her at all."

* * * * *

I left Cherry River with far less than I arrived with.

I had no Della, no flu, no backpack, no tent.

All I had was an envelope of cash tucked safely in my waistband with two t-shirts on, a thick jumper, and my winter jacket. In my pockets, I had a spare set of underwear and socks, and on my head, a beanie with sunglasses perched for all types of seasons I might encounter.

John's words kept me company as I crunched down their gravel driveway one last time, turned in the direction my heart tugged me— all the while hoping it was the right choice to find Della—and never looked back.

I struck off into a jog.

My mind locked on finding my runaway Ribbon.

I didn't say goodbye.

Chapter Forty-Four

REN

2013

I LOST HER for two full days.

The first few hours, I wasn't worried.

I figured I knew her enough that she'd head to one of her friend's from school, follow the main road, get tired, and rest along the verge.

That theory was dashed by the time I arrived at the friend's house in question, and her mother informed me with sleepy frustration that there was no reason to get her out of bed at four in the morning because Della wasn't there.

I'd waited until dawn, sitting in their deck chairs on the lawn, waiting to see if Della would turn up, hoping she would, begging her to.

But by the time the sun warmed the world, I had to accept defeat.

She hadn't come this way.

By midmorning, fear crept over my anger, and I no longer thought about her with a thinning of my lips and discipline on my mind but with an ever-fledgling panic. She was no longer the bold girl who'd kissed me without permission. She was a child lost and alone and at the mercy of all manner of creatures.

Most of them men.

Heinous, horrible men who would gladly accept a kiss and so much else.

My heart never fell below a steady race as I jogged through downtown, visited her local familiar hang-outs, and racked my brain for her favourite places and people.

By the time another evening rolled around, I hadn't eaten or drank. I raged on terrified adrenaline. I didn't need fuel because the urgency to find her before another night fell kept me pumped and focused.

I'd exhausted all my options in town.

The next place I had to search was the first place I would've gone but not somewhere I'd expect her to find sanctuary in.

Especially on her own.

Doubling back toward the outskirts of town and keeping my eye on the horizon where Cherry River Farm had once been our home, I traded paved roads for bracken paths and shed off the city veneer I'd worn while living around people.

The forest.

My *real* home.

I relished in letting the wildness inside me take over and lengthened my stride until I covered miles upon miles, ducking around trees, listening for any animals complaining at having a human amongst their midst, doing my best to track her like any good predator would his prey.

But as another night fell, slicing me from Della for a full twenty-four hours, I had to rest.

I slowed to a walk, let my eyes adjust to the crescent moon glow, and padded as quietly as I could, hoping against hope to hear the girl I would die for.

* * * * *

Another morning.

No rest.

No luck.

No Della.

My stomach growled, and my thirst had gotten the better of me around two a.m., making me drink like a beast with hands cupped to my face from the river.

I'd followed the meandering water for a while, hoping Della would be smart and do what I'd taught her.

Anything was survivable as long as you had an abundant water source.

If she wasn't near the river, and she wasn't hiding with friends…where was she?

How would I find her?

How would I keep her safe?

My legs had turned to jelly hours ago, and I half-stumbled, half-jogged forward, always seeking, never finding.

I had no food.

I had no time to find food.

I had a waistband full of money, but it was utterly useless out here in a world of trees and woodland.

If I didn't find her soon, I'd have no choice but to return to civilization and gather supplies. I would turn the pointless dollar bills into practical belongings and never rest until we were back together again.

Another lunchtime and still no sign of her.

No noise.

No hint.

No clue.

I kept pushing forward, calling her name, peering into the hazy green foliage while stripping off overheating jackets and jumpers in the spring heat.

Another evening and still alone.

No progress.

No success.

No reunion.

And by midnight, when darkness thickened to its blackest and day-dwellers traded places with nocturnal, I had no choice but to put myself first, no matter how much it killed me.

My body needed help.

I had to be smart and feed the snarling emptiness in my belly, so I could find a way to repair the howling emptiness in my heart.

It took a few hours to switch direction and leave the river behind.

I cut through small tracks made by mammals and weaved around knobbly trees. I fell over at one point, almost too exhausted to stand, but I found my final reserves, hauling myself onward into an energy depleting march.

And lucky I did.

Because at the point when I was closest to giving up, that was the moment I found her.

Chapter Forty-Five

DELLA

Present Day

NOW...BEFORE YOU judge me...
Let's talk about that kiss for a second.
It was wrong; I know that.
It was morally gross; I know that, too.

It was all manners of bad, considering I took advantage of the boy who'd dedicated his entire life to making sure I was happy, cared for, and safe. I plotted silently in the dark; I willingly waited until his breathing changed and I knew he was asleep before I swallowed back the guilt, the nerves, and the shame to press my mouth to his.

I know everything I did was wrong, okay?

So you don't need to tell me how majorly I screwed up. The instant his lips softened beneath mine, and I felt something I'd never felt when kissing Liam, I'd known just how terribly I'd screwed up.

Hugely.

Monstrously.

Life-ruiningly.

When his mouth parted, and the sweetest, heaviest sigh escaped him, and his hand came up to twine possessively in my hair, I knew I would forever punish myself for doing something so far out of permission.

Not because Ren kissed me back.

Not because he tasted so perfect or the quick flick of his tongue made a fireball ignite in my lower belly, but because, in that fleeting moment when my eyes grew heavy and I closed them to concentrate on kissing someone I never should have kissed, I grew up in an instant.

I felt things no girl should feel.

I understood things no child would know.

And I condemned myself because, as fast and as innocent as the kiss had been, it had showed me that I would never be allowed the one thing I wanted with all my heart.

Again, this is where my past knits with my present, and I can't explain the true feelings I had then because they're so tangled with my current heartache that it's hard to distinguish the two.

What I can tell you is I didn't need to be punished because I'd punished myself. I didn't need to be told how wrong it was because I'd already whipped and cursed and shouted at myself. And I didn't need anyone to tell me that it could never happen again because the moment my lips touched his...I knew.

I knew he was off limits.

I knew he would never be mine.

And the pain...ouch, even as a thirteen-year-old, it was excruciating.

Now that I'm eighteen and I've lived with that pain daily, pretending that I only think of him as my friend, convincing him—and sometimes myself—that he is far too precious to me to ever risk another idiotic move like that—I know in my heart of hearts, I don't have much left.

God, it hurts so bad just saying that.

No amount of chest rubbing or false soothing can cut away the pain growing like a cancer inside me.

I'm an adult now.

And that means I no longer officially need him.

And because I no longer officially need him, I can move away.

I can cut ties.

I can put distance between us so our interactions will reduce to what normal families with children leaving the nest reduce to: the odd holiday gathering, the occasional phone call, a half-hearted text every other day.

I will be safe from ever being this wretched every time I look at him, smell him, laugh with him, adore him.

If I don't do something soon, then my entire life is going to be destroyed. I'll never find someone I can fall for. I'll never be able to love another the way they deserved to be loved.

Those two days when I ran—the days when Ren couldn't find me—were days I needed to glue shattered pieces back together in the best order I could. It was time I needed to talk to my younger self and tell her that she had her entire life in front of her and there would be plenty of other boys to kiss, to fall in love with, to want with such desire.

I wasn't ready.

Ren would never be ready.

Therefore, it could never happen.

I'd spent a night in a friend's house who I knew was overseas, and I happened to know where the spare key lived. I'd had the place to myself, but I hadn't slept or relaxed. I'd used the space and minutes wisely, doing my best to carve out the mess I'd made of my heart and return to the Della I'd been before I'd crept over to his bed in the dark.

I'd stared into mirror after mirror, desperate to reverse the time to when I didn't destroy myself or him.

I'd stared into my eyes.

I'd clutched the ribbon from my hair.

And I'd made a vow that Ren will never know.

I knew he would find me.

He would discipline me.

He would forgive me.

And I also knew, despite all of that, I would make him believe it was all a terrible mistake. I would sell my lies. I would believe my untruths. I would do everything required to make it all go away, because he must never know that kissing him might've been the worst thing I'd ever done, but it was also the best, the realest, the most truest thing I'd ever felt, and I would never apologise for that.

I would beg for his forgiveness purely to ensure our relationship was back where it belonged, and I would nurse my dirty secrets to protect him for a change.

I've failed at many things in my life, but I'm happy to tell you, I've never once broken my vow. I've been protecting him from that secret for years. I've been lying to him every minute of the day.

And now I'm exhausted, and writing this all down has shown the conclusion I didn't want to face: I'm not ready to say goodbye.

I'll never be ready but if I don't, how can I ever move on?

Chapter Forty-Six

REN

2013

"DELLA…"

Her head snapped up from where she'd been snoozing, sitting up against a tree stump. Her eyes blinked away drowsiness, slipping from joy at seeing me to guarded with trepidation.

She should be nervous.

Now that I knew she was in one piece and not molested or dead, my panic transformed into the hottest rage I'd ever felt. The catalyst of fury replaced my insides, making my nostrils flare with hot breath and temper fire with cruel words. *"Della."*

Before, her name had been a prayer of thanks. Now it was a curse of condemnation.

She scrambled to her feet, her head bowed, contrition all over her. "Before you say anything…I'm sorry." Glancing at me between strands of curling blonde, she breathed, "I'm sorry for doing something I shouldn't. I'm sorry for running away. I'm sorry I made you worry." She licked her lips, shrugging. "I'm…just very sorry, for everything."

Her apology tried to douse my anger, but I didn't let it.

Stalking the distance between us, I crunched over twigs and foliage, coming to a trembling stop in front of her. She was no longer as short as I remembered. No longer as young. She stood subservient and entirely ready to be scolded, but her eyes burned with the same sort of fire that hissed inside me.

A fire that did its best to confuse and convince me that she didn't deserve to be told off when it was the only thing she *did* deserve. She needed goddamn boundaries, and she seemed deaf to them unless I shouted.

My hands curled, doing my best to keep control. "Are you hurt?"

I'd wanted to yell, but somehow, my fear made me check she was capable of withstanding the violence I itched to give her first. My palms burned to strike. To imprint some sort of punishment for everything she'd done.

Hoisting the backpack—*my* backpack—up her shoulders, she shook her head. She'd dressed in jeans and a thick knitted jumper with her winter jacket tucked through the straps of the rucksack. "No."

Despite studying her appearance and finding no blood or broken bones to say she was lying, I took another step closer.

Her eyes flared then dropped to the ground again, giving me permission to nurse my terrible temper. "Where the hell were you?"

"At a friend's." Her voice was small. "I knew they weren't there, and I needed somewhere on my own...just for a little while."

"Didn't you think I needed somewhere, too? To figure out what the fuck you were playing at?"

She flinched.

I'd never used such foul language toward her until the moment she kissed me.

She fucking *kissed* me!

I couldn't control my rage's spit and snarl or the pain she'd caused. "You could've been hurt, Della. You could've been kidnapped or raped or killed. Did you stop to think about that, at least? Because I know you didn't stop to think before you fucking *kissed* me."

She bit her lip, shaking her head.

Weak from hunger and strung out from everything strange and wrong, I growled. "How could you, huh? What the *hell* possessed you to do something so sick?" Not waiting for answers, I paced away, snapping incoherent things. "You're so goddamn young. You're still a kid. And I'm...I'm ten years older. If that wasn't enough, we're *family*, Della. Do you know what that means? It means you love each other, but you don't fall *in* love with each other. You've taken everything that was so right between us and destroyed it because how can I trust you to understand the difference? How can I ever touch you again? How can I ever relax around you again?"

I slammed to a stop, breathing hard, facing her with spread helpless hands. "How can we ever go back to the way things were?" Pressure built behind my eyes as I stared at the girl I loved more than life itself. The girl who'd cracked my heart. The girl who would forever have the power to break me just like she'd broken me two nights ago and every hour in-between. "Do you even know the difference between platonic love and romantic? Is it my fault that I never explained the two? Have I failed you, Della?"

I was starving for food and affection.

I was thirsty for water and someone to assure me that it would all be okay. That I could have my Ribbon back. That I wouldn't have to worry if I touched her hand or brushed a kiss on her temple. That I wouldn't ruin her by making her believe that I wanted her the way a man wants a woman when I would *never* do that.

She was mine.

She was every hope and dream I'd ever had and the fabrication of every future I'd hoped for, and if I had to say goodbye to that…

Fuck.

I cleared the squeezing misery away and coughed into the night. "I…I miss you so fucking much, yet you're standing right there."

She sucked in a pained gasp, tears welling and overflowing in a second. Wriggling out of the backpack, she sprinted toward me before it even hit the ground.

With a rush of force, she ran into me, wrapping her arms around my waist, pressing her cheek against my chest. "Ren."

Two things happened.

One, no thought was required.

This was Della.

I'd hugged her a thousand—no, a million times before, and my body recognised hers as if it was a part of me—a part I'd lost but now had found, and it hurt almost as much welcoming it back as it was to lose it.

My body rejoiced at having her home in my embrace, and I clutched her so damn hard. I curled around her, inhaling her hair and smelling foreign shampoo. I pressed my lips to her head, but then the memories returned.

The dream figments.

The real yearnings.

The forbidden responses she'd drawn from me.

Shoving her back, I held up my hand, keeping distance between us. "You've even managed to ruin a hug."

She choked on a sob, hugging herself with fierce sadness. "I know."

You've made this impossible for me, Little Ribbon."

"I know that, too."

Silence slithered between us, letting her tears fall and regret ice over my temper, until we both stood drained and empty with no place else to go.

Finally, I sighed. "I knew keeping you would be full of complications. I lived an almost daily battle when you were young not to hurt you and an even bigger war as you grew older. I've leaned on you so much. I've taken all you've had to give. And I've given you the illusion that what we share is normal. That our closeness is what others have when it's not." I looked at her, wanting to burn her with the truth. "I've never had anyone. I had no love until you taught me what it was, and even as I slowly learned the opposite of hate, I've known all along that love would end up hurting me the most." I laughed sadly. "I was right."

Her spine rolled, letting my words whip her.

I breathed hard, completely drained and ready to leave this place, to leave behind these harsh truths and put everything back into the dark where it belonged. "Come on," I whispered, "I'll take you home."

Her eyes flicked to mine with blue surprise beneath black remorse. "How can we go back? I thought Cassie called the police."

I shoved my hands into my back pockets, adjusting the wad of cash stored in my waistband. "I spoke to them. They didn't call anyone. You'll stay with them."

"But…what about you?"

"I can't go back. Not anymore."

"No!" Her cheeks dotted with urgency. "I'm not going back without you."

"You have no choice."

"I do. I *do* have a choice!"

Her anger ignited mine all over again. "Like you had a choice when you kissed me?"

Her lips twisted, and her beautiful face warred with letting me remind her of her mistakes and fighting for forgiveness. "I said I was sorry."

"It's not fucking good enough. You should never have been so stupid!"

"I'll never do it again."

"Also not good enough. How can I ever trust you?"

"You can. You *can* trust me."

I shook my head sadly. "I thought I could. And I did. I trusted you with my life."

"And I trust you with mine." She wrung her fingers, twisting and tugging. Her blue eyes darkened as some sort of resolution shoved aside her despair. "I know things will be strained between us for a while. I get that. And I also get that I'm a danger to you—that I did something outside of your control. I also get how wrong it was, and that to outsiders, it will never be permitted."

"Not just to outsiders," I snapped. "*I* will never permit such things. *Ever.* Do you hear me?"

"Yes."

"Say you understand why it will never happen again."

"Because we're family."

My heart pounded at the word. For a second, I wished she *wasn't* family. I wished we'd never met, so this lacerating torture would never find me. But then, the thought of living in a world where I didn't have Della...

Fuck.

I'd rather be dead.

But that was my future now. I had to leave her behind. I had to walk away. She had somewhere to go home to, and I did not. Our lives were about to go in separate directions. I would miss her with every tormented heartbeat, but I would rather stay away if I was the reason for her confusion.

"Family don't hurt each other," I managed to say even though I almost choked on the lie. My own family had traded me for dollars. Perhaps that was why I'd failed Della? I had no decent role models of my own.

Della tucked unruly hair behind her ear as she stood straighter. "Can I say something?"

I narrowed my eyes warily.

When I didn't give permission, she ploughed on anyway, "I kissed you—"

"Stop." I cringed, falling back a step.

Before I could interrupt her with another scathing telling off, she added, "I shouldn't have done it, Ren. I *know* that. I've learned that lesson, and believe me, I know it will never happen again. And, if I could do it all over again, obviously, I would never have done it...but I *did* do it. It happened. I can't undo it. I can't change it. And...well, I'm *glad* I did it."

My mouth hung open in disgusted shock. "*What* did you say?"

"I said I'm glad I kissed you." Her tears dried up, and every readable emotion on her face vanished beneath a cool veneer.

I fumbled with the change in her, hating the wall between us, cursing the sudden opaqueness I couldn't see behind. "What the hell has gotten into you? First, you do something you know is wrong and then you take back any apology—"

"I didn't say I'm not still sorry," she grumbled. "I said I'm glad it happened."

I spread my hands in surrender. "Please enlighten me because you've successfully confused the shit out of me."

Once again, she flinched at my cursing, but the blank shield on her face stopped me from reading anything else.

Standing tall and kissed by moonlight, she said, "I don't regret it because it gave me all the lessons you just mentioned."

"I-I still don't understand."

She sighed as if it cost her to explain. "You asked me if I knew the difference between platonic love and romantic. I thought I did. I've spoken to Cassie about her boyfriends. I know how sex works and what desire is. But learning theory is different to actual experiences."

She sucked in a breath, looking to the side as if to smooth out her tale with a script hidden from view. "In class, my teachers always encouraged us to learn with first-hand knowledge. They don't just let us read the textbook. They make us do stuff. Just like you do. You explained how to drive the tractor but until you let me change the gears and operate the thing, I didn't know what you meant."

Her argument was too well thought out. Too rehearsed. Too understandable. I hated that my hackles faded under a logical explanation.

"Love isn't the same as driving a tractor, Della."

"But don't you see?" She stepped closer. "It's exactly like that."

I schooled myself not to move, not to run as her body heat touched mine.

She looked up into my eyes. "I wanted to know the difference. And now, I do. I know you are my friend and my family. That kiss proved it. I felt nothing but warm love like I always do for you. There was nothing special from that kiss to any other we've shared over the years. I've kissed you on the lips before. Just like you've kissed me. Those weren't big deals, and this shouldn't be either."

Her voice sped up as if her carefully thought-out debate had reached the end, but she wasn't quite finished with convincing me. "I know the difference, Ren. And I know things are gonna be strange, but they'll go back to the way things were because nothing has changed. I promise. I'm still Della, and you're still Ren. I'm growing up now, and soon, you won't have to worry so much about me. I won't do anything bad, and I'll be on my best behaviour. You'll see. Just please…please…don't send me back to Cherry River if you're not coming. I know I made you mad, but I don't want to live with Cassie and Liam on my own. I want…I want to come with you. Please. Please say you'll forgive me, and we'll stay together."

Her chin tipped down as a glimpse of tangled things on her face hinted that her deliverance cost her. That there were other things. Deeper things. Scarier things inside her that she'd hidden.

The fact that she was old enough to be complex and have the ability to shield and reveal rather than blurt everything made wariness fill my blood.

What was she hiding?

What wasn't she saying?

I didn't trust her.

Not anymore.

Even if every part of me agreed with her that we'd been close in the past and affectionate in our actions, and those hadn't filled me with terror. Even if every inch howled at the thought of walking away when I truly didn't want that.

I wanted to stay with her.

I never wanted to say goodbye.

"This is too hard." I scrubbed my face with my hands. My stomach growled for the hundredth time, reminding me that making life-changing decisions with no food normally always led to bad ones.

Della stayed silent as if knowing I was in the middle of a seesaw. A lean in either direction, and the choice would crash to the ground.

The forest stayed silent and hushed. No creatures moved. No leaves rustled. We were utterly alone—away from judgment and history and the Wilsons who knew far too much about us.

This mistake was between Della and me, and, hopefully, with her promise never to do it again and my vow to make sure it never did, we could eventually find our way back to normal.

We could find another place to call home.

"What about school?" I asked quietly.

Just that one question showed her where my mind was. That I'd already come to terms with leaving. That I'd already agreed to take her with me.

She barrelled into me again, squeezing me tight. "Thank you, thank you, *thank you*." Her breath heated my t-shirt and chest.

I patted her shoulders awkwardly, prying her off me to look into her face.

The innocent girl was back.

The veiled mask was gone.

If she had any secrets, they'd sank far inside her, and I stood no chance at figuring them out now.

"Are you sure you want to leave behind your friends? Cassie? Liam?"

She nodded. "If you can't go back, then yes."

"And school? What about that?"

"I'll go to another one." She smiled. "I had to change anyway. I'm in high school now. This was my last term."

"Oh."

"But—I don't have to go back," she rushed. "I can get a job, too. I can pay my way—"

"Don't even think such things. You're finishing school, Della. University too if that's what you want."

She smiled with familiar love and devotion. "Okay."

"Okay." I smiled back, still not appeased and still tormented, but at least, for now, I didn't have to tear us apart.

That would come later.

"Come on." I strode toward the backpack forgotten on the ground. "I'm starving."

Chapter Forty-Seven

REN

2013

I'D LIKE TO say things went back to normal easily.

They didn't.

After that first night, where we headed to an all-night gas station and filled up with lukewarm Hot Pockets and processed snack foods, Della and I kept our distance.

We walked side by side but didn't touch.

We talked and laughed but didn't relax.

And when the sun rose on a new day and the decision to leave this place and the people who knew us as the Wilds cemented into reality, we headed to the local supermarket, filled the backpack full of provisions, checked over our old tent and sleeping bag, and traded some cash for another sleeping bag, rucksack, and a few other travel requirements for Della at the only camping store in town.

It felt strange not to steal the stuff we needed, even after years of earning an honest living. It felt even stranger breaking habits and saying goodbye to familiar landmarks that had been our constant for so long.

Not strange bad. Strange *good*.

I hated how easily I turned my back on everything. How I merely walked out of the Wilsons lives without a backward glance—focused only on finding Della. And now that I'd found her, I didn't care where we went.

I didn't think about Cassie.

I didn't worry about leaving John or Patricia without an employee.

Della was home to me, and there was something infinitely perfect just being the two of us again.

She might have upset me, messed up my mind, and ruined my trust, but nothing could change the fact that where she was, I was happiest, and she was all I needed.

I didn't know how to change that. And I didn't know how to make Della see that just because she was my everything, it didn't mean I wanted to be hers.

She needed to want others. That was part of life. John had advised me on such things.

His gruff voice echoed regularly in my ears: *"Show her you're human with flaws. Figure out a way to keep her as your sister, Ren. Otherwise, you won't have her at all."*

He was wrong when he said she'd ever feel more than a family bond for me. She'd told me herself, and despite my guardedness on her explanation, I tended to believe her.

She was ten years my junior, and I saw her as fresh-faced innocent and far too young to share the sort of relationship I wanted. But I'd forgotten something important. There were two sides to everything, and I'd failed to see how she must view me.

I'd been stuck-up to think she'd want me in any other way than as a guardian.

She had to be telling the truth because at ten years her elder, I was boring and surly and far too old to share the sort of fledgling romance she would eventually seek.

I didn't need to show her I was human.

She knew who and what I was.

She knew me better than anyone, and when the time came for her to meet another boy, then I'd show her exactly how flawed I was by interrogating the hell out of him before he could go near her.

John was incorrect.

Della loved me.

But it wasn't wrong or tainted. It was just as it had always been, and as the roles we'd played faded from view, and we turned toward the forest instead of the farm, I was grateful we were leaving.

Grateful to delete past expectations and remove outsider's opinions because no matter that they came from a good place, they didn't know us...not really.

No one truly knew the lives of another.

That was why I liked being alone, and by the time we reached the outskirts of the forest with our stuffed backpacks and wanderlust bubbling in our veins, I gave Della one last chance. One final choice—to admit this was truly what she wanted.

To run just like I'd done from the Mclary's.

To turn her back on everything and start new.

Unlike the last time we'd lived in the forest, Della had her own backpack with extra tools and equipment and would be expected to pull her weight. Our tiny tent would be a struggle, but at least we had separate sleeping bags. Washing in rivers would come with strict privacy, and dinners would be a chore shared by both of us.

This wasn't a vacation. This was real life. It would be hard. It would be constant. From here on out, we would be homeless until we found a new place to stay.

I needed her to understand that.

For her to accept the burden of running from people who cared because once we said goodbye, that was it.

"Are you sure?" I asked, glancing at the wind ruffling her butterscotch hair.

She didn't look at me, keeping her gaze on the beckoning trees. "I'm sure."

"Okay, then."

For better or for worse, we didn't look back as we vanished into the wilderness and said goodbye to civilization.

* * * * *

Unlike the other camping trips we'd taken over the many summers at Cherry River, this was different. What we carried was all we owned in the world. What we gathered as we wandered was all the food we'd have for that night or the next.

And slowly, gradually, the stress of living around people faded.

As a day turned into a week, and Della gave me no reason to worry, I smiled a little easier. I laughed a little louder. I didn't wince when she touched me in passing and didn't freeze when she pressed a kiss to my cheek.

The fear that she'd overstep grew less and less as our bond returned to what it had always been.

If anything, things grew better between us.

Different, yes.

Older and more grown-up, but still connected.

Before, when the stars woke and darkness descended, Della had been too young to talk before exhaustion put her to sleep. Now, she stayed up late with me.

She was older, and I finally had no choice but to see the changes in her. To notice the roundness of hips and swell of breasts. She could've become a stranger as she lost her childish angles if it wasn't for the blue ribbon she still wore either in her hair, around her wrist, or in a bow around her neck.

I still recognised the girl I'd raised thanks to the untouched joy she showed when I agreed to tell her a story, and the unsullied sound of pure happiness when I made her laugh.

Della was still Della, despite my fears of losing her, and after we'd eaten and banked the fire for the night, we lay side by side squished in our tiny tent.

As our legs brushed and breaths found the same rhythm, our natural freedom and ease with each other erased the residual mess and balance returned.

Nothing felt forced.

Nothing felt hidden.

Our ages didn't matter as much out here, only our ability to survive.

By the end of the third week, I stopped bringing up the fact that we needed to find somewhere so she could return to school. I accepted, after multiple convincing from her, that the term was almost over, and she could slip into any educational system with her current grades with no problems.

I wanted to share her optimism, but we didn't have birth records or passports or even a place to stay to enrol her. Without John and Patricia's help, I didn't know how I'd get her into class without people asking too many questions. However, I couldn't shatter her dream and figured I'd solve that complication when we got to it.

For now, we agreed to spend the summer in the forest, remembering our old way of life.

Most days, we travelled a few miles before setting up another camp. Others, we stayed in a glen and swam and sun-baked.

Once a month, she'd turn extremely private, popping painkillers and staying subdued.

At first, I worried she was sick. But by the second time, I knew.

Della was no longer a child.

Her body was an adult, even if it hadn't fully grown into one.

I offered her sympathy and tried to help with her period pain, but unlike most times where she wanted my company, she wanted nothing to do with me.

When things passed, our bond would snap right back into place and life would be simple again. Hiking, exploring, swimming.

Della hadn't packed a swimsuit, but she didn't argue when I made her wear a t-shirt and underwear before getting wet. I made sure she was never around when I bathed, and I averted my eyes whenever she'd strip—sometimes catching me unaware with flashes of her perfect skin.

We shared tasks on building a fire or erecting the tent or preparing food, and overall, the lifestyle we shared was much easier now she was older and offered more help than hindrance.

For two glorious months, we travelled on back-roads and explored the stunning countryside. Occasionally, we'd stumble onto a campsite tucked high in the hills, or hear trampers in the distance, treading the trails we'd become so sure footed on.

The money stuffed safe in my backpack wasn't needed as I allowed every aspect of our lives before the Wilsons to return—including stealing.

I didn't take from those who had nothing and did my best to only pinch a few things. Items like toothpaste and deodorant, canned food and another lighter…things that didn't cost the large supermarkets much money but kept us healthy and fed.

Della asked me to teach her the art of thievery, but that was one thing I refused. I'd teach her anything she wanted—skinning rabbits, setting traps, sharpening knives, making fires—but never stealing.

There was too much risk.

And she was far too precious to get caught.

She might not need me as much as she once did, but I still had a role to play in her life.

A role I would gladly uphold until my dying breath.

To protect her.

At all costs.

Even if it meant protecting her from herself.

Chapter Forty-Eight

DELLA

Present Day

CRAZY HOW LIFE *can change so fast, right?*

How days can blend into months, and seasons can flow into years.

That was what happened with us.

Leaving behind Cherry River was sad. Some days, I missed Patricia, John, the horses, our one bedroom, Liam, and even Cassie so much, I almost asked Ren to turn around. To admit I'd made a mistake, and I wanted to go back.

I'd never stopped to notice just how privileged I'd been living there—learning to ride, running around in open fields, swimming in creeks, and attending a school that actually nurtured my dreams instead of ruined them.

I missed it.

But as much as I missed them, I would miss Ren more, and he was no longer welcome there.

Because of me.

I'd made it impossible to go back.

I'd taken away so much from both of us.

The guilt that caused was a daily passenger. Unfortunately, I had a steep learning curve to find there were many layers of guilt. Some days, I suffered shame. Some nights, I wallowed in disgrace. Others, I wanted to flog myself with blame and dishonour and somehow purge the skin-crawling chiding that I'd done something irrevocably wrong.

I'd been selfish, and stupid, and as much as I regretted everything we'd lost, I was just as guilty for being grateful for everything we'd gained as much as I was for losing it.

For the rest of summer and most of autumn, I had Ren all to myself.

He no longer left before I was awake to work on the farm. He no longer stayed out till dark doing chores and feeling responsible for the paddocks and meadows left in his care.

He lost the edgy hardness of being relied upon and returned to the serious, wild boy I remembered.

Every story he shared. Every laugh he indulged in. I remembered how to love him purely without any of the mess I'd caused. Some weeks, I honestly didn't remember why I'd risked everything by kissing him.

What was I thinking? I'd muse.

Eww, how gross. I'd conclude.

I merely saw him as Ren—the farmyard boy who I'd watched make out with Cassie, go through chicken pox, and get all stuffy with the flu.

But then...other days...a switch would flip inside me, and I'd struggle to see him as family and only saw things I shouldn't.

Forbidden things.

Things that had the potential not only to get me in trouble but to steal Ren from me forever.

I'd focused on the glisten of his sweat, and instead of thinking he needed a bath, I'd think how salty he would taste. I'd watched him break off dead tree limbs for our fire and instead of worrying he'd hurt himself, I only noticed how strong he was. How his arms bunched and his belly clenched and how everything about him was virile and perfect and just begging to be touched.

Things were alive inside me. Heat and hunger.

Sometimes, he'd look at me before I could bury my feelings and he'd freeze. His eyes would lock on mine, understanding the look of naked need even if he didn't want to.

I'd swallow it all down, let my hair curtain my eyes, and pretend all over again that things were normal and I wasn't drowning beneath right and wrong.

One dawn, when Ren slept beside me in our tiny tent, he rolled toward me as he sometimes did and gathered me close. I couldn't help myself. I let myself be gathered, melting into the way his front cradled my back.

He was asleep. I was awake. I knew who was innocent and who was not, but it didn't stop me from wriggling closer, my belly tightening as Ren's hips jutted forward with something hard and—

Yep, stopping right there.

I can't write the horror of what happened when I gasped and woke him up. How he'd ripped himself away from me. How he'd thrown himself out of the tent and refused to talk to me for the rest of the day.

It was yet another incident swept away, dirtying our relationship in ways I didn't know how to clean.

In fact, this whole chapter I should delete, but ugh, I don't like editing, and this is so close to being burned anyway.

I won't litter the rest of this assignment with teenage awareness of how his normally comforting face was suddenly a treasure trove of harsh jawlines, straight noses, and black eyelashes. I'm not gonna remember the beard he grew or the fact that it wasn't patchy like before but full and rugged and—

Why do I do this to myself?

Why do I insist on slicing through the sticky tape on my constantly breaking heart and stabbing it over and over again?

Can you answer me because I'm honestly at the end of my limit.

I know I can't have him.

I made him believe I don't want him.

Yet...I can't forget him.

I just want him to go back to being Ren.

So why won't that happen?!

God, you're no use.

This is a waste of time.

You know what? I'm done.

This is beyond stupid. It's become a mess of words and boring.

I'd get an F for this if I turned it in.

These secrets are just stupid really. I'm sure other people have the same issues. I'm not special. Just because I've been in love with someone I shouldn't be for almost a decade doesn't mean I can justify my heartache to you.

Ugh!

Okay, that's it.

No more.

Nice knowing you, assignment.

Deleting...

* * * * *

So...I'm back.

Yesterday was a bad day.

I always have bad days remembering the forest in-between the Wilsons and what happened next. Probably because it was the last time we laughed together. The last time we could sleep side by side—when Ren wasn't hunched against the tent to avoid me—and not have every other shit I caused become a third wheel between us.

God, I don't want to write this anymore.

Not because I'm afraid of bad grades because that no longer matters, but because the end is coming. The end of everything, and the end of what I can tell you.

But before I can write those two little words and be done with this horrible excuse of literature, I have to tell you what happened in the next five years of my life.

I have to tell you why our fourth separation has lasted the longest.

I have to tell you why it's my fault.

And I have to tell you why Ren will never forgive me even though he did in the forest.

I did something even worse than kissing him.

Wow, I didn't think words had the power to make me tear up and tremble, but they did. Clever, huh? I'm making myself insane. I'm dragging everything into the light that I've done my best to keep buried in the dark.

Let's see how my hands shake typing it again. Let's do it in bold, shall we? Just for even more dramatic effect...

I did something even worse than kissing him.

Yep, that got my heart galloping.

Bet you're wondering what the hell I could do, right?

What else could I possibly do to destroy everything I ever cared about?

I'm sure you can probably imagine.

Maybe I should just let you imagine and not finish. My heart is done. I'm drained. I'm tired. I've been tired for far too long, and this is just ripping me into pieces.

All I know is, I can't write what happened in the forest.

All I can tell you is it was the best time of my life. It makes me miss him with a clawing, violent need that drives me mad. The freedom of living day to day. The joy at starlit nights full of talking and the lazy mornings with chirping birds.

It was total innocence.

Maybe one day, I'll be able to write a short story on the afternoons that stand out or try to describe the rose-coloured happiness and sun-warmed bliss we lived in. Maybe, I'll do a poem or haiku on how my love evolved all over again from crush to tenderness to fevered yearning.

Or maybe I won't.

Either way, it doesn't change how wonderful those few months were.

Ren and I found our way back to each other, and I wish, wish, wish we could've stayed in the trees and never come out. I've cried myself to sleep more times than I can count to stay in that joyful place and never slip into the Della I became.

But...it happened.

Winter found us, ice crept toward us, and snow drove us from our heaven back to hell.

And the stopwatch started ticking, inching me closer to the day when I would be alone.

The day when Ren would walk out of my life.

The day when everything would be broken.

Because I'm still here...alone...writing this sorry excuse of a story, pretending I can conjure him from nothing, desperately loving a memory, and killing myself with the knowledge that no matter how much I write about him. No matter what tales I tell you or secrets I spill, he's not going to be there to tell me off. He's not going to scold me for telling the truth. He's not going to notice or care.

I no longer need to pretend I don't love him.

I don't need to lie that I don't want him.

Can you guess why?

I've been lying to you, too, didn't you know?

I made you believe he stuck by me. That he would never abandon me no

matter what disasters I caused.
But that is another lie.
Probably the biggest one.
Because Ren Wild…he's gone.
He left me.
And he's never coming back.

Chapter Forty-Nine

REN

2015

FOR TWO YEARS, things were back to normal.

It was just me and Della against the world, but I wouldn't lie and say I didn't think about what had happened between us.

Della had shown me two sides of herself in those few days that I hadn't seen before or since. Sure, there'd been a few incidents in the forest: a few heated looks, an early morning embrace that had been instinct and not thought, and even a couple of fierce arguments.

But we'd ironed out the kinks and found a new acceptable.

As time went on, problems were few and far between.

And that worried me.

Della had revealed she wasn't just the simple blonde angel I'd raised and adored, but a girl with evolving needs; a trickster who could hide behind a mask and successfully keep her secrets.

Lately, she'd been too amenable—none of her usual fire or willingness to get into trouble for speaking her mind. But no matter how many times I caught myself studying her and no matter how often I tensed in her embraces, there was never anything more to her affection. No tension or undercurrent.

Just natural, sinless love.

It was the same as it had always been: given freely, kindly, wholeheartedly, but most of all, purely with no underlying contraband.

Her smiles were innocently genuine.

Her touches appropriately platonic.

I did my best to relax, but no matter how normal things became between us, I couldn't let it go. A niggle was always there, searching her actions and tones, knowingly putting a barrier between us that I didn't want.

She knew the wall was there, just like I did.

But we never addressed it, never tried to bulldoze it, and as time marched on, we learned to live with it. We accepted that the wariness would never fully dissolve and had become a fracture in our otherwise perfect relationship.

I hated it.

I hated that I'd lost the child I loved with all my heart and been traded a girl who had the terrifying capacity to destroy me.

Maybe it was all in my mind.

Perhaps the late-night dreams of phantom kisses with a woman I couldn't claim was turning me mad. Maybe I'd been ruined all along and that was why I could never give myself to Cassie.

Whatever caused my vigilance, I never found any reason to be suspicious.

Guilt drowned me because how could I pretend to trust Della, when night after night, I was waiting to catch her? And catch her in what, exactly? A confession that she actually loved me in a completely different way to what was allowed? A hint that she felt just as scrambled and confused as I did and couldn't find her way back to innocence?

At least, we still had each other.

That was all that mattered.

We fought against winter for as long as we could, but eventually, the icy winds and snowy chill drove us from our sanctuary and back into the cities we despised.

It took us a few weeks to adjust being around people again. And another few to figure out the rules as we navigated our way into well-oiled society where finding somewhere to stay meant paying rent and paying rent meant finding work and getting work meant providing references.

I had cash for a down payment on a rental, and I learned on the job how to walk into letting agencies, ask to view a place, and tolerate being chauffeured around, guided through the home in question, and sold on every benefit.

Even though Della and I had lived with the Wilsons, gone into town, and been around public before, this was on an entirely different level.

We couldn't hide behind the Wilsons anymore. We couldn't rely on them to find us a place to stay or talk to the smarmy salespeople on our behalf. I couldn't work my ass off and ask someone I trusted to buy everything we'd need. I had to pre-empt Della's requirements with school uniforms and stationery. I had to plan groceries and living locations so she could get to school safely without a long commute.

There were no empty farmhouses for us to borrow. No perfect villages where we could happily live off the scraps unseen.

It suffocated me, seeking places to live where no trees grew or rivers ran. My brain battled daily with my heart, forcing me to give up house hunting and focusing on why we were there.

School.

Della had to go to the best school possible.

That was the reason.

And I clutched it hard even when finding a good school proved to be as much as a challenge as finding a home.

Della helped and researched online. She narrowed her results to two, and together, we walked from our hidden shack we'd commandeered as our winter abode on the edge of a campground, and did our best to hide the fact that we were still homeless.

The cracked weatherboards and grimy windows hadn't been maintained, but it had a small stove for the extra blizzard-filled nights and it kept us from freezing to death.

It didn't help with our bathing arrangements—having to melt snow and scrub down with the other person shivering outside to grant privacy, but at least the clothes I'd bought were fresh and new and Della's hair shone gold and her eyes glowed with intelligence.

Any school would be lucky to have her.

And thanks to her skills, she managed to enrol into an all girl's high school by acing the entrance exam and telling the headmaster to call her last school for her file.

I hadn't thought to do that and used the trick when we finally found a cheap one-bedroom place three blocks away, asking the listing agent to call Cherry River Farm and ask John Wilson for a reference.

They did.

And whatever he told them ensured within the week Della attended a new school and I'd moved our meagre backpacks into a bare essential, unfurnished apartment and chewed through a chunk of my savings paying bond, first month's rent, and Della's tuition fees.

Della and I transformed its empty spaces into a semi-liveable home, thanks to flea market bargains and the odd furniture found on street corners.

I'd achieved more than I had in my life.

I'd dealt with people and hadn't been recognised for being a runaway slave or for being the man who stole Della Mclary. My fears of being taken and sold were still strong, even though I was no longer a boy, and I preferred not to be too close or talk too long to anyone.

All winter, Della caught the local bus to school, bundled up in the thickest jacket, mittens, and hats I could afford, and returned straight after class ended.

I didn't mind she didn't make friends straight away. In fact, I was glad because it meant I had her company when I returned from work after toiling away at a local building site, and we spent the evenings together with our second-hand TV, street-salvaged couch, and snuggled under a shared blanket watching whatever was on.

The job I scored wasn't perfect and didn't pay well, but it meant I could keep a roof over our heads and dinner on our table without having to hunt and gut it first.

I never grumbled as I lugged timber and dug holes.

I was the bitch on the site, gathering tools and doing the chores no one else wanted to do. The foreman who gave me the cash job said I got the dregs because I wasn't a skilled builder, but I knew it was because I refused to drink with the guys or let them get to know me.

I didn't *want* people to know me.

That was where danger lay.

Every day, I hated trudging to work and enduring yet more snide comments and rolled eyes at my reserved silence.

I missed the fields.

I missed the smell of manure and sunshine and tractor diesel.

Now, the dirt on my hands was from concrete and lime, not earth and grass. The dust in my lungs was from cutting bricks and shovelling gravel, not from fluffing hay and hauling bales.

Sometimes, even though the guys hated me, they'd offer me the odd after-work gig. The rules were: always do it late at night and always be unseen by anyone.

I didn't understand the secrecy for tasks like removing old roof sheets or cracking apart ancient walls, but I followed their stupid rules and cleared away debris. No one else seemed to want to do it, and the money was double that of day labouring.

No matter that I was grateful I had a job, some mornings, when I left for work and Della left for school, I'd struggle to continue walking to the site. Ice would crack beneath my boots and breath would curl from my lips, and I'd physically stop, look at the snow-capped trees in the distance, and have to lock my knees to stop from bolting toward them.

Days were long and hard and taxed me of everything I had.

But the nights—when I wasn't working on secret demolition—made up for the struggle.

The emptiness inside from living in a concrete jungle amongst wretches and sinners faded whenever I was near her. Her comforting voice, familiar kindness, and almost intuitive knowing when I just needed to sit quiet and have her tell me stories for a change, repaired the tears inside me.

Watching her animate tales of school and teachers allowed me to forget about everything but her. It reminded me why I'd cursed her for overstepping a boundary. And why I could never lose her. No way could I ever survive without her, and that terrified me because with every day, the remainder of her childhood slipped off like a cocoon, leaving behind new wings dying to fly.

She was evolving, and I couldn't do a damn thing but watch her morph into something I could never keep.

For two years, I held that job and paid for Della's every need. For every whisper from the wind to leave, I was held in place by the knowledge I needed to stay for her. For every tug to run, I focused on the person Della was becoming, and it was completely worth it.

A month or so after we'd moved into our apartment and I'd decorated the bedroom with purple curtains and a foam mattress covered in lilac bedding for Della—while I slept on the pop-out couch in the living room—we received our first letter.

Because we'd used John Wilson as a landlord reference, he knew where we were and wrote to us.

The letter was short and to the point, making sure we were safe and doing well and that if we ever needed anything, their door was always open. I tucked his phone number and address safely in my memory just in case.

I missed them, but I didn't know how to say such things or to convey how grateful I was for their hand in our lives—I'd fail in person, and I'd definitely fail in writing.

So Della was the one who got in touch and thanked them.

She let them know I'd found her and apologised for any embarrassment she might've caused. I approved the letter she sent, making sure it held the correct tone and gave no room for imagination that we might be doing anything wrong.

But she didn't let me read the note she sent to Cassie.

She scribbled something, folded it tight, and placed it in the envelope, licking it before I had a chance to spy.

I wanted to know what she said, but at the same time, I respected their privacy and relationship. She had every reason to stay in touch while I had a lot to stay away.

I didn't send any letters. I didn't find her online. I didn't get in touch in anyway.

What was the point?

Cassie and I were friends out of convenience. She had used me just as much as I had used her, and she no longer needed me to cause any more stress than I already had.

But with one letter came more, and Della and Cassie stayed in touch with the occasional note from Liam. Eventually, their snail mail became emails and quickly evolved to Facebook messages.

Occasionally, once Della had dragged herself to sleep and left the cheap phone I'd bought her on the coffee table, I'd swipe on the screen and scroll through pictures of Cassie at horse shows or sunsets over the fields sent by Liam.

Those moments hurt my heart for the simplicity of the world we'd all shared.

The perfection of long summer evenings and cosy winter nights. The innocence of growing up without fences and traffic lights.

I missed sharing a bedroom with Della.

I missed birthday picnics and cherished handmade gifts.

I missed holding her close on a freshly harvested meadow and hearing the birds roost in the willows.

I would've given anything to be a farmhand again.

And I knew, over the course of the two years while we lived in a city I didn't care about, and life maintained a steady stream of work, school, and evenings together, that something had to give.

Something had to change.

Otherwise, I was going to go insane.

I wasn't cut out for a job where I hated the crew and the labour.

I wasn't cut out to live in a tiny claustrophobic basement apartment.

But each spring, when the ground thawed and Della murmured that we should go back to the forest, I forbid it. She had to finish school. That was my commitment to her to pay for her education and her commitment to me to learn it.

Despite our constant desire to leave, I was eternally grateful when a letter arrived for me this time, not for Della.

A letter from John Wilson.

There was no fluff or word wastage, just a short message letting me know a friend who owned a farm not far from where we lived had recently lost his head milking harvester. His dairy herd numbered in the hundreds, and he needed someone trustworthy to start immediately.

Della wasn't home from school yet, but I caught a bus as close to the city limit as I could and walked the rest of the way to his sprawling acreage.

The farmer, an elderly gentleman with yellowing teeth and balding head called Nick March, offered me a job on the spot if I could start at four a.m. every day.

The pay was double what I was earning, and I'd get to be around animals and open spaces again.

I didn't even think.

I shook his hand and celebrated with Della that night with an expensive tub of ice cream that I couldn't really afford.

And that was how two years bled into three, and slowly, our newfound routine faded in favour of upcoming complications.

And our lives got a lot more difficult.

Chapter Fifty

REN

2016

SWEET SIXTEEN.

I'd never wanted to deny Della a birthday before, but this one…I wished we could skip right over it.

Not because she'd transformed overnight from skinny to curvy. Not because she laughed with a depth and richness that made my heart skip a beat. And not because she'd taken to wearing clothes that revealed her perfect figure, announcing to horny teens and asshole males that she was no longer a kid.

Believe me, I knew she wasn't a kid anymore.

Living with a stunning teenager when I'd turned into a surly, angry twenty-six-year-old wasn't easy. She seemed to grant life whenever she walked into a room and steal it whenever she left.

If she got pissed at me, I felt as if my world would end.

If I got pissed at her, I wanted nothing more than to punish her so she never misbehaved again.

Our dynamic became more explosive as age both bridged us closer and cracked a wider ravine. Outside appearances might have ensured she matched me almost in adulthood, but our opinions and thoughts remained divided.

She had an uncanny way of wanting to touch and hug when I wanted nothing to do with softness and connection. I hadn't been with a woman since Cassie, and it had been a long few years sleeping in a house with a girl who'd managed to flip my world upside down with a simple kiss.

I hated the fact that I still guarded myself against her when all I wanted to do was relax.

I despised the fact I'd become afraid of dreaming because, without fail, whenever I started to trust Della's lovely smile or thaw from her innocent embrace, I'd dream that night of kissing a stranger.

Of chasing her.

Of catching her.

Of kissing her until my body ached and I woke with a desperate growl for more.

I didn't know who I dreamed of. I never saw her face. And I would never admit to myself that because of what Della had done that night, I'd forever stitched her to the sensation of feeling at home the moment I kissed my dream-stranger or the heart-shattering horror when I woke up feeling dirty and wrong and in serious need of punishment.

I was desperate to taste that sensation of wonder. I craved to relive the magic of falling so deeply and quickly, I'd belonged entirely to my dream figment in a single heartbeat.

But whatever my issues were, I never let Della see.

When we first slept in separate rooms, I'd been obsessed with checking on her—making sure she was safe and no monsters climbed through her bedroom window.

Now, I was glad we had walls between us because my body never obeyed me anymore.

I woke hard.

I struggled not to release the pent-up need in my blood.

And my mind turned to ways of releasing such painful pressure without getting involved with anyone.

Cassie had made me wary, and Della had made me nervous.

I didn't like getting close to anyone, which meant I buried my needs down deep and accepted I lived in a constant nightmare.

The one saving grace to my torture was no matter Della's beauty, most days, I only saw her as my Ribbon. I could allow the comforting swell of love when she smiled at me. I could permit the way my body warmed whenever she was close.

I might forever hate myself for kissing her back while asleep, but I was insanely grateful that while awake, I crossed no boundaries in my thoughts. I didn't covert that which I could not have. I didn't confuse my dream with reality.

She was my world and home and family.

It didn't matter her long legs meant when we hugged, her head met my chin. It didn't matter her strong arms could haul things I deemed too heavy or her quick brain surpassed me in everything.

She was still little Della who I obsessed over, and sometimes, I wondered if that pissed her off.

I'd catch her glaring at me if I indulged her rather than argued. I'd get the sensation she was hurt if I played along rather than acted serious.

But whenever those rare moments occurred, by the time I turned to look closer or cocked my head to hear clearer, the smoke in her gaze was gone, the tightness in her tone vanished.

I supposed we were both keeping secrets; both hiding certain things.

But that was life.

We had our own worlds we juggled during the day. She did things at school I would never know about, and I did things at work I never bothered to tell her.

As long as we returned to each other at night, then I was okay with that.

My family was a single girl who I would happily die for, and lately, that was exactly what she made me want to do.

She might be the sweetest person I knew, but she was also the meanest, and as much as she hated me to call her out on it, I knew why she'd started testing boundaries and pushing into territories I wasn't comfortable with.

Lust.

I did my best to remember the cocktail of confusing needs and rampant curiosities I'd felt at that age, but it didn't mean I wanted her to go through it.

I wanted her to stay the forest girl, not a boy-interested teen.

Not that it mattered what I wanted.

We were no longer in sync, and when I got home from work and took her out to a local diner for our birthday dinner, I learned just how much things had drifted.

The meal started nice and normal.

We chatted about generic things, asked questions, listened intently, enjoyed each other's company…that was until a group of people arrived.

A group she knew and a boy who waved in her direction and smiled.

My gut clenched, and my fist wrapped around my Coke glass.

The four teenagers came toward our table, and Della lit up in a way she hadn't in so long with me. Her eyes met the boy's, a familiar message shared between them, and I was no longer the most important person in her world.

Nothing, absolutely *nothing*, hurt me as much as Della laughing and joking with her friends while she was so careful with me. To see her liveliness return with these strangers ripped out my goddamn heart.

I tried to be happy that she had friends, even though she'd never mentioned them. I did my best not to clutch my bleeding chest when she turned to me with blushing cheeks and bright blue eyes and asked, "Do you mind if I finish my birthday with these guys? We…eh, we have an assignment to finish and probably should do some homework."

Her lie didn't hurt me.

It was the fact she couldn't wait to get away from me.

I glanced at her half-eaten burger and remembered a simpler time when she was five and made my world come alive. I recalled how she'd taken my loveless, painful existence and showed me that not all people wanted to buy and sell you.

She was the reason I wasn't more mentally damaged and physically scarred than I was.

And because she'd been the one to save me without even realising it, I found myself nodding with a fierceness that belied my agony.

This was life.

This was what had to happen.

"Of course." I cleared my throat, waving her away. "Go ahead. You should spend your birthday with whoever you want."

She bounced up, looked as if she'd come to my side of the booth and hug me goodbye, but at the last minute changed her mind, gave me a confusing-tormenting smile, then turned and walked away.

"Be home by ten, Della," I said softly.

She looked over her shoulder with blonde hair cascading with a single blue ribbon glittering amongst the gold. "I will." She blew me a kiss before giggling at something the boy said in her ear.

Sweet sixteen.

Just like my original discomfort and desire to skip over such a birthday, my resolution solidified with another memory of my own sweet sixteen.

Cassie had said I deserved something special.

I'd had my first blow job in the shadows of a stable.

Now, Della was sixteen and laughing with a boy I wanted to punch in the goddamn face.

I couldn't stop whatever she would or would not do.

All I *could* do was celebrate my twenty-six birthday on my own.

I paid for our uneaten burgers.

I returned home to an empty apartment.

And I sat and watched the clock strike nine then ten then eleven and still Della didn't come home.

Chapter Fifty-One

REN

2016

A FEW WEEKS later, Della asked me the dreaded question.

The one I'd been expecting ever since I'd seen her happiness hanging with the group of kids from school on our birthday.

"Ren?"

I looked up from where I was trying to yank a splinter from my thumb. The bastard had gone in deep, and I'd left it for too long, ensuring a red infection and minor swelling. It was a fence's fault, catching me as I'd corralled the cows into the yard for milking. "Yeah?" I asked, distracted with a needle and tweezers.

Her bare feet appeared beneath my vision where I sat hunched at the dinged-up kitchen table. "It can wait. Do you need help?"

I smiled at her tangled hair from a long day and the pyjamas with a repeating decal of Cupid's arrows and hearts all over her arms and legs. Having her stand there ready for bed and eyes hooded with tiredness, I could almost forget she was slipping further from my reach.

Strange how you could miss someone when they were apart of everything you did.

Before I could reply, she stole the needle, pulled up the only other chair, and yanked my hand toward her.

"Careful," I warned as she prodded me with the sharp tip.

"I have to break a few layers of skin. You left it too long. It's grown over."

I groaned. "Great."

"Hold still." She bent over me, her hair obscuring her face and tickling the tops of my jean-covered thighs. I hadn't had a shower from work, and the dust and filth from working cows all day dirtied her cleanliness.

Not that she cared as she bent closer and diligently dug into my thumb.

I flinched occasionally, but somehow, she managed not to hurt me even though a bead of blood kept welling, causing her to wipe it away with her own finger, continuing her splinter hunt.

She needed a napkin or something to prevent my blood from staining her fingers, but I daren't stop her. I might not let her resume stabbing me otherwise.

The scent of vanilla rose from her hair, hinting she'd bought a different shampoo than her usual. She still smelled of the girl I'd known for sixteen years, but there was a new smell, too.

Something that made my heart chug harder the longer she huddled close.

She was so real, so fragile, so beautiful.

My fingers begged to be allowed to run through her hair, to bring her close, to hold her because I missed her so goddamn much.

As she tended to my wound, a yearning gathered that had nothing to do with her and everything to do with me.

I missed being touched.

I missed being kissed.

I missed affection that didn't come with a price of losing my soul.

By the time she finally dislodged the splinter, I struggled to breathe, and my thoughts were full of killing rabbits and tractor mechanics—anything to keep my body in check and appropriate boundaries in place.

I told myself it was because I hadn't been close to anyone in so long, all the while truth danced behind my lies.

I was waking up; seeing things I didn't want to see. Feeling things I definitely didn't want to feel.

She blew curls from her eyes as she planted the tweezers on the table with an accomplished flourish. "There you are. It's out." Scooting up, she darted down the small corridor to the bathroom and came back with some antiseptic cream from the chipped-glass medicine cabinet.

She stole my hand again, and with soft, capable fingers, spread some of the cream over the puncture she'd caused, then wrapped my thumb in a Band Aid.

She patted my knuckles like a good nurse and smiled. "Well, you'll survive. That's the good news. The bad news is you might lose the thumb."

"Ha-ha." I chuckled. "Hope I don't. Can't afford to lose another finger."

Her gaze fell to my missing pinkie, and some of her playfulness faded.

Standing quickly, I did my best not to scatter pieces of silage and grain from feeding the cows onto the floor.

I'd only recently saved up enough to buy a cheap motorbike that ensured I got to work for four a.m. without having to rely on shitty public transport. I didn't have a license to ride it—seeing as I had no proof of who I was—and even having the convenience of wheels meant I still had to get up well before dawn. "It's late. You should go to bed, and I need a shower."

She looked away but not before her eyes skittered down my body, lingered on my crotch, then dropped to the floor. Inhaling quick, tension rippled over her then was gone. She nodded quickly. "Yes. Bed. Shower. Good plan."

Twisting on the spot, her hair spun out like a gold carousel as she headed toward her bedroom. A second later, she spun back, biting her bottom lip, her cheeks pinker than before. "Eh, Ren?"

Something in her tone froze me to the floor. "What?"

She studied me with painful blue eyes, her decision not entirely formed. "Umm…"

"Umm what?" I struggled to convert air into oxygen. The way she stared hinted she knew whatever she'd ask would wedge yet another problem between us. "Tell me."

"What I meant to ask you before…. Do you think…I…" She dragged a hand through her long hair, revealing her ribbon was tied around her wrist today. "Would you mind if I—"

"Spit it out, Della." My heart rushed to know, but at the same time, warned I wouldn't like what she was about to say.

She exhaled in a rush. "Can I go on a date with Tom?"

I stopped breathing. *"What?"*

"Tom…um, you met him? At the diner? The tall guy with brown hair like yours and um…" Her gaze landed on mine before bouncing away just as fast. Deep in their blue depths other things lurked. Things she didn't want me to see.

I stepped toward her, but she tripped backward. "So…eh, can I?"

Air was still hard to come by. Everything inside bellowed to deny her request. I wanted to lock her in the apartment and never let her out. She was still too young for this. Too delicate and special and perfect to let unworthy boys touch her.

I didn't want anyone touching her.

Period.

But it wasn't my place to prevent her from growing up.

I should say yes.

I *meant* to say yes even though it slayed me.

But somehow, what I meant to say transformed on my tongue into an unarguable, "No."

Her lips thinned, and the nervousness at asking me quickly switched to resentment. "Why not?"

Just because I had to dig the knife a little deeper into my heart, I repeated her question. "Why won't I let you go on a date with him?"

She nodded.

"Because."

"Because?" She planted hands on her hips. "That's not a reason."

"I don't like him." I'd backed myself into this corner and had no way out. Why the hell didn't I say yes? I'd meant to, for God's sake. Now we slipped into yet another fight, and I was *tired* of fighting. Tired of miscommunication and walking on eggshells.

I wanted her close and caring like she'd just done with my splinter. I wanted to know where she was at all times, so I knew she was safe.

"You don't even know him." She growled.

"I don't have to know him to know what he wants."

"Oh, really?" She flicked her head to the side, her nose wrinkled with familiar temper. "Just like I know what Cassie wanted with you all those long summer nights?"

I stabbed my finger in the air. "That's none of your goddamn business."

"Just like what Tom and I might do is none of yours."

"Oh, see that's where you're wrong, Della." I moved toward her until our chests almost touched. "Everything you do is my business. You're mine to keep safe, and I have no doubt he doesn't have any intention of doing that."

"He won't hurt me." She backed up. "He's nice."

"Nice doesn't exist when hormones are out of control."

"Hormones?" She laughed condescendingly. "What do you think I am, Ren, some animal who just wants to get laid?"

I flinched.

Words landed on my tongue, but I discarded them.

She wasn't an animal, but she was getting close to wanting sex. I could see it in her eyes, taste it in her voice. She wouldn't be content with just me much longer and that knowledge kept me up at night.

Before I could choose an appropriate response, she added, "Just because you were fucking at my age doesn't mean—"

"Language."

"Oh, please. You use worse all the time."

"Not intentionally, I don't."

"What's the difference?" She curled her lip. "You swear but don't let me swear. You slept with Cassie, yet you won't let me—"

My temper snapped. "You're not permitted to sleep with anyone. *Ever*. Do you hear me?"

"You can't stop me, Ren." She crossed her arms, trembling just as much as me.

We both trembled when fighting. I didn't know how it happened or how to stop it, but with every fight, my limbs turned shaky with frustration and helplessness because I knew I could never win.

She would do whatever she wanted.

I had no power, even if I liked to think I did.

The only way to stop her from doing things I didn't approve of was to cart her back into the forest and keep her tied to a tree. And as much as that idea appealed to me, she had school to finish, a life to grow into, and I had a duty to ensure I made that as easy as I could for her.

No matter how much it destroys me.

Lowering my voice but unable to lower my temper, I seethed, "I was nineteen when I lost my virginity. You have another three years to go."

She sucked in a breath as if shocked I'd shared something so personal.

Walking past her, I grunted, "You can go out with him in a group. You must be home when you say you will, and if you leave me hanging here like you did a few weeks ago, I'll spank you so hard you won't be able to sit down for a month and then I'll ground you for the rest of your life."

Her silence shot bullets into my back as I stepped into the bathroom and slammed the door.

As the stained, chipped mirror reflected my dirty face, I whispered, "Give me a few more years, Della Ribbon. Just a few more before you leave me."

Chapter Fifty-Two

REN

2016

SCHOOL FINISHED FOR the holidays, and Della, ever the resourceful, refused to relax like she deserved after studying so hard. Instead, she wanted to contribute to our bills by getting a job.

I was too busy with the milking to argue.

After scoring the job with Nick March, I'd not only been made the head milk harvester but also the overseer for the rest of the staff on his dairy farm.

From figuring out how much protein and fibre to feed versus income per milk quart, to paddock rotation and herd streamlining, my time was booked from the moment I arrived to the second I left.

I loved being in charge and making a difference. I enjoyed working with the seven hundred head of cattle and ensuring happy stock, which in turn, made for ease of milking twice a day.

What I didn't enjoy were the long hours I had to put in and the time apart from Della.

I often fell asleep earlier due to the brutal wake-ups, and she'd stay up later texting who knew what and watching romantic programs that probably filled her head with ideas of sex and marriage and things I couldn't protect her from.

I'd wanted her to recharge during the school holidays, but in a way, I was glad she job hunted. It meant she had things to fill her days with, and no idle hands to date boys she shouldn't be dating.

And because she was intelligent and extremely capable, she landed a job within a few days, helping a local florist make bouquets and other gifts, spending her hours playing with flowers, plaiting ribbon, and turning nature into stunning works of art.

Whenever I'd come home, she'd have some sort of daisy, tulip, or rose waiting for me, tied with a snippet of ribbon on the kitchen table.

I never told her how much I adored the fact that she thought of me while at work. That she still cared enough that I was the one she kissed on the cheek and helped cook dinner with. That I still held enough importance in her life to spend time with, even if it was doing something boring like watching a movie with microwave popcorn and overly sweet cola.

Those nights were my favourite.

I could even pretend we were alone in our tent surrounded by trees instead of buildings if we pulled our curtains tight and huddled together on the couch.

Normally, I was so exhausted, I ended up dozing beside her watching some comedy or drama while she twirled and tangled ribbon, making rosettes and ribbon-flowers for basket decorations at the florist.

It reminded me of the Christmas present Patricia Wilson had given her that first year. Della had loved the colourful ribbon collection. She'd set it safely in our bedroom and never touched them because she didn't want the colours to get marked with grease and grime like her blue one had.

After a while, the ribbons were just there, seen but unseen in our bedroom until I carved her that wooden horse which then slept on the ribbons for the rest of its existence.

I supposed both gifts the Wilsons had either kept or thrown out when we left. Della hadn't taken them when she ran away, and I'd had nothing to pack them into.

It helped recalling memories when Della was still young and easily impressed. These days, she smirked rather than smiled, and sometimes I wished I could trade her with the cute little girl I'd raised instead of live another day with a beautiful brutal teen.

Some days, we were perfectly in tune—our communication effortless and easy. Others, we spoke the same language, but the message was all scrambled. I'd get on edge, and she'd get snappy, and neither of us could stop the secrets slowly driving us apart.

* * * * *

Halloween.

Just like we'd never celebrated Christmas until the Wilsons, we hadn't celebrated Halloween.

In the town where the Wilsons lived, it wasn't a huge thing, and Della wasn't interested in dressing up and door knocking on strangers. Mostly because I practically hyperventilated at the thought of her putting herself in such danger.

Humans were never to be trusted even on nights when it was acceptable to dress up like ghouls and witches and ask for candy.

This year, she wasn't a little kid with a plastic pumpkin bucket ready for sugar. This year, she was sixteen and had used her own income earned from the florist to hire a Victorian outfit with a dress that ballooned with skirts and lace, taking up the entire floor in our lounge.

The pearl-beaded corset was tight and pushed up her breasts, barely covering her nipples and revealing acres of white, perfect flesh. She'd coiled her blonde hair until the messy curls turned into corkscrews, piled on top of her head and tumbling down around her face.

Her navy satin gloves reflected the light from above as she waved an oriental-painted fan, and the baby blue material of her gown coupled with the cream bodice and Victorian lace made her eyes pop in a way that looked almost ethereal.

I might love Della unconditionally with no impropriety of lust or denial.

But that night, I struggled to see her as out of bounds. It didn't matter my body prickled or my heart pounded. I battled to remind myself that the stunning creature in finery wasn't some woman I desperately wanted to kiss, but a girl I would forever protect.

Even if it meant protecting her from myself.

"What do you think?" She spun in place, knocking over an empty water glass from the coffee table onto the threadbare carpet. It didn't break, but my stiff rules threatened to.

She was far too lovely, and everything inside begged to mess her up so other men didn't see how incredible she was.

I swallowed to lubricate my throat. "It's nice."

"Nice?" She blew away a curl that'd gotten caught on a fake eyelash—thick black frames around the most incredible eyes. "Just *nice?*" Her shoulders slouched a little. "I was hoping for more than nice. It was my entire week's salary. I should've rented a cheap stripper outfit for ten bucks."

My belly turned to a rock at the mention of a stripper.

No way in hell would that ever happen.

She looked at the ceiling with a huff. "Now I just feel like an idiot for spending so much when I should've given it to you to pay the elec—"

"Stop it." I stood from where I was sprawled on the couch. My hands tingled as I dared place them on her bare, glitter-dusted shoulders. "It's a hundred times better than nice." I squeezed her gently, ignoring the kick in my gut. "Believe me. You'll kill every boy there with a single stare."

Her charcoal-shadowed eyes studied mine, her lips parted as if searching to see if she'd killed me just like I'd promised.

And she had. She definitely had.

But I refused to let her see it.

It was better that way…for both of us.

Squeezing her again, I dropped my hands with a forced chuckle. "You're far too beautiful to go out."

She sighed as if aggravated at something I'd done but then covered it up with a giggle. "Well, I *am* going out. You can't ground me. Not tonight."

"In that case, I'm going to hog the couch and watch something gory. I'm looking forward to the peace and quiet." I stretched, reaching for the ceiling and working out the kinks in my spine. My grey t-shirt rode up my belly, drawing her gaze to my naked skin just above my belt.

She licked her lips, and my heart switched from nervous thrumming to out of control pounding.

The entire lounge filled with wildfire. The air crackled with lightning bolts just waiting to strike. My body hardened in ways it never should around Della. But I couldn't stop it. Every inch of me turned into a tuning fork, humming for something, begging for anything.

She sucked in a shallow breath as her eyes once again found mine. Only this time, they were hooded and darker, older and dangerous.

The invitation.

The *truth*.

Shit.

It was pure fucking hunger and it tore out my insides with how deeply she was starving.

For me? For sex? For anyone willing to offer pleasure?

I stepped back, combating the heavy pull to go to her, to touch her, to do things I never dared—

Knock, knock, knock.

The moment shattered as someone's fist announced guests waited outside our front door.

Della wobbled, blinking as if she'd transported far away and slammed back into reality.

I exhaled hard, dragging a hand over my face and turning my back on her.

What the fuck was that?

What had happened?

And whose fault was it? Mine or hers?

The swish of Della's skirts was the only noise as she bypassed the couch and headed to open the front door.

"Hi," she said, her voice breathy and papery, matching the shivery sensation left in my spine.

I needed to sit down. I needed to figure out what the hell happened and how to prevent it from happening again.

Turning around slowly, I ordered my body to behave as I glanced at the arrivals.

"Hi, yourself," a girl piped up dressed in another Victorian gown—hers in reds and blacks. Compared to Della, she was positively garish while Della was a powder blue angel tempting me straight to fucking hell.

The girl's gaze slipped from Della to me standing furious and dazed in the middle of the living room. She did a double take, her entire body slipping into sensual solicitation. "And hi to you too, handsome." She blew me a kiss, making Della freeze with a frosty glare. "Della didn't say how hot her older brother was."

I supposed I should be flattered, but all I felt was empty. She was so juvenile. So transparent and shallow and *young*.

Shit, she was Della's age, yet I'd never thought of Della sexually—
You did tonight.
You wondered...

My heart skipped a beat, remembering what happened between us before the knock. I was grateful for the interruption. Thankful that I'd been reminded of who Della belonged with and what my role in her life ought to be.

"Hello." I nodded politely, clearing my throat, eradicating any sin I might have committed.

Jamming both hands into my pockets, it was my turn to glower with hatred as another person entered my home.

Tom.

The boy from the diner.

Della instantly stiffened, flicking me a look before allowing herself to be gathered in a hug from the boy I struggled not to hate. She refused to meet my eyes as he kissed her cheek and wolf whistled under his breath. "Holy crap, you're gorgeous."

My hands turned into fists in my pockets.

She blushed. "Thanks."

"Are you ready?" Tom glanced at me.

My jaw clenched.

It never occurred to me that they might be an item.

That she might be dating already, right beneath my nose.

Della nodded. "Yep. Oh, almost forgot." Darting to the coffee table, she scooped up a little pearl bag and looped it over her wrist. Speaking to me, she said, "I have my phone and some cash. I can get an Uber or something home. You won't be able to pick me up on the motorbike in this dress."

I didn't trust myself to talk.

I wanted to ensure she knew the curfew and my many, many rules, but my voice refused to work. It was still a gravelly mess with things I never wanted Della to know. Things *I* didn't want to know.

"Ren?" she murmured, coming closer to me. "Everything okay?"

I nodded stiffly, stumbling back. I honestly didn't know what I'd do if she touched me. "Go. Have fun."

Even though I wanted to lock her in her room and ban Tom from ever seeing her again, I almost pushed her out the door so I could breathe again.

"Okay..." Her eyes danced over my face, a sliver of hurt hiding in them before she smiled, and it vanished. "My offer still stands. You were invited, you know. I don't know if you were listening a few nights ago when I told you about the party, but everyone is welcome."

Fuck, everyone?

"You mean...this isn't just school kids going?"

Tom grinned, self-important and making my life a lot more difficult by not punching him. "Nah, man. It's a frat party. Local uni is putting it on. There'll be booze and stuff, but I won't let Della have any. I promise."

My ears rang.

My temper slipped into an ice-cold single-mindedness.

"You're not going." I narrowed my eyes at Della. "No way."

I'd never been to a party as a guest, but I'd been to enough of the dregs when collecting Cassie on those nights she'd snuck out and called me for a ride home. Della had accompanied me enough to understand why this was non-negotiable.

The amount of used condoms and spewing kids. The reek of sex and trouble.

No. Fucking. Way.

I crossed my arms as Della looked back once at her friends then swooped toward me. Her perfume of something light and floral invaded my nose, her body heat made me sick with want, and her breath against my neck as she hissed into my ear made my knees almost buckle.

I hadn't expected her closeness or her fight, and my silence gave her the perfect battlefield to destroy me.

"Don't mess this up for me, Ren. I'm not asking this time. I'm going to this party, and you have my word I will behave. I won't drink, and I won't fool around, but this is my life. These are my friends, and I want to hang out with them."

Everything she said was for my ears only.

The two strangers lingered by the door, giving us a confused glance.

Della pulled away but not before I lashed out and grabbed her wrist.

She gasped, her eyes dropping to where I held her, her soft inhale ripping through my defences and making my fingers squeeze against my command.

I clutched her hard, unable to let go even though everything inside screamed to back the hell off. "Don't threaten me, Della."

Her eyes widened then hooded to that sultry stare I had no power against. "I'm not threatening you. I'm telling you what's going to happen. Come if you want. I *want* you to. If only to get out of the apartment and live a little."

"You know I don't like crowds."

"Well, stay then."

"You know I can't. Not now."

"Because you don't trust me." Her tongue licked her bottom lip as once again my fingers squeezed her wrist in reprimand. The feel of her tiny bones. The rush of blood in her veins. The electricity infecting both of us that wasn't there before.

Fierce.

Forbidden.

Off-limits.

She shivered, leaning closer.

It took everything I had, but I released her and stepped back, rubbing my fingertips from the residual burn from touching her. "Because I don't trust *them*."

Or myself.

"Fine." She stood tall and any hint of being affected by our whispered conversation disappeared. "Come then. I'll see you there. It's the house four blocks away toward the campus. Follow the music and pumpkins."

Without another word, she grabbed Tom's hand, smiled at the girl, then dragged them out the door, closing it with a slam.

Chapter Fifty-Three

DELLA

Present Day

AH, DATING.

So much fun, right?

Wrong.

The minute I met Tom in line at a local McDonald's of all places while I did English homework with Tina, I'd been rather smitten.

He went to a school not far from ours and regularly used our school's facilities like the basketball court and track as part of the physical education offered.

To be honest, the first thing that attracted me to Tom was his sable hair— almost the exact same colour as Ren's in autumn just before winter made it dark and summer made it bronze.

Instead of Ren's dark soul-deep eyes, Tom's were a startling green. Instead of Ren's well-honed and work-hard muscles, Tom's was gym perfected on a body still growing into manhood.

But despite his youth, Tom was cute. And compared to Ren's fine lines around his eyes and the aura of impatience and intolerance that came from hating people and growing up with the loner deep inside him, Tom was different enough to remind me I wasn't dating him to replicate my fantasies of being with Ren, but he was similar enough to ease that ache in my heart.

Sick, I know.

Twisted, I agree.

But…I always warned you I wasn't a nice person. That the more I followed this road, the worse I became.

I mean, most of the fights between Ren and me were my fault.

Shocker, right?

I know, I know, not a shock at all.

Most of the days that were full of tension and miscommunication were because those days…I couldn't hide how I felt about him, and instead of blurting out that I was madly in love with him, I made him think I couldn't stand him.

And those were the nights I fell asleep torturing myself with imaginings of what it would be like to share my first real kiss with him and be touched in places no one had touched and have him climb on top and—

Anyway, back to Tom...

He was sweet. There isn't much more to say.

I suppose, while I'm at it, I'll confess everything else I did wrong while Tom was in my life. I was cruel to him because I knew he liked me more than I could ever like him. Not that I could ever tell him why. When he texted me pages of ardent affection and how much he missed me when we weren't together, I focused on giving him something I could all while hiding the bits that I couldn't.

I couldn't give him my heart.

But I could give him my body.

But even in that way, I used him again because my physical desires...well, Ren had nailed it when he accused me of being an animal wanting to get laid.

I wasn't quite ready for sex, but holy cow, I was ready for something.

Just a kiss, a touch, a fumble in the dark.

I'd been ready for months, but something had held me back.

Ren.

Of course, it was Ren, but not in the way you'd expect.

His blurted, extremely surprising honesty that he hadn't slept with Cassie until he was nineteen had effectively dampened my libido.

I honestly thought he'd been screwing her for years as I slept stupidly in the room next to the barn. The looks they'd shared. The kisses they'd stolen—it all hinted at full blown sex.

So how had he waited so long?

Why had he waited so long?

And just how the hell was I supposed to do the same?

Look, I'm getting ahead of myself again, and there's a reason I'm going to reveal exactly what happened that first Halloween.

It was the first stepping stone to Ren walking out, and I think I'd always known it. I'd known it, and even though it lurked like a shadow between us from that moment on, I couldn't seem to stop myself.

You see...I used Tom to hurt Ren.

Another terrible confession.

What seven deadly sins does that fit into?

I'm too brain-dead and emotionally exhausted to figure it out.

Adultery perhaps? Even though Ren and I had nothing to cheat on.

I was single. He was single. And I was ready to live a little, even if living meant existing in constant pain. Even if it meant seething in jealousy when Tina hit on him. Even if it meant, eventually, I'd have to smile away my heartache when Ren found someone else.

God, I never thought I'd be so tired writing this. I didn't think memories had such a power to strangle and soothe at the same time. All I want to do is delete this and go to bed. To forget I ever started this tale and spend the last few days before my assignment is due writing something I can actually hand in.

But I also can't end here.

I'm so close.

Just a few more chapters...and then, well, then I can rest, and perhaps the past won't haunt me so much.

Are you ready?

Ready for more terrible Della?

I'm not, but let's see if I can remember exactly what happened that night. Some of it is a blur, and it's not like you need to know it anyway.

The typical party stuff.

I arrived with Tina and Tom, dressed to my eyeballs in glitter and powder and two-hundred dollar Victorian gowns, wanting desperately to feel older and wiser and irresistible to someone, and realising that no matter how much cleavage I might have or how fluttery my eyelashes were or how I stared and licked my lips, Ren was immune to me.

If anything, he just got mad and made me feel even more of a fraud than I already was.

At least, Tom seemed to love my effort, and his hands never strayed from touching me, appeasing my jealousy over Tina's constant whispering about how gorgeous Ren was and if he was available.

I tried to ignore her. I wanted to tell her he was a monk or someone who despised being touched. I threw myself into Tom's attention and encouraged his hands to rest in the small of my back and linger on my waist.

I should've shivered at having him touch me in places that sent goosebumps leaping over my skin, but all I could think about was how Ren had snatched my wrist and held it so tight and unforgiving, leaving a circlet of his fingers for minutes after he'd let me go.

Tom was so tame compared to Ren, and that taboo, forbidden factor just wasn't there, either.

Perhaps I'd become addicted to the fact that I couldn't have Ren more than the actual reality that we weren't actually compatible.

Ha!

Even now, that lie doesn't work. I tried to convince myself that if Ren was my age and available, I wouldn't truly want him. That I'd find him boorish with his rules and stuffy with his diligence.

But yep... it doesn't work.

I didn't want Ren because I couldn't have him.

I wanted Ren because he was everything that made me appreciate, adore, and burn for. He was utterly perfect from his snappish temper to his doting devotion, and yep...I'm back on the crazy torment-myself-with-falling-all-over-again-for-the-boy-who-left-me train.

God, I'm crying.

Why am I crying?

This…ugh!

No!

I haven't cried since the day he left. I didn't let myself and now…now I can't stop.

I…I can't do this.

I need a break—

* * * * *

Sorry.

Jeez, I seem to be apologising to an assignment a lot.

I couldn't finish yesterday. Not unless I wanted to drown my laptop in tears and have to buy another one. It seemed I had a weak day, made worse by a brain that refused to stop thinking about Ren, Ren, Ren.

You know? Some days, I literally do hate him. I hate his damn guts. Those days, I feel somewhat normal and can honestly say I don't want him to come back. Leaving was probably the best thing he could've done for me.

Because I now have no choice but to get over this stupid infatuation and move on.

But other days that hate transforms back into love and, holy ouch, it fills up my heart until it bursts with need, infecting my entire body until I feel as if I have the flu.

Funny, huh?

The love flu.

Stupid man has made me eternally sick, and there is nothing I can do.

Right, enough feeling sorry for myself.

Today, I'm determined to tell you about Halloween.

Where was I? Let me just skim over what I wrote yesterday and try not to roll my eyes at the patheticness of unrequited love.

…

Ah yes, okay, the party.

We arrived.

Tom got me some punch that unfortunately was alcohol free, and Tina and I bounced around in our skirts and fanned our pretty fans, enjoying the stares of young students and wiser university goers, steadily growing more and more silly as the night went on.

For an hour, I refused to let myself think about Ren.

I pretended I didn't care if he didn't come. I spun and laughed and flirted all for me, not to get back at him. So it killed me to realise how fake I turned out to be because I knew the moment he arrived.

My skin prickled. My heartbeat quickened. And everything inside me slipped from chaos to calm.

In the middle of a manic Halloween party filled with Frankensteins and vampires and zombies, I knew the second the matching piece of my heart arrived.

Sad right?

Poetic?

Star-crossed?

Screwed up?

Probably all the above.

But probably not as screwed up as the next part.

You see, I knew the second Ren arrived, and instead of going to him, being a good hostess, and smoothing over the troubled waters between us, I grabbed Tom and clutched him close.

We slow danced with werewolves and fairies, and when he gathered me closer, I mewled in invitation, and when he grinded his hips against me, I gasped in appreciation, and when his head lowered, and his eyes sought mine, and his lips crashed down, I dove my fingers into his messy sable hair and threw away all the decency and morality left inside me.

I became a husk. A chewed-up disgusting person who willingly kissed a boy all the while pretending it was someone else.

And by pretending it was someone else, I kissed harder, deeper, sexier than I ever had before. My first real kiss, and it was with a ghost of the boy I truly wanted.

I let go. I lived my fantasy.

I clawed at his hair, I tangled my tongue with his, and I fell so deeply in love with my illusion that when I opened my eyes and snuggled into his chest, I breathed the wrong name.

"Ren," I moaned with my body aching and breasts swelling and wetness gathering.

And Tom had pulled me away with a terrified look in his green gaze. We'd stood motionless on the dance floor while others swirled around us as he stared into my ripped apart secret and knew.

He knew.

And there was no going back.

* * * * *

I wish there was more to the tale.

But I've sat here for a while thinking what to write, and honestly, there isn't anything else.

I wished I could say that Ren came stalking from the mismatch dressed up crowds, yanked me out of Tom's arms, and planted his mouth on mine in punishment for ever kissing another boy when I'd always been his.

But it didn't happen.

Tom went to get us more drinks, this time with alcohol laced in its sugary depths, and Tina and I continued to dance, but my smiles were brittle and my laugh hollow.

Tom stayed close, but things had changed—awareness had been shown, harboured secrets blown wide apart. His touches were just habit, and that night, we agreed that it was fun and all, but it was better if we went our separate ways.

I wasn't sad. I was relieved. And that was yet another nail in my otherwise rotten coffin.

Meanwhile, as I was getting dumped for hurting two people in one, my heart constantly zeroed in on where Ren was.

Occasionally, he'd appear in the crowd, arms crossed and leg cocked over the other as he leaned against the perimeter, an outsider to the party, a watcher on the wall, close enough to protect me from harm but willing to let me make my own stupid mistakes.

I didn't know if he'd seen me kiss Tom.

I didn't know if he'd been hurt or didn't care—perhaps he was relieved that I was manhandling someone else for a change.

I didn't know.

But when it was time to go home, he walked with me.

He carried my high heels and gave me a pair of flip-flops he'd thoughtfully stashed in his back pocket, and guided me through streets filled with ghosts and demons back to an apartment where he went to his bed and I went to mine, and through the thin walls, I heard him tear apart the meagre furniture we had, howling at the moon.

All the while, I cried into my pillow.

Chapter Fifty-Four

REN

2016

WE DIDN'T EVEN make it to Christmas before another catastrophe found us.

For weeks, I kept the fact that I'd seen Della kissing Tom hidden. When she looked at me over breakfast of toast and cereal on the weekends, I tasted the question she wanted to ask. When I arrived home from a long day at the milking yards and she had a home-cooked meal for two, I heard the query she wanted to know.

And I ignored each look and stare.

Not because I still didn't know how it made me feel—sick to my stomach mainly—but because I worried about her. I worried what sort of person kissed another with that much heat and desire—practically making love on the damn dance floor—and then broke up with them that same evening.

I knew the feeling of not wanting to get close to someone, but she'd taken it to a whole new level. She'd used him, and as much as I loved the fact that she'd broken up with him, I couldn't get over the way she'd kissed him.

Over and over, I replayed it, ripping my heart out little by little until I was more lost and more afraid than I'd ever been.

I hadn't hugged her in weeks.

I hadn't snuggled with her on the couch.

I barely touched her.

And she didn't call me out on it or demand to know what was wrong.

We both knew what was wrong.

Lines had been crossed again, and I desperately wanted to draw more in the sand and ensure they stayed steadfast and true.

Regardless of how I felt about watching her stick her tongue down another boy's throat, she seemed to shut everything down and act normal—if we even had a normal anymore.

She never once mentioned Tom again, and I couldn't think about the kiss she'd given him without getting hot and angry and hard, and not necessarily in that order.

I hated that she'd kissed someone, but that was my own selfish reasons wanting to keep her protected. I was hot because all the men in that place watching that kiss had felt the passion dripping off Della. And I was hard because, goddammit, it reminded me how long it'd been since I'd felt the delicious friction of kissing and I was obscenely jealous.

Jealous of Della's freedom.

Jealous of Della's courage.

Jealous of Della being with anyone when all I wanted to do was lock her in a tower.

It made me sick that I couldn't entangle proper and improper thoughts anymore. I *hated* that I couldn't trust myself around her, when before, she was everything I ever needed.

I didn't know if that was her first proper kiss, or if she'd been practicing a while, but holy fuck me, she knew how to do it.

The way her leg came up to hook over his hip. The angle her head tilted to give unfettered access to her mouth, and the way her hands roamed and nails dug as if she'd drown if she didn't get more.

I could understand the awe on student faces who'd watched such a thing. Even the girls had parted their lips and wanted what Della was having, but for some reason, I didn't think it was Tom who was the excellent kisser.

It was all her, and that was what screwed me up even more.

Why was she so talented at something I wanted to shield her from for years?

And why had I only just noticed what a sexual creature she'd turned out to be?

It made my own needs spring loud and cruel to the surface, and I often thought about my experiences with Cassie. Of our kisses and thrusts; of hands in dark places and tongues wet and dancing.

I'd enjoyed sleeping with Cassie, but I hadn't felt a tenth of violent hunger as Della had shown on the dance floor that night. Perhaps, she was right and I was wrong. Some people were just more sexual than others, and I was hurting her by not letting her be free with whatever she needed to find.

Maybe she'd outgrown me in more ways than I'd ever imagined.

It fucking gutted me, but the very next day, I headed to the pharmacy while she was still in bed and bought a packet of condoms.

Afterward, I booked in a doctor's appointment for her to arrange a better in-depth sex talk than I was capable of and to discuss birth control arrangements.

Thanks to Cassie, I knew about the pill and STIs and the minefield of what sex entailed. It was time Della did too, so at least I didn't have to worry about her getting pregnant or sick.

I assumed Della found the condoms with the note I'd left on her bedside table.

Simple and to the point: *If you're going to do things outside my control, please be safe. Use these. At all times.* With a big black arrow pointing at the twelve pack of condoms.

My heart hadn't stopped pounding in agony every time I thought about her using them. But my job wasn't to prevent her from living. My job was to keep her safe while she did.

It didn't matter how I felt.

It was all about her.

And that was what I tried to remind myself when the phone call came.

* * * * *

Normally, I was the one who screwed things up. I took the blame. I shouldered the consequences. But more and more, Della was the reason things turned ugly.

Two unconnected events made one very nasty conclusion.

I came home a few nights after I'd given her the condoms to find the bathroom door wide open and steam curling down the corridor.

The scents of liquorice body wash and melon shampoo—her current favourite scents—gave me a clear path to her bedroom where she sat in the middle of her bed, dressed in innocent pink pyjamas, reading a textbook and doing science homework.

Everything was right with that picture apart from her hair.

Her gorgeous, golden hair was now a rich blue to match her ribbon.

The same ribbon tied at the end of her plait, draped over her shoulder in a vicious shade of cobalt.

"What the *hell* did you do?" I stormed into her room, barging past the door, and not caring that it slammed against the wall. She'd transformed from angel to nothing but trouble.

Trouble that I no longer knew how to handle…in so many complicated ways.

She looked up, blue eyes even brighter thanks to her new hair.

She winced at my temper. "I knew you'd be mad—"

"Of *course*, I'd be mad. Your hair is goddamn blue! What were you thinking?"

"It's not permanent."

"I don't care. Wash it out. Right now."

She shrugged, her pen in one hand and the end of her plait in the other. "It...um, it'll wash out in twenty-four showers or so."

"Twenty-four! You have school tomorrow."

"They won't mind."

I laughed, full of exasperation and annoyance at how stupid she could be. "Oh, they'll mind. There's nothing natural about that, Della. The dress code states no makeup, offensive jewellery, or embellishments of any kind."

"Why the hell do you remember the dress code?" She pouted. "Can't I have a little expression?"

"I remember because I remember *everything*." My eyes burned, sending their own message that I'd seen her kiss, and I remembered every mortal detail about it. Before she could read that stupidly sent information, I growled. "And no, expression is for after school. School is about learning to follow rules and—"

"It's stifling me, Ren! I can't be who I want to be there anymore. I can't talk to anyone about...things. I'm sick of telling lies about who we are and where we come from. They don't understand. No one understands—"

I shook my head. "I never thought you'd become one of those self-obsessed whiners like those stupid TV shows. This is *life*, Della. You need an education. You're not there to find out who you are. You're there to learn skills you'll need for when you do."

Her shoulders slouched. She had no rebuttal, and my temper stalled.

We waited in a room heavy with argument, slowly fading the more we breathed.

Finally, she murmured, "I'm sorry, okay? I just...I needed to do something. It's been a tough couple of weeks."

I did my best to relax, backing up and leaning against the doorframe with my arms crossed. "Why? What's going on?" There was no surer way to make my anger dissipate than thinking she was hurt or sad. "Tell me, Little Ribbon."

She glanced up with an unhappy smile. "Do you know you hardly ever call me that anymore?"

I opened my mouth to argue, racking my brains for a time when I last used it. Sadness filled my heart when I found none recently. "You're right. I haven't."

"Why?" Her question ached with so much more than just that one request. My bones physically throbbed to cut across the distance and sit beside her on the bed. I wanted nothing more than to gather her in my arms and crush her close. To hug like we used to. To kiss like we used to. To promise her that this might be hard for both of us, but we would never drift apart the way we seemed to be drifting right now.

The silence stretched, this time scratching my skin and drawing blood.

I forced myself to stay in the doorway, no longer comfortable to enter her bedroom with all the strangeness flowing between us. "You know why," I murmured.

I hadn't meant to say that.

I hadn't meant to say anything.

She stiffened, her lips smashed together as her eyes glowed with something that took an axe to my chest, cleaving me in two.

We stared.

And stared.

And when my body prickled and blood boiled, and I was so close to doing something I really shouldn't do, I cleared my throat and the moment was gone.

I smirked, going for light-hearted, when really, I ought to scold her for such a reckless colour. "I should probably march you to a hairdresser and get that colour stripped out, but…it suits you."

And it did. It suited her too much. It made her skin pop white and lips burn red. It made her look older, which was not a good thing.

Her shoulders fell, her tension rippling away to settle on the bedding beneath her lotus-crossed legs. "Thanks." She tugged on the end of her cobalt plait. "I know you don't understand, but sometimes…well, sometimes it feels like we're still alone in the forest, you know? Surrounded but with no one to talk to. At least, in the forest, the trees can't repeat your secrets."

"I miss it, too. But you know why we can't go back…not yet, at least."

"I know." She sighed. "But it's hard when I feel so…" She shrugged. "Look, I know I can't tell people the truth about where we came from or mention my real last name or tell people that we aren't truly related, but sometimes, I just wish I could blurt out everything." Liquid glossed her eyes for a second before she swallowed and smiled bright. "Sorry, like I said. One of those weeks."

My hands clenched into fists, holding myself in place not to go to her. "What do you want to talk about that you can't discuss with me?"

She barked a laugh as if I'd said something hilarious. Rolling her eyes at the ceiling, she chuckled in a tortured-exasperated way. "Gosh, *everything.*"

The hair on the back of my neck stood up, hating that she felt trapped and alone. "I'm always here, Della. If it's girl stuff or periods or whatever. I can handle it."

Her nose wrinkled. "I'm good. Thanks."

"If it's not that, then tell me what's bugging you."

She dropped her gaze to her bedspread, her fingers plucking the pages of her text book. "I can't."

"Why?" Despite myself, my feet stepped into her bedroom, needing to go to her when she seemed so forlorn. "What's wrong?"

Her blue hair shivered as she shook her head. "Nothing's wrong."

"Something's wrong."

Her eyes flashed with warning not to push her. "Like I said, I'm good. Don't worry about it."

My legs locked in the centre of her carpet. "Don't get mad at me. I'm only trying to help."

"Yes, and look at the great job you're doing!" She launched upright, kneeling on her bed. "Just...I can't do this right now. I need to study and you—you just—"

"I just what?"

"You make it worse, okay?"

I froze. I had no reply. Only the pain she'd caused and the knowledge that I'd somehow failed her. Nodding curtly, I backed toward the door. "Fine. Study. You know where I am if you need me."

I turned around and left before the argument could fall into trickier territory.

* * * * *

The very next day, our lives changed once again. The catastrophe hit with lashing accusations and howling consequences.

I was commanded to visit the high school where Della attended. When the phone call came, I was herding seven hundred plus cattle into the milking shed and could barely hear the snippy tone of the principal's assistant ordering me to pop in for a 'chat.'

I'd barked back, asking if Della was hurt or lost or missing. Did I need to save her from yet more Social Service agents or was it not as dire as that? The urge to run and vanish into the protection of the forest sprang into an undeniable urge.

All the woman would give me was Della had been served detention for her blue hair, and they wanted to discuss the matter.

My need to grab Della and disappear faded a little. I'd told her she'd get in trouble for such a ridiculous colour, and it turned out, I was right. Frankly, she deserved a bit of punishment, and if being detained after class and earning a stern talking-to by the principal was the price, then hopefully she'd learn her lesson.

For the rest of the day, I lived with a recipe of uncertainty and curiosity, and by the time I sped my way on a beaten-up motorbike that needed new parts and some serious care, I was wired and ready to kill someone.

I didn't care I had grass stains on my work jeans or my plaid shirt was covered in dirt. I made an honest living, and the scents of earth and cow were more acceptable to me than asphalt and metal.

Striding through the school corridors, I peeked into classrooms full of posters with correct etiquette and current assignments. A science lab smelled of sulphur. A lecture room still hummed with a projector someone had left on even though no students were there to learn.

The place was foreign, but I wondered what it would be like to attend. What did Della think when she arrived early in the morning and soaked up knowledge in different environments?

I got lost in the labyrinth of corridors and cut across the wrong campus forecourt until I found the admin building where the principal's office was housed.

The moment I stepped into the stuffy, low-ceiling building, a woman with spectacles and greying hair looked up from typing something on a computer. "Ah, you must be Mr. Wild?" She said it as a question, but with a knowing gaze that unsettled me.

"I am." My eyes drifted over the space, instinctually seeking exits and keeping a safe distance from myself and this new stranger.

"Great. Della's detention is almost over. She'll head here accordingly. Please." She nodded at a closed pine door where a bronze plaque announced a Marnie Sapture was in command of this establishment. "Ms. Sapture is expecting you."

Gritting my teeth, I strode to the door and opened it without knocking. The principal would've been pretty once upon a time, before she let stress pile on the pounds and too much makeup try to hide the heavy lines on her forehead. "Mr. Wild?"

I nodded.

"Good. We need to talk."

"As I've been told."

"Please, sit." She waved at the chair in front of her. A moment of déjà vu hit me of entering another principal's office and hearing a tale of how Della informed a bunch of five-year-olds how to skin and gut a rabbit.

The memory gave me mixed feelings of amusement and terror. She was so different to everyone else, but her differences meant we never seemed to stay in one place for too long.

Sitting down but with all my weight in my feet ready to leap up and run, I waited for Marnie Sapture to tell me why exactly I'd been summoned. The familiar weight of my goat hide knife that Cassie gave me whispered to be used.

To unholster the blade and threaten this woman the same way she was threatening me.

She ran her hand through her black short hair, shuffling paperwork with the other. Finally, she cleared her throat importantly. "I'm sure you're aware, Della came to school today with blue hair." She looked up, narrowing her eyes. "And I'm sure you're aware that our policy on uniform and conformity don't permit such unnatural colours."

It didn't matter that I'd said the exact same thing last night.

Telling Della off on my own was one thing; having a stranger do it made my need to protect her at all costs surface. "Blue isn't unnatural." I shrugged. "Blue is the colour of the sky. It's one of the most common colours around."

She pursed her lips, causing more lines to appear. "That may be the case, Mr. Wild, but blue in the clouds and blue on one's head are two completely different things."

I held my tongue, waiting for any other reason I was here. Della's detention was hardly breaking news to call in a caregiver. The hair on the back of my neck stood up as Ms. Sapture's cheeks reddened, and her righteous voice slipped into disgusted. "I'm sure you're also aware that in this state, there are rules about unnatural relationships between family."

This time, she didn't look up as if she found making eye contact with me repulsive.

"Excuse me?" I hissed.

"I said unnatural relationships between fam—"

"I heard you." I shot to my feet, hands balled. "And just what the hell are you implying?"

She stiffened but dared look up. "I'm implying that some information has come to light that you and Ms. Della's bond is more than brother and sister." She tapped some papers with a pink-painted fingernail. "This is Della's enrolment application. You signed as her brother, yet a student here informed us that a more worrying connection might be at play."

I couldn't breathe.

I couldn't see past the red haze in my vision.

All I wanted to do was grab Della and run. What had she done? Who had she spoken to? What the fuck did she say?

"Whoever said such things is lying," I bit every word as if killing them with my teeth.

"That might be, but whenever accusations like this arise, it is protocol to call Child Protective Services."

I backed toward the door. "You have no right."

She stood behind her desk, eyes gleaming. "I do have a right, Mr. Wild. In fact, I have an obligation. I invited you here today to state your side of the argument, but if you have nothing to say on the matter then—" She picked up the phone on her desk. "I suppose I might as well make that phone call now and get this over with."

Fuck.

What did I do? Waste the precious time I had trying to make her see reason or bolt now and pack up as much as I could? Where the hell was Della? I couldn't move until I knew she was safe and—

Commotion sounded outside, the receptionist's high-pitched voice arguing against one I knew better than my own.

Della.

Before I could spin and open the door, she shoved it open and stumbled over the threshold. Every nerve demanded I grab her, but I had to bury those urges because she wasn't alone.

"What the—?" I said under my breath as she dragged Tom, her ex-boyfriend, into the small office and slammed the door. She held his hand with a death grip, her fingernails making white indentations in his flesh.

"What is the meaning of this, Ms. Wild? Why is another student from a different school in my office?" the principal snipped. The phone dangled in her hand, unconnected and silent on its horrible message that Della and I did something immoral.

"I know who started the rumour, Ms. Sapture," Della said, yanking Tom closer. "And it's just that. A stupid, silly little rumour that's gotten out of hand."

I didn't understand what the hell was going on, and Della refused to make eye contact with me.

I'd been forgotten about as Tom gulped and hung his head. "It was me, Ms. Sapture. I started it. I wanted to make life difficult for Della."

The principal gave him a harsh stare. "What do you mean?"

"I mean..." He flinched as Della dug her nails harder into him. "Della and I were going out, but then she dumped me, and I got jealous and made up the lie that she broke up with me because she was in love with her brother."

Holy shit.

I stumbled backward, dragging a hand over my mouth.

Della flicked me a glance, then fixed her stare back on the

principal. "As you can see, Ms. Sapture, my brother is as horrified by this as I was. I couldn't think of a more terrible thing to say." She glowered at Tom beside her. "Jealousy makes us do strange things."

Ms. Sapture slowly sat down in her chair, her witch-hunt game-face fading in favour of the truth. The *only* truth. That Della and I weren't blood, but we were family through and through.

Aren't we?

Della let Tom go but not without a heated, warning look. "So you admit it? You and Tina have been spreading lies about me?"

Tom gritted his teeth as if he wanted to argue but nodded stiffly. "Yes."

"And you have no evidence to back up this lie? No photo or video revealing the vile things you said?" Della's eyes glittered a ruthless blue. Her blue hair matched, contrasting with the auburn and browns of her school uniform.

"None." He blew out, his tall frame sinking. "I made it all up."

Della crossed her arms, nodding once at Ms. Sapture. "You see? Stupid student gossip. I don't know why it started, but it's over now. Not a word of it was true and I'm sorry to waste your time."

Ms. Sapture looked put out, struggling to get control of the situation that Della had so successfully commandeered. Finally, she waved at the door with bored impatience. "I'll accept your explanation for now, Ms. Wild. However, I wasn't born yesterday, and I've been around enough students to understand rumours usually start from some kernel of truth." Her gaze found mine as she leaned forward almost in a threat. "One more sniff of such a thing and I'm calling CPS, regardless of your dramatics."

I glowered back, refusing to let her intimidate me.

Della brushed past me, opening the door and letting Tom step out before her.

"Oh, and one more thing, Ms. Wild," Ms Sapture clipped. "I want that colour gone by tomorrow, do you hear me?"

Della didn't answer, and with a flick of blue motioned for me to follow her.

Chapter Fifty-Five

DELLA

Present Day

I KNOW, I know.

I was stupid. Incredibly *stupid. So stupid it almost meant we were separated again, but if it hadn't have been for detention with my blue hair, I would never have heard the rumour until it was too late.*

I'd been under the illusion that Tom was trustworthy, and my minor slip after our kiss didn't bother him too much—not enough to tell people about. Yes, were dating, but he was wanted by a lot of girls, and I was nothing special.

Saying the wrong name after kissing him had been my error, but I'd apologised and believed him when he said it didn't matter. I stupidly accepted his assurances and didn't think anything more on it.

Turns out, he started making out with Tina, my so-called best friend, and she decided to rat on me. We'd gotten close over the few years, Tina and I, close enough for me to slip occasionally and reveal things I shouldn't about me and Ren.

I never came out and said I wanted him or that I was in love with him, but I supposed she read between the lines.

And yes, I know you're calling me names, and I totally accept them because it was idiotic to confide in someone, but...I had no one to talk to. No one to help settle my nerves every time the overwhelming desire to kiss Ren pounced on me. No one to be a shoulder to cry on when the wanting became too painful. And no one to offer advice on how to move past such a horrible situation and just accept that things would never change between us.

All I told Tina was there was a boy I liked.

A boy who liked me but not in the same way.

When she asked if it was one of Ren's friends, I hesitated. Tying Ren's name into any of this was dangerous but making it be an older guy who was no longer at school and who couldn't be researched made sense.

So I gave in.

I found myself spinning a tale of unrequited love with one of Ren's friends— not that he had any—and how I'd kissed him once but that was it.

Tina was sympathetic and sweet and acted as if I had a terminal case of the flu and needed constant mothering. At first, I loved it. I loved having someone nurse my achy breaky heart and be there whenever I needed to vent. But then, her questions became more prying, her eyes more suspicious, and I stopped telling her things.

I stopped muttering secrets like: when he's near me, it's all I can do not to reach out and grab him. When he's cooking beside me, my mouth waters and not for the food. When he's asleep, I wage a battle to stay in my bed and not go to his and repeat the mistake I made last time.

By the time I met Tom, Tina was sick of my wishing over a boy I could never have and encouraged my crush on Tom. He could be talked about freely, and I shared intimate details with Tina because she shared them with me. I knew she wasn't a virgin anymore and I knew she'd bled when a guy called Scooter took her to the movies and ended up banging her in the back seat of his car.

She was worldly to me, and she gave good advice on how to seduce Tom and what to expect when I first jumped into bed with him.

Unfortunately, armed with her prior knowledge of me pining for a boy who I wouldn't name, when she found out Tom had broken up with me after kissing at the Halloween party, she couldn't understand why.

She'd badgered and badgered for answers, until finally, in a moment of utter moronic weakness, I told her that I'd said the wrong name afterward kissing him. I'd said the name of the boy I was in love with. Ren's friend.

I thought I'd covered my tracks pretty good.

I patted myself on the back for keeping her away from the truth.

Funny, how it was the exact opposite.

Tina messaged Tom, telling him off for breaking up with me. They'd had some hate-lust-text-war for a few weeks before hooking up behind my back. Then, of course, it was just a matter of time before Tina mentioned my sad, hopeless situation of being in love with someone who wouldn't even notice me, and Tom told her the name I'd breathed after our kiss.

Perfect explosion.

But you know what I'm most mad about?

I'm mad that neither of them came to face me. That they didn't ask for my side of the story before they jumped to conclusions, figured I was boning my brother, and spread gossip loudly enough to get the principal involved.

So yeah, dying my hair blue was stupid. But at least it landed me in detention right next to Tina, who smirked and asked if I'd been summoned to the principal's office lately. I waved the slip in her face and she giggled. She told me to expect a certain brother waiting for me, along with a few other people who wanted to discuss our 'family dynamics.'

I'd bolted from detention without gathering up a stitch of my belongings. My backpack left opened on the floor; my pencil case on the desk, and my notebook on the page of my current homework assignment.

I left it all behind as survival instincts overrode everything and I hopped onto the nearest unlocked bike in the bike shed and hoofed it over to Tom's neighbouring school.

There, I'd yelled his name until someone pointed me in the right direction. The moment I found him in after-school woodworking, I grabbed his wrist and dragged him to my campus, all the while telling him the truth.

The only person I ever told the entire truth to.

I held nothing back. I told him my last name was Mclary, and I'd been rescued from monsters. That Ren wasn't my brother. That he was the reason I wasn't dead in a ditch somewhere. And that yes, I was in love with him, but it was fine because he wasn't in love with me and nothing inappropriate was going on. Not that it was any of his business because Ren and I weren't related, so even if we did get together, the only law being broken was the fact I was a minor and he was not.

And once I'd spilled everything, dragging my ex-boyfriend to fix what I'd broken, I made him swear to secrecy. And because I didn't trust his vow never to breathe a word, I added a threat. One that would surely put me in hell because it was yet another of the seven deadly sins. Lying. Or, at least, I think it's a deadly sin. If it isn't, it probably should be.

Doesn't matter.

The point is, I told him I'd spread a rumour how he'd fucked me against my control. How he'd gotten me drunk at that party, had his wicked way with me, then spread a different kind of rumour about me to take the heat off him.

His eyes filled with hatred, but I didn't care. All I cared about was ending this nightmare before it ruined everything.

You see, I only had one year left of high school.

The next time Ren and I ran, I wanted it to be for good. I never wanted to have to tie Ren to a new place so I could go to school. I never wanted him to feel as trapped as I did. I wanted to be free because maybe, just maybe, away from people and rules and constant reminders, Ren might slip enough to realise he loved me, too.

Chapter Fifty-Six

REN

2016-2017

FOR TWO MONTHS, our packed backpacks rested by the door ready to grab at a moment's notice. I'd never opened a bank account as I had no identification to appease the paper pushers, and the cash I'd diligently saved was hidden in a small box under the rickety floorboard beneath the couch—ready to be snatched and taken.

I'd wanted to run the day we got home from the principal, but Della had picked a fight and we'd argued well into the night. Her reasons for staying were she didn't want to move schools when she was so close to finishing, that she'd fixed it so the rumour would fade and the teachers would chalk it up to stupid teenage drama, and that I was too flighty.

I'd roared at that one.

Flighty?

How about fucking wary that even though Della was more adult than kid these days, she could still be taken away from me. Excuse me for not caring about anything other than her. Running meant abandoning my work and our apartment, but I would gladly give up everything over and over again if it meant she stayed safely by my side.

But even in the wake of my temper, she'd won in the end—just like she always did.

I bowed to her pleas to stay, just for a little while, and gamble with time to see who was right. If Tom kept his mouth shut, we would be free to stay. But if he didn't, it might be too late to run next time.

I hated it.

I hated that I didn't just grab her and leave rather than listen to her debate and bow to her conclusions. But something else made me agree and not just her excellent arguing skills.

I agreed because of the rumour that'd called me in to the principal in the first place. The rumour that Della was in love with me.

My heart had stopped and hadn't beaten correctly since. It was just a silly rumour, but I agreed with Ms. Sapture: truth lived in rumour, and if such a thing was said…

Could it be true?

Who had started it?

And how could they screw up my mind by making me fear that my love for Della wasn't pure, after all. That it was tainted and no longer black and white.

I withdrew even more from her.

I stopped using her nickname.

Whatever physical contact still existed between us, ceased all together.

She obeyed me and stripped the blue from her hair but that was about all she obeyed me in.

We became strangers living in the same apartment, and I couldn't stop it because every time I looked at her…I wondered.

I wondered what she felt for me.

I wondered what she kept hidden.

I wondered about so many things I shouldn't wonder about.

For eight long weeks, I ignored her when she was home, yet made her text me after each class. Just a quick *I'm fine* to let me know she hadn't been taken by CPS. It was the only way I could focus on my work and not get trampled by the cows. And ignoring her at home was the only way I could be civil and not tear into her, demanding answers to the sick questions inside my head.

Was she in love with me?

And if she was…where the fuck did that leave us?

The incident should've ended up with us homeless and running again, but somehow, it was swept under the rug and life continued as normal.

All of it, from the threat of Social Services to the rumour of Della's affection for me, was never mentioned again.

It made me nervous.

It made a ticking clock hover over my head, speeding up time and somehow slowing it down.

Christmas and New Year's came and went.

We didn't celebrate it.

Spring arrived, and as snow left the world a more habitable place, Della withdrew from me as I'd withdrawn from her, causing an even worse strain between us.

God, I missed her, but I had no idea how to fix something I didn't understand.

Then, two weeks before our joint birthday, I broke my wrist.

The pain of being kicked by a cow while trying to hook it up the milking machine was a price I'd happily pay all over again because it gave Della back to me. If only for a little while.

She swooped toward me after I'd driven home one-handed, turned off my bike, then stomped down the stairs and into our tiny apartment.

Her eyes widened with worry, taking in my swollen ugly wrist, instantly losing her wariness around me and fussing as kindly and as sweetly as she had with the splinter.

She bustled around, fear and affection thick in her voice as she charged to the mostly-empty freezer to find something cold for the swelling.

With jerky speed, she flew back to me, skidding to a stop and falling to her knees before me. Her focus entirely on making me better and no other mess from before.

Having her close.

Having her care.

Fuck.

I couldn't help myself.

I reached out to cup her cheek as she rested a bag of frozen peas on my skin, so grateful to have my Della back.

The moment I touched her, she flinched and melted at the same time.

The nastiness of pushing each other away vanished, and with a bone-deep sigh, she rested her cheek in my palm.

It was all I could do to stay touching her innocently. My body bellowed to clutch her tight, to stop thinking about everything, to just give in to whatever pulled us together.

The sensation of holding her was one of coming home after being lost for so long, and I *ached*.

I ached with a need so hungry, so raw, I couldn't think.

All I wanted to do was slip off the dining chair and pull her against me. Words and apologies filled my mouth with bitter regret. Why had I been so cruel to her? How had I forgotten how much I cared for this girl?

We stayed like that for far too long, me bent over her with my hand on her cheek and her curled on the floor with a heart-stealing wish in her eyes.

My lips tingled. My fingers fluttered. And Della arched up on her knees.

My attention fell to her mouth.

Her blonde hair—no longer blue or fantastical—hung over her shoulder, tickling my knuckles, and I wanted something I'd never wanted before.

I wanted things to be different. I wanted things to be innocent between us again but finally ready to accept that that would never happen.

She licked her lips, breaking the spell, inviting me to do something I desperately wanted. I needed to kiss her. But I needed it to be right. I'd had enough wrongness between us to risk losing her again.

I sat taller in my chair to kiss her forehead. To kiss her like I was allowed.

The moment my mouth touched her skin, she inhaled sharply, swallowing a quick moan. She bowed into me, pressing herself against my legs.

My thighs bunched as my body hardened against my will, and lust that I had no right to feel became excruciating.

With clenched teeth, I dropped my touch, removed my kiss, and tore my gaze away.

Standing with a wobble born from everything she made me feel, I stepped around her still hunched on the kitchen floor. Breathing for the first time since I'd kissed her, I headed to the dresser where my clothes waited, grabbed a cleaner pair of jeans and t-shirt, then walked down the corridor to change in the bathroom away from her heated eyes.

It took me twice as long, awkward and painful with only one working hand.

If things were simple between us, I would've asked for Della's help. I would've chuckled as she wrangled me from my t-shirt and teased her as she unzipped my jeans.

But things weren't simple. And that would be a complication I couldn't afford.

By the time we made it to the emergency room, taking the bus to the downtown hospital, my wrist was three times the size and an angry blue to match Della's ribbon.

The nurse checked us in, asked for a deposit up front as we didn't have documents or identification for insurance, advised I'd need X-rays and most likely a cast, and finally that the wait was long.

I told Della to go home. She had school in the morning, and who knew how much time we'd waste in this place.

She nodded to appease me but never left.

She sat beside me, reading trashy magazines, getting me coffee and water, never leaving my side for longer than a few minutes. Every so often, I felt her watching me through a curtain of blonde, her fingers tracing her lips. She'd avert her gaze the second I noticed, leaving me confused and achy and in more pain than before.

It was the longest evening of my life sitting in that room. Not because of my wrist but because of her.

It was a constant fight not to hug her close and kiss her softly. All I wanted to do was be free with my actions and affections. I just wanted to touch her to reassure myself that she was still here, despite the stress of the past few months.

But I couldn't.

I was no longer allowed to hug and touch because my thoughts were no longer clear.

When I finally saw a doctor, underwent X-rays and learned the news that a couple of fingers as well as my wrist had been broken, I wouldn't wish it away for anything.

The cow that kicked me gave me a night I'd never forget. It deleted the stilted strangeness that festered between me and Della, and I had my best friend back.

We went home together that night, me in a cast and Della with her arm looped through mine. We sat in comfortable silence on the bus home, had a midnight snack of cereal and milk, then she took my hand and instead of saying goodnight and going to our separate rooms, she led me into hers.

I baulked at the doorway, staring at her double bed, seeing it not as a place to rest but a battlefield in which I'd never stop fighting.

But I couldn't stop her when she tugged me forward, whispering, "I miss you, Ren. Please…just for one night."

I'd never been able to deny her anything.

And so, despite my better judgment, I stayed.

Together, we stripped to underwear and slipped beneath the covers.

We didn't touch, lying stiffly in the dark, but having her so close I could hear her breathing and feel her heat and smell her lovely scent…I was happier than I'd been in a very long time.

* * * * *

"Happy Birthday, Ren." Della gave me a card with one of those tinsel rosettes stuck to the envelope.

We sat in a burger joint with red vinyl and grease-stained music posters. Tradition demanded our birthday meal took place in a diner, but I ensured it was different to the last one where she left me to eat with Tom.

"I thought we agreed we weren't buying each other presents." I put down my fry and wiped salt-dusted fingers on a serviette. "Now I just feel like crap because I didn't get you anything."

"Ah, well." She shrugged. "I saw it the other day, and I had no choice. It had your name all over it."

I frowned as I tore at the glue holding the envelope shut. Sliding my finger under the seam, I ripped the paper and pulled out a card with a picture of a forest wreathed in fog.

My heart thudded harder, knowing it belonged there over anywhere; my legs tensed to run to wherever this photo had been taken. "It's beautiful." I looked up, smiling. "Thank you."

Della rolled her eyes. "Open it, you moron." Wearing a black dress with her hair slicked in a high silky ponytail, she was pure elegance. She'd grown up, and the change in her from sixteen to seventeen hurt my chest whenever I stared too much.

I'd loathed her wardrobe choices lately; mainly because they were far more revealing than before. She was beautiful in whatever she wore, but the tight shorts and skirts, the tops that clung to her...it all drove me mad trying to stop myself from hunting down the men who stared at her in appreciation.

She deserved to be appreciated—just not by them.

Not by *any* man.

Including me.

Cracking open the card, another picture fell out, this one torn from a hunting and fishing catalogue. Picking it off the table, I flipped it over until I looked at a four-person tent with a small alcove for gear and two sleeping pods off the main living. The price had been blacked out with a picture of a scribbled balloon.

"What..." I looked up. "You bought me a tent?"

She scooted her chair closer. "Uh-huh. It's the perfect size for when I finish school and we leave again. You won't have to feel awkward sleeping with me squished so close, see?" She tapped the picture in my grip. "We would each have our own wing and our stuff would be safe in the middle. It's brown like your hair, so it will disappear in the forest, and the fly screens are green. It's perfect, don't you think?" Her blue eyes danced with futures I hadn't dared think about.

My life until now had been a monotony of riding to work, cows, riding home, and staying close but not too close with Della. I hadn't dared think about what would happen when she'd finished school.

About what I wanted.

About what I needed.

The past few years had been a different chapter to our normal world—totally unrelated to who we truly were. An episode of treading water until we could go home, be happy, and figure out how we fit into each other's lives after so much.

The concept that we could leave this place...*run*.

Just us.

Fuck, I wanted it more than I could stand.

Her voice dropped when I said nothing. "You weren't planning on staying here...were you, Ren?"

I blinked, dragged into the conversation against my will. Unprepared to show her how desperate I was for something different...something better and bearable between us. "Well, no. I mean, I hadn't thought—"

She dragged a fry through her tomato sauce. "We need to start thinking about it. This is my last year of high school. We can leave soon."

Leave...

I cleared my throat as that promise did its best to wrap around my heart and free me from every restriction I'd put in place. "But what about *your* future? What do *you* want to do?"

"I want to go back to the forest. I've told you that."

"There are no jobs out there, Della. No boys to make a family with. No future apart from—"

"Apart from with you," she whispered.

I froze, studying her face and the naked desire there.

The restaurant disappeared. Silence descended, turning the world mute.

I stopped breathing.

She stopped breathing.

The only thing we survived on was the vicious, violent bond that we'd always shared but had somehow magnified from virtuous to blistering.

Her eyes filled with promises, pleas—things that filled the chambers of my heart with crucifying futures I could never have.

We stared for an eternity, drowning in each other, before I closed the card with a snap and shoved it back toward her. "I can't accept this."

She flinched. "Too late, it's in our apartment. I didn't bother bringing it with us as it's bulky, but it's already yours."

"How did you buy—"

"With my salary from the florist. I still do the odd weekend. Enough to save up some spending money."

I nodded.

I'd known that. Every time she came back from that place, she smelled utterly devine. Honeysuckle and rose petals drove me insane sitting beside her on the couch, pretending to watch TV when really I counted down the seconds for her to go to bed so I could be alone with my traitorous body.

This was too much.

My cast clunked on the table as I shifted uncomfortably, seeking something normal to say. "If you could have anything you wanted for your birthday, what would it be?"

Her eyes burned like blue coal. *"Anything?"*

I swallowed, cursing her. "Within reason." Terror at what she'd ask for locked me to the spot. This was a stupid idea.

Her forehead frowned as if thinking of every gift she'd love but knew better than to ask for. Eventually, she murmured, "A tattoo."

I coughed on a mouthful of Coke. "Excuse me?"

"I've wanted one for ages, but I knew you wouldn't approve."

Normally, I would agree with her. I'd had a panic attack when she'd come home one afternoon with her ears pierced, let alone her skin inked, but that was then and this was now. Della had once again unsettled me with talks of futures and forest freedoms. I needed to change the subject with something—anything to stop the electricity humming unpermitted between us.

"Okay," I whispered.

Her eyes widened. "What did you say?"

"I said okay. Let's go get a tattoo."

"You're—you're serious?" Her head tilted to the side, her hair swishing down her back in one long rope.

"Deadly. If you want to permanently mark your skin and regret it later, who am I to stop you?"

"I'll need a guardian who is over eighteen to sign the paperwork." She stood, inching her way around the table to stand in front of me, her tight black dress showing off every sinful curve. "Is that going to be a problem?"

I shook my head. "No problem. You want a tattoo. You can have one." Keeping my attention on her face, I stood. "Your decision."

"Yes!" She threw her arms around me, wedging her breasts against my chest, deleting space I dreadfully needed to keep between us.

I swallowed my groan as I nuzzled her against my will, hugging her fierce, missing her hard.

She trembled in my arms, her breathing quick and shallow. Her leg slipped between mine, inappropriate and far too close. "I've missed hugging you, Ren. So much." Her lips pressed against my t-shirt.

My body reacted, my heart smoked, and even though I had to fight every muscle, I pushed her away with a careless shrug as if she hadn't just crippled me all over again. "A birthday hug before your birthday tattoo."

She nodded sharply, liquid suspiciously bright in her gaze. "Right."

It physically stung not to gather her close again, but I held out my arm, the only form of contact I could handle. "Come on. Let's go get your seventeenth birthday present."

She looped her arm through mine.

And we pretended things were perfectly normal.

Chapter Fifty-Seven

REN

2017

SHE GOT A ribbon.

Of course, she did.

A long blue ribbon that wrapped twice around her ankle with one end flared on her calf while the other trailed down the bones of her foot, twisting into a shape that looked suspiciously like an R.

When she showed me after two hours in the tattooist chair, I'd almost beaten up the artist. They'd shown me the original sketch that was drawn and printed on her skin prior to inking and that ribbon had ended with a kick in its tail.

Normal.

This one, the *permanent* one, looped over itself and back across in a letter not a shape. A letter that happened to be the first of my name.

Della hadn't even tried to act ashamed, high on marking her skin with an unforgettable, unforgivable symbol.

With shaking hands, I paid the artist and was grateful when he wrapped Della's leg and foot in cellophane, blurring the design enough so I could pretend I'd seen something that wasn't there.

By the time we'd returned home, my temper was short, my mind a mess, and the tent resting in its untouched box on the coffee table just made me tip into places I could no longer run from.

Grabbing Della, I marched her to the couch, shoved her down, and kneeled before her.

"What are you—"

"Shut up," I hissed, hell bent on finding answers I was afraid of.

She gasped as I tore at the cellophane, unwrapping the plastic, revealing the slimy aftercare cream and the vibrant blue ribbon forever inked into her skin.

Two hundred dollars and she'd fucking ruined me.

My teeth hurt I clenched so hard as what I'd feared stared back at me.

Not an ordinary ribbon but one with a goddamn message. "What the hell is this?" I looked up, seething and ruthless. My fingernails dug into her foot as I held it on my thigh.

She tried to yank it away, her black dress riding up her legs, the flash of red underwear sending yet more rage into my already out of control temper.

"Nothing."

"It's not *nothing*, Della."

"It's nothing, okay?" She shrugged with a worried look in her gaze. "It's a ribbon. That's all."

My hands, despite themselves, feathered up her calf to her knee. I couldn't stop them, and I couldn't stop her reaction as her legs parted and her lips sucked in desperate air.

She should hate me for touching her.

She should leap away and smite me for even *thinking* of touching her.

But she did the opposite.

Her entire body beckoned, clouding my head, making me sick with—

"What the hell are you doing?" I groaned as I shoved her aside and stood on trembling legs.

I needed to get laid.

I shouldn't have blocked myself from other people's affection just because I preferred Della's company over everybody else's.

I wasn't naïve.

I knew Della was experimenting and testing, and this was just another push to see what I would do. Only problem was, I didn't know what I'd do if she pushed me any further.

Raking my hands through my hair, I paced the lounge as Della shuffled higher on the couch, her eyes dropping to her newly inked ankle and foot.

I couldn't look at her. Couldn't stand to see what she'd done to herself.

It hurt.

It hurt so damn much to love her so fucking dearly but be so confused. I loved her in so many ways, but here she was, trying to get me to love her in an entirely different one, and I honestly didn't know if I could.

How was I supposed to see past the little girl I'd raised?

How was I supposed to be a man with her when I would forever be her boy?

How was I supposed to be okay with the changes in my need for her?

The answer?

I couldn't.

I was projecting my desires onto her, making myself believe she sent me messages when really, they were entirely innocent.

She wasn't inviting me.

She wasn't messing me up.

This was *my* fault.

I was reading into things that weren't there.

There was no message. No ulterior cry for more.

I was the one turning innocent into dirty, and it had to stop.

Right now.

She confirmed I was the one making a mess of everything by murmuring, "Ren, I'm sorry. You're right. I did ask him to make it wrap like an R. I didn't think you'd be so mad. I thought you'd appreciate it."

I spun to face her, willing to hear the truth after my stupid mind muddied everything. "Go on."

She spread her hands helplessly. "I love you. I'll *always* love you. You're my family. Is it so wrong that I wanted a reminder of you on me at all times?" She blinked back tears, urging me to believe. "I'm sorry. It doesn't mean anything, okay? I know we never talk about it, but that kiss at Cherry River has been infecting everything between us for years. It's a toxin that I don't know how to get rid of, and it's changed how you see me and I *miss* you, Ren. I miss you so much. I miss that I can't hug you and say silly things without you tensing and thinking I'm trying to get you into bed. I miss that I can't get a tattoo that represents both me and you and explain that it's a symbol of togetherness and nothing more. That's all. That's it. If you were a girl who'd run away with me and been there every day of my life, I would feel the exact same way. I would want something permanent to remind me of all the amazing times we've shared and all the sacrifices you gave me." A single tear rolled down her cheek. "Please, it's nothing more than that. You have to believe me."

I backed up, hearing the truth beneath her shaky promises.

This was all my fault.

"I'm sorry, Della." I wanted to use her nickname, to prove to her that things hadn't changed so much that I could no longer say it. But my skin felt foreign, my heart a stranger, and I needed to fix myself before it was too late.

Stalking to the front door, I grabbed my keys and my phone.

Tonight, I'd reached my limit.

I needed companionship that would hopefully clear my head. I needed to be away from Della in order to do that.

Not looking back, I said, "Don't…don't wait up for me."

I slammed the door before I could fall before her and beg her to forgive me.

Chapter Fifty-Eight

DELLA

Present Day

THAT WAS THE *beginning of the end.*

If I could, I'd rewind time and never get that ridiculous tattoo. I couldn't explain what came over me as the artist bent over my foot and dug his needles into my virgin skin. Ren had paced the front of the shop, studying blown-up pieces on the wall, flicking through books with tattoo designs.

I'd thought I would be happy with the simple design, but the longer the tattooist dragged his needles, the more it felt like only half of the puzzle. The ribbon had been a part of my life since the day I could remember...just like Ren.

It wouldn't be right to draw myself without him there to weave into the tale, too.

With Ren's back to us, I'd whispered to the tattooist to flow the ribbon into a capital R. He'd given me a strange look, glanced at Ren who'd signed the paperwork with his matching last name to mine, and shrugged as if it wasn't his business.

He'd finished the piece quickly, and my heart swelled as the formation of the first letter of the word I loved most in the world came into being on my foot.

Only, I hadn't thought ahead.

I didn't guess how rattled Ren would be or understand how much he was cracking beneath the constant mixed messages I sent him.

He was right to doubt me.

I promised myself I kept my secrets about loving him hidden. I lay in bed congratulating myself on being able to lie to his face and laugh about something silly when all I wanted to do was climb into his lap and pull his lips to mine.

But...I wasn't as good an actress as I believed.

I couldn't have been because if I had, Ren would never have suspected any other meaning than sweet connection thanks to the freshly finished tattoo.

It was my fault he demanded to know what I meant.

It was my fault I couldn't answer him truthfully.

It was my fault he went out that night.

And it was my fault he stayed out until dawn and when he came back, lipstick stained his t-shirt and his hair was mused from another's fingers.

I didn't know if he'd slept with someone, but he'd definitely made out, and it ripped me apart.

I'd been hiding for years and I'd finally reached my limit.

I stayed away from him the next day and the day after that.

I made sure to wear socks long enough to cover my new artwork and even wondered if there would be a way to laser it off so I could pretend I'd never been so stupid.

For a week, our conversations consisted of stiff hellos, goodbyes, and how were your days, but it all came to a head on a Friday evening when his phone chirped on the coffee table.

He was in the shower after a long shift at the milk farm.

Normally, a Friday meant pizza or takeaway and a chilled evening in front of the TV, recharging after a long week.

Not this Friday.

This Friday, I picked up his phone and brought up the notification.

Ren Wild, the boy from the forest and avoider of company, had joined a hook-up site.

He'd been matched with three women in the area and had obviously messaged one because her reply was a simple: I'm interested for no strings. I don't want commitment, either. I'll meet you at Paddington's at ten p.m. Bring a condom.

* * * * *

Can you understand why I did what I did next?

Can you put aside your judgment just for a little while and give me some slack for being a bratty, stupid teenager who didn't grow up fast enough? Who chased away the one person she'd ever loved? Who ruined everything when it had all been so good?

If you can't, then I don't want you reading anymore—not that you will as I'm burning this in a few short days, anyway.

But if you can, then keep torturing yourself because it only gets messy from here.

Super messy.

End of the world, Ren leaving me, kind of messy.

Let's see…first there was Tom.

Then there was Larry.

After that…some boy I didn't get his name but tasted like blueberries from the lollipop he'd been sucking on.

The nights that Ren left and didn't come back till late, hopping in the shower almost the second he walked in the door, and unable to meet my eyes the next morning, were the nights I stopped wishing.

I stopped hoping that one day...Ren and me...well, I stopped being so young.

I finally accepted what he was telling me. There would never *be a Ren and me, and it was time I stopped killing myself over it.*

The best way to do that was to find a replacement.

I only kissed the boys.

Or at least, I did at the start. By the time Blueberry came around, I was itching for more, if only to erase the blistering emptiness inside me.

I let him touch me.

I let him kiss my breasts and press his fingers inside me.

And I felt nothing.

I think that destroyed me the most.

Here I was doing my best to move on, but my body was just as broken as my mind. The things Tina told me should happen like the tensing and the quickening and the sparkling orgasms never happened.

All I felt was the probing of unskilled fingers and the swirl of tentative tongue.

Some nights, when Ren stayed out super late, I'd feel so rotten, so sick, so twisted, that the next evening—regardless if it was a school night or not—I'd find a party somewhere and crash. I'd dance like a slut and encourage like a whore, and when a boy finally kissed me, I'd want to vomit with tearful disgust.

For almost a year, we co-existed in shame.

Him doing whatever it was he was doing, and me doing my best to move on.

I didn't want to be this doormat. I didn't want to be this weak. When I hooked up with a guy, I pinned all my hopes and dreams on him and truly listened to what he had to say. I laughed at his jokes, even if they weren't funny. I answered his questions, even if they were hard, and I truly did my best to make a connection so I could find some self-worth after so many years of self-hate.

But it never worked.

No matter how much I tried to release myself from Ren, returning to him every night, living with him, loving him...it tied me up into knots I could never be free from.

I often thought about leaving.

Of running away so I could stop being so weak.

But every time I thought about waking up without him, of living in a world without him, I couldn't do it. I'd unpack the bag I'd hastily stuffed in the darkness and accept that this was my punishment for every sin I'd committed.

The one saving grace was Ren never saw a woman twice.

Believe me, I knew.

I became a master of reading his phone when he was in the shower, skimming over past messages and investigating new ones.

For some reason, even knowing he was running to these women to fuck, I still felt better than them because he returned to me afterward. They might borrow his body, but I ruled his heart, and he was still mine.

Until...one day, that assurance and kingdom that I'd always treasured was threatened to be invaded by infidels.

A second date.

A woman who went by the name Rachel989.

Her message carved out my heart with an ice-cream scooper: I had fun last night. I know we agreed it was a one-time thing, but there's something about you. I'd love to see you again.

I would've deleted it and hoped Ren never saw it.

If it wasn't for his reply: Okay. Tonight. Same place.

I'd rushed to the sink and thrown up.

Dramatic right?

Yep, I said so to my body. I schooled it for the long minutes that Ren was in the bathroom, and I plastered on a fake smile when he came out dressed in a black button-down and faded jeans that hugged him like a second skin. His sable hair was tussled from rough towel-drying. His lips pouty and almost sad. His eyes dark with unshared things.

He was drop-dead gorgeous, and he didn't even know it.

Of course, this Rachel989 would want a second date. She would want him for a third and a fourth and marriage, too. And I'd finally been slapped in the face with my reality.

Ren was twenty-seven, almost twenty-eight. He was at the age when people settled down and started families of their own. He would eventually replace me with his own sons and daughters…and wife.

And as he kissed my cheek and asked what I had planned for the evening, I marvelled at how steady my voice was. How I could fib so effortlessly when every piece of me was breaking. How I could stand there with my bones shattered and organs splattered on the kitchen floor.

That was my true performance because he never knew how much I sobbed the moment he closed the door, promising to be home soon.

I sobbed so much I couldn't breathe, and my tears were no longer tears, but great heaving, ugly convulsions where hugging myself didn't work, where lying to myself didn't work, where promises that it would get better definitely didn't work.

I'm sure you can probably guess what I did next?

If you can't, then you've never been in love with someone who was off making a future with someone else.

Wiping away my grief, I crawled to my phone and went on the Facebook group listing campus parties in my area. There was one that a student at the local university that I'd considered applying at for their creative writing course was hosting.

It was late.

The party was probably winding down by now, but I stripped and climbed into the shower. I shaved every part of me. I styled and painted and slipped into the little black dress I'd worn on the night of my seventeenth birthday.

Unlike that night, when I wore new red lingerie that I hoped peeked out beneath the black straps, tormenting Ren at dinner, this time, I wore nothing.

I wasn't playing games anymore.

I was done, and this was war.

I caught an Uber to the party as my killer heels would break my ribbon embroidered foot before I could arrive, and I sashayed my way into the tipsy crowd, looking for a particular kind of prey.

A boy of pretty origins, slightly drunk, single, and up for fun.

And when I found him, I pulled him to the side and told him the truth. I hid my cracked voice behind a sultry beg and said, "I'm in love with someone else who doesn't want me. I'm a virgin who doesn't want to be innocent anymore. I want to forget...about all of it."

I'd pulled away, expecting him to run but needing him to understand that I wasn't going to be an easy lay. I would be skittish and jumpy and most likely cry at some point, but I'd chosen him and all I expected him to do was relieve me of the one thing that I'd started to hate.

I didn't want to be a virgin anymore because Ren most definitely wasn't.

He'd waited until he was nineteen but on the cusp of my eighteenth, he'd well and truly ensured I had a fair number to sleep with before I caught up to him.

Any idiotic concepts I'd had of saving myself for him—of him waking up one day and climbing into my bed with words like how stupid he'd been and how much he loved me and wanted me and needed me and then he'd kiss me and touch me and fill me and...

I sighed, blinking with my freshly painted eyelashes and waited for this pretty stranger to save me.

To make his life easier, I opened my beaded bag and pulled out a condom.

The first condom from the box of twelve that Ren had bought for me. Inside my bag, all I had was some cash, my phone, and two more condoms. Because who knew if once would be enough to ease the agony in my soul?

"What's your name?" the pretty stranger asked.

I paused, wanting to use a fake one to protect me from any future pain but determined to ruin myself as much as I could, to prove I was brave enough to survive anything. "Ribbon. Della Ribbon."

He rubbed the back of his neck, disrupting his dark blonde hair, blinking with baby blue eyes, looking the exact opposite of Ren.

I was glad.

I wanted to look into this stranger's face when he was inside me and have no doubt that he wasn't Ren.

"And his name?" he murmured as he stepped closer, cupping my chin and studying me. "The guy who's just thrown you away?"

My eyes burned, but I kept the sobs away. "Wild. Ren Wild."

It was the first time no one believed we were related. Two different last names. Two different futures.

"Well, Della Ribbon," the stranger said. "He just made the biggest mistake of his life." Drawing me close with his fingers on my chin, he kissed me sweetly.

I suppose I should stop there.

I should fade to black and let your imagination fill in the blanks, but I'm feeling extra martyr-ish today, so I'm going to tell you what happened.

It was nice, really. Exactly what I'd asked for.

First, I kissed him back.

I willed my mind to blank and gave everything had into his control. The kiss was innocent to start with, warm lips and soft touches, but then he took my hand and guided me through the stragglers still lolling on couches and drinking against walls and led me upstairs.

My legs shook and the draft from not wearing underwear reminded me exactly what I was about to do.

Part of me screamed not to do this, that I wasn't ready, while the other stabbed her pitchfork into the dirt of my soul and screeched that it was.

I was ready to be an adult.

I'd been ready for so, so long.

"Don't you want to know my name?" the pretty stranger asked as he guided me into a room with a queen bed, white bedding, and a mountain of pillows.

It was a girl's bedroom.

I didn't know whose house this was or where this room's owner was, but I didn't care as the stranger spun me around and pressed me against the wall.

"Do you?" he asked again, his eyes blazing blue, his lips wet and waiting.

"Is it wrong if I say no?" I dropped my gaze, expecting him to leave. I didn't know why I didn't want to know his name. After all, I needed something to remember him by. He would forever be part of my life—taking my virginity would tie him to me regardless if I wanted it to or not.

But he smiled softly, nodding as if he understood. "Are you going to pretend I'm him?" He kissed me gently, waiting for me to reply.

Against his lips, I murmured, "I don't want to, but I can't promise anything."

How lucky was I? How incredibly lucky to be honest and not have to pretend to be brave and sexy. I didn't have to hide my shakes. I didn't have to fake my fear.

He kissed me again, and I opened my mouth, licking him. When he pulled away for a breath, I moaned, "I don't want to think about him. That's the point."

"Well, think about me then. Think about where I touch you..." His fingers trailed down my face to my breast, cupping me with a pressure that wasn't enough. "Think about where I kiss you..." He pressed his mouth to my neck, sending coils of desire through my belly. "Think about where I'm going to fill you..." His fingers drifted down my thigh and hooked under the hem of my dress. With locked eyes, he shoved aside the material and skated his touch, up and up.

I bit my lip, breathing fast as he touched me between the legs and found I wore *no underwear.*

A firework of surprise showed in his blue gaze as his fingers feathered over my newly shaved mound. "You truly came here to do this…didn't you?"

I nodded as he pressed a finger inside me.

The condom in my hand fluttered to the floor as his mouth found mine again and kissed me deep.

I sighed, clutching at his shoulders and letting my bag drop to where the condom landed.

The stranger could kiss.

His fingers felt better than other boys who'd touched me.

And it didn't take long for my body to shed its sadness and welcome any other feeling but heartache.

I spread my legs, pressing my spine against the wall and hooking my fingers into his belt.

He groaned as I cupped his erection, tracing the hardness, learning that his length and girth were impressive and would most likely hurt me.

I shivered harder, a mix of terror and lust making me jumpy. My mind was nothing but fog—a mist where no thought could find me apart from touch.

Kiss.

Finger.

Sex.

No Ren.

No breaking hearts.

No Rachel989s.

My hand worked harder on his belt as he made me wet. His one finger morphed to two, stretching me in all the right ways. My head turned heavy, my eyes hazy as I struggled to free him.

Ducking to his knees, the stranger hooked my leg over his shoulder and kissed me in a place no one else had before.

His tongue ran over my smooth seam, flicking on the clit I'd been told did wonderful things but still had yet to learn them.

My knees almost buckled as lightning bolts appeared from nowhere. I latched my fingers into his hair, a flash of Ren filling my head with his sable copper locks.

I bashed my head into the wall behind me, wanting him out, needing him gone so I could enjoy this.

This wasn't because of him.

This was because of me.

And he was once again ruining it.

"Della Ribbon…" the stranger moaned as his tongue entered me, and I collapsed into his arms. Pressing me against the carpet, he climbed on top of me, his hips thrusting between mine, his metal zipper cold against my heated wetness.

I squirmed beneath him, needing more, instinct making me reach for him and unbuckle his belt.

His hands fumbled for the condom on the floor as I successfully unbuckled his belt then unzipped his jeans. The minute I shoved them down his legs, followed quickly by his boxers, I gasped at the size.

I didn't want to get hurt, but ouch, I couldn't imagine how he'd fit inside me.

"It's okay," the stranger murmured as he arched his hips and rolled the condom on. Once sheathed, he cupped my cheek again. "I'll do my best not to hurt you."

I nodded. I didn't know what for, but I was grateful. Out of all the horny teenagers I could've chosen, this boy wasn't like them. He took his time. He kissed me sweet. He smoothed my trembles and wiped a rogue tear away as his kisses swept me away from Ren and delivered me to Ren at the same time.

"Do you want me to stop?" he whispered as my legs tried to clamp around his hips, feeling the strangeness of hard man against the soft yielding of me.

I paused, biting my lip, staring at the ceiling with a chest full of icicles and dread.

Did I want him to stop?

Not really.

Did I want him to hurry?

Yes.

Pulling his head back down to mine, I kissed him with heat and demand. "I want you to finish this."

His eyebrows knitted together as if I'd hurt him, but his lips sought mine again as his hand wrapped around my hipbone. "I should do this in a bed for your first time." His other hand disappeared between us, guiding the tip of him to my entrance.

I stiffened as the first press of him warned that this wasn't a joke.

This was happening.

"I don't care."

I was about to lose every shred of innocence I had left to a boy I didn't know his name.

"Wait." I pushed at his shoulders.

He gritted his teeth but didn't try to enter me. "You changed your mind?"

Resting my hands on his ass, I pulled him into me, making his eyes widen and mouth pop wide. As he sank into me, I shook my head. "No. But I want to know your name."

He groaned as his length slid inside me, then hit an obstruction that pinched and burned.

He looked at me, looked through me, looked right into the person I was and said, "My name is David."

David.

Della and David.

It had a nice ring to it.

We poised on the point of no return, his elbows jamming into the floor beside

---

my ears, holding himself above me. "Do you want me to finish, Della Ribbon?"

My heart gave one massive kick of denial before I nodded. "Yes..."

And the rest is history.

He thrust inside, tore apart my virginity, and tried to be as gentle as he could. All the while, tears leaked from my eyes, and I kissed him with a ferocity that ended up with us rolling around on the floor as I fought him for power.

I wanted him to pin me down and take everything I had to give. Instead, he let me manipulate him. He allowed me to roll him onto his back and ride him on top, not caring that my insides hurt or the pleasure in my blood was mixed up, screwed up, and so far away from heaven that it sent me plummeting to hell where I surely deserved to live.

It lasted longer than I thought it would.

His thrusting sent ripples through me, his harsh breathing and tattered groans made me feel powerful and wanted, but when his pace increased and his fingers tightened and his kisses deepened, I didn't leap into the void with him.

He came.

I didn't.

He kissed me.

I kissed him back.

And then my cell phone rang, putting a full stop on one of the strangest paragraphs of my life.

Funny how Ren knew the exact moment to call. Almost as if he had some sixth sense telling him what I'd just done.

I ignored it.

Most of the time, I got home before Ren even noticed I was missing.

But not that night.

Unfortunately, or fortunately—depending on how you look at it—he caught me on the worst one, ringing me again, just as I was wiping a Kleenex between my legs and marvelling at the smear of blood.

Once again, I let it ring as I exited the bathroom attached to the bedroom where I'd lost my virginity and padded barefoot to David.

He pulled me into his arms, kissing my temple and hugging me close. "I'm sorry I wasn't who you wanted."

I kissed his chest before letting him go to put his t-shirt on. "You were the best person for me to lose it with. I'm glad it was you."

He smiled. "Well, I'm honoured." Buckling his jeans, he stood awkwardly by the door as I rearranged my dress. "Do you want to...eh, stay in touch?"

My heart fluttered at the way he looked at me. At the fascinated puppy dog crush that no doubt made him feel all protective and smitten with a girl who begged for sex in such a sad, pathetic way.

I smiled, picking my beaded bag off the floor and stuffing the two unused condoms inside. "It's fine. I knew what I was doing. You don't have to worry about me."

My phone danced around again, chirping its annoying little chirp.

"Are you going to get that?" he asked.

"Why? It only hurts."

He held open the door for me to exit the room. "Want me to talk to him?"

I laughed. "That would be interesting."

The chirping grew louder, and I sighed. "He'll be concerned about me."

"In that case, you better answer it." Tucking a curl behind my ear, he murmured, "Come find me after. We'll have a drink. Get to know each other a little."

The fact that he liked me enough to want to hang out even though he'd already gotten me into bed made me warmer than I'd been in a while. "Sure."

With a handsome smile, David left me alone as I sucked in a steadying breath and smoothed down my dress one last time.

I pressed accept on the call. "Hello?"

My voice was empty and flat like it was most of the time these days, and I didn't have time to fix on the Della false brightness and strength that Ren was used to hearing from me.

"Della?" His tormented tone slipped into my ear making tears stab my eyes. "Where are you?"

"I'm safe, don't worry."

"That's not what I asked."

I let silence gather between us as I stared at floral wallpaper in some stranger's house.

"Della?" His voice dropped to a whisper. "Tell me where you are. What happened?"

Now, there were two scenarios I could've done and knowing the outcome of the one I chose, I should've gone for the other one.

I should've told him I was fine, and that I'd be home soon. I should've kept my secrets just a little longer, hidden my heartbreak for just a little more, but with my insides bruised from another man and that same man actually wanting to spend time with me, I was done playing this part.

I was through pretending and wanted to ensure the canyon that'd formed between us could never be repaired.

And I had the perfect way to do it.

"Della, answer me," Ren commanded.

So I answered him.

I told him things I should've taken to my grave because who wants to hear about another being so vindictive and lost they'd practically do anything for a sliver of happiness.

"I'm at a house party a few blocks from home. I Ubered here in my little black dress with no underwear, and I selected a boy from the dwindling crowd."

His harsh inhale sounded like thunder in my ear.

"Do you want me to continue?" I breathed, rubbing at the fiery ruin of my

heart.

"*Yes,*" *he strangled.* "*Finish. Tell me.*"

"*This boy kissed me and took me upstairs, and I told him I was a virgin who was tired of being a child. I asked him to relieve me of it.*" *Tears cascaded down my cheeks as I confessed, knowing full well I broke his heart as well as mine.* "*And…he did.*"

Ren hung up.

Chapter Fifty-Nine

REN

2018

IT WASN'T HARD to find her.

Whatever Facebook group she joined, I joined too.

Whatever event she tagged as interested in attending, I clicked the button too.

Thanks to social media, I knew more about Della's schedule than she thought, and tonight was no different.

I killed my bike outside the house.

Music still filtered from cracked windows with a few shadows of people dancing in the living room. I wanted to stab out my heart that this was the place where Della had come for comfort instead of confiding in me.

I'd failed her so fucking much.

When she'd answered on the third call, I'd been relieved but furious. I'd wanted to tear into her to delete some of the panic in my blood, but that was before I heard her voice. Before the hollow defeat replaced her normally beautiful tone, hinting that tonight…something had happened.

I'd wanted to yell at her for leaving me. I'd wanted to demand her excuses why I'd come home to an empty apartment after meeting a girl I'd met online for the second time.

I'd come home early.

I should never have gone.

It was a mistake.

Every meeting was a mistake.

I'd had a drink with her and let her down gently, my only thought of returning to Della and laughing with her at something stupid on TV or debating the pros and cons about a new camping device.

Each woman I hooked up with was just buying me time, even

though I felt it running out. I told myself things between me and Della would go back to the way things were if I got my rampant desire under control. That it wasn't her I dreamed about but some nasty side effect of not having sex for so long.

I'd done my best to believe my lies. I'd honestly wished they were true as I smiled at faceless women and touched unwanted places.

It didn't matter that my lust was being controlled, it didn't stop my dreams becoming more graphic or my days become more difficult the deeper I fell into Della.

I could fuck every female I could find but in the end…no one could cure me but her.

And now, I'd hurt her so much she'd snapped just like I had.

She'd willingly chosen self-harm because it was the only way to leach out some of the pain.

So yes, I wanted to be livid with her. I wanted to strike her, grab her, kiss her with every red-tinted rage, but hearing such desolation from the girl I loved, I couldn't do it.

All I cared about was her safety, her happiness.

All I needed was to get her home.

I clutched at my hair, digging fingernails into my scalp, doing my best to get myself under control. I didn't want to think about what she'd told me. I didn't want to visualise what she'd done. And I daren't focus on how crippled I was knowing she was no longer a virgin.

"Yo, man, party's over." A tipsy boy waved my way, his arm slung over some brunette as they made their way down the garden path. For a house party, the place was well tended with manicured bushes and lush grass.

I didn't know why that bothered me. Why this place was ten times nicer than the apartment Della and I shared or that whoever had accepted her invitation to sleep with her might come from much better stock than me.

He might have money, manners, and mansions.

And what did I have?

Fucking nothing because Della had deliberately torn out my heart and ensured nothing would ever be right again.

Swinging my leg over the bike, I ignored the leaving couple and marched up to the front door. Pushing it open, I entered the cream foyer and narrowed my eyes at the reek of booze and weed.

Only a few lights were on, scattered like islands in the darkness as I made my way through the living room to the kitchen to the den.

No signs of a blonde girl in a black dress.

With sick despair, I followed more rooms, past making out

students and giggling girls until I stumbled upon the one thing I couldn't live without.

Curled up in another man's arms, her cheeks pink as he murmured something in her ear.

His hand on her thigh. His lips on her throat.

It was more than I could fucking bear.

Della ran a fingertip along the rim of a champagne glass looking every inch an adult. There was nothing girlish about her with her sex-tussled hair, tight dress, and jaded look in her stunning blue eyes.

I stumbled at the sight as the man grabbed a blanket from the back of the couch and draped it over her lap, stroking her softly. She smiled in thanks, tucking it behind her, hiding the long expanse of beautiful legs, sneaking away the ribbon tattoo complete with its R.

I thought I couldn't stand seeing him touch her before. But it was nothing compared to the shredding, slashing sorrow now.

"Della," I breathed, marching as steadily as I could toward them.

She froze. Her eyes round and shooting to mine. "Ren...what—what are you doing here?"

My hands curled as the man looked me up and down, studying me, judging me, waging war with just one glance.

Tearing my eyes from my enemy, I said, "I came to take you home."

She sipped her half-full champagne. "I'm not ready to go home yet."

Anger sneaked over my pain, granting me safe haven from my misery. I latched onto it, desperate to feel anything but the grief I had no right to feel. "Don't argue with me."

"Don't command me then."

"I'm not commanding you."

"Yes, you are." Her eyes narrowed. "I'm a big girl, Ren. Run along back to Rachel989."

I stiffened. "What?"

"You heard me." She slugged back the rest of the drink in one mouthful.

"I can take her home. Don't worry about her," the man dared to say.

I didn't look at him, keeping my eyes fixed on Della as I tried and failed not to see the change in her. The new knowledge in her gaze. I'd hoped...

Fuck, I'd hoped it was a lie.

That she'd said something so hurtful on the phone just to punish me, but now, I knew.

She was telling the truth, and she'd fucked the guy currently holding her close like I wanted to do.

And *shit*...that fucking hurt.

"Della. Now." I growled, quickly losing my temper. I'd never beaten someone up before, but if I didn't get her out of his grip soon, I would.

Shoving off the blanket, Della swooped upright. Fire blazed in her eyes as she stalked in bare feet and stabbed me hard in the chest with her finger. "You don't get to boss me around any longer. I'm almost eighteen, Ren. You don't get to baby me anymore."

Grabbing her wrist, I jerked her through the space and toward the front door. "You and I need to talk."

"Hey!" She struggled. "Let me go." Her fingernails scratched my skin, but I didn't release her.

The front door beckoned, night sky and streets to get lost in before we had a conversation that would probably end us forever.

"Oi!" A hand landed squarely between my shoulder blades, shoving me forward.

Stumbling, I instinctually let go of Della so I didn't make her trip with me then spun to face who'd dared touch me.

The man.

"David, don't!" Della called, tripping to get between us.

But it was too late.

All the pain and regret manifested in my fists, and I swung without thinking.

David ducked, his blond head narrowly missing being hit.

He rammed his shoulder into my chest, sending us both slamming to the ground.

"Stop! Both of you!" Della screamed.

We didn't listen.

I kneed him in the ribs, sending him rolling to the side. He shot to his feet, trying to punch me again.

I punched him first.

I wanted to *kill* him.

My broken wrist, long healed from being cow-kicked, twinged as I swung hard and true and connected with his jaw.

He reeled backward, right into Della.

Oh, fuck no.

I charged forward, intending to throw him off her, but she pushed David to the side and leaped in front of me.

Slamming on the brakes, I managed to avoid bowling her over. "*Move*, Della."

She crossed her arms. "No."

David stood behind her, his eyes glittering with malice and

triumph. He knew he'd won because he'd had what I couldn't. He'd taken the most precious thing in the world to me, and fucking gloated about it.

I couldn't help it.

I couldn't walk away from this without making him bleed. He'd fucking destroyed me; it was the least I could do.

I swung again, aiming over Della's shoulder at the bastard's face. Only, she shied the wrong way. David bumped her, sending my fist half into his jaw and half into Della's temple.

"Fuck!" Catching her as she fell, I choked on worse pain I could've imagined. I'd come here wanting to hurt someone, and I'd ended up hurting her.

She moaned, cupping her head with a wince.

David tried to grab her, but I snarled in his face. "Touch her and I'll kill you." I wasn't joking. I didn't need any other reason to murder him. I *wanted* to kill him. Needed to.

He heard the raw truth in my tone.

He froze, allowing me to hoist her into my arms like a groom would carry a bride and stumble through the house to the front door.

Della mumbled something under her breath, her fingers tangled in blonde curls as she rubbed where I'd hit her.

"I'll make it better. I promise," I groaned as I carried her down the steps and across the garden to my bike.

Standing on the threshold, David didn't follow us as I gently placed her on the back of the bike, mounted, revved, and sought her arm to latch it tight around my waist.

She still had strength even if I'd dazed her, and the feeling of her hugging me even if she didn't want to sent my heart smoking with sadness.

"This is my place, Della Ribbon," David called over the rumble of the engine. "Come by anytime."

I fed gasoline to the rumble, turning it into a snarl, ripping from the curb and away from all manner of agonies.

The entire time I drove, all I could focus on was David calling Della by *my* nickname.

She'd allowed a stranger to share something so intimate.

She'd allowed a stranger to take her innocence, and all that was left between us were past mistakes and future heartbreaks.

* * * * *

Home.

A word that was supposed to mean contentment, safety, and love.

Now, it meant nothing as Della leapt off the back of my bike the moment we arrived and cleared the stairs to our apartment before I'd even turned off the engine.

I sighed heavily, killing the rumble and locking up.

Coming home to an empty place before had been a nightmare, but heading inside with a pissed off female who had every right to be angry was even worse.

My boots thumped on the steps as I went to her, stalking over the threshold before closing and bolting the door.

I found her sitting on the couch with a bag of frozen peas held against her temple.

Shit.

Raking hands through my hair, I lingered by the coffee table, not knowing how to fix this. "Della, I'm...I'm sorry."

"You're sorry?" Her eyes flashed as her head snapped up. "Sorry for ruining my night, sorry for punching my date, or sorry for hitting me?" She threw the peas at my face. "What *exactly* are you apologising for, Ren?" She laughed coldly. "Maybe you're apologising for sleeping with half of the female population over the past year? Maybe you're apologising for walking out night after night and leaving me here alone, wondering where the hell you are and who the hell you're doing." She crossed her arms tightly as if warding herself against me. "What do you want to apologise for because I'm confused."

"I didn't sleep with them. Well..." I rubbed the back of my neck. "Not all of them."

"Oh, excuse me for thinking you'd turned into a man whore." She flung up her hands. "Really, you're just a regular male, aren't you? Sleeping around, looking for someone to make you happy."

"You. *You* make me happy."

"Ha! Yet you've never tried to sleep with me."

"*What?!* No, of course not. You're Della! You're—you're—"

"I'm what? Too innocent for you, Ren? Too young? Do you look at me and still see a child because you better open your damn eyes. I haven't been one in a long time." She smiled thinly. "And now I've joined the ranks of adulthood. I'm not a virgin—"

"I don't want to hear it." I held up my hand. "Stop."

"Oh, you don't want to listen? You don't want to know how he took me or what it felt like? Then again, I'm sure you don't need to know. I almost forgot. You have enough experience of your own to fill in the blanks."

"Della, just stop."

"No, how about *you* stop, Ren. You know what I realised tonight?" Her cheeks flamed red as her eyes welled with furious tears. "I realised I hate myself. I hate what I've become. I hate everything I stand for, and I'm done. You hear me? I'm *done*. School is almost finished and instead of moping about wishing for things I can't have, I'm focusing on my future. Did you know David goes to the college who hosted the party tonight? I told him I'm interested in creative writing...that I might want to be a storyteller like you used to be or maybe a journalist or writer or I dunno.... All I know is, I'm moving on. No more thoughts of running back to the forest with you. No more make believe. This is real life, and I'm letting it pass me by. I'm going to enrol next week, so I know where I belong."

Her shoulders slouched with weariness I hadn't seen until now. "I'm weak for giving up, but I tried. I really did."

I stepped toward her, hesitant, wary. "Tried what? What aren't you telling me?"

Her fatigue faded with yet more crackling rage. "Are you really that blind? Do you honestly not know? Or maybe it's because of me. Maybe because you raised me, you can't see past the mess of being sole guardian to an entirely reliant child. And maybe that's my fault for not realising that sooner; for believing that the love we share wasn't just one-dimensional but could grow into something different."

She glowered at the ceiling, tears trailing paths down her cheeks. "God, I've been so *stupid*."

Every inch of me begged to go to her, to hug her close and do my best to shield her from her unhappiness, but I couldn't move. I daren't do anything because right here, right now, the end gaped wide between us, and I didn't want to fall into the abyss.

I didn't want to be faced with the reality that had been slowly gathering ever since Cherry River.

"Della...don't," I begged. "Don't do this."

I didn't understand what I pleaded for, only that I wasn't ready. I'd *never* be ready.

She cocked her chin, shaking with blonde hair wild and a red mark I'd graced her with on her temple. Her ribbon tattoo flashed on her naked foot, snaking up her ankle.

She was gorgeous, and she was wrong that I'd been blind.

I'd seen her changing. I'd watched her transform from sweet girl to stunning woman, but I was responsible for her well-being. I was the one who had all the power whether she acknowledged it or not. And having that sort of power was a terrible burden to bear.

I would always be hers, but I couldn't be what she was looking for. I couldn't block her from growing into who she needed to become. I couldn't put my own hopes and dreams onto her and read between lines that weren't really there, hoping that there might be some way, some chance, that our friendship could be something more.

Something that wasn't sick and twisted.

Something that wasn't morally wrong.

"Let's go to bed. It's been a long night. We can finish this in the morning." I wanted a truce, a peace treaty until daylight chased away this corruption.

But Della pinned me to the floor with an angry sniff and a flash in her blue eyes. "No. I'm done waiting." Grabbing the hem of her dress, she yanked it over her head.

I stumbled back as she tossed the scrap of material to the floor and stood naked before me.

My heart hissed with possession. My body hardened with need. And my eyes feasted on curves and shadows of the most beautiful woman I'd ever seen.

I was utterly spellbound and trapped. If she moved toward me, I wouldn't have been able to run. If she kissed me, I would've have been able to stop what I desperately wanted to do.

The end would've come in a totally different form.

And who knows where that path would've led us.

But she didn't chase.

She didn't try.

Instead, she held her head high as if proving to herself that standing naked before me wasn't as poignant as she'd believed. That it wasn't anything special when it was the most special thing in the world.

My heart cramped with so many things as she planted her hands on her hips, pinned me to the floor with a merciless glare, and said coldly, "Take a good look, Ren Wild. See for yourself what you've been trying to deny. I'm not a girl anymore. I haven't been for a long time, and now…it's too late."

I couldn't breathe as she added, "You know…for so long I was terrified that I'd strip in front of you and you'd scold me like a little girl. That I'd bare everything I've become and you wouldn't see. But the way you're looking at me…you *do* see. You see but it's not enough. It will *never* be enough."

Stepping with willow legs and fairy grace, she closed the distance between us and whispered, "I lied to you, Ren. I've been lying for years, but this time, this time I'm speaking the truth when I say, I don't need you anymore. I don't want you. I can survive without you no matter what life throws my way. Isn't that what you wanted to hear? To know I'm self-sufficient? That I won't make your existence any harder than I already have?" Cupping my cheeks, she breathed, "Cherry River was a mistake but not in the way I led you to believe."

I trembled beneath her hold.

I was so fucking close to snapping.

Her fingers so soft and sinning on my face.

"I made you believe that I kissed you as an experiment and maybe I did, but that wasn't the real reason." Her tormented gaze drifted to my mouth. "I kissed you because I wanted to. I deliberately waited until you were asleep to have *you*—the boy I loved above everyone—give me my first kiss." She laughed under her breath, tortured and hollow. "Up until tonight, I'd stupidly hoped you'd be the first of so many things. That can never happen now."

I swallowed back a wash of grief, once again slammed with the knowledge she'd slept with someone else. Someone had been inside her. Someone had loved her who wasn't me.

I wanted to punish her for that.

I wanted to touch her, kiss her, press her against the fucking wall and screw the consequences, but then I was crushed beneath mental pictures of her naked, back arched, and lips kissed as that bastard traitor from the party thrust inside her.

I stumbled backward, burning beneath hot jealousy. I gulped back every need and looked at her sternly. "Go to bed, Della."

"Oh, don't worry, Ren. I'm going. But not before I prove to myself I'm stronger than I thought." Her touch reached for me again, softening to a caress as her thumb traced my bottom lip and she stood on her tiptoes, bringing her mouth to mine.

I froze as she kissed me.

Innocent.

Sweet.

It was the hardest thing I've ever done not to kiss her back.

Not to ruin that innocence.

Every muscle turned rigid at the invasion, the seduction. My eyes begged to close. My lips pleaded to part and give in.

I was seconds away from throwing it all away and taking what I wanted, but then she was gone, dropping her touch and smiling with every nightmare in the world. "Goodbye, Ren Wild. Goodbye to fallen dreams and impossible fantasies."

When she turned her back on me, I couldn't tear my eyes off her perfect ass as she walked bravely across the lounge to the corridor.

Every part of me wanted to follow, still spellbound and broken.

Just before she disappeared into the darkness, she looked back.

Her eyes locked on mine.

Her lips parted.

Her breath caught.

And we stood trapped in a physical embrace even while apart.

My willpower cracked enough to put one foot in front of the other as I *begged* to have her.

Then she shattered it by smiling soft and sweet like she'd done since she was a girl and dropped her eyes. "I'm sorry, Ren…for everything. But things will be better now. I promise. I'm done making life difficult…for both of us."

She left without a backward glance, leaving me in the rubble of our lives, stupidly believing anything could be better now everything had been destroyed.

She didn't come back even though I stood there, silently screaming her name over and over for her to find me.

This couldn't be it.

This couldn't end.

We couldn't end.

But…we had.

We'd been honest for the first time in years and it had successfully proven what a dangerous game we'd been playing. We'd been willingly hurting each other. Twisting all that was good between us until there was nothing left.

My chest ached. My body throbbed.

I stood there for far longer than I should have.

Long after she'd headed to her bedroom.

Long after I heard the springs of her bed bounce and the click of her light signal she'd cocooned herself in the dark.

Only when my legs threatened to collapse did I trip across the lounge and grab her dress discarded on the floor.

I hugged it as I fell heavily on the couch.

I rocked with it as my mind flickered with images of her fucking another while flashes of her as a child made me sick.

I couldn't untangle the two. I couldn't accept the Della I loved with all my soul was now an adult. And not just any adult, but a woman who'd torn out my heart.

I switched from filthy obsessions to a racing track of warning.

Dawn wasn't far away.

A new day where even sunshine couldn't fix what was broken.

Della didn't need me anymore, but somehow, I needed her more than ever. I needed her more than I could stand. More than I could ever let her know.

She'd been honest with me tonight, and it was time I was honest in return.

We were both miserable. Both searching for answers when we only gave each other questions. Both looking for permission to circumstances no one could understand.

I had no excuse for my behaviour. I was haunted by a dream-kisser. In love with a figment of my imagination that disgustingly believed Della was my fantasy.

When really…she could never be.

Della was mine, and I was hers.

I was her protector. She was my best friend.

I'd seen her grow from baby to child to woman, and no matter how I felt about her, I would never be allowed to have her in any other way but family.

I would burn in hell before I did.

I should be able to happily stand by as she found a lover, a husband, and be proud that I gave her such a life.

So why did the thought of her finding such gifts make me want to tear out the remainder of my heart and deny her everything? Why did I want to trap her in this one-bedroom apartment for the rest of our lives, never letting her see others, never letting her be happy unless she was happy with me?

That wasn't right.

That wasn't healthy.

I would end up smothering her, and I loved her far too much to destroy her.

I couldn't have her, and I couldn't watch her walk away.

So there was only one thing I could do.

She was right.

She didn't need me anymore.

I'd done my part; I'd given her everything I had to give and now, I had to give her her freedom.

Once the idea manifested, I was grateful for the guidance. I didn't second-guess as I pushed aside the couch and pulled out the cash I'd saved under the floorboards. I moved quietly as I checked the contents of the forever-packed backpack and lashed the new tent Della had bought me to its bulk.

I wanted my removal from her life to take years. For something to say we were so entwined, so tied together that there was no possible way for me to walk away. But I didn't come across any knot or rope that couldn't be undone with the simple choice to leave.

Within thirty horrible minutes, I had everything I needed.

I stared at the corridor where she rested and took two steps toward her before I grabbed control again and nodded with determination.

This was what had to happen.

I'd hurt her.

I continued to hurt her just like she continued to hurt me, and we both shouldn't have to live in agony any longer.

Placing the cash on the coffee table, I looked around the apartment one last time. Grabbing a spare pen and a Post-it always housed next to the TV remote, I wrote the hardest letter of my life.

Della Ribbon,

I love you so much it hurts—

My hand paused.

My brain full of everything I wished I could tell her.

There was so much to say. So many confessions to share.

But in the end, I couldn't write any of them.

Goodbye, Della.

I put the pen down next to a years' worth of rent, picked up my backpack, and walked out the door.

Book Two

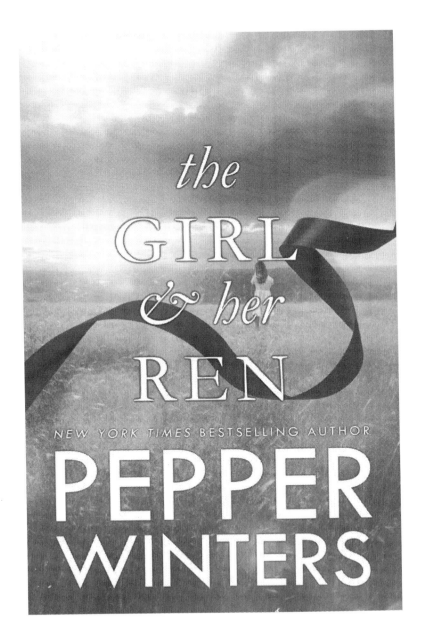

the GIRL & her REN

NEW YORK TIMES BESTSELLING AUTHOR

PEPPER WINTERS

DELLA

2032

FIRST, I WANT to say thank you.

Thank you for falling in love with Ren just as much as me. Thank you for allowing me to share our journey. Thank you for forgiving my youth, my jealousy, my possessiveness; but most of all, thank you for understanding what our story has always been about.

It wasn't about two children falling for each other.

It wasn't about sex or hunger or selfishness or want.

It was about love.

True love.

Love that spans decades, infects souls, and turns you immortal because, when you love that deeply, nothing can ever die.

It transcends time, space, distance, universes.

A love like this isn't confined to pages or photos or memories—it's forever alive and wild and free.

Love.

That is what our story is about.

Romance comes and goes, lust flickers and smoulders, trials appear and test, life gets in the way and educates, pain can derail happiness, joy can delete sadness, togetherness is more than just a fairy-tale…it's a choice.

A choice to love, cherish, honour, trust, and adore.

A choice to be there when arguments occur, and agony arrives, and fate seems determined to rip you apart.

A choice to choose love, all the while knowing it has the power to break you.

A choice, dear friend, to give someone your entire heart.

It's not easy.

No one ever said it was.

Some days, you want it back, and others, you wish you had more than just one heart to give.

Love is the hardest thing we'll ever have to do because love, as miraculous and *wonderful as it is, is also cursed and soul-breaking.*

Because of love, life is a war of moments and time and bargaining for more of everything.

But in the end, love is what life is about.

And love is the purpose of everything.

So, thank you.

Thank you for sharing our love.

Thank you for living, for choosing, for being brave enough to fall.

Chapter One

REN

2018

WHEN I RAN from the Mclary's, took a baby that wasn't mine, and chose to keep her against all odds, I never stopped to wonder...how.

How did we survive all those years?

How did I keep myself alive, let alone baby Della?

How did one choice change my entire world—not only giving me a family of my own, but teaching me, before it was too late, that not everyone was evil.

Della Mclary successfully stopped me from going down a very dark and lonely path by forcing me to know the opposite of hate. I supposed, if someone were to judge the kid I was against the man I became, they'd say she saved me.

They'd say, without her, I would be a very different person.

Probably one a lot less forgiving, understanding, and most likely violent, angry, and dangerous.

They'd be right.

Those tendencies were still there, born from being abused and unwanted, forever a part of me whether I wanted to admit it or not. But I was also so much more, and those parts, the *better* parts, were stronger.

I chose kindness over cruelty, honour over disgrace, and propriety over indecency.

And it was the last one that made me leave.

The last one causing my current state of unhappiness.

It also made all those previous wonderings of *how,* completely irrelevant. Because who cared how it happened? Only that it did, and it was the best thing that could've ever happened to me.

But now I had nothing, and I couldn't stop scratching at the scars, wondering what caused me to deserve seventeen years of heaven with a girl I'd give everything for, only to endure the worst thing I'd ever imagined by giving the greatest sacrifice I could.

Her.

She was my greatest sacrifice.

And I did it to protect her from so many, many things.

But the question was back. Taunting me. Tormenting me.

How.

How did she get into that backpack in the first place?

It was night. She was a baby. I didn't know where she slept, but surely, she had a crib with bars or a room with a door. The backpack was discarded where it always was by the door. It wasn't a plaything for a child and it wasn't sanitary for a baby.

But somehow, she'd ended up in it.

How had Della been in that bag at the exact same time I decided to run?

Was it purely coincidence? Did fate know far more than we did, understanding that Della wasn't born for the Mclary's but for *me?* For me to learn how to love. For me to have someone to hold. For me to protect and treasure and focus on rather than spiral into a place I shouldn't go?

Or…had Mrs Mclary put her there?

Had she seen my test run the night before, watched me steal the meagre rations I'd managed, and somehow put her darling daughter in the stuffy, weathered ex-army bag?

And if she did, that changed my question from how to why.

Why did she give up her only blood?

Why did she tell her husband to shoot me and specifically mention what I could have in my stolen bag as I ducked and bolted through their cornfields?

The only two answers I could come up with were:

One, she wanted me and Della dead and figured she could kill two birds with one stone, blaming me when they walked to my gunshot body and noticed the bullet that killed me also killed their daughter.

Or two, Mrs Mclary wasn't as evil or as complacent as I thought. Maybe she knew I was about to run and figured I was a better chance for Della than her husband ever was. The same husband who raped young girls when he believed his wife was upstairs asleep. The same husband who went to church and sang before God and donated at least an acre of produce every season. The same husband who was pure filth decorated in small town trust and lies.

Regardless of my questions, it didn't change the fact Della ceased being theirs that night and became mine instead.

Every year from the first to the last, I loved that girl as if she were my very own blood, sweat, and tears. Girl made from my bones. Child made from my heart. Woman made from my soul.

The perfect mirroring piece that reflected everything I'd never had, loving me as unconditionally as I'd loved her, making me believe that questions didn't matter when it came to us.

We were too important. Too perfect for one another. Too connected.

There was no argument. No denying. No elaborating the absolute truth. It didn't matter if she was six or sixteen; our bond was unshakeable.

Which was why leaving her was worse than the worst thing I could do. Why walking away wasn't just painful, it was suicidal.

I'd come alive the day Della became my family, and I died the day she ceased to be.

And it was my fault.

For so many years, I'd told myself my love was innocent.

I'd clutched onto my lies.

I'd hoped I could keep her, regardless of how my heart silently changed from protector to traitor.

But then, I woke up.

I saw the truth.

I understood the facts.

I tore out my godforsaken heart.

And my questions didn't matter anymore.

Because all I knew, all I wanted, all I could bear was redemption from everything I'd done wrong.

And for the first time in my life, I wished she'd never been in my backpack, after all.

Chapter Two

DELLA

2018

LET ME ASK you a question.

Why exactly are you still here?

Didn't I vow never to write in you again? Didn't I close your document, bury the file, and shove aside all memory of Ren Wild and the secrets I was stupidly sharing with you?

Yet…here you are, still lurking on my desktop, a judging little icon begging me for an ending.

But I manage to ignore your taunting. I keep my mouse pointer well away from your pain and open a new file labelled Assignment Version 2.0.

Or that's what I did for the past little while, at least.

I earned an extension when I had nothing to hand in to Professor Baxter. I blamed the flu—which normally wouldn't be a homework-delayable excuse—but I have a bit of a reputation at college, you see.

The reputation of being a quiet, diligent student who enrolled the very afternoon she finished her high school exams. The moment I was free, I walked out of those halls and marched to the university a few blocks away. They weren't open for new admissions yet, and I didn't have my results from English, math, and science—not to mention any legal identification.

But that didn't stop me.

I practically got on my hands and knees for a chance to attend. To know I had a place to go, an institution to hide in because I no longer had anyone to call my own.

They were strict on no special treatment, but something in my desperation must've swayed them because my pleas were answered nine days later, and I was accepted into the creative writing course that I'd coveted for a while.

And, thanks to skills used to fibbing about our truth, I was able to extend the deadline for providing personal documentation, enrolling without proving who I was.

All I cared about was a new adventure that would keep my thoughts far from

Ren—for however long it lasted.

Not that anything had that power…but I had to try.

The second I entered campus, I gathered a reputation that stuck.

I was known as the earliest arrival and last to depart. I studied with sheer-minded focus. I never answered back. I was hardworking and didn't make trouble.

Along with an academic reputation, people made assumptions about me as a person. They knew me as slow to smile and last to laugh. A reputation for being a loner who would rather celebrate her upcoming eighteenth birthday on her own, rather than risk her heart by asking friends to fill up the hole inside her.

They say I'm lonely. They call me sad. They murmur sympathies when they find out I'm almost eighteen, live alone, and have no family—

Anyway…why did I even open your file?

I have no ending to give you.

He hasn't come back.

It's been two whole months since he left.

One graduation in the past.

One birthday in the future.

And no one to love or kiss or—

You know what? That's not important.

What is important is I didn't die when he walked out the door.

Bet you thought I slept through him leaving. Did you picture me waking up after a good night's rest thinking everything would go back to normal after I'd stripped naked and kissed him?

Are you insane?

Of course, I didn't sleep that night.

I know Ren. Or at least, I knew Ren.

I knew I'd pushed him to his limit and there were only two places he could go.

One, he would stew all night. He'd weigh the pros and cons. He'd blame himself, his parenting skills, his lack of discipline, and beat himself up for doing something wrong. And if, by the dawn, he hadn't figured out there was something between us that wasn't mere unconditional love, then he wouldn't have been able to look at me again—for fear of what he'd become—and he'd leave.

Or two, he'd watch my naked body stroll bravely away after kissing him, and think for a moment. Just a moment. A delicious awareness-crackling moment when he realised he loved me too. And not in just a brother-sister kind of way, but an earth-moving, I-have-to-have-her-right-now kind of way. He'd run after me, shove me against the wall, and his lips would taste so sweet because it would be the first kiss he bestowed instead of the other way around.

Two options.

But I knew in my heart which one he'd choose.

And I'd known the instant the door clicked, and I padded in my cupid pyjamas to stare at the money left on the coffee table, the unfinished note *explaining nothing, and the woodsy, broody smell of Ren fading in the air, that I was right.*

He'd chosen option one.

My heart didn't know how to beat anymore. My lungs didn't understand what air was.

But tears?

They'd vanished.

Not one droplet escaped as I stared at the door, wishing, begging for him to return, and gather me in his arms.

I waited all night until the sun slipped through the curtains, gently kissing everything awake. Its kiss wasn't kind to me though, because it gave me the first day of many without him.

If someone had touched me that first dawn, I wouldn't have been able to keep it together. I would've broken on the outside as spectacularly as I broke on the inside.

But there was no one to touch me.

No one to tell me it would be okay.

I couldn't be a child and scream until my heart stopped suffocating. I couldn't destroy everything so I could purge the destruction inside me.

All I could do was cling to routine and head to the bathroom for a shower. I dressed in my school uniform. I ate some peanut butter toast with the crusts cut off. I gathered my school bag and walked the three blocks to school. I paid attention in class. I smiled at fellow students. I escaped the moment the bell rang. I slung my backpack up my shoulders and strolled to the supermarket close to our—my—apartment. After I chose a two-day-old lasagne that was discounted in the deli, one packet of Oreos, and an iced coffee, I walked back home. I ate, I watched TV, I did some homework, and I went to bed.

I did all that.

I, I, I.

Me, me, me.

And not once did anyone suspect that my world had just fallen apart.

Not once did I cry.

Not once did I scream.

I bottled it all up—the heartache, the agony, the bone-deep cracking—and I swallowed it down like a pill I didn't want to take.

And there it sat—a breathing, seething thing dark in my belly, blocking my usual appetite for adventure, food, and love.

Blocking me from feeling.

Blocking me from screwing up again.

The next day, I repeated the day before.

And the tomorrow after that.

And the tomorrow after that.

Until a week had passed and I hadn't died.

My worst nightmare of Ren leaving me had come true, and I was still alive.
And I hadn't cried.
Not once.
Not even a little bit.

Chapter Three

DELLA

2018

I CAN'T SEEM to go on my computer without somehow clicking on your icon and exposing a nightmare.

I should've deleted every word I ever typed, but last week, when I wrote to you against my wishes, I slept a little better.

I didn't wake drenched in sweat, fearing someone had stolen into the apartment while I rested. I didn't lie in bed in the morning, frozen solid with the thought of yet more faking, more living, more existing without him.

It was as if I had a friend again.

Two months and one week is a long time to be on your own with no one to talk to. I'd started this assignment with a new lease of hope. I'd stupidly believed by writing about him, I could make him come back. Every day I gave you my secrets, I clung to a fantasy that he'd somehow feel me spilling our life story and come back to reprimand me.

But when the due date with Professor Baxter came and went, and I claimed the flu to write a hasty tale of a girl with two parents who weren't monsters, I shut up all that pain again.

And I suppose you caught my lie, right?

I said I never cried.

And I didn't.

Unless you count the times I cried while writing this stupid assignment.

Anyway, I don't have the energy to type anymore today.

These memories are too painful. My tale too familiar.

I'm no longer part of a pair.

I'm singular.

Just Della.

And I have a life that I'm wasting.

A life that Ren gave me.

As much as I hate him for leaving, I can't destroy what he gave me.

I'm going to move on.
For him.
Even if it's the hardest thing I've ever done.

Chapter Four

DELLA

2018

IT'S BEEN ANOTHER three weeks.

Three months since he left, and it hasn't gotten any easier.

But...I actually have something to write about other than Ren.

To be fair, my life has been pretty mundane since the night Ren walked out the door. I've crammed as much as I could into daylight and night-time hours, doing my best to delete Ren piece by piece.

I've stopped asking myself ridiculous questions as I fall to sleep in an empty apartment.

I've given up trying to find answers I'll never earn and accept that what I did was unforgivable.

I shouldn't have kissed him.

I shouldn't have tried to change us.

I shouldn't have demanded more.

I'm nothing but numb bones, dazed heart, and paralyzed soul.

Who knows...maybe I'll always torture myself with that night. Maybe I'll always feel wretched for hurting him.

I just had to push and push, and when he had nowhere else to go, he did the one thing he was best at. He'd run from the Mclary's because they were monsters who tortured him; now he'd run from their daughter because she'd hurt him too much to repair.

I have nothing.

Nothing but regret and minutes upon minutes of time to contemplate the What Ifs. *The* What If *I'd let him go to bed and given him a few days to analyse how he felt? The* What If *I'd just been honest and said,* 'Ren...you know I love you, but what you don't know is I'm *in* love with you. Now, before you freak out, it's nothing to be afraid of and I understand if you don't feel the same way, but just in case you do...just in case some part of you that feels a tiny spark like I do, then let's figure it out. We always figure things out—together.'

And he'd say... 'Okay, Della. You're right. I do love you. Now, get naked.'

And we'd live happily ever after.

That's the worst kind of torture, isn't it? The horror where every outcome and scenario delivers a happier one than the life you're currently living.

But it all comes down to choices.

I chose to sleep with David, and I chose to slug back a few glassfuls of wine to dull the ache of entering womanhood. I chose to embrace my recklessness, strip, and yell at Ren.

I was tipsy and hurt.

And I wish I could take it all back.

But you already know all this, so I'll stop.

The real reason I wanted to write is...I needed someone.

Summer is well and truly here, and Ren is not, and that's left me empty to the point where I'll do anything to fill up the darkness inside me.

I'm ill-equipped for adulthood where I return to an empty apartment every night, the couch still smelling of him, the air still laced with his voice, and the night still warm with his hugs.

The memories nick my heart with their tiny, painful blades—giving me a thousand cuts until I bleed out slowly.

It's so slow, I don't even notice I'm dying.

I've run my immune system down. And the week after I handed in my assignment, I got sick.

Just a simple flu—karma for lying about being ill—but it knocked me on my butt. I could barely get out of bed from the body aches and fever. I had no food and no way of getting to a doctor without sneezing over some Uber driver.

I stayed in bed for two days, eating dried Ramen noodles because I couldn't stand up to put the kettle on from shivering so bad, and sipping tepid tap water for my raging sore throat.

In the middle of the second day, I honestly thought I would die, and no one was left to care.

Ren...ouch.

God, the pain never gets any easier to bear.

Thinking of him is a syringe full of poison to the heart. Dare murmur his name and it's a mallet to my bones. Risk imagining him sitting here, wiping away fever-sweaty hair and kissing my brow while feeding me chicken soup, and it's a cannonball to my entire chest.

By the third day of curling up with chattering teeth, I knew I couldn't keep doing this. I wasn't dead, but it wouldn't take much to finish me if I didn't stop grieving.

Ren would be furious if he knew I'd gone from chasing everything to uncaring about anything, especially after all the sacrifices he made for me.

That was the only reason I managed to grab my phone, log in to Facebook, and look up all the Davids close to me.

It took a few page refreshes and an hour of stalking social media, but I found him.

The man I lost my virginity to.

Technology connects all of us and, for some reason, I despise that.

I hate the fact there's no barrier anymore. No corner to hide from prying eyes.

David was easy to find, but not Ren.

He's no longer in reception.

He's returned to the wild that lives in his blood.

I have no way of contacting him and, believe me, I've tried. I've tried everything but smoke signals.

And thanks to that butcher's blade to the heart, I needed someone even more.

His Facebook page said his full name was David A. Strait. His birthday was New Year's Day, he was four years older than me, and according to his relationship status, he was single.

Funny that I'd willingly searched for the man who took my girlhood—a man I knew nothing about—yet almost cried in relief when I found him.

My message was lacking and needy:

Hi David,

You probably don't remember me, but I'm the girl who pathetically asked you to relieve her of her virginity. You took me up on the offer, and then got beaten up by the guy I was trying to forget. Remember that messy evening? If by chance I've jogged your memory, I hope it's not too forward to be honest with you again.

That guy? He walked out on me twelve weeks ago. I thought I was ready to survive on my own, but then I got sick. I hate that I'm asking you this and fully expect a hell no, but if you don't mind being kind to me one last time, I need your help. My address is Apartment 1D, 78 RuBelle Ave. I'm just a few blocks from your place actually— walking distance really...

I coughed wet and ugly as I pressed send.

It showed as delivered a few seconds later.

For a few hours, I dozed with congestion in my nose and a continent the size of Africa sitting on my head.

I almost forgot I was waiting until my phone chirped with new correspondence.

Even though I knew it wasn't Ren. Even though I knew, knew, knew I'd never get a text from him again; it didn't stop my ridiculous heart from jumping off a building and hurling itself onto painful concrete.

It wasn't Ren.

But it was the next best thing.

I'm on my way.
Love, David.

Chapter Five

DELLA

2018

SORRY IT'S BEEN so long.

I meant to tell you what happened when David appeared at my apartment, but the guilt…

The guilt of welcoming him inside, letting him sit on the couch Ren used to sleep on, offering him water from glasses Ren used to drink from, sharing the space that Ren used to share with me…

The guilt hurt even worse than the bone aches from the flu.

Not that I have anything to be guilty for.

I'm single. I'm alone. I've committed no crime.

So why does it feel like I've cheated so many times on Ren in the past few weeks?

Let me explain.

David arrived with store-bought mushroom soup, fresh ciabatta, and a pharmacy bag full of painkillers, decongestants, and throat lozenges.

I welcomed him in, almost hyperventilated having him in Ren's space, paid by Ren's money, made possible by Ren's sacrifices, and stiffened in his arms as he hugged me and said, "You can't stay here on your own. Pack a bag. You're coming with me."

I gave him complete control as he bundled me into some sort of Chrysler, and drove us silently to the very same house I'd lost more than just my virginity in— I'd lost Ren.

He guided me inside, past the tastily decorated lounge with wall stickers of life quotes, up the stairs and past the bedroom where we'd ended up screwing on the floor, to another at the end of the hall.

He welcomed me into his bedroom with its charcoal and black colour scheme, pulled back the sheets on a king bed, and cocked an eyebrow until I crawled exhausted into the offered cocoon.

He set up a tray and let me eat the soup in private and swallow a few pills before he returned with a box of tissues, a hot water bottle, and passed me the remote control for the large flat-screen above his dresser on the wall.

I camped in his bed for two days.

And this is so hard to admit, but…I felt something for him. Something warm and grateful and, when I could breathe through my nose and showered away the stickiness of sickness, I wanted to repay him for his unbelievable kindness.

So, when he asked me to stay, when he said he'd thought about me a lot and wanted to see what else was between us other than just a one night thing, I said yes.

I knew what I was doing.

I wasn't stupid to think I liked David enough after two days of him playing nursemaid to move in with the guy, but I was lonely, I was lost, and just like the first time David made me feel wanted, he had a knack at making me feel it again.

So…here is my latest confession.

For the past three weeks, I've been living at David's house.

Actually, right now I'm typing this ridiculous never-to-be-read assignment at the breakfast bar in his kitchen.

It feels like yet another betrayal to admit that.

But why should I suffer in a place that stabs me over and over again with memories of Ren when he left me so damn easily?

Why can't I run, just like him?

After I felt better, David took me home to gather some clothes, toiletries, laptop, and school gear, and we returned to his place, slightly awkward and a little afraid of what we'd just committed to.

I had no intention of letting the lease on my apartment go.

It wasn't just an empty home.

It was the last place Ren had shared with me.

I wasn't ready to say goodbye.

I only left because I was more afraid of sleeping another night on my own than sharing a house with a kind-hearted stranger.

If you're shaking your head, thinking I leapt straight into sleeping with him—you're wrong.

Three weeks and we haven't even kissed.

I'm innocent.

But at the same time, I can't lie to you.

I can't type the words that pigeon-hole David into the friendship-only box.

Just like that first night, there's a chemistry between us that simmers rather than burns. It heats up my blood just enough to melt the frost Ren left inside.

In the past three weeks, I've learned the A in David's full name stands for Alexander. That his dad is rich from aluminium manufacturing, and his parents bought him this house close to the university so he'd be warm and safe to study. The three-bedroom place is all his, but he opted to share with a girl whose room we'd shagged in that night.

She'd been away for the weekend, and David's room had already been stolen by other party-screwers.

The third bedroom was storage and a gym—the same gym that kept David's body trim and taut rather than fierce and strong like Ren's, thanks to a life of physical labour.

The first night I met Nathalie—who went by her favoured nickname of Natty—my hackles rose. After all, I'd gate crashed her cosy love nest with David.

But my worries were for nothing.

Natty adopted me as her sister and had a flair at finding the worst movies but making them the best with commentary and snacks.

Turns out, I'm not the only one nursing a chronic case of a broken heart.

We all were.

A house of rejected losers all banded together, banishing—or doing our best to banish—the nightmares who had scarred us.

Natty had been cheated on by her fiancé.

Me, you all know my story.

And David…well, he'd been jilted by the girl he'd fallen in love with while working the confectionary stand at the local cinema a few years ago—he didn't know she was married and he was the other man.

It destroyed him.

And, it destroyed me too because their tales ended with someone cheating on another.

Was that the only path for romance?

It hurt to hear their sad stories, but it also helped because I was no longer alone. I had two misfits to help heal me, and for the first time in my life, I stopped analysing everything I said and learned the novelty of telling the truth.

I held nothing back.

What I've told you, dear assignment, is what I told Natty and David over the course of three weeks.

They know who I am.

They know who Ren is.

They know my pathetic tale and life moves on.

Chapter Six

REN

2018

LEAVING HER WAS the hardest thing I'd ever done.

Harder than living in the city.

Harder than existing at Mclary's.

The *hardest* thing, and I'd done it voluntarily.

Walking away with my back aching beneath a rucksack full of tins and bottles, tents and sleeping bags, I physically fought myself every step.

What the fuck was I doing?

This was *Della.*

We'd never been apart except for three incidents in our past, and each of those only separated us for the shortest time possible.

I loved her.

I *needed* her.

So why the hell did I walk away from her?

The forest ought to have filled me with relief, being back in nature's sweet embrace. The warbles of birds and clear air, far from city smog, ought to slip the stress off my shoulders like an unwanted coat.

But I found no pleasure.

I found no sanctuary.

Because I was alone.

Della was my home. She was it for me. She was my *everything.*

And I'd always known she'd leave me eventually—as she should. As it was meant to happen when a kid outgrew their mentor. I used that excuse over and over.

Me leaving her was merely quickening the inevitably of *her* leaving *me.*

But it didn't stop the pain.

It didn't stop the regret.

It didn't change the fact I no longer had the most important thing in my life, and I was slowly dying without her.

* * * * *

That first day, I didn't get far.

Trees weren't just landmarks guiding me deeper into their midst, but supportive friends, holding me up as I stumbled beneath heartbreak.

I'd travel a mile with my thoughts full of disgust at my response to seeing her naked. I'd stride onward with fists clenched and teeth clamped against nausea for ever thinking about Della the way I had these past few years. I'd punch a sapling for the lust masquerading as love and beg for a way to be free—to somehow find simplicity again.

But then, my thoughts would change, and all I'd see was the little girl I raised. The sweet, trusting blue eyes gazing at me with uncomplicated love as I brushed her blonde hair or fed her a piece of crisp apple straight from the Wilson's tiny orchard.

My confusion would vanish, and I'd backtrack at a jog, staring at the city line below where Della existed without me.

She was my responsibility.

She was mine, and I'd left her all alone, undefended, uncared for.

Who *did* something like that?

Who put themselves first when their entire life had been wholeheartedly promised to another?

I'd hate myself the most in those moments.

The moments where my love was once again pure and full of self-sacrifice.

I was being an ass.

I was reading into things that weren't there.

How the hell did I think I could abandon her?

She was my kid.

My best-friend.

Fuck, she *needed* me, and I ran away like a thief. A thief who stole her protection, familiarity, and comfort all because he couldn't handle his own demons anymore.

I thought I'd protected myself from the vile whispers in my head. I thought I'd found a suitable outlet for the prohibited dreams about a blonde goddess who kissed me, loved me, and told me it was okay to fall and fall hard.

The one-night stands had helped curb my desires but each one left me emptier than before. Each one, I itched with guilt. Each one, I thought of Della.

Della.

Della.

Della.

Fuck...

I couldn't do this.

I couldn't leave her alone, unsafe, uncherished.

But as I'd race to the edge of the wilderness, riddled with remorse, and inhale the stench of cities and humans, I'd freeze.

Flashes of naked skin and come-hither eyes would turn my body traitorous.

And I'd remember all the mistakes and sexual tension that'd been building between us for years. I'd finally admit that the buzzing awareness was more than bonded connection but unpermitted chemistry.

It wasn't right. It wasn't allowed.

Della was no longer a little girl I'd die for.

She was a young woman destined to kill me.

Kill me with the absolute unacceptable ability to switch my pure love into dirty lust and destroy any chance at being close again.

On the fifth time of returning to the forest's edge and getting nowhere, even while covering more miles in one day than I'd normally do in two, I had to stop.

I had to admit that I'd left to save her.

I'd run because what I was feeling wasn't fair to her. I'd promised to pave her future with everything she could ever want, but by staying, I was confusing her.

She owned me heart and soul, but she needed more than me.

She'd *always* needed more than me, and the countless times we'd grown up together, the many incidents that proved just how much I lacked and she excelled, meant my determination to do the right thing was a vicious dictator.

I'd been with her every step—literal and figurative.

I'd stolen a lot of her independence.

I'd been the one smothering her, and *of course,* her feelings toward me would morph into something neither of us could have.

She hadn't had the freedom to learn who she was without me there to teach her. I'd screwed her up. I hadn't been fair. I'd been selfish and possessive, ensuring I was the most important person to her—just like she was to me.

That was wrong.

I saw that now.

John Wilson was right. I'd ruined any chance at keeping her as my sister, and now, I couldn't have her at all.

I'd promised to raise her to the highest heights she could achieve, and I'd sacrificed everything I could to achieve that.

That was all this was.

My final sacrifice to ensure she'd forget about this puppy crush, delete her teenage confusion, and find true happiness.

She'd no longer be brainwashed or subconsciously pick up on my corrupt thoughts. She'd be free to make up her own mind.

That resolution gave me enough willpower to turn and finally leave the city lights behind. Tree silhouettes welcomed me, looking like a ribcage where my empty heart hung lifeless and torn.

Della had a crush.

That was all.

But my feelings...they were deeper than a crush, harsher than a fling. My feelings were dark and complicated and yet another reason why I had to leave.

I strode quicker with heavy boots, turning my back on Della, vanishing into the forest I would always call home and the only place that could make me miss her even more.

Chapter Seven

DELLA

2018

EYES.
Yep.
Eyes.
I feel them on me.
Everywhere.
At the supermarket, at college, at the park—even at David's house.

It's been four months since Ren left, and I'm going insane. I think I catch a glimpse of him, but nothing's there. I smell him in the air, but no one's around. My skin prickles like it did whenever he was close, but I'm all alone waiting for the bus to school. I'm in class, and my fingers trail across my paper as if touched by a phantom caress. I'm in bed, and my body heats as if worshipped by sinful lips.

I feel him everywhere.
I think about him **all the time**.
And yes, that had to be in bold because it's a nightmare I can't stop.
I thought I'd accepted his disappearance. I thought I was stronger than this.
But, I'm not.
If anything, I'm getting worse.

Instead of feeling alone like I once did—utterly abandoned and unwanted and lost, I feel…connected.

The scattered pieces of me are re-centring, thanks to the illusion of him watching me.

Every night for a month, I've called his cell-phone.

I'll wait until David is in the shower so he doesn't see me feeding my addiction and send Ren a message. A simple: 'Where are you?' Followed a few hours later with silent tears: 'I miss you.'

No call has been answered.
No message delivered.

Ren is still out of range, still deep in his beloved forest, as far away from me as possible.

So, these eyes I'm feeling?

They're not his.

They can't be.

But it doesn't mean I'm not constantly aware of something. *Perhaps my heartbreak has infected me and made me sick? Maybe my mind has finally snapped, and instead of choosing to forget him, it's making up stories to keep him close.*

Either way, I hate it.

I can't win.

I wanted to be so much braver than this. So much stronger.

David and Natty moved on when their hearts were broken, so why can't I?

Why can't my dreams of him returning home and falling to his knees in forgiveness stop haunting me? Why can't I exist one day—just a single day— where I don't want to tell Ren what happened at school, or laugh with him about something stupid, or ask his advice on something important?

He was a part of my life ever since I can remember.

And I have to give myself some slack.

I haven't just lost a lover, because we were never lovers. I haven't just lost a friend, because he was never just a friend. I've lost a parent, a home, the only person I ever loved and relied on and my grief is crying out for all of them.

But, at the same time...my grief is changing.

I know I pushed him away.

I'm the one who needs to ask for forgiveness, not him.

But I am angry.

God, I'm angry.

Burning, growling, fist-shakingly angry.

Summer is well and truly here, and it's the hardest season because it's Ren's favourite. It was the time of returning to the forest—either permanently or just for weekends away. It was swimming together, and picnics, and horse rides, and hay baling, and browned skin, and sweat, and long nights with just a sheet, side by side in bed.

These days, summer means nothing special, and my routine of school, homework, and chores remains the same.

However, David asked me a few weeks ago when my birthday was. He knows enough about me that I was honest and said I didn't know the exact date. That Ren would pick one during summer and we'd go out for burgers and fries to celebrate a long-standing tradition of sharing an unknown birthday.

My heart stabbed me with its well-honed blade, only to patch itself up with yet another hastily applied and totally ineffective Band-Aid when David took my hand, smiled in sympathy, and said he'd take me out to dinner himself to celebrate.

He's willing to be a substitute.

He knows how much I miss Ren.

I tell him.

And if I don't, he hears it in my voice and sees it in my eyes.

He'd be blind and stupid to think I wasn't trawling the streets with my heart on a platter, looking for its rightful owner to come claim it.

I have another confession to make.

I'm still living at David's, but I moved into the spare room where boxes have been pushed against the walls and the gym equipment relocated to the garage. I didn't bother bringing my own furniture over, and I bought a cheap bed and dresser on sale that David helped transport home for me.

The apartment I shared with Ren is my dirty little secret.

David thinks I terminated my lease and sold everything I didn't need.

I lied.

I go there on the days when the loneliness and anger hurt the most. I sit on the couch where Ren kissed, hugged, and wiped away my tears, and rock around the never ending ball of sick, sick sorrow.

The rent money Ren left behind has been diligently used to ensure the space remains untouched by others.

I don't know why I do it.

I know he's not coming back.

It's a waste of money to hold on to something I haven't lived in for months.

So why is there this inability to move on?

Why do I keep distance between David and me?

Why do I cringe whenever he takes my hand?

And why…why did I push him away when he kissed me last week? Why did I freeze on the stairs as he caught my wrist, pushed me against the wall, and apologised just before pressing his lips to mine?

We've kissed before.

We've slept together once, yet he apologised as if he knew what he was doing wasn't what I wanted.

Home life has been a little strained since then.

Natty knows what happened because I told her. She encouraged me to go for it. That David was a good guy: sweet, kind, loving.

I'd laughed and faked interest.

While she was encouraging me to jump into bed with David, I wasn't picturing the boy she spoke about, but the boy from my past. I lived in my little fantasy where the man I went home to at night—the one I kissed in the dark and let enter my body—wasn't a sweet, kind boy like David but a tortured, determined man like Ren.

So, you see?

That's why I'm writing to you for the first time in a month.

David is taking me out for my birthday tonight, and I already know what he's going to ask.

He's going to see if we can go from room-mates to lovers.

And...

And this is so hard to admit...but I know what answer I'll give him.

Are you judging me?

Do you know what you'd do in my shoes?

Would you forever pay rent on an unlived-in apartment just because it's the only thing you have left of a boy who would forever own your heart? Or would you terminate the lease, accept the inevitable, and try to find happiness in any place you could?

I'll tell you what my answer is going to be.

It's yes.

I'm going to move on.

Or at least, I'm going to try.

If only it wasn't for those eyes.

The eyes that follow me.

The eyes that know me.

The eyes that somehow, somewhere, belong to the boy I'll never be free from.

Chapter Eight

REN

Previous Month

I TRIED LEAVING for three interminably long months.

Every morning, I'd pack up my tent, snuff out my fire, and stride from camp toward the horizon. And every evening, I'd end up at the same ash-scattered, tent-crushed earth I'd left nine hours before.

A perfect boomerang—unable to break from the forgone conclusion that I couldn't take another step farther from Della.

I was bound to her in sickness, health, love, and distance, and I physically couldn't survive with more miles between us.

After the initial few weeks of mindless wandering, I didn't even bother packing up the tent anymore.

I'd leave my belongings and hike all day, exhausting my body so I might find some reprieve in sleep from the never ceasing desires and mistakes in my head. I'd deplete every ounce of energy, so I didn't turn my cell-phone on and climb the largest tree for reception. I'd barely hunt or eat, so I didn't have the energy to message her things I should never say out loud.

I ate my secrets, and my unpermitted desires sustained me…barely.

Away from Della and free from the authoritative position I held in her life, I allowed myself to remember her in so many different ways.

I smiled when I recalled her as a baby, and her stubborn attempts to copy me.

I grimaced when I remembered her as an eight-year-old, desperate to know about sex and the terribly uncomfortable talk we'd shared.

I sighed when I relived the perfection of the long nights when she'd help me learn in the hay loft, and we'd sit so close, laughing by starlight, studying until she fell asleep against my side.

Innocent memories.

Memories I was permitted. Memories I was proud of because back then…I'd been true in my love for her. I'd been allowed to touch and kiss her because there was nothing more than the everlasting need to make her happy and keep her safe.

It was the years after that had me tossing in my sleep and dreaming things I wished I could stop.

The dream goddess who always opened her arms to me.

The blonde woman I wanted more than anything who always kissed me as deeply as I kissed her, who tumbled to the forest floor, who ripped off my clothes with the same gut-shredding passion I felt and cried out as I filled her violently.

Those dreams woke me hard and hurting and more tormented than I'd been in my entire life.

I only wanted to remember her as my Della, yet my mind kept plying me with fantasies that she could be my future, too. A future I'd never contemplated until the day she'd kissed me. The day she'd tangled herself up with my dreams and my heart—my stupid, *stupid* heart—shed its capacity at only seeing her as a child and saw her as so much more instead.

"Fuck!"

The trees were the only ones who heard my distress, who witnessed my disgrace as I fisted myself and worked out the disgusting desire from my body. I felt sick to my stomach as I came, not because I masturbated, but because my mind fixated on Della and that was a line I should never fucking cross.

Even though I struggled with two memories of baby Della and sexual Della, I knew in my soul there was only one journey I could take.

It was as if Della had an invisible hold on me.

There hadn't been any rope or knot binding me to her as I packed my bag and left the apartment that awful night, but there was now.

An invisible lasso that tightened every time I tried stepping farther away, yanking me back, keeping me firmly stuck.

Was this limbo or purgatory?

Was it punishment for leaving her so callously when she needed me the most?

Those questions kept me company on my long treks through the forest until I'd memorised every trail and recognised every tree.

More questions came at night. Questions I had no right to ask.

Was she with someone?

Was she happy with someone?

Had she forgotten about me when I could never, *ever* forget about her?

But it was the questions that sprang on me, heavy with guilt, festering with shame that meant I would never be able to move forward.

Not like this.

Not without checking on her.

Not without convincing myself that she didn't need me anymore.

I would rather be crushed knowing she'd deleted me from her world, than forever wonder if she was okay.

I couldn't handle the unknown, the never ending need to see her, the almost manic desperation to clear the air between us and somehow find closure to this entire convoluted mess.

I'd lost weight.

I'd forgotten how to breathe.

My bones were glass and my chest a forge.

True love was a vicious monster, feeding on my reserves, breaking me beneath its resolve to either kill me if I didn't obey or destroy me if I did.

I was glad the forest didn't have mirrors because heartbreak had not been kind to me.

But just because I'd made a mistake by leaving, and it'd taken me three months of mentally punishing myself for all the misguided, impure thoughts I'd been having, I could finally admit what I couldn't before.

Away from the city, free from society's judgment, I had no choice but to be honest with myself.

I wished I could stop it.

I begged for it not to be true.

But…the reality was, I was in love with Della.

Not just platonic, parental, brotherly, friendship love but bone-crunching, heart-pounding, air-stealing, delicious fucking love that broke me down until I no longer knew who I was.

All I knew was I couldn't keep doing this.

I couldn't keep living without her.

I needed her in my life in any capacity that she'd let me.

Even if it meant I'd have to walk her down the aisle as she married some undeserving prick, I would do it.

I would take whatever she gave.

I didn't make a conscious decision to pack up my tent that morning or turn toward the city instead of away. I didn't mean to leave my campsite or haul my possessions onto my back.

I wanted Della, but I still didn't know how to deal with that even as I struck off on different paths, passed unfamiliar trees, and weaved my way from wilderness to city.

The closer I got, the more my worry escalated.

Was she even there?

Was she still at our apartment, or had she moved?

Had she sought out Cassie's help and returned to Cherry River?

My boots travelled faster as scarier questions chased me.

What if she'd been hurt? What if she'd been taken or sold or abused while I'd been having a personal crisis? What if I'd put myself first, and she'd suffered because of it?

I would die.

By my hand or heartbreak's if that was the case.

How could I say I loved her when I'd done the exact same thing to her as my mother had done to me?

My mother had sold me because I was worth more to her as dollars than I was as her son. And I'd walked away from Della because I chose propriety and martyrdom instead of burying my own pain and focusing on giving her everything I had left to give.

I'd been so fucking selfish.

And I stopped walking.

I ran.

I ran as fast as I could.

I ran all the way back to the apartment, to Della, to fix this.

* * * * *

She wasn't there.

For two weeks, I stalked the street where we used to live, returning to the dilapidated shed Della and I had slept in when we first arrived in town, watching for any sign of her.

No one entered our apartment.

No landlord or new tenant.

No Della.

Rain or shine, I'd leave my temporary shack and travel into the congested suburbs and find a place in the shadows to watch.

And every day, my heart would sink a little more.

I'd focused on the wrong questions.

I hadn't stopped to ask the most important one.

If Della had moved on and left…where had she gone, and how could I find her? Would it be as simple as turning on my cell-phone and calling her? Would she talk to me? Or had she changed her number?

I'd left every dollar I had on the coffee table when I'd gone, so I had no funds to purchase credit for my phone. And for now, I had no intention of finding a job. I could hunt what I needed to eat or I'd steal if long hours in the city meant game was scarce. Not that I had an appetite these days.

I ran purely on confusion and regret.

Money didn't matter to me, and besides, I couldn't stop watching the apartment, hoping against hope that someday, some hour, she'd turn up.

On the fourteenth day, when she still didn't show, and no one else entered the space, I crossed the street, checked I went unnoticed, and descended the stairs to the claustrophobic basement apartment.

It took fifteen minutes, but I managed to pick the lock with the two knives from my boot, and my steps sounded criminal as I crossed over the threshold for the first time since saying goodbye to the love of my life.

The first thing that hit me was the smell.

Must and un-use and un-want. Dust bunnies sat together in corners as if the unsealed windows had encouraged a breeze to enter and do some cleaning. The kitchen tap dripped like it always did into an empty sink. Dishes sat on the rack waiting to be put into the paint-chipped cupboards.

After living so free in the forest where nature decorated with sunsets and moonlight, the space was abysmal and poky.

How had we lived so long in this small place?

Then again, everywhere seemed better when Della was around. We were happy in a garden shed or under the stars as long as we were together.

Rubbing at the sudden blistering burn where my heart lived, I strode through the tiny home. My hands clenched as my eyes fell on the coffee table where the note I'd scribbled Della still sat unfinished.

She hadn't moved it.

The cash was missing but that was the only thing changed in the entire room from its faded brown couch to its ugly striped curtains.

No noise came from the bathroom or Della's bedroom, but I couldn't stop myself from following the corridor—memories of Della naked haunting my every step.

I sucked in a painful breath as I pushed open the partially cracked door to her bedroom. Her bed was unmade, like usual. Her bedside table droplet-stained from glasses sipped sleepily in the night.

Prowling to her wardrobe, I wrenched it open. Sucking back another pained breath, I noticed the clothes she favoured and often wore were no longer there.

One of the only signs that she no longer lived here.

Her toiletries in the grout-stained bathroom were gone. Her subtle scent of petals and flowers from working at the florist no longer noticeable in the stale air.

She hadn't been here in a while.

Yet she still paid rent; otherwise, our furniture would've been evicted and a new tenant living in our home.

Why?

And if she still paid rent but didn't live here, where was she?

My boots echoed off the corridor walls as I headed back toward the living room, and my eyes fell on the front door.

A sequence of events unfolded in rapid fire.

Of Tom arriving that Halloween to take Della to the dance.

Of her kissing him in the dark amongst witches and vampires.

Of my jealousy finally starting to make me notice my feelings for Della were changing.

Of yet more jealousy and absolute excruciating heartbreak as she called me the night she lost her virginity.

Of me storming over there, snatching her as if she were mine to snatch, and beating up the guy she'd chosen over me.

I couldn't remember his name. I couldn't remember much about that night other than my roaring agony.

I didn't know what I'd do if I saw him again.

Wait...

Something inside me bellowed with possession. Something that whispered the answers to my questions.

Where is she?

I knew.

I didn't know how.

I didn't know why.

But I knew where to start looking.

I bolted out the door.

Chapter Nine

REN

Current Month

I'D BEEN CALLED many things in my life.

A boy.

A belonging.

A bastard.

But this was a new low.

I was a pervert, a peeper, an obsessed watcher who didn't have the power to stop.

For two weeks, I stalked Della every second of every day.

I knew her schedule. I knew her friends. I knew she had English on Mondays and lit class on Wednesdays. I knew she studied until late and watched movies with the guy she'd slept with—who I remembered was called David—and some black-haired girl I didn't know.

I knew she slept alone in her own room in a new bed, new sheets, new pyjamas, and genuinely laughed when David whispered in her ear at breakfast and smiled softly when he clutched her hand goodbye.

I knew she was sad and lonely and angry.

I recognised the tightness in her shoulders, the blaze in her blue eyes, and the stiffness of her step.

We'd been apart longer than we'd ever been, but I knew her better than I knew myself.

I might not be fluent in many things, but when it came to reading Della, I was a master. Every nuance and twitch, I understood. Every flick of her hair and sniff of her petite nose, I read the hidden message.

And the language she shouted was of serious rage.

She was a part of me, and her anger became my anger because I understood it.

I felt it, too.

I was angry that I'd driven us to this point.

I was angry that, until a month ago, I had full intentions to track her down, approach her, and get on my knees in apology. I had an entire script planned, written in my mind not on paper, burned into my memory as if scribed in fire.

I was going to pledge myself to her all over again.

I was going to beg her forgiveness for breaking my promise never to leave her like I did when she was a baby playing on that comfy rug with glittery goldfish and opinionated cats.

I'd left her even when I promised I wouldn't.

I'd done that.

She hadn't asked me to go, and despite the mess between us, my leaving was inexcusable.

But my carefully planned speech had faded the longer I watched her.

I couldn't take my eyes off her, loving her the way I was meant to with pride for her excelling at life without me, joy that she was studying something she loved, affection for the messy blonde curls, and warm-hearted sentiment for the ribbon fluttering in her strands.

The first day of watching her went too fast and, before I knew it, my stalking reached creepy levels until I couldn't leave unless her bedroom light went out and sleep meant she'd be in bed for the rest of the night.

I'd slink off, hidden in my shadows and shame, crawling into a sleeping bag and dreaming inappropriate dreams full of need, love, and passion.

At dawn, I'd return to her, an itch in my blood commanding me to be close after so long apart.

The next morning, I found her hugging David goodbye on the stoop of the white picket fenced house I could never afford, and her bare legs flashed me where I hid in the trees across the street.

She wore flip-flops, and wrapped around her ankle was the same tattoo I'd paid for on her seventeenth birthday. The one with its matching blue ribbon trailing into its capital R.

A year old and the ink was just as bright, just as damning as the night I cupped her foot and demanded an explanation—begging her to put me out of my misery, all the while knowing she was about to condemn me even more.

The tattoo sucker-punched me with so many things, and I didn't have the courage to approach her that day. Instead, I drowned beneath everything I'd done wrong and everything I didn't know how to fix.

The day after that, David kissed her.

It'd been the slap to the face I needed.

It woke me out of the trance I'd fallen into, shaking me with truth that I'd left her for months, but she wasn't a wilting flower entirely reliant on me to thrive. She was tenacious and brave and fiercely independent. Always had been—always looking after me just as much as I looked after her.

Of course, she wouldn't wait for me.

Of course, her anger would drive her to find other things…other people.

My insides wanted to curl up and die, but I refused to be weak. I refused to think of myself as the injured party when I'd been the one to walk away.

I'd done this.

I'd pushed her to find comfort from some other man. A man she'd already given herself to. A man who had every power to destroy me, and he didn't even know it.

When he kissed her, every muscle seized.

She didn't exactly kiss him back—not the way she'd kissed Tom at the Halloween party—but she didn't push him away, either.

She nodded to something he said while they stood on the garden path, and he cupped her pretty cheeks like I wanted to, her eyes glowing with a mixture of affection and tears.

I wanted to kill him.

But I was also grateful because he'd kept my Della safe when I had not. I wanted him gone, but I wouldn't hurt her again.

She'd chosen him.

I had to respect that.

That was my punishment.

I returned to my borrowed shack on government land, unable to stop reliving her kissing him. Kissing the boy she'd lost her virginity to.

Just like when I'd run, I was only thinking of myself.

I should be happy she wasn't writhing in matching misery.

She was alive.

She was healthy.

She was living.

Who was I to ruin that all over again?

If she'd moved on, then I would do everything in my power to spare her any more pain.

So, I settled in to watch, to study, to make sure what she'd said to me that night—the way she'd stared, and stripped, and kissed me—had been what I'd feared all along: a puppy crush. A silly infatuation.

Nothing more than innocent flirtation that I'd turned into something messy and untrue.

I needed to see that so I could let go of these tragic needs driving me into an early grave.

But…if she loved me the way I was learning I loved her…could our relationship evolve? Were our foundations strong enough, our morals good enough, to risk losing everything just for the hope of something more?

A few months ago, my answer had been no. I wasn't willing to risk it.

But now…now, I knew I'd fucked up everything and lived with the daily torture of what it was like to exist without her.

I wanted her back.

Emotions had been the glue that sewed us together, and I refused to let them be the crowbar to pry us apart.

I'd lost Della the moment I'd walked out the door. I'd decimated her trust, her faith, and her affection, all because I wasn't brave enough to admit I felt something, too.

And now, watching her kiss men from a distance was all I had left, and as much as I despised myself, I couldn't stop.

I just *could not stop.*

I couldn't be away from her.

I couldn't survive not seeing her.

I wasn't proud of it.

I knew she'd become a sick addiction.

And for the first time in my life, I wasn't fighting to better myself but letting myself slide into a deep, dark place I didn't know how to climb out of.

Even at Mclary's, I'd never let self-pity destroy my hope that one day I would be free—either in death or by running away.

I knew what I should do.

Leave.

Like I said I would.

Stop this madness and let Della find her place in the world without me messing it up even more.

But…I couldn't.

I gave in.

I kept watching.

The days became a blur.

I couldn't stop myself trailing her to school, to the coffee shop, to the pricey house she shared with David and the girl.

My heartache robbed me of yet more weight because I couldn't tear myself away to eat. I had no money for vitamins I sorely needed.

My body didn't feel right...it felt sick.

I truly was the villain and slid into even worse territory for stalking her.

It all became much worse the night of a muggy summer's evening when David led her from the house dressed in baby blue shorts and white open-necked shirt, holding my Della's hand as her cream sundress with a lacy collar fluttered around her bare legs.

Once again, her ribbon plaited in her hair and inked around her ankle reached into my chest and tore out my pathetic heart.

She was so fucking beautiful.

He led her to a Chrysler parked in the driveway, opened her door, then hopped into the driver's seat and drove off.

I couldn't follow them, so I waited in the street-shadows, wishing for something to chase away the time, bowing beneath the weight of constant jealousy, plaguing myself with worry about what she was doing.

I wasn't a smoker or a drinker, nor did I have money for cigarettes or alcohol, but I would've gladly given away every worldly possession to have something to numb my self-inflicted pain.

They returned a couple of hours later, the warm breeze blowing scents of grease and bacon across the street as they climbed from the car, laughing at some joke they shared.

On the quaint garden path, David grabbed her hand and spun her into him. "Happy birthday, Della Ribbon. I hope you were okay with sharing a burger with me and not with him."

Goddammit, my chest cleaved in two.

Her nickname.

Her birthday.

She'd told him.

I stumbled with a mixture of despair and starvation.

She gasped as David clutched her close.

I winced as my fingers burned to touch her like he was.

She flinched as he bent his head to kiss her.

I barely controlled my growl as his body pressed against hers.

Their lips met, and this time...Della kissed him back. Hot and wet and needy—the same way she always kissed when trying to deny the truth and buy into a fantasy.

The same way the woman from my dreams kissed me. The same way I kissed her: with naked desire that sprang from desperation for love as much as a lust-filled connection.

With wet lips, he kissed his way along her jaw, then whispered something in her ear.

Her back straightened, eyes widened, and indecision flickered over her face.

But only for a moment.

Just a single moment where I knew she thought of me before pushing me out of her life like I'd pushed her out of mine.

And then, she nodded. "Yes."

Yes to what?

Yes to ripping out my heart?

Yes to tearing apart my love?

They vanished into the house, leaving me in pieces on the pavement.

That night, her bedroom light never turned on.

However, two shadows danced over David's curtains until late into the evening.

Two shadows having sex.

Two shadows of two people where one who meant the world to me had taken my hopeful heart, tore it out with reality, and left it to bleed out alone on the street.

I'd stalked her for long enough.

I'd seen enough to understand I no longer stood a chance.

As their birthday night of fucking finished, and their bedroom light went out, I turned and walked away.

I was twenty-eight.

She was eighteen.

And it was over.

I sent a prayer for her eternal happiness—the only thing I could give her for her birthday—and walked away.

I didn't go back.

Chapter Ten

DELLA

2018

I SLEPT WITH him.

How could I?

How could I sleep with someone when my heart still belongs to another?

How can I be so cruel by leading David on when I might never be able to return his feelings?

I have no answers for you. I have no answers for me.

The blistering truth is, the night I slept with him, I sat in the shower once he was asleep and sobbed my damn eyes out.

The worst part?

I felt like I owed him when really, I wasn't ready.

He was so sweet, taking me out for a birthday burger and fries. So understanding when he let me list each and every diner Ren had taken me to, including the last one when he'd agreed to let me get a tattoo—the same tattoo I can't look at now without wincing with agonising regret.

He was so gentle as he took me home, kissed me, and asked if he could give me my present in his bedroom.

It wasn't an invitation for sex even though he'd touched me all night—grazing his hand with mine, kissing my cheek when I made him laugh about my five-year-old birthday and the incident at school about skinning Frosty the bunny.

Natty gave me a Cheshire cat grin when we returned, and David guided me up the stairs with our hands entwined. She winked and gave me a big thumbs-up as she slowly vanished from view as I reached the landing. Her encouragement made me feel semi-normal, as if entering David's room wasn't a direct slap in the face of Ren's memory.

But Ren wasn't here.

Ren had never kissed me the way David had.

Ren had never been interested in me the way David was, so I did my best to push him from my mind and planted a grateful kiss on David's lips as he gave me a jade green scarf and matching nail polish for my birthday.

That kiss turned to another.

Which evolved to another and another until the nail polish and scarf fell to the carpet and David whispered, "I want you. Do you want me?"

His voice wavered with uncertainty and need; a potent combination of authority and fear. Knowing he was as terrified as I was allowed me to be braver than I might've been. It allowed me to thank him in one of the only ways I could.

I nodded—not trusting my voice—and moved toward the bed.

As he stripped me, kissed me, touched me, rolled on a condom, and slid inside me, I did my best to keep my heart and mind with him.

But I wasn't successful.

For weeks, I'd hoped I would be able to move on, that the gentle affection I had for David would suddenly explode into the all-encompassing craving I've had for Ren for as long as I can remember.

But the simmer never became a burn.

If anything, it grew less and less as I acknowledged that I wasn't ready for anyone who wasn't Ren. I wasn't being fair because I was so far from the realm of being okay it was laughable.

The sex was fine.

But his hugs made me empty, and his kisses made me lost.

Afterward, David spooned me and my chest ached unbearably. My tears slowly trickled inside me until they clogged my throat with silence. And when his breathing finally slipped into slumber, and I was free to be honest with myself, I tore out of his embrace, bolted to the bathroom, and barely contained my grief as I wrenched on the shower and hurled myself under the hot spray.

My theory was the water would hide any escaped sobs and camouflage the sadness pouring down my cheeks.

To be honest, I didn't even know why I cried.

It wasn't like I'd cheated on Ren. It wasn't like I had any other sexual experience to judge other than sleeping with David on Natty's bedroom floor.

I was eighteen and so messed up by the boy who'd raised me that I was a wreck after having such a lovely evening with a man anyone would be lucky to date.

But you know what?

You know what I've kept tucked inside where all dark, disturbing secrets live?

The real reason I cried that night?

It was because I felt him.

I've felt him for weeks.

Every day, the sensation of him being close gets worse.

Eyes everywhere.

On the street, in my class, in my dreams.

A yearning that matches mine. A pleading that mirrors mine.

And I know it's just my mind playing tricks on me, but dammit, I have this feeling that if I turn quickly enough, I'll catch Ren behind me. This constant awareness that if I just breathe his name, he'll miraculously appear, just won't let me move on.

I'm stuck in limbo.

I'm becoming unhappier instead of happier.

I'm becoming lost instead of found.

And I need to do something…soon, because if I don't, I'm afraid of what I'll become.

I say I'm strong, but the reality is, dear assignment, I'm not.

I'm brittle and fragile and made of spun glass where my insides are nothing more than swirling smoke looking for a crack to escape, to hitch a ride on the wind, to fly into the forest, desperate to find the boy who stole my heart and beg him to make me whole again.

* * * * *

Six months.

Six eternally long months.

Nothing much has happened. I haven't slept with David again. Things are a little weird, but we continue to co-inhabit well enough.

I haven't had the energy to write.

But something changed, and I have news.

Funny, how honesty is always the worst weapon, isn't it?

I've turned to you as a sounding board because I have no one else to talk to. Natty is on David's side—as she should be. David is doing his best to date me— as he should with our history. And all along, I keep my secrets until I can tell you.

Normally, I write on a park bench while waiting for the bus after school, or in a coffee shop during lunch hour, but the other night, I stupidly left my computer on standby in the lounge, not password protected like normal, and David read everything.

He saw what I wrote about sleeping with him.

He saw how sad I was.

How empty and angry and confused.

I offered to leave, but David didn't kick me out. He didn't walk away from me, but he has withdrawn his offer of dating.

He said it was his fault to push for something he knew I wasn't ready for. That he understands I'm not over Ren, but will continue to support me as a friend.

He's correct, of course, but having him confront me so calmly with no blame or ridicule made me feel even worse.

He knows what it's like to love and not be loved in return, and to my utmost horror, I've done it to him again. Not that he's in love with me, but there is something there. Something that could become something, *if you know what I mean.*

Anyway, I'm running out of time, my Uber will be here soon, and I'm taking you to my old apartment. I'm going to print off every stupid word and burn you like I should've done the moment I knew I couldn't hand you in.

I've told David I'm having the afternoon away to get my head and heart on the same page. That I'll return in better shape and ready to stop moping around his house.

My printer is still gathering dust in my old room.

The clothes I don't wear still in my wardrobe.

The bed I don't sleep in still waiting for a dreamer.

It's time, don't you think?

Time to stop this—all of it. Time to cancel the lease on somewhere I'm not living, time to patch up the heart I'm not using, and finally put the past where it belongs.

Behind me.

Oh, my Uber is here.

I had other things to say, but I suppose they're unimportant now.

Farewell, assignment.

This is the last you'll hear from me, and I want to say thank you before I let you go.

Thank you for being a shoulder to cry on. Thank you for being the only one who truly understood how I felt about Cassie, Ren, David…everyone.

Just thanks, for everything.

Chapter Eleven

REN

2018

THE EVENING DELLA slept with David I forced myself to stop being ridiculous.

I sucked up my pride, rubbed out my bruises, and trekked the few blocks to the abandoned apartment that my cash still paid for.

The lonely space breathed a sigh of relief as I jimmied the lock again and stepped into the musty, unloved lounge. It needed someone to comfort, just like I needed someone to comfort me.

I meant to do some dusting, return to the borrowed shack, and grab my backpack. To have my first shower in a while—if the water hadn't been turned off—and eat if the pantry still stored food.

But that was before my feet guided me to Della's bedroom, and my eyes fell on her unmade bed. Images of her sitting cross-legged while doing her homework slammed into me. The memory of her blue-dyed hair so glossy and bright. The sounds of her laughter as I pulled her ponytail. The feel of her arms around my waist and her cheek on my chest—

Fuck, it was too much, and every chore and task faded beneath the immense blanket of exhaustion.

I wasn't proud of it, but I fell face first onto Della's bed, wrapped myself up in her blankets, and inhaled her pillow.

I slept for two solid days, waking briefly to drink water straight from the tap and gnaw on a few stale crackers from the kitchen. All my body cared about was dreaming, and I woke angry and hard when my dream goddess refused to visit me—almost as if being in Della's domain meant my loyalties to her returned to loving her as a brother, rather than the complicated tangle I now accepted.

Unfortunately, once my body caught up on sleep, it became determined to reveal how badly I'd neglected it. Rundown immune system and no weight reserves meant a simple cold found me a very comfortable host. Within a few hours, the congestion and headache turned to fever and coughing—cursing me with the flu.

I got sick.

And I couldn't do a damn thing about it.

I spent a week combating lungs full of oppressive agony, and hugging a burning chest that charred me to ash.

At some point, I feared I wouldn't get better. That I'd fall down the sickly slope into pneumonia like I had when I was fifteen.

But, through some miracle, the hacking coughs slowly abated and the burning slowly cooled, morphing to a wheeze I could cope with.

When I felt semi-human again, I returned to gather my things in the forest. Afterward, I cased out a local convenience store for staples, and spent two full days spring cleaning the apartment.

To start with, I didn't want to spray the tropical scented disinfectant just in case I deleted any smells of Della, but she hadn't lived here for so long that no whiff or note of her was left.

Della had paid utilities as well as rent, which meant I had hot water to wash and gas to cook with. I wanted to thank her for wasting money on something she no longer used—almost as if she'd known I'd return and need a place to stay.

When I wasn't staying busy with chores, I tailed her.

I'd promised myself I wouldn't go back.

I broke that promise.

Countless times.

I couldn't help it.

After I was better, and more publicly acceptable, I walked to her shared house in much cleaner clothes than before, and watched her go to college. I waited outside like all those years ago when she first went to school, and followed her home again.

I slowly drove myself insane, keeping her constantly in my thoughts, all while she returned to David every night.

By the end of the second week, I couldn't do it anymore.

Any of it.

I couldn't keep stealing supplies so close to home unless I wanted to get caught. And I couldn't keep stalking unless I wanted to keep sliding into that dark, dismal place I couldn't climb out of.

I needed money.

I needed to learn how to exist without her so I could put myself back together again and be the parental figure Della needed, not the off-the-rails, rejected lover I had currently become.

The next day, I headed to a supermarket two blocks away that I hadn't stolen from and read their advertisement board for employment. I wasn't deluded to think I'd find a perfect farmhand role, but I was prepared to do what was necessary to get my life back on track.

The only two positions available were a window cleaning gig or a barman at a local nightclub. No way could I be cooped up in a darkened cesspit with writhing bodies and pounding music.

That left the window cleaning job.

I memorised the number then asked to use the supermarket manager's phone to arrange an interview. I knew nothing about washing windows, but I needed cash, so...

The owner was a spindly looking pothead whose dad had bought him a franchise once he'd dropped out of school with no prospects. He wanted someone to run the bookings and basically handle the entire business.

I bullshitted enough that I got the job, earning cash under the table with a bonus for each new contract I signed.

My first pay cheque was used to purchase a cheap pair of jeans and a couple of t-shirts, replacing the holey, discoloured things I'd lived in for far too long in the forest.

The next lot of cash went to topping up my long-suffering cellphone, and it became a thing of torture as I stroked the buttons and read old messages from Della that I'd never seen.

At the start of our separation, she wrote to me often. Telling me stories of classes, exam results, how much she missed me, how much she cursed me, how much she was sorry.

Then they became less and less. Until now, she didn't message me at all.

Now, it was my turn to curb the all-consuming need to get in touch. Lying in her bed, I wrote text after text that I never sent.

I'm in town.

I'm in our old apartment.

I miss you.

I want you.

I love you.

I'm in love with you.

I deleted them all, needing more time so I didn't do something I regretted, something we couldn't survive.

Before I knew it, another two months had passed, pushing me over the six-month anniversary of leaving Della. Even though I still saw her every day—if only for snatches of time between window washing jobs or after work before dusk fell—I still missed her more than food, shelter, and freedom.

At least, she had a routine and friends. She had movie nights and dinners out. She had a life that I didn't want to ruin, and it gave me all the more incentive to stay out of it.

I hated that I watched with horror every night until her bedroom light turned on, not just his. I held my breath to see if she'd sleep with him again, and exhaled in utter relief when she didn't.

It was sick.

I knew that.

But it didn't change anything.

And, as much as our distance slowly robbed me of life and purpose, I didn't let her know how much I wanted her.

How much I missed her.

How deeply I cared.

How fucking screwed up I was…over everything.

Chapter Twelve

DELLA

2018

DAMMIT, THE APARTMENT still smells of him.

I haven't been here in so long, but the moment I opened the door, it felt as if I'd never left.

It feels lived in.

I was expecting dust bunnies and cobwebs, but the floors are freshly polished and the corners neatly clean.

I know I said I wouldn't write to you again, assignment, but I had to tell someone.

I think I might have to go see a professional. Admit I have a problem. Talk to a doctor, maybe.

This level of delusion can't be real, can it?

I feel him watching me. I prickle for no reason. I stiffen at the slightest noise. I believe, no matter how insanely impossible, that he's close by.

And now this?

I truly am losing my mind.

My bed was made when I came home, and I swear I left it a mess.

The bathroom smells like tropical disinfectant, not the faint must of mould that lingers in the grout around the tiles.

How is that possible?

Why do I keep deluding myself this way?

He's gone!

He's gone!

I need someone to scream that in my face and then maybe the folded threadbare towels will make sense, or the fact that if I stand still and inhale, my nose fills with his woodsy, wild scent instead of stale passing of lonely time.

I smell him.

And I don't know what to do anymore.

I came here to put things behind me, yet everywhere I turn, the past keeps dragging me back.

I haven't said it out loud since he left—not that I ever said it out loud—but sitting here in my bedroom that Ren helped decorate, looking around the apartment Ren helped make a home, I can't pretend anymore.

I'm still in love with him.

Even more than before.

I'm still furious at him.

Growing hotter by the day.

And I'm afraid.

I'm so afraid I'll never be able to get past this, that my future is a merry-go-round of prickled skin for no reason, smells of Ren in the air, and the unnerving sense that he hasn't truly gone, after all.

Maybe he died out in the forest, and his ghost is haunting me.

Maybe this is what everyone goes through when they lose someone so damn special.

Either way, I can't do this anymore.

I came here to burn you, and that's what I'm going to do.

And then, I'm going to sell every piece of furniture and leave.

I can't be in this town another moment.

Screw my creative writing course. Screw being brave. Screw lying. Screw everything.

I can't do it.

I can't stay.

I'm running…just like he did.

It's finally time to say…goodbye.

Chapter Thirteen

REN

2018

STEPPING INTO THE place I used to live with Della was excruciating.

Every day was the same; the pain never got easier, or the sensation that I was missing something fundamental any gentler.

She was the reason I went to work.

She was why I remained in a city I couldn't stand rather than return to the forest I loved.

And she didn't even know I was back because I was too much of a pussy to face her. I wasn't ready to accept her anger at my weaknesses, to bear the brunt of her disappointment, or to stare into her eyes as I lied about what I felt for her.

I wanted that lie to be truth when I next saw her.

I wanted to hold love in my heart and no lust. I wanted to hug her hard and feel connected and comforted and not consumed with the desperation of spilling everything.

Of confessing that I loved her in a totally different way.

That I couldn't exist without her.

That I was willing to do anything to have her back.

I hated how incredibly wrong it was to fall for the girl I'd raised, yet my body said it was unbelievably right. That it had been waiting for that moment to finally come alive and shout *yes* to finding everything I never thought I'd find.

My eyes glued to the carpet where she'd fearlessly stripped and offered every secret and vulnerability. And just like every day, I cringed in horror knowing that, despite the fact she'd moved on and my vow to pretend my love hadn't changed for her, if I could rewind time, I would gather her close and kiss her.

I wouldn't wait for her to kiss me.

I wouldn't make her put her entire heart on the line.

I would meet her halfway because our entire lives had been a partnership, and it was up to me to carry half her burdens.

My boots were heavy and droplet stained from washing windows as I trudged down the tiny corridor to her—*my*—bedroom.

Wait.

I froze as the sounds of splashing water came from the poky bathroom at the bottom of the hall. Light glowed beneath the door.

What the hell?

I'd grown so used to having sole use of this place, I hadn't considered what I'd do if she suddenly returned.

I backed up, my heart racing into overdrive.

Shit.

I'd caught her in the shower.

I didn't know her to shower at dusk—she was normally a morning person—but if she'd had a long day at college or a fight with David or whatever other reason had brought her here, I supposed it was only natural. Then again, I had no right to know her routine anymore.

I'd *left* her.

I wasn't privy to her heartaches. She wasn't a virgin, after all. She had the man she'd chosen warming her bed at night.

Once again, that knowledge harpooned me, and my steps faltered. She'd grown up beneath my nose and, by the time I'd noticed, it was too late.

Everything was too fucking late.

A painful cough ripped from my lungs.

Turning around, I meant to head back to the living room and out the door, but a stack of papers sat on her desk beside the cheap laptop I'd bought for her birthday a couple of years ago. A few of the keys were missing and the Wi-Fi capabilities were shit, but the thing was well used ever since Della decided to take her skills at telling stories, and my past of sharing tales, and enrol in creative writing.

The laptop hadn't been on her desk when I left this morning.

She'd brought it with her.

Was it an assignment?

Was she hard at work on a project, and this was the printed results ready to hand in tomorrow?

Looking back at the bathroom door, the sound of running pipes and groaning water pressure said I had enough time to spy.

I shouldn't.

I should run before it was too late.

Just the action of stepping into her room uninvited—the same room I'd slept in for the past few months—and glancing at the discarded bra on her dresser, the pink panties on the floor, and strewn jeans on her bed made my hands clench and belly knot with dangerous things, but the fat stack of pages and bright green Post-it note on top beckoned me forward.

My eyes widened and my heart beat with a different panic as I noticed my old lighter propped on top with a sketch of a fire and the words, *'It's been fun cutting out my heart, but it's time for you to burn. I'm ready to leave and be done with this.'*

The words were written in marker, deep and black and full of sharp pain.

Leave?

She couldn't *leave.*

Where would she go?

Who would be there to keep her safe?

I stopped breathing as my eyes fell to the title page beneath.

The Boy & His Ribbon
by
Della Wild

My heart froze as the title harpooned me in the chest.

She didn't.

She couldn't.

She *promised.*

Our secrets were our lives.

No one must know.

No one must guess.

I'd taken her against the law.

I'd kept her from everyone's knowledge.

I'd fallen in love with her even though she was practically my kid.

And yet...she's written it all down.

Every sordid, broken, pure, delicious thing.

I couldn't stop my shakes or urgency as I grabbed the paper, tossed off the lighter, and ripped over the first page.

Chapter Fourteen

REN

2018

I'D NEVER BEEN the best reader—no matter how much time Della spent teaching me—yet reading that manuscript, I absorbed the words through my fingers as well as my eyes.

The story leapt from the pages, latching sharp fangs into my heart. Every emotion and carefully fabricated lie ripped apart my life, dousing me in blistering honesty, pouring its black and white truth into the wounds it left behind.

It wasn't just words that sliced me, but Della's voice. Her vibrant honesty. Her fierce tenacity reading aloud the secrets she'd written.

...that was what he did to me, you see? He made my entire life a jewellery box of special, sad, hard, happy, incredible moments that I want to wear each and every day.

*

I can honestly say Ren is my favourite word.
I love every history attached to it.
I love every pain lashed to it.
I love the boy it belongs to.

*

To me, Ren was magical.
He might not have been able to read and write, but he was the smartest person I knew.

*

I wish I could paint a better picture of how much I looked up to him.
How much I worshipped him.
How much I loved him even then.

*

Amazing what love can make someone do, right?

In my toddler brain, I associated him calling me Ribbon with his admittance of loving me. He'd accepted me as his own. He no longer needed to remind himself that I wasn't born to be his.

∗

Sometimes, and don't judge me for this, but sometimes, I would do something naughty just to have him yell at me. I know it was wrong, but when Ren yelled, he drenched it with passion.

∗

How many times do you think a person can survive a broken heart?
Any ideas?
I would like to know because Ren has successfully broken mine, repaired it, shattered mine, fixed it, crushed mine, and somehow glued it back together again and again.

∗

I was jealous that he was close to another when I was supposed to be the only one. I was angry that he turned to another for comfort and didn't come to me. But most of all, I was in shattered pieces because I wasn't enough anymore.

∗

I'm in love with Ren Wild.

It looks even worse in bold, doesn't it?
It looks like a life sentence I can never be free of…which, in a way, is exactly what it is.

∗

But what I do know is I will always love Ren.
I will always be in love with Ren.
And I also know I will never have him.

∗

Why do I do this to myself?
Why do I insist on slicing through the sticky tape on my constantly breaking heart and stabbing it over and over again?
Can you answer me because I'm honestly at the end of my limit.

∗

The next time Ren and I ran, I wanted it to be for good. I never wanted to tie him to a new place so I could go to school. I never wanted him to feel as trapped as I did. I wanted to be free because maybe, just maybe, away from people and rules and constant reminders, Ren might slip enough to realise he loved me, too.

∗

That was my true performance because he never knew how much I sobbed the moment he closed the door, promising to be home soon.
I sobbed so much I couldn't breathe, and my tears were no longer tears, but great heaving, ugly convulsions where hugging myself didn't work, where lying to myself didn't work, where promises that it would get better definitely didn't work.
I'm sure you can probably guess what I did next?

If you can't, then you've never been in love with someone who was off making a future with someone else.

My breath roared in my ears. My limbs turned shaky and liquid.

I only had minutes to read, but I skimmed as fast as I could, absorbing letters of pain, heartache, and confusion.

I recognised the moments she wrote about.

I remembered the attitude she gave me around Cassie. The jealousy she tried to hide. The possessiveness she never stopped nursing. The obsession of keeping our family just us and no one else.

I had no fucking idea her withdrawal and moods were because she thought I'd replaced her with Cassie. I was so naïve to think she hadn't seen me sneaking off to make out time and time again.

Fuck.

Even with the kiss she'd given me when she was thirteen, I'd believed her when she said it was purely growing pains and learning what attraction was.

An experiment, she called it.

I'd *believed* her when she lied point-blank to my face.

I'd chosen to trust what she said rather than focus on what her body language told me. What her eyes screamed. What her sighs whispered.

How could I be so fucking *stupid?*

How could I be so blind?

How had I not seen how distraught she'd been the night I went out on that second date with some woman I couldn't remember? How had I not heard her tears or run back to her to stop her from losing her virginity instead of forcing myself to believe I was doing the right thing by finding comfort in arms I was allowed rather than dying for the ones I wasn't?

My hands curled around the pages, wanting to wring her neck for years of bullshit, while at the same time, wanting to clutch her close and say I finally understood. Understood the unrequited pining. Understood the burning jealousy at the thought of anyone else having her but me. Understood the epic heights of such sweet agony and the almost addictive properties of loving someone you just can't have.

The night she lost her virginity, I'd done that. I'd pushed her into doing something final by believing I was the only one hurting. That I was the only one struggling with right and wrong.

Fuck!

I spun around, one hand latched around the pages and another tangled in my hair.

I needed to get the hell out of here before I did something

unforgivable.

But…everything locked into place.

My heart stopped beating. My body stopped shaking. I swallowed a groan as Della stood dripping wet in a towel, glowering at me in the doorway.

We stared.

And stared.

And *stared*.

I didn't move.

She didn't move.

I hadn't heard the shower turn off.

I didn't feel her arrive.

I'd been too focused on learning the years of pain I'd put her through to focus on the present.

She'd been in love with me. Was she still? When did she know? How long had she lied? How badly had I ruined this?

Slowly, my heart tripped into beating again, wary and worried, quiet and quick.

With blazing blue eyes and wet blonde hair plastered against creamy shoulders, she padded barefoot toward me.

I stumbled backward, my knees giving way at the delirious perfection of seeing her again, of her seeing me, of us being alone together—away from others and judging opinions.

My lips parted to speak, to say something that could delete the years of agony, soothe months of hardship, and have her love me the same way she did before I'd stupidly run.

But my voice no longer worked, my lungs no longer operated. She closed the distance, bringing familiar smells of vanilla and melon until she reached out and snatched the pages dripping with secrets from my hands.

I flinched as if she'd punched me in the gut.

Tears glittered in her gaze as sadness so deep and cloying seemed to blur her before me. "You read them…" Her whisper fissured with soul-breaking disbelief.

And for the first time…I saw her.

Truly saw her.

Not as a baby.

Not as a toddler.

Not as a child.

I saw her as Della.

Herself.

Her own creation.

A creation I'd had no hand in, no part in nurturing or raising. She was no longer mine; she belonged only to herself, and she'd utterly crushed me beneath her written honesty.

"Ribbon," I breathed. My voice shook. My hands curled into fists as I took in her wild, wet, blonde hair, the sharp wings of her collarbone, the swell of her breasts beneath the towel, and the long willowy strength of her sun-kissed arms and legs.

The first time I'd used her nickname in far too long.

But I had no choice.

The word was torn from my entire being as I stood staring at the most stunning creature I'd ever seen.

How had I prevented my eyes from seeing?

How had I believed she was merely pretty—just my little Della who needed me to survive?

How had I convinced myself that she loved me only as a friend when everything between us flared hot and forbidden with years of pent-up desire?

She was never innocent like I believed.

She was never pure like I hoped.

She was *none* of those things.

Not anymore.

She was sin and sex and such sizzling chemistry, my entire body burst into flames.

I couldn't take my eyes off her.

I couldn't breathe as explosion after explosion hit me, realisation after realisation, acceptance after acceptance that I'd loved this girl since I'd stolen her yet…here now, this very fucking moment, I fell head over heels, madly, desperately, horribly in love with her, and it fucking *ruined* me.

Her words…her confessions…I didn't stand a goddamn chance.

I shot forward, grabbing her tight and clutching her to me.

A hug.

Our first hug in so damn long.

Her body was unyielding—no longer open to my touch. She was braver, stronger, sexier, and having her in my arms, my body shook off the shackles I'd always locked tight and fell away.

I hardened, I groaned, I buried my face in her hair and allowed myself to shake with fear of losing her.

She didn't move in my embrace. Her back bowed as I pulled her closer. Her breath caught as I wedged us tighter, no longer keeping propriety between us, allowing her to feel how affected I was having her in my arms, wanting her to know I was done lying to her and myself.

That I felt something I shouldn't feel.

That I'd felt it for years, and this was my confession after reading all of hers.

My hips rocked against hers, seeking an answer, desperate to know it wasn't too late as I burrowed my nose into her hair, inhaling her, kissing her, wanting to kiss her lips but unable to let go long enough to pull her face to mine.

I was close to breaking.

Emotionally, physically, sexually.

My mind was full of heat and sin, a clawing hunger that had nothing to do with sex but everything to do with finally showing her how I felt about her—how tortured I was because of it.

Holding her again, hugging her after years of miscommunication, bullshit, and dancing a dance we didn't understand, I felt as if I'd returned home, and the one person who was home no longer knew me or invited me in.

I was cast out into the cold, and my fingers dug harder into her skin as I shook my head against her rigidness, the coldness, the unbreakable ice she bristled with.

Pressure tingled in my spine, goosebumps prickled my skin, and a heaviness that could only be described as regret filled my eyes.

Tears distorted my vision for all the waste, all the mess we'd put each other through by not talking to one another. Not being brave enough to admit there was something more.

There had *always* been something more.

There had always been fate puppeteering our lives as if we were its own personal entertainment where survival fell away in favour of sex and two people who loved each other more than life itself were forced to break apart to stay bound by society's rules.

"Della." I forced myself to unwrap my arms and step back. My body howled at the distance, but I couldn't touch her when she didn't want to be touched.

"Please, Della..." I didn't know what I asked for, but the brittle unhappiness on her face snapped into rage-filled indignation. "I'm sorry."

"Sorry?" She laughed once, shattering the shocked silence between us, deleting her tears, and choosing rage over disbelief. Instead of stepping into my arms like I needed her to, instead of kissing me as I was begging her to, she hefted the heavy pages of her manuscript and threw them at my face with all her might.

They hit me square in the jaw, shredding my chin with paper cuts, sending me reeling backward as A4 snow fluttered to the floor.

"What the—" I rubbed the impact zone, wincing in pain.

"How *dare* you!" she seethed. "How *dare* you walk back in here and think you have any right to read what is mine? How dare you touch me after years of avoiding my hugs? How dare you, Ren! How fucking *dare* you!"

Her fury roared in my ears, and I backed up as she hit my chest with fist after tiny fist. Tears streaked down her face, mixing with errant droplets from her shower. Her bare toes dug into the carpet, pushing her forward, giving her power to defeat me.

"Get out!" Her cheeks turned red with hatred. "Get out. *Get out!*"

"Della! Wait—" I tried to grab her wrists as she pummelled me, but I didn't succeed. "Let me explain." Every time I touched her, my fingers seared with need. Having her so close made my body crave and harden and do things I'd always forbidden it to do around her.

It was a traitor, but then again, so was my goddamn heart.

She continued hitting me, her hair flying in damp curls. "There's nothing to explain. You left! You left me alone. You *left* me, Ren! I've cried myself to sleep, desperate to earn just *one* more hug from you, and now you're somehow here and I want nothing to do with them! You have no right to hug me. No right to read something that was never yours to read. How *could* you? That wasn't for you! That wasn't for *anyone*. It's not yours. It was *never* yours."

"Stop." Finally, I managed to grab her furious fists, gulping against the heaven of touching her. "What was never mine?"

Her eyes flashed, turquoise fire and navy brimstone. "*All* of it. None of it. It doesn't matter. Just...*get out!* Go back to wherever you ran to. I don't need you anymore. I *can't* need you anymore. This is too hard as it is." Her lips twisted into a grimace. "You're making this impossible for m-me—" Her voice broke as a sob stole her breath.

"Della. Fuck." Tugging her closer, I lost the ability to talk.

Words evaded me. Apologies and explanations and questions.

Only my heart functioned, and that was full of newness.

"You might not need me anymore, but I need you more than ever," I whispered, holding tight as she struggled. "I've been so blind. So fucking blind."

She stilled, her sudden frozenness unnerving. "*What* did you say?"

"I said I'm sorry. So unbelievably sorry."

"*Ha!*" She wriggled out of my grip, pushing me away. "I don't want your apology. I don't *accept* your apology. You leave after promising you never would, then come back at the worst possible time? No. Nuh uh. I won't let you make me feel as if I've lost my mind. I won't let you do this to me, do you hear me?!"

"Do what? Come back because I can't survive without you? Come back to tell you the truth that's been fucking tearing me apart every day since I left—"

"Stop it!" She clutched her hair. "This isn't real. I'm imagining this. I've finally lost it, and you're just a figment—"

"I'm not. I'm real." I grabbed her wrists, yanking her hands from her golden strands. "I'm here. You're here. And I want to tell you that what I read in those pages...fuck, Della. Why didn't you tell me?"

Her gaze fell to the scattered paper by our feet. Her face twisted with another complex recipe of hate and horror. "God, you *did* read it. How much did you read? That wasn't yours, Ren! None of it was. It was mine, and you've taken that just like you've taken everything else from me!"

My heart imploded into a black hole, sucking everything into it until my insides hollowed out with grief. I'd not only hurt the woman I loved, I'd ruined her.

Just like I ruined myself.

"I didn't mean to hurt you. I didn't mean—"

"But you did! You left."

"But I'm back now."

"Yes, and you read something that was private!"

"But it's *us.* You wrote about us. Me and you. If I'm not allowed to read it, then who is?"

"Anyone but you!" She threw her hands toward the ceiling. "Literally anyone—" Her rage abandoned her with another rib-quaking sob. "God, why does this hurt so much?!" She stifled her sobs as fast as they appeared, but not before slicing my heart with their razor-sharp agony. "Just...go away."

"I'm not leaving."

"Well, I don't want you here."

"Too bad." I crossed my arms even though I trembled with every urge to sweep her off her feet, gather her close, and rock her on the bed. She was angry, yes, but beneath her anger was heart-shattering pain.

Pain I'd caused.

Pain I needed to repair.

Wiping away wet tears, she narrowed her eyes. Her chest rose and fell with temper as she bit out, "What are you doing here anyway? Why now? Do you know how hard you're making this for me? I thought I was going crazy when I came back here. Everything smells of you. My bed was made. The shower clean. I thought I'd lost it. But now...now it makes sense." Her anger smoked into something new and condemning. "Wait. You were here before...weren't you? Oh, God." She froze, flinching with ice. "How long have you been back?"

I squeezed the back of my neck. I wanted to discuss anything else but that. She hated me enough without giving her another reason.

"*Ren?*" She stepped closer, bringing her fury until it gnawed into my flesh. "How long, Ren?"

I swallowed hard before admitting, "A few weeks."

"Weeks!"

"Maybe a couple of months."

"*What?!*" She spun around, her towel loosening around her fuming frame, teasing me with glimpses of skin as she snatched it tight and jerkily re-did the knot by her breasts.

I gulped back a wash of insane hunger.

This was dangerous.

Our fights always made me feel out of control, and this one was no different. Yet this time, my desire to rip off her towel and force her to understand what I was saying overshadowed my desire to stop arguing.

What I'd been trying to say all along.

If only she'd fucking listen!

"I couldn't leave you," I snapped, my own temper building to match hers. I hated that she'd turned this moment into something violent instead of the homecoming I desperately needed. I hated that I'd hurt her so much she couldn't forgive me like she usually would. And I hated that ravenous appetites did their best to unhinge me and make me forget that I might be ready to accept that I wanted her in so many indecent ways, but first and foremost, I was her friend, protector, and caregiver, and she had every right to hate me for doing exactly what I said I'd never do.

"I abandoned you. I know that." I stepped forward, chasing her as she paced the small bedroom. "And you have every right to hate me. But, Della, I need you to listen. I came back because I couldn't stay away. I tried. I really did. I did my best to leave—to let you live your life without me ruining it even more—but each time I packed up my gear and hit the trail, I ended up doubling back until I found the same camp. I-I couldn't go. I couldn't stop what I feel for you."

If I expected a thawing in her temper at my inability to walk away, I was sorely disappointed.

Her cheeks glowed with a brighter red, her chest pink and flushed. She faced me head-on, scorn painting her face like vicious makeup. "You couldn't what? Go through with it? Turn your back on me? Your only family? Or you couldn't leave the comforts of the city after having running water and a salary for so long? Because I sure as hell don't think you came back for me!"

"I did. I came—"

"Don't you *dare* lie to me, Ren. Not anymore. I'm *done* with lies."

"Good, because so am I!"

"Fine!" she screamed. "So tell me what you came here to say and get lost!"

My gaze tripped to the floor where I stood on a page with the bold words **I'm in love with Ren Wild**, and my body jerked with hypocrisy. My own rage unfurled to treacherous levels as I pointed at the damning letters. "You're done with lies, huh? How do you explain this then? How do you explain every line you wrote and every confession you shared? You stand there judging me for leaving; you yell at me for daring to come back to tell you what I've wanted to tell you for years, and you pretend you have nothing to say in return."

I bent and snatched the paper, shaking it in her face. "How long, huh? How many years did you live with me, laugh with me, love me all while lying to my goddamn face? Was everything fake between us, Della? *Was it?*" I threw the paper at her, watching it flutter and float to its fallen friends on the floor. "I don't know what's real anymore. I don't know what to do. I don't know how to fix this. All I know is...you're as much to blame for this as I am."

"How do you figure—" She huffed in disgust. "Are you saying I *didn't* love you? That I pretended to care about you even though you've been the only person in my life since I was a baby?"

"No—"

"Are you saying that I lied to you when I was a kid and told you I loved you? That I made it up when I said I was happiest teaching you in the hayloft or that my heart didn't splinter when I watched you with Cassie? What, Ren? What part of our life together am I lying about?"

"I'm not saying—"

"You are." She planted hands on her hips, showing off the swell of her breasts and the tormenting shadow of her nipple so close to being revealed if the towel slipped just a little more. "Then again, maybe you're saying that for seventeen years, I didn't care about you? That you weren't the most important person to me?" Her tears started anew, fresh and glittering. "That you weren't my world, or that I didn't need you, or that I didn't miss you every damn night since you left? That I didn't curse myself for everything I'd done, every mistake I made. That I didn't wish I could turn back the clock and change so many things. That I didn't beg for a chance to make it all better, to find a way to stop my heart from switching in its affection, to somehow seek a way to stop all the pain and—"

Angry sobs interrupted her tirade, giving me time to grunt around my own agony, "I'm not saying any of that—"

"Then what *are* you saying?"

"I'm saying you lied about how you loved me! A-and I…I lied, too."

Silence plummeted us into frigid waters, causing the fire between us to smoke and billow.

Her chest rose and fell as breathing bordered hyperventilation. We glowered at each other, truth bright and fragile and hesitant—almost as if disbelieving this was the moment we came clean.

The moment.

The moment we'd been running from for so fucking long.

Our eyes locked, clutching hard with the knowledge that this time…this time, we weren't shoving it under the rug, or pretending we hadn't just confessed, or running from the truth that none of this meant anything other than teenage hormones and miscommunication.

We were through with bullshit.

And it hurt to understand we'd both been hiding for so long. Both forgotten how to be honest. Both missing in a sea of deception.

Her eyes downcast, argument raging and fading while honesty made her hiccup just once. She glanced at the bold line I'd pointed at, the printed permanent reminder that I wasn't making this up. That for years, I wasn't picking up on signals that weren't there. That I wasn't going slowly insane.

I'd been reading her truth. But I'd been too afraid to face mine.

"Oh," she finally whispered, shrugging sadly. "Yeah, that."

My heart fucking shattered.

This time, I swooped toward her with more than just the need to touch her but with the desire to fix everything. To tell her she wasn't alone. Not anymore.

Grabbing her cheeks, I ran my thumbs over her cheekbones as I pushed her the final distance to the wall where her back pressed and her breath caught, and I lowered my head to nudge her nose with mine. "Yeah, that," I murmured.

My heart.

Fuck, my heart.

It cried at finally touching her in a way I'd wanted to do for so incredibly long. My body cursed for so many incidents where we could've solved this with conversation and not ran away.

Her teeth chattered beneath my fingers as she shook as much as I did. We'd always shook when we fought. Always been so affected by the other's temper that our worlds were in disarray until we stopped.

The familiarity of such a thing. The realisation that this wasn't just a girl I was in love with but the one person who'd been there every step of my existence made it hard to breathe.

I sucked in air greedily, lungs useless, panting against so many things while doing my best to chase away my trembles even as my entire body went weak and wobbly for finally holding my Ribbon this way.

The fallen papers crunched beneath my boot as I shifted my weight, leaning into her, seeking an answer. "Why didn't you tell me?"

She flinched, her eyes closing beneath an avalanche of pain.

This hurt.

Everything hurt.

"Della...please." My calloused thumbs caressed her silky-soft skin, catching on her young perfection with my older imperfection.

Ten years separated us.

Ten years was an eternity when she was a babe and I was a boy, but now...it no longer held such power. I refused to let it because I didn't know what I'd do if I couldn't touch her the way I was touching her now.

She laughed quietly, full of torture and tragedy. "I did tell you. In a roundabout way."

"You didn't."

"But I did." She dared meet my eyes. "I never understood how I could touch you, hug you, kiss you, and you never knew. I didn't know how I could hide my jealousy when you were with Cassie or later with your one-night stands. I lay awake at night analysing every sentence I said to you, amazed that you never heard what I'd been shouting for longer than I could remember."

She pressed her face into my right hand, daring to donate a kiss on the edge of my work-worn palm even as her eyes flashed with resentment. "Is that what you came back to hear? To hurt me a little more? To force me to admit that I've been stupidly in love with you for years, and there was nothing I could do about it?" Her blue gaze burned. "Is it, Ren? Because fine, you got your wish. Whatever you read...it's true. I started writing it for college, but then I realised you were right all along. I can never tell people our story because they won't understand. To start with, I was more afraid of them seeking you out and putting you in prison for kidnapping, but now I'm more afraid that I'd be judged for falling in love with someone who raised me. I'm horrified of what they'd say, the looks they'd give, the disgust on their faces because, even though I understand it's morally wrong, I can't help how I feel."

She kicked a foot-trodden paper, her body wriggling against mine. "I'm sick of feeling like I have to hide. From you and everyone else. I'm sick of lying to David that one day I'll get over you. I'm sick of watching you self-destruct by sleeping with a parade of women when

I was there all along. Wanting you. Waiting for you. Begging you to just open your stupid eyes and *see* me—"

My boot thudded heavily as I took the final step into her. My leg between her legs. My hips to her hips. My body against her body. My heart pounded as I cupped her cheeks harder, willing her to understand. "They're open now. Believe me. I see you." My fingertips burned as I forced myself to be gentle.

She froze, inhaling quick. Her eyelids fell to that sultry stare I had no power against, and this time, I didn't fight it. This time, my gaze latched onto her parted mouth, and I couldn't do anything else. I collapsed against her, I breathed in her delicious, familiar scent, and I pressed my lips—

She tore away, ripping her face from my hold and ducking beneath the cage of my arms.

For a second, my brain couldn't figure out what had just happened. That the kiss didn't connect. But as I spun around to face her, my jeans tight with unrequited desire, and my mind a fucking mess, I gulped back pure agony as she shook her head, wrapping tight arms around herself as more tears cascaded down her cheeks. "I-I don't know if you do. If you truly saw me, Ren, you'd understand that this—"

"This what?"

"Whatever this is won't fix what you've been running from."

"Don't you think I don't know that? That's why I'm here, Della. Aren't you fucking listening? I'm in love with you, too. Goddammit, can't you tell? Can't you see how much I'm breaking?"

That dreaded stifling silence fell again, numbing everything as she gawked at me. My words didn't seem to register, bouncing off a force field designed to protect her heart, but then they stabbed into awareness, and she crumpled in place, wincing and crying, shaking her head with panic. "What sort of cruel joke is this? You missed me in the forest so figured you'd get me back by telling me what you think I need to hear?"

There was no hope in her gaze, no joy like I hoped; only resignation and age-old grief. "I know you, Ren. I know you'd never let yourself think of me any differently than the way you always have. I'm your Little Ribbon. Untouchable. Protectable. Something to be adored but never touched. Oh no, *never* touched."

I closed my eyes briefly, unprepared for the depth of pain her mistrust caused. "I don't know how to make you believe me. I'm *in love* with you. I'm head over fucking heels for you. I have been for years. How can I make you see that?"

I spilled my darkest secret with my eyes still closed, and when I

opened them again, she was closer to the door and farther from me, her gaze tormented with new thoughts. The same dangerous light she'd had when she cornered me with the idea of going to school the first time, of the suggestion we share a last name, of the fight when she didn't want to go back to the city after months of bliss in the forest—glowed bright and savage, ready to destroy me.

I knew that look.

It was a look that petrified me because I never won against it.

My hand rose, imploring her not to run or do something we'd both regret. "Della…"

She shook her head again. "Don't."

"Whatever you're thinking…stop it."

She licked her lips, her forehead furrowing deep. "I just remembered what you said."

"That I'm in love with you?"

"No. Before that. The truth."

"That is the goddamn truth. I love—"

"Stop it, Ren! Okay, just *stop* it!" she shouted, her tone snippy and sharp. "I can't deal with this. You're spouting nonsense that makes me think you hit your head. And that's after you admitted that you've been back for months. *Months!*" Her voice thinned until it was soundless. "You've been watching me, haven't you? I wasn't imagining it."

I hung my head. "No, you weren't."

"Every day?"

"Yes."

"How could you? How could you do that to me?"

I didn't understand how I'd hurt her, but I put aside my questions and bowed to hers. "Because I couldn't stop myself. I couldn't stand to be away from you."

"But you *left!*" Her voice rose with a breakable octave. "You left me. You walked out that door."

"I know."

"Ugh!" She blinked back tears, her body wobbling with sadness and rage. "Want to know why I don't believe that you're in love with me? Because if you were, there is no way you could wait so long. Months, you've been back. Months where you watched me and made me think I was going insane. Remember all those times growing up when I knew you stared at me and I stared at you? Remember how in-tune and aware we were of each other?

"I knew that day when you needed help counting and charging up those hay-buying customers. I felt you looking at me over acres of paddock. I've woken up at night to you watching me. Just like you did with me. I've spent a lifetime learning how my skin prickles when you think of me. Did you forget that, Ren? Did you forget that I might have been lying to you for years, but you've just tried to do the same with me in the *worst* possible way?"

I shook my head. "I-I don't understand. I needed time to figure out how to tell you—"

"No, you needed time to do your best to convince yourself it wasn't real."

"If you know it's real, why are you arguing?"

"Because you didn't come to me the *moment* you returned. The difference of loving someone and being in love, Ren, is loving someone can be full of obligation and self-denial. But being *in* love makes you selfish and greedy and *hungry*. It turns you into a self-serving monster because you can't breathe unless you have the one person you need."

She laughed coldly. "I know because I've lived in that emotion for so damn long. I've hated myself for how much I wanted you. What I did to myself thinking about you. How I used other boys to scratch the itch that was you. But you? You watch me from afar. You selfishly know I'm safe, watching me, studying me, all while I'm left wondering if you're even still alive! How could someone who says they're in love with another do that, huh? How could you stay away when it's taking all I have not to rip off my towel and pull you down onto my bed even while I hate you?"

I staggered under her condemnation and the mental image of her tumbling naked on her bed. "Fuck, Della."

I didn't know what I cursed at. The brutal honesty of her latest confession or the barbaric, almost primitive need to climb on top of her and force her to believe me. To crawl inside her body and soul and growl into her ear while I took her violently. *'See? I am telling the truth. I do love you. I love you so much you make me goddamn insane.'*

But I shook away the dark brutality, taking my turn to be the sinner with secrets. "Regardless of what you think, I *am* in love with you, Della. And I stayed away because I-I—"

"What? *Tell me!*" she screamed, her sudden outburst ratcheting up my temper to uncontrollable levels. She'd successfully threaded lust with rage, and it was a cocktail I no longer had any power over.

"I wasn't ready, okay?! *Fuck*, I don't think I'll ever be ready to accept that I've fallen in love with the child I stole. That even now, I struggle seeing you as Della, grown-up and filled out, an adult in your own right, and not buckle beneath the image of you when you were five years old with your beautiful blonde hair and fascination with your ribbon."

I dug my hands into my scalp. "It makes me sick, okay? It makes me want to burn out my eyes for ever seeing you naked as a kid or hugging you when you were a teen. It makes me want to cut off my own cock for ever getting hard around you, for all the inappropriate thoughts I had about you, for despising the boys you dated, for wanting to die knowing you let another fuck you when all I ever wanted was the freedom to love you in that way."

My temper cindered into exhaustion, leaving me breathless. I shrugged brokenly with palms spread in surrender. "How can I admit such things to you, Ribbon? How can I stand here and confess that I've jerked off to images of you? That when you were still innocent, still untouched, still so fucking young, I was using other women to somehow find a way to remain honourable and not crawl into your bed? Do you know how many times my willpower almost failed? Do you know how many dreams I've had? How many times I've had you in my arms and on my lips, only to wake up and find it was all a fantasy?

"It was everything I could do to hide such things from myself, but you...I could never tell you because I couldn't stand for you to think of me as a monster. For you to see me as others' would. A paedophile. A beast. A twisted-up son of a bitch who would rather put himself first than the child he'd sworn his life to."

My breathing came ragged as she took a hesitant step toward me.

However, this time, instead of disbelief, there was a sliver of something, a fledgling hint of hope, an aura of satisfaction of finally, *finally* hearing my truth. "How long?"

I shook my head. That was one secret I wanted to take to my grave.

But she came closer, her towel slipping farther, her eyes getting softer. "How long, Ren?"

"It seems like forever," I moaned, shaking my head again, begging her to let it go.

Her fingers fluttered on my overly hot forearm. Sweat covered me from fighting and declaring. My energy was gone. I was more exhausted than I'd ever been in my entire life, but still, she didn't let it go.

"Please...I need to know."

I looked up, flinching at just tasting the words. My tongue burned with wanting to lie, to add on a few years, to not make myself such a child-stealing savage. But she'd been honest with me, and now, it was my turn to be honest with her.

Hesitantly, I raised my hand, cupping her cheek for the second time, grazing my thumb once again over the delicate bones that swooped up toward stunning blue eyes. This time, she didn't jerk away, and I stared so damn long into her that I became lightheaded and terrified.

My voice was barely a whisper as I admitted, "Since you kissed me."

She tilted her head, biting her lip as if her emotions threatened to drag her under, but not before she got her final answer. "Which time? The kiss that drove you away or the kiss in the stable at Cherry River?"

I closed my eyes.

I'd been given an opportunity to hide the worst of my transgressions. I could say it was the kiss she'd given me when she was seventeen—so close to eighteen that it was no longer illegal to fall in love with a minor.

But...I couldn't do it.

Tonight had been a truth-tearing hurricane, and I had no choice but to murmur, "When you were thirteen." I sighed with every sickness and shame I'd carried for five interminably long years. "The night you woke me up kissing me."

"*Oh.*"

One tiny sound as she jerked and fell.

I wasn't prepared for the way she crumpled. The way her legs gave up supporting her. The way her body shoved aside her anger and tumbled pliant and welcoming into my arms. And I definitely wasn't prepared for the way her eyes welled with a different kind of tear.

A tear full of heartache and years of hiding; a glistening, glittering joy that infected my heart until I felt forgiven. Understood. *Redeemed.*

Somehow, without saying a word, she gave me absolute absolution.

"I thought you hated me for that."

"I did." I pressed my forehead to hers, needing to be close, needing to sit down. "But not for reasons I made you think. Not for reasons I made myself believe."

"You saw me that night? Truly saw me."

"I saw that my feelings toward you were changing. That there was something unsaid between us. Something that wasn't allowed. Something that only grew bigger and more incessant as we grew older."

"Is this real?" she breathed. "Did you honestly just say you fell in love with me the night I fell in love with you?"

My knees quaked as I backed toward her bed, holding her tight and forcing her to trip with me. "I think I fell in love with you the day I returned for you in that house where I'd left you as a baby. The moment you saw me, you crawled so fast. You knew you were mine, and I was yours, even then. I'd never had anyone be so excited to see me. So innocent with their affection. So trusting that I'd keep her safe."

I sat down heavily. The instant the mattress held my depleted weight, Della spread her legs and climbed onto my lap, her towel opening indecently, revealing naked heat-flushed skin that I desperately wanted to drink.

But I forced myself to keep my eyes on hers, adoring the way her legs wrapped around my back and her arms looped around my neck and our foreheads remained glued together, our eyes so close, our lips so near.

This was all so new, and yet, so heartbreakingly familiar.

This was Della.

She was my home.

"I'm not saying I fell in love with you in this kind of way," I murmured as our lips inched closer. "I'm saying there are so many ways I fell in love with you. Most of them pure and utterly unconditional, but that night in the stable, the night you entered my dreams and made me plummet...that night was different."

Her chest rose and fell, her nipples pink and tight in my peripheral vision as her towel fell away, draping damply over my arms where I hugged her.

She breathed quicker, harder, as our mouths crept ever closer, quietly, tentatively, afraid that any moment this perfection would shatter, and we'd wake from yet another life-tormenting dream.

"I'm sorry I made it impossible for you to stay," she whispered, looking deep, deep into my eyes, all that trust and affection and connection back in place.

She was home, just like me.

She'd returned to being the girl I would kill for and the woman who had every power to kill me. Only this time, there were no shields. No blockage of honesty. No slurry of lies. The way she looked at me was unlike anything she'd done before.

I'd caught glimpses, sure. The nights in the forest after she'd run away. The moments before I'd head out for a shallow night of pleasure with unknown women. The seconds before I'd climb into bed and she'd stare at me from the corridor as I turned out the lights.

Glimpses and glances—windows into the world of just how desperately she loved me, the same world I'd been hiding from her.

"You didn't make it impossible. You were trying to make things better by pushing me to admit what I was afraid of." I brushed back her hair, my body hardening, heating. My mouth watering, tingling.

Our lips drew closer still, magnets intent on connecting.

A new kind of energy crackled around us—just as dangerous and potent, but this time, it was passion, not rage.

Passion I never believed I was permitted to feel around her.

Passion I never thought I could earn.

I basked in it, loving the spark and sizzle of her body pressed against mine. Of the wondrous anticipation of where this was going, the build-up of seventeen years of living in each other's pockets, of being each other's everything, of finally coming full circle from friends to possibly more.

More than I could ever deserve.

The first graze of mouths was barely there. A whisper of touch. A kick of taste. But my heart ran away, galloping and pounding as wild as our shared surname and just as feral.

Della jerked in my arms, sucking a shaky breath. Her legs squeezed around my waist, her arms twitching around my neck. "Ren?"

My eyes were too heavy to keep open. They went half-mast. My body aching. My mind messed and incoherent. "Yeah?"

"I want to kiss you."

I licked my lips, groaning beneath my breath. "Yeah, me too."

"But...you need to know something."

The back of my neck strained with pressure, desperate to press my mouth to hers and devour any more words. I no longer wanted conversation. I wanted something so much less innocent that damn conversation. "What do I need to know, Della Ribbon?"

She shivered as I ran my fingers up her naked spine and ducked to press a kiss on the very same collarbone that had tormented me for most of my life.

Old memories crackled like ancient TV channels, overlapping the Della I had in my arms with the baby I'd carried in my backpack.

I jerked and shoved the disgusting comparison away, doing my best to silence the voice hissing that this was wrong. That I had no right. No permission.

"You kiss me," she murmured, her back bowing, pressing more of her skin into my mouth. "And that's it. There's no going back. No way I can stop loving—"

I didn't let her finish.

My arms banded tighter, and my chin arched up.

And I kissed her.

Hard.

Deep.

Wet.

Long.

I kissed her for all the nights I'd wanted to kiss her but couldn't.

I kissed her for all the years I'd needed her but daren't.

And she kissed me back.

Just as hard, deep, wet, long.

Her taste.

Her softness.

Jesus Christ.

She moaned into me, her tongue darting out and licking mine. Her body writhing on my lap, her weight and movement rubbing against the rigid hardness in my jeans.

I wanted so fucking much to shove aside my clothing and consummate this newfound acceptance. I wanted to propose to her and marry her and never let her go again.

But as our kiss turned from exploration and newness to uncivilised grinding and gasping, the same crackling, snowy memories came back.

Of Della laughing as I cannonballed naked as a fifteen-year-old into the lake.

Of Della crying when she was stung by a bee and my seventeen-year-old self sucking out the stinger and kissing her wound all better.

Of Della reading aloud the sex education book when I was eighteen and just as lost as I'd ever been, finally realising that she was so far above me I could never get her back.

Boom, boom, boom.

Reminder, reminder, reminder.

I tore my lips from hers and shot up.

Twisting sharply, I placed her on the bed and yanked out of her embrace before her eyes had fully opened and her lips fully noticed they were no longer being kissed.

"What?" Her eyes instantly filled with blue terror. "Ren...no." She scrambled to her knees. Naked as the day she'd torn off her dress and forced me to see that she was no longer a virgin. No longer untouched. "Don't do this. You promised."

I backed away, pinching the bridge of my nose, unable to stop the torrent of recollections.

Of Della riding Cassie's horse for the first time and falling off.

Of Della giggling at something Patricia said only to stop laughing when I went in hearing distance.

Of Della watching me with a heart-stealing look as I chopped firewood shirtless.

Della.

Della.

Della.

Always there, always mine, and now, I didn't know how to separate past from future.

"I-I—" I balled my hands, forcing myself to look her in the eye. "I want you, Della. You know that now, and I have no intention of lying to you. I'm in love with you. I want to be with you. But right now…right now, I need to work through this, okay? Can you give me time? Can you understand how hard this is for me?"

She stood, fumbling for her towel and holding it as a barricade in front of her. "I understand because it's hard for me, too. Don't you think I have the same memories? Of you kissing Cassie? Of you younger and softer and nothing more than an uncomplicated farm boy who made me fall in love with a single smile?"

I held up my hand. "I know this is unfair, but our situations are nothing alike."

"They're *everything* alike."

"No." I shook my head firmly, scolding her like a child when, only seconds ago, I'd been kissing her like a man. What role did I play in her life anymore? Disciplinarian or partner? Father or husband? "They're not alike. At all."

Stalking to the door, I wrenched it open before saying softly, "I raised you, Little Ribbon. In my heart, I hold so many elements of love for you. I've fed you from my own fingers. I've washed your body. I've held you tight while you cried. I know we aren't siblings, but somewhere along the way, I did love you as a brother. I need to untangle that love before I can move on as…as—"

"As my lover?"

I winced. "Yes."

"Are you sure you want to be? This isn't just you running away again?" Her eyes sparkled with another wave of unshed tears.

I hated that I'd let her down all over again, but I wouldn't be honest with her if I didn't tell her how hard this would be. How difficult I found it separating all the Della's I knew, and *somehow* learn to allow myself to love all of them after she'd been off-limits for so long.

But I also knew if we were going to do this, we couldn't do it here.

We couldn't do this where people knew us as relatives.

We couldn't do this where we might be caught.

"Do you still have the same phone number?" I asked, my fingers clutching the doorknob, holding myself in place, stopping me from running back to her and shoving her down on the bed.

From this distance, all I wanted was her, but I knew the moment I touched her my world would shatter, and I'd drown beneath memories determined to make me vomit for taking a sweet, innocent girl and turning her into something sick with want.

"Yes." She hung her head. "But I won't be here when you get back. I have to go back to David's. I only came here to burn that." She arched her chin at the scattered forgotten papers, trodden and crumpled on the floor.

My chest ached at the thought of her going back to him, but I had no choice. "Don't burn it. And give me a few hours. I'll text you, okay?"

She looked up, forlorn and afraid but resilient just like I knew her to be. "A few hours? I thought you were going to say a few days."

I smiled sadly. "I've wasted more than enough days not having you. I have no intention of wasting anymore."

She smiled, wider than before. "Okay, I can accept a few hours."

"Thank you." My eyes drank her in, imprinting this Della, the *new* Della into my mind first and foremost as I backed out the door, promising, "I'll be in touch. And when I do…we're going to talk. You're going to help me understand that there was no other path for us. That it was always going to be this way. That we were always meant to be. And then…we're going to leave."

I didn't wait for her reply.

I had some soul searching to do.

I had some compartmentalizing to sort.

And I needed to do it now.

Because once I did.

I could have her.

And my complicated world would finally be complete.

Chapter Fifteen

REN

2018

DELLA: *ARE YOU ready to talk about this?*

The glow of my cell-phone screen lit up the night-shrouded park where I rested. The bench made my ass flat from hours of sitting, watching the sun go down. Pruned bushes and carefully controlled trees granted a sense of home, but nothing was wild about their regimented flowerbeds.

I'd meant to move. I'd meant to text Della hours ago, but once I'd opened the gates of so many stored memories, I couldn't rush it.

It was a curse to have a good memory.

I didn't have to strain to pull up image after image of Della as a two-year-old, five-year-old, ten, fourteen, sixteen. I knew her body and scars from falling off horses and clumsy incidents better than I knew my own. I knew more about her than any lover should. And I didn't like how that made me feel.

Was it right for me to want her body that I'd seen grow from so small to so stunning? Was it disgusting to admit, even though I'd carried her as a child and cared for as a baby, I saw her as more than just my responsibility and legacy now? I saw her as my other half. My future. Everything I'd ever been searching for.

I guess I'd *always* seen her as my other half; I just didn't have the lust component to go with it. It made sense now why I'd always felt lonely even when she was in my arms—because some part of me knew it wanted more but couldn't have it.

Sighing heavily, I pressed reply. The alphabet spread out on an on-screen keyboard, waiting to transform thoughts into messages.

Thanks to Della, I could read, write, spell, and wrangle technology enough to be proficient. Even when we'd moved away from the

Wilsons and our regular study sessions were replaced with long hours at the milking shed and Della traded me for other boys, I hadn't stopped learning.

Instead of Della being the one to choose which textbook or subject I'd study, I merely went through her school rucksack on the nights I wasn't exhausted and read science books, math, English, then stole a few pieces of paper to work out the answers before checking mine against hers.

She'd caught me once or twice and had rushed over to kiss me. But then, she'd remembered that kissing wasn't exactly permitted anymore and would pat my shoulder with a strained smile instead.

I knew she was proud of me for continuing my studies, but I didn't do it for me. I did it for her. I did it so I could converse and calculate and not have to rely on her because I knew my job as her caregiver was almost over, and she would leave me for better things.

And when that day happened, I couldn't afford to be illiterate without her.

Then again, I'd left her before she'd left me.

And now...now there was a chance we would never be apart again.

My heart cramped with a hope so vicious it made me shake.

My fingers typed slowly, deleting my regular typos, hoping my spelling was on point. I wanted to be honest with her. I needed to be. She needed to know just what she was getting into because this was me putting everything on the line. This was me ripping up my world when I still didn't fully understand if I could.

Me: *I don't know if I'll ever be fully ready. If this was happening to someone else, and not you and me, how repulsed would you be if you knew the man was contemplating sleeping with his own kid?*

Goddammit.

I sat forward, digging my elbows into my knees and wiping my mouth with my hand.

Fuck.

Seeing it in black and white, reading how foul that sounded, I very almost dry-heaved. What the hell was I doing? I'd been driven by my desire for so long that I'd forgotten what this actually entailed. What sort of sins we were about to commit. What sort of mess we were about to create.

This wasn't me.

I wasn't this self-obsessed.

I ought to be her father figure.

I ought to be better—

Della: *First, I'm not your kid. I never felt like you were my father, and there was never any confusion about what we meant to each other. Second, forget about everyone else. They don't matter. I couldn't judge on another's life just like I don't want them to judge us.*

My head hung as I ran my fingers over the touchpad. She was right, I supposed. For some reason, we'd always clung to the boundaries that we weren't blood or related, almost as if we knew eventually we'd want more than just friendship.

Before I could reply, she sent another.

Della: *You told me this afternoon that we were going to talk. And we're talking. But if I'm honest, I don't think this can be rationalised by text message. You asked me to help you understand that there was no other path for us. That it was always going to end this way. That we were always meant to be. I'm not just saying what you want to hear, Ren. I truly believe that. And the only way to come to terms with it is to just…trust me, trust you, trust us.*

I sighed.

Her message was a lot kinder in black and white than mine had been. She'd successfully thrown my own words in my face, making me see there was no other choice for us. Even if she hadn't kissed me and firmly imprinted herself into my dreams, I would have eventually fallen for her because a man like me, I didn't love easy. I didn't trust easy. It'd taken me seventeen years to even admit I was ready to put my heart on the line in a romantic sense rather than family.

Cassie had known that about me. She'd sensed that I would never care more for her than gentle affection because I was too afraid to open myself up to pain.

Della was the only one worth risking such agony.

And as much as I'd vehemently deny it, I'd already been hurt by the Mclary's which sort of gave Della permission in a strange, unfathomable away.

She was the only one allowed to hurt me in the future.

I opened a new window and typed slowly:

Me: *Are you willing to let me work through this? Do you understand it won't be an overnight switch for me? It's going to take time.*

The moon hung heavy above, reminding me that it had been too long since I'd been in the forest. As much as I needed to live in the apartment to stay close to my addiction of stalking Della, I'd had my fill of cities.

I hadn't liked living here when Della was finishing school. There was no way I wanted to live here while we figured out whatever we were about to embark on. We'd had a near miss with her principal with rumours of her being in love with me. A mere rumour almost separated us. Now it was fact, we stood every chance of being ripped apart.

This had always felt like a temporary place. A chapter that didn't quite fit.

If it was over and we could go home...*thank God.*

Della took her time replying, and I reclined against the pigeon-crapped bench, exhaling hard.

Della: *I can't promise I won't get frustrated. I can't say I won't get mad if you kiss me, then pull away. But what I can promise is, I've wanted this since I was thirteen, and if you need another thirteen years to accept that I was born for you, then so be it. I'll be patient.*

I chuckled quietly, wincing as it turned to a cough.

I doubted she meant to be funny, but even now, her temper came through something as impersonal as a text. Somehow, it made me feel better—as if I wasn't such a monster to contemplate such a crazy idea as taking her for my own.

Me: *If we do this, we can't do it here.*

Della: *I know.*

Me: *Don't say you know as if nothing else matters. We need to think about this. You're in college. When does your course end? You're with David. How will he take you breaking up with him? What about your job at the florist? We have an apartment and furniture to get rid of. Are you prepared to say goodbye to another home?*

It took much longer for me to type such long sentences than Della, and my leg bounced as I pressed send, nervousness trickling through my blood. It wasn't a simple matter of running like previous times. We had things holding us here. We had bills and people. Or at least...Della did. She was more adult than I was in this scenario, and once again, my mind tripped down memory lane, feeding me images of her young and innocent and untouchable, doing its best to unhinge my resolve that this was what I wanted. No matter how hard.

Della: *I've already written regarding my course and withdrawn, stating a family emergency. I used part of the rent money to pay for the first semester—which I doubt I'll get back. But where we're going, we don't need the cash. I quit my job a while back. I'm not dating David; he turned me down when he realised I wasn't over you, and the apartment is easy. Terminate the lease, put our furniture back on the street corners where we got them from, pack a bag and…let's go home.*

My heart pounded as a breeze kissed my cheek, tugging me toward the black spaces where the city lights didn't reach. The darkness full of leaves and rivers.

Home.

I knew where my home was.

Did she?

Me: *Home means no running water, no supermarkets, no roof. Are you sure you want that?*

Della: *I don't know if reminding you of a younger me is a good idea, but on the night of my seventeenth and your twenty-seventh, I gave you that tent. Remember what I said?*

I groaned under my breath. That was one memory that wasn't just remembered but polished daily and treasured. She'd let me see behind her fakery that night. She'd painted a future that I'd desperately wanted, even while believing it could never happen.

Me: *You asked if I intended to stay here and said we had to start thinking about our future. That you wanted to return to the forest, and that's why you bought me that tent.*

Della: *And you asked if I was sure. You made a point to tell me there would be no boys, no jobs, no school. No future out there in the wilderness.*

Me: *And you set me straight by saying there was no future apart from with me.*

I looked at the moon again, tension slipping away. I was torturing myself about wanting Della as deeply as I did when, for so many years, I'd already been living with the same sin. I'd already accepted the mess, even then. And I wouldn't do anything to jeopardise it now. Not when we were so close.

My lips curled into a hesitant smile as my mind raced with everything we'd have to achieve. Every goodbye we had to finalise. Every beginning we were about to embrace.

Standing from the bench and striding toward the apartment, hopefully for the last time, my fingers flew, and I sent.

Me: *Pack a bag. We leave in two days.*

Chapter Sixteen

REN

2018

TWO DAYS

Forty-eight hours to delete our entire existence as the Wilds.

Della and I kept our distance while we systematically dismantled our world. She focused on selling, donating, and sorting through her stuff at David's house, while I lugged our fifth-hand couch up the steps of our place, and dragged it to the same street corner we'd salvaged it from.

My body proved just how badly I'd treated it the past few months and the residual cough from the flu made tasks last longer than I wanted.

I didn't like that Della had refused to sleep at our apartment, insisting that she owed David too much to abandon him without explaining and they needed a proper goodbye.

The urge to forbid her—the desire to beg her to be with me instead, proved I needed to keep my possessiveness in check. I'd never stopped her from hanging with her friends before.

I wouldn't start now.

Instead, I threw myself into my tasks, doing my best to tie up loose ends quickly so Della was mine and we could leave.

Scrawling a hasty poster, I announced a one-day garage sale and opened our apartment to anyone who wanted cutlery, crockery, bedding, an ancient TV, decrepit motorcycle, and anything else we couldn't carry.

I made sure to wash and pack clothes for both Della and me. Winter jackets, summer t-shirts, and every season in between. She still had her bag that we'd bought when we left the Wilsons, and I studiously ensured our rations and belongings were evenly distributed, even though I put all the heavy stuff into mine. The two pots for cooking, the many lighters I couldn't function without, the multiple knives I carried even though I constantly had at least three on my person at all times.

Della messaged me on the first day of our self-eviction from this city and said she'd called the landlord, cancelled our lease, and asked for our returned bond to be paid in cash. We didn't have a fixed contract anymore, so we weren't breaking any rules, and I left her in charge of cutting off the electricity and gas, leaving the apartment as dark as the forest on my last night in so-called civilisation.

With Della staying one last night at David's, I bunkered down in the empty space, lying on a thin yoga mat I'd stolen a few months ago in the very same sleeping bag I'd washed and prepared for our upcoming disappearance back home.

All that existed from the life we'd created in this apartment were empty walls and lonely carpet. Not one plate left in the cupboards, not a single blanket left in the laundry.

All gone.

My phone buzzed in the darkness.

Della: *I know we said I'd swing by our place and stuff the rest of my clothes into the backpack you have prepared for me, but…David has requested you come here.*

I shot upright, jack-knifing off the floor.
What the fuck for?
Ignoring my chugging heart, I wrote back:

Me: *What did you tell him? Is he planning on killing me? Does he have a gun?*

Della: *What? Don't be ridiculous. He won't kill you. And I told him the truth. He already knew it anyway.*

Me: *Goddammit, Della. I feel sick about this already without being judged by him. I'm the guy who raised you, who is now stealing you into a life of uncertainty, and who stole you from him. Of course, he wants to kill me.*

Della: *He wants to understand. That's all. Love hasn't been kind to him either, Ren. And you did beat him up, after all. You kind of owe him an apology.*

Me: *I beat him up because he stole you from me.*

She took a long time to reply, and I could hear her thoughts as if they were my own. *He didn't steal me. You pushed me into his arms. He didn't take my virginity. I gave it to him as I was over being hurt by you.*

My shoulders slouched, and I reclined back into my sleeping bag, cursing myself all over again. By the time her message buzzed in the dark, I was ready to agree to whatever she wanted if only to try to make amends to her, David, and frankly, even to myself.

Della: *Closure, Ren. I think we both need it. I think you need to understand what we're doing. You need to accept that we're leaving together—just like old times. But unlike old times, we know exactly what we're going to do out there...alone. You can't lie to yourself anymore. You can't imagine a life of happiness with us side by side and believe it will be like before. It will be better. Because this time, we aren't lying. We ARE going to sleep with each other. We ARE going to learn about each other on an entirely different level. And if you can't accept that in front of David, then...I'm actually terrified that you'll never be able to accept it. What's to stop you from changing your mind if this gets too hard? What if you can't stop the images of me as a kid when you see me naked? What if you break down the moment you slip inside me and can't go through with this? Where does that leave me? What will that mean for us? I want this, Ren. You have no idea how MUCH I want this. But I'm also so scared because if this doesn't work, if you can't accept it, then I'll lose so much more than just a lover. I'll lose you all over again, and not having you was the worst thing I've ever endured.*

My breathing was loud and heavy. My eyes flying over her message again and again. We were no longer talking about David. She'd somehow opened the vault of her terrors and shared them with me. I hadn't stopped to think how hard this would be from her point of view. I'd returned to her, told her I was in love with her, flipped her entire world upside down, and asked to take her away from the people who knew her, all with only a vague promise that we would try for more.

There was no guarantee this could work.

I couldn't promise I could get past my ethics.

Of course, she panicked and didn't believe me.

Of course, she doubted me when I'd kept so many boundaries between us for so long.

I didn't know if I'd ever be able to make her see that my mind was made up—even if there would be struggles along the way. I was willing to work through them because I'd do anything required to keep her.

Once again, before I could put my thoughts in order, she sent another message.

Della: *Sorry, Ren. I…I don't know where that came from. Just please, tomorrow when we leave, come collect me from David's. Say goodbye to him and Natty. Hug me in front of him. Tell him what I've been telling him for months. Let him be the first to see you do mean this. That I'm not imagining it. That this is real. Please…*

The glowing phone lit up the empty bedroom where Della had slept innocently for so many years, all while I'd banished myself to the pull-out couch, desperate for distance. Certain that if I could keep physical distance between us, it would manifest into emotional distance, too.

It never did.

It'd only made my need for her increase because all my life, I'd been used to sleeping with her beside me, of her breathing in the night, of her warmth in the dark.

And I'd forbidden myself to have that comfort the moment her kiss changed everything.

Was it weak to admit that I'd been living a half-life since the day we left Cherry River? Was it twisted to acknowledge that I'd gone from having affection and kisses from the one person I loved more than anyone, to months on end of no touch, all because I couldn't understand how a hug could hold so many different languages and complications?

I wasn't fluent enough to hug her while pretending it was platonic.

I wasn't brave enough to touch her while masking every unsaid craving between us.

And now, Della wanted me to hug her in front of David.

But that wasn't what she was asking.

She was asking me to stop pretending. Begging me to stop fighting, to finally permit myself to sink into those cravings, knowing full well I would never be able to swim back out.

She was afraid I could walk away from her after this.

Afraid I was about to steal her entire life and leave her broken when I realised I couldn't do it, after all.

But it was the wrong thing to be afraid of.

What she should fear was the part of me I'd kept hidden from her.

For seventeen years, she'd brought out the best in me. She'd nurtured my sense of honour, duty, and devotion to the point where she didn't know any different.

She never glimpsed the other part of me.

The part that had steadily grown worse the longer I denied myself what I wanted.

The savage part.

The violent part.

The first person to see it was Cassie.

After our first time having sex, she'd chuckled and told me I was far more dominating than her other lovers. That the boy who used to flinch when she kissed him was no more.

She said I had a tornado wrapped around my heart—tightly coiled and mostly contained until it came to sex.

At the time, I'd denied it.

It made me sound like a monster, even if she tried to assure me it was just a primitive part of me taking over. That it was normal. That some men were more aggressive than others. But as we sneaked into the stables again and again, I'd learned something new about myself.

She was right.

I couldn't stop it.

The Ren who would give his own life to save Della's vanished during sex when he no longer thought about others but himself. Only himself.

I hated it.

And as I shared hollow fucking with faceless women to rid that steadily building desire for Della, I couldn't ignore it any longer.

I wasn't as noble as I liked to believe.

In all aspects of my life, Della came before me. I sacrificed everything I could for her. I gave her the clothes off my back, the sweat off my brow, and the promises from my heart.

Nothing was too much.

No request too crazy.

But when it came to sex...I wasn't giving.

I wasn't selfless.

I wasn't soft.

And that was yet another thing that kept me awake at night, because even if I could come to terms with sleeping with Della, how the hell could I ever tell her that the Ren she knew would not be the Ren she loved when I was inside her?

I trembled in my sleeping bag as I shoved aside such thoughts and focused on putting her mind at rest even while mine rode a stormy sea.

Me: *Okay, Della. If you need a public display of affection, I'll do it. I'll come to his place tomorrow once everything is done, and I'll hug you in front of him. I'll lay claim to you. I'll kiss you if that's what you need. But then, we're leaving, and we're never coming back.*

I didn't mention my rapidly building concern that, once we were in the forest, surrounded by all-seeing trees and all-knowing birds, things would change once again.

That the fight to see her as my...*lover*...and not just my friend, was just the first of our many problems.

Hopefully, by the time we were alone and ready to do whatever it was we'd do, I'd have that part of myself under control. And she'd never have to see me as anything other than her sweet, protective Ren.

My phone vibrated just as I rolled onto my side, ready to rest so I wasn't wired from lack of sleep tomorrow.

It would already be hard enough; I didn't need to be fighting exhaustion.

Della: *I never want to come back. Kiss me. Hug me. Let him see that this is real, and you can take me wherever you want, for however long you want, any way you want. And yes, that's a thinly veiled sexual innuendo. The kind that I've been dying to say to you for years. To be free to finally do it...I have to keep pinching myself to believe it's real. Until tomorrow, Ren. Xxx*

My body hardened at the thought of kissing her again, followed immediately by the nauseous feeling of doing something wrong.

Here she was messaging me things we'd danced around for years, all while sleeping in the same house as the boy she'd lost her virginity to. Strange how actions had driven us to this place, and they were about to drive us to somewhere new entirely.

Sighing heavily, I adjusted myself before typing two words.

Two terrifying, exhilarating, life-changing, heart-winging words.

Me: *Until tomorrow.*

Chapter Seventeen

REN

2018

MY BACK ACHED from carrying two sets of camping gear.

One clinging to my shoulders, the other dangling from my hands.

Two over stuffed backpacks. Two sleeping bags. Two wardrobes for two people about to say goodbye to buildings and bills and people.

Unlike when I was a kid—fearing I didn't belong and would be noticed—I boldly wore my earth tone t-shirt and cargos. Wanting them to see that I didn't bow to fashion or conformity, that I only wore clothes for one purpose: practicality.

My pockets were full of matches, lighters, knives, and first-aid kits.

I had enough snares and traps to ensure we didn't need a supermarket for weeks and enough packets of rice, pasta, and other easy-to-cook things that meant we could vanish into the woods and never been seen again.

Not by this city or its inhabitants, at least.

Good riddance.

Coming to a stop outside the house I knew well, the same street where I'd stood and watched Della with despicable shame, I couldn't take another step.

My boots—complete with yet another knife tucked by my ankle and tramping socks protecting toes from blisters—froze to the pavement. I physically couldn't open the white picket fence or stride up the pretty garden path.

The same path where David had hugged and kissed my Della. The same path where I'd carried Della from accidentally punching her the night I tore her from David's bed.

Fuck.

The front door swung wide as Della bounded from the house, her blonde hair secured in a ponytail, her lithe body encased in sturdy jeans, dusky pink t-shirt, and matching hiking boots.

No dresses or stupid sandals.

An outfit to run.

A dress code of living in the forest.

We're really doing this.

My stomach clenched for the fortieth time since I'd handed back the key to the apartment, done one final sweep of the place, tossed out the last of our accumulated junk, and made my way here.

Early afternoon and our lives were about to swerve into terrifying territory—not because we were homeless again, but because I was petrified of what would happen the moment our tent was erected and the stars announced our bedtime.

Would we sleep together tonight?

Was I ready?

Would I ever be?

She didn't stop until she flew to the gate and unlatched it, granting me invitation to step onto another man's property. "You came."

"Of course, I came." I scowled, unable to stop my stress from tainting my voice. "This is hard enough without you doubting me and acting surprised every second."

She smiled, dipping her head. "You've been gone for six months, Ren. You'll have to get used to me poking you at random times just to make sure you're real. I missed you." Stepping toward me, she ducked around the backpack I held in front of me, slotting her body into mine. "I missed you so much—you have no idea."

My fingers tightened on the rucksack straps, desperate to drop it, but propriety still commanded I keep it as a barrier between us, even as my heart yearned to gather her close.

My temper softened at the pain on her face. "I have some idea, Della." Ducking to kiss her swiftly on her cheek like I'd done for years—an innocent peck that was permitted—I murmured, "I missed you, too. Enough to make me face things I never wanted to face."

She stared into my eyes, studying me. "In that case, I'm glad you left."

"What?"

"I'm glad because if you didn't, maybe you'd never have..."

"Been brave enough to admit it?"

She nodded.

My fingers clenched on the straps, begging to release so I could cup her cheek.

But then, I looked up.

And there he was.

David.

And all my tenderness vanished beneath seething temper.

Arms crossed, lips thin, eyes narrowed as he glared at me from the front door. He judged me in ways I'd already judged myself.

Paedophile.

Sick fuck.

Blasphemer.

It didn't help that I agreed with him.

The urge to hit him all over again thrummed in my fists. Della noticed my quaking, turning to look over her shoulder. But as she twisted against me, I remembered what I'd promised her last night.

A hug.

A declaration.

A vow to this new direction.

She wanted me to accept this. *Us.* Well, I wanted to make him pay.

My fingers released the straps and, as the clunking sound of a survival-filled bag tumbled to the pavement, I reached for her in ways I'd never reached before.

My arms latched around her, holding her deep against me, forcing her to inhale me, feel me, accept me as my boots nudged against hers, and I hugged her so damn hard.

She made a noise of surprise as I deliberately slipped one hand to the back of her head and one to the bottom of her spine. Once I had such a dominating grip on her, I splayed my fingers through her hair, fisted the ponytail dancing down her back, and spread my touch along the top of her ass. In one seamless move, I pulled her hair down to tip her head up and pressed her hips shamelessly into mine.

She gasped as I held her prone and helpless, but I didn't kiss her.

I captured her in ways I ought to go to hell for.

And I looked up toward the man watching my every move. The man who'd had what I never could. And I let go of everything decent as I waited for him to understand he'd never have her again.

Not a single touch.

Not another *anything.*

This wasn't about me.

This was about some caveman insanity driving me to stake ownership in absolutely terrible ways.

My fingers tightened in her hair, fighting off the whispers that this was wrong, ignoring the man I truly was—the man who would *never* lay a hand on Della this way.

But then David's eyes flared with surprise and darkened with rage, and nasty triumph spread devil-hot blood through my veins.

I couldn't stop myself.

After all, I was only doing what Della had asked me to do. To lay claim on her. To prove, once and for all, that I was hers. What a shame that I lost sight of that and used a moment that ought to be pure as a weapon to destroy my competition.

And once David was fully aware how Della melted in my arms, submitted to my harsh hold, and feathered her breath with lust, I ignored him and looked down into the blue, blue gaze of my Little Ribbon.

She trembled hard, her chest panting, her gaze wild.

Images of her, young and innocent, tried to delete the pinpricked red cheeks and sinful invitation.

I shook my head, squeezing my eyes from the messy double imagery. I focused only on one Della. The one I held. The one who begged me to finish what I started.

And then, I kissed her.

Right there.

In public.

Where anyone could see.

And something brittle shattered between us.

Something that wasn't wholesome but filthy and twisted and held shades of black and grey and red, red desire all wrapped up in punishment.

I was punishing her for making me need her this way.

And she was punishing me for making her wait so damn long.

The kiss started with a crush of lips and bruise of mouths, but it quickly turned from explosive to desperate.

My fist yanked down on her hair, forcing her mouth open as I struggled to hide that violent side of me.

She groaned long and low as I kissed her deep and dark, full of disgust for what I'd done and drowning with desire for what I needed.

My body tightened, tingled, tangled, and my mind went from a single thought to crazed with memories of threading my fingers through Della's hair in simpler times. Of brushing back curls as she slept as a four-year-old. Of wiping away sweat as she battled chicken pox as a seven-year-old.

And fuck, I was *appalled* with myself.

I pushed her away.

I wiped my mouth.

I picked up her backpack, forgotten on the street, and shoved it into her arms.

She stumbled, blinking back passion, dazed with being taken, and licked her lips as worry and fascination and that strange light I didn't like assessed me as if she didn't know me but very much wanted to.

"What was that?" she breathed, stepping toward me, forcing me to trip back.

"What was what?"

"That kiss."

"The kiss you asked for." I cleared my throat, choking on yet more lies. "The promise I made to show you that I won't go back on my word."

David strode down the path toward us; Della rushed in a whisper. "That was more than that, and you know it." She cocked her head; her ponytail messed from where my fingers had ruined it. "That wasn't you. That was—"

David arrived in hearing distance with blond hair and distrusting blue eyes, and she cut herself off, smiling sweetly at him. "Hi."

I wanted her to finish. I wanted to tell her that it *was* me. Just a me she'd never seen before.

But David looked me up and down, his arms crossing harder over his preppy-boy chest. Ignoring Della, he grunted, "Hello."

My spine straightened, muscles tightened. "Hello."

We glowered as if we were about to go to war to win the hand of some maiden we both could never hope to deserve.

Della inched between us, closer to me than to him but still playing mediator. "David, I want to re-introduce you to someone. Now, before you say anything, you already know my story, and at the time, you said you understood. I'm asking you to remember your understanding and not—"

"It's okay, Della." David let his arms uncross and dangle by his sides. "I get it." His jaw clenched in a way that said he didn't get it, but to his credit, he held out his hand for me to shake.

I studied him, not quite ready to let bygones be bygones. Della inconspicuously kicked my boot, and I flicked her a glance.

This meant something to her.

And my entire life was based on the undying need to give her whatever she wanted.

No matter how hard.

I shook his hand firmly, friendly, and my anger swirled into shame. "I know what you must think of me." David opened his mouth to say something, but I snapped, "And believe me, you have every right."

We broke apart as he said, slightly surprised, "Look, I only need to know two things, and then I can let what happened between us go. I can overlook how sad Della was the night she came to me for...comfort, and I can accept that she'll be safe...out there." His eyes trailed to the city's horizon where the barest glimpse of trees beckoned.

"All right." I nodded. "But first, I want to say something." The words tasted sour, but I forced myself to continue. "Thank you for being the one Della ran to that night. I caused her pain and, out of anyone she could've chosen, I'm glad you were the one to help soothe it."

I glanced at Della, my heart kicking at her wide shock and besotted disbelief. "I never told Della, but I blamed myself. Every damn day. And I left because I was selfish. I only thought of *my* pain, not the girl I'd promised to keep safe." I tore my gaze from Della's, glaring at David once again. "You kept her safe when I didn't. And for that...I'll always be grateful."

I owed him that.

A thank you and an apology.

But I also owed him a warning.

My ability to accept that I was the reason Della ran into his arms only stretched so far. I could be magnanimous because we were leaving. We would never see him again, and that was the only reason I could lower myself to second best before him, to curb my anger and play meek.

But if we *ever* crossed paths again, if he ever tried to take what was mine...it wouldn't end so civilised.

David shared a look with Della before clearing his throat. "Eh, thanks."

I nodded sharply, the heaviness from my backpack reminding me that streets weren't my home, and it was time to leave.

Holding up his hand, not as judgmental as before, he said, "Okay, the two things I need to know are—"

"David, we talked about this last night." Della butted in. "And I told you, time and time again, nothing inappropriate happened. You know that. That's the whole reason I came to you in the first place. He refused to do anything inappropriate. *Please*...don't bring it up again."

"I know what you said, and I trust you. But I want to hear what he has to say." Pinning me with a glare, he added, "So, Ren. First thing I need to know is did you ever touch her improperly? Ever. In all the years you grew up together. Not an 'oops' as you were helping her from the pool or a 'whoops' when you were tucking her into bed?"

I stood taller, disgusted. "What sort of sick bastard do you think I am?"

"The one who's taking a child he raised and hiding her in the jungle to do whatever he damn well wants."

My chest puffed up, my hands clenching. "First, it isn't a jungle. Second, she's no longer a child. Third, I never *once* looked, touched, or thought of Della in any way other than brotherly affection until she—"

I cut myself off.

A kiss at thirteen was still a terrible thing to admit. It didn't matter that the moment it all changed, it wasn't my fault but hers. *She'd* been the one to ruin us, destroy me, and corrupt every day from there on.

And who knew?

If she'd never kissed me at the exact same second when I was having the most incredible dream of my life, I might never have had to fight changing thoughts and switching needs.

But she had, and I couldn't confess her age or mine when it'd happened.

Della put her hand on my arm, squeezing gently. "Ren, it's okay." Turning to David, she sniffed. "You know enough. You don't need to know anymore. And as for your second thing, I can guess what you're about to ask."

"You can?" He raised a fair-coloured eyebrow.

"Of course, she can guess," I interrupted. "Everyone can guess what you really want to know. I want to know, too. But there isn't an answer. Not yet, anyway."

Della gave me a sad look, her fingers feathering on my arm again, this time in worry rather than consolation. "Does it scare you?" she murmured.

I completely forgot about David as I drank her in, saw her panic, tasted her concern. Unable to stop myself, I cupped her cheek softly. "I'm fucking terrified. But...we don't have a choice now. We've gone too far to go back."

She pressed her face into my hold, her gaze glassing liquid before she nodded. "I know."

David sighed. "I guess you have just answered my question."

We both turned to him, my hand dropping from her cheek. I'd forgotten how in-tune Della and I were. I didn't know what it was—a lifetime lashing us together, heartstrings knotted together, or just a sixth sense.

Our connection used to wow me as a boy and now undid me as a man.

"You want to know what happens in the end," I said quietly, staring him down. "You want to know if I'll keep Della happy for the rest of her life. That this isn't a mistake. That we aren't doing something sick just for the hell of it. Am I right?"

David swallowed, his face falling in a way I hadn't expected. "I care for Della, and for the past six months, I've hated you for hurting her. But you're right. It *is* sick, and I don't agree with it. And I hope to God I'm wrong, but I don't think it will work between you. However, I also know you care for her. I see that. I just hope you understand what you're getting into."

My stomach clenched. "I know."

"No, I don't think you do." Anger turned his voice sharp. "You share the same last name. How's that going to work now you're no longer able to be called brother and sister? You know Della better than anyone, but how is it going to feel when you can't separate the past from the present? What happens when it all goes wrong? What about when people find out?" He forced out a breath, reining himself in. "Look, you're right. There is no answer. And I can't protect Della from future heartache. It's not my place. I just hope you know what you're doing. Seeing as you're supposed to be the parental figure in this scenario."

Fuck.

His words rang in my head.

It wasn't anything I hadn't thought about before, but he'd returned all my revulsion and fear. What *would* happen when we could no longer use the same name? Was that why I was forcing her to leave? So the next town we came across, I could introduce her as my *wife* and not my sister?

Christ.

I spoke the truth when I said it was too late to go back, but maybe it was suicide if we continued going forward.

Dread settled acidic in my belly as David shrugged at Della. "Sorry, Del. I know I said I'd just say goodbye, but I couldn't help it." Gathering her in a hug, he kissed her cheek. "Forgive me?"

She sighed. "Nothing to forgive. I'm sorry I put you in this situation."

"Don't be." His eyes glistened. "I'm really glad you found me that night."

My hands curled, reminded yet again that David had touched her.

"I'm always here if you need me. Just please...be careful. Okay?" He kissed her one last time, then stepped back. "I want you to be happy, regardless if I don't agree with how you find it."

Giving me a cool look, he pointed toward the road. "Now, get off my property."

Snatching Della's hand, I helped her slip her backpack onto her shoulders and yanked her through the white picket gate. "Be my pleasure."

Letting her go, I expected Della to take her hand back. Instead, she latched her fingers around mine—five of hers to my four—and tugged me forward. "Come on, Ren. Let's go home."

Chapter Eighteen

REN

2018

WE'D WALKED FOR miles.

At the start of our journey, we'd cheated and used our remaining coins to catch a bus to the city limits. Another few miles up the road, and we would've passed the dairy farm I used to work for. Even this far away, the air was tainted with the smell of silage and cow manure.

Instead of heading that way, we'd cut across some farmer's paddock, jumping over fences and ducking through wire until we approached the outskirts of the forest.

The trees were thin and sparse on the border, steadily growing thicker and taller as shadows swallowed them up. Fallen leaves scattered on the ground while the scent of must and mulch soothed a little of my heartache, welcoming me back.

Della paused as I stepped into the embrace of bracken and branches. We hadn't talked much since leaving David. Our conversation stuck to impersonal topics such as where I'd stored the rest of our cash, if I gave the apartment key back, and how many supplies we had before we had to return to a town.

My answers had been soft and monosyllable, my mind still hung up on David's questions. I needed to do this. We had no choice but to try. But what if...?

What if we realised we didn't work as lovers?

Where would that leave us? How would we ever go back to being family?

I waited for Della to look up at the towering trees, glance over her shoulder, then stride toward me with resolution.

Joining me in the shadowy world, she asked quietly, "Are you happy, Ren?"

I jolted, my heart forgetting its own woe and focusing on hers.

"What?"

She dropped her eyes. "Are you happy?"

"What sort of question is that?"

She looked up, annoyed. "One that you're not answering."

"Of course, I'm happy. You're here. I'm happy whenever you're around."

"That wasn't my question, and you know it."

I sighed, dragging a hand through my hair. "I *am* happy, Della. But if you're asking if I'm happy about what we're doing, I can't give you that."

Her shoulders slouched. "Why not?"

"Because I don't know if I am yet."

"Oh." She flinched, breaking me all over again. I wanted to hug her, but after years of denying myself, I didn't remember how to just reach out and take her.

"I don't want to lie to you, Little Ribbon." I closed the distance between us, capturing her hand. "We both need to adjust. I'm sure if I asked you if *you* were happy, you wouldn't be able to give me a direct answer."

"I could." Her fingers twitched in mine. "I am. *So* happy. But I'm also petrified that any second now, you're going to say this was a terrible mistake and march me back to David's."

"Believe me." I chuckled darkly. "I won't ever take you back to David. You're mine. You always have been."

"Phew. I thought you forgot that part." She half-smiled and walked into me, wrapping her arms around my waist.

"Never." I allowed my embrace to envelop her, pressing my chin on the top of her head, smelling the subtle scent of melons. "You'll always be mine, and I'm beyond happy to have you with me in the forest again. Is that enough for now?"

She nodded against my chest. "It's enough."

We stood together for a long while, once again committing to this and gathering courage to continue. Once we'd settled our heartbeats, we broke apart, striding deeper into the forest.

Our boots snapping twigs and backpacks creaking were the only sounds as we ventured farther. We didn't talk—almost as if we were afraid of conversation and its power to make us wonder what would happen when we stopped for the night.

And now, we'd stopped.

For the past twenty minutes, Della had gathered firewood while I'd erected the tent that she'd given me on my twenty-seventh birthday. The same birthday she'd gotten her ribbon tattoo and I'd started a year's disaster of sleeping with women I didn't like, want, or need.

I'd despised myself for being so weak I'd sought companionship with women I couldn't even remember.

Della dumped her armful of branches beside a fallen trunk I'd dragged into a small clearing to be a bench. Strolling over to me as I fixed the final tent peg into the ground, she put a hand on her hip. "Did you use this one while you were gone or our old one?"

"This one." I stood, stretching out the kink in my back, cursing the aches in my chest. Just like old times, her gaze drifted to the bare flesh below my t-shirt and above my belt.

And just like old times, my heart smoked in desire and I shut down the aching in my blood.

But...I didn't have to shut it down.

Not anymore.

How long would that habit take to break?

Della licked her lips as I lowered my arms. "I want to kiss you again, but I don't know how."

She seemed to melt into the forest floor. "Yes, you do. At least, you did before." Her gaze darkened. "You still haven't answered me about that, by the way."

"And I'm not about to answer you now." Closing the distance between us, I gathered her close, used my forefinger to tip her chin up, and pressed my mouth gently to hers.

Technically, our third kiss, but it punched me in the chest just as violently as our first.

I kept my mind locked on her. This Della. Right now. No Little Ribbon. No childhood recollections. No memories of anything but *this.*

Her breath caught as I kept the pressure soft and coaxing, even though everything inside said to crush her to me and let go of my control. No one was around. No one would know. But *I* would know, and that was the main issue we'd have to overcome.

Her tongue crept along my bottom lip, making my body harden. She arched up on her tiptoes, kissing me deeper as she slipped her tongue into my mouth.

My thoughts tried to flicker, a hologram of a little blonde angel laughing in the hay.

I groaned, licking her in invitation, killing the image.

"God, Ren." Her arms looped around my neck as I dropped my finger from her chin and hugged her flush against me.

Our heads switched sides as our tongues danced and lips slid. Magic sparked from everywhere, electricity hissing, chemistry burning.

I couldn't catch my breath as we clung to each other, kissing and kissing, losing track of time, not caring our boots crunched leaves as we stumbled together and righted, tripped together and stabilised.

And even though we attacked each other with a kiss, even though my mind threw memory after memory at me, and Della's hands clutched my hair and tugged, and my fingernails dug into the soft curves of her hips and yanked her closer, we didn't try for more.

We were happy conquering this small but unbelievable task. Learning each other, recognising each other's flavour, remembering each other's body in an entirely different way than the way we'd known before.

I sucked her bottom lip, biting gently as her leg pressed against mine, wedging against my hardness.

Her control snapped, and she tried to crawl into me.

I responded.

I couldn't help myself.

Wrapping my arms tighter, I somehow marched her back and back, kissing and kissing, until her spine wedged against a tree, and I leaned into her.

Her fingers tugged viciously at my hair. My hips thrust in response, disobeying me. Her teeth nipped at my bottom lip, like I'd done to her, her tongue frantic for more.

Our kiss became frenzied and so fucking hot, I couldn't stand it.

Breaking away, I held her at arm's length as I struggled to get my breath back around the sudden vice of my lungs.

Her eyes were so dark they were navy, her pupils as wide as a cat's. "Wow." Tracing her mouth with a trembling finger, she shook her head. "I always knew kissing you would be extraordinary, but I had no idea how much."

I coughed, then murmured around a throaty groan, "Kissing you is better than I could've imagined."

"You're saying you imagined kissing me?" She looked up beneath thick eyelashes.

I dragged a shaky hand over my face. How could I answer that?

"The truth, Ren. Did you?"

I laughed under my breath, tortured with honesty. "Yes. I imagined it."

"And?"

"And what?"

"Is it like you imagined?"

My voice thickened as I swallowed hard. "Better. So much better."

She gave a flicker of a smile, slightly nervous, kind of shy, but entirely sexy with the utmost power to drop me to my knees. "I'm glad."

"Glad you're destroying me?"

"Glad I'm not the only one feeling this."

"You're not." I took a hesitant step toward her again, brushing aside a wild curl like I had so many times in the past. "I feel it too. I have for years."

She rose up, kissing me innocently on my stubble-covered cheek. "I can't tell you the relief it is to hear that." Ducking away, she headed toward the four-person tent she'd bought me. The brown siding and green stitching camouflaged it perfectly in the rapidly falling dusk.

Dragging her backpack toward her, she sat on the fallen tree trunk and pulled out a packet of pasta and carbonara sauce to make an easy dinner. I wasn't fooled by her calmness. She acted as if our kiss hadn't just scrambled her up, but her body couldn't hide the jerky motions or shaky breaths.

Yet another reason evolving our relationship came with pitfalls. We couldn't hide. We knew each other too well.

"You still haven't told me, by the way." She looked up as she tossed me a lighter from the bag, pointing at the piled firewood to start a fire. "About what happened at David's."

Fisting the fire-starter, I strode toward the pile, dropped to my haunches, and set about making a stack with kindling. "Told you what?"

I knew fully well what.

The kiss.

The way I held her.

The mistake.

I cringed. I hadn't been myself. I ought to have stared David in the eye, told him to mind his own fucking business, and carted Della away. But she'd asked me to stake my claim. How could I deny her that when she obviously needed it?

"Ren..." Her tone raised my eyes.

I sparked a flame, holding it to the dried leaves and tiny twigs. I didn't know how to reply, so I shrugged instead. "There's things about me that—" I cleared my throat. "Look, I was jealous. You asked for a public display of affection, and I gave you one. Can we just leave it at that?"

She narrowed her eyes. "What things don't I know about you?"

I groaned under my breath, hating that she could finish my sentences. "The same sort of things I don't know about you."

This was turning out to be as awkward as talking to her about sex that first time. That damn book and its pornographic images. The stilted, strange conversation about penises and vaginas.

Once again, my heart suffocated with repugnance for what I was doing. How was any of this right when I'd taught her what sex was only to contemplate showing her a decade later?

"What don't you know about me?" Her nose wrinkled. "You know everything there is to know about me."

I pinned her with a stare. "Not everything, Della."

It took a moment for my pointed words to land, but when they did, she blushed. The pink flush wasn't something I often saw on her, and it made my body crave to touch her all over again.

"Oh."

"Yes, oh." I focused on nursing the baby flame into a cheery blaze before falling back onto my ass and resting my elbows on my knees. Twirling the lighter in my fingers, I said carefully, "I know you intimately, but not in…that way. I don't know what you like. I don't know what you need to find…" I coughed. "Pleasure."

Her cheeks reddened even more. "Do you want to know?"

It was my turn for my skin to heat. "Is that a trick question?"

She laughed quickly. "I can tell you…or show you."

I fisted the lighter, squeezing it hard, remembering exactly how the night had gone when she'd begged to be enlightened on sex. She'd taught *me*, not the other way around. She'd read words I couldn't read and explained things I didn't understand.

No fucking way would I repeat that embarrassment or be reminded how far out of my league she truly was.

"I'll learn for myself." I growled. "I don't need a lesson."

"I'm not saying you do."

"I know I've leaned on you a lot in the past for reading and maths and things, but in this topic, I don't need any guidance. Got it? I won't be able to handle this if you start teaching me—"

She held up her hand, worry painting her face. "I didn't mean—"

"Leave it, Della." I stood, swiping at leaves stuck to my jeans. "Let's just focus on dinner, okay?"

"No, not okay." She stood too, her chin arched. "I get that this is hard for you, but it's hard for me, too. You say there are things about you that I don't know? Well, guess what? There are *so* many things I don't know about you these days. You've been steadily pulling away from me and hiding so many parts of you that this feels wrong. I have all these memories of you where you're covered in sunshine, an open book, but now you seem in the shadows and covered in clouds. You say you leaned on me, but you never did. I taught you because of my own selfish desires, not because you needed help. So don't withdraw into yourself and paint this any worse than it already is."

Striding toward me, she balled her hands. "You've taught me so much, Ren. You've literally taught me everything I know. Don't you think it feels weird knowing you'll have to teach me what you like, too? How you like to be touched? How rough, soft, deep, and fast you like it?" She sucked in an angry breath. "This is new for both of us. Just because I've accepted the idea of being with you for far longer than you have of me doesn't mean I'm not having the same thoughts as you. Not struggling with memories of you teaching me how to drive the tractor or your innocent face before you earned hard edges."

She stopped, breathing hard.

Time ticked on as our argument faded, but we didn't make a move to patch up the wounds left behind.

Finally, she whispered, "I'm tired. Can we just go to bed?"

Bed?

I gulped, eyeing the tent.

Unlike the previous one we'd shared, there was more than enough room for two adults without touching. The double wings meant we could be entirely separate while our bags were in the middle.

She caught me studying the two pods and huffed painfully under her breath. "Don't worry. I have my own sleeping bag this time; you don't have to sleep so close to me."

Ripping a tawny-coloured bag with highlighter pink zippers from her backpack, she ducked under the tent awning and threw herself into the left wing.

I stood there wondering what the hell happened and how the fuck it all went so wrong.

I hated that we'd had yet another fight, but that wasn't new. Our tempers always seemed to ignite around each other. But the fact that she'd curled up tight, fully clothed and hurting made me wince because she was right.

I'd been wrapped up in myself once again. She was Della. She was the reason I was alive—the sole purpose for why I'd been placed on this earth: to protect, cherish, and care for.

And I'd just made her upset.

Again.

Moving our belongings away from the fire and placing the pasta back into its pouch, I bent and undid my laces before kicking off my boots. I didn't strip anything else. Not my belt, socks—nothing.

If I did this, I needed to be fully clothed.

Tonight was not the night we fell into sex. Neither of us were ready.

Unfurling my own sleeping bag, I crawled into the centre pod, unzipped it and spread it over the two yoga mats I'd brought with us. Once it was flat, I reached into the wing where Della lay curled up tight and grabbed her ankles.

"Hey!" She squirmed as I yanked her through the small alcove and into the main one. "Let go."

Ignoring her, I didn't stop until she lay beside me, then unzipped her sleeping bag, all while my eyes burned into hers, daring her to stop me.

I kind of wanted her to stop me. I wanted her to hit me because I deserved to be hit. I wanted her to curse me because I warranted being cursed. But most of all, I wanted her to fight because if she did, I could fight back and release some of the hissing lust in my veins.

Almost as if she sensed how close I was to snapping, she stopped wriggling as I rolled her out of the warmth, smoothed the now-open bag on top of us, pushed her onto her side facing away from me, then lashed my arm around her waist and yanked her firmly into my front.

The moment her solid, familiar weight kissed mine, I groaned under my breath.

Right.

Wrong.

Home.

Pulling her as close as I could, I didn't hide the fact that I was hard, shaking, and fighting the hardest I'd ever had to fight not to tear her clothes off and teach *her* a lesson for a change.

A lesson about me.

A lesson about how much I wanted her.

She moved in my embrace, and for a dreadful second, I thought she was trying to get away, but then she moaned softly and pressed her hips deeper into mine.

My fingers dug into her flat stomach as I buried my nose in her hair.

I couldn't stop myself from rocking into her, allowing that one element of sex to manifest where I thrust fully clothed, hinting that in that moment, the way I liked it was torturously slow and tormentingly erotic.

She shivered as I nuzzled her ear, breathing hotly. "Don't run away from me again, Della. Got it?"

She brought her arm up, her fingers threading in the hair at the bottom of my neck. "Only if you promise the same."

Nipping at her earlobe, I grumbled, "Never. Whether this works or not, I'm not going anywhere. You have my word."

Chapter Nineteen

DELLA

2018

THEY SAY LOVE can be the worst test of all.
I tend to agree with them.
First, Ren left me.
Then he came back for me.
Second, Ren stalked me.
Then he told me he loved me.
Third, Ren told me to pack and leave.
Then he warned he needed more time.
My heart...wow, it had been given its every wish and fantasy in one painfully, truth-filled argument, only to be told to press the pause button.

I hope you don't mind me scribbling this in a notebook instead of on my laptop—I sold it, you see. I wiped it clean and got a couple of hundred dollars for it from a fellow student. No point bringing it with no socket to charge and a backpack already heavy with important things.

Not sure why I'm writing, really.

Then again, what's happening between Ren and me is all so new, I want to keep some structure in my life, and writing things down is it.

After a manic couple of days getting rid of the things I had at David's, cutting off utilities, and assuring Natty and David that I knew what I was doing, I'd believed the test would be over.

I thought stepping into the forest would be our fresh start.

A new beginning where we could forget the past and be two adults and not two children. Where love would finally nod with pride and say, 'Okay, I made you suffer enough, now crawl into that tent and get busy.'

It didn't quite work that way.

When Ren had said he had it harder than me accepting this new us, I hadn't agreed. We'd both grown up together. We both had memories and love and connection that no amount of time or distance could steal.

I'd been hurt that he could say that, to be honest.

But now, after tasting his kisses and knowing the exact moment when he stopped kissing me and started thinking of the past, I agreed he did *have it worse than me.*

He was right.

He'd raised me. He'd seen me in every stage of cute, embarrassing, plain disgusting, and everything in between.

And that was the difference.

I'd been raised by him; therefore, I worshipped him.

I'd seen him in every mood of possessive, angry, distrusting, hardworking, and forever untamed.

Two very different ways to see somebody.

One practical and parental. One fantastical and fanciful.

Funny, how my memories don't just see a skinny boy with nine fingers, dirty and wild—I only remembered power and strength and the undeniable safety I felt in his presence. I didn't remember Ren as a teenager with a zit on his forehead and the Mclary cattle brand on his hip—I saw him as lanky and incredible and not afraid to plough an entire field on his own.

I'd never seen the ugly messiness of life that he had by raising me.

So, yes. He was right.

I didn't have to overcome as much to be able to kiss him.

I had no fear we were doing something wrong.

My only fear came from his fear and, for once, I wouldn't make it worse on him.

I wouldn't push him.

Not this time.

Or not for as long as I could help it, anyway.

Chapter Twenty

REN

2018

FOR TWO DAYS, we learned how to be friends again.

Mornings, we ate breakfast of squashed bread and jam, packed up our gear, and walked until exhaustion made our backs sway and bones creak. Nights, we'd stop, set up our home, then cook harmoniously, eating pasta and canned supplies by moonlight and sharing tales of the past few months as we caught up with what we'd missed.

It was exactly what I needed.

To find my friend again.

To accept that there was no place, no person, no scenario I would rather have than this, right here, with her.

By the time we found the meandering river that had been our faithful friend since leaving Mclary's all those years ago, we were both ready for a bath and itching for clean clothes.

Summer was still in the air even though autumn was only days away. Muggy temperatures and no breeze found us deep in the forest. The sun teased low in the sky, not quite ready to go to bed as we finished putting up the tent.

Della wiped her brow with the back of her hand.

Blonde curls stuck to her sweaty neck. Heat glistened on her upper lip. Leaves clung with foliage fingers to her ponytail, choosing her over their branch and willingly committing suicide.

The polish of house living and city conveniences had faded from her skin, leaving her as wild as I remembered, slipping back into the surname she'd given us.

"Ren?" She waved a hand in my face, snapping me back to the present and out of my daydreams of licking away her heat, pushing her onto the ground, and stripping her free of every sweat-wet piece of clothing.

---

x

Clearing my throat, I ran a hand through my hair. "Yeah?"

"I asked if you want to go for a swim."

Glancing at the narrow river, the babble and bubble hinted it might be too shallow to do anything more than sit and sluice.

Pointing downstream a little, she said, "The current is calmer there. I reckon there's a place deep enough to submerge, at least."

"Okay." My heart picked up into a pounding tempo. Bathing had been a regular thing with us even when we were young. When age didn't matter, we'd skinny-dipped with no thought of doing anything wrong. But then, my body had changed and become a master over my mind, and I'd refused to be naked around Della.

And now…what was the correct protocol?

She saw my wariness, laughing gently. "Underwear stays on. Is that what you were about to say?"

I half-smiled. "Would you be shocked if I suggested naked?"

She blinked. "Were you?"

I swallowed. "I don't know."

Her shock faded under a thin glaze of disappointment. Ever since I'd hugged her two nights ago, keeping her trapped in my arms almost the entire night, we hadn't discussed when or how we'd leap over the divide from family to lovers.

I didn't know how to bring up the subject and didn't know what to say if I did. Della had relaxed around me but only on topics we both knew were safe. The moment we stared too long, or that sneaky, burning lust became too painful to ignore, we suddenly found other tasks that urgently needed doing.

I knew why we'd gone nervous.

We'd missed each other so fucking much, and here we were, living the life we'd clung to, all the while about to jeopardise it.

I had everything I could've dreamed of, and it made me hate myself because not once had I asked how she felt about quitting her writing course or if she missed any of her friends.

I couldn't bring myself to ask either because I wouldn't survive the answer if she admitted she wanted those things more than she wanted me.

"I'll make the decision for you." Grabbing the hem of her t-shirt, she ripped it over her head, dislodging her ponytail and its decoration of leaves.

My breath caught in a sharp cough as my eyes drank in her slim figure and black sports bra. The fullness of her chest was a perfect handful, the shadows of her belly enticing me to touch, trace, and torment.

Never taking her eyes off me, she kicked away her boots,

unbuttoned her jeans, slid them down long legs, and pulled them off with her socks.

Standing in black bikini briefs, looking athletic and strong and so fucking gorgeous, I very nearly stumbled with desire for her.

The scraps of material were the only things keeping me from seeing her—*all* of her—and I both thanked them for their discretion and cursed them for their barrier.

"Your turn," she whispered, swaying a little as her hands reached up and undid her ponytail, letting rivers of gold pour around her shoulders. The flash of blue ribbon beckoned me forward, and I stole it from her fingers, wrapping it around the back of her neck and pulling her toward me.

"You're beautiful," I murmured, pressing a kiss to her mouth. "I don't know how I ignored that fact for so long."

She gasped, surprised by my swift affection; a step behind my lust.

Before she could catch up, I broke the kiss and dangled the blue ribbon in her face. "This looks familiar." I smirked. "Not a day went by that you didn't wear this in some way." My gaze drifted to her bare foot where the inked one with its cursive R still caused my heart to clench. "Didn't you ever wonder why a piece of satin lasted eighteen long years?"

Her forehead furrowed. "Huh?"

"Think about it." I stroked the blue, dragging it through my forefinger and thumb. "It lived in the elements, got wet, dirty, knotted, and crushed. Yet it never fell to pieces. Never tore when I tied it in your hair, never unravelled when you wound it around your wrist."

Her head cocked. "What are you saying?"

"I'm saying, I couldn't exactly let your favourite thing fall apart now, could I?"

Confusion shadowed, then was chased away as comprehension lit up her face. "You replaced it?"

I chuckled. This was one secret I *could* share with her. Giving her back the ribbon she so desperately treasured—even now as an adult—I headed to my backpack that rested against a gnarly looking pine.

Throwing her another smirk, I reached into the side pocket sewn tight for protection of wallets or other important things and pulled out a circle of cardboard that had well and truly seen better days. The printed label and name of the colour had long since worn off, the edges frayed and torn, but there, in the centre of the wheel, was a depleted length of blue satin.

Her eyes widened like an owl's as she dashed toward me—careful where to put her bare feet on the bracken-littered ground—and snatched it from my grip. "Where did you get this?"

Spinning it in her hands, she pulled out the pin holding the ribbon from unravelling and compared it to the one wrapped around her fingers. "Oh, my God. It's the same. Mine is faded and marked, but it's the same colour."

I chuckled, loving her disbelief. "My longest secret. I've had that since I was fourteen. I'm guessing there's only a few years left before it runs out."

"What? *How?*"

"We were living at Polcart Farm, remember? I'm not sure you will, seeing as you were so young—"

"I remember," she interrupted. "I remember Snowflake, our cow, and the TV channel with the puppets."

I ignored the squeeze of my ribcage and sharp stab of my heart as I recalled Della bouncing in front of the TV with her chubby toddler legs growing each year to an adorable little girl chasing after Snowflake in the field.

A crest of simple affection and absolute unconditional love made me feel wretched and wicked all over again for thinking of her in the ways I did now.

Squeezing the back of my neck, the enjoyment of sharing my secret faded somewhat. "You were four. That ribbon of yours was falling apart. It tore in half one night when you were learning how to tie a bow around my arm. My ears are still ringing with how loudly you cried."

Her shoulders rounded. "I don't remember that."

"It's because I never told you that particular story. I didn't want you to think your ribbon was an imposter." Pinching the wheel back, our fingers kissed and I stroked her softly. "I adored how much you loved that silly piece of blue. And when you finally went to sleep with your face all blotchy from screaming and your breath all short from bawling, I snuck out to find you a new one."

"Where did you go?"

"Into town. It took all night to find a house with two old folks, a man who liked to tinker with cars in his garage and a woman who liked to scrapbook and had a room full of ribbons, buttons, beads, and stickers." I smiled sadly, remembering the treasure trove of stuff that Della would've adored. "I wanted to steal everything for you, but I only took what was most important. It wasn't a perfect match. But it was close enough."

Holding up the ribbon, I let memories paint my voice. "That night, I took the two torn pieces of your ribbon, measured out a new length the same, then spent the rest of the darkness hours doing my best to make the bright blue of the new one look as weathered as yours. I stomped it into the gravel on the driveway. I dragged it through mud and washed it semi-clean. I crumpled it and abused it until it didn't look so perfect anymore."

I shrugged. "You woke up the next morning panicked, tears already welling, but I told you it was just a bad dream. That nothing had happened to your ribbon. See? There it was, intact and looped through your hair. The relief on your face, Little Ribbon." I sighed. "It was worth the sleepless night and dirt beneath my nails to be able to take that sadness away. I didn't know what it was like to love something that fiercely—not until you came along—and I didn't want you to know what loss felt like. Not then. Not when you were still so young."

Tears welled in her beautiful blue gaze, tumbling down her cheeks like the babbling river behind her. "I had no idea."

"Why would you? I never told you."

"But...how did I never notice?"

"Because I didn't wait four years to give you a new one next time. Every year, a few days after our birthday, I'd cut a fresh strand, rub and fade it, then swap it while you were sleeping. Sometimes, the blue was brighter, and you'd study it as if confused. But you never thought to ask why."

Her arms came up, her fingernails scratching my scalp as she grabbed my hair and yanked me down to her mouth.

Her kiss wasn't soft with desire. It was sharp with gratefulness.

Born from innocence, tainted with confusion, but wholeheartedly flavoured with love. Deep, blistering, *endless* fucking love.

"I didn't think it would be possible to care for you any more than I already do," she murmured against my mouth. "You've just broken my heart, Ren." She kissed me again, mixing salt from her tears.

I wrenched back, fear icing my insides. "What?" Grabbing her biceps, I demanded, "Why would you say something like that?"

She hung docile and crying in my hold. "Because you were always so damn selfless. You *always* put me first. You sacrificed everything you could for me. You would've done anything I asked, and it wasn't enough."

Swiping at her tears, she growled as if furious with herself. "It wasn't enough that I was your everything. I wanted more. I wanted no other woman to have you. No one ever to own your heart. I was so *selfish* compared to you, and I made you unhappy in your own home. I pushed and pushed you. I dropped hints I knew you would refuse to acknowledge. I never thought about how I made you feel.

All the while, you were replacing my ribbon every year because you loved me so—" She couldn't finish, her tears coming fresh and fast.

Crushing her to me, I kissed her brow, her hairline, her ear. "Caring for you was the easiest thing I've ever done, Della. Raising you was the best thing I've ever achieved. I'm so fucking honoured to have had that privilege."

Pushing her away a little, I bowed my head to stare hard into her eyes. She needed to hear this, and she needed to hear it now.

Before I did what I could never undo.

Before I broke the final filament of my self-control.

"I might have been selfless when it came to you, but I promise you I am no saint. I'm hungry, Della. So fucking hungry, and I need you. But you need to know that the Ren you know—the boy who would kill himself if it meant keeping you safe—that Ren has a flaw. His selflessness comes at a price."

Her gaze danced in mine, desperately fishing for what I struggled to tell her. "What price?"

"I don't think I can be that selfless anymore."

"I'm not asking you to."

"You're not getting it." I dug my fingers harder into her arms. "When it comes to sex, I'm not...gentle. I only think of myself."

Heat drenched her eyes, making the blue turn to sapphires. "I'm glad. You deserve to put yourself first for a change."

I shook my head, sharp and quick. "You still don't understand."

"I don't need to understand." She ripped herself out of my hold, swooping up to kiss me again. "I need you to show me." Her lips bruised mine, her tongue tasted me, and her breathless beg undid me. "I wasn't going to do this. I promised myself I wouldn't push you again. But please, Ren. Show me. Don't be so nice to me. I need you to do that." She kissed me harder, wetter, faster. *"Please."*

Fuck.

I very nearly snapped.

I attacked her back, kissing her brutally, swept up in her pleas, drowning beneath vicious desire, but...just like a couple of nights ago when she'd slept stiff in my arms as if unused to being touched by me, we weren't ready.

I was hungry; that wasn't a lie. But beneath my hunger lurked childhood memories just waiting to pounce and condemn me. Under no circumstances did I want to feel sick while making love to Della the first time.

I hadn't told her my flaws to give myself permission to treat her without care or attention. I was selfish, yes, but then again, I'd never had sex with Della, and I wanted it to be different.

I wanted it to be special.

I needed it to be the best goddamn thing we'd ever experienced, and until I was mentally more stable and Della more trusting that I wasn't going to run again, it would be a mistake.

Her tongue stole into my mouth, licking away the remaining shreds of my willpower.

She made sleeping together seem like the easiest thing in the world, while it felt like the hardest thing I'd ever have to do.

I kissed her back—I couldn't help myself—but my thoughts tangled once again, taking the sting out of the whip of urgency.

We'd spent our entire lives together.

And, if I had my way, we'd spend the rest of eternity.

There was no rush if I never planned on letting her go.

I *couldn't* rush.

Because I hadn't fully come to terms with this.

I hadn't found a truce between the old me and the future me. The brother and the husband. And I needed to because it wouldn't be fair to either of us if I didn't.

"Della..." I groaned as she hooked her leg over my hip, doing her best to climb me.

"Kiss me back, Ren." She licked my bottom lip before sealing her mouth on mine again. "I want you. Now. Please."

"Christ..." I melted and hardened and wanted so damn much to give in to her. I might have spent a lifetime looking out for her, but she'd mastered the art of commanding me. Whatever she asked for, I found it extremely hard to deny.

But this...it had to be right.

"Stop, Della." Grabbing her shoulders with harsh fingers, I put distance between us, making her stagger back before finding her balance. Her face was wild and wistful and tugged on every heartstring I possessed. "Not tonight."

"Why not?"

"Because I need more time."

"To do what?" She blew a curl from her eyelash in a frustrated puff. "To torture yourself a little more?"

I scowled. "No, to find peace. To accept the fact that I have so many memories of you at every stage of your life, and to find a way so they don't drive me insane when I finally do let go."

"I know those are legitimate concerns, and I understand because I understand you...but you need to get over that, Ren." Swatting away my hands, she crossed her arms. "The past isn't going anywhere. It's always going to be a part of us."

"I know. But do you honestly want me to take you when I'm not emotionally ready?"

"I don't think we *will* be ready until we've had sex."

I coughed, hating the need in her voice. She'd always been braver than me—always willing to leap before looking. But I wasn't wired that way. I hadn't had that privilege when raising a kid at barely ten years old. "Well, I think it would be rushing if we did it now."

"And I think we're just tormenting ourselves by waiting."

"Unfortunately for you, it's not your choice." I stood to my full height, glaring her down. "Don't push me until I'm ready, Della."

"Push you? I'm trying to *help* you!" Her arms uncrossed only for hands to plant on her deliciously curvy hips. "You're turning sex into this huge thing, when really, it's just an act."

"Just an *act*? Is that what this is? A quick fuck to you? How stupid of me to treat it as the biggest thing in my life. I didn't know I was just some guy you wanted to screw to get out of your system."

"You know that's not what I meant."

"Do I? You're the one getting mad at me for being honest." Once again, our romantic moment spiralled into a fight.

Were we always destined to clash?

I didn't remember fighting this much before. I didn't like it then, and I despised it now. But I wouldn't bow to her temper. No matter how much my body agreed with her to get it over with.

Sex between us shouldn't be a 'get it over with' kind of thing. It should be the best fucking thing in the world.

My anger swirled hotter, annoyed she couldn't see that sleeping with her was something I never believed I could have. It was the one thing I didn't feel worthy of. The one gift I didn't know how to take. And to have her give me permission so flippantly, well, it hurt.

It killed, actually.

She cheapened it when I wanted it to mean so much.

"You said you'd be patient," I said coldly.

"I did. But I also said I'd be frustrated." She sighed again, looking up at the purple slashed sky as if beseeching perseverance. "God, I'm sorry, Ren. I promised myself I wouldn't do this, yet here I am making a mess of everything again." Her voice softened, regret tightening her eyes. "You call yourself selfish…but look at me." She chuckled a little. "Okay, you need more time. How much time?"

"I don't know."

"But it won't happen tonight?"

"No." I shook my head firmly. "It won't."

"Can't blame a girl for trying." Her shoulders slouched. "Ugh, I'm being a bitch." Rubbing her face, she moaned, "Forgive me, Ren. I don't know what came over me. I just…I thought we'd come out here, and I dunno…act like a pair of bunnies." She shrugged with a roll of her eyes. "I should've known it wouldn't be that easy. I even understand *why* it's not that easy, so just put this moment of weakness down to the fact that I'm madly in love with you, and it's taking everything I have to keep my hands to myself."

I laughed quietly. "Madly, huh?"

"Completely." She smiled shyly. "Utterly. Totally."

"I'm madly in love with you, too."

"Now you're just teasing me."

A small smile tilted my lips, glad our fight had vanished, leaving us drained but connected. "There's plenty of time for that. Teasing. Kissing. Fucking. I'm not going anywhere, and neither are you."

"Well, a girl only has so much patience before she goes a little crazy."

"You're already crazy. Crazy for me." Moving closer, I pulled her into another hug, loving the familiar simplicity, grateful she swooned into me. "Believe me, Little Ribbon, this is the hardest thing I've ever done. Saying no to you when you're so damn beautiful and willing? God, it's pure agony." I nudged her chin up with my knuckles, staring deep into her eyes. "But when I take you, Della. I want my mind to be clear. I want to be with *you*, not the past. I want to fully accept us, not feel torn between right and wrong."

Kissing her softly, I murmured against her lips, "When I'm inside you, Della Wild, I want to only have one thought, and that's how much I fucking love you."

She sighed into our kiss, snuggling closer. "When you say things like that, I can be patient. For just a little longer."

And she was.

For a few more days, at least.

Chapter Twenty-One

REN

2018

SEVEN DAYS SHE gave me.

One week to accept the unacceptable and change our entire relationship.

We didn't end up swimming that night; the river was too shallow, but we did manage to bathe and wash a few pieces of clothing. Although I wasn't ready to sleep with her, it didn't stop my eyes from roaming over every inch as she soaked herself in the swift current.

I'd stupidly blocked myself from finding the best pleasure in the world, but I clung to the hope that when I finally did let go, it would be entirely worth it.

That night, we slept in just our underwear, sandwiched together in the tent, nuzzling and kissing as if we'd always been so close. I loved that each time we kissed, it was a little easier, my mind a little quieter, my heart a little less confused.

In the morning, as we packed up our camp and headed back on the trail, I grabbed her and pressed her against a tree. My hands roamed to her breasts as I kissed her hard, driving myself against her, drowning with a sudden crippling need to take.

Her moan snapped me out of what I'd done purely by instinct.

Backing up, I waited to be persecuted beneath memories of Della as a baby and Della as a child. But…nothing came.

No sick sensation. No regret. Only awareness that, for the first time, it'd felt perfectly normal to grab and manhandle her because I wanted to, and she was mine.

There was nothing wrong with that.

In fact, there was everything right, and I froze because I'd held her, kissed her, and touched her—in ways I never thought I could— and not once had my thoughts tried to ruin me.

My capacity for change had finally started, and the sick sensation was taking a back seat to the rapidly growing lust I struggled to control.

"You can do that again…if you want." Della smiled behind a golden curl, her lips still pink from my kiss.

"If I do, I won't be able to stop."

She groaned, "Say that again and *I* won't be able to stop."

Taking her hand, I chuckled. "Patience is a virtue."

"Not when it's making my heart work overtime and my body behave like a horny cat."

Tugging her into a walk, I chuckled. "A horny cat? I have no idea what that feels like."

She gave me a dirty look. "Oh, really? You want me to believe you've never felt like you want to jump out of your skin at the barest touch. Never wanted to scratch someone or pick a fight just so you can be attacked and have it lead into the roughest, sexiest moment of your life?"

I stared at her dumbfounded.

I'd known Della was passionate—I'd seen her kiss other men, for God's sake—but maybe my waiting wasn't just about putting the past in the past and accepting our new dynamic, but also about figuring out who she'd be in bed before I got her there.

Was she like me?

Was she aggressive or tame?

Did she expect our first time to be beneath a blanket of stars with gentle snuggles and sweet missionary, or did she secretly crave what I did?

A messy, filthy, violent affair that left us bloody and oh-so-fucking satisfied?

Letting her go, I stepped in front of her, following the narrow animal track. "I've been many things, Della, but I can't say I've been a cat."

More like a wolf.

A starving one.

Clearing my throat from thoughts full of thrusting and wetness, I said, "Let's get going. Think you can keep up?"

She snickered behind me. "Think you can keep avoiding this subject for much longer?"

I scowled into the trees. "I'm fully aware I can't."

"Good." She sniffed with a mixture of smugness and joy. "Because I'm going to be a good girl and not push you, but it doesn't mean I'm not going to make you fully aware just how much I want you. How watching your butt right now turns me on so much. How your boots cracking twigs makes me hot. How your smell makes me we—"

"Della," I snapped, spinning on her and pointing a finger in her face. "Thin ground, Little Ribbon. Behave yourself."

With a flash of mischievous blue, she stood on tiptoes and bit my finger, running a warm, silky tongue around the tip.

I groaned.

Loudly.

My cock instantly sprang into the hardest, most agonising erection I'd ever had.

I dropped my hand as if her saliva was gasoline and her teeth the match. My entire finger burned and, *fuck*, it wanted more.

She licked her lips, her eyes hooded and hazed. "Okay, Ren. I'll do what you say."

The temptation and invitation behind that innocent, obedient phrase almost had me yanking off my backpack and shoving her onto her knees right there in the middle of the forest.

Brushing past me, incinerating my body with hers, she whispered, "I'll behave. Guess we better get hiking, huh? The sun won't last forever."

Words vanished.

Humanity disappeared.

I was an animal, pure and simple, so damn hungry for the girl I'd always loved.

I couldn't take my eyes off the way the sun dappled her hair, glinting on her ribbon, or the way her body glided through greenery as if she was part forest herself.

A quick flash of her bounding through the trees when she was nine or ten came and went, but instead of defiling the new love I had for her, it layered my heart with a heat that unravelled me and stitched me back together in an entirely different way.

Someone who was okay with this.

Someone who could finally admit Della Mclary never *was* a Mclary because she'd always been a Wild.

I wanted to tell her just how much I loved her. Just how much I would *always* love her. How I'd had an epiphany, and I knew within my very bones I'd never leave her, hurt her, or do anything other than defend, cherish, and adore. I pitied anyone who ever came between us. I feared what I'd do if anyone ever tried to—

"Coming, Ren?" She looked over her shoulder, nonchalant and willowy.

Her gaze met mine, playful and happy before they darkened in response to the shadows swirling inside me. The shadows of possession and dominion that clenched my fists, already angry with phantom ideals that might try to ruin this.

"Ren?" Her voice lowered, the expression on her face one of seriousness and trust. "Everything okay?"

I might've grunted something in response, but she'd well and truly won. She'd shown just how right she was. Sex *was* just an act. Because we'd already surpassed mere pleasure and flesh. We were joined on so many levels, and nothing else mattered but that.

"Fine." Marching toward her, I coughed and pointed ahead. "Let's keep going."

I was fucking captivated by her.

Utterly bewitched.

But I wasn't prepared to spill the contents of my heart when I didn't fully understand it myself.

"Okay…" Her forehead furrowed, but she obeyed, and I spent the rest of the day in agony, eyes fixated on her gorgeous ass as she strode ahead, my body in a perpetual state of thick, black desire.

Served me right.

I wanted her.

I could have her.

So *why* was I waiting again?

* * * * *

Every day, we travelled deeper into the forest, following the river and leaving behind the city we'd called home for so long. At night, we were pleasantly exhausted and returned to the ease of before when Della would ask for a story, and I'd willingly conjure past events we'd shared.

Even though I'd fully accepted the inevitable and just how screwed I was by falling in love with this woman, I hadn't initiated anything past a kiss.

And Della remained true to her word and didn't push me.

It'd become a silent joke, kissing, grinding, driving each other to the pinnacle of tearing off clothes and consummating but then pulling back at the last second.

Making out with Della was the best and hardest thing I'd ever done. Best because I never knew kissing could be pure fire, that a tongue could make me lose myself, that a fingernail dragged down my spine could almost make me come. And the hardest because I couldn't let go…not yet.

We'd had almost two decades together, yet this element of touching and kissing was entirely new, and I wanted to learn everything I could before I jumped a grade. I wanted to be fluent in her moans. I wanted to know her levels of need.

Already, I knew her legs spread whenever I grazed my fingers along her lower belly. Her gasps became heavy whenever I'd tuck aside a curl and murmur in her ear how much I wanted her.

But it wasn't enough.

I wanted to know what made her snap.

And on the fourth night, I found the spot as she spread out her sleeping bag while I kneeled at the bottom of the bed and pulled off my t-shirt. Her bare leg flashed me, her ribbon tattoo with its R, bright blue and taunting.

Without thinking, I flipped her onto her back, grabbed her ankle and dragged her freshly river-washed foot to my mouth.

She froze as I pressed a kiss on the ink, brushing my nose against her soft skin.

"Ren…" Her head fell back as I kissed her again, slipping my tongue out and licking the length of the ribbon all the way to the cursive capital of my first name.

I nipped her.

"Holy…" Her entire body crackled and sizzled with desire.

My fingers tightened on her ankle, holding her still as I licked the length again. "You got this to torment me."

Her foot arched in my hold, her legs widened, her hands fisted in the sleeping bag. "No—"

"You got this because you were in love with me."

"Y-yes." Her breath caught as I nipped at the R again, scraping my teeth over the fine bones of her foot, fighting the feral part of me that wanted to clamp down and bite hard.

"You fantasied about me touching you."

"Every night." Her eyes met mine, blazing. "All the time."

I almost gave up there and then.

My body had never felt so wired or hot or greedy.

The little boy shorts and t-shirt she slept in could so easily be removed, and her body feasted on.

But as much as I cursed waiting, I fucking adored the anticipation, and I licked her tattoo once more before placing her foot down gently. "You very nearly ruined me, Little Ribbon."

Unzipping my jeans, I slipped out of them and didn't bother hiding the raging erection I sported.

She licked her lips, eyes locked on my tented boxers. "And now you're doing the same by teasing me so badly."

I didn't say anything.

I just wanted to bask in the heady drunkenness of lust and the unbelievable knowledge that I'd earned everything I'd never dared hope to earn.

Crawling beside her, I wedged her back into my front and breathed as hard as her.

And we just lay there.

Trembling with need.

Cooking with desire.

Fully aware we were playing a very dangerous game.

And we were utterly addicted to it.

Chapter Twenty-Two

REN

2018

BY THE SEVENTH day, that intense desire meshed with carefree laughing. We'd found a balance of friendship and chemistry that made me trip even deeper into love.

Every day, we tramped until our bones ached, and we'd make our home in the wonderful heart-warming high of being just us again. Whenever I looked at her, I wanted to explode with affection. Whenever she looked at me, my body begged to override my hesitation.

Her eyes had the power to send electricity fizzing down my spine and between my legs. Her laughter had the magic to make my chest ache and body throb. And when she stopped in a small clearing at twilight and shrugged off her backpack, she turned to me, not with relief at finding somewhere to rest, but with a demand I could no longer ignore.

I knew.

Even before she opened her mouth.

I *knew*.

With suddenly shaky hands, I pushed at the straps and let my bag slam to the forest floor.

The air changed. The trees froze. The creatures silenced.

"Della…" I didn't know if I spoke in warning or acceptance or denial. Whatever I was feeling was drowned out by the overpowering appetite in my blood.

I wanted her.

I wanted her more than I could stand.

Taking a step toward me, Della reached up and undid the blue ribbon in her ponytail. The gold mass plunged around her face, making my mouth dry and my cock pay utmost attention.

"We haven't put up the tent," I groaned, breaking beneath the heavy pressure in my chest. The pressure that was done waiting. The pressure I'd been living with for so fucking long.

"I don't care." She bent and undid her laces, kicking her boots away, not fussed where they landed.

My knees trembled to move—either to her or away from her, I couldn't quite decide. Thanks to the week of teasing, I didn't trust myself around her. I didn't know my limit of self-control anymore. I didn't know how spectacularly I'd snap and what would happen if I did.

She'd always been my Della, but right here, right now, I was hers. Well and truly hers.

A slave to his queen, enraptured and caught and begging for her mercy. I was ready to kneel before her, but that final part of me that didn't fully trust he could have this perfect life, the tiny sliver that still believed he ought to love her the way he always had, gave one last attempt at propriety.

"We're dirty. We need a bath." I spread my hands, revealing the mud-smudges and grime from hiking all day.

"I don't care about that, either." Her voice lost its sweet melodic tone, slipping straight into sin.

Goddammit.

I couldn't compete with that.

I couldn't deny her or myself any longer. She'd put a curse on me, deleting any other arguments or delays, keeping me pinned in her stare.

She stepped again, and my cock swelled to an agonising hardness. I coughed around a groan. "Della…you're making this impossible for me."

"Good."

"What if we're rushing—" Even to my ears that excuse was empty.

I was ready. So fucking ready.

"We're not." She wrapped the ribbon around her wrist, tying it quickly.

"At least let me put up the tent."

"No."

"We only get one first time, Della."

"And I can't wait any longer."

"I'm not sleeping with you without a bed." If there wasn't something soft to support her, I didn't know what sort of state she'd be in once I'd finished.

"Too bad we don't have one."

"If you gave me a few minutes, I could set it up." I pointed helplessly at my bag. "At least let me—"

"I can't wait another minute, Ren." Her hair glittered in the fading light as she shook her head. "All day, I've been counting. Just another minute, just another minute. And now, we're here. And I have no more minutes.

My heart lurched. "Our minutes seem to be up."

"They do."

"What does that mean for us?" My voice was smoky and hot.

"It means you made me do this. You made me this way. I promised I wouldn't push you, but Ren…you've been torturing me. When you licked my tattoo…? *God*, I can't stop thinking about it. I'm in a state of permanent wetness."

I choked on the sudden avalanche of lust. "Della—"

"Too much for you? Too honest?" Her cheeks burned with the same sexual fever I suffered. "Too bad. You're to blame."

I chuckled darkly. "Me? It's you I can't keep my hands off. It's your fault I constantly need to touch you, kiss you."

"So do it."

"I don't know if I can be gentle." I shook my head. "No, I *know* I can't be gentle. Not after—"

"I'm not asking for gentle." She smiled thinly, almost angry with me in her desire. "I'm asking for you to put me out of my misery. No more teasing. We face this. Together. Right now."

I gulped as I stepped toward her, already lost. "Face what we've been running from for years?"

She nodded sharply. "No more running."

I sucked in a lust-heavy breath, coughing once. "No more running." I stepped again. Entirely entranced by the violent hunger lashing us together. It was so damn powerful it muted everything else.

No thoughts. No accusations. No fear.

Just us.

As it had always been.

My mind raced, already drunk on images of how good we'd be together. Of how she'd feel as I slipped inside her. Of how hot and wet and—

I was too far gone for more memories to find me. Too twisted to let echoes pull me back. But in some shred of rationality, a voice entered my ears with warning.

Not Della's or mine, but Cassie's.

Protection.

The night I'd lost my virginity. The night I'd learned about condoms and STIs and unwanted pregnancies. Thanks to that lesson,

I'd never slept with a woman without a condom. It was paramount. It was law.

Christ.

It took every strength, and then some I borrowed from the devil himself, to step back. "Shit, we can't do this."

"What? Why?"

Pinching the bridge of my nose, I did my best to swallow back hot, hungry rage. The rage that very much wanted to forget about the rules and take her anyway. "We don't have protection. I didn't bring any."

What was I *thinking*?

Why did I forget something so important—almost as if I'd banished the very idea of sleeping with her, believing it would never happen no matter how much I wanted it to.

I'd done this deliberately, even if I denied my moronic logic.

Della blinked calculatingly, holding up her hand. A single condom rested in her palm. "I did."

"Where did you get that?"

"Does it matter?"

I ought to feel absolute horror that my last attempt at ensuring this was right had just been eradicated. But all I felt was relief. Sheer, indescribable relief.

It was the final straw.

The last hint to show I was ready.

So, *so* ready.

I dropped my hand, giving her a grateful smirk. "Thank fuck for that."

She laughed unexpectedly, her lips spread over perfect teeth. "Even if we didn't, I wouldn't have been able to stop. Not now."

"Me neither."

"Good."

"God, you've made me hard."

She sucked in a breath. "And now you've just made me even wetter."

If I thought the forest was quiet before, watching us shed away every shackle we'd imposed, I was wrong.

Now the trees vanished, the river disappeared, and all I saw was Della. We'd just been graphically honest, yet a joke mixed present with past, making me chuckle under my breath. "Thank everything holy, I taught you to always be prepared."

Her laugh turned to a breathy moan. "Ren…if you don't touch me soon, I'm going to combust."

I lowered my head, watching her with half-hooded eyes. "I like

---

seeing you like this."

"Like what?"

"Desperate."

She took another step. "So, so desperate."

"You have no idea how filthy my thoughts have become."

"If they're anything like mine, I have some idea."

"Fuck, Della." I balled my hands, matching her step with one of my own. "Is this real? Are we really going to do this? It isn't another dream? Because I've dreamed of this. So many times."

"Touch me and find out."

My hand raised, crossing the final distance, tingling with intensity to touch the one girl I'd loved forever.

I'd always known Della was special. But what I hadn't known was every year I fought to keep her safe, I was ultimately protecting every dream I'd ever had. I'd had the privilege of raising her, but really, I'd been creating a future I'd never be able to deserve. Every winter snowstorm and summer rain shower, forest adventure and paddock picnic had all been leading to this.

I'd been searching for something all my life, and it had been under my nose the entire time.

Her.

My past, present, and future.

The only path I could have taken.

It wasn't a choice anymore.

It had *never* been a choice.

I stumbled toward her as she stumbled toward me, both starving for touch. Even before my fingers landed on her arm, they stung with electricity so sharp it crackled between us.

Our eyes locked as I whispered, "If we do this, it's no longer just a fantasy."

"I know."

"We do this, and everything changes. Forever."

"I know."

"If I touch you, I'll never be able to stop."

"God, touch me then." Her eyes fell shut as we met in the middle of the small clearing.

Having her that close undid me to the point of forgetting everything else.

I didn't care about the repercussions anymore.

I'd literally exhausted myself to the point of not being able to fight.

There was nothing to fight against…only something to fight *for.*

"Open your eyes, Della." I growled as the savage part of me licked its lips for what it was about to taste.

I was seconds away from giving her every disgusting sin I'd lived with. I needed her to understand that by tempting me this way, I would no longer have any control.

Her eyelids fluttered upward, her gaze heavy and heated.

We stared into each other, stripping ourselves bare.

"Tell me to stop," I begged. Even on the cusp of no return, I pleaded for salvation.

"I can't." She bit her lip, looking me up and down with such pain-filled greed, my belly clenched. "I'll never be able to do that."

Everything about me burned. On fire. Seconds away from erupting into fury. "You've always pushed me. Forever tested me."

"And you've always indulged me. Forever protected me," she breathed shallowly, her gaze locking onto my lips. "I'm sick of you protecting me."

Our chests brushed as I sucked in a breath, knowing it would be my last one for a while. I was about to drown in her. And I didn't care if I damn well suffocated. "If I kiss you now…it's all over."

"Stop trying to scare me off and do it."

"So bossy." I smirked.

"I don't know how else to tell you I want you, Ren." Her eyes flashed with temper. "I don't want to talk. I don't want to stop. I don't want you to treat me kindly or gently or softly. I want you to show me. I want you to take me, just like you said you—"

I snatched her into my arms and kissed her so damn hard our teeth clacked.

I showed her.

And then I showed her again.

And again.

I kissed her harder than I'd ever kissed her.

I let our week-long foreplay drag us down and down, deeper and deeper where heartbeats and blood reigned and the only thing we needed to do was connect.

Connect in the most primitive way possible.

She cried out as I plunged my tongue past the seam of her lips, forcing her to accept me, commanding she dance to the same feral song.

We fought to get closer—her wedging into me and me bowing over her. My hands turned to claws, holding her cruelly.

Nothing was enough.

No scratch intense enough. No bite painful enough.

There was nothing civil about us.

We were animals.

Dirty, filthy animals that had reached a dirty, filthy level and had nowhere else to go.

Teeth and nail and sullied, snarling lust.

Lowering her to the ground, I didn't care we had no tent or shelter. I didn't care sticks and leaves would be part of what we were about to do.

I didn't care.

I had no *capacity* to care.

The only thing that mattered was getting inside the one person I needed more than air.

Della went without a fight, letting me brush aside as many twigs as I could before pressing her onto her back and smothering her instantly with my weight.

She squirmed beneath me as I grabbed her jaw and kept her still so I could deepen the kiss to exquisitely harsh.

With my free hand, I shoved up her t-shirt and cupped her bra-free breast with eager fingers. Her back arched, revealing the perfection of bare skin. Her legs kicked out wide, welcoming; her hips raised off the ground, seeking.

My brain short-circuited.

A flicker of persecution needled me as my hand drifted down the delectable length of her belly, ripped at her belt, and tore at her zipper. Image after image of Della in similar undress. Of her changing after late night baling and getting covered in prickly dried grass. Of her sitting on a rock by the pond in her swimsuit, pretending to be as worldly as Cassie but failing for being so young.

Bang. Bang. Bang.

Caution. Caution. Caution.

Even though I loved that little girl with all my heart, I no longer bowed to her.

I bowed to this new mistress instead.

I wasn't clutching that child or kissing someone I shouldn't be kissing. I wasn't committing some heinous act, or stepping over lines that should never be crossed.

This was Della.

Girl and woman.

A girl with a ribbon in her hair, and now a woman with a tattoo on her foot.

I was kissing my goddamn soulmate, and who fucking cared how we'd met or how long we'd known each other? Fate had decided to throw us an unconventional beginning by giving her to me the moment she was born.

Her lips parted as I kissed her with renewed violence, ignoring sudden breathlessness and overwhelming heat.

Moaning, she slung her arms over my shoulders as I managed to unzip her jeans and yank at them without finesse. Frustration bubbled as the tight material refused to move. "Are you trying to kill me?"

She smiled beneath our kiss, her lips stretching tight with the same kind of delirium I suffered. "You mean…you need help stripping me?"

"Don't taunt me, Della. Now is not a good time."

"Why? Because you're a little worked up?"

"Because I'll die if I don't get inside you."

"Oh." She blushed, pleased and sexy. "In that case…"

I glowered as she pushed me away and hooked her fingers in her jeans. With a coy, almost shy look, she shoved them down her legs, leaving baby blue bikini briefs.

I groaned.

"Do you have to be so fucking gorgeous?" I fell on her again, kissing, attacking, worshipping. Her heat promised me all kinds of sinful things as I ran my hand between her legs, just once, unable to stop myself from claiming.

She jolted as my fingers trailed over her inner thighs, wrenching her knees apart to give me more room to settle between them.

Keeping my weight on my elbows, I fisted her hair, morphing the kiss from deep to downright devouring. My body ached with a fever born from needing her so badly. With our mouths locked, I pressed my hips into hers, surging upward, searching for every part she'd give me.

My hand lassoed around her neck, squeezing for that perfect taste of submission.

The flash of surrender that I so desperately needed.

Her mouth popped wide as I held her tight.

Our eyes locked.

For a second, she stared as if she didn't know me then, in a wash of pure acceptance and obedience, she corrupted me with bliss.

She licked her lips, arching herself deeper into my control.

"Fuck." I fell on her again, holding nothing back, driving her into the dirt, squeezing her gorgeous throat, stealing everything I could.

I wanted to treat her as kindly as I'd always done, but she knew me now.

She knew enough to understand I wouldn't be sweet.

Not in this.

I reached between us for my own belt. "Don't move. I won't last much longer if you move."

But she disobeyed me, wriggling a little higher to slip her hands over mine and grab the buckled leather instead. "Me."

That simple possessive word made me harder than I'd ever been. "*Christ*, Della."

A thunderstorm percolated in my blood. Rumbling thunder and crackling lightning gathered like eager sinners in my lower belly, howling at her to do whatever she damn well wanted.

I couldn't breathe as her shoulders bobbed, her hands busy below. The tug of her yanking the leather through the buckle, the slight give as it fell to the sides, the incineration of her fingers on my sensitive skin as she unhooked the button and eased my zipper down.

And when she touched me…when her fingers feathered over my hardness for the first time. When she bit her lip as if shocked and awed that I'd finally, *finally* permitted such things. When her touch turned from feather to forceful and she wrapped her fingers around me, I motherfucking broke.

My mind fractured, and I sucked in lungsful of tainted air.

And by breaking, memories I'd been ignoring drowned me.

Of Della teaching me to read.

Of Della smacking a kiss on my lips under the mistletoe that first Christmas at the Wilsons.

Of Della…

Della…

Della.

Fuck.

I panted as if I'd run to Mclary's and back. My eyes saw double. My heart beat triple. But even though I bordered obsession filled with disgust for what I was doing, I couldn't stop.

For a week, I hadn't remembered.

Now, those memories were determined to play a part—to ensure we were prepared for the aftermath of pleasure. To prove we were ready to accept that we could never go back, only forward.

I accepted.

I wholeheartedly flung myself into the future and fisted both hands into her hair, smashing her lips to mine.

I stole her breath as my tongue dove deep, tasting her, condemning her.

She writhed, her legs scissoring tight around my waist, caught up in the whirlpool of erotic thirst and carnal hunger.

Our bodies strained with violence, already grinding, punishing, needy.

For years, I'd suspected Della was just as volatile as me when it came to sex, and now, I knew. She was just as unleashed. Both of us dangerous. Both highly unstable.

A fatal recipe.

Beasts driven to mate on the forest floor.

She nipped my lip, digging her nails into my scalp.

With a rumbling groan, I attacked her again, twisting in a vortex of young Ribbon and the present. My touch turned nasty, bruising her as I tried to take and take.

We kissed hungrily, savagely.

I wanted to hurt her for the power she had over me.

I wanted to punish her for making me this crazed.

Della slid a hand between our tight, overheated bodies and grabbed my cock, jerking me with vicious command.

I snapped and kissed her again, teeth and tongue and torment.

Deeper and deeper, over and over.

She cried out as twigs and debris scratched her while I devoured her. Thorns and sticks were nothing compared to the delicious pain her nails granted as she fought me back, bruise for bruise.

There was nothing gentle about any of this.

Both of us drunk on wildness and frenzy.

And when our battling wasn't enough, I bit her bottom lip.

Hard.

Too hard.

She cried out, pulling back with a look of fiery desperation and a thread of wariness.

I'd told her I couldn't control myself. But as fresh air filled my nose and common-sense returned, my heart became master over my traitorous body, dousing my lust with ice. "Ribbon...I-I'm sorry."

She breathed as hard as me, quicksilver desire in her eyes. "I'm not." Rearing up, she captured my mouth again, enslaving me to her for life.

Our mania reached a new level of velocity.

All the years between us, each precious in their own way, were now barriers we had to smash apart *immediately*.

I needed her instantly.

She needed me urgently.

I loved that we both raced to the same chaotic beat.

Her body wriggled beneath mine as she shoved her underwear down her legs.

I froze, knowing she was naked, and I only had to lean back to look.

I wanted to look.

I *desperately* wanted to look.

But if I did, this would be all over.

Everything about this was too much.

Too much.

Della didn't pause, moving to undress me fast and ruthless, almost as if she wasn't sure I'd go through with this. Grabbing my jeans and boxer-briefs, she inched them down my ass.

I shivered as her fingers kissed my bare flesh and couldn't stop my hips from arching, giving her room to shove aside the unwanted clothing. Once they were mid-thigh, she fell back, then wrapped slim arms around me, pulling me tight.

I hissed as my eyes snapped closed against the most *incredible* thing I'd ever felt.

Her naked against my naked.

Her heat against my hardness.

I groaned low and loud as she burrowed closer, my hands balling where they wedged into the ground.

Her arms looped around my neck, her lips on my ear as she breathed, "You didn't look."

I knew exactly what she meant. "I couldn't."

"Why not?"

"Because I'm barely holding on as it is." Inhaling her gorgeous scent of wilderness and melons, I grunted, "Seeing you naked…fuck, Little Ribbon."

Her right hand slid from my shoulders, following the contours of my chest, leaving a trail of fire in her wake. "You didn't let me look, either. Can I?"

All my life I'd given her what she wanted. How could I deny her now?

I gulped as I pressed off her a little, her eyes searing my cock as she melted into the ground. "Look at us, Ren."

My jaw clenched as I looked down to the trimmed dark blonde curls and glisten of Della and the steely hard cock of me.

It didn't matter I'd seen her body grow through every stage. It didn't matter she'd seen me go from boy to man. All that fucking mattered was how perfect we looked together now.

"You're making me lose my mind." My hips dared to press closer, making me hiss again against the blistering heat of her.

"I lost mine years ago." She sucked in a breath, her hand shaking as it continued its path down my chest.

My heart suddenly crucified me, hating me for all the wasted moments we could've shared. "Why was I so blind?"

"Because your morals were killing you." She smiled softly. "But also because you knew it wasn't right. I was too young. I wasn't ready."

"And you're ready now?"

"This is the best moment of my life. Does that answer your question?"

I bent to kiss her, my back tight with tension, keeping me aloft. "I love you, Della."

"I know."

"I've loved you since that first moment I found you."

"Liar. You hated me."

I chuckled. "I wish someone could cuff me around the head as a ten-year-old and tell him his entire world was in that backpack."

"Well, your entire world wants you to stop talking and touch her."

She successfully stole every word, slamming me back into the swirling speed we'd shared before.

Her fingers locked around me, making me jolt. She shivered as if touching me affected her more than any summer breeze or dusk-shrouded forest ever could.

I'd had a lifetime of being held by her, loved by her…but this? It was fucking *everything*.

My hands moved as she touched me harder. Digging my left hand into the dirt, I ran my right down her side, my thumb kissing the side of her breast.

I wanted to mark her, brand her.

She moaned, her hand twitching around my cock.

I wanted to take my time and fondle her, lick her, bite those perfect nipples, but there was a demon in my blood howling for other things.

Dropping my touch down her waist, I marvelled at the shape of her, then lost my goddamn mind as I found the pulsating heat between her legs.

No barriers.

Just satin and silk and everything Della.

I disintegrated.

Everything ached.

My thumb found her clit, and my finger, shit, that drove into her with no sweet sonnets or requests. I couldn't help myself from spearing deep, twisting my existence with how perfectly hot and wet she was.

Her back arched as I withdrew, smearing her slipperiness against my other finger, rubbing her clit just once before I drove both into her.

I drove so hard, her body inched higher up the bracken littered ground.

Her mouth opened wide. "Holy fu—"

"Enough talking, remember?"

Leaves crackled as she squirmed. Breaths panted. My mind was awash with greed.

The wondrous sensation of being inside her ought to be enough. I ought to linger in this magic and take my time learning what she liked.

But it was too late for that.

"Condom. Where is it?" I bit out, thrusting my fingers deeper.

She searched blindly in the dirt beside us, finally holding up the foil packet.

"Put it on me," I snarled, thrusting fingers into her body while my cock wept with punishment. If I didn't get inside her now, I'd come. I was so close. *Too* close.

Her hands trembled as she ripped the foil, grabbed the rubber, and cupped my length.

I growled under my breath as her tiny touch rolled the condom over me, squeezing my base as if determined to make me explode.

Knocking her hand away, I ripped my fingers from her and angled my hips.

"Tell me to stop, Della." My voice wasn't my own. It was black and dripping and demonic.

"Never." Spreading her legs, her hands landed on my ass, pulling me into her.

A small ribbon of blood decorated her arm from a sharp twig.

A shadow of a bruise marked the creamy flesh of her throat.

I wanted to feel bad.

I didn't.

The first welcome of her body blew my existence into tiny smithereens, and I no longer cared about the pieces. I didn't care if I'd be the same person after this. I didn't care about right and wrong.

This was right.

So, *so* right.

I fell on her, crushing her into the earth as I pushed inside her. I wasn't slow. I wasn't gentle. I was everything she'd made me become.

She tensed beneath me, her body tight, unyielding.

Parts of me cried for what I was doing, for the desecration of the purest thing I'd ever loved, while most of me rejoiced at finally finding the one person I'd been searching for.

"I'm sorry." My mouth slammed on hers, and my hips shot forward, driving through that tightness until her body gave way in a rush of welcome, her legs wrapped around my hips, and her moan filled my lungs.

She wanted me.

And I took her.

Hard.

Fast.

Ruthless.

My eyes snapped closed as everything inside wanted to erupt. Her heat. Her scent. The fact that this wasn't some faceless, nameless woman I couldn't stand but the girl I'd loved my entire life. The girl I'd die to deserve.

My heart swelled to four times its size, suffocating in its ribcage, desperate to sacrifice itself to her.

I was the luckiest bastard alive.

Connected.

Finally.

Together.

Finally.

Shock crashed over us that we were no longer separate, but one.

Tearing my mouth away, I locked eyes on hers and begged to see what I needed to see. The same violent fire. The same undeniable desire. Plucking a leaf stuck to her cheek, I groaned, "Look at what you're making me do."

"I don't care."

"I'm inside you."

"I know."

"I'm fucking mad for you, and you're wedged on the forest floor. You're bleeding for fuck's sake."

She smiled as if I'd given her the best gift in the world. "I know."

I laughed, groaning under my breath as my cock throbbed in her body. "What else do you know, Della Ribbon?"

"I know that you're inside me. And you're just delaying what you truly want to do."

My eyes hooded. "And what's that?"

"You want to fuck me."

My entire body rippled in impending release. "Quiet. You'll make me come."

"Well, you shut up and fuck me."

I thrust once, both of us hissing with searing pleasure.

"I can't believe—" My voice hitched as I thrust again. "—we're talking at a time like this."

"I can't believe you're *still* talking." Her hips rocked up, rubbing herself on me. With a sexy moan, she dug nails deeper into my ass. "Shut up, Ren."

I kissed her, speaking into her lips. "You're such a menace."

"And you're a tease."

I laughed again, awed that even in this new act we could joke like old times. "Tease? Oh, I'm many things, Della, but I'm not a tease."

My knees dug traction into the leaf-littered earth, driving into her again, deep, so deep.

Her head fell back, and her fingernails dug into my ass, yanking me harder into her.

I stared at her in total fucking awe.

How had I never seen?

How had I never known?

She was my other half, not just in friendship and family, but in everything else, too.

"You want me, Della Ribbon?" I murmured, my cock throbbing inside her.

"Yes. God, yes."

I moved.

I thrust hard, driving her into the ground. "Have me." *Thrust.* "Have all of me." *Thrust.* "You already have my heart. Now you have my soul."

I thrust in anger for how true that was.

I bent to kiss her again, and something snapped inside her. The same thing that'd snapped inside me. She bit me, pushing my shoulders and fighting against me to roll me onto my back.

For a second, shock rendered me pliant, and I rolled over, staying inside her, pressing her hips down onto mine. I coughed, unable to comprehend why I was on the floor instead of her.

She sat on top of me, her eyes heavy and lips swollen, and although she looked absolutely stunning with leaves crowning her tangled hair and dirt smudging her cheek, she didn't belong up there.

She belonged beneath me.

Rolling again, I pinned her to the ground, grabbed her wrists, and slammed them above her head. My hips rolled, locking her in place. "I call the shots, Della. Not you."

Something flared in her eyes as she struggled to free herself.

I only fucked her harder, my fingers tightening around her wrists as I thrust fast and deep. "Argue and I'll argue back." My face contorted with black agony as I let go a little more, biting her neck, arching my hips until every inch of me pounded into her. "Then again, fight. Let's see what happens if you do."

A look of rebellion etched her face, then melted into pure, glittering lust. "You think you're punishing me?" Whatever fight had been there siphoned into utmost surrender. "Ren, you're giving me exactly what I need."

Something hot twisted in my belly, bathing in her submission.

The need to own every part of her made me slip straight into the animalistic aggression I tried to hide.

I couldn't stop it.

I'd *never* been able to stop it.

But with her so beautiful and aroused beneath me—fighting back, matching my thrusts, biting me, scratching me—I'd found my equal.

I'd found home.

"What are you doing to me, Della?" Rearing up, I ploughed into her. Not caring she inched upward, dislodging twigs and leaves with each thrust. My knees burned from digging into earth. My back cramped for bowing into her, forcing everything I could inside her. "I promised I'd never hurt you. And now you've driven me to the worst."

I was a rough lover, but this...seeing her come undone in the most basic way possible, covered in earth with the scent of nature all around us, I lost it.

Dropping on top of her, I didn't care she bore my full weight or that I'd trapped her, smothered her, captured her.

She was mine, and she'd take what I gave her.

"Hurt me because nothing has felt this good in my *life.*"

Grabbing her around the neck, I kissed her furious and vicious. My fingers twitched to squeeze. My nails ached to mark.

"Make me come, Ren. *Please* make me come." She moaned as I drove into her with all the finesse of a raging bull.

Burrowing my face into the crook of her neck, I drove again and again. "You've ruined me. Fuck, you've ruined me." Harder and harder I rode her until the forest was full of skin slapping and animals rutting.

She cried out as I thrust faster, crueller, driven by her fight and surrender.

"Della." My forehead crashed against hers as I panted and raged, wanting to climb deeper, cursing her and myself. *"Fuck."*

Pinching her wrists with my left hand, my right soared down her body, squeezing her breast with nasty fingers before finding the place where we were joined.

We were wet and messy and scorching hot.

It turned me on.

Christ, it turned me on.

I couldn't catch my breath as I found her clit and rubbed.

Her back snapped up. "Oh, God!"

"Shut up. Just shut up." I rubbed harder, all while plunging my tongue into her mouth in time to the plunging between her legs.

Her nails punctured my ass, riding with me as I rode her.

Every roll and twist and thrust of my hips, she matched me until I didn't know who fucked who.

Leaves flew. Birds scattered. And it was no longer about love but war.

"Ren!" Her body tightened, her legs spasmed around my hips, and the delicious heat of her pulsed with release.

I lost everything that made me human.

I only lived to make love to this woman.

I only existed to be hers.

My orgasm brewed full of pain and exquisite intensity, pushing me over the edge.

We clawed and cried and thrust and fucked, and my entire world changed being inside her. My soul switched owners as the thunderstorm that had teased me from the beginning finally found its matching cloud and erupted into existence.

My release ripped howls from my chest, vows from my heart, and promises from my soul. And I knew, without a shadow of a fucking doubt, I would never be whole again unless I had Della.

She was it for me.

I belonged to myself no more.

I'd officially handed over my life, and I was done fighting.

Forever.

Chapter Twenty-Three

DELLA

2031

A NEW MANUSCRIPT, a new page, a new story.

It's been a long time since I wrote down our tale. Too long since I've felt the keys of a laptop beneath my fingers and sat alone with my memories.

So many, many memories.

To be honest, I don't even know where to begin.

I did scribble now and again into that tatty notebook I took with me, but once Ren and I slept together, I forgot about everything else.

I didn't need anything else.

It was like the past story of our lives was over, and we had a new story to look forward to.

Does that make sense? It was the end of an era. Forbidden, unrequited love no more.

I will admit that I worried a little once we finally 'did the deed.' I worried that Ren would struggle with our new connection. I worried we'd still have roadblocks to overcome.

I needn't have worried.

Once Ren took me on that forest floor, filling me so full and hard that I had external and internal bruises for days, he committed himself to everything he'd been fighting.

His protectiveness became fiercer. His love deeper. His commitment truer than it had ever been.

That first time—that magical time—we both walked away (or rather limped) with cuts and scrapes and a togetherness that meant we could barely stop touching long enough to put up the tent.

From that moment on, we were insatiable.

Desperate and hungry and crazily in love.

Being in love with Ren Wild...words can't do it justice.

When he finally took me—when he finally woke up and saw he wasn't the only one with a wildness inside him—we reached a level that sometimes scared me.

The depth of love I felt for him.

The depth of love he felt for me.

It demanded our hearts beat to the same rhythm, our bodies be near, our minds be in-tune, our breaths be in-sync. I'd never felt anything like it. And I still feel it today.

His fears that he was selfish and unkind when it came to sex were totally unfounded. He couldn't accept that, after a life of doing his utmost to protect me, it was okay to be rough.

Wanting me as savagely as I wanted him didn't make him any less of a saint.

In fact, his darker desires made perfect sense. He bent over backward to put my needs before his own, but when it came to sex, he took his own pleasure too.

And there was absolutely nothing wrong with that.

Sleeping with Ren that day in the forest was my third sexual experience, but it might as well have been my first. Where Ren treated me like a queen in every waking moment of my life, when he got me beneath him—I was his to use as he saw fit.

He snapped and growled and dominated. He swore, which he painstakingly never did. He bruised me after making a vow to protect me from everything. He took control over what he wanted rather than sacrificing everything. When he thrust, he forgot about me and became obsessed with me at the same time. And when he made me come, that was the true gift because I'd never come before.

I craved—even before I knew what I needed—to be punished.

I needed to be punished because I'd fallen in love with a man I shouldn't, and a part of me always needed that discipline.

Only Ren understood because he had that same sin. Ren was the only one with the power to make me feel wholeheartedly female, and I worshipped that man with every inch.

I look back, and I'm actually jealous of myself. Jealous of that perfect time. Jealous of everything we were about to enjoy, endure, and explore.

There is so much I need to tell you. So many, many things.

And I will.

I'll get around to it because I'm not leaving anything out.

I can't, you see.

I have to write it down because I never want to forget. I never want to forget every minute of every day—not just passing flashes that make an impression.

Flashes like sleeping with Ren that first time.

Flashes like every day thereafter and every day in between.

Life is so fast and stuffed full of surprises that I'm afraid if I don't write them down, they'll disappear just as child amnesia deletes your earliest memories.

And it's more than just a drive to immortalize Ren with ink on paper. It's a necessity because these pages are our photo album.

Back when we were younger, we didn't have the luxury of cameras and video recorders. There are no pictures of us as we grew side by side. But there are words. And they are just as special because they're painted with all the love and connection I was feeling at the time. They not only show an image but let me borrow those emotions and relive it.

As for the other assignment—the one I was going to burn just before Ren walked back into my life? Well, that's here beside me. Almost two decades later, and I still have it. Ink smudged and paper torn but still intact and treasured.

Ren never let me burn it.

He tucked it safe and kept all three-hundred-and-ninety-seven pages wedged in his backpack the entire time we travelled.

This story is no longer about a baby and a boy who were never meant to be family, but a woman and a man who were always destined to be soulmates.

But before I get started, I want to say a few things.

First, I'm well aware I'm breaking another writing rule. Not only am I shattering the fourth wall, but I'm also talking to you from the future. I have the benefit of knowing how this tale turns out.

I know the ending.

I know the journey we take.

And you'll have to excuse me if I slip now and again. You'll have to forgive me for any spoilers because it isn't intentional. It's hard keeping things tucked up inside, desperate for their time to shine, my fingers cramping with desire to fly over the keyboard and release sentences and descriptions of the best man I've ever known.

But as much as I want to just blurt out everything, to let you know what happened when we travelled back to Cherry River, to whisper the name of someone so unbelievably special, to reveal if Ren and I got married...I can't.

It wouldn't be fair, because like any story, there is a beginning, a middle, and an end.

You know our beginning.

You're about to know our middle.

And our end...well, that's not finished yet, so you'll have to be patient.

What I can give you are incidents.

Five incidents that are crucial to this tale.

Just like I teased you with the four times Ren and I were apart, this time...there are moments.

Wonderful moments.

Horrible moments.

Moments that make up a life.

Five of them.

One, two, three, four, five.

Some I loved.

Some I hated.

One that hasn't happened yet.

My advice?
Watch out for them.

Chapter Twenty-Four

DELLA

2018

"STOP," I COMMANDED, slipping from the tent and stretching out the kinks in my spine. My entire body felt used and abused and oh-so-delicious.

Sex was my new favourite activity.

And I wanted a second round immediately.

But first...there was something that'd been bugging me since I saw Ren bathe in the river that first night.

"Why?" Ren turned to face me, his t-shirt dangling in his hands, low-slung cargo shorts already hiding the parts of him I wanted to explore. "What's happened?"

Padding barefoot toward him, I ran my fingers along the visible ribs interrupting the perfect shadows of strong stomach muscles. "I've wanted to ask you for the past week. When did you lose all this weight?" My heart clenched, suddenly terrified. "You're not sick, are you?"

He cupped my chin softly, his gaze molten caramel mixed with coffee. "No, I'm not sick." His hair was longer, teasing his forehead with sable bronze thanks to summer turning the strands light.

I could stare at his perfect face with its strong nose, powerful jaw, and thick eyelashes for an eternity and still find things to love about it. "Then why can I see your ribs?"

"Because I didn't exactly have an appetite when I left you."

I accepted his fleeting kiss before he let me go to sling his black t-shirt over his head, hiding the skinniness that wasn't there before. To be fair, he hadn't eaten as much as he normally did these days. I'd put it down to the sexual tension between us and the fact that my own belly was tied up with string.

But I didn't like seeing Ren skinny. I didn't like feeling as if I hadn't taken adequate care of him.

Following him as he wandered around camp, I asked, "You're saying you didn't eat the entire time we were apart?"

"I'm saying love was cruel, and my mind fixated on other things." He stopped and faced me. "I didn't want food, Della. I wanted you."

My skin burned with pleasure.

I knew it shouldn't, but in a way, that made me feel better. I hadn't forgiven him yet for leaving me, or for stalking me for months and not letting me know he was back in our apartment.

Three months we wasted.

Three long, horrible months where I lived unhappily with David, unable to stop the sensation that Ren was close by, all while he crashed in our apartment alone.

"Is it bad if I say you deserved it?"

He chuckled, running his hands through his hair. "Is it wrong that I love hearing you say that?"

"Say that I'm glad you suffered?"

"I deserved to suffer." He gave me a rueful smile. "I made you suffer by breaking my promise and leaving."

"We both know why you did."

"Yes, and I was selfish. I was only thinking of myself. I didn't know how to deal with what I felt for you, and I was weak enough to run." He coughed a little then gathered me in a hug filled with electricity and desire.

His soft lips pressed a kiss to my hairline. "Never again, Little Ribbon. You're stuck with me."

"And you're stuck with me." My smile faltered a little—just a flicker—but enough for Ren to frown.

"You okay?"

"Yes, just...*you're* okay, right? You're happy and healthy and you'll put on weight again and stop that little cough you do sometimes?"

He grinned. "I love it when you care."

I swatted him. "I care all the time."

He nodded, falling serious. "Look, I had the flu while we were apart and I haven't fully shaken the cough, that's all. And as for putting on weight, I've already filled out. You make my appetite come back because I need all the energy I can to keep you satisfied."

My cheeks pinked. "You kept me satisfied well enough last night."

His chocolate gaze turned dark and rich. "You too." He licked his lips. "Last night was..." He sighed with a little huff of indescribable bliss. It made my stomach flutter and heart leap for joy. "It was amazing, Della."

He kissed me again, distracting me from another niggling

question.

He noticed, nipping my bottom lip before pulling away with a resigned look. "Something else?"

"Umm..." I shrugged. "I need to ask you something."

His frown spread. "Ask me."

"I know we're both surviving on no sleep with no small amount of shock for what we've done but..."

"But..."

"Well, after fighting your feelings for me for so long. Now we've, eh, crossed those boundaries, are you still happy?" I ducked my gaze. "Are you happy you—"

"Ah, Della." Scooping me into strong arms, he rested his chin on my head. "I was honest with how I struggled to come to terms with loving you this way, and now, I'll be honest again." His voice dropped to a smoky murmur. "For the first time, I don't care about any of it. I can stand here with my head proud and tell the sun to go guilt-trip someone else for a change. Last night was the best night of my life with the only person I have ever loved. As far as I'm concerned, it was the first time for both of us. No one else compares because no one else ever came close to how I feel about you. And now that I know who you are beneath that bossy, brilliant girl I raised, you're in trouble because having you once won't be enough. Having you twice or three times or even a lifetime will never be enough, do you hear me?"

Pulling back, he stared as deep as he could into my heart. "I'm not just in love with you, Della. You're the only reason I'm alive. Loving you gave me purpose. And now you've completed me by giving me something I never dared dream of, so to answer your question, yes, I'm happy. So fucking happy I'm going to explode."

I shivered in his arms. "Okay then. Good."

"Fine." He grinned.

I raised my chin, my eyes fixating on his beautiful lips. "You know...after a declaration like that, you can't expect me not to want to get you back into bed." Standing on my tiptoes, I brushed a soft kiss on his mouth. "Take me into the tent, Ren."

He groaned, "Don't tempt me. It was hard enough untangling myself from you this morning."

Last night—after we'd orgasmed and slowly realised the enormity of what we'd done half-undressed, smeared in mud, and scratched with leaves in the middle of an empty forest—we'd petted and stroked and laughed at the sudden glorious freedom of being together.

That dazzling freedom drenched us in a high that made us shake and laugh and giggle like silly children as Ren pulled free, disposed of the condom, then plucked me from the gound.

The river was too shallow to swim, but we were able to wash off the stickiness and wilderness before eating a simple dinner of roasted fish, then snuggling up like we always did in the tent that took forever to put up, thanks to him grabbing me or me kissing him with our constant need to be close.

It was the best day of my life, but for some reason, we couldn't fall asleep. Too in awe of what had happened, too afraid that if we closed our eyes, we'd wake and it would all be a dream.

All night, Ren cupped my breast, rocked his front into my back, and wrapped his leg around mine. Our touches were allowed to be sexual. We were allowed to include our bodies as well as our hearts.

By the time dawn stole the midnights of darkness and used a different palate of shell-pinks and mandarin-golds, Ren and I were well and truly smitten.

Thank God, no one else was around because we were completely wrapped up in each other to the point of eye rolling.

"We have nowhere to be. No deadlines. No appointments. Why can't we just have sex for the rest of our lives?"

Ren chuckled, warming my heart with its husky melodic sound. "Because you didn't let me prepare. You pounced on me yesterday, remember?"

"I did nothing of the sort." I smirked, knowing full well that when I'd found that small clearing, I couldn't hold off the urgency anymore. The tingling, sparkling urgency that had steadily grown from painful to excruciating.

If Ren hadn't given in last night, I very well might've attacked him against his will.

"You won last night, Little Ribbon. Now you have to do what I say." Throwing me a heated look, he commanded, "Help me pack up camp. We're heading down river where the current isn't so fast and it's deeper to swim."

I followed him as he pulled the sleeping bags from the tent and started to roll them up. "And then what?"

He threw me a cheeky, deliciously dirty look. "And then, it's my turn."

Chapter Twenty-Five

REN

2018

DELLA HAD CHANGED my world.

And now, I wanted to change hers.

As we strode through the fading light to yet another campsite, I spotted a natural clearing where no sun was welcome, and no trees grew.

The river babbled in the distance, glistening in the twilight with invitation to wash away our exhaustion and relax. It wasn't as loud or as swift as our last stop. The surface calm and serene instead of choppy and chaotic.

The small cuts and grazes from sex last night marked Della's creamy skin as she strode ahead of me, her backpack heavy, boots crunching purposely, unaware I'd made my choice.

I wanted to feel bad about hurting her, but all I felt was absolute satisfaction and weird male pride.

"Stop," I said quietly hiding a cough as I slipped my bag to the ground and once again became bombarded by the tingling, incinerating chemistry that'd set up a constant vigil between us.

Della brushed away a sweat-sticky curl, breathing shallowly as she slowed to a halt and turned. She didn't say anything as our eyes locked, and we became caught up in a vortex of need.

"Don't." I kept my distance. "I'm doing my best to have camp set up before we give in this time."

"And how's that going for you?" She laughed as I tore at my bag's zipper and wrenched out almost every belonging in a rush.

"Good." I fisted the tent and shook it out.

"If you say so."

"Hold that tongue of yours, Della. I'm having you. Just give me a few minutes."

She smiled sweetly as I began the process of erecting somewhere to sleep—somewhere to take her where it was soft and safe so I could take my time and make her fall apart as spectacularly as she'd made me.

Disposing of her own bag, Della rubbed her lower back as she came to grab two sides of the tent as I unrolled it. She held it taut while I hammered in the pegs. Together, we inserted the poles, bending them until the nylon sprang upward, creating a roof.

The entire time we worked, my skin never stopped prickling at her proximity. And once we'd finished, she moved away and stripped off her t-shirt, leaving her in just a black sports bra and jeans as she twisted up her hair to encourage a breeze to cool her down.

My gut squeezed, my heart pounded, my mouth went dry.

All my life, she'd cared for me. She'd done chores I didn't ask her to, cooked food I didn't request, been there every step of the way. I no longer looked at her as two people—girl and woman—just her.

Della.

Mine.

Dappled in twilight with tiredness clinging to her skin, she looked so damn young. Too young to withstand the hurricane of lust in my blood.

But she *had* survived.

She'd fought me back.

She'd woken me up to the temptress she truly was, and I couldn't wait anymore.

We had a bed.

That was all we needed.

As she kicked off her boots and removed her socks, her ribbon tattoo with its capital R filled my vision, no longer condemning me but welcoming me.

I wanted to lick it again.

Bite it for good measure.

Stopping beside her as she turned to face me, I hovered like a love-struck fool, drinking her in, licking my lips at how I wanted to suck the sweat on her chest and run my thumb over the perspiration on her upper lip.

I was so fucking in love with her, I could barely stand it.

She looked up, shielding her gaze from the final light streaming through the trees. "Why are you looking at me like that?" She narrowed her eyes. "You don't look well. In fact, you look hungry." She stepped toward the bags. "I'll make you something to eat. You need to put on weight—"

Grabbing her around the waist, I shook my head. "I'm not hungry for food, Della."

She blinked, whatever tiredness she suffered vanished. "Oh."

"Yes, oh. You've turned me into an addict."

"I don't mind."

Nuzzling her nose with mine, I breathed softly, "It's my turn to ask you something."

"Okay..." She didn't help my concentration or self-control by fixating on my mouth. "What?"

"Last night...was it okay for you? Not emotionally, but physically?"

She laughed under her breath. "Seriously?" She melted in my hold, her eyes soft and glowing. "Good? That's a very underwhelming word for how great it was."

"I was rough with you."

"And I loved every second of it." She tilted her head. "What's this really about?"

Honestly, I didn't truly know. I'd shown her quick and explosive, but I didn't want her to think that was my only trick. And I didn't want her to think I was some idiot who needed affirmation that he'd performed well.

This wasn't about me.

This was about her.

This was about pleasing her, so she never looked elsewhere again.

This was about me ensuring my heart would never be broken when she realised I wasn't everything she hoped I would be.

"Last night was the best night of my life, Della. Is it wrong that I hoped it was the same for you?"

Her body tensed. "It was."

"Can I try to make it better?"

"There's no need. I loved every—"

"I had you pinned in the dirt while rutting into you like a savage. Tonight, I need to show you I'm more than that."

"I know you are." She pressed a kiss to my cheek. "I love you as a savage. That savage made me come for the first time, so believe me, I loved it just as much as you did."

"Wait." I reared back, holding her at arm's length. "What do you mean, the first time you came?"

She blushed. "I'm saying...I'd never come before."

"But..." My mind whirled on all the times she'd thrown hints and secrets in my face, daring me to rise to the bait, tormenting me on a daily basis. "You implied. You said—"

"That I'd made myself orgasm to thoughts of you?" She sighed. "Yes, I know. I wanted you to have that mental picture. Sorry." She winced a little as I glared at her. "The truth is, I *did* try. I've touched myself while thinking about you, but even though I wanted you enough to overlook certain rules, I could never get past the fact that you didn't want me. Every time I got close, I…I couldn't do it. The shame would be too much to bear, and I'd stop."

I rubbed my face with a hand. "So you're saying you've spent your entire life frustrating yourself and never finding a release?"

She laughed under her breath. "I guess you could say that."

"No wonder living with you made me on edge." I chuckled painfully, coughing once. "Every time I looked at you, Della, the way you stared at me almost brought me to my knees. The amount of times I lectured myself that I was imagining it, picking up on things that weren't there." I shook my head, reliving the agony of sharing a house with the one person I couldn't have. "You made my life a lot harder than it should've been."

She smiled sinfully. "Yes, but it meant I got you in the end, so I have no regrets."

I fell quiet, letting the past crash over me but no longer suffering the same guilt as before. Maybe Della was right, and everything had happened for a reason. Maybe I'd never let myself care for anyone else because I knew I'd never be able to share my heart with anyone other than her. And maybe she'd never made herself orgasm because all along she'd been waiting for me to—

I groaned, wedging my fingers against my temples as yet another tormenting thought appeared.

"What? What is it?" Della scooted closer. "You have that look again."

"What look?"

"The look that says you want to whip yourself for ever thinking about touching me."

"First, I'll never feel that way again. Ever. As far as I'm concerned, your body is mine just like mine is yours. And second, just because you know me doesn't mean you can predict everything about me."

"Well, you should accept that last night needed to happen the way it did. It was never going to be slow and sweet, Ren. We'd been edging to exploding for years."

I nodded, picking up on her wavelength just as I used to do when she was young. "It smashed through our perceptions. Changed the relationship between us."

"Exactly." She shifted to kiss my stubble-covered cheek. I hadn't shaved in a few days and didn't have the urge out here. "And now, stop changing the subject and tell me what you're truly thinking."

She was right. Last night was never going to be anything more than a feral battle because we had far too much history between us. History that held different dynamics and ages and pent-up secrets we hadn't shared.

Now, things were out in the open.

And we had so much to look forward to.

Cupping her cheeks, my touch sent goosebumps ricocheting down her arms. "I've taught you almost everything you know. Just like you've taught me."

Her breath came feathery and light. "Yes."

"Would it be sick of me to teach you something else?"

Her gaze hooded as she leaned into me. "Teach me what?"

I licked my lips, drawn to her, unable to stop the way her heart hooked mine. "How to come. Not just when being ruthlessly taken but with my fingers inside you, my tongue licking you, my cock fucking you. So many different ways. I want to be the one to teach you all of them."

She gasped, then shook her head slowly. "I-I wouldn't mind."

The shy happiness in her tone undid me.

Bringing her close, I kissed her hard. "Good answer, Little Ribbon. Let's start now."

Chapter Twenty-Six

DELLA

2018

REN'S KISSES WERE something made of fantasy.

Hard and rough. Swift and sexy. Deep and lingering. Whenever he kissed me, it didn't matter if it was a peck or a meal, he completely hijacked my thoughts and body.

And that was how I went from standing in my jeans and bra to him undoing my belt and zipper, pushing the denim down my legs, then reverently removing my black bikini briefs before pulling the sports bra over my head.

Once I was naked, he kissed me harder, plucked me from the ground as if I weighed nothing and carried me in arms that bunched and trembled with an intoxicating mix of love and lust.

My legs automatically wrapped around his waist, our lips never unlocking as he toed off his boots, kicked them aside, and marched fully clothed toward the gurgle and chuckle of the river.

He licked me deep and clutched me strong, trading dry land for a water-world as if he outran echoes from our past and bravely stormed into our future.

"What are you doing?" I gasped when he continued walking. Water sucked at his socks, saturating his jeans. His steps became wades as we traded the shallows to a darkened pool where the current didn't disrupt the crystal clarity of the surface.

Once there, he ducked to his knees and pulled me down into the cool, crisp embrace of the river.

His breath caught from the chill, a tiny rattle roughening his voice. "Making love to you."

Somehow, it felt as if he bowed to me. Worshipping me all while his tongue said he planned to corrupt me with an evening of ecstasy.

The coolness of the running water stole the remainders of our breaths as it flowed between us, making our bodies tense. His eyes caught mine, hooded and heated as he grabbed my chin and pulled me back into a kiss.

I gasped into his mouth, shuddering from the sudden temperature change and the refreshing lick of liquid.

"You're sopping wet," I murmured, tilting my head as he kissed me deeper, and his fingers found their way into my hair.

"And you better be too," he whispered, hot and dark. "Because I'm sure as shit hard."

A lash of lust travelled from my heart to my core, tugging on strands and sensuality, preparing my body for whatever he wanted. "All you have to do is smile at me, Ren, and I'm wet."

He attacked me with unbridled need. His kisses were pure velvet violence. "Don't say things like that. I want this to last, not be over in seconds."

"Then stop seducing me so well."

We laughed together even as his hands stroked skin sore with cuts from last night's war. His palms explored my back and spine, fisting handfuls of my ass as he yanked me forward and onto the straining erection in his jeans.

"Do you know how often I've stared at this?" His fingers kneaded me. "How I'd dream of seeing you naked and in my bed?" His lips parted wider over mine, directing the kiss from shallow hello to deep dance.

I moaned as he kissed me like all women wanted to be kissed—hungrily, fondly, passionately.

We kissed all night.

We kissed for a second.

And as we kissed, he rocked up into my bare core, his zipper as cold as the river, his hands holding me firm.

We were in perfect alignment for sex.

Pity he was still so encumbered.

Our thoughts vibrated to the same frequency—just like always—because he pushed me down his lap, giving him room for his hands to fumble at his belt.

"Let me." I panted, partly from cold and mostly from need.

He clenched his jaw as I found his buckle and unthreaded the leather. I didn't tease; I was just as starving as him. Popping his button and drawing down his zipper, my hand vanished into his boxers before he could push me away.

Satin-covered steel and sheer power. Holding Ren so intimately was like being given the keys to immortality.

His head fell back on a groan, nostrils flaring, hips rocking, granting me all the magic in the world.

"I'm always so damn close with you."

"Is that a bad thing?" I gasped as his fingers trailed over my goose-pimpled thighs and dug into my flesh.

"Bad that I find you unbelievably gorgeous and can't help how much I want you?" He kissed me with a twist of silk and softness. "Never."

Rearing back a little, his arms criss-crossed as he grabbed his hem, and with eyes dripping with chocolate promise, yanked his sodden t-shirt over his head. With a grunt of strength, he tossed the wet material toward the shore.

"Thought you'd wash your clothes as well as yourself, huh?" I snickered as he gathered me to his hot, naked chest. His cock wedged against me, making both of us hiss in that deliciously depraved way.

"Everything about me is filthy, so yeah." He smirked. "Just trying to cleanse myself from needing you so badly."

"I don't think the river will help with that." I melted as he kissed me again, adding bruise upon bruise, rasp after rasp from all the other kisses we'd shared.

"I think you're right." Pushing me away, he ordered. "Go get the soap. Let's see if that works."

I swiped hair from my eyes, the ends floating in the water like kelp. "Now who's being bossy?"

"Only because I want to stare at you while you get it." His eyes glowed. "Go. Before I change my mind."

Burning up from the desire between us that even the chilly river couldn't douse, I turned and waded back to the shallows. Self-consciousness descended as water sluiced off me, preferring to stay with its friends than on my skin.

With my spine straight and belying the nervous butterflies in my stomach, I swayed my hips, revealing my back and bottom to Ren.

It wasn't like he hadn't seen me before, but this...it was different.

Without a backward glance, I headed toward the bags standing sentry at the tent's entrance. It only took a second to unzip the side pocket where painkillers, toothbrushes, and soaps lived, then spin to face the only man I'd ever love.

His arm was above his head, cocked back to toss his soaking jeans to the bank.

They landed with a loud splat beside me, his boxer-briefs on top, letting me know he was as naked as I was.

My heart fluttered as I stepped into the water.

Ren bit his lip, his right shoulder rocking up and down. I knew exactly what he was doing, and it made yet more lust bubble in my belly.

Reaching him, I kneeled and ducked my fingers beneath the surface. Sure enough, his right hand was latched around his cock, stroking himself. "Couldn't wait?"

He didn't even look ashamed, more like tortured. "You are far too stunning for mere mortals. Are you truly mine?" He took my hand, wedging it beneath his on his stiff cock. Squeezing both of us, he grumbled, "Feel what you do to me, Della? See what I've been hiding from you for years?"

I couldn't catch my breath at the raw honesty in his tone. The knowledge he'd hurt just as much as I had. The shared pain we were well acquainted with.

I'd seen Ren naked so many times.

His body was as familiar to me as my own.

But this was entirely new.

He'd shed the brotherly side of himself, allowing me to see him as a man and not just my protector.

He couldn't be any more handsome or tempting, and I wrapped my fingers tight beneath his, making him half-groan, half-snarl.

Desire snapped and crackled, making its way to form a fireball in my core.

Ren surrendered to my touch, wrapping his arms around me, dragging me close. "Come here." Our skin slipped and slid over each other as I floated onto his lap, and my legs wrapped around his waist.

Releasing his erection, I moaned as he rubbed against me, and we both almost buckled with pleasure. The soap in my left hand wasn't wanted as Ren purred into my mouth, rocking against me, fucking me even though we were still apart.

His fingers threaded through my hair, tugging my head back as he broke the kiss and nipped his way down my throat. He didn't let me go as my back bowed and water lapped over my head, drenching every inch of blonde.

His mouth was hot as he trailed kisses down my chest, then latched onto my nipple with furious need.

I cried out as he wrapped one arm around my waist, driving against me as his tongue swirled and teeth teased, slipping from one nipple to the other.

"God, please..." I writhed against him, needing him inside me. *Now.*

But he didn't bow to my command. Instead, he sucked my breasts one more time before kissing his way up my throat and ending at my mouth with the longest, sexist kiss I'd ever been given.

I gave up trying to figure out what he would do next.

"Turn around," he murmured. "Turn around so I can wash you."

With a quick inhale, he unwrapped my legs, then spun me on his lap, pushing me outward until I floated on the surface. Gathering the thick weight of my hair, he lathered the soap and ran his strong fingers over my scalp, massaging gently, breathing a little easier thanks to familiar pastimes and recognisable comforts in the sex-storm we lived in.

My body didn't know if it should orgasm or melt. I was tangled with lust and trust, remembering all the other times Ren had washed me, tended to me, cared for me.

It made my heart burst and tears prickle as I whispered, "That feels so nice."

"And you feel too perfect to be real." Lathering more bubbles, his large hands worked over my shoulders, under my arms, over my breasts, and down my belly.

"Kneel," he ordered, pushing my body deeper into the water so I switched from floating to kneeling. "Turn to face me."

There was something so erotic about following his curt commands.

Once I faced him, he rubbed the soap once again, then trailed his hand through the water to the curls between my legs.

I jolted as he washed me gently, the slipperiness of soap washed away by the river, leaving me so much wetter than before.

Never looking away from me, he spread me apart, then inserted two fingers inside me.

I froze and tightened and quaked and liquefied.

He might've only given me two fingers, but it felt like two pieces of his soul. Two pieces that Cassie had bemoaned she would never have. Two pieces that no one else would ever own.

Just me.

Only me.

My mouth fell wide as he sank deeper. He hooked his touch inside me, pressing, rubbing, igniting the fuse that would eventually explode into a toe-curling orgasm. He didn't give me a moment to breathe, analyse, or decide if I wanted to fight back, submit, or melt into a puddle in his hand. All that mattered was I was his, and he was touching me in ways I'd always begged him to.

"Ren," I breathed as he gathered me closer.

"Shush." Never looking away from me, he studied my every twitch and sigh as if learning exactly what made me simmer.

And he found it with his thumb on my clit.

My back bowed, and a low moan spilled from me as he drove two fingers deeper.

He smiled, satisfaction glowing in his dark eyes. "You like that?"

"Uh huh." I nodded with desire-lethargy, my head heavy and eyes struggling to focus.

"Good to know." Pulling his touch from my body, he lathered yet more bubbles and dragged them over the sparse hair on his well-defined chest, swiftly washing himself before the soap disappeared to clean other areas.

I wobbled before him, shocked that he'd touched me so spectacularly, then acted as if nothing had happened.

"Oh, that's just mean." I pouted as ripples of pleasure still worked through my core, begging him to come back.

"It would be mean if I didn't plan on doing more." His hands finished washing, tossing the soap toward the shore. "But I do. An entire night of more."

"I would've done that," I said.

"What? Wash me?" He shook his head, jaw tight and eyes black. "Della, I'm seconds away from forcing you onto my lap. I couldn't stand you washing me. I barely have any control left as it is."

"I don't care. It's about time you let go of that lifetime of control. You just teased me. It's only fair I tease you." Wanting to make him as wound up as me, I pushed off the pebble-littered riverbed and floated onto his lap. "I need you, Ren." Wrapping my arms around his shoulders, he was too slow to push me away.

My core connected to his cock, and we stiffened.

"You're making me insane." He growled around a cough.

"All you have to do is give in." I ran my tongue around the shell of his ear, adoring the way he trembled. "You want me? Then take me. Right here."

My heart thrummed as his possessive hands splayed over my back like panther paws—velvet and heavy with a touch of claw. "You're a minx."

"And you're a martyr." Pulling back a little, I kissed his cheek and chin and finally sought his lips. "Please, Ren. Just a tiny thrust and you'd be inside—"

His hands shot to my hips, angling me perfectly so the tip of him hovered over my entrance. "Such a demanding little thing." He breathed as if he'd run for days, his eyes hotter than I'd ever seen. "Ruining all my plans."

I didn't know who made the first move—me with a quest of my hips or him with a probe of his, but somehow, we went from two people to the precipice of becoming one.

Nothing else mattered.

No other thoughts entered.

The world had vanished, and it was just us in our forest like always, on our own like forever, fighting the undying need to merge into one.

"You want this?" Ren strangled, slipping another inch inside me.

My forehead slammed to his wet, cool shoulder, unable to stop my teeth from latching into his skin. "Yes!"

"Goddammit, Della." He surged deep. "*Fuck*, you feel incredible."

Hard.

Fast.

Consuming.

My legs spread wider as my feet rubbed on pebbles and flotsam, not caring about anything but his hard length slamming inside me.

My hips rocked back, driving him deeper to that wondrous place.

"Don't move," he snapped.

Prickles of rejection kissed over my skin. "Why not?"

"Because I'm so fucking close to coming, and I forgot to put a condom on. You feel *far* too amazing bare."

His fist wrapped in my hair, pulling my head back until he could meet my eyes. I expected him to kiss me hard, to drive into me harder, but his face blackened with self-control. "I can't believe I broke that rule."

"What rule?"

"Never have sex without protection."

My shoulders fell. I knew enough from sexual education at school and what Ren had taught me that STIs were a big reason rubbers were important.

But we'd been safe with others. Surely, we could be free with each other. "You're inside me. It's already too late."

He swore under his breath as I rocked on him.

"Stop, Della." His hand landed heavily on my hip. "It's never too late." The hardness of him throbbed inside me, his heartbeat matching the thick craving of my own.

Pushing me, his length slipped out torturously slow. Once we were two people again, he burrowed his face into his hands and yelled into his palms. *"Fuck!"*

I gave him a moment, hating the separation but familiar enough with Ren to know he followed rules—especially ones that protected me—religiously.

He stood upright, and the river went from lapping around his shoulders to barely covering his proud erection. "Let's get inside the tent. I'm assuming you have more condoms with you?"

I stood on lust-wobbly legs as Ren swept me into his arms. His eyes softened with regret. "I'm sorry. I didn't mean to ruin the moment."

"You didn't."

Kissing me softly, he whispered, "I'm just so terrified of hurting you. It would kill me, Little Ribbon. If I ever did anything to—"

"You won't." I wrapped my arms around him, sucking in a breath as he swung me into a horizontal position like a groom would his bride and carried me from the river. "You never will."

Pressing his nose to mine, he chuckled. "You always manage to bring out the best and worst in me. One moment, I don't care about anything but fucking you; the next, I want to lay you on a throne and pledge everything I can." He carried me toward our bags with hardened feet used to walking on twigs and prickly things. "Being in love really is a disease."

Placing me reverently by my backpack, I got my balance by clutching his biceps. "Love's a disease?"

He nodded, brushing aside my wet hair and palming off excess droplets from the river. Even brusque, having his hands on me was pure cashmere and desire. "When I'm with you, I have the cure. I feel stronger, happier, invincible. But when I'm not, I feel as if life itself could delete me, and I wouldn't care."

The intensity of such a strong moment infected both of us, and our eyes locked with oaths and vows. "I'm never leaving you, Ren."

"And I'm never walking away again. No matter what happens. We stick together."

Our lips sought each other, sealing our promises with silky sweeps of our tongues.

The heat of our skin helped dry us a little, but we didn't care about the rest as we pulled apart and I bent to unzip my bag. The sound of the zipper in the gloom made Ren wince, his senses on high alert.

Dropping my hand into the dark rucksack, I rummaged for a second before pulling out a box.

A familiar box with a familiar note stuck to the top.

"What the—" Ren snatched it from my hands. Squinting to read in the final threads of light, his basic handwriting decorated the top: *If you're going to do things outside my control, please be safe. Use these. At all times.* "Is-is this the box I bought you?"

My cheeks glowed pink. "Yes."

"But…how?"

I could guess what ran through his head. How many condoms had I used? Had I replenished the box? Had I used David's instead? I didn't want him having those thoughts. He'd end up on the moral seesaw again, wondering if he was wrong in taking me. We were in such a good place and I refused to let anything from our past ruin that.

My heart hiccupped as Ren battled beneath his mental struggle, and I stole the box back, cracking it open to reveal a neat regimented row of foil wrapped condoms glinting in the gloom. There were too many to count quickly or guess how many were missing. But Ren wouldn't need to guess. I would tell him.

"I only used two. Well, three, counting last night." I kept my fingers locked tight on the box.

"What?" He coughed. "How is that possible? I saw you kissing Tom at the Halloween party. I'd seen how passionate you were. I lived with you, for God's sake. As you slowly awakened to the idea of sex, it drove me mad every time you went out with your friends, not knowing what you were doing."

My insides smarted for how much I'd hurt him over the years, but I stayed brave because I owed him this. I owed him an apology. "You're forgetting that most of the time, I was in agony over you, Ren. I only used two; you have my word. One the night I lost my virginity, and one the night of my eighteenth birthday." I didn't want images of me sleeping with others in his head, but he needed to know the truth—that I wasn't some harlot, even if I made him think I was.

I never looked away from him. He deserved to be able to read the honesty on my face, not just hear it. "Yes, I lost my virginity because I was messed up over you. But I chose not to have sex again because I wasn't emotionally ready. I didn't sleep with anyone until that second time on my birthday. And I didn't do it because I wanted him. I did it because I wanted *you*."

He sucked in a noisy breath.

"For months, I'd felt as if you were near. My missing you was at an all-time high. I never wanted to be with anyone else but you. I'm a terrible person for using David when I never stopped loving you."

He made a sound as if I'd kicked him in the gut. "Della—"

"I don't say any of this to be cruel, Ren." I shook my head, wet strands clinging to my shoulders. "I'm telling you out of pure honesty because you never truly accepted that I could love you as much as you love me. You are my entire world. You ran because of me. And in some part of my mind, I'm worried you'll run again if this is too much to accept."

Sick, sick shame filled his face. "God, Della. You let me take you so roughly—you have cuts and bruises all over you—and it was only your third time?" He dug fingers into his hair. "Why didn't you...I don't know...?" He looked at me with pain and self-disgust. "I should've taken you gently. I should've remembered you are so youn—"

"If you call me young, we'll have a problem."

His lips thinned. "But it's the truth. I raised you, for God's sake. I should've been more careful." Backing away, he wiped his mouth with a trembling hand. "I pushed you into losing your virginity by being an asshole, and I'm the reason you did it a second time by watching you instead of having the balls to admit I was back in town. I-I don't know what to say."

"I don't want you to say anything. Words only get you into trouble."

"But I should have—"

"What? Waited until we were in some motel and gone slow? Ren, I love you. But when you start second-guessing yourself, you're really a pain in the ass, you know that?" Holding up the back of my arm where a pretty decent scratch had scabbed over, I said firmly, "I wear these with pride. Every second of last night was better than any fantasy I've ever had of you, and believe me, I've had a lot."

A twisted half-smile decorated his face.

"I was only able to come because you gave me exactly what I wanted, when I wanted it. Your strength. Your aggression. I need that because all my life you've been strong and aggressive in keeping me safe, and somehow, I've come to associate that with you loving me. If you dare touch me with kitten gloves and feather kisses, I'll just rile you up until you snap again." I chuckled under my breath. "And we both know how easy I can spark your temper. Don't make me prove it."

He rolled his eyes, tension slipping down his spine. "I always knew you were trouble, Della Ribbon."

"And I always knew you were it for me, Ren Wild."

He closed the distance, tugging the ends of my dripping hair, his knuckles brushing my nipples. "How is it that you turned out like me when I did everything I could to prevent it?"

"How is it that you see that as a bad thing when it's the best thing in the world?"

"It's not a bad thing." He gathered me close, one hand going between my shoulder blades and the other on the top of my bare ass. "It's a miraculous thing. We're so similar that I swear if I didn't have memories of being sold that day, or vague images of my mother, I'd be terrified we were actually brother and sister, and Mclary was my father, too."

I fake shuddered. "God, can you imagine it? A lifetime of lying about being siblings only to find out we actually are?"

His face darkened as troubling thoughts filled his gaze. Bringing me flush against his nakedness, he whispered against my ear, "Even if that were true, now I've had you, I wouldn't be able to stop."

Molten heat swelled between my legs.

"Now I've been inside you and found the girl of my dreams, I don't care if our blood runs the same. We share the same heart anyway. I'd live in sin and go to hell because I literally could never give you up." Ren tugged my hair, arching my neck so he could latch his lips and teeth onto my throat. "I thought I was sick before—wanting you after so many years between us—but I truly must be the devil if I can admit I would fight every law, rule, and enemy if they ever tried to take you away from me."

His lips made their way to mine, planting firm. A swift, dominant tongue slipped into my mouth.

My knees gave out as I surrendered absolutely. In that second, I felt entirely like a girl and not a woman. I felt young and being kissed by a much older, braver, purer person than I could ever be.

"Ren…" I moaned against his lips as his hand trailed down my body, dipping between my legs and finding how wet I was.

He growled beneath his breath, driving two fingers inside me as he wrapped his arm around my hips, holding me steady.

"Tent, Ren." I stumbled backward, wanting so much to continue what he was doing but quickly losing my eye sight to galaxies and shooting stars the longer he stroked me.

Ripping his fingers from me, he spun me around and pushed my back. "Get in."

As I tripped forward, he stole the condom box from my hand, fisted a single one, and tossed the rest to the side.

Slick sweat sprouted over my skin, full of needle pricks of anticipation as I ducked under the awning, and Ren followed me inside, almost as if he were as dazed as me.

Our sleeping bags were unzipped and ready to cocoon us.

"Lie down, Della."

Ren's command was full of wood smoke and kindling. "Now."

I had a physical reaction to him commanding me—a rippling squeeze of pure lust from my heart to my core.

Flopping onto my back, I looked up as he kneeled above me, his cock jutting out, his eyes wild as the feral cats we'd seen stalking us for our scraps.

"Open your legs." Ren sucked in a breath, biting his bottom lip when I did as he asked. He was as naked as a heaven-sent prince ready to corrupt me.

I didn't care I was exposed to him. I didn't care we hadn't fully cleared the air. All I cared about was Ren and the clawing hunger rapidly filling the tent with hailing fury.

"What am I going to do with you, my dear Little Ribbon?"

Opening the foil packet, he plucked out the slippery condom and, without tearing his gaze from mine, rolled it down his impressive length before squeezing the base and hissing between his teeth. "You've seen me at my worst, my sickest, my angriest, and my saddest. But you haven't seen me when I'm so fucking hard I have no control." Letting himself go, he crawled toward me, settled between my legs, and bowed until his mouth hovered just above my core.

Every muscle in my body locked.

He smiled; his lips swollen from prior kisses, and his jaw covered with dark stubble. "No one has because no one has pushed me as much as you do. I'm weak against you, Della."

I licked my lips, loving his honesty. I was jealous of his past lovers, but I pitied them too because Ren never gave them what he was giving me. He wasn't just giving me his body; he was giving me his life, heart, mind, breath, and soul. He was giving me everything, and I took, took, took. I took all of him because he'd already taken all of me.

"You made me," I breathed. "I only exist because of you."

"No, you exist because the universe knew a ten-year-old kid with nine fingers and hate in his heart was lonely."

I cried out as his tongue licked me for the first time, stealing language, maths, history, and every other knowledge I possessed, leaving me empty apart from one thought. "Ren."

"Enough talking." His whipping whisper came just before his mouth sealed over me.

He didn't ease me into this new sensation. He didn't test and probe. He dined on me. He devoured me. He drove two fingers inside me all while his teeth nipped my clit, and the burning heat of his mouth never stopped.

I didn't stand a chance.

I had no control over the typhoon swirling and building, sucking up debris, cleansing my heart from all its maybes and uncertainties and blowing them around, focusing the eye of the storm into my belly.

Up and up, I flew.

Tighter and tighter, I gathered.

And when his voice shared his tongue, spearing into me and murmuring against my searing flesh, he smashed the old Della apart and gave this new one wings. "Remember that wish—" *Plunge, lick, bite* "—you made when you were five years old?" *Twist, tease, nibble.* "At the diner with the cupcakes?" *Thrust, consume, worship.* "Answer me, Della."

I shivered, unable to talk but desperate to reply. I nodded. I remembered, or at least I remembered the stories he'd told me. "I wished for us to never be apart. For you to take me everywhere."

"I'm ready to ensure that wish comes true." He licked me again. And again. "You're mine, Della Wild. I'm going to take you places you've never been. Starting with making you come on my face."

The crude snap, the dirty vow, the darkness of his voice—they all added matches to the swirling wind inside me.

His mouth settled over my core again as his tongue laved and fingers hooked and those tiny flying matches inside turned into a spark, a flame, a roaring fireball that took me with no warning.

"*Oh*—" It was the only word I knew as Ren dug fingers into my thighs, holding me down and wide as he gave me no safety, no sanctuary, no reprieve from the torture he brought between my legs.

"God, you taste—" He bit me again. "You taste like Della. Like everything I've ever dreamed of."

And that was it.

I did what he said I would.

I exploded.

I unravelled.

I came and came and came.

And before the final breeze blew the fire out, Ren crawled up my body, slotted his hips into mine, and thrust inside me in one long, delicious impale.

We both cried out. Him low and guttural. Me high and needy.

This was truth.

This was us.

This was everything.

His hips pistoned into mine, driving me deep, shoving me into the sleeping bags, and the tent shook and creaked, and we clawed and snapped and bit, our hands never empty, our legs never untangled, our bodies as joined as they could ever be.

On and on, he fucked me.

On and on, I rode him.

And when a matching fire-breathing typhoon found him. When his body couldn't withstand the pleasure. When our hearts exceeded too much love and thankfulness and joy, he reared up on his hands…

…and roared.

Chapter Twenty-Seven

REN

2018

IT TOOK A MONTH.

A month for me to trust that this was real.

That I hadn't died and found my version of heaven. That I wasn't asleep and living in my dream. That I wasn't fantasising that Della was mine only to find I'd gone insane.

For four wondrous weeks, we stayed in the forest, swimming in chilly rivers, making love in glades, and eating the rest of our supplies before brushing off our hunting skills and living off the land.

Autumn well and truly arrived, turning the final mugginess of summer into the warning chill of impending winter.

T-shirts became sweaters and we snuggled for warmth as much as for sanity.

We walked far, sometimes leaving the river to climb up a hill for a better vantage point, and sometimes doubling back to a campsite where we'd shared a night beneath the stars, naked and writhing on a sleeping bag beside a cheery fire.

We didn't care what time of day it was or where we were—when the urge to be close overtook us, we didn't fight it. We'd spent far too long fighting it and were now making up for lost time.

Most mornings, I woke with Della plastered to my side—just like she did when she was little—her face tucked into my chest, her legs wrapped in mine. Those moments stabbed my heart with memories of a blonde cherub who always made me melt.

I found it hard to let such thoughts in—of Della playing with Liam when she was six or seven. Of Della launching on my back while I raked freshly cut lucerne when she was eight or nine.

The guilt was still there, but not because I'd slept with her. The guilt was because she was so damn pure and had an entire life ahead of her. By accepting what had always been between us, I'd stolen that future from her. I'd shackled her with me, and I still struggled to believe I would be enough.

She'd always been so bright and brave and capable.

I'd always been distrusting, untalkative, and stubborn.

I'd given her everything to ensure she had an education, enjoyed fellow humans, and was prepared for a career she could be proud of. But by giving in to my feelings for her, I'd made all those sacrifices obsolete. I should've noticed just how similar we were. I should've stopped to *look* at her, not just manhandle her into a life people were told they should want.

As far as I was concerned, I would never live in a city again. I doubted I could. I'd reached my people quota the day I ran from Mclary's, and that hadn't changed just because I'd fallen in love.

But I also couldn't deny, I would live in a high-rise poky apartment if that made Della happy. If she wanted to work in an office and have overpriced drinks with her colleagues and become the bread winner, then I would agree, because I meant what I said: I was hers.

We'd stepped over every line we could, and there was no going back now. She was stuck with me, and no matter what sort of life she wanted—city or farm—I was limited to what I could offer her.

Wherever we ended up, I would forever be an unskilled labourer with no accolades to my name. I knew hard work, and I lived to cultivate and tend, but I would never be a man to wear a suit, own a laptop, or host dinner parties in his home.

At the moment, Della was as wrapped up in me as I was in her…but things always had a way of changing. When she grew sick of my overprotectiveness, or when she turned away my need to have her in my arms…what would happen then?

She was still so damn young—still forming into herself; unaware of her true wants and dreams. Compared to her, I'd always been the surly old man who would rather growl at visitors than welcome them. Would Della love me when she was my age and I was pushing forty not thirty? Would she still find me handsome with sun-weathered skin and a body that had seen better days?

At least those thoughts were few and far between—I could forget about any future worries because when I was with Della, she made me exist purely in the now. When her fingers touched my arm or her lips landed on mine, nothing else mattered.

Nothing.

And that was the best gift she could give me because for the first time, I was free from worry. Free from the weight of responsibility and concern for her future and mine.

"Ren?" Della cocked her head, her hands glittering in scales as she rasped the silver fish I'd caught.

I put down the snare I was making to catch dinner, giving her my undivided attention. Her hair was lighter from living outdoors, bordering white gold instead of sunshine. The blue of her ribbon peeked between the glossy strands, dangling a little over her shoulder.

"Yeah?"

"I know we agreed not to discuss it again, but…it's all I can think about."

I groaned, leaning heavily against the sapling I'd chosen to sit by. "Della, you know why I can't—"

"It's not enough. It doesn't feel complete."

I wouldn't admit that I felt the same way. That whenever I was inside her, I hated, *hated* having to pull out before I came. We'd gone through her box of condoms—the box I'd bought her and probably close to their expiry date—within the first few days of sleeping together.

Once they'd run out, we had no other alternative. To start with, I'd adamantly swore I wouldn't touch her again until we had more. That had blown into a massive argument where she threw logic in my face and made me agree that since I'd never had unprotected sex before her and she hadn't either—we were safe in that respect. However, I wasn't just worried about that.

I didn't want to hurt her, and I knew what would happen if we continued sleeping together with no protection.

She'd get pregnant.

And as much as I loved her, she was far too young to be shackled with a kid—I should know after dedicating my life to a child I hadn't planned—and far too naïve to think it wouldn't happen.

And out here? If she got pregnant, so many things could go wrong. Even if we headed back into town, we had no insurance or money to pay for hospital stays and baby check-ups, and I refused to put her in danger when it was avoidable.

"You got your wish. We're still having regular sex. It doesn't matter if I come on your stomach or inside you, it still feels incredible." I lowered my voice, giving her a dark smile. "Believe me, Della, that first time I felt you without anything between us, it took everything I could not to come that very second."

She huffed, not buying my attempt to redirect the conversation. "It doesn't feel complete, and I struggle to come, knowing you can't finish with me." She brushed away a tumbled curl with the back of her hand, decorating her forehead with a fish scale.

Seeing her in a stretched sweater hanging over her shoulder, jeans with holes and frays, and dirt beneath her nails with mess upon her face made me hard.

So damn hard.

I loved how wild she was. How the last name she'd baptised us with matched us perfectly. And because she was wild, she wanted our sex to be wild.

Three weeks ago, she'd crawled onto my lap while I was turning a spit-roast of rabbit and undone my shorts before I could stop her.

She'd been naked under one of my t-shirts, and it only took a second for her to squeeze me, jerk me, and make me hard enough to slip inside her. I'd become her prisoner the second I felt her wet heat, allowing her to take from me until…she stood as suddenly as she'd sat on me, her eyes harsh and dangerous.

It had been the night after our fight about the condoms, and she still hadn't forgiven me for not giving in.

Well, she won. And she won again when she looked me in the eye, then dashed away, barefoot and hair free, disappearing into the woods.

I wasn't responsible for what I did next. I wasn't myself as I tossed good meat into the cinders, clutched my open shorts to keep them on, and took off after her.

So many times we'd played chase when she was little. So many times I'd run after her when she was angry or cheeky or pissed, and because of those games, I knew how to play this one.

I knew how to track her. Knew the weaves and ducks she favoured. Never staying in a straight line, she used the undergrowth to hide her.

The small hitches of her breath and snaps of bracken as she navigated the gloom led me directly to her.

She didn't see me until it was too late.

And when I did…my behaviour was abominable.

Pushing her to the ground, I let out a savage groan as she landed on all fours, then, because she insisted on fighting me like an animal, I fucked her like an animal.

I speared into her from behind—just like all the farmyard creatures did—and the scream she made? Holy shit, I lasted mere seconds.

I thrust savagely until her entire body rippled with her release, and then I pulled out, fisting myself hard as I came all over her back.

The shame that crashed over me was entirely new. It wasn't about taking more than I deserved but going too far—for letting her push me until I snapped and only thought of myself. For getting so caught up in whatever war we'd been fighting that I'd hurt her.

But of course, Della hadn't let me stew, and once we returned to our camp in stony silence, she'd climbed my body and kissed me deep, murmuring that having me behind her, driving into her like a monster had been the best experience thus far.

I hated to admit that I'd fucking loved it too, and unfortunately for both of us, we became hooked on pushing our limits. Of using trees to stand against and rocks to bend over and riverbanks to writhe on. Nothing was safe from our insatiable love, and even now, the minor scratches from this morning's lovemaking still glowed on her palms from where I'd shoved her to her knees after she'd returned from washing in the river.

She made me a terrible person, but she also freed me in ways no one else could.

Sighing, I shrugged. "What do you want me to do? Get you pregnant?"

She froze. "Is that what you're afraid of?"

Why did this conversation sound eerily like the one I'd had with Cassie the night I lost my virginity?

Putting the snare down, I hoisted my ass up and went to her. Brushing away the fish scale on her forehead, I sat down and murmured, "I'm not afraid of it. I'm afraid of losing you to something that's full of complications and pain."

Her eyes searched mine, deep and almost wary. "I know it's early days, but we've never actually discussed our future."

"Our future now that we're together?"

She nodded shyly, looking back at the fish in her hands. "I know it's technically only been a month, but it's been so much longer than that. As far as I'm concerned, I've been yours for eighteen years. But I never thought about having children until the exact moment you said you were afraid of it."

I clasped my hands between my knees, very aware how dangerous this subject could be. Before my dreams came true and I earned Della, I was adamant I didn't want any more kids. It'd taken a lot out of me to raise her right and fix all the things I did wrong. I wasn't exactly the best father figure for her. Look at us. We'd fallen in love despite everything telling us not to.

But in that moment, sitting beside her on a dead tree with the smell of smoke swirling around us and the sounds of happy birds serenading us, I had a flash of what life could be like if Della gave birth to my child.

Of another girl.

A girl who would once again own me completely, make me stress, make me proud, give me purpose—a legacy I could utterly adore. A legacy of both me and Della—a little girl who had her blue eyes and my dark hair and our cynicism of society.

And I wanted that.

Very much.

Just...not right now.

Tipping her chin up with my forefinger, I kissed her gently. A simple press of lips and love, not asking anything more than a quick connection. "I'm not afraid of it, Della. But I am selfish."

"Oh, please." She rolled her eyes. "Is this like when you said you were selfish in sex? Because you got that wrong. You never leave me wanting. You always—"

"I'm selfish because I've only just found you. I want to keep you for myself for a little longer. I want to share a world with you. I want to marry you. I want to give you everything you've ever wanted, and only then, once I've had you all to myself, will I be ready to share."

Her shoulders slouched as love glowed on her face. Love I still couldn't get used to. Love I would do anything to deserve. "Ren, we could have a hundred children and not one of them would steal me from you. I know women aren't meant to admit this, but you would always come first for me. I wouldn't be able to help it."

I chuckled against her lips as I kissed her again. "You've just proven you're not ready, either. You're the one being selfish, Little Ribbon. When the day comes that you love me so much that your heart has expanded for more, that's the day we'll start a family. But not before."

Standing, I held out my hand to pull her to her feet. "Because one thing is for sure. Our child will steal our hearts entirely, and I wouldn't have it any other way. I would want you to love our daughter more than you love me. I'll happily come second."

She weaved her fingers with mine until there was no space between us. "You have my word, Ren Wild, that I will forever love you. But if and when we have a family of our own, I promise they will be loved just as much as I love you." Walking into my embrace, she hugged me hard. "But I don't want a daughter. I want a son. I want a son exactly like you."

Chapter Twenty-Eight

REN

2018

"DO YOU KNOW this is probably only the third or fourth time we've been shopping together?" Della grabbed a can of nectarines from the supermarket shelf and placed it into the basket I carried.

"Supermarkets aren't exactly a rare occurrence." I smirked. "I happen to be well-versed in how to get into most of them undetected."

"Yes, and you didn't let me go on those adventures, did you?" She smiled, her blue jacket, jeans, and boots faded from forest-living, and her hair with its requisite leaf hidden amongst the gold.

"I didn't want you to be in danger," I said.

"No, you didn't want me cramping your thieving skills."

"That too." I reached for a packet of pasta, placing it on top of the canned nectarines. "Then again, when we lived in the city and we had cash to pay for things, you did most of the shopping."

"Only 'cause you worked such stupid hours. I mean, really? Who gets up before dawn?"

I rolled my eyes. "Are you forgetting I'm a farm boy? At Cherry River, I was up with the cockerels, and at Mclary's—well, it was be up before him or your ass would be beat and you'd have to spend the day in agony as well as exhaustion."

Her face fell a little, her gaze trailing to my missing finger. "You know, I don't think I ever apologised for what my father did to you."

I froze to the spot. "Why would you? You weren't responsible."

"I know, but now that I'm not so self-obsessed, I can see how hard it would've been for you to love me. Not only love me but keep me when you were running for your life."

I went to her as she turned to stare blankly at brightly boxed taco shells. Wrapping my arm around her, I kissed her temple. "What's really going on, Della? Why are we talking about the past when we're both so incredibly happy in our present?"

Wedging herself into my chest, she breathed me in, shaking a little. "I don't know. Being back in a town? Having other people watch us? Wondering if they know? Afraid that we'll be caught and the past few wonderful weeks will be over?"

Putting the basket down with our carefully chosen supplies, I hugged her close, breathing into her ear. "No one sees us. We're invisible."

Other shoppers strolled past, some looking at us and others not caring at all. I wouldn't deny I'd felt the same fear Della did as we left the forest, backpacks, and tent and followed the animal tracks out from the trees toward the country doorstop where the only things on Main Street were a bar, pharmacy, doctors, pet store, diner, and supermarket. Oh, and a knickknack store that claimed to have more junk than K-Mart at half the price.

However, we wouldn't be here if it wasn't for Della's insistence. We didn't need food, but fresh fruit and baked goods would be nice. And we didn't need medicine, but we had come to see a doctor.

The prickle of being around people again was worse after being on our own for so long, but Della had insisted, and I couldn't refuse.

Besides, I wasn't against getting some more painkillers for the ache that hadn't left my chest. It'd been months since I'd had the flu yet an occasional cough still lingered, annoyingly persistent.

"Della, look at me." I pulled back a little, waiting until her chin popped up, and her eyes met mine. "No one knows who we are. We're just two strangers to them. Two strangers kissing in a supermarket."

Her lips parted in a gasp as I bent my head and captured her mouth with mine. Her back rippled with tension under my palms, her eyes wide and worried. But then I deepened the kiss and her tension melted away, trusting me to keep her safe, slipping into the lust we always suffered.

Her eyes closed, and my body hardened, and this was a bad, *bad* idea because I couldn't just keep the kiss at publicly acceptable; I had to lick her, taste her, clutch her as close as I could so she felt what she did to me.

Only when her breath caught and someone cleared their throat in disapproval did I let her go. The kiss upset my balance. I expected trees around us not shelves with overly sugary cereals. I was all the more aware we were in a place I hated. But at least I'd helped Della with her anxiety, and she gave me the biggest smile with pink-pleased cheeks.

"Kiss me like that again, and we'll be arrested for indecent exposure." She looked me up and down as if she'd rather eat me than the food on display.

"Look at me that way for much longer, and this town expedition will end as quickly as it began."

She laughed softly. "Thank you. I needed that."

"I know you did." I wiped my bottom lip where her taste still lingered. Honey and chocolate from the Toblerone bar she'd opened and snuck a piece before we'd paid.

"Okay, so we're done here, right?" I coughed once and picked up the basket from the floor. Another tube of toothpaste, sunblock, painkillers, and a range of perishable and non-perishable foods. We used a basket to select what to buy so we didn't fill up a cart and forget we had to carry it for miles.

"Oh, almost forgot!" She dashed back to the toiletry aisle while I made my way to the checkouts. At least today I wouldn't be stealing. The cash I'd saved before leaving and the deposit on the apartment we'd had refunded were more than enough to keep us going for a couple of years before the dreaded concept of employment knocked on our strange holiday-honeymoon.

As I placed the basket on the conveyor belt behind an elderly woman counting out coupons, Della tossed three boxes of condoms on top of our innocent fruit and veggies.

"Three?" I raised my eyebrow, flicking a quick glance at anyone who might've seen. I didn't care that we were buying condoms. I cared that they'd figure out Della was the one person I should never be sleeping with.

"Tina told me a couple of years ago that the pill takes up to a week to become effective, and if I have a tummy upset, secondary precautions are needed, too." She gave me another coy I-want-you-right-now kind of look. "I won't last a week, Ren. And don't pretend you will, either."

I gritted my teeth as the checkout girl stole our basket and started scanning things before tossing them into plastic bags. "You're forgetting I exercised self-restraint for years. I can manage a week."

She pinched my ass as I pulled out a bundle of cash from my back pocket. "That was before."

Before.

Such a simple word, but it held so much history.

"You're right." I smiled, loving the way she stood close, her eyes twinkling with joy—joy for just sharing something as mundane as shopping with me.

Clearing my throat, I tore my gaze from hers and looked back at the cash in my hands. Handling the money shot me back to the time Della had helped me tally up and charge for the hay bales at John Wilson's place.

Not for the first time, I thought about him. How he was? Did he get another farmhand? Was his family okay?

And not for the last time, I wondered what he'd say now that I'd broken that self-restraint and claimed Della.

Would he understand?

Would he condemn me?

Would he say *I told you so*?

His warning of finding a way to keep Della as my sister ran through my head as the teller reeled off a figure, and I handed her a bunch of notes. I'd failed in that respect, but really, looking back…I think he knew. He knew there was something more between us, and that was why he'd sent us away.

Because eventually, even if we'd stayed there, we would've fallen into bed, and things would've gotten messy. Especially with Cassie in the mix.

"Have a pleasant day," the checkout girl said blandly, already scanning items of the customer behind me.

I grabbed two bags and Della took one as we left the supermarket with its annoying beeps and bright lights and stood on the pavement where the sun reminded us we were wasting one of the last days of camping weather by being cooped up inside concrete and steel.

"I don't want to be much longer, Little Ribbon."

"Me neither." She placed her well-used and scratched aviators on to avoid the glare and strode purposely toward the doctor's. "How is this going to work, do you think?"

I shrugged. "Same way we've always done it. Our name is Wild. We'll pay cash. We lost our driver's licenses, so have no identification, yada yada."

Slowing to a stop, she looked at me, biting her lip. "Hey, Ren?"

My heart pumped faster—as it always did when she looked at me like that. "Yeah?"

"On the form, if they ask what our relationship status is…um, what do I put?"

Goosebumps scattered over my arms as the answer I'd always given her delayed upon my tongue. *'I'm your brother.'* That wasn't just incorrect anymore, it was undermining everything good and perfect that'd happened between us.

Putting the groceries down, I tugged her bag free to join the rest, then ran my fingers through her hair until I fisted two handfuls right there on the street. "I never got to give the speech I'd prepared when

I came back to find you. I had a whole promise laid out. How I'd come back because I couldn't live without you. That even if it meant I couldn't have you, even though it would rip my heart out and leave me bleeding until the day I died, I'd gladly walk you down the aisle on your wedding day. I would've given you away to another man, Della, because that was my job in your life. To ensure you had everything you ever needed in which to *live*. To be happy."

I trembled as I kissed her softly. "But then I read your manuscript, and I realised *I* could be the one to make you happy, so I said other things. So much more important things." Digging my fingers harder into her hair, I murmured against her mouth, "So, if they ask who I am to you...there's only one thing you can say."

"What's that?" she breathed, shivering with matching goosebumps.

"That you share my last name. That you own my heart." I kissed her hard and fast, long and lingering. "Tell them...you're my wife."

Chapter Twenty-Nine

DELLA

2031

WHEN REN KISSED *me that day on the street, he didn't know it, but he gave me every hope I'd been nursing since we'd fought with the truth and gave in.*

Our last name was as much his as it was mine, and I didn't want to change. But how could we not when Wild had been a sibling address, and these days, we were so much more than that?

I'd teased with the idea that it could be our married one, sure, but until Ren said the words I'd been fighting, I didn't think it was possible.

He successfully made me float on air, wrapped me up in daydreams, and sent me gooey with desire.

After that, I didn't really care what we did as long as he was always near.

We went to the doctor, filled in forms, ignored side glances when we said we had no I.D, and proudly ticked the 'married' box without an ounce of shame.

To start with, the doctor refused to see us without some form of identification.

But Ren quietly took him aside and had a few words. I didn't know what transpired, but after an hour or so wait, I was ushered in to see a doctor who asked my sexual history, if I was aware of the health risks, and prescribed me the pill to prevent pregnancy.

I asked for more than just three months' supply, but he was adamant my blood pressure should be checked before a refill was given.

At the time, it frustrated me, but then I remembered it would be winter, and we'd most likely be holed up somewhere close enough to a town not to be a nuisance.

After we'd filled the script at the pharmacy next door, taken another handful of condoms from the fishbowl on the counter saying 'Free: help your frisky selves,' *my stomach growled, and the diner with its sun-bleached specials in the window and paint-chipped green door reminded me of all the times Ren had found ways to make simple excursions into life-affirming treats.*

Looking back, it was yet another moment I had no choice but to write down. Mainly because of what happened next.

I'd dragged him into the grease-infused restaurant all while he grumbled and kept his eyes glued on the horizon where the tips of the trees waved at us in the chilly breeze. I'd forgotten how unsociable Ren was. After living in the city for so many years, he'd relaxed enough not to hanker for freedom or give the impression he was a trapped animal amongst a cage of glass and brick. But he'd been in his element for too long, and it was a visible chore for him to stay away for long.

I felt the same tug to leave, but I also had the tug of hunger. Taking pity upon him, compromising like a good couple, we agreed to order takeaway cheeseburgers and curly fries, eating the naughty but oh-so-good meal in the tiny park across the street.

Once our bellies were full and fingers salt-dusted from french fries, I stood and expected him to march directly back into the wilderness with me trotting to keep up.

However, his eyes landed on the junk store with its vow to beat K-Mart with its merchandise and prices and, with a determined look, he dragged me into the overly cluttered store with its scents of candle wax and plastic toys, smiling as if he had a secret.

This is why I had to write this.

This is why I was so madly in love with him.

"I want to buy you something."

"Okay…" I narrowed my eyes. "What do you want to buy me?"

"Something you're not allowed to see until I've found it."

I looked around at the overflowing baskets of tea-towels and dog collars. This place had everything from shampoo and cookies to Easter and Halloween decorations. "And you'll find it in here?" I raised an eyebrow. "What exactly are you up to?"

"Call it…a gesture of a future eventuality."

I laughed, drawing the attention of the mid-twenties cashier sucking on a lollypop. "I think we need to get you back into the forest. The city is infecting you with retail therapy and commercial advertisement."

"You did say shopping with me was a novelty." He smirked. "While I find what I want for you, you find me something."

"Like what?" My heart sprang into action, acting nonchalant but already rushing with images of finding the perfect gift. We'd shared many birthdays, but apart from my ribbon tattoo that Ren paid for, and the willow horse he carved back at Cherry River, we had no keepsakes or mementos. Not that we had space.

"Go on." Ren pointed down an aisle full of ugly porcelain vases and weird bachelorette party gimmicks—let me tell you there were a lot of penises: penis straws, penis shot glasses, penis aprons, and unicorn horns shaped like dildos. "You trying to tell me I'm missing an appendage you want, Ren?" I couldn't stifle my snicker. "Cause you know, I rather like playing with yours so I can see the

allure—"

"Honestly, Della." He grabbed my bicep, yanking me into the aisle and away from the nosy sales keeper. "You always know how to get a rise out of me, don't you?" His voice was brash with temper, but his eyes glowed like chocolate syrup.

Things with wings erupted in my heart as I stood on tiptoes just as Ren's mouth crashed down on mine.

He kissed me so fierce and swift, I stumbled backward, directly into a shelf of penises with wind up legs that all bounced and whirred from the unwanted collision.

We broke apart, laughing as penis after miniature penis committed suicide off the shelf.

"You break it, you pay for it!" a voice yelled from the front of the store.

Ren and I only laughed harder.

Funny how memories like that—the ones that are so simple and stupid—are the ones that stick in your head with such clarity you can transport back to every smell, heartbeat, and yearning.

I want to share every detail, but I also want to rush and tell you what Ren bought for me and I bought for him. Because, honestly, they were two gifts that became our most treasured belongings. No mud, snow, dust, or grime could make us remove them. Even now, I still wear it. Even now, after so long.

"Ten minutes, Little Ribbon." Ren kissed the tip of my nose. "And no peeking at where I go."

"I have no idea what to get you, so I'll be using those ten minutes wisely, not stalking you."

"Good."

"Fine." I grinned. "See you at the cash register."

"No, see you outside. Here." Forcing a twenty-dollar bill into my hand, he kissed my cheek as if he couldn't not kiss me whenever we were close. "Pay for what you find and meet me on the street."

* * * * *

Sorry, I let memories take over and forgot to type.

Who knew writing about something so silly would be so utterly heart-breaking—not because it was sad but because it was so good?

So perfect.

So sweet.

I was so incredibly lucky, and I'm just glad I recognised just how *lucky, rather than take Ren for granted.*

The older I get, and the more I grow, I'm always struck by two things:

One, no matter my age, I always feel the same. No more adult than child or wise than stupid. I keep expecting myself to snap into a grown-up, but it's never happened.

And two, nothing beat just hanging out with Ren.

Nothing.

No trip or gift or fancy new experience.

Nothing could beat just existing with the love of my life.

Remembering is almost bittersweet, but I suppose I better finish this particular chapter before I close my laptop and go in search of the very man I'm writing about.

I'll skip over the mad rush through the carnival ride of junk and pointless figurines and

not bother to mention the adrenaline rush of finding such a random, childish, and exquisitely perfect gift that Ren would no doubt roll his eyes at and laugh in that affectionate, perfect way of his. The way that opened his entire face from suspicion and ruthlessness into a window of trust and devotion.

I couldn't stand still as I waited for him on the curb and spun to face him when the junk store bell jingled.

In his hand rested a small, brown paper bag.

He gave me a half-smile. "This feels like a ridiculous idea now."

"I think it's the best idea you've had in a while."

"You're saying I lack good ideas, Della?" He narrowed his eyes, but behind his fake annoyance, laugher bubbled.

"Well, you have to admit the best idea we've ever had was sleeping together— and that was mine, so you're welcome. You can thank me later, but right now, you're handing over my present."

"You're saying all of this, our relationship, the fact that I told you to call yourself my wife, was your idea?" He put the shopping bags on the ground, delaying giving me the gift just like he had when he'd presented me with that tea-towel wrapped horse.

Delay tactics were Ren's way of pretending he wasn't nervous by covering it up with bluster and brawn.

"Yes, all mine. Been my idea for years." Shooting my hand out, I held up my own paper bag. "Stop changing the subject and swap."

He huffed dramatically, playing along with the familiar way we joked and ribbed. "I don't know why I put up with you most of the time."

"Too late now. You married me."

His face lost its joviality, slipping straight into steely sternness. "Not yet I haven't. But I'm working on it."

My tummy let loose a torrent of floating balloons, filling my insides with helium.

"Here." He passed me the gift, taking his in return. "It's not much. But it's a promise of more."

I don't mind telling you—mainly because you'll have figured it out for yourself—but I wasn't good at delayed gratification. I should've clutched that paper bag and paused in that moment. That delicious, perfect moment where the happiest future I could've ever imagined teased.

But I didn't.

I was too impatient.

I ripped at the bag and tears instantly appeared as I tipped out a ring with a blue gemstone dancing in the sun.

It wasn't real.

It wasn't silver or gold or sapphire.

But it was the best thing I'd ever received.

Ren's shadow fell over me as I swiped at the tears trickling down my cheeks. "I didn't mean to make you cry, Della Ribbon."

"I know. Sorry." I looked up with a watery smile. "I just...Ren, I—" I shook my head, grasping for words on just how perfect he truly was. How grateful I was that I had his heart. How I'd never take him or his thoughtfulness for granted. Ever. "I just...I love you so much."

He smiled, tilting his head like an eagle would while pitying a poor mouse for falling in love with him. An eagle who could soar away at any moment and kill that little mouse with just one talon. "I know."

Taking my hand and the ring, he slipped it onto the finger where engagement rings belong. "This is exactly what it implies. We've messed up the usual steps of a relationship. We met young. We loved each other in so many different ways before the one that truly mattered. But now that I have you, this is the only way forward. If it's too soon, tell me. If you're having second thoughts, better put me out of my misery now. But if you want me as much as I want you, then you don't even have to give me an answer because I've already made it for you."

Tugging me into his arms, he kissed me sweet. "Will you marry me, Della Wild?"

I shuddered in his embrace, more tears falling. "I gave you my answer the day I was born, Ren Wild." Standing on tiptoes, I met his second kiss, deepening it until the street vanished, leaving only silky tongues, hitched breaths, and hands straining to touch secret places. "Yes. A thousand times yes."

I could finish this chapter on that line. It holds quite a punch, and you all know how much Ren's random proposal meant to me. But I want to tell you what I got Ren.

Pulling back from his arms, I was the one to open his bag and pull out the baby blue leather band with nine diamante letters threaded onto it—letters I'd chosen from tiny boxes full to the brim with alphabets and shapes, painstakingly deciding the best, simplest message for him to wear. For everyone to see.

He burst out laughing as I opened the clasp and hoped it would fit his large wrist.

It did.

Barely.

Stroking the glittery word-charms, he gave me a look so completely humble and awed I felt as if I'd given him the keys to my forever rather than a simple gimmicky bracelet.

And in a way, I had.

Because forever would never be enough. Not with Ren. Not with my soulmate.

Cupping his wrist, I kissed the springy hairs of his skin right above the bracelet. The charms blinded me with their crystal glitter as I breathed, "Della Wild Loves Ren Wild Forever."

DW ♥ RW4EVA

Chapter Thirty

REN

2018

WE STAYED IN the forest until the second snowfall reminded us that as much as we'd adopted the wilderness as our home, we had yet to find ways to grow fur coats and hibernate in warm burrows.

The cold ruined everything, making bones ache and lungs burn and bodies bow to nasty viruses.

The sooner we were warm and out of the elements, the better.

We had cash for a rental, but without furniture and other belongings to furnish it, we didn't bother putting ourselves through the stress of real estate agents and reference checks.

Not to mention, we didn't want to lock ourselves into a long lease when we had no intention of staying past the last frost.

I suggested finding another government owned hut on a tramping trail, or searching for an uninhabited building like we did with Polcart Farm, but Della took my ideas and one-upped them, suggesting we could have a toasty, furnished place away from main cities and only pay for the months we wanted.

I didn't believe her, but the day we headed to yet another tiny town to buy thicker jackets, she topped up her phone credit, and showed me an online site that rented holiday homes that usually fetched a premium in summer but were offered at great rates during winter.

Together, we sat in a cosy coffee shop beside a gas fire and ate delicious apple and cinnamon muffins while scrolling through housing options.

We were there for hours, searching, discounting, debating pros and cons of each. Some were too close to the city, others were semi-detached or had the owner living on site. Most were totally impractical for loners like us, but finally, after a second muffin, we narrowed it down to three.

One was a few miles from a local town and decorated in country chic with yellow everything; two was a rambling big place with weathered furniture and bare wooden floors; three was a two-bedroom cottage with whitewashed floors, handmade daisy curtains, and the comfiest looking couches with a fireplace.

For four months' hire, it would take a big chunk of our cash, but if the two-bedroom cottage lived up to the pictures, it was totally worth it.

Della—ever the resourceful and happier to deal with strangers—called the number and arranged to view the property the next day. We spent the rest of the afternoon heading back into the forest, packing up our belongings, and having a final dinner of fish and rabbit.

The next morning, we left the trees and met with the agent.

The moment we stepped inside, we knew.

This was our winter nest, and we paid cash upfront in lieu of not having credit cards. The round, blue-rinsed hair woman asked for a bigger bond seeing as we didn't have the necessary paperwork, but after chatting to us and showing us around the quaint, cosy cottage, she handed over the keys and happily gave us instructions on how to work the oven and washing machine.

That night, Della and I made love for the very first time in a bed.

The foreignness of clean cotton and soft springiness of a mattress added a sensual element to our otherwise rough encounters. Our thoughts were on the same wavelength once again, and our touches were softer, our kissers longer, and when I slipped inside her, our connection was deeper than it had ever been.

I adored her to the point of stupidity.

I'd wake in the night with horrors of losing her. I'd stare, completely bewitched at odd times during the day, even if she was doing something as mundane as washing the dishes.

I had no power over myself anymore—she had it all.

And I was glad.

I was glad whenever the fake blue gemstone gleamed on her finger. I was glad whenever the diamante letters on the leather bracelet she gave me caught my eye.

I was glad for all of it.

I was grateful for everything.

I was so damn lucky.

Normally, I despised winter.

But that one…I didn't mind it so much.

Not with warm beds, roaring fireplaces, and Della.

In fact, I didn't mind it at all.

Chapter Thirty-One

REN

2019

SPRING ARRIVED WITH a vengeance, thawing the frosts and banishing the snow as quickly as they'd arrived. The weather reports said it would be one of the hottest summers on record, and both Della and I couldn't wait until the last day of our agreed cottage rental where we could leave for the forests we loved so much.

Living in the cottage had been an experience I wouldn't forget, and we'd become a little too used to having a comfy house with a pantry full of food and a freezer crammed with everything we could ever need.

The first week after moving in, we'd spent a few days setting up with supplies, so when the snow fell, we wouldn't have to leave unless we wanted to.

And sometimes, we wanted to, despite the cold.

On the mornings when the sun twinkled on virgin snow and birds sang in white-capped trees, we'd slip into warm clothing and go for a walk. Sometimes, we'd kiss by the frozen river, and others, we'd tease and torment until we practically ran back to the cottage and couldn't tear our clothes off fast enough.

Those were my favourite days.

The ones where we forgot about ages and education and futures and society.

A simple existence where we ate when we were hungry, slept when we were tired, and fucked at any time or place we wanted.

Nothing in the cottage had been free from our escapades. Not the smooth bamboo kitchen bench—where I'd hoisted Della onto it, bare assed and panting. Not the claw foot bathtub that was big enough for two—where Della had gotten on her knees and blown me.

Not even the woodshed was free from us screwing like the

bunnies Della wanted us to become. I'd ended up with a splinter in my ass, but I didn't care, seeing as Della was a master at tending to my injuries.

A couple of days before we were due to hand the keys back, we washed all our clothes, sorted through our supplies, ate the rest of the food that we couldn't take with us, and prepared to hike for the rest of the season.

I felt like a creature crawling from its den after a winter of bunkering down.

I was itching for exercise. I was ready for adventure.

I wanted to be a wanderer again even though I also wanted other things.

Things like being able to officially call Della my wife. Things like officially making our last name Wild and not just a word we'd chosen.

My belly clenched whenever my attention landed on her hand and the gaudy blue ring I'd bought. The promise I'd made and the need to make her mine was a constant desire.

I hadn't told her, but one night, while she slept beside me, I'd used the final internet credit on her phone to research how to get married. The information bombarding the screen made my brain bleed, and the prices some people were willing to spend made me sick.

The thought of a party with hundreds of people watching a very private moment turned me right off, but even the civil service ceremony with just a single witness wasn't open to us.

Basically, we couldn't get married.

Not unless I found a way to get us birth certificates, and we became real people and not just lost kids in the system.

It was a complication that had always been on the back of my mind, but I had no clue how to rectify it. It also didn't help that the diamante letters of my bracelet had already lost some of its glitter, the tiny gems falling from their metal surroundings.

In the dead of night, deep in my nightmares of losing her, I feared it was a sign that if I didn't find a way to make her my wife soon, my entire future would be in jeopardy.

I didn't care the jewellery couldn't stand up against time, I would wear it until it disintegrated and then somehow resurrect it because it'd become almost a good luck charm, promising me a future where Della would always love me, just like she promised.

Despite my desires to make her mine on paper as well as in my heart, we left behind the cottage where we'd found so much happiness and, for the first time, I was open to the idea of putting down roots.

A place to call our own.

A bed to keep Della warm.
A house we could raise a family in.

Chapter Thirty-Two

REN

2019

2019 WAS ONE of my favourite and equally unfavourite years.

Summer was spent skinny-dipping, travelling, fucking, learning, laughing, and living in every precious moment.

It didn't matter we had no life luxuries. We didn't care our bathroom was open air, our shower was sometimes shared with fish, or our bedroom was a flimsy thing that was useless against storms— nothing could scare us away from the joy of being alone, entirely self-sufficient, and free to love how we wanted to love.

Our need for each other seemed much more accepted out here, rutting against trees and rocks, driving each other to pinnacles I doubted a house with pretty painted walls could contain.

We had solar lanterns that lit up our tent when we wanted light and solar chargers for phones we didn't care about. We made do with what the sun wanted to give us and only ate what we foraged and hunted for months on end.

I never asked if Della missed her friends or school. I never regretted spending a lifetime ensuring she had an education, only to yank her away from one the moment I fell in love with her.

We belonged together.

End of story.

And I'd take on the entire universe if it ever tried to take Della away from me.

Then autumn arrived.

Bringing with it more than just its pretty colours of copper and bronze—it heralded my worst nightmare and the reason we left the forest much earlier than we planned.

It all started with a storm.

A particularly terrible storm that ripped our guy-ropes from the ground and scattered our tent pegs in the undergrowth.

Trees cracked as they were uprooted from the earth. Animals screeched as their homes were destroyed. And at some point in the howling, slashing rain, Della crawled into my arms and I hugged her close, keeping her safe from whatever crime we'd committed against Mother Nature for her to hate us so.

It took thirty-six hours for the worst to pass, and everything we owned—including us—was soaked.

The nylon of the tent and its rain sheet couldn't withstand the torrent and I worried keeping Della from a sturdy house was the right choice.

Eventually, she'd want more than this.

And she'd be fully within her right.

What if she'd gotten hurt?

What if *I'd* gotten hurt?

What if I wasn't around to protect her?

As we sorted through our littered and destroyed campsite, nibbling on things we salvaged and drinking fresh rainwater, we did our best to find the tent pegs and tangled guy-ropes, and at some point with our bodies muddy and spirits dull, I made the decision that we needed to be closer to civilisation and not a week's walk from anywhere.

And thank God I did.

Because a day after we arrived at a campsite, only a few hours' walk from a town, Della got sick.

Really sick.

Fucking terrify me and make me bargain with the devil sick.

We didn't often get viruses, and if we did, it was mainly from our quick excursions into towns and touching coins and menus contaminated by other sick people.

But this was different.

For days, she vomited every morning, stayed grey for most of the day, and complained of aching stomach pains that even copious amounts of painkillers couldn't stop.

I didn't understand how Della got the stomach flu and I remained untouched. We ate the same things. We were careful about what we cooked. But whatever illness struck, it chose her and chose her hard.

By the end of the fourth day of watching her vomit, and suffering fear and utmost helplessness, I couldn't handle it anymore. Her assurances that she was getting better were bullshit, and I'd had enough.

I couldn't listen to her being so ill or watch her gorgeous body become gaunt with malnutrition from not being able to keep anything down.

She had to see a doctor.

Now.

Della was so weak her protests had dwindled to nothing apart from the occasional groan when her tummy hurt and a half-hearted swat when I helped her into a jacket and jeans and tugged her from the camp.

I left behind our belongings, not caring about a single thing.

Nothing mattered.

Only her.

All I took was a smaller rucksack we had for emergencies and stuffed it with our cash, Della's manuscript, toothbrushes, and a spare set of clothes in case we were delayed for a night or two.

Della followed me slowly, her steps laboured and her skin ghostly. I tried to help her. Tried to offer support and even carry her as we headed down the steep animal tracks to the rye paddocks of some farmer and cut through his land.

But each time I reached out, she pushed me away with a shake of her wobbly head. "I'm fine, Ren. Don't worry about me."

But I did worry.

I worried a whole fucking lot and had never been so grateful to see a road when we finally travelled four hours and found a painted path and not a muddy track.

My temper was short from fear, and my patience at her unwillingness to let me help depleted. I was furious at her for getting so ill—as if this were her fault—but mainly I was livid at myself for letting her assure me it would pass, when obviously, it was only getting worse.

If anything happened, I'd never forgive either of us.

"Come on, Della." My voice was clipped as I held out my hand, hoping now she was on the road she'd quicken.

But if anything, the opposite happened. The moment her boots found level concrete, her shoulders slouched, and she seemed to fade before my eyes.

"Fuck." Marching to her, I scooped her off the road and cradled her close. "I'm never going to forgive you for this."

She smiled weakly. "For getting ill?"

"For not letting me help."

Her head thudded against my chest and stayed there as she closed her eyes, no longer even pretending she was strong enough to fight me. "You're helping now."

"Yes, and you're about to pass out on me."

"Nuh uh." She yawned as she clutched her lower belly. "I'm still here."

"You better stay here too, Della Ribbon. Otherwise, I'll—" I cut myself off, drowning beneath vicious promises and violent vows.

"What? Otherwise what?" Her eyes opened to a dull blue laced with pain.

I coughed hard, averting my mouth until I stopped. "I'll murder and cheat and steal and commit any crime imaginable if it means I find a cure for you."

She smiled, her hand cupping my cheek briefly before it tumbled back into her lap. "I love you, Ren."

"And I love you, even though I despise you right now."

Laughing softly, she stayed content in my arms as I lengthened my stride and marched toward the larger of the towns we'd been in recently. I didn't care sweat rolled down my spine beneath my jacket, or my heart beat in terror at the colourless sheen on her face and the sticky temperature of someone unwell.

I was used to walking. I was fit and normally had good endurance, but each step my chest seemed to switch from its familiar ache to a discomforting twinge.

I coughed and strode faster, ignoring my pains and focusing entirely on Della's.

It took too long.

It didn't take long at all.

She was too light and motionless in my embrace.

The town welcomed us up ahead as we passed road signs stating speed and population. "We're almost there, Little Ribbon. You'll be fine soon; you'll see."

I coughed again, cursing the breathlessness of panic.

Please let her be fine.

I kept my thoughts on pleas rather than the curses I wanted to shout.

As I stalked down the main highway, the tiny buildings slowly became recognisable landmarks of a church and hall and convenience store.

With every step, I bargained with fate not to take her from me.

I wouldn't hesitate to kill for her if it came down to it.

If a sacrifice was needed, I would deliver with no hesitation.

I would sell my own soul.

Maybe I'd put this curse upon her by loving her too goddamn much. Maybe I should feel regret for stealing her away and keeping her all to myself. Perhaps I should repent in some way.

If I should, then I would go to church and apologise to God while we were in this town. I wasn't a religious man, but if it meant Della was cured, I would do fucking anything.

Glancing at Della, I hugged her closer.

Doctor.

Fast.

My legs lengthened again, ignoring my fatigue. I would walk until I was dead if it meant I could save her. Keeping my chaotic thoughts to myself, I didn't speak as bare farmland gave way to congested streets, hazy in the hard-to-see dusk light. Streetlights suddenly turned on, ready to combat the darkness as I climbed the curb and scanned the shop fronts for a doctor.

Nothing.

Only a row of clothing stores, hairdressers, a florist—which reminded me of the one Della used to work at—and a few other stores with knick-knacks and magazines.

I had no intention of wasting time walking up and down, searching.

More sweat ran down the inside of my jacket as I coughed and spotted help.

"Excuse me." I stepped into the path of a blonde woman pushing a red stroller. "Where is the nearest doctor?"

She peered up, the fading light behind me blinding her a little. Her lips pursed as she looked at Della in my arms. "She okay?"

"I'm fine." Della clipped weakly. "He's just—"

"She's not fine. That's why I need a doctor." This woman had precisely two seconds to tell me what I needed. Otherwise, I was asking someone else who wouldn't waste my time. My heart palpitated strangely, starving for air and salvation. "Where can I find one?"

"Ren. Manners," Della hissed.

My back stiffened as I glared at her, then spat out. "Where can I find one, *please?*"

Della snickered, somehow deleting a little of my horror at her being ill and absolutely helpless to help her.

"I'll deal with you later," I said under my breath. "Behave."

Della blew me a kiss, then winced and clutched her side. "Ow."

Instantly, any patience she'd granted me flew down the goddamn road. My lungs became blades, puncturing my chest. "Do you know, lady, or are you just wasting my time?"

The woman sniffed as the baby inside her stroller grizzled. She rocked it softly. "I'm thinking. Look, you won't be able to see a general practitioner. It's past six p.m., and that's when they all close around here. But there is an urgent doctor's and afterhours surgery."

"Where?"

"Two streets over on Jordan Road."

"Which way?" Moving out of her path, I waited until she pointed to her right down a road where shopkeepers carried in signs and pushed racks of merchandise back into their stores.

"Down there. Take your second right. It will be on the left side of the street halfway down."

I remembered to be polite before Della told me off again. "Thank you." I broke into a jog, following the woman's directions.

My heart skipped a beat.

I looked down at Della and my entire body churned with sickness. Her skin was a ghostly pallor, her lips thin as she winced again.

Christ.

Please, please let her be okay.

I coughed and ran faster.

Chapter Thirty-Three

REN

2019

"MR. WILD?"

"Yes?" I looked up from where I had my face buried in my hands in the waiting room of the afterhours. It had cost a small fortune, countless explanations why we had no I.D, and finally, nasty threats for someone to treat her regardless that we didn't have the necessary paperwork.

If my threats hadn't worked, I was prepared to hand over every dollar just to have someone examine her and tell me how to fix this.

"Can you come with me? Mrs Wild asked if you could join us."

Terror shot down my limbs as I stood and stumbled after him. The long hours spent waiting in the yellow plastic chair had numbed my ass and made me stiff. "Is she okay?" I coughed into my hand. "She's been away for ages."

"I know. I'm sorry for the wait." The doctor had thick black hair and tanned skin, hinting he had Indian blood somewhere in his lineage. "We had to do a small procedure."

"Wait, what?" I slammed to a halt, dragging the attention of other worried husbands, wives, and parents from their own woe to focus on mine. My blood drained to my toes. "What procedure?"

The doctor narrowed his eyes, looking me over. "Are you quite well yourself, Mr. Wild? You look a bit under the weather."

"Forget about me. I'm fine." Stepping into his bubble, I growled. "What about Della? Where is she? Tell me what you did."

"I think it's best if we discuss this in private, don't you?" The doctor smiled encouragingly, waving away my temper as if he was used to husbands losing their shit.

He wasn't that much older than me, which didn't help with my trust issues. What the hell would he know? What was his experience?

"Where's my wife?"

Such a strange but perfect word. A word I had no right to use in the eyes of church and law, but every right in the eyes of our togetherness.

"Just this way, please." Buzzing his badge against a locked door, he guided me down a white corridor smelling strongly of disinfectant until we reached a room four or five doors down. Pressing the handle, he pushed another door wide, letting me enter first.

I eyed him carefully as I stepped inside, only to break into a jog the moment I saw Della.

She smiled the instant I arrived, holding up her hand for me to grab. "I'm sorry you were stuck out there, Ren. And I'm sorry for making you worry the past few days."

"Nothing to apologise for." Brushing aside her hair, my fingers came away hot and clammy from her skin. "What's wrong? What's going on?"

My heart couldn't figure out what pace it wanted to settle on. Fast and furious, braced for bad news, or slow and sedate, buried beneath hope that all of this was a mistake.

"Please, Mr. Wild. Take a seat." The doctor motioned at a grey vinyl chair in front of his desk. The ugly wood was wedged against the wall with apparatus and a computer blinking with important scans and who knew what else.

There was no earthly way I could leave Della's side where she lay on a starched bed hoisted high. "Tell me. Immediately." I squeezed Della's fingers, my heart choosing fast and furious as the doctor nodded.

"Mrs Wild has mentioned all her symptoms, and we've done a few tests."

"Tests? What sort of tests?" I glanced back at Della, my vision going wonky with worry. "Ribbon?"

"It's okay, Ren. Just calm down. I'm fine. Let him explain. Okay?" She brought my hand to her lips and kissed my knuckles, somehow injecting me with a much-needed dose of serenity. "You're all sweaty."

"Yeah well, you got me worked up."

"Well, I'm fine so relax, okay?"

My heart leapt on a trampoline instead, double bouncing and triple beating. "I'll relax when I know what's going on."

All I could think about was the nightmare of her being in the hospital with complications from chicken pox when she was younger. I couldn't do a thing to take away her pain or make her heal faster.

I hated it then, and I *despised* it now.

Della murmured gently as if I was the one in peril. "I wanted Doctor Strand to tell you because he'll do a much better job than I could."

Forcing myself to stay rational, I turned to face the doctor. "You have my word, I won't interrupt. Tell me. What's wrong with my wife?"

Doctor Strand cleared his throat, giving Della a gentle smile. "Technically, nothing should be wrong in a couple of days, but we will need to monitor her until that time. Mrs Wild has chosen outpatient therapy, so I expect to see her daily for the next seventy-two hours to ensure things are okay."

"Fine." I wouldn't focus on the complication of such a request or the deeper concern of why we had to stay in town. Obviously, whatever was wrong with Della was worse than I feared. "It's not stomach flu, is it?" I cringed, not wanting an answer even as I craved one.

"No. I'm afraid it's not," Doctor Strand said. "It's an ectopic pregnancy."

"What?" My world tilted, sending me stumbling against the bed holding the most beloved thing in my life. "What does that even mean?"

"It means a fertilized egg is growing outside the uterus. The baby can't survive and it will lead to life-threatening internal bleeding if we don't stop it."

I couldn't focus on the words life-threatening without wanting to be sick.

"How? How did this happen? She's on the pill." Frowning at Della, I asked, "You've been taking it, right? We had an agreement—"

"I know. And I am." She squeezed my hand. "But about a fortnight ago—just before the storm—I had an upset tummy. Just once. I didn't think anything of it, and we didn't have sex that night. By the time you woke me up in the morning—"

She blushed, flicking a glance at the doctor and saving him the details of just how I'd woken her up by slipping inside her warm, soft body as she moaned, still half asleep.

"Anyway, I didn't remember that we should probably use alternate protection." She hung her head. "I'm sorry, Ren. I know this is my fault."

"Don't, Della." I shook my head. "It takes two to cause this. I'm just as much at fault as you."

She smiled gently. "Regardless, it was enough for me to get pregnant." She winced. "I'm truly sorry."

"Stop saying that." Looking back at the doctor, I commanded, "Why has she been so ill? Women get pregnant all the time. Why is my wife struggling so much?"

"It's a possibility she has another condition called hyperemesis gravidarum, but those symptoms don't usually show up until week four or five. And she's not that far along. We'll cross that bridge when she next wants to have children, but for now, we need to deal with this. Unfortunately, the pregnancy can't be permitted to continue."

My mind didn't know which word was more important to latch onto, so I let them all go in a stream of incomprehensible gibberish.

Della was pregnant.

But she couldn't continue to be?

"I-I don't understand." I sounded like a fucking idiot.

Doctor Strand clasped his hands. "I don't want you to concern yourself with her vomiting. Sometimes these things just happen."

"How can we make it un-happen?"

"By removing what the body is obviously trying to reject." He gave Della a supportive smile. "The small procedure we've done is an injection. I've given her methotrexate, also known as trexall. It will stop the cells from growing and allow the body to reabsorb the pregnancy."

He rushed as I opened my mouth to ask more questions. "I think she's only nine or so days along, so the medication should be effective. There's always the risk of it not working, in which case laparoscopic surgery is our next option. However, we prefer to use mexthotrexate to prevent damaging the fallopian tubes, which may cause complications for future conceptions.

"I require Mrs Wild to come in daily to monitor her hCG levels until they're back to normal. The good news is she isn't far along, and I have confidence she'll make a full recovery once the pregnancy is terminated."

Clearing his throat again, he threw a kind look at Della before focusing on me. "I have already advised Mrs Wild of the side effects, but you should be aware, too. The injection can sometimes cause cramping, some bleeding, nausea, and dizziness. I recommend she take it easy and spend a few days in bed. Think you can keep her there?"

I didn't know if he was trying to make a joke to cut through the tension or if he was serious. Either way, Della wouldn't be leaving a bed the moment I found her one.

"Is she free to go?" My mind already leapt ahead, problem solving and planning. Where the hell would we sleep tonight?

"She is. I've made an appointment to see her in the morning."

Della swung her legs over the bed, her feet dangling high off the floor. "I'm fine, Ren. Honestly. We'll just treat it as a mini-vacation, and then we can go home."

I smiled and let her believe I accepted that, when in reality, I was already committed to staying close to town for the next few months. Autumn had already arrived. We only had another six to eight weeks of chilly weather before we would've been driven into civilisation by the snow anyway.

We were here now.

We would stay until spring.

Pushing me away a little, Della sprang to the floor, wincing and grabbing her stomach.

"Goddammit, let me carry you." Wrapping my arms around her, I tried to pick her up, but she shoved me back. "I can walk, Ren. Don't even think about it."

My jaw locked, but I wouldn't argue in front of a stranger.

"Thank you, Doctor Strand. I'll see you in the morning." Della took my hand, and together, we headed from the strong-smelling room and back to the waiting area.

I settled up, paid yet another small fortune, and accepted a card with a new appointment time for eleven a.m. tomorrow.

By the time we were on the street, thick darkness had fallen and even the restaurants were closed. I doubted we could find a similar cottage like our last one at this time of night. I doubted we could even find something to eat.

Della pointed at a quaint sign up ahead. "Look, it's a Bed and Breakfast. Let's crash there and sort out better accommodation tomorrow."

I froze.

The thought of sleeping in a house with strangers. Of seeing those same people in the morning. Of hearing them through the walls and sharing their showers.

God, no.

I honestly didn't think I could do it.

My feet actually backed away as everything inside me repelled against the idea.

I would rather sleep on the street. Naked.

But then Della flinched and hissed between her teeth, her face going white and hinting she wasn't as okay as she pretended.

She was ill.

She was tired.

And it was no longer about me.

It was *never* about me.

"Okay, Della. Bed and Breakfast it is."

Chapter Thirty-Four

REN

2019

I DIDN'T SLEEP.

Of *course*, I didn't sleep.

After we'd checked into the last available room in the five-bedroom Bed and Breakfast, I'd paced the small flower-decorated space like a caged rat. Thanks to my idiosyncrasies, I didn't have a hope in hell of relaxing in this place.

Just as I feared, the sounds of pipes groaning as another guest had a shower and the flush of a toilet a wall away drove me nuts.

I wasn't claustrophobic, but living so close to other people was past my very limited tolerance when it came to my fellow human race.

I didn't know how Della stood it, considering we both preferred trees and silence to buildings and chaos. Then again, she'd spent her childhood in noisy school classrooms and busy malls. Her natural habitat included both, while mine was firmly set in wide open fields with only a tractor and wind for company.

Doing my best to stay calm, I pictured emptiness all around me with no threats to listen to and no people to suspect.

But it didn't work.

I despised being so close.

I hated that we weren't free to go where we wanted.

I cursed how, even now, even though almost two decades separated me from Mclary, I still had the occasional panic attack that demanded I run.

The day I'd had my first attack—when John Wilson closed the door at Christmas to give me my first pay packet—I'd wondered if I'd outgrow them.

And I had, to a degree.

But my childhood had made me distrustful, and the loner who had run when he was ten was just as happy on his own with Della now that he was twenty-nine as he had been as a boy.

I was simple.

I needed Della.

That was it.

Nothing else required.

And the thought that she could be taken from me by something as idiotic as this?

It made me fucking *rage*.

It was exactly what I'd feared happening. It was why I never wanted her pregnant in the first place.

I paced again, checking the bathroom for intruders—as if they could climb through the tiny window—doing anything I could to stop my temper from building and latching onto the one person I shouldn't be angry at but was suddenly insanely furious with.

By the time I entered the bedroom again, my fists were clenched, my heart beating chaotically, and I itched for a fight—anything to expend the sick-fury and never ending need to keep Della safe.

I couldn't fight her body from hurting her.

But I could fight—

"Ren." Della noticed my unravelling self-control. How could she not with my pacing and jumpiness and longing looks out the window?

"Ren, come to bed."

Bed? Lie down? Sleep? Let my guard down when other people slept so close? In the same *building* as us?

"Can't." I flung myself into the high-backed chair with an orchid decorated ottoman, swallowing a cough.

The meagre supplies I'd brought with us meant we'd at least been able to clean our teeth after the landlady kindly brought up some ham sandwiches and a few chocolate cookies as an evening snack.

She seemed nice enough, but so did anyone who wanted to lull you into a false sense of security.

"Ren, the door is locked. We're safe."

I narrowed my eyes at the flimsy lock and the flimsy door and its flimsy hinges. If someone wanted to come in, they could. No problem.

Conversation was good, at least. It gave me something else to think about instead of the undying need to scream at Della.

She huffed as if she didn't quite understand me even though she should. Of all people, she should understand *exactly* what I was struggling with.

She cocked her head. "You didn't have a problem sleeping at the Wilsons, and they were just across the driveway."

I clutched the armrests hard, forcing myself to stay on this subject and not yell a totally different one. "To start with, I was sick and didn't have a choice. And by the time I was better, I'd learned to trust them."

"Well, trust that nothing will happen here. We're just guests like everyone else. We'll checkout in the morning, and everyone will go their separate ways. No one cares who we are."

I did my best to relax, but the tingling anxiety continued to zoom in my veins. Needing to change the subject—to prove to myself I wasn't a monster who screamed at Della when she wasn't well—I asked gently, "How are you feeling?"

Her face fell as she plucked at the pansy bedspread with its copious amounts of pillows.

"I'm okay. I just keep hearing the words 'you're pregnant.' You know?" She shrugged, a gleam of tears springing from nowhere. "I thought I'd feel happy if I ever heard those words. But all I felt was terror. The pain...if this is what it feels like to be pregnant, I don't know if I can—"

"Stop it." I leaned forward, digging my hands into my temples and wedging fingers into my hair as if could prevent her from speaking. "Just...go to sleep."

Her gasp spoke volumes of how I'd shocked and upset her. "What do you mean? Wait. Are you *angry* with me?" Shifting higher in the pillows, dressed in just her t-shirt and underwear, she demanded, "Why are you acting like this?"

"Like what? Pissed off that you're in pain and there's nothing I can do about it?"

Stop it, Wild.

Just stop it. Before you go too far.

"Forget about it." I raked my fingers through my hair and let them fall to my knees. I'd been the one to work myself up. I'd made myself feel sick and out of control. Not her. "I'm sorry. Go to sleep, Della. Get some rest."

A long pause before she muttered, "I won't be able to sleep unless you get into bed with me."

"I can't."

"You can. It's just a bed, Ren. They've washed the sheets. They've—"

"It's not that."

"Then what is it because your temper is driving me—"

Swooping to my feet, I growled. "I can't touch you. I can't lie beside you. I'm the reason you're in agony. Why did I put so much responsibility on you, huh? To not even bother supporting you with

568

taking the pill at the right time every day, making sure you were okay, ensuring that things like this didn't happen. You're so fucking young. Far too young to get pregnant, let alone a complicated one. What does that even mean? Is it because I carted you out to the wilderness and thought I could keep you healthy and happy? Is it because I didn't give you what you needed as a kid and your body is all messed up now? *What?"*

My roar found every corner of the room and bounced back amplified. "I mean it, Della. You're only nineteen. How did I think it was right to touch you? Let alone *sleep* with you?! I'm sick. I'm perverted. I'm the reason you're in agony and…and, I don't know how to make it right."

I stalked to the door, then back to the window, needing open spaces and trees. My lungs begged for fresh air. "I'm *furious* at you for putting yourself in danger this way, but it's me I should be angry at."

Punching myself in the chest, I seethed, "All me. I knew getting involved with you would be a bad idea. I'm ten years older. I should know better. Maybe it was me, huh? Maybe it was my screwed-up sperm that made you pregnant where it can kill you. Goddammit!"

Breathing hard and struggling, I stood in the centre of the room, desperate to pick up the confessions I'd just littered all over the floor, but unable to move.

Most of my issues didn't even make sense. All I knew was I was horrified, terrified, and pissed off at everything.

Della sat stonily in bed, her chin high and eyes bright. "How can you say that? How can you say *any* of that? Loving me was a bad idea? Screw you, Ren. It's not your job to make me swallow a damn pill every day! It's not your fault that the pregnancy is ectopic. None of this is your fault!"

"I didn't say loving you was a bad idea. I said *sleeping* with you was."

"And I said *screw you!*"

"Della—" My heart punctured for how my worry twisted my words. "Look, all I'm saying is, I should've kept myself in check. I shouldn't need you the way I do. I shouldn't expect to have you every day. Sex is a health risk. Especially when you're still so young."

"If you say I'm young again, we're going to have a serious issue, Ren Wild." Della sat on her knees, the blankets discarded. "Girls have babies when they're fifteen, for God's sake. Sometimes even younger. I'm not young. I'm fully grown, and you're forgetting it's not just you who wants sex every day. I initiate as much as you do. It's not your job to treat me with silk gloves and hold me at arm's length when you need me as much as I need you!"

My temper roared back into cyclonic heat. "No, *Della*, it's my job never to send you to the goddamn hospital!"

"And you didn't! What happened is a freak thing. Even the doctor said these things happen randomly with no rhyme or reason. It's not your fault."

"Not my fault?" My temper coiled and snapped. "*Not my fault?* Okay, let's just see what *isn't* my fault." Holding up my fingers, I counted on them as I spat, "You grew up with no parents. You lived a lot of your childhood totally homeless with a kid who knew nothing about nutrition or health. You trusted everything I did when most of it was wrong—"

"Why the hell are you re-counting the past now? This has nothing to do with any of that!"

"Shut up and let me goddamn finish, Della!" My snarl was the harshest I'd ever been with her, but I couldn't control it anymore. We'd been together for a year and a half, and in that time, I'd remembered the past often. Most of the time, I loved thinking of her as younger and older. Proud rather than disgusted to have the privilege of loving her in so many different ways.

But now?

Now that reality had slapped me in the face, I crippled beneath blame.

Heavy, *terrible* blame.

I'd always believed my choices had been made with her best interests at heart. I'd always put her first. Always fed her over me if there wasn't enough food. Always wrapped her in my jacket if hers wasn't warm enough.

I'd screwed up many times raising her, but I'd like to think I'd been honourable and true.

But...I hadn't.

My choices had always been about me.

And that had never been more obvious.

"You were happy at your creative writing course. You were working on your future. You had everything I wanted you to have, and what did I do? I took you away from all of it!"

Pacing again, I struggled for air. "I didn't ask if you wanted to live in a goddamn tent. I didn't discuss with you what you thought about abandoning everything. I ran the moment it got hard between us, and I snatched you for mine the moment I knew I couldn't survive without you."

Della shifted again, her forehead furrowed, and hands balled.

I didn't know if it was from pain or anger, but I had no hope of stopping everything I'd bottled up. These dirty, awful conclusions that had whispered cruelly in my ear as I'd sat in the doctor's waiting room. Waiting and not knowing if I'd be told good news or bad. Waiting and not knowing what was wrong with my Della and what I'd done to cause it.

Because it had to have been me.

Because I should've known better and not been so fucking selfish.

"I love you, Della. And I'm so fucking sorry I did this to you. I'm sorry I have no money to keep you healthy. I'm sorry I have no career to build you the house you deserve. I'm sorry I somehow got you pregnant and now you're sick and in pain and there's absolutely *nothing* I can do about it. I'm sorry for all of it, but you should know that when it comes to you, I'm useless. I wanted you, so I stole you. I loved you, so I kept you. I didn't stop to think that by making you mine, I owed you more than I ever did before. I owe you a life that everyone else has. I owe you a stable environment. I owe you a man who can fucking provide and who isn't afraid of humanity, for God's sake!"

"Ren, stop—"

"No!" My eyes narrowed to sniper scopes, a cough exploding from my lips. "Let me finish." My chest rose and fell, spikes stabbing my lungs as I inhaled with even worse admittances. "With you, I'm the rawest form of myself. I obey no laws, I follow no rules. If someone hurts you, I *will* hurt them back, ten times worse. No, a thousand times worse, because you mean more to me than anything. I would *kill* for you, Della. My entire purpose on this earth is to love and take care of you. I've been doing it for almost twenty years, and I plan on doing it for another twenty and beyond. But how the fuck can I mean that when *I'm* the problem? All this time, I believed I was protecting you from them when I should've been protecting you from myself!"

Dragging a hand over my mouth, I shook my head as a future I'd always wanted incinerated into dust with reality. "What if we do end up having a family, huh? What happens when you're in labour and about to give birth? Do I expect you to suffer on your own and deliver in a forest that hides your screams? Do I think I can just drop you off at the hospital when it's time with no I.D or money, and a few hours later, we'll walk back to our tent with a goddamn new-born? A new-born who needs shelter and safety and a mother who is healthy and happy and has a bed and a shower and a fridge and a roof—"

"Ren!" Della climbed off the bed, flinching as another wash of agony worked through her. "Enough. None of that matters. We're not having children yet. It's fine—"

"But don't you see? It's *not* fine. It's shown me just how precarious all of this is. How I've been so fucking blind and wrapped up in this fantasy that we can stay wild and not suffer any consequences. How did I not see this? How did I not understand that this life can never be permanent? It's too risky. I need a job. I need to provide for you. I need to stop being a creature who thinks a tent is a suitable home and be a man instead and build you the life you deserve—build you a future we both want and a future we can't have unless I grow the fuck up."

My pacing ended by the chair, and I collapsed into it, all my rage depleted. All my terror shared. All my worries tainting the air just like they'd tainted my mind.

Pinching the bridge of my nose, I murmured, "I just can't stop thinking that I did this to you, and you're the one paying for my mistakes. That this would never have happened if we'd just stayed in our old apartment and figured this out in a place where humans are meant to live, not drag you halfway across the country with nothing."

"Ren." Della cut in. "Ren, look at me."

It took a monumental effort, but I did.

She sat on the side of the bed, whitewashed and tear-streaked.

Our eyes locked, and the love I felt for her poured free in painful waves, obliterating my anger, commanding I go to her.

I couldn't fight it.

I'd never been able to fight it.

I needed her as much as she needed me, and I'd fucking shouted at her while she was ill.

Christ, I'm a bastard.

Storming toward her, I climbed onto the mattress—boots, knives, and all—and pulled her into my arms. Tucking her back under the covers, I kissed the top of her head and breathed in her delicate scent of pine and earth and air. "I'm sorry, Little Ribbon. I didn't mean to say all that. I'm just…I'm so scared of losing you."

Snuggling into me, she wiped her tears on my chest. "I know this is hard for you. I guess it would be hard for anyone when they first hear they're pregnant and what it all means. But you can't believe that you took me into the forest against my will, Ren. I love our life. I love our tent and simplicity and freedom. If I didn't, I would tell you."

My breath still came fast and haggard, but the crazed terror faded a little as I hugged her harder. My heart stopped its fanatical beating, slipping back into a rhythm I knew.

She kissed my t-shirt, whispering, "You didn't do this to me, and you *do* provide for me. You've provided for me all my life, and no one could've done it better. So please don't worry about the future,

Ren. And please don't think you'll ever lose me because you won't. I promise."

"How can you promise something like that?"

"Because I know love transcends blood and bone. Yes, eventually we will die, but we're bound to one another. For eternity." Kissing my t-shirt again, she worked her way to my collarbone and whispered into my feverish skin. "You have my word if, heaven forbid, anything happens to me, I'll wait for you to join me. Death isn't our ending, Ren. Promise me you won't stop sleeping with me or prevent us from having a family one day because you're afraid of life itself. And all the rest of it—the house and money and things—it will work out. You'll see."

I held her for a long time, her heart thudding against mine, imprinting her shape and curves against me, allowing our connection to eradicate my fury and accept that I wasn't truly angry, just petrified.

Finally, I kissed her hair. "Thank you."

"You don't have to thank me."

"I do. I don't know what I'd do without you."

She smiled up from my arms. "Well, lucky for you, you'll never have to find out."

Echoes of her promising that we'd always be together, even past death, made me clutch her as hard as I could.

She squeaked a little in protest, but I tipped her chin up with my knuckles and kissed her lips. I'd wanted to keep the kiss tame and sweet, but the moment I tasted her, my tongue crept into her mouth and hers met mine in invitation.

A quick kiss turned into a sensual make-out, our lips gliding, tongues dancing, hearts kicking.

And when I finally pulled back, my chest burned with the same promise she'd given me. "You have my word in return. If anything happens to me, I'll wait for you to join me. You're mine, Della. Always will be."

She relaxed, breathing easier. "Good."

"Fine," I murmured, like we usually did at the end of an argument, releasing the final tension.

Reclining into the pillows still fully dressed, I waited until Della found a comfortable position with her head on my chest and body spooning my side before I stroked her hair with shaking fingers. "Now, go to sleep, woman. I'm not going anywhere."

It was a promise I kept all night.

I didn't undress, and I didn't sleep, but as I held the girl who was my everything, and she slipped into slumber and her body went lax against mine, I whispered into her moonbeam painted hair, "I hope to be the man you deserve, Della Ribbon. I hope I can give you everything your heart desires. And then, when we've lived a life rich in so many things, I hope I die before you. Because if I don't, I know I won't survive a day without you. I can't."

My voice hovered like smoke as I sucked in a gasp with how true that was. It wasn't an empty sentence. It was every truth imaginable, and, in some inexplicable way, I hoped whatever rules of fate governed our lives heard me and understood how deadly serious I was.

It was my prayer.

My penance for taking Della all those years ago.

She gave me a life and taught me how to be happy. And if she left me, I would no longer want that life without her.

It was selfish and cruel to wish such a thing, but I knew who was stronger out of the two of us, and it wasn't me.

Cradling her in the moonlight, I looked out the window at the stars.

I was her watcher and protector.

And I never let her go...all night.

Chapter Thirty-Five

DELLA

2031

THAT WAS THE *turning point for us.*

The moment where life got in the way of our fantasy, bringing us both back to earth with a crash.

Still, to this day, I get mad at myself for ruining such an idyllic existence.

I wish I could rewind time and remember to use alternate protection. I should've told Ren that we might not be safe.

An honest mistake was the biggest catalyst of our lives.

But really...it turned out for the best.

Things were about to happen that meant our past and future blended in a way we never expected.

Surprises that we never wanted inched closer to being known.

Wishes would come true and promises would be kept.

And one of those life-changing five incidents crept ever nearer.

Chapter Thirty-Six

REN

2019

THE NEXT DAY, I was better equipped after my meltdown the night before.

I kissed Della good morning, showered away my sleeplessness and worry, and focused on being the strong one and not some nutcase who wished upon a star, asking for something as morbid as death before another.

That was my secret, and she would never know just how fundamental she was to me.

That sort of pressure wasn't fair to anyone, and it was my fault I felt that way. My fault that she'd turned from my charge to my friend to my lover.

She didn't have the luxury of entering my life when I was fully developed with other significant relationships to lean on. *She* was my significant relationship in every way, and that sort of connection wasn't exactly easy.

Once I was dressed and Della comfortable with the TV on and painkillers in her system, I popped out like any normal city dweller, and bought her a chocolate croissant and coffee from the bakery two stores over, rather than eat with other guests.

At least, my body was back to being mine again with no breathlessness or palpitations. Stress had almost killed me last night and I refused to let it happen again. I would remain calm and reasonable, so I could provide the best possible care for Della.

When I returned, we ate breakfast in bed, laughed at some kid's cartoon, and reminisced about the bad reception and street-salvaged TV at Polcart Farm.

It was simple and lovely and filled me with false belief that she was on the mend.

I'd hoped she'd be able to keep her breakfast down, but ten minutes after finishing, she rushed to the bathroom and retched it all back up.

My temper built, cursing myself all over again, begging for a way to fix this.

Once she'd purged her system and her skin was once again the colour of a corpse, she protested weakly as I stripped her and myself, and for the second time that morning, turned on the shower and dragged her into it with me.

Running hot water was a novelty, and I didn't care how much we used if it granted Della some comfort.

I took my time washing her gently, massaging her scalp until she moaned, feathering my hands over her curves until her lethargy showed a spark of sexual interest.

When she plastered her naked, water-drenched body to mine and kissed me, I turned off the shower, bundled her in a towel, and helped her dress.

Sex was not something either of us should be indulging in right now.

By the time we sat back in the doctor's office and he checked her temperature, took a blood sample, and asked how she was feeling, his face went from kind to guarded, and my worry went from simmering to roaring.

My lungs imitated tiny sickles again. My breath catching with pain. *So much for staying calm.*

With professional silence, he scanned the readings of her blood test, smiled a little too brightly, then said he'd like to give her another injection as her hCG levels hadn't changed and he'd expected at least a small drop.

It took everything I had to stay sitting and permit him to jab her with that needle. In a way, I wanted him to jab her with a thousand needles if it would make her better, but I also wanted to murder him for the bead of blood as he pulled the injection free and patted a Band-Aid over the puncture while Della kept her eyes tightly closed.

After another hour of monitoring, Della was cleared to return to bed.

Walking slowly, hand in hand, to the Bed and Breakfast, total strangers smiled at us seeing a couple in love, not a man distraught by his lover's pain.

At least we had a room and a bed, and after I'd ensured she was safe and warm, lying down with a glass of water close by, a bucket just in case she vomited again, a hot water bottle courtesy of the landlady, and the TV remote, I left her for the afternoon, taking my phone and hooking into the free Wi-Fi of a coffee shop, searching the same site where Della had found our previous winter accommodation.

I'd reached my limit staying with other guests.

But I couldn't go back to the forest.

Not now…maybe not ever.

Not after my epiphany last night.

I owed Della so much more, and I didn't want to return to her until I had a solution to our unknown future.

It took longer than I wanted. I wasn't nearly as adept with using a small screen with big thumbs and reading the descriptions as quickly, but just before dusk, I managed to narrow my search down to two suitable places that I wouldn't be tempted to bulldoze or bolt from.

An old manor house that offered cheap rent in return for physical labour to do repairs and a one bedroom container house planted on a hilltop where a local farmer grazed his sheep.

The idea of being close to livestock appealed to me. But the fact that the owner would pop around often to check on them turned me off. Besides, if snow was heavy this year, getting up and down a hill might be tricky.

Leaving the coffee shop as the sun painted the sky in a swirl of reds and coppers, I called the manor house number and spoke to a gruff older woman who said her husband had died five years ago, and the house was falling apart.

I told her I was happy to renovate, that I had experience with tools and was a diligent worker, but only if she agreed not to pop by and check on us.

She'd grudgingly agreed, mentioned something about writing a long list so we wouldn't have to be in constant contact, and gave me a time to meet the following day.

I spent yet another sleepless night in the Bed and Breakfast holding Della close, wincing when she winced and holding back her hair when she vomited. The sooner whatever drug the doctor had given her worked, the better, because I didn't know how much longer I could stand seeing her like this.

* * * * *

"Isn't it too big, Ren?" Della asked quietly as we drifted away from the grey-haired bat who'd met us at the manor house to give us the 'grand tour.' Not that there was anything grand about the place anymore.

The roof had partially caved in in the dining room, the eight bedrooms upstairs had a roost of pigeons sharing one and a nest of mice in another, and the kitchen was straight out of a time warp with a coal range to cook on and a sink that could fit an entire pig.

It was cold and drafty and frankly, I'd already made up my mind to say no. It wouldn't be fair of me to expect Della to camp inside a house all winter because we'd literally have to pitch a tent inside to ward off the breeze and bird shit.

But that was until the owner caught us coming down the impressive winding stairs and said, "There is, of course, an annex next door where I've been living for the past couple of years. It's got two bedrooms, warm and dry, which is where you can stay. I'm moving in with my daughter and just want to get this place sold but can't afford a builder to do what's needed."

"So you thought you'd rent it out, get money, all while your tenant fixes it up for you?" Della asked sharply. Her patience hadn't been the best, and I couldn't blame her with feeling the way she did.

The old woman narrowed her eyes, her spectacles perched on the end of a hooked nose. "It's a nice house. I was told people do this type of arrangement all the time."

I jumped in before Della could piss her off. "Look, thank you for your time, Mrs Collins, but I think—"

The woman held up her hand. "You seem strong, and I don't know about you, but winter can get awfully boring without a hobby or two." She crossed her arms. "Tell you what. You can live here all winter for free, and we'll work out what you owe me in rent once I know what sort of renovations you're willing to tackle. Fair?"

I hadn't let Della know how tight funds had become. What with her doctor's bills and the Bed and Breakfast, we barely had enough to cover one month's rent, let alone four or five.

At least, I could earn the roof over our heads. I could do enough work that ensured my labour ought to cover our stay. The place was far enough from the city limits not to be disturbed, and there was somewhere warm to go to at night.

"Can you give us a moment?" I smiled politely at Mrs Collins.

"Of course." She turned toward the large engraved front door. "Take your time."

"Della?" Cupping her elbow, I pulled her into the large lounge, coughing at the dust swirling from the floor. The moment we were out of earshot, I told her the truth. "Money is running out. This might be our best hope at avoiding another winter with some coin left over to buy food."

"But, Ren. Have you seen the amount of work required?"

"I know. It's a lot but—"

"Do you really want to be working all winter?"

I laughed, running my thumb over her cheekbone, so damn happy there was some colour there for a change. We'd had another doctor's appointment, and he said her levels were dropping, which was a good sign. He still insisted she should be in bed, and the fact that she'd argued until I'd brought her with me to see this house had added a bit of friction, but it wouldn't be just me living here. She had every right to weigh in on the decision.

"Not sure if you remember, but I was happy working on Polcart Farm. Tinkering kept my mind off the short days and cold nights. I think this would be good for me."

"Would you let me help?" She smiled, kissing my hand as it cascaded from her cheek.

"Of course. I'd adore your help."

"Even up ladders and things?"

I frowned. "Within reason."

"Fine. You do the hard yards, and I'll paint and plaster and wallpaper and do whatever else you'll deem safe enough for me."

"So…you're okay living here?"

"As long as there is somewhere with a working toilet and a warm bed, then yes." She nodded. "Be kind of cool, actually."

"Should we go tell Mrs Collins?"

Della clutched my hand and stood on her tiptoes, pressing her mouth to mine. A faint line of sweat appeared on her upper lip, revealing she needed to be back in bed and resting. "Make sure we can move in tomorrow. I'm sick of you not sleeping in that Bed and Breakfast."

I chuckled, kissing her back. "Deal."

* * * * *

We moved in the next day after Della's doctor's appointment. Her hCG levels had once again dropped, and Doctor Strand finally looked more relaxed than tense around her. The cramps in her stomach weren't as bad, and the minor bleeding had stopped along with her vomiting.

The relief at seeing the cheeky spirit in her eyes and the sheer gratefulness at her quick kisses and sarcastic comments made my heart glow with happiness.

I didn't even care we wouldn't be returning to the forest.

Della was okay, and I wouldn't ask for more than that.

While we wouldn't be heading back into the trees we'd called home for so long, I did travel back to our campsite and collected our backpacks and belongings.

Della wanted to come, but I'd put my foot down before an argument could start.

Her hipbones stuck out and her flat stomach was concave from vomiting so much.

She was on the mend, and no way would I let her risk her health after the nightmare we'd just survived.

The return trip took me over eight hours, not to mention the pack up time. And I'd never admit—even under pain of death—but I had to stop a few times due to a frustrating case of breathlessness.

I feared by not having antibiotics to ward off the flu so long ago, I'd scarred my lungs a little. I kind of wanted to take Doctor Strand up on his offer to take a look at me, but our funds were strapped, and I wanted to keep what we had just in case Della needed more treatment.

Besides, I was used to long journeys, and had far too much to do than worry about an occasional cough.

* * * * *

One week turned to two, and we settled in.

In the cosy annex, we washed the curtains to remove any scent of its previous inhabitant, dusted the cute figurines of pumpkins and snow peas above the TV, and cleaned the tiny kitchen with its white countertop and wooden cupboards.

Della had a few more doctor visits, which ate into the final reserves of our cash, but she was finally given the all-clear along with a fresh prescription for the pill.

It'd been the longest we'd ever gone without having sex, and the night we celebrated her recovery—trying not to think about the fact that she'd actually been pregnant—we fell into bed together and finally gave in to how much we'd missed each other.

We made it last as long as we could, long and slow and deep.

And when it grew too much, we came together, hard and fast and wild.

Only to do it all over again a couple of hours later.

* * * * *

Two weeks melted into three, and I started working on the house.

By day, Della and I roamed the large corridors and bedrooms, making notes of what to tackle first, and reading through the list Mrs Collins had provided.

By night, we crossed the overgrown lawn, went past the weed-dotted tennis court, and hid in the small annex where the open fireplace crackled and popped, and I raided the terribly untended veggie garden by the old kitchen, pulling up long overdue broccoli and kale, leaving Della to use her internet trawling to turn them into a feast.

We'd become more adaptable—not just to outdoor living but to city living, too. When it was on our terms, neither of us felt trapped or ridiculed or afraid.

The town was nice enough with a couple of supermarkets, cheaper restaurants, and plenty of houses that looked like they kept their doors unlocked—if it came down to needing to 'borrow' a few things if our money ran out.

Mrs Collins was true to her word, and a week after moving in, she had three trucks deliver timber, paint, and fixings. The materials were stored in the old garage at the back, and that was one of the last interactions we had all winter.

She trusted us in her home and we trusted her to leave us alone.

Our bargain meant I had no intention of letting her down.

Her late husband's tools, stored in the workshop behind the four-car garage, were a candy box of ancient cranks and rusty hammers—a history lesson in gadget evolution, but they did the job.

Six weeks flew by, and I tackled the roof first.

Before the weather turned entirely disgusting, I ripped off the broken tiles, removed the rotten joists and bearers, and began rebuilding the ancient girl to survive another century.

Those were some of my favourite days—working in the attic with Della perched on old trunks, reading me stories from ancient diaries and dusting off porcelain-faced dolls and patching up bug-chewed teddy bears.

It did something to me watching her cradle the toys so lovingly, almost as if imagining the kids who had once played with them before time turned them to adult, then to dust.

I didn't have the guts to ask her how she felt about pregnancy after the pain she'd endured. Then again, I knew Della was a fighter and determined, and despite what had happened, she'd still want a kid…eventually.

And although I was still well acquainted with the terror of losing her, I couldn't deny I already loved her for the mother she would become. The way she'd hold our son or daughter. The way she'd kiss them and read to them and introduce them to the world that we viewed as harsh but would be so fantastical to them as we'd ensure they'd forever be protected and cherished.

That winter was just as good as the previous one in our cottage.

As we grew familiar with the manor house, we'd run the halls, have paint fights that turned into tickle wars, chase up the rambling stairs and indulge in still-dressed sex, rutting against a wall or over the arm of a hundred-year-old chaise.

Della was my other half, and the magic that existed between us meant the sad old house slowly shed off her cobwebs and stood from her ruins, prouder, prettier, braver than she ever had before.

Chapter Thirty-Seven

DELLA

2020

CHRISTMAS.

New Years.

Another year.

I wasn't exactly sad to say goodbye to 2019, thanks to the still sharp memories of an ectopic pregnancy, but there was so much good about the year, too.

Ren skirted the topic of what happened in a way that made me suspect he took it a lot harder than I had. Respecting his fears of losing me, I never truly described the pain to him. Never told him that as he carried me from the forest, I felt as if my ovary was trying to claw its way free, determined to drag my entire uterus with it.

Thanks to him, I was still alive.

Thanks to him, we had a chance at a family in the future.

And that was another reason I never told him what I went through when Doctor Strand said the words 'You're pregnant.'

How could something so good be so excruciating?

How could something I wanted be so utterly terrifying?

And how could I admit to Ren, that even though I knew the termination had to happen, I felt as if I'd killed our child in cold blood? What sort of life did we end? Was it a girl like me or a boy like Ren?

Sometimes, in those first few weeks, I'd stroke my phone with the urge to message Cassie. She was the one who'd helped me during my first period, and the only girl who'd confided in. I wanted to share my feelings. I wanted someone to understand that, even though I knew it had to be terminated, it still didn't stop the occasional nightmares of some ghost-child condemning me for choosing my life over theirs.

But I couldn't message Cassie because I hadn't told her about me and Ren.

Sure, I'd spoken to her since we'd gotten together but I always directed the conversation away from her questions of my love life and if David was still in the picture.

What I really wanted to talk about was the shadow slowly building inside me about Ren.

A shadow full of worry.

He'd put on weight since we'd been back together. He laughed and joked and ran and played and worked.

But he still coughed.

Not often.

Not all the time.

Just occasionally.

But my ears hated the sound and my heart twitched like a frightened rabbit every time he did.

Just like I never told him what I went through with the ectopic pain, I didn't confide my growing concerns over his own health.

To look at him, he glowed with vitality and hardiness...but when that cough appeared?

The shadow inside me grew bigger.

I was used to not having a sounding board to share my concerns, so our separation from society was nothing new, but sometimes I did wish I had someone to assure me that from here on out, life would be kind to us and grant long healthy days and never ending happy nights.

Despite the fact I kept a few things from Ren, and my worries chewed like tiny mice inside me, winter was great fun in that rambling, ramshackle mansion.

Ren had always been a hard worker, and that part of him came out loud and proud as he took it upon himself to renovate the entire property and not just the long list Mrs Collins had provided.

One month turned to two, then three; snow fell, ice formed, and we stayed warm thanks to physical labour. Some days, we'd focus on the bedrooms, lugging timber up the stairs to rebuild rotten walls, both of us learning how to plaster so it didn't look like Play-Doh slopped on the wall, and figuring out that paint didn't dry in the cold and caused ugly streaks that meant we had to sand and try again.

Other days, we cleared the overly cluttered living rooms of old magazine boxes and discarded dresses from a century ago, ready to rip up threadbare carpets and buff ancient floorboards beneath.

I loved every second because it meant Ren and I were together, like always.

Life couldn't get any more perfect.

Until spring arrived, of course.

And then it just got better.

We stayed far longer than usual, but whenever I brought up the subject of returning to the forest, Ren refused.

What he'd said at the Bed and Breakfast still governed him, and he was determined to provide more than just a tent even though that was all I really wanted.

Just him and long, hot days of freedom.

Summer came knocking with a vengeance, giving us an easier job of tackling areas of the house we'd left until last. And as ramshackle slowly became regal once again, the urge to move on returned, despite not knowing where we would move on to.

That traveller's itch and wanderlust was vicious once it arrived, and it hung a countdown clock over our heads, tick-tocking for a departure.

Almost as if she heard our growing restlessness, Mrs Collins left us a neatly penned note in the repaired letter box asking for a tour in one weeks' time.

We'd stayed longer than any place in two years, but even though Ren didn't want to make me homeless again, another reason we hadn't traded walls for trees was that he felt as if he hadn't done enough.

The house was immaculate compared to the state it was in when we first arrived. The roof was solid and watertight. The bedrooms rodent and pigeon free with fresh paint, beautifully sanded floors, and furniture that I'd painstakingly washed, waxed, and restored.

The downstairs was just as impressive with its polished chandeliers, spotless—if not still ancient—kitchen, and the lounge had a full makeover with new walls, re-tiled fireplace, replaced chimney flu, and an emerald rug the size of a small country we'd found in the attic and spent weeks airing out.

We were officially down to almost nothing in our wallets, but I didn't think I'd ever been so happy. Ren had even stopped coughing as often, thanks to having a proper house to protect us and regular vegetables in our diets.

Things were good.

Better than good.

But by the time Mrs Collins arrived for her tour, Ren and I grew nervous about showing her around.

It was her home, after all.

The photo album of her youth and scrapbook of her twilight years. Had we trespassed on those memories?

To start with, she'd listened as Ren explained what we'd done and nodded as we showed her room after room. Toward the end, though, her nods turned to trembles and the curt replies from a gruff woman became silent tears from a grateful widow.

We feared she hated what we'd done. That somehow, we'd overstepped.

But of course, we worried for nothing.

It took two hours and forty-three minutes to show her around, bypassing the gardens and tennis courts that we hadn't had time to tackle, and as we all stood on the repaired front veranda with peach roses perfuming the muggy breeze, she pulled out her cheque book and wrote us a figure that, even if we could've cashed the cheque, we wouldn't have felt comfortable taking.

Ten thousand dollars.

Probably her entire retirement kitty, judging by the patched-up blazer she wore.

Obviously, we insisted we couldn't take it.

Not just because it was too much, but because we had no way to cash it. No bank would touch us, no loan office would trust us—not without identification.

But even though it was a gift we couldn't accept, there was something special about being offered that cash.

Ren and I stared at the cheque all evening after Mrs Collins had gone, and somehow, in that moment of feeling worthy and valued, we turned to each other and said, "It's time to go."

The next day, we called to let her know the annex was free, and it wouldn't take a gardener much to tidy up the outside in order to sell the old girl for a tidy sum.

We left with freshly packed backpacks and aired out sleeping bags, leaving the cheque on her kitchen bench with a simple note saying thank you.

We were penniless and homeless, but our happiness made us richer than we'd ever been.

Chapter Thirty-Eight

DELLA

2020

"ARE YOU SURE, Della?"

I leapt into Ren's arms right there in the tiny office of Lo and Ro's Fruit Picking. "I'm sure. But only if *you're* sure."

He chuckled into my hair, holding me close, making my legs dangle off the ground. "Well, we just spent our last dollar, so unless you want to be in love with a thief, I suppose we don't have a choice." Letting me go, he smiled at Lo—a middle-aged woman with a baby boy tugging at her skirt and a sun-burned button nose. "We'll take the job. How long was it for again?"

Lo—short for Loraine—pushed a clipboard toward us with a pen. She, along with her husband, Ro—short for Ronald—owned a farm that grew apples, pears, and berries.

"Five to six weeks, depending on how quickly we strip the orchards before working on the greenhouse berries. We like to pick later in the season because we can charge more as fruit gets scarce with colder weather."

"Makes sense," Ren said as I grabbed the clipboard and began hastily filling in the boxes. Names? They were easy. Phone number? We had one of those. Date of births? Fine, we could fudge that. Most details were easy apart from three things.

"Eh, Lo?" I looked up, tapping the pen against the form. "We don't have a bank account or an address, and recently we were robbed, and they took our driver's licenses, so we don't have any I.D. Is that going to be a problem?"

I hated lying. I also hated how not having a piece of paper with our name on it had become a hazard in day-to-day living. But I wanted this job, and Ren needed some cash in his pocket in order to feel as if he was taking adequate care of me, so I fibbed and hoped for the best.

Lo looked us up and down, judging our tale.

I'd never been the best liar and hated to do it to a woman who'd caught us counting our last coins on the dusty highway where she had a small wooden stall selling freshly picked apples and pears. She'd taken pity on us when we'd settled on buying three instead of four, mentioning if things were tight, she had a few fruit-picking jobs open.

We'd only been on the road a couple of days since leaving the manor house, and we'd yet to embrace the thicker forest as we didn't have the cash to fill up our backpacks with supermarket food. As comforting as it was to know Ren could hunt enough to keep us alive, I wanted more to my diet than just meat and the occasional wild vegetable.

When I'd seen the fruit stand, my mouth had watered, and I couldn't stop myself tugging Ren across the road and drooling over a gorgeous pear.

"Ah, gotcha. You're one of those." Lo finally nodded.

"One of what?" Ren asked, his hackles rising, a slight cough falling from his lips.

My heart instantly froze, and I studied him.

Searching.

Seeking.

Desperate to know why he coughed, so I could stop it once and for all.

Perhaps it was just allergies.

Maybe it was from living in storms and traipsing through snow for so many years.

"Backpackers." Lo pointed at our well-used bags. "I've had a fair few from overseas come through and want to be paid in cash as it violates their visa."

Sighing, she picked up her baby son from the floor and plonked him on the small desk amongst the boxes of pears, blueberries, and apples. "Okay, I can do cash. And your hourly rate will be a dollar more, seeing as I don't have to pay tax. I'll pay you every Sunday, cash in hand. Got it?"

Ren cleared his throat, hiding any remnants of his tension. "Wow, thanks. We appreciate it."

"Meh, don't mention it. Government takes too much these days and doesn't do anything worthwhile with it. Rather help out people who need it." Taking my unfinished clipboard, she scanned it. "Married, huh? So you want a co-cabin with no one else?"

Ren stiffened. "You mean, you offer accommodation, too?"

Lo smiled. "'Course. We're expecting dawn wake-ups and out in the orchard plucking by seven a.m., lot of transient folk don't want to pay for motels seeing as fruit-picking isn't exactly a long-term thing or pays the big bucks." Bending down, she rustled below the desk before pulling up a key with a carved apple keychain. "Cabin six. It's the only double free. Some people don't like it as it's the farthest from the communal showers and kind of on the forest edge. Heard it gives some tender-hearted folk the heebie-jeebies, but me? I love wildlife, and there's nothing to be scared of." Dangling the key, she raised a dark eyebrow. "So, you want it?"

Ren looked at me, and I looked at him.

This was entirely his choice.

I would happily live in the tent farther in the treeline if that was his preference, so he surprised me when he held out his hand and waited until Lo dropped the key. "We'll take it. Happen to like wildlife too, so think it's the perfect fit."

And it was.

For the final weeks of summer, we tackled yet another kind of job, and Ren—who seemed to glow with the dawn—relaxed back into the wild, serious, incredible man I knew and loved.

Together, we'd pluck ripe, plump produce and sneak one or two on our way to the weighing and packing station. By day, we'd work with other staff—some young, some old—and by night, we'd walk the rows between the orchard trees, inhaling the scent of life, lying on our backs in the grass and watching the stars with the songs of cicadas serenading us.

Occasionally, if we stayed out late and crept back through a sleeping, silent farm, Ren would snag my hand and pull me into the massive greenhouse. There, surrounded by strawberries and raspberries and every other berry imaginable, he would push me into the shadows, press me against a wall, and hoist up my skirt to slip inside me.

For a man who loved waking with the sun, his nocturnal activities never failed to steal my heart and make me melt. His kisses were as hot as the greenhouse, his fingers coarse from picking fruit, his harsh breath as sweet as the sugary berries around us.

Together, we'd rock in the dark in perfect harmony, faster and harder as bodies demanded more, and fingers bruised, and teeth nipped, and hands clamped on mouths to silence our moans.

We were completely untamed and unashamed.

Utterly in tune and bonded.

Even with long hours and early wake-ups, Ren and I smiled often, laughed regularly, and fell into a pattern that only comes from being with someone for so long. We'd always been able to finish each other's sentences, but now, we barely needed to talk.

I knew with just one look if he needed a drink or quick massage to loosen the knot in his back. He knew with just a glance if I needed a kiss in the shade or more sun cream on my skin.

The long days equalled blissful dead-to-the-world sleep. I even grew accustomed to the delightful ache of hard work in my lower back and moaned in gratitude when Ren massaged the cramp in my hands from twisting apples off branches all day.

Our tiny cabin was perfect in its basicness with its whirring mini fridge, lumpy queen bed, and small discoloured sink.

Lo didn't just give us a job; she gave us something incredibly raw and pure, teaching us the ease of working the land and cultivating. Eating straight off the trees, sharing our skills to help each other, working our muscles until sleep was no longer a luxury but a necessity.

Not that Ren wasn't a master of that already with his past, or me, thanks to my chores of helping on a farm in my childhood, but this was something else.

This was Ren and me in Utopia.

It was how humans were supposed to exist.

I could've lived in fruit-picking paradise forever, but unfortunately, our life had a few bumps up ahead.

If I had known what was about to happen, I would've prepared myself.

But that was the thing about life.

You didn't know what to expect until it happened.

Chapter Thirty-Nine

REN

2020

THE PHONE CALL came on a Sunday.

I knew it was a Sunday—unlike most of my life when I had no idea what day or even month it was—because we'd just been paid for our fifth week of fruit picking, and I'd agreed to take Della out to a diner down the road to celebrate having some cash saved up again. Plus, we hadn't enjoyed our shared birthday yet, and that tradition was one we did our best not to break—especially as she was no longer a teenager, and I was officially thirty.

I was old.

And some days, I felt it.

Especially when I recalled a TV show we'd watched a few years ago with men who claimed their first million before they were thirty. The show interviewed entrepreneurs and successful business owners, making me doubt I had what it took to be anything more than what I was.

I'd never been number savvy or have any desire to be rich.

I *was* rich.

I had Della.

But just because I had everything *I* ever needed, didn't mean Della did, and that put pressure on me to find a way to be more.

At least we had some cash again—not much, but enough to fill our backpacks with food, and travel in the final patches of warmth before winter arrived all over again.

We were late hitting the road, and we still didn't have a clue where we were going. I'd tentatively thought of finding another farmhand job or a milking foreman position—something I knew I was good at and paid fairly well—but I didn't know how to go about finding those.

Of course, those worries became obsolete the moment the phone rang, diverting our journey onto a totally different path.

I had a razor in my right hand and a face cloth in my left, staring into the grainy mirror in our fruit-picking cabin, combating terrible lighting to shave the couple-of-month-old beard that I hadn't trimmed in far too long.

Poor Della earned red lips instantly from kissing me these days, and I was sick of itchy cheeks when I got too hot from working.

Della looked up from where she sprawled on the bed, already to go in a black flower print dress with her gorgeous hair loose and curly.

The phone rang again and again in her hand, all while she continued to stare at it rather than answer.

"You going to get that?" I asked, swishing my blade in the sink, ridding the hair it had already shaved from my throat.

"It's Cassie."

I spun to face her. "Why would she be calling?"

She shrugged. "We messaged last week. She said everything was fine. Just shot the breeze about unimportant stuff." She bit her lip, nerves dancing over her face as if she didn't trust Cassie even now.

The phone seemed to ring louder. "Maybe you better get it."

Swallowing, she shot me a look and pressed accept. "Hello?"

Instantly, her skin eradicated all colour, leaving her white. A hand plastered over her mouth. "Oh, God, Cas. I'm so, so sorry."

Abandoning my razor, I rubbed off the soap from my cheeks and crossed the room to her side. The tinny voice of Cassie drifted from the phone. She was crying, but I couldn't understand what she said.

Della's eyes welled with tears, spilling over and hurting my heart. Clutching her hand, I sat heavily on the mattress as she sniffed and nodded. "Yes, of course. We'll be there." Shaking her head at whatever Cassie had mentioned, she said firmly with a little wobble of tears, "No, not at all. We're family. We want to be there."

Another few seconds ticked past before Della sniffed again and straightened her back. "Okay, let me talk to Ren. I don't know where we are exactly or how long it will take to get back to you. Just…let me talk to him, and I'll let you know, okay?" Her eyes shot to mine, then more tears fell onto our joined fingers. "Okay, sure. Here he is."

With a shaking hand, Della passed me the phone. "She wants to talk to you."

I wanted to ask what had happened, but I had no time as I took the heavy cell and held it to my ear. "Cassie?"

Instantly, her cries became sobs, and the part of me that cared deeply for her sprang into an all-out blaze. "What is it? You okay?

What can I do to help?"

I winced, glancing at Della, afraid she'd be jealous or hurt that I'd leap to Cassie's aid if she needed me. It wasn't romantic entanglement; it was purely friendship, and the knowledge that I owed her family not just my life, but Della's, too.

Only, Della just looked at me with adoration and trust, nodding for me to continue.

Cassie swallowed back her sobs, long enough to splutter, "Please come home, Ren. Please."

Before I could assure her that we would do whatever she needed—regardless if I knew why, she told me.

And broke my damn heart.

"It's Mom. She died this morning."

And nothing else mattered.

Not how we'd get there or how long it would take. Standing, I looked for the backpacks, but Della was already ahead of me, flinging open the single wardrobe and shoving our clothes into each bag.

"We're coming, Cassie. We're coming home."

Chapter Forty

REN

2020

IT TOOK US six days to cross the miles we'd travelled since leaving the Wilsons.

Between paying for bus tickets and hitchhiking, we managed to trade the still sunny skies of whatever small town we'd been picking fruit in for the cooler clouds of the Wilson's territory.

Della and I barely slept, and when we did, it was in a hastily erected tent with a muesli bar for dinner or something just as quick and easy.

Cassie had called twice since we hit the road. First, checking in to see where we were, and second to let us know the funeral had been arranged and we better hurry if we wanted to attend.

We travelled as fast as we could, even though I still felt bad about ditching Lo and her fruit-picking job after she'd helped us out. I'd broken my honour, and I hated that I'd do it all over again because Patricia Wilson had died.

Gone.

She was the only mother I knew.

The woman who'd shown me that not all mothers wanted to sell their children.

I couldn't think of her as…dead. It just didn't compute. It hurt too much.

"She's been keeping things from me," Della murmured, her head on my shoulder as the overnight bus trundled us the final distance.

"Hmm?" I opened my eyes. I hadn't been sleeping, but my brain was fuzzy enough not to follow. "Say again?"

"Cassie. I didn't want to pry as I've been keeping things from her, too. But…now I wonder if she was hiding the fact that Patricia was sick along with all the other stuff."

"What stuff?"

She shrugged, jostling me a little in the small, squished together bus seats. "I think she and Chip have had a rocky time. Some messages they're back together, others they're apart again." She sighed, deflating beside me. "I haven't been a good friend to her."

Moving my arm, I looped it over her, forcing her to rearrange before resting her head on me for a pillow. "The fact that you stayed in touch shows you're a better friend than me."

"You wouldn't say that if you knew what I've thought about her over the years."

I chuckled under my breath, halting a cough. "I think I have some idea."

"Believe me. You don't."

"Believe me. I do." My hands curled, reliving the suffocating rage and stomach-clenching helplessness when Della ran to David. "You're forgetting I've been in love with you for a long time, Della. I just kept it hidden. Just because I didn't let on, doesn't mean I wasn't in pain when I saw you with another boy."

"I put you through that just a couple of times." Her voice turned sharp. "Whereas I lived a constant nightmare with you and Cassie."

I flinched.

I'd wondered when this subject would come up.

For years, I'd felt the strain between Della and me back at Cherry River. At the time, I'd been too blind and stupid to understand that the discord between me and my tiny best friend was Della's heart breaking. When she was a little girl, it was broken because she thought she'd lost me by having to share me. And as a young woman, it was broken because she fell for me long before she should feel such things.

Kissing her hair, I cuddled her close. "I'm sorry for hurting you, Little Ribbon."

Her body stiffened in my hold. "You didn't—"

"I did. Countless times. I was just too clueless to see it."

She laughed softly. "I was five and you were fifteen when we first met the Wilsons. We couldn't have been expected to vocalise how we felt when we had no clue ourselves."

"You have a point, but I'm still sor—"

"Don't apologise." She snuggled nearer. "There was no other path we could've taken. Our ages don't make any difference now, but back then, ten years was an ocean apart."

"It still doesn't change the fact that I hurt you. Then again, I don't fully understand why you were jealous."

"What?" She twisted to look up at me, her eyes a condemning

blue. "How could you *not* understand? I was *obscenely* jealous."

"But you should've known there was nothing to be jealous about." I kissed the tip of her nose, braving her temper. "I remember telling you once that you were it for me. No one else ever came close. You've had my heart since you could barely say my name."

"Ugh, and that just makes me feel even more wretched." Her face fell as she tucked herself back against me. "Did you know Cassie once admitted she was in love with you? On a ride together. It was one of the things that pushed me into kissing you that night." She winced, a deeper blush working over her skin. "That was the day of my first period. I didn't have the courage to tell you, but Cassie…she looked after me."

"She loves you, too, Della."

"Not the way she loves you."

It wasn't news that Cassie was in love with me. I'd seen it—admittedly too late, but by the time I did, I hadn't slept with her in a long time. And I hadn't given it any thought because I had Della, and no one else mattered.

But I also understood why this conversation had happened. Della was feeling nervous.

And to be fair, so was I.

Not just because we were about to say goodbye to one of the best women we knew, but because we hadn't addressed the past.

Bracing myself, I asked, "Did you tell her? About us?"

My heart pounded for her answer, which didn't make sense as it wasn't like I wanted to keep our love a secret, but…Cassie wouldn't understand.

"Are you crazy?" Della shuddered. "That sort of information isn't something you announce via text."

"I agree it's something she needs to hear in person."

"I know." She rested her fingertips on my chest. "But it's even harder because her Mom just died. What sort of people would we be if we hurt her even more when she's been hurt enough?"

"Honest people." Staring ahead, I worried just what sort of shit storm we were about to walk into. "You're my only family, Della, but the Wilsons…they come a close second. We owe them a lot, but don't think for a minute I won't tell her. I won't spare anyone's feelings from the truth."

Even as I gave her that assurance, I couldn't stop the thread of fear.

John Wilson had sent us away for a reason.

That reason being the town had seen Della and me grow up as brother and sister. Did we still run the risk of being separated by

Social Services now Della was twenty? Could I still be arrested for keeping her, even though the crime had no doubt been filed with unresolved cases and not on a local cop's radar anymore?

Della's tension slowly crept back, chasing the same thoughts I did. "You said you couldn't go back. Do you think that still stands?"

I wanted to smile and shake my head and tell her not to be so silly. But I couldn't because I honestly didn't know. And not knowing was tantamount to danger.

I coughed and closed my eyes. "We made our choice. We're almost there. Guess we'll face any consequences together."

* * * * *

My phone was almost out of battery by the time we crossed the town boundary, and memories bombarded me of the last time we were here. The night of panic as I ran down streets and investigated houses, thanks to Della running away.

The night she'd kissed me for the first time.

The night everything changed.

Della weaved her fingers through mine as our boots crunched on the road and our bags creaked on our backs. "The night I kissed you..." She gave me a sad half-smile in the pink light of a new day. "I felt something, Ren. I didn't quite understand it at the time, but I felt *everything* when I kissed you."

Bringing her hand to my lips, I kissed her quick. "You destroyed me that night."

"Would you have noticed me differently if I hadn't?"

It was a question I'd asked myself before, and even though I would never know for sure—never fully know if I would've continued loving Della the way I was supposed to or if she was always meant to be more—now our lives were entwined, it was hard not to believe all of this wouldn't have come true anyway. Kiss or no kiss.

"I wouldn't have been able to keep my hands off you."

She laughed quietly. "You know, two years ago, you wouldn't have been able to say that. You would still be hung up on how wrong it was to want me."

"That's true." Looking down the road with only a few more steps separating us from the Wilson's driveway, I murmured, "But life is too short. Patricia just showed us exactly how short."

Della's shoulders rolled in grief. "I can't believe she's gone."

"Me neither."

"Cassie said the funeral is today."

I sighed, rubbing the grit from my eyes and exhaustion from my mind. "It's dawn. We have time to have a quick shower and dress appropriately."

Not that we had anything appropriate to wear. I didn't own anything black that wasn't riddled with holes, and the closest thing Della had to a somber dress was her charcoal-flowered one.

I coughed a little as we traded public road for private driveway. It ought to feel different, stepping back into a place where we'd grown up, but nothing happened.

No bells.

No fanfare.

Just a farm that I knew so well with tractors tucked up in bed and paddocks I'd explored a thousand times before.

The familiar blue and black letterbox proudly stated the Wilsons lived here. A manila envelope wedged in the slot, delivered by a postman who didn't know the tragedy that'd happened inside.

Della let out a heavy sigh as we crunched on gravel and moved toward the barn where we'd lived for so many years. The barn where I'd had my first blowjob, lost my virginity, talked about sex with Della, and every other nonsensical moment in between.

"Ren?" Della tugged on my hand, removing her fingers from mine. "I didn't finish saying what I wanted on the bus, but…I don't think we should tell anyone about us. Not yet."

I scowled. "It doesn't matter if we tell anyone or not. They'll know."

"How will they know?" The farmhouse came into view with its beautiful gardens and flowers that would no longer be tended to by Patricia. "People are used to us being affectionate. Nothing has changed in that regard."

"Oh, they'll know, Della." I rolled my eyes at her naïvety. "The way you look at me, and the way I look at you? That isn't something that can be ignored. It's obvious we're not just brother and sister. And besides, I'm not going to hide that I'm in love with—"

"Oh, my God!" a familiar, husky voice cried as the front door slammed open.

Cassie gawked at us for a second, her hair still the same colour of her bay horse, messy and long. Her figure was trim and toned, encased in cream silk pyjamas.

She was older than before.

Time worn, just like me.

"I can't believe it." Shadows etched her pretty face and grief gnawed her body. "Ren? Della? You're truly here."

Charging from the doorway, she winced and hobbled as her bare feet danced over gravel, then she threw herself at us. "You're both so much bigger than I remember!"

She clutched us in a three-way hug, both Della and I soothing the girl from our past. The girl who'd made our worlds difficult and taught us so much.

"Cas!" Della hugged her back.

My arms wrapped tight, breathing in a foreign smell of a woman I no longer had any feelings for apart from sadness for her mother and gratefulness for her friendship. "I'm so sorry, Cassie."

She squeezed us tight, her body quaking as she fought tears. A few seconds passed before she composed herself enough to pull away and smile fake-bright. "I couldn't sleep. There I was, staring out the window and thought I was dreaming when you guys appeared. At first, I didn't recognise you." She nudged Della. "You've grown so much." Her eyes landed on me with a flash of history and heat. "And, wow, Ren. Age has been kind to you."

I stiffened, but her quick assessment vanished as another tear welled and rolled down her cheek. "I'm so sorry for dragging you back here. I just...I really needed to see you both."

"Don't be sorry." Della shook her head. "We want to be here. We loved Pat so much."

Cassie's bottom lip wobbled. "I know. She was the glue of this family. I don't know how Dad is going to cope." Waving that concern away as if we were strangers to entertain and not family who understood, she looped her arm through Della's. "We have so much to catch up on. Any guys on the scene? What happened to that last one? David, was it?"

Her voice was too jovial and forced, hiding just how much she was hurting. "Wait, where have you come from? You're filthy. You been on vacation during school holidays or something?" She looked us up and down, growing suspicious.

Right there.

This was the moment to tell her.

To admit the truth that Della and I were in love, that I'd gotten her pregnant and almost killed her, that I was seeking a future that was everything she deserved.

Cassie ought to be told point-blank rather than wonder, because it was obvious *something* was going on.

I cleared my throat, cursing as yet another damn cough rattled my lungs. I daren't glance at Della. "We, eh—"

Della cut in. "David and I broke up, and I decided that I'd done enough study for a bit. Taking some time off." She kept her eyes averted as if ashamed to tell Cassie that we were together. Then again, ashamed wasn't the right word. Worried, perhaps? Afraid? "Ren kindly agreed to take me travelling for a while."

What the hell?

I could kind of understand omitting the truth, but outright lying? That would spiral out of control and fast.

"But you love school." Cassie pouted. "And sorry about David."

"I'm not." Della smiled. "He was never the one." Sneaking me a quick look, she focused again on Cassie, but Cassie's attention had fallen on me. The way she studied me said she figured out something was different but couldn't understand what.

Giving me a soft smile, she said, "You look even better than you did the night you left, Ren."

I flicked Della another glance, assessing her level of acceptance and how I should respond. I nodded. "You, too."

Even in her grief, she blushed. "That's kind of you to say. I can't believe it's been so long." Jostling Della's arm, she whistled under her breath, brushing aside whatever tension had sprung up between us. "And you, little lady. You were thirteen when you kissed, um, well, when you guys left. I know you sent me pics, but you're stunning, Della. All grown up." Pecking her on the cheek, Cassie sighed. "Can't believe we're not all kids anymore."

I wasn't opposed to reminiscing, but there was a time and place, and dawn on the driveway, a few hours before Patricia's funeral, was not it.

"Liam home?" I looked at the farmhouse, not seeing any lights on in the bedrooms. "John?" I missed that old farmer. I wanted to offer him my condolences and thank him again for all he'd done for us.

"Dad isn't doing so well. I think he finally had a sleeping tablet last night after the doctor said he'd fall sick if he didn't rest. And Liam, he's okay. He lives in town now with his girlfriend, not here. You'll see him at the funeral."

A fresh wash of tears filled Cassie's eyes, and she smiled brighter. "Anyway, sorry. I'm sure you guys have travelled a long way. I mean, look at you, almost as dirty as the day you first arrived." Laughing at her joke, she let Della go. "Go on. Your room is still made up. Feel free to shower, and I'll bring one of Dad's suits over for you, Ren, and you can borrow one of my dresses, Della. Once we're all dressed, we'll have breakfast, and then...we'll go say goodbye to Mom."

* * * * *

Stepping back into our old one bedroom off the stables filled me with nostalgia and claustrophobia.

Nostalgia for all the precious memories I had of hugging a tiny Della, of telling her stories, of holding her when she was sad.

And claustrophobia for all the feelings I now had on top of those innocent ones. The memories of thrusting inside Della, of her cries as

I made her come.

So many ways I knew her, and sometimes, it felt as if I knew too much. That I didn't deserve to know what she looked like as a ten-year-old as well as twenty. That I wasn't meant to hear her childish laughter blend with her adult chuckle.

Crossing the room and shrugging off her backpack onto her old single bed, Della was quiet as she stared at the dresser where we'd kept our things. The ribbon box from her first Christmas present Patricia had given her, and the willow horse I'd carved, still rested together.

A time warp to another era.

This room might've had guests stay in the years since we'd left, but it still smelled of hay dust and summer sunshine of our youth.

"Oh, wow." Della kicked off her boots and padded in her socks to a little shelf by the bathroom door. Picking up a silver photo frame with ducks waddling on the bottom, her voice wavered with tears. "It's us."

My temper wasn't exactly calm, thanks to Della refusing to tell Cassie the truth about us, but curiosity got the better of me, and I headed to where she stroked a time-bleached picture.

Looking over her shoulder, something reached into my chest and squeezed. Something pure and innocent and young.

I didn't remember John or Patricia taking a lot of photos around the farm, and this one had been taken without our knowledge, capturing a moment of utter simplicity that only made it all the more perfect.

"You're so pretty," I breathed, drinking in the sight of young Della with white blonde hair, blue ribbon tangled in whatever breeze had danced in her strands, and the yellow daisy top and skirt she favoured. Knobby knees and white sneakers and the most gorgeous heart-warming smile as she hung on the moss-covered gate, staring at me as if I held her every wish and promise.

And then there was me: lanky and awkward, still a teen with an aura of aloneness beneath the vicious veil of protectiveness for the little girl beside him. I had my hand on Della's shoulder, laughing at something she said, my entire body turned to face her as if I had to be wherever she was to survive.

Hay covered us, pink cheeks, and sweaty heat. Everything about the photo said summer fun without a care in the world but also throbbed with love.

So much fucking love between two kids who not only adored but needed each other past common-sense.

My anger vanished as I wrapped my arms around Della, hugging her back to my front and resting my chin on her head. She smelled of earth and travel and sleepless nights but she was still the girl I'd known for two decades. "I love you as much as I did then. Even more."

Twisting in my arms, she reached up and kissed me.

I expected my usual reaction.

The undeniable desire to give in to her, to grant permission, to take the kiss she gave me and deepen it into something more.

But familiarity gave way to a different kind of reaction.

I couldn't help it.

I reared back just as our lips connected.

And my heart that loved her as a woman threaded with a heart that had once loved her as a child. A heart that knew its boundaries. Knew its boundaries so well, it scrambled behind them and trembled in disgust.

It happened in a split second, but Della froze. She gasped, stumbling back as if I'd slapped her. "Ren…"

"I didn't mean—"

"Don't." Her hands balled. "Nothing has changed. Just because we're back here—"

"I know." Raking fingers through my hair, I coughed around the sudden tightness in my chest. "It-it just happened. I didn't mean to pull away. I—" I dropped my hand. "I'm sorry, Little Ribbon."

Even her nickname in this place sounded blasphemous for all the knowledge I now had of her. The knowing of every dip and curve of her body—the same body I'd washed and healed.

Fuck.

My heart raced as more nausea filled me.

I'd raised her, for God's sake.

I'd lied to every person in this town and told them she was my sister.

Stepping onto the Wilson's estate, I'd been waiting for some sort of homecoming, some sort of nudge of welcome. But I hadn't expected to be bombarded by every emotion I hadn't dealt with before Della kissed me and ran away. Every emotion from a teenage boy struggling to keep his thoughts in check and honour intact.

My boots thudded as I took another step away from her.

And it broke something between us.

I hadn't meant to do it.

Even now, I wanted nothing more than to move toward her, kiss her deep, and assure her that nothing had happened.

But something *had* happened, and I didn't know how to fix it.

Della shook her head as if denying what I'd just done.

I raised my hands, wishing I could ignore the memories, the strict unbreakable laws I'd erected in this place.

But then Cassie's voice sliced through our agony. "Ren? Della?"

I spun to face the door where Cassie stood on the threshold holding an armful of clothes. Her hostess routine and sweet welcome was immediately blackened as she tasted tension on the air, assessing the complications throbbing between me and Della.

"Um...I brought you some clothes." Stepping gingerly into the room, she placed them on the bottom of the bed that had once been mine. The same bed where I'd woken up with my fist in Della's hair and her mouth on mine. The same bed where I'd dreamed of a girl I wanted more than anything, gotten hard thinking about, and never dared admit it was the thirteen-year-old asleep in the dark beside me.

Shit.

"Everything okay?" Cassie asked as she made her way back to the door.

If she didn't know something was going on before, she sure as fuck did now.

Sucking in a heavy breath, I growled. "Fine, sorry. Long trip." Marching toward her, I grabbed the door and began to close it. "We'll have a quick shower and be with you soon, okay?"

I shut it before she could reply.

I'd been an asshole to a woman whose mother had just died all because I couldn't control my thoughts from past and present.

By the time I turned to face Della—to try to fix what I'd broken—the bathroom door slammed and the lock clicked into place.

I barely made it to my old bed before my legs gave out, and I collapsed onto it.

Chapter Forty-One

REN

2020

THE FUNERAL WAS crowded with almost everyone from the small town paying their respects to a well-liked, wonderful woman.

As we stood beside the Wilsons on the church steps while they welcomed people to the service, Della and I stayed stiff and hurting, unsure how to breach the sudden gap that had appeared between us.

I was achingly aware of her.

She was flinchingly aware of me.

Our connection had switched from steadfast to fragile.

I wanted to grab and hold her. I needed to talk to her away from prying ears.

We had no time to clear the air and standing at the entrance to a religious service to say goodbye wasn't the time or place—not because Patricia was the one we ought to be honouring, but because the town insisted on giving us its own welcome.

Person after person smiled and said hello as they trailed into the church.

Exclamations of how big we'd grown, how pretty Della was, how tall I'd become. Along with questions of where we'd been, what we'd been doing, and if we were back for good.

Della's old teacher hugged her, then looked at me with strange curiosity, acting as if she knew why Della kept flicking me nervous glances.

Other so-called friends narrowed their eyes as if they knew a secret, and some girls from Della's grade seemed to find answers to their questions in Della's obvious tension.

I didn't like any of it.

I didn't like being noticed, and I didn't like being judged. And I definitely didn't like being estranged from Della at the worst possible time when we both needed each other.

Once the larger part of the crowd had entered, I inched closer to her, brushing her hand with mine.

Our skin sparked; the electricity between us crackling.

But she stepped out of my reach as one of Cassie's friends who'd offered to hop into my bed with no strings attached smiled at me and pressed a fake kiss to my cheek before heading inside.

Out here, away from our old room where so many memories clung to the curtains and the photo that immortalised two children who didn't know any better no longer condemned, I was clear-headed and disgusted with the way I'd acted.

I needed Della to understand I hadn't meant to pull away, and things were still exactly the same as before. Not letting me touch her made me almost suicidal with the need to drag her away from nosy townsfolk and demand she talk to me, to accept my apology.

But then the service started, and it no longer felt right to be hurting over a relationship I still had when the relationship I'd shared with Patricia was gone forever.

The Wilsons, Della, and I headed somberly into the church.

Halfway down the aisle, Della tripped on the carpet runner, stumbling in Cassie's borrowed heels.

I caught her.

The touch was purely instinctual to protect her from falling—cupping her elbow, lashing my arm around her, pulling her close.

I steadied her, fighting the urge to kiss her, all while standing in the aisle surrounded by busybodies.

Had I just revealed I was more than just an overly attentive brother? Would people know we were more?

My worries were answered as knowing eyes brushed over us, making my heart fist and lungs burn.

Of course, people noticed.

We weren't strangers here.

And our arrival back into their midst wasn't unseen.

John was right that people wouldn't understand, and Della was right to keep our relationship hidden.

Giving me a grimace, Della pulled away, and I coughed as if nothing had happened.

More eyes followed us as we continued to the front and the pew reserved for close family. My back prickled as people stared at us. It was nobody's business, and I wanted to growl for them to stop, but I swallowed my temper, pushed the wariness from my mind, and focused on Patricia.

She deserved to be focused on.

Nothing else.

Sitting down, I kept my hands to myself and didn't reach for Della's as we listened to the priest give his spiel then, one by one, the Wilsons got up to speak.

Liam—no longer a silly boy who'd gotten naked with Della under the willow tree—delivered a speech of love and thanks that brought tears to everyone's eyes. Adam—the oldest son we hadn't met but was the reason for John's charity toward us—painted a picture of a mother he adored. Cassie—dressed in black and shaking with sadness—did her best not to cry through her delivery, and John...

The big, gruff farmer who took us in and gave us shelter. The larger than life, generous man who'd become my only father figure, managed two sentences before breaking into a sob.

It fucking hurt to see a grown man who seemed utterly invincible shatter into pieces before the coffin of his dead wife.

I never wanted to live through that torture.

I never wanted to bury Della and live alone, just waiting for the day I could join her.

Tears danced over my own vision, not for Patricia's loss but for John's pain at being left behind. I was selfish to be almost grateful that, thanks to the ten-year-age difference between Della and me, I would logically be the one to go first.

I'd spent my entire life protecting Della from sadness and agony, only to admit in this matter, I couldn't protect her.

I'd be a wreck, just like John.

Dressed in a too-big black shirt of his and too-short borrowed black slacks, my fists clenched as John held up his hands in surrender, shrugged an apology at the gathered crowd, then stumbled off the podium and crashed from the church.

Della flinched as the doors slammed closed, leaving everyone a little shell-shocked and slightly afraid.

The priest stood, saying the final words while Della chipped at the ice between us and touched my hand. Just a flutter, but it made me inhale as if she'd just given me air after a day of suffocating.

She wore a borrowed dress from Cassie—a black one piece that hugged her every curve, making her seem older, wiser, sadder. "You should go to him."

I bent my head so I could whisper in her ear, "I don't want to step on Liam's and Adam's toes." They were his true sons, after all. However, looking where they sat next to Cassie, neither of them could console their father; the Wilson children were wrapped up in their own sad world of losing their mother.

John was on his own.

My heart hurt even more.

"You're right." Inhaling her scent of vanilla and caramel—recognising a shampoo she used to use as a child that was most likely still in the bathroom, restocked by Cassie or Patricia, I slipped from the pew as a hymn started. "You'll be okay?"

She smiled softly, her standoffish behaviour gone. "I'll be fine. You'll find me after?"

"Of course. We need to talk."

"I know."

Holding her blue eyes for as long as I could, I stepped from the church and winced as the heavy doors cut me off from her.

The day was overcast and grey, matching the melancholy mood.

Striding forward in my weathered boots that didn't match the black dress code, the top of my sock glinted with my well-used knife. Searching the graveyard with stone and cherub headstones, it didn't take long to find John on a bench beneath a tree with white flowers, his head in his hands and large frame quaking.

Was it right to intrude when he was obviously suffering? Would I make it better or worse?

Before I could make up my mind, John looked up, his red-rimmed eyes heavily lined and wrinkles more pronounced than before. His hair was whiter, his body not as fit, but the quick flash of power and authority he'd always had made him sit up straighter and clear his throat. "Ren."

We'd seen each other this morning after Della and I had finished getting dressed in borrowed clothes and joined the Wilsons in their kitchen. We'd all shared an awkward reunion over toast and jam with strong coffee. Conversation hadn't exactly been flowing, and apart from a clasped arm and bear hug, John hadn't talked to us.

I'd understood his silence.

His grief was a physical thing, throttling his voice and heart.

But now, his face lit up, focusing on me and not on his dead wife—grateful for a reprieve. "Sit with me, my boy." He snapped his fingers. "Sorry, not boy." Wiping away the moisture on his cheeks, he chuckled softly. "Della would kill me for calling you that. She was rather adamant your name was Ren."

I matched his chuckle, hiding a cough. "You're right. It was a pet peeve of hers. Probably because I told her over and over again that my name was Ren and never to use anything else."

I didn't think I'd told him much of my sale to the Mclary's, but sitting beside him, I offered up a piece of myself. "Her parents didn't care what my name was. As a baby, she would've heard them call me boy. I guess something deep-seated like that can have strange consequences."

John nodded, his eyes clearer, happy to focus on other things. "Sounds like that might be the case."

We sat in silence for a bit. Apologises and kind words danced on my tongue, but nothing felt right. I didn't want to hurt him deeper by saying the wrong thing. So I said nothing at all, hoping he knew how sorry I was in our shared silence.

Finally, he sighed heavily. "You lost, didn't you?"

"Excuse me?" Glancing at him, I raised an eyebrow. "Lost what?"

"The battle on keeping her as your sister."

Heat flushed my skin as I dropped my gaze to the ground. "Ah."

"Yes, ah." Reclining, he rubbed his mouth with his hairy hand and shook his head gently. "How long have you two, eh…"

"Two years."

"Are you happy?"

I looked at the sky with an almost wistful exhale. "I was until this morning." Looking at him, I shared my idiotic fears. "I screwed up a little. I guess being back here has tangled my thoughts somewhat."

"Understandable."

"I hate it. I hate this feeling of distance. I-I'm so afraid of losing her. I love her so much, but no matter how much I want to, I can't protect her from everything. One day I'll lo—" I cut myself off, horror drowning me. "Fuck, John. I'm sorry. I didn't mean. *Shit*—"

"It's okay." He patted my shoulder. "I get it. I feel the same way about Patty." He buckled as if someone had shot him. "*Felt*. I *felt* the same way about Patty." He swallowed a few times, getting his grief under control. "I loved that woman, and I know the fear you're living with because I've felt it myself. I think everyone feels it when they love something so much."

I slouched, cupping my hands between my legs. "How are you coping now the worst has happened?" It was a terrible thing to ask, but I had to know. I had to understand how broken I would be if Della ever left me. Either by choice or death.

John took his time, staring at the headstones in front of us. "I'm still alive, against my better wishes, but I have a family relying on me. I can't give up because I owe Patty to keep going. You can't fear the end, Ren. Not when you have so much to look forward to."

His words hovered between us.

I should've continued to let them hover. Instead, I blurted, "Della got pregnant. Ectopic. She got sick. It showed me just how much I've been avoiding the future, and that I can't anymore."

"I'm sorry." His gruff voice calmed me somehow. "You know, I never liked seeing Patricia pregnant. I know some men say it's the best thing they'll ever experience—seeing their wives fat with their unborn child, but not me." Shaking his head, his tone thickened. "I never relaxed until she'd given birth and was back at home happy, and bossy, and just as full of life as normal. Only then did I let myself focus on my new child."

I'd forgotten how easy it was to talk to John.

Forgotten how nice it was to have someone to confide in when I wrapped myself up in knots. Even on a day like today.

"Thank you." I nodded, coughing again. "That helps. Especially when I keep thinking I'm the worst man alive for hating the thought of Della getting pregnant, only to crave a family with her one day."

John smiled sadly. "You're not the worst. If you're anything like you were before, you're the opposite of worst." Slipping back into a reclined position, he asked, "So, I'm guessing your last name...you've kept it? Do you introduce her as your wife instead of your sister?"

My heart skipped. "Look, we can talk about this another time. I-I don't feel right. Today should be about—"

"Pat would want to know how you two are doing. Same as me. My grief isn't going anywhere, Ren. Believe me. It's nice to have a reprieve." He cocked his chin. "Go on. Fill me in."

I sighed again, amazed that in a few minutes of conversation, John had successfully brought up all my greatest fears and somehow given me freedom to discuss them. "Well, I put her through high-school. I watched her date assholes who didn't deserve her. I hurt her by sleeping with women, all while doing my best to fight what I felt for her—"

"And when did you know what that was?" His bushy eyebrow rose.

I cleared my throat, unable to look him in the eye. "The night she ran away."

"Yeah, I thought as much."

"That was why you said not to come back, isn't it?" I rubbed the back of my neck, unable to delete my tension. "You knew people wouldn't be able to accept that we'd lied after we went so far to make it the truth."

"I sent you away because you both needed to figure out who you were away from people who thought they knew for you." He looked at the rain-threatening sky. "I fell for Pat when I was young. Fifteen, to be exact. I knew I wanted to marry her the second she smiled at me, but it took almost a decade to convince her father I wasn't just trying to get her into bed."

I laughed under my breath, smothering yet another cough. "Seems you won."

"I did." He smiled smugly. "I was married to my soulmate for forty-eight years. And I didn't take a single year for granted."

I kicked at a pebble, wanting so fucking much to have what he had. "I want to marry Della. And I'm going to somehow. But no one knows who we are. We don't exist. We have no birth certificates or passports. How can we get married without that stuff?"

John flicked me a glance. "That will make it tricky."

"But…not impossible?" I hated that my heart beat quicker, tasting hope.

"Nothing is impossible." Giving me a watery smile, John patted my knee with his heavy paw. "I'm happy for you, Ren. I always knew you kids loved each other, and I'm not above admitting I was worried once or twice when I believed you were true relations. I'm glad you chose to fight for her and not go your separate ways." Tears glistened again. "True love is a blessing and so damn hard to find."

Placing my hand on his, I shared his grief. "Patricia loved you, too. You guys were a perfect example of a happy marriage when I didn't have any role models. She helped me and Della so much."

"That's nice of you to say." Letting me go, he stood with a weary sigh. "I suppose we better get to the wake, and then…you should probably tell my daughter that you and Della are no longer just siblings before she figures it out like I did."

Standing, I coughed harder than I had in a while. My eyes watered as I cupped my mouth, waiting for it to pass.

"You okay?" John asked, worried.

I smiled, shoving the episode away. "Yeah, sorry. Damn cough just keeps lingering."

"You were sick?"

"A while ago. Need some good ole' home cooked meals to get my immune system back in working order."

John's face fell. "Well the cook of the family has gone, so you'll be stuck with chargrilled things on the barbeque from me, I'm afraid."

I winced. "God, I'm sorry—"

"Don't. I know. Let's just keep talking about other things." He waved his hand as we slipped back into a walk. "So, when are you going to tell Cassie?"

"Della thinks we should wait."

"Wait?" He shook his head. "No, waiting doesn't work in this world, Ren. She'll be shocked, I'll admit, and maybe a little hurt, but she's in a good place now. Her and Chip are giving their relationship another chance, and little Nina will be coming in a few days. You can meet her. She's adorable. Patty loved that little tyke."

Following him through the graveyard, I asked, "Nina?"

"Cassie's daughter." He raised another eyebrow. "Her and Chip share custody right now while they figure things out. She's six, almost seven."

I froze, my inability to do fast math once again my downfall.

How long had Della and I been gone?

When was the last time I'd been with Cassie?

John must've understood the sudden whiteness on my face as he held up his hands. "She's not yours, Ren."

To go from shock to relief so quickly made my knees liquid. "Oh."

"I will confess, I did ask her. She got pregnant not long after you guys left. But she said you two hadn't been together in a while. That you'd pulled away from that part of the friendship, and had always used, eh, protection."

"Protection doesn't always seem to stop such things," I muttered, thinking of Della's complications.

"That's true but rest assured, Nina isn't yours. Even if Cassie didn't do a paternity test, you can see for yourself she's Chip's, purely thanks to the flaming red hair of her father."

Clasping an arm around my shoulders, he guided me into the church as if he were the one consoling me and not the other way around.

I let him be the patriarch—the role he played so well, for a little longer, but once we got to the wake, I stayed close by, monitoring his drinking, doing my best to change the subjects when his face grew blotchy and tears streamed silently down his face as he hung in the shadows.

He might have his own children, but if he let me, I would be there for him as much as they were.

We hadn't discussed if we should stay or go or what the Wilsons expected, but by the time nightfall smothered the farm and the wake was over with a fridge full of casseroles and leftovers, Della and I cut across the driveway, pushed our single beds together, undressed without speaking, and reached for each other.

We were too emotionally exhausted to talk.

Too physically drained to do anything more than hug.

We returned to an age of innocence, where skin on skin contact was purely for comfort and nothing else.

We fell asleep in our old room, entangled and entwined.

Just as before.

Chapter Forty-Two

DELLA

2032

DEATH IS NEVER easy.

And it wasn't any easier just because we hadn't seen Patricia in a while or that we weren't truly her children. Patricia had been a large part of our lives, and Cherry River didn't feel the same without her.

Being back in that place...I wish I could warn myself.

Wish I could whisper what was about to happen.

It's so obvious from where I sit in the future, but of course, with the complications between me and Ren, the residual childhood jealousy toward Cassie, and the overwhelming aura of grief on the farm, all of us were preoccupied with other things.

Things like accepting John's invitation to stay and for Ren to resume his role running the fields.

We had no place else to be and no rush to leave and really, Ren had been searching for an answer to our future, and found a temporary one by brushing off his skills to work the land.

That first afternoon when he cleaned the rusty tractor from its cobweb jacket, greased ancient gears and cranks, and kicked her into a growling, diesel-coughing start, my heart fluttered with so many memories of him. So many memories of so many different Rens. Child Rens, teenage Rens, early twenties Rens, right to the thirty-year-old man I adored.

For a week, we spent our days alone, toiling in paddocks and debating what to do with grass long past its prime. Ren's frustration grew thanks to the lack of care since we'd been gone, and his determination to take on the workload now that John could no longer handle it burned with need.

He announced war on nature, pulling up weeds that hadn't been there before, liming entire meadows and harrowing others.

For seven days, we didn't discuss what had happened when we'd first arrived at Cherry River, nor touched more than a sweet hug to go to sleep. There was always either someone too close or something more pressing to deal with.

Somehow, my request to keep our relationship hidden had backfired, and without thinking, walls were built and timelines crossed, so there was nothing to hide, after all.

No kisses to secret. No sex to avoid.

Cassie's suspicions faded as more days passed, and Ren and I acted no different than we had when we were thirteen and twenty-three.

Plus...I was worried.

God, I was so worried.

Ren's coughing hadn't stopped.

And I didn't know what to do.

I did my best not to hover or freeze when a small cough sounded and was almost glad of something else to think about when Cassie shared her own pain, revealing how Patricia had died of a sudden stroke.

No warning.

No signs.

Just woke up one morning, made breakfast as usual, and by the afternoon, she was gone.

She also confided in me about Chip and her daughter, Nina.

To say it was a shock hearing she had a daughter was an understatement.

I was angry she hadn't told me.

Hurt that after years of messaging, she'd kept her a secret.

But then again, I had no right to be jilted. I'd done the same to her.

I hadn't told her about me and Ren. I'd kept us a secret, too.

I'd spent my childhood knowing she was in love with him, just like I was.

I'd spent countless nights in tears while she touched him, just like I wanted. And, although we were all adults now and I knew Ren was mine, that sort of fear was deep-seated and nonsensical even as age made me wiser.

So, you can see why I asked Ren to keep our relationship hidden. Yes, I didn't want to hurt Cassie at her mother's funeral, but I also needed time to figure out how to apologise for thinking the worst of her all those years apart.

To admit that I was weak enough to be threatened by her.

She was the only one who truly understood what it was like to love Ren and not have him, and we would always share that in common.

But keeping the truth quiet was never going to work.

And on the seventh night, we were caught.

In more ways than one.

Chapter Forty-Three

DELLA

2020

I'D BEEN DRINKING.

Not a lot, but a couple of glasses of wine with Cassie had made my fears over Ren amplify until I sat on the pushed together single beds in our bedroom to wait for him.

Seething.

Stewing.

Spiralling into terror that the reason he hadn't touched me in a week was that he remembered what he had with Cassie. He remembered me as a little girl. He remembered too much to be with me.

Time had strange properties here. It had taken the seven years when Ren and I had lived alone and folded it so the two ends touched, forming a bridge from past to now and blurring everything in between.

I'd grown up a lot in the two years since Ren had claimed me. I'd grown to like myself more and stand up for the things I believed in. I'd blossomed into someone worthy of him, and I hated, positively *hated* that confident Della now bowed to a less confident one.

That my fears over his coughing made me mad at him.

That my concerns over his blasé attitude made me rage.

I knew what was happening.

My anger was founded entirely in terror, but it didn't make ignoring it any easier.

I'd started the week off blaming Cassie for my doubt, but sitting in the dark waiting for Ren, my heart showed the truth.

I loved Ren with every fibre of my being. There was no part of me that would survive if anything ever happened to him. My entire life he'd been everlasting and indestructible.

And to have that faith punctured every time he coughed…to have panic fill me, drop by drop, until I was close to overflowing…it made my hands ball and heart quake and an almost manic desperation to have him touch me, hold me, convince me that my mind was running away with me and everything was fine.

I'd tried voicing my fears before, but Ren didn't tolerate my mother hen routine and he'd just kiss me, smile, and brush me off as if it were me with the problem.

However, this morning I'd woken with a new resilience and spent the day working beside him, holding oil cans and rags as he maintained the tractor's decrepit engine, helping thread the twine through the baler when it snapped on the overly thick grass, and generally proving to him that I wasn't a child he needed to be afraid of or a kid who couldn't handle life.

As always, we'd fallen into a comfortable pattern working together, and by evening we were so tired it didn't take much convincing for Cassie to get us to dinner.

The dining room looked the same as all the other times with one key thing missing.

Patricia's place setting and presence.

It was a wound that still bled, and conversation stuck safely on subjects of the farm.

Adam had returned to his wife and two children, and Liam had stayed in town with his girlfriend. So it was just the four of us, and John kept looking at where Patricia would sit, and Cassie kept looking at her father.

Once our meal was finished, I stood with renewed purpose, ready to tackle my concerns with Ren, but John asked for Ren's opinion on a new grass seed, and Cassie dragged me to her room where I learned yet more about her on and off again relationship with Chip the accountant.

From proposals to pregnancies to births and break-ups, I saw how much she cared for him and how glad she was they were giving it another chance.

The entire time she spoke, all I could think about was Ren. How he'd never once let me down, even when things weren't perfect between us. How he'd always put me first, even when we'd had nothing to our names.

And how, here in a place that meant so much to both of us, everything that we'd created had been threatened, all because the past dared mingle with our present, making me wonder and worry.

And so, I'd had a third glass of wine before bolting from the farmhouse and cutting across the driveway—the same driveway I'd run across so many times before—and paced our bedroom, needing to end whatever distance was between us.

I *missed* him.

I missed him more than I could stand.

For twenty minutes, I'd paced before resorting to sitting on the beds.

I'd been waiting for an hour.

Waiting for a way to stop feeling so lost and alone and cast aside.

The door opened fifteen minutes later, swinging wide as Ren prowled in with a hand buried in his hair as if already stressed about sleeping in a room with me.

"You're back."

My voice wrenched his eyes up, squinting in the dark. I hadn't bothered to turn on a light as dusk steadily became night. I knew I seemed creepy, sitting cross-legged, hands tightly linked in my lap, my heart terrified and temper fuming, but I couldn't help it.

I'd reached my limit and we needed to talk.

"Della, what the hell are you doing?" Ren flicked on the overhead light, shutting the door behind him. "Why are you sitting in the dark?"

"I've been waiting for you."

"Okay." He frowned. "I'm here."

"You are." Unravelling my legs, I hopped off the bed and moved toward him. "A week ago, you refused to kiss me. Since then, you've barely touched me. I feel like you're avoiding discussing—"

"I haven't been avoiding anything." He straightened. "And I *have* touched you. We fall asleep touching every night. Plus, you know why we haven't talked—there just hasn't been the right time."

"Now is the right time."

He sighed. "Look, you're tired, I'm tired. Let's wait until morning so we don't say things we might regre—" A cough interrupted him.

My heart grew hot with dismay. "See? There you go again. Avoiding this. What are you so afraid of?"

"I'm not afraid of anything." His nostrils flared. "I think you've wound yourself up and should calm down before—"

"Don't tell me what to do. I'm not a child anymore, Ren. You can't command me and expect me to obey." Storming toward him, I stood on my tiptoes and slammed my lips to his.

I wanted to fight.

The frightened part of me needed it.

His mouth yielded to mine for just a second before he pulled back...just like before.

My heart cracked.

"Della. Stop." He had the audacity to raise his hand and wipe his mouth as if what I'd done wasn't permitted. As if the past two years of countless sex, endless kisses, and numerous I love you's had never happened.

For a second, I wanted to run.

Another second, I wanted to hit him.

And then, in a final second, I nodded, accepted my hurt, and prepared to fight for what was mine.

"I won't let you do this." Stepping into him, I grasped his belt, tugging quickly at the leather. "I miss you, Ren. I want you. I'm worried about you and feel like you're not—"

"Della…" He tripped backward as I worked on unbuckling him, crossing the small room until his back smashed against the door, and I trapped him. "*Della—*"

I didn't stop until I unthreaded the leather and yanked the buckle free, discarding both ends the instant they were undone. "Don't 'Della' me. You know what you're doing, and it isn't fair." My fingers attacked his button then reached for his zipper in record time.

"What *I'm* doing?" His large, warm hand landed on mine, stopping my progress, gripping me hard. "How about what *you're* doing?"

"I thought that was obvious."

"You're upset." His fingers twitched around my wrist, his eyes shouting their love but his body rigid with refusal. "I get it. I know it's my fault, but whatever you're doing isn't the way to fix—"

"Please." I bit my lip, stemming sudden tears. "Please prove to me that nothing has changed when it's all I can worry about. Please let me make love to the only man I've ever wanted. Please convince me that this fear inside—this fear that is slowly growing—is completely crazy and irrational. I need to know you're okay. I need to know *we're* okay. I need—" I stopped as a cry spilled from my lips, revealing just how knotted I was over this.

Over our distance.

Over childhood fear that he didn't want me anymore.

Over adult terror that life wasn't infinite like fairy-tales but a war for every moment.

"Fuck." He let me go only to wrap me in his strong embrace. "Nothing has changed, Little Ribbon. I promise."

"Prove it." I stayed stiff in his arms. "Sleep with me."

A tormented chuckle bubbled in his chest. "I'm not taking advantage of you when you're like this. We should talk. Why didn't you tell me you were so worried?" The softness of his worn, blue sweater was warm, the thud of his heart familiar. My body responded to what it had always considered safe, and my spine relaxed even as I fought to stay angry.

"You know I love you. How many times have I told you that? Nothing can drive us apart, Della. I know I hurt you with my knee-jerk reaction when we first arrived, but nothing has changed."

He ducked and kissed me sweetly, tasting my tears. "See? I love you. I'm *in* love with you. Everything is fine."

I blinked, lips tingling and heart smarting. "Kiss me again."

"Not tonight."

"Why?"

"Because you're worked up over something I don't understand. I'm sorry about before, I truly am. But anything else you're worried about is completely ridiculous, and I won't be pushed into sleeping with you. Not when you're like—"

"My fears aren't ridiculous, Ren."

"I didn't mean they were."

"Is it ridiculous that I love you so much I can barely breathe at the thought of losing you?"

"What?" Temper lashed through his voice. "Why the hell would you lose me?"

"I don't know. You tell me."

"Is this about Cassie?" His eyes blackened. "Don't you trust me?" His question was soft but lethal, daring me to give light to my terrors when, up until a few days ago, I trusted him with my life.

I sighed, defeated and fully aware I was at fault. "Of course, I trust you."

"So, you're not driving yourself insane thinking I'm going to leave you for Cassie?"

I flinched. "I won't deny it was hard at first, but I know what we have supersedes all that."

"Then..." His head tilted, hair caressing his forehead. "What is this really about?"

"It's about us." I shrugged helplessly. "It's about me needing you and...and I don't like this distance between us." I looked down. "I was wrong to keep our relationship a secret. The longer we don't tell people, the more I worry it's even real."

His finger tipped my chin up. "It's real, Della. More real than anything in the world."

"I needed to hear that." I half-smiled.

He tucked a curl behind my ear. "You're forgetting *you're* the one who wanted to hide. I wanted to tell everyone the truth."

"I was wrong." Reaching for him, I brushed my mouth on his. "Please...take me to bed. Let's just forget I made a mess of this."

I chickened out.

I'd picked this fight to address that annoying little cough.

I'd stewed in stress so I would have the guts to order him to see a doctor.

But, somehow, none of that mattered anymore.

I just wanted him.

Inside me.

Around me.

With me.

Our lips touched before he shook his head with a soft groan. "I can't sleep with you in this room, Little Ribbon."

My eyes snapped wide. "Why?"

"There are too many memories here."

My heart fluttered, tasting progress. "So? Memories are just memories."

"Memories have a way of driving me insane." His tongue wet his lips, his gaze drawn to my mouth. His voice denied me, but his body reacted. "So many memories of so many things between us."

"But don't you see?" My hand landed on his chest, sliding down until I pressed my palm against his erection. "That's why we need to make new ones."

He hissed between his teeth. "Stop."

My bravery at addressing so many things had flown out the window, but I wouldn't let him deny me. Not in this. Not when we desperately needed to connect.

"I want you, Ren." Sinking to my knees, I tugged his jeans and boxers down in one smooth glide. They bunched around his knees as his cock bounced free.

I didn't hesitate.

I licked him, inserting him into my mouth.

"Fucking hell." His hand fisted in my hair, holding me tight as he crippled under my control. "Della." His belly clenched as he rolled over me, hugging my head as I licked and sucked, doing my best to shatter him.

For a second, I thought I'd won.

He sucked in a wobbly breath, his body swelling in my mouth.

But then that damn side of him that protected me at all costs resurfaced and, with a savage growl, he pushed me away. "Della...no." He staggered sideways, tripping to the centre of the bedroom, doing his best to hoist up and rearrange his jeans. "Are you trying to kill me, woman?"

His anger and denial hurt, but not the same as before.

I kind of understood now.

I sort of finally saw.

This wasn't about me at all.

This was about this room.

This place.

I thought I'd had it hard here.

That lying in bed jealous and petty was painful.

But really...I hadn't.

Yes, Ren had always been forbidden, but at least, he hadn't been a mortal sin.

Me...on the other hand.

If Ren had felt the *slightest* tug toward me—a tug that overstepped even the smallest of margins...then I could understand why this room wasn't just a room.

Because I hadn't just been a girl he wanted; I had been a child.

A child who meant more to him than anything else in the world.

A living, breathing nightmare.

This room had become his judge and executioner, its very walls, furniture, and windows condemning him for every dream he might have had, for every fanciful wish, for every fleeting thought.

God, I'm sorry.

Pushing off my knees, I let go of my anger. I drowned in apology. I moved toward him as gently and as carefully as I could because he was spooked and hurting, and I'd been the one to do it.

"You truly did love me, didn't you?" I whispered.

His gorgeous coffee eyes widened, his chest rising and falling. "Of course, I love you."

"That wasn't what I said." Pressing my fingers to his heart, I hated that he flinched. That his sun-bronzed hair shivered as he stayed tight and wound as if he'd bolt at any moment. "You loved me more than you should, even before I kissed you."

His face contorted. "I-I loved you as a brother."

"No, you loved me as something more." Tears trickled down my face at the truth—the exquisite, agonising truth. I wrapped my arms around his waist, not caring he still had his jeans bunched in one hand, hiding his decency. "I'm sorry, Ren."

He rippled with stress, not hugging me back. "Della, I—"

Those two words were an arrow, shooting from the bow of his mouth, ricocheting around the room until they punctured us through the heart.

In their simplicity, they admitted everything.

His head came down and his lips sought mine with a level of devotion and need that transcended time and logic. His arms banded around me, fierce and possessive. And the ice in his muscles cracked, melted, and cascaded away in a waterfall of released tension.

"I didn't realise until we'd left." Burying his face in my hair, his entire body quaked as if this was his true confession. "I didn't know. You have to believe me. I was a kid. You were mine. There was no other future I could think of that you weren't there beside me."

"It's okay." I stroked his back, being the rock he'd always been for me.

How had I not seen it? It wasn't me or my kiss that made him realise there was something more.

There had *always* been something more.

Our love hadn't honoured boundaries fashioned by age or circumstance. Our love had thrown us together and told us the truth way too early.

It had laughed in our face and said, *'This is the person you will adore forever. This is the person designed, crafted, and perfected for you. But you can't touch them. Not yet. Not for decades. Not until you're worthy of the gift I've given you.'*

Time, it seemed, had a nasty sense of humour.

Time had hurt Ren far worse than it had me.

"Being back here makes me wonder if I ever overstepped," Ren murmured. "It makes me second-guess e*verything*. Every time I touched you, what was I thinking? Every time I kissed you, what did it mean? Every time I saw you naked, was I averting my eyes like I thought, or was I watching you when I shouldn't?"

He exhaled with a ragged groan. "I don't know anymore. I don't know if I did right by you, or if all along I was some perverted—"

"Stop."

He sucked in a breath, his chest heaving as if he'd run miles.

"Trust me when I say this, Ren Wild, you were and are the most honourable man I've ever known. I understand how you could second-guess. I know how time can play tricks and make you remember different things. But I need you to listen now because not *once* did you make me feel awkward around you. Your touches were strictly brotherly. Your kisses perfectly pure. I grew up so safe and happy because I knew you adored me. I knew we were special. I knew we had something that no one else could ever steal or share. So please, Ren. Please don't let the past damage what we have or make you fear you did anything wrong. Because you didn't. Not a single moment was wrong. Not a single—"

He kissed me.

He clutched me close and kissed me deep, shutting me up, telling me he trusted me, assuring me he was okay.

I crumpled in his arms, submitting entirely to his hot mouth and skilful tongue.

His fingers slid into my hair, cradling me as he bowed over me, tucking me into him, doing his best to join us together in all the right ways.

On and on, we kissed.

Heads dancing.

Tongues licking.

Hearts racing.

Ren had always been a masterful kisser, but something was different about this one. Something new and honest and true.

He held nothing back.

He tasted me and let me taste him.

He commanded possession and let me possess in return.

And the entire time we kissed, I didn't tell him what else I remembered.

How, when he was eighteen, I knew he dreamed of someone he wanted because he'd cry out in his sleep, waking me to see his young face straining with want and misery.

How, when he was nineteen, I knew he pleasured himself in the dark once our beds were separated and we could no longer touch, and I'd hear his soft groan as he came—the same groan I now recognised as a woman.

Ren had kept everything he was going through a secret from me, but it didn't mean I wasn't aware.

He was a boy.

He was human.

He was perfect.

My lips tingled from his as I reached for his undone waistband.

He shook his head, rubbing our lips together. "No—"

"Yes."

His heart pounded harder as I pushed the material down. His face drained of colour as I broke our kiss and looked between us. There, on the bare flesh of his hipbone, with his boxers and jeans pushed low enough to reveal the splattering of hair but not enough to reveal his cock, was his brand.

The same brand I'd kissed before, licked before, pressed my cheek to and cursed my parents for what they'd done to him, all while thanking them because, in a way, they'd bought him for me.

Time had used them, too.

Time had ensured they brought us together.

The oval brand with its *Mc97* glinted cruelly in the light. Running my fingertip over the scar tissue, I whispered, "This room is nothing more than a room. The only thing that means anything is you and me." My fingers drifted to the dark warmth of his underwear, ducking down and fisting his hard length. "You *can* touch me, Ren. You *can* kiss me. There's nothing stopping us. I *want* you to touch me. I need it...and I think you need it, too."

He shuddered again, his breath short and fast, eyes wild and black. "You're pushing me too far, Della Ribbon. I don't know how much longer I can keep saying no."

"Good because I want you to say yes."

"But it's not right."

"It is."

"I can't stop thinking, ah—"

I squeezed him, making his head tip back, revealing a long, powerful throat with its five o'clock shadow and Adam's apple bobbing as he swallowed. With his eyes closed, he strangled, "But I nursed you when you had chicken pox in that very bed. I sat in that chair as you learned about sex, and I hid just how much I didn't know. I watched you sleep when you were still a kid. I had dreams that—"

"None of that matters now." Pushing firmly, I backed him toward the single bed that used to be his. The one with black sheets and no colour. The one I'd curled into, when he wasn't looking, to smell his pillow.

He tripped backward, his jeans slipping to half-thigh. Landing on his ass, he snapped out of whatever trance I'd put him in and shook his head. "No." Standing up again, he begged, "Let's go rent a room somewhere. Or pitch the tent. Somewhere it's just us. I want you, Della. And you're right, I need you. But...this place is too much."

"Please, Ren." Colliding with him, I dug my fingers into his hair and wrenched his mouth back down to mine. "Please." I kept my fingers lashed in the soft copper strands, piercing my tongue into his mouth.

And finally...he snapped.

His hands clamped on my ass, hoisting me up with impressive strength and encouraging my legs to wrap around his hips.

The moment I latched on, he moved until he slammed me against the wall. My spine bruised as he wedged me tight, rocking into me, his lips harsh and dominating as the kiss I'd given him turned into one of crushing need from him.

His hands trailed upward, squeezing my breasts before cupping my cheeks and holding me steady.

And then he kissed me.

Truly, deeply, *deliciously* kissed me.

His mouth opened wide, his tongue dancing with mine, our heads shifting and breaths hitching as he consumed my every thought.

"You just had to push, didn't you?" He nipped my lip, biting and licking his way down my jaw to my throat. There, he sank sharp incisors into my flesh, making me cry out and claw at his shoulders. "Had to make me do this. Had to make me accept."

My hands fell to his hips while he continued to rock into me, making me wet, ensuring my entire body throbbed for his.

Luckily, I wore a skirt. My one and only skirt with a grey sweater with silver thread.

His touch found my thighs again, swatting the material away, hooking his fingers into the cotton between my legs. "I can't stop. I doubt I'll ever be able to stop."

I expected him to put me down and wait until I'd removed my underwear, but I'd pushed him too far, and he merely yanked the fabric aside and drove two fingers deep, deep inside me.

"See, Della?" He withdrew and plunged inside me again. "This is what happens when you push me." He wasn't gentle. He wasn't kind. He was ruthless and merciless and I *loved* it.

His hand cupped me as his fingers pulsed, dragging heat from everywhere. "Is this what you want? Tell me this is what you want. Tell me this is okay. Goddammit, Della, tell me you need me as much as I need you because I'm going out of my goddamn mind."

I convulsed as he rocked his fingers so deep, a sliver of pain cut through me. Pain that only made my pleasure all that more intense. "Yes. God, yes."

"This is what you pushed me for? This is what you've broken me for?"

"*Yes!*"

His touch rocked up, pulsating in the perfect way he knew I loved. I moaned as my body responded with tingling, tangling bliss.

"You've always driven me wild." He kissed me again, his tongue lashing and cruel. "Always been too bold." His kiss turned deeper still, making me breathe him, ensuring my body wasn't just made up of my cells, but his too. A synergy of bodies. A blending of him and me and past and present and the lovely, lovely knowledge that whatever distance had been between us was no more. "Always been too much for me. So much braver than me."

"No," I cried out as he thrust his cock against my leg in time to the fierce drive of his fingers. "You've always been braver. I understand now how hard it would've been—"

"Hard?" His teeth found my neck again, biting, licking, consuming. A small cough nudged my fear. "Hard is nothing compared to how hard I am now. How fucking hard I am for you."

I had no reply, only a boneless sigh and a desperation that had a will of its own.

A desperation I'd always had.

A desperation that had always wanted Ren in any way it could have him.

This had always been our future.

There was no way we could fight an attraction like this. No way of denying a connection like this.

This was destiny.

Pure and simple.

Dragging my hips closer to his, Ren broke the kiss and stared down. His lips were red, skin flushed, hair a mess. He looked savage. Clothes were wrong on him when he seemed so primitive and free.

In a flash, I saw him naked in rippled resplendent glory, standing in his chosen home—the forest where we'd shared our childhood. With the trees we called friends, and the river we called parent, behind him.

That was where Ren belonged.

That was where a man so much more than human should be.

With fingers inside me, he cupped my cheek with his free hand, trembling even now, but this time with lust so vicious it tore pieces off our hearts.

We stared at each other.

Him and me.

Us.

And he said, "I told you I loved you, Della."

"I know."

"I told you I always have."

"I know."

Withdrawing his fingers, he grabbed his cock and lined up with my body. "Are you happy knowing I can't deny you? Are you pleased with yourself that I have you pinned against the wall and can't stop? Are you happy that after this, I'll never know if I loved you the way I should have? That I'll forever wonder? Forever think of fucking you here, in this room, and no longer care about any of it?"

"Yes. So many times yes."

"Good."

I smirked. "Fine."

He thrust, filling me with one quick impale. "This is what you make me become." He didn't wait for me to adjust, just rocked deeper again and again. "This is the power you've always had over me ever since I woke up and saw my soulmate and not just my friend."

My fingers clawed at him.

I gasped as he sought my lips and kissed me as ferociously as he took me against the wall. "This is what I was hiding from you as well as myself." He thrust. "This." He drove deeper. "Fuck." He roared as he tried to climb inside me. "This. It has *always* been this. Always been you." His forehead crashed on mine as his rhythm lost any melody. "Fuck, it's always been you, Della."

Tears sprang with the heartbreak in which he admitted such a thing.

Love melted my soul with the shock in his eyes that he'd finally seen.

"Ribbon…" His gaze glittered as he blinked in disbelief. Disbelief that it had taken him two years of being together to finally snap and admit to himself.

"I-I don't care anymore." He smiled with sharp teeth and sharper joy. "I don't care what people think. I don't care if they judge. I." *Thrust.* "Don't." *Thrust.* "Care."

"Finally." I laughed as he suckled my neck, driving into me again and again. His lips were poisonous and his tongue venomous, slowly killing me as I scratched him, marked him, begging him to treat me worse.

And he did.

We raged and fucked and claimed.

A battle.

A war.

Love at its rawest.

And it was right.

Unbelievably right.

Threading my fingers in his hair, I moaned, "It's always been you, Ren. It will *always* be you." My oath triggered the rest of his undoing, and whatever gates he kept locked blew wide apart.

"You're mine." He growled.

"I know."

"And I'm yours."

"I know."

"Fuck." His breathing turned to heavy grunts, a cough rattling just once as he rode me faster, climbing higher, driving and demanding.

Our kisses were messy and out of control.

Our hands heavy and greedy to touch.

His lips bruised mine, injecting need and desire into my blood until I shivered uncontrollably.

His body hardened inside me until he groaned in pleasure-pain.

He thrust faster.

On and on, affirmation after affirmation, love after love.

And when he pressed his fingers to my clit and rubbed in perfect rhythm to his thrusts, I was no longer fighting but sprinting toward the promise only he could give.

My body spun and spindled and shattered outward, rippling around his invasion, making tears prickle my eyes.

The second my orgasm finished, Ren buried his face in my hair, swallowed a howl, and drove so hard, so deep, I was sure we'd end up in the stables beyond.

"I can't stop. I'm-I'm…" His rumbling, hungry groan tore from his throat as his body quaked in mine. He went taut, dangerous. Then his body pulsed over and over, hot splashes marking me as his, finding his release as quickly as I'd found mine.

For a long moment, neither of us moved.

Our hearts clanged like church bells.

Our limbs throbbed like pounding drums.

And then a softness replaced the madness, and Ren scattered feather kisses all over my face as we clung to each other, coming down from our addictive high.

He coughed quietly, making yet more tears swell in my eyes.

Sweet, fuzzy feelings battled with scared, timid things, and I wanted to hug him close and fight every hour, every year and stay right there, together.

Accepting another kiss, I whispered, "Ren…will you do something for me?"

He smiled, dazed and satisfied. "Anything."

"I want you to see a doc—"

But a knock sounded on the door.

The unlocked door.

And it opened.

And Cassie walked in.

And she saw.

Everything.

Chapter Forty-Four

REN

2020

"SHIT." My hand flew up as if I could stop her mid-step. "Cassie. Out!"

She froze, drinking in the sight of me with my jeans around my thighs, Della sex-mauled and panting in my arms, and our semi-naked bodies joined in a way that needed no explanation.

"Holy shit." Cassie clamped a hand over her mouth, spinning around. "What the—"

With her back turned, I winced as I disengaged from Della. Stepping back, I dropped her gently to the floor. Once she was steady, I hoisted up my jeans and tucked my still hard flesh into my jeans.

The sound of my zipper and clink of my buckle sent my cheeks blazing, made worse by Della rearranging her underwear and smoothing down her skirt.

Clothes might cover us, but they didn't stop the raging heartbeats, tangled hair, or swollen lips of what we'd just been doing.

Of all the fucking times.

Of all the fucking places.

I felt as if I'd been skinned alive and every organ left on display. I felt butchered and broken and bruised, and it was all Della's fault. But I also felt awed and amazed and absolutely stupefied that I hadn't known what fears lurked inside my heart.

That I'd avoided coming to terms with what we'd done for two years, and it'd taken a stupid bedroom full of our youth to make me snap.

I hated that she'd pushed me.

But I loved her for it too, because I felt lighter than I had…in, well, *ever.*

I was centred and calm, and I didn't want a fight with Cassie messing up that special connection that had sprung between Della and me. I wanted to bask in it. I wanted to forget about everyone else for a while and just love her. I needed to reassure her that I was fine and the fear she'd been nursing was completely unfounded.

Dragging shaking hands through my hair, I did my best to put myself back together.

Giving me a guilty look, Della checked me over, found I was marginally suitable for company, then said softly, "You can turn around, Cassie."

Cassie peered over her shoulder warily, eyes narrowed. For a second, she stared at us, hurt and hating. Then she spun around, her mouth falling wide with shock. A few squeaks came out before she cleared her throat and snapped, "I mean...I suspected *something* was going on but...to actually know it's true?" She crossed her arms tight. "I-I don't know what to say."

I didn't want anything to do with this.

I was sorry she'd seen us together, but that was her fault for walking in unannounced.

I was sorry she had to face the truth that I was with Della, but it wasn't like I was hers. We were kids when we hooked up. It meant nothing.

I cleared my throat, hiding yet another cough. "Cassie, I think you better go— "

"Wait." Della held up her hand. "There isn't anything *to* say." She glanced at me before finishing, "We're together. It's that simple. I'm sorry I didn't tell you, Cas."

Cassie's eyes narrowed, flitting to me, then back to Della, then back to me. Her anger only increased. "You're *together*? Well, that just makes it all fine and dandy, doesn't it?" She rolled her eyes. "Don't you think it's a little...I dunno? *Disgusting* to do something like that in your old room? A room where you told me and my family you were brother and sister?"

"That's in the past." Della's face hardened, prepared to take on Cassie in a way that worried me. "It's none of your business what we do or don't do in whatever place we choose."

"It kinda is, seeing as this is my home!"

"It was ours, too!" Della shouted back.

"Yeah, and you were kids!"

"And now we're not, so get over it!"

Cassie sniffed. "It still doesn't make it right."

"I don't care. I'm not looking for your approval." Della crossed her arms. "This has nothing to do with you."

Cassie faced me, her temper zeroing in on me instead. "You promised me when I saw you guys that night in the stable that you hadn't kissed her before. That you'd never touched her. You stood before my parents and assured us all that there was nothing going on."

I wanted to leave. The walls were too close. The door too far. But this wasn't just Della's fight. It was mine too, and I'd always known we'd have to face it, sooner or later.

Standing taller, I wished I could shed the scent of sex from my skin. "I told the truth. Nothing was going on." I winced. "Then."

Cassie pursed her lips, eyes full of storms. "How long?"

Dangerous, dangerous question.

"Two years," I muttered.

"Two *years*?" Cassie's face blanched. "Della..." She looked at her as if her heart was broken.

Della's own heartbreak painted her features as she shrugged helplessly. "I-I couldn't tell you. I'm sorry."

Cassie put up a hand, blocking Della from view as she locked eyes on me. "You expect me to believe you've only been fucking her for two years? You guys suddenly vanished into the night. Who's to say you didn't do what I just witnessed the *minute* you were away from here? Who's to say you weren't fucking—"

"Don't you *dare* accuse me of something I haven't done." My jaw clenched with disgust. "What sort of person do you think I am?"

"One who was obviously lying to himself."

"If you think that low of me, then leave!" I pointed at the door. "Like Della said, this has nothing to do with—"

"He didn't touch me until I was eighteen." Della leapt to my defence, standing in front of me like a shield. "He left me, actually. For six months, he put distance between us, but it only showed we'd been running from the truth and couldn't anymore."

Cassie cocked her chin, not giving an inch. "The truth about what?"

"The truth that I was in love with her, and she was in love with me." I growled. "We didn't plan it. Believe me, I tried to fight it. But...she's mine. So, are we done here?"

Silence fell.

Tempers cooled a little, only for Cassie to turn her attention back on Della and fire up all over again. "It still doesn't change the fact that you didn't tell me."

"Well, we're telling you now." I did my best to keep my patience. "We're together and engaged and—"

"Wait. *What?*" Her skin whitened. "Oh, my God. You're *engaged?*"

Cassie shook her head. "And you didn't think I deserved to know? You didn't think my friendship valued a heads up? You didn't think our past, Ren, gave me some sort of right to know?"

"Our past meant nothing. We fooled around, that's all."

Cassie pressed a fist to her heart. "Wow, Ren. Just wow."

Regret swamped me. "Look, I'm sorry, okay? I just meant, Della was always—"

"Yours." Her eyes glossed. "I get it. Can't say I'm even surprised. There was always something more between you two. Sleeping in the same bed? Joined at the hip all the time? It wasn't normal." She rolled her eyes. "Dad told me to let it go, that you'd both had a rough start to life, and it was understandable that you'd found family in each other and overcompensated...but I always had my suspicions."

"You never said anything." Della frowned.

"I didn't know how. I tried to joke about it a couple of times, but Dad overheard me and told me to give you a break. He said who cared if you loved each other so much that it was a little creepy? I should be happy you had each other." She laughed. "But you have to understand, I have two brothers, so I know what siblings are like and, I'm sorry, but you two? You were never siblings."

I froze.

All along, I'd believed my lie was ironclad and impenetrable.

Turned out, the only person believing it was me.

Everyone else was just waiting for us to wake up, grow up, and admit it.

"Fucking hell." I coughed.

She hugged herself tighter, giving me a helpless shrug. "It's done now. Secret's out."

"I can explain." Della stepped forward, her fingers twirling the cheap gemstone ring I'd bought her. The ring that promised a marriage, a life, a forever.

It was a testament to how distraught Cassie had been at her mother's funeral and how grief-blind she'd been this past week that she hadn't noticed Della's tattoo, her ring, or my bracelet with its missing diamantes.

We hadn't taken them off—not that a tattoo *could* be taken off.

They screamed the truth even when Della didn't want to voice it.

Cassie's eyes tracked her, narrowing at the glint of fake sapphire. "When are you getting married?"

"We can't. Not yet," I said.

Before Cassie could ask any more questions, Della jumped in. "I know we hurt you, and I wanted to tell you...so many times. I just didn't know how without coming across as cruel or vindictive or proud."

Cassie softened a little. "I knew how you felt about him, Della."

"I know."

"Walking in and seeing you guys together is worse than being told point-blank."

"I know that, too." Della's shoulders fell. "We didn't plan it. It just…happened."

"Well, I'm never coming in here unannounced again." She gave a wry smile laced with hurt. "God, the images…I can't get them out of my head."

"I'm sorry," Della said softly. "Truly."

Cassie looked at the ceiling before shaking away her anger. "I just have one more thing to say and then I'll let it go."

"What?" Della asked.

"You didn't tell me the biggest thing in your life—when we'd all practically grown up together—but you acted miffed that I didn't tell you about my daughter. Kinda hypocritical and it made me feel terrible. I get that you're together—I even accept it and saw it coming, but I'm hurt that you hid it."

Della balled her hands. "I agree. It was my fault. Ren wanted to tell you, but I…I was nervous."

"Nervous. About me? Why?"

Della looked away.

"Ah, I get it." Cassie laughed sadly. "You thought I'd try to steal him from you, is that it?"

Della flinched, twirling her ring again as if it could invoke a spell and fix this mess. She looked as if she didn't trust that promise on her finger. The proposal I'd made. The conviction that one day I *would* marry her.

I stepped forward, taking the heat off Della. "I'm the one who's made a mess of this. Not her."

Cassie chuckled softly. "Same ole' Ren, taking the blame when it isn't his fault." She gave me a smile that wasn't cruel or sarcastic but honest and hurting. "You didn't make a mess of this; *we* did."

Moving toward Della, she stood before her awkwardly. "I guess I owe you an apology, too. I know what I was like in my youth, and I'm not proud of some of the choices I made. I hate that those choices made it seem like I would take Ren away from you."

I scowled, pissed off that they spoke as if I were some possession to be passed around. As if I had no say in the matter.

Della nodded slowly, looking younger but sterner and far more regal. "You don't owe me anything, Cas. So many times I wanted to tell you the truth. I'm sorry for not trusting you like I should have."

Cassie sighed. "I just wish I'd known sooner."

"I wish I'd told you sooner." Della gave her a tentative smile. "So...you're okay with this?"

Cassie nodded. "Of course. It's not like it's even a shock. We're family and I love you both."

Della wrapped her arms around Cassie, hugging her hard. "Thank you."

They clung to each other for the longest moment before Cassie pulled away. "I grew up the moment they put my daughter in my arms, and that's why I can honestly say I'm happy for you guys. I'm overjoyed that you figured it out and are together but...not everyone is."

"Wh-what do you mean?" Della threw me a worried look.

"I mean...I didn't come here to catch you guys doing, um—" She waved her hand. "I came to tell you something, and I've already taken too long." Casting a look over her shoulder, her entire body stiffened. "You don't have a lot of time."

My system leapt into high alert, adrenaline flooding me as she glanced at the open door again. "What do you mean?"

"I mean...Liam just called. He's doing work experience with the local police to see if he wants to join."

"Why is that a problem?" I clipped, doing my best not to let my mind run away with nasty conclusions.

"It isn't." Cassie rubbed her arm. "He'll do great at it. But it is a problem when he calls me in a panic because he overheard a conversation mentioning you."

"Mentioning Ren?" Della asked sharply. "What did they say?"

Pacing in front of us, Cassie twisted her loose hair into a rope until it draped over her shoulder. "God, I don't know how to fix this. Having you guys back has meant the world to Dad. He can grieve without worrying about the farm. And I know he wants you to stay on indefinitely. But...I don't know how that's going to happen."

"Why?" Striding toward her, I grabbed her shoulders and spun her to face me. "Spit it out, Cassie. What's going on?"

"They're on their way over here."

"Who?" I growled. "*Who* is on their way?"

"The police."

My insides turned to ice as Cassie gave me a terrified look. "The town's been talking, Ren. They know something's going on. There's been rumours for years about how fast you disappeared and theories about why."

Letting Cassie go, I stormed toward Della, staying close to her side, sensing a threat but unsure how to protect her from it.

"Theories are pointless. Besides, it's none of their goddamn business."

"I agree, it's not. But Liam, bless his heart, overheard what you told Mom and Dad that night. He was hiding on the stairs."

"What?"

She winced. "He knew you'd been bought, and the people who kept you were called Mclary. He heard Della was theirs and how you ran away with her."

I tripped backward. "Oh, fuck."

"Oh, no." Della turned white.

"Goddammit!" Raking a hand through my hair, I glowered. "I only told John and Patricia, so I could prove she wasn't my sister— not for that information to become public knowledge!"

"I know. And he feels sick about it, but he was a kid, Ren." Cassie's face etched with apology. "All he heard was a story about cattle brands and fingers being cut off and you saying the police were probably after you for kidnapping Della. It was too juicy *not* to tell his friends."

"Shit." I hung my head. "I should never have said anything."

"But Ren never kidnapped me," Della said, strained and stressed. "He didn't know. And anyway, my parents weren't exactly the best people in the world. He did me a favour taking me from them."

"I know that." Cassie nodded. "And Liam knows he screwed up. I've yelled at him—many times. Only, the gossip he shared when he was in school has circulated enough for it to reach the ears of parents and teachers, and now...well; now you're back in town, and I guess it got them talking again."

Squeezing the back of my neck, I paced the small room. At the time, when I'd stood before Patricia and John and given them enough information to ruin my life, I'd been fully prepared to be waltzed out of there in handcuffs.

Back then, I didn't care as I would've sacrificed my freedom to ensure Della could stay with them.

But now...now, I had too much to lose.

My eyes met Della's. "We need to leave. Right now."

Della didn't speak, just nodded and immediately turned to the backpacks we'd unpacked by the dresser.

Cassie stood by the door, watching as we prepared to pack up any hope of staying here for winter.

John was right when he sent us away.

We shouldn't have come.

"You-you can't leave. Not again," Cassie murmured. "Dad needs you, Ren. We all want you to stay."

"We can't." I grabbed a bag from Della and wrenched open a drawer where we'd stuffed our clothes, fighting a cough. "I won't lose her. Not now. I didn't do anything wrong—"

"Stop."

Everything inside me slammed into a brick wall.

My head shot up, eyes locking onto the two shadows behind Cassie. They morphed from the stable gloom, two uniformed officers who I recognised from selling a couple of hay bales to on and off over the years.

Della froze, dropping her bag. "Wait. No."

"Sorry, ma'am." The older of the two with a greying moustache stepped closer, scanned all three of us, then said, "Ren Wild, you're under arrest for the kidnapping of Della Mclary and you're coming with us."

Chapter Forty-Five

REN

2020

I'D BEEN TRAPPED before.

It was so long ago now that time had healed me from a lot of it, but sitting in a brightly lit room with a locked door, two-way mirror, and handcuffs that had been removed from my wrists glinting silver on the table, shot me straight back to a different type of captivity.

Here, I wasn't expected to work until I passed out or eat scraps before the pigs could get them, but I *was* expected to give them something.

Something I didn't know how.

The door opened, depositing a visitor into my tiny prison. The officer with his greying moustache and skinny frame sighed wearily as if working through the night was about as fun for him as it was for me.

He scuttled into the spare chair on the opposite side of the table.

The manila folder in his hands slapped against the table, and he gave me an exasperated smile.

I didn't buy it, but I did buy his exhaustion and the fact that he was old, tired, and wasn't out for a witch hunt...just doing his job as an upholder of the law and protecting his town's citizens.

"So..." He cleared his throat and splayed his hands flat on the table on either side of the folder. "I know we asked you before, but you have to give us something."

I leaned back in the chair, stiff and slightly chilled from sitting there for so long. My lungs ached and the slight rattle in my chest pissed me off. "I'm not evading your questions. If I knew the answers, I would give them."

He frowned. "So, you still don't know where the Mclary's farm is? You don't know your mother's name? You can't prove anything of what you told me? That you were bought for labour and ran away when you were ten?"

"I have no evidence. I don't even know my real last name. All I know is I didn't cut my finger off—Willem Mclary did. I didn't brand my hip—Willem Mclary did. The only crime I'm agreeing to is I *did* take their daughter, but not by choice. I was a kid running for his life. The *last* thing I wanted was a baby."

I chuckled, remembering the juvenile hate I'd had for her when I'd first found her in my bag. "She'd squashed all my rations and drained me of all my strength. If I wasn't so sure they'd have killed me, I would've gone back and dropped her off."

"But you didn't."

"I didn't."

He tapped the table with a fingernail. "But that was nineteen years ago. You could've dropped her off at any other point. To any police station in any town."

"I tried."

He sat up taller. "Ah, yes. In the town you didn't know with a family you can't name."

"That's right."

"You left her for a couple of days?"

"Yes. Like I told you, I only went back because I saw her on TV. Some news reporter said she'd be put in foster care if no one claimed her. I might've hated her back then, but she didn't deserve to be lost."

My heart pinched a little with memories. Of her blistering joy when I'd gone back. Of my profound connection knowing I would never leave her again. That I would do anything it took to give her the life she deserved. That I was in love with her as deeply and as truly as anyone could love another—regardless of age.

Silence fell as the cop stared at me. His name was Martin Murray and he was a good man. Honest and hardworking and I wasn't afraid of him. I wasn't afraid of being coerced into confessing something I didn't do. I was only afraid of the repercussions that I legitimately deserved for taking something that wasn't mine.

I wasn't trying to deny that fact.

I was merely trying to make them see that I'd never hurt Della. I'd done everything I could to raise her right. And just had to hope that that offered some leniency for my crime. And I also had to hope that Della forgave me if I ended up in jail and left her on her own.

At least she had the Wilsons again.

At least she was safe.

Is she thinking about me?

What sort of panic was she going through since I'd been marched from our bedroom and stuffed into the police cruiser?

I coughed, missing her so damn much.

Finally, Martin Murray laughed with a thread of frustration. "You know, I've seen you grow up. Not that often, but I walked the beat when you were busy picking up Cassie Wilson so she didn't drive home drunk. Wherever you were, Della was by your side. It was stranger seeing you two apart rather than together. I know you treated her well. And I know in your mind, it wasn't kidnapping. I'm not trying to throw you in jail, Mr. Wild. I'm only trying to solve this case."

"You know my name is Ren. Use it."

He nodded once. "You have to understand how difficult you're making this investigation."

"Not my intention." Sitting still, I waited for the next question—yet another thing I couldn't answer. But he sighed again and opened the file. "I have something to show you."

"Okay…" I shifted forward, leaning closer. My eyes locked on the typed front page of whatever document he had. A bunch of numbers decorated the top, along with the words *unsolved* and a date and then a name.

Della's name.

Missing Case of Della Donna Mclary.

She had a middle name.

I never knew.

My mouth went dry as he flicked over the page and slipped out a glossy photo of the place that haunted my nightmares. "Is this their farm?"

Words vanished down my throat, leaving me mute.

I nodded around a harsh cough.

The same dilapidated farmhouse with its rotten veranda and haphazard shutters. The same barn in the distance where I'd slept with other stinky, starving kids. The machinery and tractors and animal feed all scattered uncared for in the muddy yards.

I hadn't forgotten anything about it.

Not a single thing.

Not the sweat on my back or the pain in my muscles or the fever in my blood.

Not the soul-crushing feeling of abandonment and abuse.

Martin held up another image. "This them? Willem and Marion Mclary?"

Again, I hadn't forgotten a single thing.

From the dirty dungarees Willem wore to the faded sundress his wife preferred. Everything was grimy and unloved and held an aura of perpetual greed.

I nodded again.

"And this?" His third photo showed Della.

A rosy cheeked baby who didn't belong. A baby with inquisitive blue eyes and a ribbon twisted around her chubby fist. All she wore was a diaper and a food splattered purple bib.

She sat in her highchair in the same kitchen where I'd scurried like a cockroach and stolen crumbs from the floor when they weren't looking.

My voice returned, its volume restored thanks to the baby who taught me how to read and write. "That's her. Della Mclary."

"Why do you call each other Wild now?"

"Because she chose that for us to share."

"But it's not a legitimate name?"

"No."

His forehead furrowed. "How have you gone this long in life using a fake name with no documentation?"

I shrugged. "Luck?"

He chuckled. "I think you make your own luck, Ren."

"I make my own way, if that's what you mean."

We made eye contact and smiled.

I'd found an unlikely friend in this cop. This cop trying to persecute me for a nineteen-year-old unsolved crime.

Pulling a wad of papers out, Martin skimmed the text before giving me some information, for a change. "Della was reported missing by her father. When the local police went to their farm to write up the report, they made a note of lack of sanitation and signs of other inhabitants in the barn. You said that's where you slept with the others?"

"Yes."

"Why didn't the police see them when they went over?"

"There was a bunker." I flicked through the rolodex of things from that time. "Mclary was a doomsdayer. Had a bunker full of food and supplies. He'd stuff us all down there if he got whiff of a visitor coming." I laughed, not that it was a laughing matter. "It was a monthly occurrence, thanks to the pastor having a drink or two with Willem. He donated to the church, you see…keeping up his image."

"And how many children were there with you?" Martin picked up a pen, holding it above a blank piece of paper.

"Not sure." I frowned, doing my best to count when, back then, I didn't know how numbers worked. "Ten. Fifteen, perhaps?"

"And all boys?"

"No. Not all boys." My black look gave him all he needed to know. "The girls were Mclary's favourite."

Martin whitened, scribbling something down. "And you don't know where they went after they were burned out on the farm?"

"A few were killed, I know that much. And a man in a black suit came and took others away. Another sale. Another transaction. Don't know what happened after that."

The cop, whose entire career was probably based on writing up DUIs and sorting out domestic disputes, put down his pen and rubbed his eyes. Those sort of images weren't the kind you could rub away.

Slowly, he sifted through the file again and pulled out another document. "What I'm about to tell you may or may not have power over what your future holds, but after your arrest, we did our best to track down the Mclary's. To tell them the good news that we've found their missing daughter."

I kept my emotions hidden about that.

I would kill them all before they took Della away from me.

"They're dead. Both of them."

I jerked in my chair. "How long?"

Turned out...I didn't need to kill anyone.

"Six years."

"How?"

"Marion Mclary shot Willem point-blank with a shotgun, then turned it on herself."

My mouth fell open. "What?"

"Murder and suicide." Martin shrugged. "The case was open and shut. Their estate was placed into the hands of the bank that'd been threatening foreclosure for years, but it never sold."

"What does that mean?"

"It means the farm is untouched, and we might find evidence of what you're saying."

"And if you do?"

"Then there is no crime as far as I'm concerned."

"Are you authorised to make that call?"

Martin stood. "This is my town, and you're my citizen. I've known you since you were a teen, and John has been ringing my phone every ten minutes, demanding you be released. He vouches for you. We can't hold you for longer than twenty-four hours without evidence, and hopefully whatever evidence we do find absolves any wrongdoing, and this will just be a minor inconvenience."

I looked up at him, towering like a praying mantis. "So...now what?"

"Now, you and me are taking a little road trip. And hopefully, when we come back, all this mess will be sorted out, once and for all."

Chapter Forty-Six

DELLA

2031

INCIDENT NUMBER ONE.
The first of the five I warned you about.
Ren's arrest for my supposed kidnapping.
I don't need to explain the level of panic I faced as the police took him away. How I sprinted after the cruiser, hammering on the window until I couldn't run fast enough. How I collapsed on the road with my knees bitten by gravel, and my tears tearing air from my lungs. How Cassie picked me up and dragged me into the house and how John got on the phone and made an absolute nuisance of himself demanding information on Ren.

It was the longest night of my life.

Three times, I tried to steal John's Land Rover keys and drive to where they'd taken Ren. And three times, John had taken them from me with a stern look and sterner wisdom that attacking a police officer and making threats wasn't the way to end this smoothly.

By the time dawn arrived, everyone was exhausted and still in yesterday's clothes waiting for news—any news.

And then, the phone call came that Ren was being taken out of town for a while, and I well and truly lost it.

I grabbed the phone from John and threw curse words down the line to whomever was unlucky enough to listen. I threatened and pleaded and cried, only for the stoic voice of authority to say it was a matter that needed to be concluded, and this was the fastest way.

I was hung up on.

I should've breathed deep and centred myself.

I should've allowed John to talk sense into me and calm down enough to understand that they couldn't really separate us.

Could they?

I didn't know if they could. I didn't know how the law worked, or what they could charge him with, or how long they'd keep him from me.

All I knew was I'd lived the worst time of my life when Ren left me, and I couldn't do it again. I couldn't sit by and let them do this to us. I couldn't let them take his freedom.

So, I bolted across the driveway to the disarray of our room and dumped out Ren's backpack onto his bed.

The last thing to fall out was my manuscript, wrapped in plastic and bound with string, protected at all costs.

It was my only piece of evidence that Ren hadn't taken me maliciously or held me against my will. My only way of proving this was all a massive misunderstanding.

I despised my parents for what they did to him. As far as I was concerned, they were dead and always would be. They were despicable human beings, and Ren was a freaking saint in comparison.

I expected a fight when I slung on some clean clothes, tied my hair with my ribbon, and flew back across the drive. I anticipated having to run to the police station with no car to make my journey swifter.

But I shouldn't have doubted.

Cassie and John stood by the ancient Land Rover, keys jingling in anxious hands, a look of going to battle on their faces.

I didn't burst into tears again, but I did hug them fiercely and climbed into the back seat where Cassie kept flicking glances at my manuscript but didn't dare ask what it was.

And when we arrived at the police station, we were almost too late.

Ren had been given a clean black t-shirt and black coat that came to his thighs. With his scruffy jeans and weathered boots, he looked like a surly detective about to go study a corpse. He strode from the station with an officer beside him, face unreadable and hands balled.

"Della."

His look of shock unravelled me, and tears spilled down my face. All I wanted to do was leap into his arms and offer up anything to trade his life for mine. But I did the only thing I could.

Ignoring him, I locked my attention on the grey-haired officer beside him and ran at full speed with my manuscript in outstretched hands as if it held all the answers.

"He didn't kidnap me. He was a minor. He didn't know any better. Please—" Shoving the heavy paper into the policeman's arms, I demanded. "Read it. It has everything you need to know. The only way I can prove I was happy with Ren. Happier than I'd ever be with parents who bought and sold children for their own gain. Please, you have to believe me. Release him."

Ren pulled me to the side. He wasn't wearing handcuffs, and his fingers were soft on my cheek. "It's okay, Della. I agreed to go with them. It's all right."

"What do you mean?"

"I mean…something has come to light, and this might be the fastest way to clear this up."

John stepped forward. "Wherever you're taking Ren, we're all coming."

The officer shook his head. "Sorry. It's over an eight-hour drive. Mr. Wild has agreed to accompany us, but no others."

Ren lashed an arm around me, kissing my temple as he turned to face the policeman. "Bring her."

"What?"

"Please," Ren said. "She has a right to see it."

"See what?" Cassie asked.

The officer ignored her, staring at Ren. "I don't think that would be wise."

Ren pointed at the manuscript weighing heavily in the cop's hands. "That is our tale. That is our truth. Della is my truth. And she deserves to know."

I couldn't stop shaking, cuddling into his side. My future hung in the balance, and the officer looked at John as a friend rather than a law enforcer. "I can't take you all. There isn't enough room."

John's chest puffed up. "We'll drive ourselves."

"No." Ren shook his head. "This is something Della and I need to do on our own."

"Do what?" Cassie asked, finally earning the attention of everyone.

The officer shot a look at Ren then me, before he admitted, "The Mclary's are dead. Their estate is still untouched, and Mr. Wild has agreed to help us with this investigation."

Dead?

I shuddered harder.

Parents who gave me life.

Parents I hated more than anything.

Gone.

"She's coming." Ren straightened. "Or I'm not."

How were they dead?

How long had they been dead?

All this time they'd been a dark, devilish stain chasing us across the country.

Before I could ask what any of this meant, the officer slowly nodded. "Okay. She comes."

Marching toward the cop car with my words in his hands, and the second officer who'd arrested Ren last night sitting patiently behind the wheel, he added, "Let's go. We have a long drive ahead of us."

* * * * *

I can't explain the feeling of being chauffeured in the back of a police car for eight hours.

Every traffic light we stopped at, people peered inside, sneering at us, believing we were criminals. Every bathroom break and snack grab were met with leery stares and confused looks as to why we weren't handcuffed.

Six hours into the trip, we found a diner on a lonely stretch of road and shared an awkward dinner. As we ate our meals, the waitress couldn't take her eyes off Ren as if he were some infamous outlaw that only made him all the more attractive.

I don't want to mention how jealous that made me. How petty I was, even then, to be angry with women for finding Ren as handsome as I did. Little did they know I still had his kisses on my mouth and his orgasm inside me.

Those were my secrets, and I clung to the knowledge…doing my best not to fear what we were driving to, and what would happen when we got there.

Martin Murray, who introduced himself as we pulled away from the police station, was quiet in manner and talk, leaving his fellow officer, Steve Hopkins, to fill in the gaps.

Not that there were any gaps to fill as no one was in the mood for conversation.

Ren and I shared a few lingering looks, a few whispered sentences, but silence had infected us, too, our thoughts already in the past—the past we were driving across country to.

When we finally arrived in some quiet country town with a bedraggled Main Street, sparse unloved houses, and a church with a wonky cross, Officer Murray drove straight to the small satellite office of the local law enforcement, and together, we all sat down with Bob Colton and Remy Jones—two more officers who were the first to the scene of my parents' death—and chatted about tomorrow's adventures on no sleep, lots of coffee, and a long journey.

Bob Colton had already collected the keys for the Mclary farmstead from the bank who were looking at possibly demolishing the house and sub-dividing the land—seeing as no one was interested in buying such a big place that needed so much work.

Then again, we were there to enlighten everyone on what truly happened at that farm. And it would be yet another reason it wouldn't sell.

On the drive over, Martin had filled me in on what he'd told Ren.

About what my mother did to my father.

About the empty house where two corpses had lain rotting for weeks before someone reported the stench.

About how, when the forensic team combed the house for clues on why my mother had murdered my father, they hadn't found a single shred of missing children, malicious abuse, or a barn full of bought employees.

That worried Ren. I could tell.

The crease between his eyes never stopped frowning. His eyes dark and turbulent.

If they'd been alone when they'd died, where were the kids? Had they sold them or killed them?

Those questions squatted in my mind, making sleep impossible as we were put up for the night in some dingy motel with only cold water in the shower and a single towel to share.

At least, they'd given Ren and me the same room.

There was no talk of what we were to each other, or if it was illegal for us to stay together, or what the hell all of this meant. For now, everyone was focused on finding out where we'd truly come from and just what Ren had endured.

A policeman sitting outside our door was the only sign we weren't just guests on this little foray and Ren was still a suspect.

When Martin had surveyed our room and stepped outside to leave us to it, he pointed a finger at Ren and said, "I'm trusting you not to run, boy. You came here freely. Continue to be cooperative and this will be smoother for all of us."

Ren nodded as the door closed, and I whispered under my breath, "His name is Ren...not boy."

Chapter Forty-Seven

REN

2020

THE FIRST STEP onto Mclary's property filled me with a complex recipe of emotions.

Hate.

Horror.

Rage.

It felt as if I'd only left yesterday, yet the house was smaller than I remembered, the tractors not as scary, the barn not as huge and hungry for tiny children.

With our entourage of two officers from home, two officers who'd overseen the murder/suicide, and another two for good measure, Della and I were as popular as we'd ever been.

We all moved down the muddy driveway past rotting bales of hay and around a pile of scrap iron to the front door where I'd bolted with a baby Della clinging unseen in my stolen backpack.

Della slipped her hand into mine as we crossed the threshold into the house, and just like that, I was a ten-year-old kid again.

My world narrowed to terror.

My throat constricted.

My body reacted.

Bruised and beaten, starving and sad. Ghost images of a screeching Della ripped my head toward the kitchen. Long ago echoes of a TV program showing what a real family was wrenched my head to the decrepit lounge.

Della felt my tension and squeezed my fingers, dragging me back to the present.

Coughing, I gave her a grateful look, forcing myself to stay in the now.

"How do you want to do this?" one of the officers asked. I didn't know which one, and I didn't care. I merely drifted forward, clutching Della's hand, taking comfort in the thud of my boots and the reminder that I wasn't ten anymore.

No one could hurt me again.

They were dead.

Good fucking riddance.

"Where's the box of evidence that you guys gathered in the murder/suicide investigation?" Martin Murray asked, leading the officers into the kitchen where notepads came out, and a box was brought in from a cruiser and placed on the well-used bench.

"This is all we took. Some bank statements. A few IOUs from a local feed store. An unpaid invoice for a tractor service, along with this." Remy Jones, a middle-aged pot-bellied man held up a red notepad that had been curled and rolled with an elastic band and a pen jabbed in the pages. "We figured she killed him and then herself because they were up to their eyeballs in debt, and it was only a matter of time before they lost everything. She blamed him for their lack of fortune; couldn't be bothered struggling anymore. *Bang, bang.*"

My eyes locked onto the notepad as he waved it around with his stupid conclusions. Mrs Mclary didn't shoot her husband for something as useless as money. She shot him because she'd had enough of him raping girls. Maybe in her twisted mind, she thought he cheated on her, or perhaps, she'd finally woken up to how fucking horrible they were and what they were doing to kids.

Either way, she'd killed pure evil and then done the world a favour by eradicating herself, too.

I tried to look away from the notebook as the officer flicked through its pages with a scowl. "This thing makes no sense, though. It's just a bunch of numbers with prices beside it. Four hundred here. Two hundred there. A thousand dollars a few times, but that's rare." He shrugged, tossing it back onto the counter with a slap. "Must be another IOU book, or maybe how much they paid for stock?"

No one seemed interested in answering him, but I couldn't tear my gaze off that damn red notebook.

Something familiar...something tugging me to tumble backward through time.

Red.

Pages.

Pen.

The farmhouse fell away, replaced with an older version—a version where Marion Mclary still lived, and she sat rocking on her rocker by the grimy window, her spindly hand scribbling.

I'd been tasked at lugging in firewood. Load after load until my arms shook and my shoulders threatened to pop from their sockets.

She hadn't cared.

On and on she rocked, writing in that little notebook before creaking her way toward the bookcase that lived in a shadowy part of the living room.

The past and present blended as I followed the tug of my feet, leading me toward the bookcase that still groaned under the weight of cookery books that were never used and auto mechanic magazines that were torn up as fire kindling.

"Ren?" Della asked softly, but I wasn't really there with her.

I was in an in-between world. A place where I was neither thirty nor ten. I was plasma, merely a figment as I reached for the book where I'd seen Mrs Mclary stuff cash that afternoon before swatting me around the head for spying.

Pulling the Bible free, a few coins tinkled inside as I released Della's hand and flopped open the Book of God. Inside, instead of silky pages of testament, someone had hacked away and created a box—a carved out section for secrets.

Martin Murray came up behind me, muttering something to his colleague as I gingerly reached in and held up a matching notebook to the red one he held, except this one was black, sinister, and dripping with filth.

Someone reached over and pinched it from my fingers, leaving me to stare at a few measly bucks and a chewed-on pencil in the Bible. Placing it back on the shelf, I shook my head clear from memories and re-settled into my current existence.

I expected the same hum of conversation from before. The same beat of footsteps as cops trawled the house. The same knowledge of safety that comes from hustle and bustle when you aren't the main attraction.

Only, I kind of was.

Bob Colton scanned the notebook pages then gave me a strange, almost scared look. Snapping his fingers, he commanded, "The red notebook. Now."

An officer scrambled into the kitchen, darting back with the matching notebook to the black one he held.

The moment Bob had it in his hands, he strode to the sideboard, shoved aside an old candelabra with decades' worth of dripped wax, and spread out both booklets, his finger trailing one line of text before matching it with another.

"Oh, my God." He flicked me another look. "Do you know what this is? How did you know where to look? You've been in this house five minutes and already found more than we did."

Della gave me a worried glance, staying silent beside me.

This was the house she was born in, yet it was as foreign to her as it was familiar to me. I shook my head, swallowing a cough. "I saw her one day. Writing something. She stored cash in the Bible."

"There are two hundred and seventeen names here." Bob's face turned to chalk.

"What do you mean?" Martin brushed up to him, skimming the same text.

I didn't understand why both men suddenly looked at me as if I was some unknown specimen. Some sort of thing that shouldn't be standing before them.

Martin swallowed hard, his face matching Bob's in chalkiness. "You said there were ten or fifteen."

"Ten or fifteen?" I questioned.

"Children. You said there were ten or fifteen children in captivity here."

"Yes. At any one time. I have no idea how many came and went on top of that."

"Holy fuck." Bob Colton clamped a hand over his mouth and spun to look at his team. "Call for help. Cadaver dogs. Diggers. As many hands on deck as you can."

Della asked nervously. "Wh-what's going on?"

Martin's grey eyes landed on hers, wide as full moons. "The two notebooks are a ledger."

My heart sank to my toes. My lungs stabbed with pain. "She kept records?"

He nodded, beckoning me forward to glance at the two spread apart notebooks. "See? The red one has the line number and price. The black one holds the name." His voice became unsteady with fury for all the children the Mclary's had bought and hurt. "Number eight in the red notebook correlates to a girl in the black one called Isabelle May." His uniform creaked as he murmured sickly, "They paid two hundred dollars for her."

Della sucked in a gasp, her eyes dancing over text faster than I could, latching onto names, breathing them like a chant. "Duncan Scott, Ryan Jones, Jade Black, Monica Frost." Her blue eyes glittered with malice for her mother and father as she snatched the notebooks and flicked the pages faster and faster, skimming and skimming until she finally froze, face tight, body stiff, hands shaking. "Ren Shaw."

Icicles replaced my heart as my feet locked to the floor. "What?" My question was barely audible as Della read the number beside my name and tracked it to the number in the red notebook.

Tears spilled down her cheeks as the notebooks fell from her hands, and she threw herself into my arms. "Seven hundred and fifty dollars."

And the farmhouse vanished.

And all that mattered was holding Della as we trembled together.

Because I finally had answers to whom I was.

I was Ren Shaw.

And my mother had sold me for a measly seven hundred and fifty dollars.

* * * * *

I suppose I had something to be thankful for.

For the past six hours, the Mclary farmhouse had become a hive of activity with cops buzzing and machinery humming and dogs sniffing.

I was no longer the suspect of a kidnapping investigation. I was the kid who should never have survived and, instead of side glances whenever I touched Della, I received thumbs-up for taking her away from this morgue.

Because it was a morgue.

In the past few hours, the cops who'd brought reinforcements from every county they could, who'd strung up police tape, and blocked off every way onto the property, had already found four tiny skeletons.

One beneath the veranda just tossed like one would a mouldy potato.

Two in the offal pit, boy bones with sheep bones and pig.

And one behind the house that had at least been partially buried with fingers sprouting through the grass like a new species of weed.

No one noticed us anymore.

No one commanded us to leave or get back.

We were invisible as I led Della out of the farmhouse and toward the fields I'd toiled in for two years.

Funny, how two years had felt like an eternity back then but were nothing in the scheme of a life. Odd, how two years had scarred me so spectacularly, leaving gorge marks in my soul and unfilled holes in my psyche.

We didn't speak as we walked hand in hand, ducking past digging cops, keeping a wide berth of dogs as they galloped from one side of the yard to the other, barking warnings that there were yet more bodies below the earth.

We bypassed two police who studied discarded building materials on the ground. One kicked a partial fallen wall with his foot, making it break into dust. "Shit, that's asbestos." Talking into a crackling walkie-talkie, he said, "Get a contractor here who's qualified in contaminated removal."

Spotting us, he pointed away, indicating to give the crumbling wall a wide berth. "Hazardous substance. Stay back."

We didn't speak, just merely drifted away, letting the farm guide us where it wanted to.

I didn't know where we were going.

I didn't care.

I just had to walk; otherwise, I'd explode with the tumbling, tearing feelings inside me.

I felt guilty.

So fucking guilty that I'd run and not tried to help the others.

I'd been selfish and afraid, and I should've done something.

But I hadn't.

And now, the hundreds of missing children files would be stamped deceased and their families notified. Whether it was parents who'd sold their kids, or an evil uncle or aunt, someone would have missed the lives that the Mclary's had bought, abused, and ultimately snuffed out.

At least, I hoped someone would because it was too sad to think otherwise.

Della's hand twitched hot and tight in mine. We didn't just hold hands; we held ourselves together as we traversed the fields and somehow, some reason, my feet turned toward the barn that had been my bedroom for so long.

Where fleas had made me itch and hessian sacks made scratchy blankets. Where nightmares had tormented me just as surely as life had.

"Ren..." Della said. "I don't think—"

I squeezed her fingers and marched onward, keeping my face blank as a cop to our left shouted with dismay that he'd found another body.

How many did the ground contain? Was this still a farm or a cemetery?

The first touch of shadow from the large creaking barn was a physical scratch on my skin, making me prickle with goosebumps. The soaring ceilings and musty scent of hay cloying with memories.

I *hated* this place.

I hated it as fiercely as I'd hated Mclary.

I wanted to burn it to the goddamn ground, but I swallowed my pyro tendencies and weaved my way through stables, past pallets that had been beds, and into the metal crush where Mclary had drenched his stock.

And there...

Shit.

My jaw clenched, and a wave of bile scalded my throat.

Della cried out, planting herself in front of me and shaking her head. "Don't, Ren. Let's go."

"No." Pushing past her, I walked heavily until I reached the rack with Mclary's tools. The rack where I'd stolen a knife and let some other poor kid take the blame. The rack that most likely held the tool used to cut off my finger. The rack where a long metal brand waited for its next victim.

For once, my hand didn't shake as I pulled the heavy rod with its oval *Mc97* stamp off the wall and hefted its weight.

Today, it was dull, cold metal that could do no damage.

Back then, it had been a molten-glowing weapon that turned me into a possession.

Della crept to my side, resting her head on my arm. "He was a sick fuck, and I'm so sorry."

My lips twisted into a smile. "Language, Della Ribbon."

"Oh, I'm sorry. He was a *fucking* sick fuck, and I'm glad he's dead."

I sighed, shaking my head. "How can you make me smile at a time like this?"

"Same way you make me the luckiest girl alive even when we stand in a place like this." Her voice caught. "To know I came from these people..." A tear ran down her face. "I'm disgusted. I-I'm *appalled.* I feel like I'm going to be sick for what they—"

"Della." Turning to face her, I let the brand clatter to the concrete floor and gathered her in my arms. "Stop."

She clung to me, her fingernails digging into my back. "I'm so sorry, Ren." Her tears soaked into my t-shirt. "So sorry for what they did to you."

"I'm not." I kissed her brow, pushing her away with a quiet cough. "I would live it all over again because it gave me you."

Her face contorted with love and abhorrence and everything in between. "We shouldn't have come here."

"We didn't have a choice." Looking past her to the innocuous barn that had been the stage for so many vile things, I murmured, "I don't regret running that night, but I do regret not coming back and trying to help. For not going to the authorities and telling them what I escaped from. For not doing *something.* If I can do something now...even if it's too late, then I have to try."

Her slender frame wedged against mine again, gripping with a fury that made my heart leap with love and gratitude. "You saved two lives that night, Ren. Two lives that wouldn't have made it if you hadn't taken that chance."

"Is it enough? Is it enough to be grateful that we have each other when so many kids died here?"

"It has to be." She pressed a kiss to my chest, snuggling into the borrowed coat I wore. "I love you, Ren Wil—" Her head came up, forehead furrowed. "Shaw. Your real last name is Shaw."

I shook my head and kissed her nose. "No. It's not."

"Who are you then?"

"I'm Ren Wild, protector of Della Wild.

"A boy who survived."

* * * * *

Night had fallen by the time the mayhem slowed down.

A building crew had arrived to remove the asbestos, a trailer was parked up to catalogue the corpses they'd found, and the farm crawled with trespassers.

Officers set up spotlights for the evening crew, while fellow workers handed out takeaway cups of coffee and store-bought sandwiches.

I was hungry, tired, and ready to leave this place.

My bones ached and my lungs throbbed. I couldn't get rid of the pressure inside me, the ever constant rattle these days.

I wanted nothing more than to sneak away in the dark and vanish with Della.

But I didn't know if we were allowed.

Was I still under arrest?

Was I free to go or bound to stay?

Another eleven bodies had been found throughout the farm, all in various states of decay and mutilation.

Della had refused to eat an offered muffin, and my stomach was a snarling mess of snakes.

When dusk crept over the overcast day, we'd sat on the steps of the veranda watching, always watching, as tarps covered freshly dug up bones and dogs panted with a job well done on their leashes.

Della stayed close, sharing body heat as the air chilled both of us. I opened my coat wide, welcoming her against me.

"Mr. Shaw?"

My eyes tracked a young detective as she stomped past in muddy boots with a clipboard.

"Mr. Shaw?"

I glanced at the beagle slurping up water in a stainless-steel dish that its handler had put down for him.

"Mr. Shaw?" Someone tapped my shoulder, wrenching my head to look behind me. Martin Murray bent over me, his eyebrow raised.

"You want something?" I asked, my voice gravel and soot from lack of rest.

"Yes. We found something you might want to see."

Standing on creaking legs, I helped Della up and shrugged out of my coat, so she could keep its warmth. I coughed as my heat dispersed.

She tried to refuse, but I merely bundled her tighter, did up the button, and kissed her forehead. Turning my attention to Martin, I ran a hand over my face, trying to wake myself up.

"Miss Mclary? Mr. Shaw?" A female officer with long black hair in a plait appeared from the house. "Can you come with us, please?"

Della padded toward her, but I stopped short. "That is not my name nor Della's. We're Wild. Use it."

Martin scowled. "But it is. You finally know your real name."

"It ceased to be my real name the day I was sold."

He studied me, finally nodding. "You know, all records and proceedings going forward are going to be under the name Ren Shaw and Della Mclary. You have to get used to it."

"What proceedings?"

He looked away, embarrassed. "Well, I still don't know what will happen with the kidnapping charge. Whether it will become a state crime now Willem and Marion Mclary are dead, or…or if it can just be ignored."

"When will you know?" I asked, following him and the female officer into the gloomy house with its feeble lighting in cobwebbed shades.

"Once this mess has been sorted out."

"They're dead children, Mr. Murray, not a mess," Della said sternly. "And if you bring a case against Ren, I'll contest it. I'm the only living Mclary left. And I say I wasn't kidnapped."

Martin squeezed the back of his neck, indicating his stress levels were as strained as ours. "Another topic for another day. For now, let's focus on what we found."

Together, we moved deeper into the house toward the narrow staircase leading upstairs.

The steps groaned and cracked as we trailed single file up and up, then followed obediently down the dingy corridor. I'd never been upstairs, and I guessed one of these rooms had been Della's nursery once upon a time. Now, they were just store rooms with junk and miscellaneous boxes with a master at the end with a stripped mattress and stained carpet.

The sweet smell of decay hinted that this was where Marion Mclary had decided to do the deed.

"We found this," the female detective said, marching to her colleague who was taking photos of a hidden panel in the wardrobe. "A cubby full of documents."

"What sort of documents?" Della asked as we moved deeper into the room, peering at the scattered paperwork all over the bed and yet more coming from the secret hole in the wall.

"Birth certificates."

I inhaled sharply, stalking toward the bed and fisting a few stained pages. Some were hand scribbled, and others were computer printed. Some girls. Some boys. Too many to count.

"They asked whoever sold their child to give them their birth certificate too?" Della stood next to me wrinkling her nose in disgust. "That's not just sick. That's…diabolical. It's as if they fully believed they were buying an animal and had the bill of sale to prove it."

Martin Murray nodded. "I agree. A case like this can't explain the rationale of the people who committed the crimes."

"How many?" I snapped, doing my best to rein in my hope that mine existed in the pile.

The female officer said, "We've counted. There's one hundred and sixty-seven. Compared to the two hundred and seventeen names, I'm guessing some kids were born and never registered, some didn't have their birth certificates, and a few were sold with the child, if what you say is true, Mr. Shaw, and they were moved on once they could no longer do the work required."

"Have you found mine?" I asked quietly, wishing I didn't have hope bubbling in my chest because I already tasted bitter disappointment.

But to finally have that piece of paper? To finally be free to marry Della? It would be a gift after such a grotesque day.

"No, I'm afraid not." The female officer scanned the pages in front of us. "I mean, there's always a chance we'll find more, but not at this stage. However—" She turned to a colleague and collected a page protected by cloudy cellophane. "We did find this one."

Della was the one to take it. Only right, seeing as it had her name on it.

In shaky calligraphy, her name, Della Donna Mclary, stated she was born on 27th of June to Willem and Marion Mclary.

She gave me a weak smile. "I'm going to scribble that out and make it Wild instead."

I chuckled softly. "Or I could just marry you and make it legally Wild."

Her face fell. "If you can somehow make Wild legally yours, first."

"I'm working on it."

She smiled sadly. "Work on making your birthday the same as mine, too. Can't break a lifelong tradition now, can we?"

I ran a finger over her birth certificate, stopping on the date. "I don't care when I was born. I'm sharing yours forever."

Martin looked away as I glanced at him, he'd been listening but pretended to give us privacy and another moment or two to study her birth certificate before holding up yet another document.

This one was dog-eared and had been written on something soft, so the pen had almost pressed through the page, leaving embossed letters and not just ink. "This was in the secret cubby, too." Passing it to me, he nodded for me to take it.

I did, gingerly.

I didn't want to touch what they'd touched. I didn't want to read what they'd written, but as my eyes fell to the top line, and I understood what it was, I passed it to Della.

I couldn't have it against my skin.

And besides, something this important should be read correctly with no pauses or stumbles. Something this important should be burned and never read at all.

Della flinched as she took it from my hands. "A suicide note."

"Yes." Martin Murray nodded. "One that explains a little but not a lot. But one that I feel will mean more to you than to us."

With that cryptic comment, he left us to talk to the team by the wardrobe, and Della and I drifted to the window where torches and spotlights shone through the darkness, illuminating skeletons of those who weren't as lucky as us.

I coughed and swallowed, my hands balling. "Should we read it?"

Della skimmed it. "I don't know."

We stood there for a moment, soaking in the ramifications. Finally, I stood taller. "Read it."

"You sure?"

"I'm sure." Crossing my arms, I waited.

Slowly, she smoothed the page and began.

"To whomever finds this.

"My name is Marion Mclary and I have ten minutes left to live. When my husband returns from the fields, I'm going to take the shotgun and shoot him in his heartless chest and then, I'm going to put myself out of my misery."

Della glanced up, her face whitening before her eyes locked back on the page.

"The kids are gone. Half of them sold at rock bottom price to Kyle Harold

and half poisoned by the creek. At least none of them will escape and tell the world what we've done.

Then again, I don't care what happens after I've gone. I don't care that everything will come to light, and the church will turn on us, and our friends will know the truth.

I don't care because I stopped caring the day I married into this evil and went along with my husband's plans.

I'm not entirely to blame. After all, I did become the buyer and seller of our little worker bees. As far as I was concerned, we needed labour and labour ain't cheap...unless you buy it young.

I could've continued with what we were doing. This isn't the kind of letter where I confess to my crimes and beg for forgiveness.

There is nothing to forgive. We lived our life the way we wanted.

I don't care Willem raped those little girls. I don't care he mutilated those little boys. Everyone needs discipline in their lives. Even if those lives were short.

I know I have a one-way ticket to the devil, and I'm not gonna fill this page with lies.

But I am going to admit a secret that Willem never knew. The secret that's the reason why I'm pulling the trigger.

Della Donna Mclary.

My baby girl.

She wasn't supposed to be born. I tried to kill her. I tried to starve her out. But the church says thou shall not abort, so I let her come into our dark world.

And for a time, I didn't feel any different.

I didn't see her in the girls screaming as Willem molested them. I didn't see her in the kids starving in the barn.

She wasn't like them.

But then one day, I did see her like them. I saw her eyes flicker as Willem booted that boy from the kitchen. I saw her scream when Willem shot the kid for letting the sheep out.

And I knew she'd either end up in her father's bed, or worse, become like us.

Just because I'm not apologising for what we did, doesn't mean I didn't know it was against the Lord's teachings.

And for once, I wanted to do right by God rather than just sing pretty hymns in church.

I was going to do the world a favour.

I was going to kill her before she became me.

For weeks, I tried to do it.

Holding her under in the bath until she blew bubbles.

Clamping my hand over her nose and mouth until she kicked.

I could inspect a child from some white trash family and offer money for their offspring, yet I couldn't kill my own daughter.

Then I saw that skinny runt of a boy think about escaping. He snuck into the *house one night, scurrying like a rat in the dark, stealing food and placing them in Willem's backpack by the door.*

Normally, I would've told Willem to shoot him. To kill him dead before the sun rose.

But…he was my chance.

My one chance at killing my daughter without having her blood on my hands. So…I let him believe he wasn't noticed.

I held my tongue when he looked at my Della, and I watched that scrawny toad make his move.

When he slipped from the locked barn the next night—revealing a security issue—I knew it was time and grabbed my sleeping daughter and stuffed her in the backpack where his rations were ready to escape.

She was a good girl. She didn't wake up as I zipped her in and hid her in the darkness.

That little rat poked his head into my house, sniffed around, then slung on the backpack with surprise in his eyes from the extra weight.

He looked as if he'd take it off again and check his supplies.

I couldn't have that.

So, I yelled for my sleeping husband. I told him we had a runaway and to get the shotgun.

And then, we had some sport as that little boy took off in the corn, bounding like the rat he was, carrying my daughter with him.

I hoped a bullet would take them both out.

I hoped two mistakes could be fixed with one.

But Willem missed.

And to this day, I don't know if the boy and my baby are dead.

I like to think they are because she was born to evil, and he was sold to the devil. Nothing good can come of them surviving.

But now, my secret is on paper, and I'm ready to kill my husband. I blame him for not knowing if she's dead or not. I blame him for this life of dirt and destitution. I blame him for everything, and I've had enough.

I've had enough of the raping, killing, and struggling. We have labour, yet the farm doesn't grow food anymore. We have stock, but they get sick and die.

Consider this my intent to cancel the missing person's report that Willem filed. Turned out, that man rather loved his daughter. He loved her enough to want her in all the wrong ways. I knew. I saw it before he could touch her.

At least I saved her from that fate.

I am Marion Mclary, and I don't apologise for what me and my husband are.

I only apologise for letting my spawn run away and not knowing if she'll grow up to be like us.

She deserves to die.

Just like that boy who took her."

Chapter Forty-Eight

REN

2020

A WEEK PASSED where we returned to Cherry River, kept our heads down, and tried to move on. I wasn't arrested with the strict provision I stayed in town and didn't travel.

John hired a lawyer on my behalf—just in case the state decided to go ahead with prosecuting me for Della's disappearance, and I did my best to repay him by preparing the fields for a good rest over winter for a bumper crop come summer.

John and Cassie asked questions that first afternoon, but Della and I didn't know how to answer them.

Our minds were still messed up from what we'd seen. Images of dirt-smeared bones, time-tattered clothing, and the bay of cadaver dogs replayed on a loop inside my head.

What happened back at Mclary's had affected both of us.

Della more so than me.

She'd learned she hadn't, by some miracle, chosen to belong to me by crawling into the backpack, after all. She'd been placed there by her homicidal mother.

I finally had answers to my how and why of how I ended up with a baby.

And she'd learned she'd been unwanted in a sea of mistakes and, despite her rage when we were at the farm watching police exhume such horror, a heavy shame and thick depression cloaked her.

She withdrew into herself, and there was nothing I could do about it.

The day we travelled the eight hours back to Cherry River, we barely talked. The day after, she didn't want to discuss it. The day after that, she snapped at Cassie to leave it alone.

For a week, I let her stew and put up with her half-hearted smiles and weak assurances.

But she couldn't hide from me because I understood more than she knew.

I understood she was searching.

Searching deep inside herself for a hint that she might be what her mother said.

A devil.

A monster.

Just like them.

And how could she not after seeing what they'd done?

But I also knew she'd find no trace of evilness because she was as pure and as perfect as they were vile and villainous.

On the eighth day of her despondency, I packed up the tent and sleeping bags and told John we'd be back in a night or two. Cassie was staying in town with Chip and her daughter, and Della fought me a little on leaving John on his own, but we needed to reconnect, and I needed to remind her of something.

As we walked, just the two of us, over the fields toward the treeline we knew so well, I clutched her hand hard. The fake sapphire I'd bought her had gone smoky with age and chipped from wear, but she still wore it religiously, just like I wore my leather band with its metal letters with a single diamante remaining.

As we walked, I struggled not to cough.

I was fully aware how Della flinched whenever I did. It was an annoying sound, I agreed, but that was all it was—an annoyance.

I felt okay in myself. Nothing stopped me from living a life of physical activity and labour.

Her worry was a tad frustrating, but I could understand, just as I could understand her quietness now. They were circumstances outside her control, yet they affected her wholeheartedly.

Hopefully, I'd be able to reassure her on both accounts.

Once in the forest and far enough away from the farm, I pitched the tent, gathered her close, and made love to her like old times beneath the glittering stars.

At first, she resisted, claiming a headache. Then she lied and said she wasn't interested.

Her refusal didn't annoy me because yet again, I understood. "Della…"

She refused to meet my eyes, staring into the fire I'd built and coaxed into a warm blaze.

"Nothing has changed, Little Ribbon."

Tears she'd bottled up cascaded down her cheeks as I went to her and cuddled her close. "Let me help…please?" Kissing her, I guided her onto the sleeping bag I'd spread on the ground, slowly undressing her, not making any sudden movements in case she ran.

My voice didn't speak, but my body did.

It assured her that she was still who she believed and I was still who she knew. It convinced her, slowly, gently, that what we had outweighed any pain or terror from the past.

Hesitantly, she responded to my kisses, purred into my touch, and when she spread her legs and I slipped inside her, her gasp was full of sorrow.

We moved together, hands always touching, lips always kissing, our bodies thrusting in affirmation of life and love.

The cool air didn't stop us. The owl hoots didn't scare us. I didn't care it was late in the season and snow seasoned the air. I didn't care we shivered as we moved together, chasing an orgasm that wasn't just about pleasure, but a declaration that we might have been touched by evil, but it hadn't claimed us.

We'd chosen our own path, and we always would.

Afterward, with my body still in Della's, I smoothed back her hair and cupped her cheeks. Lying over her with her trapped beneath me, I murmured, "You have never been, nor will you ever be like them, Della Ribbon."

She flinched, the fire dancing in her eyes with golden spirals. For a second, a flash of ire said she wouldn't talk to me. Then torment drenched her voice. "But how do you know? How do you know I won't snap one day and—"

"I know because I raised you."

"What if that filth can't be changed? What if I'm lying to you and myself? What if I'm not a good person and could kill—"

"You *are* a good person."

"But how do you *know*? Truly know?" Her gaze searched mine, desperate for an answer. "I'm so afraid I have no control. That I am what they made—not what you guided. That I have no choice."

"You *do* have a choice. We all have a choice."

"But genetics—"

"Have nothing to do with it." I stared deep into her, needing her to believe me. "I know you are good and sweet and kind because I *know* you. I've known you your entire life."

She squirmed beneath me. "That's not an answer."

"It is. It's the best one. I've seen you grow, Della. I've seen you uncensored and undisciplined and uncivilised. I've seen you in every mood there is, and not once did you hurt anyone or anything. You weren't malicious. You weren't cruel. You were—"

"I was, though, don't you see? I was cruel to you."

I chuckled, hiding yet another cough. "You were never cruel to me."

"But—"

"No buts." Running a thumb over her pink lips, I whispered, "They had you for a year, Della. I've had you for almost twenty. Whatever they taught you or said to you is drowned out by the endless conversations and love we've shared."

She frowned, running her tongue over my thumb. "Did you ever look at me like she did? Did you ever think I could be like them?"

"Never."

"Not even when you didn't want me?"

"Not even then." Kissing her softly, I added, "And not wanting you lasted for a heartbeat before I became yours."

"I'm sorry, Ren."

"Nothing to apologise for."

"I know...but I need to. Seeing that place. Seeing those bodies. Seeing how *real* it all was."

I pushed those memories aside, just as I always shoved memories of that farmhouse away. "I accept your apology if it makes you feel better, but only if you accept mine."

She frowned. "Why are *you* apologising?"

"Because I always blamed you for making my running all that much harder. I cursed you for being in my bag when all along, I should've been thanking you." Pressing my forehead to hers, I hardened inside her, comforted by her body heat and already desperate for more. "Without you, I would've been shot before I ever crept back into the house to collect my supplies. My escape was all down to you being in that bag. You are the reason I'm alive, Della. Not the other way around."

Her eyes softened, and the shadows that had lurked inside her dissolved. "Kiss me, Ren Shaw. I'm sick of apologies."

I raised an eyebrow, my lips thinning in reproof. "Ask me again with the correct name."

She smiled. "Kiss me, Ren Wild. Make love to me. Promise me you'll never let me go."

So I did.

And I promised.

And I never let go.

* * * * *

Another week passed, slipping us back into routine.

Della spent more time with Cassie discussing horses and Cassie's future dream of one day opening an equine business, and I returned to my odd jobs around the farm.

The air was cooler now, making the frustrating ache in my chest three times worse.

Some days, I barely noticed it.

But then some days, like today, I felt as if lunch lodged in my throat and wouldn't swallow. I willingly coughed, trying to eradicate the obstruction, forcing deeper coughs and longer barks, begging for a reprieve from the pressure.

It was there, while I hung onto a stable door, bent over trying to clear the weight in my lungs, that John found me.

I thought I was on my own.

I refused to cough so badly in people's presence because I knew how annoying the noise could be.

But as John stomped toward me in his dirty overalls and a rusty tool kit to lend a hand, I'd destroyed any hope of stopping, thanks to willingly encouraging a coughing fit.

His eyes tightened as I held up my hand, swallowing back wracking heaves, clamping my other hand over my mouth and doing my best to stop.

"Ren?" John placed his tool kit on the cobblestones, coming to put a hand on my back as I rode out the final waves of affliction. "Take it easy." His gaze travelled to the hose in the corner, his body swaying in its direction. "Want some water? Choking on something?"

I shook my head, smothering yet another cough and standing up with a gasp. "I'm—" A couple more coughs caught me unaware, lashing my chest with pain. Finally, when I could breathe again, I said, "I'm fine." Smiling with watery eyes, I inhaled deep, fighting the tickle to cough again. "Just hay dust."

Turning, I reached for the nails that I'd been using to fix a loose hinge only for John to fist my wrist.

"What is that?" His fingers latched tight, cutting off my arteries.

"Don't touch me." I tugged, feeling a residual thread of panic from being held against my will. No matter how many years passed, I doubted I'd fully have control over my attacks.

"Goddammit, Ren. What the *hell* is this?" He held up my palm, shoving it under my nose.

Red.

Liquid.

Blood.

My blood.

Fuck.

I froze, running my tongue over my lip and tasting the nasty flavour of copper. My eyes met his, and I broke beneath the love there. The love he had for me. And the worry. Shit, the worry.

"It's okay, John." I yanked my hand free, wiping the blood on my jeans. "Don't—"

Fisting his keys from his overalls pocket, he grabbed my bicep, once again layering me with a fissure of fear. "We're leaving. Right now."

"Leaving? To go where?" He pulled me from the stable.

So many parts of me wanted to shove him to the ground for manhandling me, but I understood his violence came from panic just like my panic came from violence.

"Doctor." His eyes welled with fury and impatience. "You've been coughing ever since you got back home. I'm not putting up with it anymore."

"But what about Della?" I twisted my arm free, raising my eyebrow when he tried to hold on to me. "Let go, John. I won't ask again." My gritted teeth and feral tone hinted I wasn't coping.

He dropped his hand but didn't stop his fast pace to the barn doors. "She's with Cassie. They popped into town to see Chip at work. We have time."

"I-I can't make her worry."

He stopped, turning to face me. "And you can't make me worry, Ren. I'm not losing you like I lost Patricia. I love you like a son, but if you don't see a doctor, I will kick you out of my house, so help me God."

I smirked. "Winter is close. You wouldn't dare."

He didn't smile back. "Try me. Now get your ass in the truck."

* * * * *

It was as if my lungs knew they had an audience because I hadn't been able to ignore the tickle and wheeze since John drove me above normal speed limits to his local practitioner.

There was no discussion over identifications or money.

No discussions period as his regular doctor called his name ten minutes after we arrived, and we were ushered into a small white office with posters of body parts and skeletons on the wall.

To start with, I resented John for dragging me down here.

I worried if Della was safe and what time she'd be home.

What would she do if she found scattered tools and no workmen to use them?

What the hell would I tell her about John's kidnapping and the blood stain on my jeans?

But then those questions switched to others that made my heart pound a little bit harder.

What if I'm in trouble?

What if...it's serious?

"How long have you been coughing, Ren?" The elderly doctor with jowls from losing weight clicked his pen, waiting for me to reply.

"Two and a bit years, give or take."

"And this is the first time you've coughed up blood?"

"Yes." I rubbed at the red stain on my clothes, then placed my hand over it as if I could stop it from being real. I didn't want to reveal my ever-growing fear, but I couldn't stop my question. "Is that bad?"

"Well..." The doctor stroked his jaw. "Sometimes, yes. Sometimes, no. If you were coughing a lot, you could've just irritated the lining of your throat and burst a few blood vessels. However, if the blood came from your lungs, it's a different matter."

"Oh." My heart skipped a beat.

"First, before we go down scary roads like that, let's just see how your health is in general, okay?" He narrowed his eyes. "Do you exercise? Eat well?"

"I'm active and try my best."

"Okay, have you ever been on medications or dealt with long-term illnesses?"

"No." I massaged the back of my neck. "Never."

"Any heart palpitations? Lack of appetite? Abdominal pain? Chest pain? Shortness of breath?"

Shit, I'd had all of those on and off over the past few years.

I glanced at John who sat beside me.

Just like there hadn't been any discussion about money or I.Ds, there'd been no discussion if he would accompany me into the appointment.

"Go on, Ren. Answer the man." He scowled, angry with me but also afraid. I understood his fear came from Patricia dying—that he'd leap onto anyone ill because he'd lost someone. But just because I understood didn't mean I liked being smothered or being told what to do.

The doctor probed me again. "How old are you?"

"Thirty-ish."

"You don't know your date of birth?"

"No."

"So you don't know your family history and if lung issues are common?"

"No." I crossed my arms. "Can't you just give me some antibiotics and clear it up? I probably should've had some a couple of years ago when I got the flu. It turned into a chest infection."

His eyes narrowed as if I'd given him a clue. "Do you often get chest infections?"

"He had pneumonia when he was a lad. Fifteen, I think," John said gruffly. "Occasionally, he'd get a cold, and they'd stick on his chest for a while, but he was healthy apart from that."

I threw him a look. "Didn't know you were keeping such close tabs on me."

He smiled sternly. "I notice when all my kids are ill."

I swallowed hard. I knew John loved me like his other sons. Hell, he'd often called me son and treated me no differently.

But to have his concern overflow, to have him bristle beside me and force me into this all because he was worried, made me feel warm and cared for—despite my temper.

Tapping his pen against his lips, the doctor re-read his notes, the wrinkles on his forehead growing deeper. His blue eyes met mine with an intensity I didn't like. "Have you ever been around asbestos?"

"The building stuff?"

"Correct. Sometimes it's blue, brown, green…white."

"Not that I recall." I snapped my fingers. "No, wait, that's not true. The police said there was asbestos at the farm I visited last week."

"Did you inhale any of it?"

I shook my head. "No, we weren't close enough."

John went dangerously still. "He lived there. When he was a boy."

"Ah." The doctor nodded, his face falling. "How long did you live there?"

My insides went cold and still. "Two years."

"How long ago?"

I bit my lip, begging my brain to do simple math. "Um, twenty years ago, I guess."

His pen scratched on paper, wrenching hope from my achy chest. For a moment, he didn't say anything, studying me as if he had X-ray vision and could see my lungs and the secrets they hid.

Finally, he glanced at John before asking me, "And in that time, did you play with any building supplies or have contact with such things?"

I laughed before I could stop myself. *Play?* There was no play. I'd been beaten with a piece of lumber, had wall debris smashed over my head, and a hot brand driven into my skin.

If that was play, I didn't want to know what abuse was.

The doctor, whose name hadn't been provided, pursed his lips. "Something funny?"

Swallowing a twisted chuckle, I said, "Sorry. No. I didn't play, but I did use the tractor to break apart an old shed that Mcla—the farmer didn't want. I buried it."

"And have you done any other work around suspect buildings?"

I went to shake my head, only a horrible thought appeared. "I did. In 2015 when I got a job as a menial labourer. I was paid cash to dismantle unwanted structures at night. It seemed…shady, and no one else wanted to do it."

Fuck.

I'd been so happy to take the extra cash.

I didn't have a clue back then about contaminations or that man-made materials could be so deadly.

My ignorance had given me extra pocket money, but at what price?

John put his head in his hands, elbows wedged on his knees.

I wanted to pat his back and assure him that whatever conclusions his doctor was cooking were wrong. I wanted to say I'd worn masks and gloves and knew what the hell I was dealing with.

But the lies solidified on my tongue and terror turned into stones inside me.

No one spoke.

All of us dealing with ramifications, deep in separate thought. Shakes infected me the more I fell into the pit of despair.

"Right then." The doctor shattered the taut silence, scribbling more notes. Spinning in his chair, he faced the computer and started typing with two fingers. "There are numerous explanations for your symptoms, so we're not going to worry just yet. You're young and fit, which is always a good thing." He threw me a look, stabbing his fingers on the keys. The process was laborious and not at all smooth like Della's typing.

"However, I've dealt with a lot of claimants over the years and learned that jumping to conclusions can sometimes be a good thing." His eyes burned into me. "Sometimes, they can save a life."

Hitting enter, a printer whirred into action.

Grabbing the document, he signed it then passed it to me. "You need to go to the hospital. I've referred you for blood tests, X-rays, and possibly a CT scan."

"What? Why?" The stones inside me manifested into rocks, weighing me down, pushing a painful cough from my lips.

"I'm not wasting time testing for bacterial infections or immune deficiencies. I've dealt with too many cases not to see the warning signs. Once I know the answer to this question, then we'll look at other possibilities."

"The answer to what question?" John asked, his voice tight, face harrowed.

"The warning signs of what?" I blurted at the same time.

Giving us both a grave look, the doctor answered us in one go, announcing the nature of my death. "Mesothelioma."

Chapter Forty-Nine

DELLA

2031

HE NEVER TOLD *me.*

After decades together, unbreakable trust, and a never ending connection, he didn't tell me.

He

didn't

tell

me.

Just writing those words breaks my heart into smithereens.

It breaks me in so many ways. It makes me sob, rage, beg, curse, and scream.

For so long now, I've shown you how pedantically Ren protected me all my life. Revealed how he would do anything for me, in any circumstance, time, or place.

I've painted his picture over and over, showing you exactly what sort of man he was, and how his greatest quality was also his biggest flaw.

He was selfless and careful and kind.

And in this...he was no different.

He decided to carry the burden alone.

I hated him for that.

I cursed him every day for lying.

I never knew what he went through that night.

How John drove him straight to the hospital, signed with his insurance, and sat with Ren for hours, waiting for the tests.

All I knew at the time was Cassie received a phone call as we were on our way back from spending the afternoon with Chip and Nina, saying they'd gone into town for a beer and dinner.

It was a tad unusual, but John had treated Ren to a meal out—just the two of them— before, so I wasn't overly concerned.

I wasn't concerned when Ren came home later than normal and tossed his jeans into the wash straight away.

I wasn't concerned when he ran more 'errands' with John a few days later, leaving Cassie and me sketching out stables and arena concepts for her horse business.

I wasn't even concerned when the phone rang for Ren and he took it alone in the farmhouse, returning a little while later subdued and quiet but still willing to kiss and laugh when I poked him to liveliness.

All that time.

All those minutes and hours and days.

I didn't know.

How

did

I

not

know?

How did I not see?

I loved him past sanity.

I loved him more than anything else in the world, so…how?

Chapter Fifty

REN

2021

I WAS SICK.

Sick of lying.

Of hiding.

Of holding Della late at night, listening to her soft breathing, all while fighting the terror that'd set up home inside me.

The lies I'd told the past few months.

Fuck.

The lies I'd told over and over again.

I wished I could take them all back.

I wished I could kill my mother for ever selling me to a place that had tried to kill me when I was young and didn't succeed until I was older.

I'd run with Della, so full of hope and boldness for life. I'd protected her by any means necessary. I'd sacrificed everything for her. I'd given her my heart and soul.

Yet…I couldn't protect her from this.

I'd believed I was just like any ten-year-old kid the day I'd escaped from hell.

I'd fallen in love and grown up and planned a future with the woman I wanted.

And the entire time we'd plotted course and travelled through time, I'd been a dead man walking.

I might have run from Mclary's. I might still live and breathe and exist, but I'd died there.

I was a ghost.

Della had fallen in love with someone who was already dead….He just didn't know it yet.

God, the pain.

The torment.

The undying *yearn* to somehow reverse the clock and forbid such tragedy from happening.

I thought I was prepared to die. I believed I would accept when my time came because I would've had an entire lifetime with Della by my side.

I wanted kids with her.

I wanted the privilege of growing old with her.

I wanted to marry her.

Now…that lifetime was no longer an option.

No one knew how long I had.

Statistics had been thrown around until I had to stop listening. I refused to let depression latch onto one answer while hope clung to another.

How fucking twisted that I got my wish?

I would die before her.

It was a guarantee now, not merely a possibility.

And I would die so much earlier than I wanted.

That was the worst part.

Lying in bed, warm and cocooned in the dark—that was when the aching, quaking grief found me. Tears would leak from my eyes as I squeezed them shut against the agony of what existed in our future.

I'd clutch a sleeping girl close, stifling my urge to cough, hating the curse in my lungs.

The tests had come back positive.

Stage one mesothelioma.

John had been there when I'd heard the news. When the phone fell from my hand and the doctor on the other end asked us to come see him for further information. When I'd heard words such as latency period, chemotherapy, radiation, and surgery, I'd shut down.

I couldn't help it.

I turned blank inside to prevent pure, undiluted rage from consuming me.

Rage at life.

Rage at injustice.

Rage at unfairness.

Rage at love itself.

Life, it seemed, had decided I'd loved too deeply and for long enough. I'd had Della for longer than most couples, and we were still so young.

But I was greedy.

I didn't want to die.

I wanted more and more and *more*.

I wanted everything I would never have and it fucking tore me up inside that I couldn't.

So, when doctors hemmed and hawed about my prognosis, I said nothing.

John cried.

I didn't.

When treatment plans were discussed, John demanded all of it, any of it, immediately.

And I'd stared into silence and wondered.

How?

How would I ever tell Della?

How would I ever break her heart the way my own heart was breaking?

How could I protect her from all of this while ensuring she would be safe once I'd gone?

Being given that diagnosis was the start of a war between John and me.

He wanted to pay for surgery straight away.

I wouldn't accept charity.

He wanted to hook me up to drips and lock me in the hospital.

I needed to be outside.

Both of us wanted a solution, but I refused to accept the money he had from Patricia's life insurance, and I had no intention of letting Della see me frail and weak post-surgery.

John was willing to condemn me to a life of sickness if it meant extending that life by a few years.

But I had no intention of being bedridden.

I was incurable.

We both heard that truth.

And now, it was the hardest decision of my life to gamble on what option would give me most of what I wanted.

Rushing into it wasn't going to happen.

I needed to think.

To plan.

To strategize.

For a month, we argued while I researched, and he rang every hospital in the country. Not having any money or insurance, my choices were slim.

But then, John's doctor referred me to an oncologist who dealt with mesothelioma and agreed to see me for free, considering I was one of the younger patients to show symptoms, and I wasn't on death's door just yet.

I had time.

I had the potential to be studied.

I lied to Della once again, claiming I was inspecting a guy's farm for new fence lines, and headed to the appointment on my own.

I didn't want John there. I needed to do this alone. I wanted the luxury of showing my fear to a doctor rather than acting brave around a friend.

And that was how I found out two things that didn't save my life but definitely gave me hope.

There were off-label trials for men like me. Two drugs that had shown success in later stages but had yet to have conclusive evidence in stage one.

Keytruda—an immunotherapy that was administered by intravenous injection for thirty minutes every three weeks, and a listeria-based vaccine called CRS-207 that had shown promise.

One was a passive immunotherapy and one was an active, meaning my already pre-loaded immune system that had adapted and grown with me would have help in fighting the cells that were slowly killing me and be taught to recognise those cells.

I liked the sound of that.

I enjoyed the thought of my body becoming its own weapon instead of its own enemy.

I nodded along as the doctor advised there were still side effects, but not nearly as many as chemo, and accepted the fine print. And besides, the side effects were almost identical to the symptoms I already had—coughing, breathlessness, and lack of appetite—that I didn't care anyway.

Every three weeks was doable, and I could lie to Della about an hour trip away from home—either to the lumber mill for barn supplies or some other made-up excuse.

The oncologist suggested I think about it, but I knew I wanted to fight and fight hard, so I signed hundreds of waivers, put my life in his hands, and started the first round of treatment three days later.

I'd never been good with sharp things.

And needles?

Fuck, it was a nightmare.

Sitting in a low-ceilinged ward with dying people while chemicals flowed through my veins made claustrophobia press on me until my breathing turned shallow and my coughing became worse.

By the time it was over, I already dreaded the next appointment—glad I had twenty-one days to grow some balls to face it.

But at least I'd done something to give myself a chance. I hadn't just curled up and accepted the inevitable like John believed I had. I wasn't being a martyr by refusing to worry Della with this shit. This was my problem, and I would fix it.

Hopefully.

When I went home that night, I felt a little nauseous but overall fine, and I took Della to a diner, making sure I joked and acted perfectly normal.

Her eyes were sharper and attention closer, suspecting things but not sure what. But by the end of the meal, after seducing her with rich food and making her drunk with kisses, she slipped back into our trust and her wariness floated away.

That night, I made love to her with a passion bordering painful.

I refused to turn on the light, hoping she could feel me bruise her, love her, consume her, and always remember me as strong and *alive.*

Turned out, life was a slippery thing, but I grasped onto it with all my strength.

There was no way I was dying.

Not yet, at least.

I couldn't—not until I had my ring on Della's finger and her last name forever stitched to mine. And that was how a wet day in spring brought at least some answers to my prayers, along with a threat to my time-restrained freedom.

Martin Murray knocked off slushy snow from his boots and strode into the kitchen with a red nose from icy breezes. John had invited him onto his property with the taut wariness of a soldier being drafted for battle.

Ever since I'd been told what lived inside me, John had been overly protective of me.

Della sometimes raised an eyebrow at the way he layered my plate with vegetables and filled my palm with vitamins. He'd overstepped a few times, but I didn't have the heart to tell the old man to back off.

He'd done so much for me.

The lawyer he'd arranged—in case I was still prosecuted for Della's kidnapping—had now been given other duties, including drawing up my Will and Testament—leaving everything I had to Della, even though I had nothing of value—and arranging my funeral so it wasn't yet another burden when I was gone.

Rain turned to snowflakes as we all sat at the well-used dining table in a fire-warmed house and prepared to find out what happened with the Mclary case.

Nerves danced down my spine. Worry that I might be thrown in jail filled my broken lungs, granting a rattling cough. What if the investigation had finished, and I'd still been found at fault?

Della sensed my tension, running a gentle hand over my lower back.

Never again would I take her touch for granted.

Never again would I be annoyed at her or be short-tempered or argue.

It was a struggle not to count each time she touched me, keeping tally of how many I could earn before I wasn't there to earn more.

Shaking my head, I banished those thoughts as Martin cupped his hands around a cup of steaming coffee and looked at John as he lowered his big bulk into the chair at the head of the table.

"Thank you for seeing me." Martin cleared his throat, his eyes catching mine, then Della's.

Long ago, Della and I had sat here and been interrogated in a different way. I'd been coughing with pneumonia, and a five-year-old Della had tried to fight my battles. That had ended in a happy conclusion.

Would this?

"Why are you here?" I asked, not impolitely but with a reminder that the sooner this was over with, the better.

"I have news." Martin reached to the briefcase by his chair leg and pulled out a file. "Here." Skidding it across to us, he waited until I'd opened it and pulled out a page. It looked like gibberish full of police terminology, dates, reference numbers, and findings.

"What is it?" I looked up, stifling a cough.

"It's a summary of the report finalising the case of Mclary versus Mclary."

"And am I still in trouble?"

The thought of dying in prison?

Of living my last ticking time without Della?

Fuck, it was more than I could bear.

Della stiffened beside me, ready to leap up and strangle the detective, just like I was ready to commit murder to ensure I stayed out of jail.

Screw treatment and houses and towns, I'd take her back to the forest and live for however long I could, happy and content, just her and me.

"You can't blame him," Della snapped. "He didn't do anything—"

"Ribbon." I placed a rough hand over her soft one, keeping her steady. "Quiet."

She flashed me a look, her gaze lingering on my mouth.

I had an insane urge to kiss her, to kiss her as much as I possibly could before...I couldn't.

Martin shook his head. "No. We've ruled Miss Mclary was placed in that backpack by her mother, and you were unaware. Under that proviso, we aren't calling it a kidnapping."

"What *are* you calling it?" I asked around a slight cough.

Della narrowed her eyes, her fingers flinching under mine.

"A rescue." He smiled gently. "A miracle that two kids survived against all odds."

"Wow." John cleared his throat, tears glittering in his big eyes. Ever since losing Patricia, and now my secret malady, he wore his emotions on his sleeve—a gruff, grizzly bear turned into a teddy.

He was against me not telling Della. He hated that I'd forbid him from informing anyone.

But that was my choice, and he had to honour it.

Otherwise, well—I'd promised he'd never see us again if he did.

It was my secret to tell...when I was ready.

John flicked me a glance before asking the officer, "So...what does that mean?"

Martin grinned. "It means he's free."

My shoulders sagged as if someone cut my strings. Della slouched too, a massive sigh exploding from her lips and making the pages dance.

"Now that there's a surviving heir to the Mclary estate, I advise you to get in touch with a lawyer to see what value you'll receive once the bank has claimed the outstanding debt. You'll have to undergo a DNA test to confirm you are their descendent, but that's just a formality."

I stiffened, recalling what poison existed on that farm and that I hadn't been the only one living there. "Should she undergo any other tests? To make sure she's healthy?"

John smothered a heavy sigh laced with sadness. "Shit, you don't think she has—"

"Quiet," I hissed.

"What's he talking about?" Della asked. "Ren?"

"Nothing." I clutched her hand in mine. "That house wasn't exactly sanitary. It might be best if you have some tests to ensure you're healthy and nothing infected you when you were a baby."

Things like asbestos...a killer that took ten to forty years to make itself known.

She could've been infected by me and second-hand contamination. Or by her father or mother or crawling around in silicate minerals and fibrous crystals in the dirt.

I'd researched.

I'd studied.

I knew my enemy intimately.

Della had taught me the power of education, and I knew enough to understand what risks she faced and what conclusions I'd have in my future.

How I would die.

How it would feel.

How I would look to Della as I slowly traded life for death.

That was the hardest part.

Knowing how much it would hurt her…seeing me that way.

Martin raised an eyebrow. "Um, I can ask. I know a few officers found asbestos onsite, so it might not be a bad thing to rule out."

I froze.

I hadn't meant for him to blare the damn word.

John tensed in his chair as we both looked at Della.

Pleading that in this, she wouldn't be too smart.

That in this awful, awful matter, she'd not see the truth.

Martin scribbled something down. "Heaven forbid anything comes back positive, but there are open litigations and settlements for anyone who may have been exposed."

Please…don't let her know.

Della studied the table, her mind racing before she bit her lip and asked something that made my heart gallop for different things. "What about the other kids? Are you tracking them down? Have you found any of them who were sold to that Kyle Harold my mother's letter mentioned?"

Martin took a sip of his coffee. "We've sent the names to a larger police force and, as far as I'm aware, they're in the process of going through missing persons and wanted offenders. I'll ask for an update and get back to you."

"Okay." Della nodded. "Hopefully, a few can be found before it's too late."

Too late.

Too late.

The words echoed in my skull.

Despite my anger at my body's desire to kill me, I couldn't be greedy.

I'd had so much longer than those kids.

I was the lucky one.

Once again, the guilt that I never went back settled heavily.

"We're also looking for your mother, Ren."

"Don't." I balled my hands. "As far as I'm concerned, she's dead. I never want to hear about her again, got it?"

Martin looked taken aback but slowly nodded. "Fair enough." Clearing his throat, he said, "Oh, I almost forgot." Reaching into his briefcase again, he pulled out a thick bunch of papers. "This is yours." Sliding it to Della, he waited for her to read the title and glance up.

"Did you read it?" Her fingers traced the words *The Boy & His Ribbon by Della Wild.*

"Yes."

I winced. "Please don't tell me you're going to arrest me for falling in love with a minor or incest."

He chuckled. "No. As much as society thinks we're out to ruin lives, we know when we come across good people, and you are good people. In fact..." His hand disappeared a final time into that damn briefcase, coming out with a framed piece of parchment. A matte black frame and simple glass, but as he pushed it toward me, it became my most precious thing in the world.

Utterly priceless because it finally allowed me to do what I'd been wanting to do for years.

It gave me a wish before I could have no more.

"I-I don't understand." I didn't dare touch it.

I couldn't.

Is it real?

Della started to cry. John welled up again. And I just kept staring, afraid, ecstatic, disbelieving.

"It's not going to bite you, Ren." Martin laughed. "It's legitimate. You have my word. It also means you'll have to start paying taxes now we know you exist."

"I-I don't know what to say." My hand tentatively stroked the glass, the reflection of the lights above dancing over the letters below.

"Don't need to say anything. You deserve it. I'm sorry it took almost thirty-one years to have one." He cleared his throat when no one said anything, adding, "You guys love each other. It's obvious to anyone who meets you. I suggest you do something about making the name Mclary a thing of the past."

Standing, he picked up his briefcase and strode to the door. "Oh, I also took the liberty of doing something I overheard about birthdays. I hope you don't mind." Tapping his temple, he smiled. "I'll let myself out. But if you ever need anything, you know where I am."

I barely managed a goodbye before my attention locked back on the birth certificate in front of me.

My birth certificate.

The birth certificate registered and legal in the name Della gave me.

Ren Wild.

And his birthday?

27th of June.

The same day as Della's...just as it should be.

For a second, all I could do was stare.

I was legal.

I was *real.*

I never believed something so simple could be so damn bittersweet.

I had permission to marry, all while serving a death sentence.

Pressure wrapped around my lungs with black affliction, but then my heart drowned it out with red affection. I was still alive, here and now. I still had Della, today and tomorrow. I still had a future, shortened but valued.

Time was never on our side.

It didn't matter then, and it didn't matter now.

Nothing mattered but *us.*

In a rush of daring, reckless true love, I stood so fast my chair toppled to the floor.

Eyes widened at my explosive behaviour, then gasps fell as I sank to one knee before the ribbon-hearted girl I'd loved forever.

Her blue eyes became twin puddles of tears as I grabbed her hand, kissed her knuckles, and whispered, "Della Donna Mclary…"

She flinched in my hold, and John's hands curled on the table.

My voice caught as I couldn't hold back my desperate, *desperate* need to have her as my own. Selfish, yes. Sad, absolutely. I would make her a widow before long, but even that couldn't stop me.

She was mine.

It was written in the stars and scribed in the galaxies, and nothing on earth could change that.

This was true inevitability, utter undeniability.

I didn't even need to ask a question.

"Marry me."

Chapter Fifty-One

DELLA

2034

DO YOU HATE *me?*

Do you hate me for taking you on this journey, making you fall in love with Ren, all while knowing how it ends?

Do you hate me for telling the truth?

Believe me, I've often wondered if I should change our ending. If I should lie and create the perfect happily ever after—just like Ren wanted me to.

But...whenever I type a chapter full of happy fakery, it seems so forgetful, so cliché, so counterfeit.

At least, I gave you a warning. If you read the words I chose and saw the message I shared, you'd know.

You'd know more than I ever did.

In fact, you know more than I did back then, and I sympathise with the pain you're going through.

Ren.

My Ren.

The answer to my puzzle, the conclusion to my journey, the man I was always meant to belong to.

He wasn't immortal, after all.

But...I have to be honest. I have to make you see.

This was never that sort of tale.

This wasn't a romance—I was blatant about that from the start.

This wasn't even a love story—even though love is the only thing that matters.

This is a life *story.*

And life includes good times and bad.

It includes birth and growth and...yes, even death.

This is a story of truth.

This is a story of my heart.

A story we all go through because eventually...we all die.

Some before others, some quick and fast, some in their sleep far from now.

But before you give in to those tears and believe you know our ending, stop.
Keep reading.
Keep enduring.
Because I can promise you, the ending...it's better than you think.

Chapter Fifty-Two

DELLA

2021

I SHOULD HAVE been on cloud nine.

Ren had proposed.

Ren had a birth certificate.

Ren wasn't arrested.

Ren was also lying.

His eyes lied. His voice lied. His body lied.

And it hurt.

So much.

Funny, how hiding the truth could hurt more than a fist or cruel word. Funny, how a person you trusted above everything could suddenly become so dangerous.

He was *lying*.

I knew.

I knew the signs because I'd lied to him often enough while he still cared for me as a sister. I knew how a lie festered inside you. How it sank its hooks in, dragging you deeper into its web, whispering in your ear that your lies came from a good place, a worthy place, a place of protection.

Ren was lying.

And because of that, my heart that was normally so open toward him fashioned a little gate—not a door blocking him out, but a small barrier that wasn't there before.

I hated it.

I hated him for making it happen.

I grew up faster in two months than I ever did in two years. I felt it happen. My rosy outlook on life, the childish belief that nothing could tear us apart, the idealistic notion of perfect happiness...they'd been threatened, questioned, and found wanting.

All those 'errands', those 'work' phone calls—they were poisonous barbs digging into my skin, layering me with pain, punishing me for loving someone so much when they were only hurting me.

At least I knew he wasn't cheating on me. At no point did such a ridiculous thought enter my mind. Ren was mine. He was *still* mine. Even if he was being a bastard lately.

Did he think I was stupid?

Did he think I was too weak to know?

I didn't need a degree to know his lies stemmed from his cough.

A cough that, to start with, I'd hoped was just bad allergies. Ren, after a lifetime of dealing in grass and animals, had built up an immune system that didn't often feel the tickle of hay fever, but occasionally, if the wind blew in a different direction or if the season had grown a different spore within the grass, he'd have a few days of watery eyes and a stuffy nose.

It never lasted long.

It left as quickly as it arrived.

But this...it hadn't.

It had gotten worse.

It'd morphed into a cough that woke me up at night and made me cry silent tears in the dark.

I supposed it was my fault that he believed he could get away with such fibs. I didn't push him to see a doctor even though terror chanted in my blood every second of every day. I didn't sit him down and stare him in the eye and ask point-blank what he was keeping secret.

It was my fault as much as his; he didn't tell me because he was protecting me. And I didn't hound him because in a way...I *wanted* protecting. I wanted to continue believing in the fantasy that he was invincible.

But I also wanted him to trust that I wouldn't break, that I wouldn't leave, that I was strong enough to carry whatever burden he dealt with.

Of course, I didn't share my worries with anyone, and, as I slipped from the farmhouse where Cassie and I had been calling contractors and arena surface companies for her equine set-up, my shoulders rolled with tiredness.

I hadn't been sleeping.

I was sick of pretending.

My smiles were fake, and my tears hidden when Ren held me close last night and whispered about making me a legally married woman. His murmurs of togetherness and forevers were full of hypocrisy, and I'd turned my back on him.

I was tired.

So, *so* tired and I couldn't pretend anymore.

I just wanted the truth, so my mind could stop conjuring nightmares.

Pushing open the barn doors, I strode into the comforting shadows where splinters of light danced with hay dust and horse hair.

I wanted to go for a ride to clear my head, but as I moved toward the tack room, a voice caught my ears.

A voice I knew better than my own.

"...and when will you know?" Slight pause. "Ah." Another pause. "Yeah, okay."

My steps turned to tiptoes as I crept toward the stables and ducked behind some stacked bales. Through the stalky, golden grass, I spotted Ren.

My heart kicked like it always did.

He was so handsome with jeans slung low on narrow hips, a grey and black plaid shirt rucked up to his elbows, and boots that had travelled miles covered in dirt. He had one thick glove on his left hand and the other tucked into his back pocket as he held his phone with his right.

He leaned on the stable door, his head bowed, handsome face grim. "Yeah, I've had two so far." He closed his eyes. "Actually, that might be true. I haven't been coughing as much lately."

My hands balled beside me. *Who the hell is he talking to?*

He listened to whomever was on the phone for a long moment, before kicking the stable door softly as if he wanted to rage but wasn't prepared to pick up the aftermath of ruin. "I have another treatment in two weeks or so." He shook his head, his dark, unruly hair tumbling. "No, no side effects."

I crumpled word by word, unable to tear my eyes off him.

This was worse than my nightmares.

This was real.

"Yeah, I know. A test would be good. I want to know if I'm responding, too." He raked a hand through his hair. "Okay, sure."

I pulled back into the shadows as he turned to face me, his eyes landing on the bales I hid behind. His chocolate gaze glittered, but his jaw was tense and strong. "If it works...how long do I have?"

My heart.

God, my *heart*.

It was no longer beating and pumping inside me.

It was bleeding and gasping by my feet.

I wanted to scoop it up. I wanted to stop it growing cold and discarded and covered in old manure, but I couldn't because Ren pinched his nose, then looked at the ceiling as if he stared at God and cursed him.

"That's not enough," he groaned. "I'm-I'm getting married—"

Whoever he spoke to cut him off, and his gaze fell to the ground. "I know. Yeah, stay positive, I'll try." Running a hand over his face, he murmured, "Thank you." He punched the disconnect button, threw his phone to the floor, and collapsed against the stable door.

With his knees up around his ears, he picked up a piece of hay and twirled it in the most dejected, terribly broken way that my heart crawled from its manure grave and hauled itself back into my chest, desperate to go to him even smeared and dirty and dying.

"Fuck," Ren whispered. *"Fuck."*

* * * * *

Staring into my reflection, I let the tears fall.

A girl I didn't recognise stared back at me. A girl with eyes the colour of grief and hair the pigment of sorrow.

Ren was already in bed, watching something on TV, waiting for me to finish my shower so we could snuggle together and lose our troubles in a movie that would never have the power of forget.

I'd left Ren in the stable.

He didn't know I'd heard.

He didn't know I knew…

Knew that he was sick enough to no longer look at the seasons as four adventures but four wheels pushing him closer to the one thing I never thought would be our enemy.

Not until decades from now.

Not until we'd raised children and grown sick of each other and became cranky and grey.

Death.

My fingertips pressed against the glass, tracing the tears on my cheeks in the coolness of the mirror.

I was naked.

Hair drenched from my shower and water still dripping over me.

I was cold.

Nipples pebbled, and skin raised with goosebumps.

I was empty.

Silent on the outside, screaming on the inside.

The mirror lied when it painted a picture of a girl just standing there crying. It should show the truth—the reality that I was hair tugging, skin bleeding, nails scratching, voice yelling, fists flailing, and knees bruised from begging for salvation.

I was chaos not calm.

A sob caught in my throat as I reached into the medicine cabinet and pulled out my nightly ritual.

Face cream applied.

Teeth brushed.

Pill...

The tiny pill sat in my palm—no longer just a drug designed to keep me free from pregnancy but a small, ticking explosive.

Time had once again screwed us.

It had given me to Ren too young.

It had granted only a few wonderful years when we could touch and kiss and love.

And now...it'd taken away our future as cruelly as it had shoved us into one before we were ready.

The pill.

The magical little pill that stopped things from happening.

And time, the demonic power that sped up all things.

Ren had asked how long he had.

When you asked that question, the answer was never good.

We were on borrowed days now, on bartered minutes, and bargained seconds.

My palm tipped sideways, and the pill scattered down the plughole.

Our dreams were slashed...all but one.

We didn't have the luxury of waiting.

Catching my eye one last time in the mirror, I dressed in the boy shorts and cami I wore to sleep, turned out the light, and went to bed where, for now...my lover still waited for me.

Chapter Fifty-Three

REN

2021

"I DON'T THINK I can do this anymore."

Another week of lying, sneaking, and hiding.

Outwardly, Della still smiled at me, accepted my kisses, and talked to me, but inwardly...she'd gone.

I didn't know how to explain it.

The empty feeling whenever I touched her. The heartache whenever we kissed—she'd pulled away even while her body was still mine.

I'd hurt her enough to shut down, and that fucking tore me into shreds.

John raised his head, his big paws curling around his coffee cup.

We'd started at sunrise today, thanks to spring arriving overnight with warm air, bright sun, and grass sprouting from the ground at a visible rate.

The farm had woken up from hibernation, demanding to be tended.

"I told you from the start to tell her." He gnawed on his inner cheek, his wrinkles tightening around his eyes. "She knows something isn't right."

"I know." I sighed heavily.

She'd always been too aware of me. Too smart for her own good.

John smiled sadly. "I know you're trying to protect her, but you're only hurting both of you." His eyes drifted with memories. "I didn't know Patty was close to leaving me—none of us did. The suddenness was what made it so hard. The fact that we didn't have time to say goodbye or look for hope or tick off a bucket list. She was here, and then she wasn't." He gulped, his knuckles turning white around his coffee mug. "You aren't going anywhere, Ren. Not for a very long time—"

"You heard what the doctors said, I only have a few—"

"Stop. You didn't let me finish. I was going to say...you aren't going anywhere, but we're realistic to know you have a fight ahead of you, and you need her by your side. We *all* want to be by your side. Liam, Cassie..."

"I know." I slugged my coffee in one gulp.

What the hell am I doing?

The distance between me and Della wasn't worth any price.

I needed to fix this.

I needed to tell her.

Somehow.

I stood from the table. "You're the best boss in the world, John, but I'm gonna stand you up today." I coughed a little. "Gotta take a few days off."

"Told you you didn't need to work while you're—"

"I'm not an invalid," I snapped. "Not yet, anyway. I want to work...just not when I've fucked up and need to fix it."

He chuckled. "Well, I'm docking your pay."

I smiled at his joke. "Wouldn't have it any other way." Marching to the back door, my legs filled with nervous energy. I'd woken this morning with an itinerary of fertilizing and weed-killing the back pastures. Nothing on that agenda said I'd finally have the guts to tell the love of my life I was dying.

But I couldn't keep lying anymore.

I had another treatment next week. Depending on how well it went, I'd be tested to see if I'd responded. Either good news or bad...I wanted Della to be there.

"Before you go." John lugged his bulk from the chair and moved toward the shelf where Patricia had grabbed the sex education book for an eight-year-old Della all those years ago. Pulling an envelope free, he came toward me. "No arguments, Ren. None, you hear me?"

I eyed him. "Depends...what is it?"

"I know you've been lucky enough to enter an off-label trial for your age group. But we don't know how long that'll last." Shoving the envelope into my hands, he muttered, "This is for after. Just in case."

Tearing it open, I didn't find cash like I had on my first pay packet.

Instead, I found a contract.

A contract written up between Cherry River Farm and me, its employee.

John had found a way to pay for my treatment by legally making me his worker—someone who now paid tax with a notable salary. Someone who could receive healthcare.

My eyes met his. "How many times are you going to meddle in my future, John?"

He chuckled. "As many times as it takes." Patting my shoulder, he nudged his chin at the door. "Go. Find your girl. Make it right between you."

"This discussion isn't over." I shoved the contract into my back pocket. "I'm not putting you in debt. No matter how you word it in fine print."

"Yeah, yeah. Go."

I gave him a final look, amazed that in my short life I'd been victim to the worst of evil and son to the best of them.

Stepping outside, I squinted against the rays of fierce sunshine. Yesterday, it seemed as if winter would never leave, and this morning, spring had well and truly kicked its ass.

I hoped the nice weather stuck around for a while because where we were going, we'd have enough to deal with to worry about snow.

Jogging into the barn, I tried not to get my hopes up that my usual breathlessness was better today. That I hadn't coughed as much. That the ache had faded somewhat.

I'd had two treatments of Keytruda, and, so far, I was lucky.

Barely any side effects and if possible…already some signs that the experimental immunotherapy was working.

Please, please, God, let it be working.

Tossing the gear we'd need into one backpack, I ensured we had water and snares and my knives were sharp and ready. Slipping on a black jacket that had seen better days, I hoisted the backpack onto my shoulders and made my way over the cobblestones to our one bedroom.

The Wilson's guest bedroom was all well and good for now, but soon I'd need to figure out a way to give Della the house she deserved. A home of our own…before it was just hers.

Opening the door, I caught Della perched on the end of the bed dressed in her riding gear. Jodhpurs that clung to curves and a tweed coat that brushed her thighs.

Her hair was plaited down her back with her blue ribbon in a bow at the end. "Ren." Guilt echoed in her tone as she slammed the laptop closed and tossed it onto the unmade sheets beside her. "What are you doing back so soon?" Her eyes travelled over me, making my body harden. "And why do you look like you're going camping?"

"Because we are." Moving toward her, I grabbed her wrist and pulled her from the bed. "What were you looking at?"

"Nothing." Her eyes narrowed with her lie.

"Were you researching something?"

Her head tilted. "Should I be?"

"Depends."

"On what?"

"On how much you already know."

She gasped. "Are you going to tell me *what* I should know?"

My heart pounded. "I can't keep lying to you."

Tears welled in her gaze. "Does that mean I can stop hating you?"

I walked into her, slotting her body against mine. "I think it will only make you hate me more."

She flinched, burrowing her face in my chest.

Squeezing her tight, we shared a hug full of sadness before I coughed gently and ruined it.

Her eyes met mine as I pulled away, reaching for her hand. "We need to talk."

"I was afraid you were going to say that." Her tongue licked as a tear rolled past her lips. "What if...what if I'm not ready? For weeks, I thought I was. I've been so angry that you've lied...but now?" Her face drained of colour. "I don't know if I'm ready, Ren."

Kissing her sweetly, I stared into her, wishing I could protect her.

Wishing I could change our future.

Wishing I could stop this.

"Let's go home, Della Ribbon. And then...we'll talk."

* * * * *

We set up the tent in silence.

The once familiar tasks a little rusty as we grabbed nylon and inserted poles.

Firewood had already been collected. A snare already set. Our camp as homey as I could make it.

The tent was the last thing, and the minute it was up and pegged securely to the ground, I spread out our yoga mats and made up a sleeping bag bed.

Della didn't enter the tent. She drifted around the camp with an aura of loss and fear, kicking at pine cones and tugging her braid.

I let her drift because I needed the camp to be as perfect as I could before I told her...because once I did? Nothing else would matter.

Time was no longer relative.

Some days dragged with hazards and peril—every second doing its best to remind me that I no longer had the privilege of old age. And some days flashed past with peace and positivity—every heartbeat doing its best to assure me that I could beat the timeline the doctors gave me.

I'd been in Keytruda forums.

I'd read miracles and tragedies.

I aimed to be a goddamn miracle because there was no way I could leave Della yet. She was still so young; so pure and perfect. I didn't want to be the reason she faded and found life anything less than extraordinary.

Once my chores were complete and I had nothing left to distract myself with, I looked up to where Della hovered.

It was as if she knew before I spoke a word. And I was stupid to think she didn't. So idiotic to believe she hadn't figured out something was wrong...seriously fucking wrong.

The forest became thick with everything we couldn't say. Birds quietened. Trees stilled. Time itself slowed so we stood in a nucleus where nothing could touch us.

Her gaze shouted, her body swaying a little in disbelief to whatever she saw on my face.

Finally, when the strain grew too much to bear, I spread my hands in surrender with a dismal shrug. "I'm so sorry, Della."

I expected a fight.

She was angry and hurting and, whenever those two emotions combined, she was vicious. But instead, she folded in on herself as if some beast crumpled her like a discarded piece of manuscript—erasing part of our story, deleting all the chapters that could have been.

With the softest, saddest cry, she broke into a run and slammed into my arms.

I stumbled backward, holding her, hugging her, stabilising both of us as her heart pounded against mine.

"I don't know what I was thinking," I murmured into her hair. "How I thought I could protect you from this. Please...forgive me."

She shook her head, face wedging against my shoulder. "Don't. Please don't."

"Don't what?"

"Don't tell me. Don't make it real."

I sighed, pressure banding and pain throbbing. "It's real. Whether I tell you or not, it's real."

Her arms squeezed me harder. "But you're mine. You're *mine*."

"And I'll always stay yours." My lips feathered on her temple, gulping back my first taste of bitter honesty. "No matter where I go."

Another bone deep sound came from her, making me rock on my heels as she wriggled closer.

How the fuck could I do this?

How could I voice something so tragic when all I wanted to do was pretend I was fine?

But a cough reminded me I *wasn't* fine.

I was slowly dying.

I didn't know how long we stood there—both of us petrified, both of us understanding what this meant. Every touch from here on out would have a different flavour. Every smile would be treasured and counted. Every laugh would be hoarded and noted.

Nothing would be taken for granted.

That sort of connection and awareness could make life utterly exhausting—doing our best to scribble down memories and strive for more achievements.

But that was the thing, I didn't want to race the clock and fill our lives with empty meaning. I didn't need to complete a bucket list or travel or seek cheap thrills.

I had everything I ever wanted, needed, and valued right there in my arms.

There was only one thing I needed, and it would be the hardest thing I'd ever ask of her. "Della..." Pulling away so I could see her face, I cupped her cheeks. "I'll tell you anything you want to know—everything I know, at least. But before I do, I need to know something from you."

Her tears dribbled over my fingers, my thumb running softly over her lips. "Ask me."

I closed my eyes, hunting for strength. When I opened them again, her tears had stopped, but her sadness still glittered bright.

"I need..." I shook my head, jaw locking. I looked to the side, fighting the crush of despair.

"Ren." Her fingers dug into my waist. "Ren...look at me."

It took a monumental effort; her beautiful face danced as liquid dared fill my eyes.

She smiled joylessly before sweeping up and pressing her mouth to mine.

The second she kissed me, I threw myself into her.

I groaned and gathered her close, frenzied in my desire for connection.

We stumbled again, but this time in undiluted lust.

Yet another thing that would become so much more. So much more than just sex and kisses and thrusts. Even as my mind imprinted her subtle minty taste and inhaled her light melon fragrance, I did my best to stop.

To stop kissing her as if I were already gone.

To stop remembering her as something I'd lost when she was alive and willing in my arms.

Her teeth teased my bottom lip, making my thoughts scatter. Hunger for her coiled in my belly, and I latched onto the simplicity of desire.

I'd wanted to be honest and clear the air.

But Della had once again given me something I didn't know I needed.

I missed her so fucking much.

I'd hurt her and driven her away and deserved her coldness.

But standing there, surrounded by nature and no one, all that existed between us was heat and passion and devotion.

There would be time for talking.

After.

Scooping her into my arms, I somehow managed to traverse the campsite with its leaf litter and hazardous tripping and carried her into the tent.

Placing her onto her feet, we kicked off our boots in synchronization before slamming to our knees, praying to each other, sacrificing our hearts, offering up everything we had to be worthy of one more day.

Her fingers landed in my hair, pulling my head to hers.

I obeyed, kissing her hard and fast, deep and long.

How was I supposed to stay strong when I had a girl like Della? How was I supposed to be okay with this?

I had so many things I needed to do before I went.

I needed to find a way to provide for her. To protect her future and know she was safe. I needed to have a family with her. To at least see one or two wrinkles on her flawless face.

Our tongues met, then retreated. Our lips connected, then paused.

Out of all the things I'd miss, kissing Della was the most.

"Ren?"

Her whisper physically hurt me. "Yeah?"

More tears scattered down her face while she kneeled before me. "Promise me we'll always be together." Her hands clutched mine with crazed urgency. "Promise me this isn't over. Promise me like you promised five-year-old me that you'll never let me go. Never, ever leave me."

Jesus Christ.

My heart squeezed, and I wrapped her in my arms, dragging her onto my lap.

I wanted so fucking much to be able to promise. I would've given anything to assure her we had forever. That there wasn't a guillotine already poised above my neck.

I should do what I'd always done and *protect* her.

Fuck, I should protect her.

But my lungs burned, my back ached, and my body prodded me to be brave. "I will always love you." My avoidance of her promises wrenched a sob from her lungs. Her legs squeezed around my waist, her breath hitching with sorrow.

"I'll never stop, Della Ribbon." Her curls stuck to my lips as I inhaled her sweet scent. "Not until life rips me from your arms. And even then…it's not goodbye."

A cough tumbled from my mouth. A cough that made her stiffen and arms tighten.

Kissing her, I murmured, "I promise that every breath I take is for you. I've never loved anyone else and I never will."

She crawled closer, kissing me with a fury that threatened to make me snap. "My heart has always belonged to you."

"I know." My voice broke, and I fisted her hair to kiss her hard.

My body tightened, my heart pounded, and by the time the kiss ended, I was lightheaded and out of breath, and I didn't know if it was from her or the disease inside me.

The doctors had warned me that as I progressed, my strength would go. I'd lose weight. I'd struggle to breathe. I'd fade away piece by piece.

That was my utmost terror.

That Della would remember me that way.

"I need you to promise me something." I didn't tear my mouth from hers, speaking directly into her. "Promise me that you'll remember me like this. That you'll stay with me. That you won't hate me for dy—"

"Stop. I-I can't." Her lips twisted beneath mine.

"Can't promise you'll stay by me while I go through—"

"Can't hear you say the word dying. *Please*, Ren." Her eyes met mine, so close and somber.

The knowledge I was the one causing her so much pain crippled me. "I thought I could do this." My neck bowed, my forehead touching hers. "But I can't. Not yet."

"Me, too. I'm not ready."

"I need you, Della."

Her hands fumbled on my belt, ripping open the buckle and unzipping my fly. "You have me. Always."

I half-smiled, repeating what she said as if it were a vow. "Always." As if that one word linked us beneath the eyes of nature, binding us better than any wedding ceremony.

Her hand dove between us, slipping into my boxers and fisting me.

My breath caught at the sudden shot of pleasure, and all I wanted to do was give in. We needed to lose ourselves from reality for a while, but I placed my hand over hers.

"Wait." I coughed quietly.

Her eyes met mine, wincing. "Why?"

Why?

Because we had so little time.

Because I needed so much more than I already had.

I never looked away even though it was the most vulnerable I'd ever been around her. "I know it's soon, and we agreed to wait…but I'm ready to come second best."

Her lips parted.

I waited to see if she understood.

Of *course*, she understood.

She was my intelligent, beautiful Della.

She bit her lip, her chest heaving with tears. "A-are you going to leave me that fast?" Her fingers twitched around my erection. Her eyes closed tight as if barricading herself against my answer.

"I—" I groaned, fighting yet another cough. "I don't know how to do this, Della. Don't know how to hurt you when it's the last thing I ever wanted to do."

"Then don't." She looked up. "Lie to me. Tell me this is all a terrible mistake."

"You know I can't do that. I've tried. I can't hide from you. Not anymore."

"I know." Her face held no colour, blood sinking inside to protect her heart. "Just…after. Tell me after."

"Fuck, Ribbon." I kissed her, tasting salt and misery and an end we both weren't ready for.

As we kissed, my hands undid the buttons of her jacket and pushed it off her shoulders. Our lips disconnected as I fumbled for her jodhpur zipper. She hadn't changed before trekking with me. She hadn't done anything apart from follow me dazedly from the stables and over the fields to the forest.

Popping the button against her flat stomach, she watched my fingers undress her.

"I stopped taking my pill a week ago. I—" She gave me a guilty half-smile. "I didn't discuss it with you. I threw it down the drain. I'm sorry."

"Sorry?"

"For making that decision alone."

I kissed her, jerking her close. "You made the right one. You made the only one."

"I want your baby, Ren. But...I don't know if I'm ready to share you. Especially now."

My heart sank. "Then we'll wait. I'll respect that."

I'd respect it and hope to God I survived long enough to make a child with her. Hope to heaven the drugs that would extend my life wouldn't make me sterile before it was too late.

Her hand moved again, pulling me free from my jeans and boxers until I stabbed upright between us. "How long, Ren?"

"Della..." Using my knuckle, I nudged her chin upward. "Please, stop." I bent to press my lips to hers, expecting a refusal but earning a soul-blistering kiss instead. "After, remember?"

"After." She nodded, her fingers stroking hotly.

My body became corrupted by her touch. Part of me was no longer interested in sex after talking about such morbid things, but the larger part was ever more desperate.

Desperate to live.

Desperate to start a new life.

Desperate to tell the Grim Reaper to fuck the hell off.

Ignoring the unsaid things between us, hiding the secrets dripping with pain, I whispered, "I want a child with you. Even if it will drive me insane the entire time you're pregnant. Despite what happened with the ectopic scare, I want a daughter like you. I'm selfish to risk everything to have that."

She smiled sadly. "And I want a son like you."

"Guess we'll have to have both, then."

"Do we have time?"

I winced, swallowing on my shortened longevity.

Do you want to know? Are you so eager for me to break your heart?

I sucked in a breath. "I—"

"Wait. Don't." She pressed her lips to mine. "Just kiss me."

So I did.

I kissed her, undressed her, laid her on her back, and slid from my clothes. Snuggling into one sleeping bag, I pulled the other up and over us, trapping our body heat.

My hand disappeared between her legs.

She jerked as I touched her, feeling her silky flesh, hot with want. Her eyes glowed sapphire as I pressed a finger inside her.

I wanted to make this last. To touch her for hours and lick, taste, and worship, but a baser desire lived within me. The knowledge she wasn't on the pill. The idea that we could create something bigger than ourselves.

I wanted to leave her with a legacy that was more than just money or possessions. I wanted her to have a piece of me. A child with my blood in its veins and a shred of my soul in its heart.

I stupidly wanted to find some way to always be there...even when I wasn't.

Her hips arched up, welcoming me to touch her deeper. I inserted another finger, making her wet, encouraging her to forget her grief and only remember pleasure.

I found her lips again, kissing in time to my pressure, my tongue in rhythm to my finger, my body winding tighter the longer she fondled and stroked.

For so long, I'd known her body as intimately as anyone could. I'd seen her legs grow from chubby to elegant. Her chest from flat to full. And now, I knew exactly what pleased her and how to make her submit entirely.

As I thrust deeper, she gasped into my mouth. "If we're lucky enough to have children, I promise to love them." She cupped my cheek, holding me steady. "But I also promise I'll love you more. I won't be able to help it."

My fingers stopped, wedged tight inside her. "That's something I can't agree to." Sorrow balled in my heart. "Don't you see? I *need* you to love them more, Della. I need someone else to hold your heart when I can't."

Her breath caught, body flinched, the precipice we'd been dancing over yawning. "I hate you for this." The fierceness in which she said it broke me.

"I know."

"I hate you *so* much, Ren."

"Hate me if you must but love me, too. Please..." Withdrawing my fingers, I climbed over her, slotting my body into hers. When I felt her damp warmth, I pushed, spreading her, filling her, invading every last piece she could give me.

Tears cascaded down her cheeks, soaking into the sleeping bag below.

I rubbed away the droplets I could and licked at the ones I missed, cradling her as I made love to her.

How many times would we have this?

How many more moments of connection?

We rocked together—gentle and almost apologetic. Our touches safe and kisses guarded. But slowly...the hurt dissolved, leaving only lust and our bodies burning with desire.

Our pace turned faster, tame blending into violence.

Carnal hunger ripped through my veins, kicking my heart, coating my skin with need.

Della writhed beneath me, meeting me thrust for thrust.

Her face wasn't soft or open but angry and revengeful. Without speaking, she ran her fingernails down my back, deep and deliberately mean.

I bowed, groaning in pleasure-pain, my cock hardening to excruciation.

A blackness encroached my mind, filling me with a mad kind of savagery.

She felt the change. She matched it with her own.

Our lovemaking turned to war, and my thrusts switched from rocking to fucking.

"Goddamn you, Della." Fisting her hair, I held her down as I bucked inside her. She moaned as I yanked on the strands—the same strands I'd washed and braided and brushed. The hair I'd seen wet and tangled and even blue. The hair I'd inhaled while sleeping beside her in the tent and fought a love that couldn't be fought.

"I hate you," she whispered as I pulled out and pushed her onto her stomach. Gripping the back of her neck, I thrust back inside her, keeping her pinned and imprisoned. "You. Already. Said. That." I growled, sweating and aching and forever fighting a cough.

"I hate you because I love you," she cried as I hit the button inside her that added mind-bending intensity.

"Ribbon—" I grunted as her back arched, forcing herself onto me, ramming herself down my length.

"I hate you because I won't survive."

My body was stiff and awkward, every neuron locked inside her. "You will. You have to."

"I don't want to." Her mouth opened wide as I yanked her hair back and kissed her. My chest pressed to her back, riding her, knees digging into sleeping bags, and tent shivering with our speed.

I grunted, "You have no choice."

"I *do* have a choice."

I drove harder, deeper, crueller. "You don't. I can't face this if I believe otherwise."

Her face twisted into anguish. "Fuck you."

"I'll fuck you instead." Thrusting faster, I nipped at her ear. "I'll always be inside you, Della."

I rippled with the need to release. The toxic blend of punishment and pleasure was a dangerous place to be. I couldn't treat her gently. I couldn't keep my touch soft. I couldn't be *nice* anymore.

She felt me losing control and tried to make me come, teeth snapping at my mouth, back hollowing as she speared herself deeper onto me.

I tried to kiss her, but she merely bit me, utter wretchedness tumbling from her soul. A second later, she moaned with joy as I gave her the fury she wanted.

I fucked her harder.

"Is this what you want?"

She moaned. "I want you forever. That's what I want."

"And you have me forever."

She wriggled beneath me, activating predator instincts that planted a fist in her lower back, keeping her prone and open.

She groaned, guttural and feral, just like me. Fighting me for no other purpose than to piss me off.

She looked over her shoulder. "If you loved me, you'd stay."

What a horrid thing to say.

What a *disgusting* slur to utter.

"Don't you think I'm trying?" My anger turned to rage, and I fucked her with contempt instead of everlasting love. "You've pushed me too far, Della."

She bucked and pleaded, and I lost myself to her.

I'm sorry.

So goddamn sorry.

She made me angry, so fucking angry. She made me sad, so eternally sad.

And I didn't want to be either of those things because I had to be strong for her.

She squirmed as my rough palms caressed her spine, massaging with possessive strokes.

Grabbing handfuls of her ass, I forced her legs to spread wider, her feet kicking, flashing me her ribbon tattoo, drowning me in memories; painful, shard-filled memories of our shared childhood, stabbing me over and over, craving, wanting, *begging*.

A cough caught me unaware.

Another cough followed that one.

And I bent over, clamping my teeth into her shoulder, stifling any more.

I *refused* to be ill.

I refused to be a faulty clock deciding how many minutes I could have with her.

"I love you, Della." My cock throbbed, hard as wood; my mind raced, a mess with desire. I looped an arm around her stomach, holding her tight as I thrust into her from behind. "Forever."

Rage drenched my blood. Anger at life and love and loss.

My hips pistoned faster, taking out my sadness on her—letting her taste a little of the fury inside me. The grief and yearning for more.

Her head snapped up as my fingers found her clit, rubbing fast and hard. "God—"

Her body tightened around me, preparing for a release.

I loved taking her like this. Loved dancing on the border of animal and human, right and wrong, sexy and sadistic.

There were so many things I wanted to do to her.

So many, *many* things.

Would time give them to me?

"You've broken me, Ribbon. And now, I have to break you." I reared up on my hands, driving my body into hers, unapologetic, untamed, unforgiving.

She wanted me rough.

She had me.

I was jerky and fierce.

I was lost and afraid.

I was in love and utterly in pieces.

I wanted to punish her for the life she'd have after me. I wanted to free her from the pain I was about to cause her.

I hated her.

I loved her.

I missed her so fucking much already.

"God, Ren." Her cry unravelled the final parts of me, and I lost the remaining pieces that made me hers.

I fucked and thrust and layered her with bruises upon bruises.

And still, she begged for more.

My teeth found her skin, and my body answered hers. And our hearts clanged and pounded to the same song, the melody giving way to a crescendo, the crescendo exploding to the finale, and we rode that song until sweat glistened and moans echoed, and our bodies found the same pleasure as our hearts.

We came together, fast and spent.

We loved each other, even though it hurt.

We were bonded, so there would be a forever.

And not even death could stop us.

Chapter Fifty-Four

DELLA

2021

"WHAT ABOUT JULIE?"

I cracked open my gaze, shaking my head on Ren's naked chest. "No."

"Holly?"

"Nah."

"Daphne?"

"Definitely not." I peeled my face from his skin and rolled my eyes. "You're bad at baby naming."

"Those are common, nice names."

"Yes, and they're all girls."

He smiled even though it didn't erase the melancholy in his eyes. "We're having a girl, Della." His gaze travelled down my exposed breasts to my flat belly. "We made one. Today."

Goosebumps sprouted over my arms. "Could it happen that quick?"

He pulled me back down onto him, our shared heat slightly sticky and too hot, but I had no intention of leaving his side.

We'd calmed from our orgasms and separated enough to lie side by side until Ren gathered me to spoon against him as if he needed me to touch him at all times.

"After the short straw I've been dealt, we better have made a baby today. I think I deserve that much." He narrowed his eyes at the tent roof. "Hear me? Whoever you are? Impregnate this girl if you feel a shred of guilt for what you've done to me."

Tears stung my eyes all over again.

I'd forgotten how much I'd cried in the past week, and I'd only shed more because we'd been avoiding the monster in the room.

The monster we came into the forest to face.

How long?

But before we did, I wanted to exist in light-hearted baby planning a little longer. "Okay, say I'm pregnant. Say you have magical sperm, and *bam*, I'm knocked up—out of wedlock, no less." I tapped his chin, making him chuckle. "Say all of that happened? Well, I'm telling you, I'm having a boy."

"Why do you want a boy so badly?"

"Because I want another you."

He sucked in a breath.

The comment was meant to be blasé, but no truer words had been spoken. I wanted another Ren to replace the one who was dying. I wanted Ren to somehow clone himself, heal himself, and never die—not until he was one-hundred-and-two and ready.

Our joking bled away.

We sighed heavily with no small amount of misery.

Oppressive silence smothered us, and we made no move to lighten it.

Exhaustion spread over me even though it was still light outside. I felt as if I'd run every marathon there ever was and still had so many to go.

I suffered no anger anymore. No rage or fury.

Just heart-weary desolation.

I didn't know how much time passed, but Ren squeezed me, rousing me from a strange, stressful doze. "Jacob."

"Huh?"

"If you're pregnant with my son. I want to call him Jacob."

"Why?"

He shrugged. "I just like the name. It feels…right."

My heart splashed into my stomach, annihilated by acid and circumstance. "Okay, Ren. I can live with Jacob."

He gave me the sweetest kiss, his lungs inhaling and exhaling with a gentle cough.

A cough that couldn't be ignored anymore.

We tensed, once again on the same tattered wavelength.

"Della…"

"Ren…"

We spoke together and stopped together.

"You go," I whispered.

He flinched. "I don't know what to say. You've guessed the hardest part."

"I didn't guess. I overheard you. On the phone in the stable." My voice wobbled. "You asked how long. I knew we didn't have a lot of time."

"Shit." He kissed my forehead. "And you dealt with this for a week on your own?"

I brushed his concern away. "It's nothing compared to you. When did you find out?"

His tone strained. "Does it matter?"

"No." I burrowed into him. "Nothing matters now."

"I'm so sorry, Della."

"Don't do that. Don't apologise for something that isn't your fault."

"But how can I not? How can I not hate myself for what—"

"Stop, Ren." Every muscle clenched. "Just tell me. Tell me what's wrong with you."

He froze, his heart racing against me. "I've had it for twenty years."

I squeezed my eyes as if that would protect me from goblins.

"At Mclary's. I was put at risk..."

I wanted to tell him to stop, to never tell me, to laugh this awfulness away. But I nodded and held on with all my strength.

"You'll need to be tested too—just in case. But I'm hoping you weren't exposed like I was."

"Exposed to what?" I wanted to go deaf, to never listen to what devil hurt my love, but instead, my ears rang...waiting for his answer. And even though I knew it was coming. Even though I'd heard it in my head and watched it happen over and over in my nightmares, it still had the power to change my world.

To change me as a person.

To strip aside my remaining youth and make me so much older than I ever wanted to be.

"Asbestos poisoning." He swallowed hard, his chest working. "I have stage one mesothelioma."

I tried to speak, to be brave and ask questions, but I left him totally alone to explain.

A foreign word I didn't know.

A title to a host of unrecognisable evil.

I was clueless.

I was shell-shocked.

I didn't know myself anymore.

I only knew a canyon of vast quaking emptiness with a river of the roughest, churniest despair.

Ren swallowed again, chewing on tears. "I've had two treatments with a drug called Keytruda. It's been proven in other studies to be very successful. Some even call it the miracle drug, and it doesn't cause as many side effects as chemo."

He struggled to continue, before clearing his throat and saying matter-of-factly, "It's an active immunotherapy method that stimulates my own immune system to work harder. It gives it a new code…kind of like a computer update to seek out the cells that are bad and attack. I've read forums of people who had cancers reduce—positive responders, they're called. There are some people called total responders, who, after treatment, show no sign of having cancer at all."

He squished me close. "I'm hoping to be one of those."

My voice caught in my throat. I had so many questions, but I was weak; sobbing silently into his chest, feeling his heart pound, hating it and its limited beats.

"I go again soon and want you to come with me. I'll be re-tested…we'll know then if there's hope."

There were so many things I wanted to know, but I couldn't think of a single one. Only the worst thing. The thing I didn't want an answer to, but suddenly was desperate to know.

Inhaling his smoky, wild smell, I asked around my tears. "How long?"

Ren groaned, rubbing his hand up and down my arm. "I don't want you worrying, Della. I want you to focus on the fact that I'm going to outlive every prediction. You have my word I'll—"

"And I'll support you every step of the way. But…how long, Ren?" Looking up, I stared into his deep, sorrow-filled eyes.

And he stared back at the heartache in mine. "Twelve to twenty-four months."

I gasped.

One to two years?

That was *nothing*!

That was torture.

That couldn't be allowed.

"Finding it at stage one is rare, so I'm already ahead of the game. No one really knows how long I'll have. I'm unusual, and that's why I've been given access to this trial even though the drug has already been approved. I promise you I'll have longer than two—"

"Stop." I shook my head, my hair sticking to the sleeping bag and crackling with static electricity. Electricity that I'd feed into his blood if it meant it could eradicate every inch of whatever disease was inside him.

Three seconds ago, I'd been broken beyond repair, destroyed and drowning beneath the knowledge that I couldn't handle this—I wouldn't be able to watch Ren die and stay strong.

But now…now I had a timeline.

I had an enemy.

I had the name of the weapons we'd use to fight it.

Kissing him, I filled with resilience, tenacity, hope. "No."

"No?" he whispered into my mouth.

"No." I nuzzled close, already planning healthy food regimens, study, research, and second opinions. My mind no longer had time for tears. I had a lover to save and ensure he became one of those total responders because there was no other ending for us.

"Not so soon. I won't let you leave me so soon."

He grinned softly. "I'll do everything in my power to obey."

"You better, Ren Wild." Grabbing his hand, I planted it on my stomach and, with a conviction that came from somewhere else, somewhere all-knowing and elemental, I vowed, "I'm pregnant with your child. And I refuse to raise him or her alone. You got me into this mess, and together, we'll find a way for you to survive it."

Chapter Fifty-Five

DELLA

2032

THE SIGNS WERE obvious...now I knew where to look.

The hints that we'd been given too much happiness and now deserved a dose of despair.

I wish I could put your mind at rest.

I want to shout 'surprise' and announce a nasty, practical joke.

But it isn't a joke...it never was.

Life had banished us into the struggle of fighting to stay together, and even if we'd seen the signs earlier, we wouldn't have been able to change fate.

Just like it'd been fate that made us fall in love.

It was fate that would ultimately kill us.

We weren't miracle workers or immune to normality. Our love didn't make us safe from adversity...if anything, it made us more susceptible to catastrophe.

Our hearts were linked.

If one went, so would the other.

If one hurt, both felt it.

A ripple effect that wouldn't just end when Ren died but would continue to haunt me until the day I died, too.

As we lay together after Ren told me, I swung between bravery and cowardice.

I wanted to head to the doctor's straight away and demand every treatment, drug, and trial. I wanted to assure him that I would be strong, and he could lean on me—that he wouldn't face a single piece of this alone.

But I also wanted to stay in that forest and never leave. I wanted to hand my hope to the wind and beg it to rewind time to when Ren was eight and he was never sold to my parents.

I was willing to give up an entire lifetime with him—to prevent us ever meeting, to stop true love from forming, to end all of it—if it meant he would never have been exposed to asbestos.

I would accept he'd love another, marry another...that was how frantic I was to heal him.

I was willing to exist and grow up in that hell-house with a murdering mother and raping father if it meant Ren survived. Because, at least that way...I would never have known what I was about to lose as I wouldn't have had him to start with.

Was that selfless or selfish?

Selfless to want him to live or selfish not to want to face the pain?

No matter what happened in the future, I would keep fighting. I would keep clearing the carnage and carrying a sword into battle.

There was no other way.

Because I was Ren's.

Yesterday, tomorrow, for always.

By the time night had fallen, casting us in moon glow and star shadows, Ren and I were steady enough to venture outside and cook a simple meal.

Watching him boil water for pasta and use his knife to whittle a stick into a stirrer, I made up a story of enchantment where he was part seraph and indomitable—where the inescapable power of age held zero sway.

And that was the moment that I knew, just knew that love would be the hardest thing I'd ever have to endure.

It wasn't my origins or the fact I was never meant to exist. It wasn't seeing what my parents did or the dead children they'd tortured.

It was something only a lucky few enjoyed.

Something that was said to be worth any pain or price.

Love.

I was no longer a silly girl who idolized her prince and saviour.

I was a woman born to darkness and now, I bargained with that darkness for hope. Hope for the boy I was created for.

A boy I wanted to marry.

A boy I did marry.

A simple, perfect marriage that was the third largest incident of our lives.

Three out of five moments.

Wonderful moments.

Horrible moments.

Moments that make up a life.

One, two, three, four, five.

One, Ren was arrested, which led to a domino river of birth certificates and closure.

Two, Ren told me he was dying and began a nightmare we would face together.

Three, Ren married me a week after and made me the happiest and saddest girl alive.

Four...?

Well, four arrived eight and a half months later, bringing joy and sorrow in equal measure.

And five?
Ugh, five...
Five will come last.
Once our story is over.

Chapter Fifty-Six

REN

2021

THERE WERE MANY things I'd experienced in my thirty or so years.

Some mundane and some uncommon, but I'd never felt more aware of my fragility and timelessness than when I said, 'I do.'

When I joined the ranks of husbands.

When I entered the community of marriage and swore my life to serve, protect, and adore.

Up until the moment I'd heard the word 'incurable,' I'd been a patient man.

I didn't rush. I weighed up the pros and cons before I leapt. I enjoyed knowing every outcome before I committed.

But now…

Now, I was the opposite of patient.

I was thirsty and unrepentant and impetuous.

And I didn't wait for anything.

Not that Della wanted to. She was just as hasty as me to bind our souls together.

After a few days in the forest, both discussing and skirting the subject of my impending demise, we returned home as a united front and braved the storm of telling Cassie and Liam together.

John had helped.

Tissues had been used.

Curses had been uttered.

Hugs had been given.

John was right when he said this would be easier with people by my side, and I stood a little taller, a little braver for tomorrow.

It also meant things got done a hell of a lot faster.

Between all of us, we arranged a simple gazebo in the garden and a reverend to marry us. I gave up my concepts of marrying Della in a simple meadow, relinquishing planning to the grandiose ideals of Cassie and letting her invite Adam and his family.

While she plotted our wedding, Della and I visited oncology and the doctor who'd kindly put me on the off-label trial of Keytruda.

Rick Mackenzie was an old Scot who'd been away from home for decades but still had a burr of Scottish accent. He'd been gentle, explaining what I couldn't to Della, and answering her unsteady questions.

I'd held Della's hand, flinching when she flinched and soothing her when she cried.

I chose to have another treatment of Keytruda before my tests to see if I'd improved, and Della hissed between her teeth as the nurse pricked me with the needle and began the thirty-minute siphon of man-made magic into my body.

Once again, claustrophobia clawed, but it was thirty minutes of hell for hopefully a lifetime with my wife.

Afterward, with no side effects to speak of, Rick arranged for another CT scan, blood work, and X-ray, and also took samples from Della...just in case.

Our results were due any day now, and it'd been the hardest thing not to get my hopes up about my own prognosis and keep all fear away from Della's.

On our way back from the hospital—only a couple of days before our wedding—I pulled into town and parked, and just like that day in the junk store in a town I didn't remember, I had the undeniable urge to buy Della a ring.

A ring she would wear for the rest of her life.

"I need to go shopping." I turned to her, my hand on the steering wheel.

"I think I can guess what for." She smiled, opening the door. "No peeking?"

"No peeking." We climbed from the vehicle, and I locked up. "Meet back here in an hour?"

An hour had turned to two as I couldn't find the perfect ring.

My budget was tight and my wishes too lofty.

But at least, in the end, I got something that would hopefully trump her milky, fake sapphire.

I coughed a little, clearing my throat as Nina appeared at the top of the silver-carpeted aisle, scattering flower petals and dragging my mind to the present.

Wedding.

Marriage.

I was getting hitched today.

The fire-haired little girl Cassie had created with an equally fire-headed country boy. When we'd first been introduced, Nina had been shy and scuffed her sneaker into the dirt. That childish uncertainty reminded me so much of Della growing up that my heart had overflowed with echoes from my past.

Of Della smacking a kiss on my lips in the fields when she was nine.

Of Della squealing as I'd blown raspberries on her stomach when she was eight.

Of Della always there, always gorgeous, always mine.

It made standing at the top of the aisle beneath a flower coiled archway—a groom waiting for his bride in a new pair of jeans and white shirt—all the more poignant because finally, *finally* my dreams had come true.

I no longer had to fall asleep to find her. She was there in my every waking moment.

Raising Della had been my biggest challenge and my greatest honour and, as she appeared—blonde hair loose and simple white dress kissing her ankles, her tattoo blue with its ribboned R—I fell even more.

My heart no longer resided in my chest.

It made a home in her hand.

It settled content in her hold.

And it would stay there, even when the rest of me was gone.

My mouth went dry as she drifted toward me, looking ethereal and so damn young.

I never wanted to forget.

Not a single thing.

Not a fraction of a moment.

I'm so sorry, Little Ribbon.

So sorry for marrying you with an ending already close.

I should annul this marriage, never consummate it, and leave her untouched so she never knew the pain of being a widow.

But there were things I could do and things I couldn't…and this was one I couldn't.

I *had* to marry her.

I'd wanted to marry her since I'd found her.

John walked beside her—our joint father who'd adopted us heart and soul—while Cassie trailed behind her—a sister to us both.

Funny, how the two women who'd been in my life the longest had switched roles.

Once, Della had been my sister, while Cassie was my lover.

Now, Della was my almost-wife, and Cassie was my family.

And when Della arrived before me and John gave her to me with a smile and a look that cleaved my contaminated chest in two, I'd never been so happy or so sad.

All my dreams had come true and, because of that…my life was almost over.

I clutched her hand as we faced the reverend together. We shook equally, afraid and eager, nervous and sure.

The reverend smiled and nodded and spoke about the sanctity of our union.

I didn't listen.

I couldn't.

My entire attention locked on the stunning girl beside me, on the perfect way her hand fit in mine, and the knowledge that after this, she would no longer be a Mclary.

She'd be a Wild.

Her five-year-old suggestion no longer fake but so, so real.

With our eyes joined and love flowing, the reverend gave us state regulated verses and offered up church approved vows, waiting for us to parrot them after him.

Simple and uncomplicated.

No penned poems or scripted sonnets.

Just the bare essentials to bind us.

I couldn't tear my eyes off her as she repeated after him, "I, Della Mclary, choose you, Ren Wild, to be my lawfully wedded husband. For richer, for poorer, in sickness, and in health, for as long as we both shall live."

Sickness.

The worst one.

The one I was about to drag her through.

I'm so sorry, Della.

My voice shook as I struggled to hold myself together. "I, Ren Wild, take you, Della Mclary, to be my lawfully wedded wife. For richer, for poorer, in sickness, and in health, for as long as we both shall live."

Disguising the grief in my throat, I pressed a kiss to her ear, closing my eyes on the tears that threatened. "And long past that. Forever, Ribbon. Forever."

She shivered and laughed quietly as I pulled the ring I'd bought from my pocket. Her eyes widened at the solitaire diamond with an italic inscription inside:

Wild forever and always. I love you.

She shook her head, another emotional chuckle falling free. "I-I can't believe this."

I brushed aside a curl, imprinting the feel of her soft cheek. "What can't you believe?"

"That once again, we shared the same idea." Opening her palm, she revealed a glossy gold band with the same promise from my dinged-up leather bangle stamped inside.

DW ♥ RW4EVA

I wanted to curse.

To swear.

Profanity seemed the only cure to release the overwhelming pressure and love inside me, but with God watching us become man and wife, I just drew her close and kissed her deep, all while John chuckled, and Cassie swooned, and the reverend cleared his throat with reprimand.

"You're supposed to wait until *after* you've said the words 'I do.'"

With Della's lips on mine, we smiled and laughed, teeth clacking as we both murmured, "I do."

"I do."

My fingers fumbled on hers, switching her chipped sapphire to her other hand and sliding the diamond over her wedding finger. Once I'd trapped her with vows and jewellery, she trapped me.

I never thought a piece of precious metal could transfix me, but as that ring settled cold then turned warm, I no longer felt alone.

I felt an overpowering sensation of home and heart and hearth.

"You may kiss the bride." The reverend clasped his hands and stepped back.

There would be many things I remembered on my death bed.

So many wonderful things.

But that kiss?

That first kiss where Della was my wife would always be the brightest.

That kiss was our beginning, middle, and end.

That kiss bound us past life and death, sickness and health.

That kiss was life itself, never ending, forever existing, two souls entwined...

...for eternity.

* * * * *

"Are you sitting down?"

My fingers tightened around my phone, my eyes tracking Della as she packed a few clothes for us to return to the forest for a small honeymoon.

Only a couple of days, just enough to consummate—more than once—and to forget our future. If we could.

"No. Should I be?" My voice was gruff, belying the injection of panic.

Rick Mackenzie, my oncologist with his Scottish calmness, said, "Let's get the important stuff out of the way, shall we? Let's start with Della Mclary."

"Della Wild now. As of a few hours ago."

Della threw me a kiss, folding a t-shirt neatly.

"Congratulations."

"Thanks." My knees wobbled, depositing me onto the pushed together single beds of our youth. "Is she okay?" My eyes never left Della's as she plopped the t-shirt into the small pile we were taking with us and came toward me.

Slotting herself into the V of my spread legs, her fingers curled in my hair, and I held her waist to my nose.

I inhaled hard, smothering a cough as Rick said, "She's fine. No signs of any asbestos related diseases."

A cry that could only be described as tormented thanks fell from my lips, soaking into her belly button. "Oh, thank God."

Della hugged my head, trembling. "I love you, Ren."

Her whisper scattered around me as Rick continued, "As for you...I really should ask you to come into my office so we can go through any questions you might have, but...well, I can't wait. I wanted to tell you straight away."

Blackness slithered its way through me, blotting out my hope, tearing up the calendar pages of my heart, deleting the months I thought I had. His urgency created pure terror. "What is it?"

You have one month to live.

Kiss your wife goodbye.

Hope you have your casket sorted.

I planted a hand over my eyes, begging the depression to stop.

Rick's voice cut through the medley. "You're a positive responder, Ren."

For a second, I had no idea what that was.

All my research and knowledge, gone.

Poof.

Then the words deconstructed and reassembled into a sentence I could understand. *You're not dying...yet.*

The phone slipped through my hand. It bounced on the carpet like an undetonated bomb.

Was it real?

Was it true?

Not only had I gotten one dream by marrying Della today, I'd earned an extension from leaving her too?

"Ren?" Della's worried voice cut through the buzzing in my head. "You okay?" Ducking, she collected the phone and held it to my ear. "He's still talking."

I cupped her hand with mine, ignoring the phone.

My lungs blazed with pain, but I didn't trust that pain anymore. It was trying to make me believe in a lie.

I'm not dying...yet.

Gripping her hard, I breathed fast. "It's-it's good news. Fuck, it's *excellent* news."

For all my positive thinking, I hadn't dared hope for this.

It would fucking break me if it turned out to be bad.

She nodded frantically, tears sparkling. "Thank God." Urging me to take the phone, she said, "Find out more. Talk to him."

Licking my lips, I obeyed, still shell-shocked and disbelieving but ready to listen. "Sorry. Minor accident. Wh-what did you say?"

"What happened? You drop the phone?" Rick chuckled. "You wouldn't be the first. But...be happy. You didn't mis-hear. I said you're showing signs of improvement. As you know, mesothelioma is aggressive, and the tumours are small and dispersed throughout your lungs and abdomen. However, the treatment has halted any from multiplying. In some areas, they've even decreased."

"Holy *shit*."

Della whacked me on the shoulder. "Language."

I laughed, daring to grab a piece of lightness in all of this. "Sorry, Doctor Mackenzie."

"Bah, I've heard worse. And call me Rick. Think we're on first-name terms now that I'm healing ya."

Della bent and pressed her head against the phone, trying to hear. I pulled it away and put it on speaker so we both could listen.

Coughing just a little, I asked, "So...what now?"

"Now? We keep you on three weekly treatments and watch for more progress. If, in a few months' time, your lungs show significant improvement, you come off the drug and are announced in stable condition."

Don't ask.

Don't ask.

"And my prognosis?"

I asked.

Shit.

This was a happy time.

The best of times.

I shouldn't ruin it by asking for the new date of my death.

However, Rick laughed encouragingly, light-hearted even,

infecting me with his optimism. "Screw one to two years, Ren. You've just bought yourself a few more. I don't know how many more, but you're young, only stage one, and prepared to do whatever it takes. That in itself puts you miles ahead. As far as I'm concerned, we'll keep you alive for however long you decide."

"Forever." Standing, I pressed a kiss to Della's lips, talking more to her than my doctor. "I choose forever."

She kissed me back, breathing, "Forever, Ren. A hundred forevers."

"On that note, I'm gonna leave you two newlyweds to enjoy the good news. See you soon, Ren." Rick hung up.

Tossing the phone onto the bed, I swooped my wife into my arms and spun her around. "I hope you didn't marry me thinking I'd be dead in a couple of years, *Mrs* Wild."

Her head tipped back, blonde hair flying, diamond ring glinting. "God, you calling me that does things to me."

"Things?"

Her lips crashed down on mine. "Bad things. Wet things."

I stumbled to the wall, wedging her beside our old dresser. "I mean it, Della. I'm going to fight. Every fucking day."

"And I'm going to love you, every fucking day." She plastered my face with kisses like she used to do when she was a kid and excitement overflowed.

"Language." I nipped at her lip.

"Kiss me, husband." Her lips kissed every part of me, from chin to throat to ear.

I loved she still retained that childish enthusiasm.

I loved that she was giddy with joy, celebrating the best news of all.

Her lips gave up their flurry of kisses, seeking my mouth with sweet desperation.

I matched her with a different kind of fury.

One of bittersweet relief and explosive gratefulness.

I'd sworn my life to this woman.

We no longer had to play pretend husband and wife.

We were *real*.

As real as any other couple and just as permitted to love unconditionally.

And yet, I would forever be more than just a husband to Della. And she would forever be more than just my wife.

Our relationship would always have a different depth to it.

A unique connection that had been formed thanks to so many facets of love.

Love that had already been tested in so many different ways.

Breaking the kiss, I grabbed her hand and twirled her wedding ring.

"Wild forever and always." I quoted the inscription. "Time means nothing when it comes to true love. Promise me you understand that."

She searched my eyes, finding nothing but my soul bare and hers for the taking.

Death would still come for me.

But for now...we were hiding.

Hiding out of its reach, creating a life that would be so infinitely precious and pure.

She blinked back tears. "I understand, Ren."

"Good."

She smiled softly. "Fine."

The familiarity of such a silly phrase meant we didn't end up camping that night.

We fell together and consummated our marriage in the very same beds where we'd denied such a future from existing.

From children to adults.

From friends to soulmates.

Forever.

Forever.

And always.

Chapter Fifty-Seven

REN

2021

"REN?"

John lugged his big body from the couch where he'd been nursing a beer. "Can I have a word?"

Liam sat on the floor with his very pregnant girlfriend, and Adam had his wife, Carly, on his lap while their two kids played on the carpet.

Since Della and I hadn't made it to the forest for our honeymoon, the Wilsons had improvised and hosted an all-day affair of just hanging out. And for once, I didn't mind being around people.

These weren't just people.

They were *our* people.

Family.

Cassie had hired a last-minute caterer to feed us, seeing as Patricia's culinary magic was no more, and the Wilson grandchildren did a good job at pegging up the hole left by her missing presence—even though nothing could replace such an amazing woman.

Della and I were planning on going away tonight. We'd have a few days to ourselves before I threw myself back into my farm chores, saved some cash, and planned where we would live.

The one bedroom in the stable was too cramped, and although I'd had such good news yesterday, I wouldn't take any bonus years for granted.

I needed to sort out our future...soon.

"Sure, what's up?" I asked, swigging the final mouthful of my own beer—just one to celebrate—and catching the ever watchful, always loving eye of my wife.

Della had been Mrs Wild for twenty-four hours, and I couldn't stop looking at her or my ring on her finger.

She gave me a smile from where she sat with Cassie and Nina on the floor doing a puzzle. Pieces were scattered everywhere with Nina giving directions to her mother and aunt.

Cassie looked up, grinned at me, then glanced at her father and nodded secretly.

What the—

I didn't like that.

I didn't like secrets.

My hackles rose.

"Come into the kitchen." John tipped his white head toward the scuffed, well-used table and chairs. "Bring Della. This concerns her, too."

Whenever we had conversations at that table, things happened.

Big things.

Life-changing things.

I wanted to groan. What had he done now, the meddling ass? I still had his Cherry River contract tucked in the dresser in our room. I'd read the fine print, and sure enough, he'd given full insurance to all my health-related incidents.

I'd made a mental note to call the lawyer who had my Will and Testament and ask him how much John would stand to lose by covering me. I'd heard horror stories of some drugs costing thousands per week, sometimes tens of thousands.

I didn't want to die, but I wouldn't put anyone into destitution to save my life, either.

John was worth a lot with his land. If he were to sell, he'd be a millionaire without a doubt. But all that equity was tied into his legacy, and I never wanted to be the reason he'd be forced to sell.

Della cast me a look, climbing to her feet.

"Go on," Cassie whispered. "You'll want to hear this."

My eyes skipped over the Wilson children and grandchildren before Della clutched my hand and tugged me toward where John had sat down. The entire vibe of the place had changed. Everyone was in on this, whatever it was.

I narrowed my eyes warily. "What's going on?"

"Sit." John pointed at the chairs beside him, waiting until Della and I obeyed.

We sat, and my tension wound even more. "Okay, we're sitting. Now what?"

He smirked. "Always so suspicious."

"Always justified around you."

He chuckled, his large paws linking on the table top. "One of these days, you're going to learn to relax, Ren. Mark my words."

Phrases like that were double-edged swords. 'One of these days' implied a timeline that stretched into infinity. We both knew I didn't have infinity—not that anyone did. We all died...eventually.

But just because I'd had incredible news that I wouldn't be going anywhere for a while, it didn't stop the bitter-sweetness that it would be sooner than I liked.

"One of these days, you'll stop surprising me with your harebrained ideas." I smiled. "I mean, who gives a fifteen-year-old kid a place to stay and makes him family? Who hires a lawyer for a supposed kidnapper—"

"Yeah, okay. I'm a saint. I get the point."

Della laughed, making my heart wing as I reclined in my chair.

I chuckled under my breath. "Yeah, a saint who interferes."

He held up his hand. "Guilty."

"Once Ren has stopped giving you a hard time, John...what is it you wanted to talk to us about?" Della asked quietly, blonde hair scooped over her shoulder. Her ribbon around her throat today.

The same throat I'd squeezed from behind and pushed down while I took her.

Tearing my gaze away, I cleared my mind from inappropriate thoughts.

John grinned. "First, I want to say a very happy marriage to you two. It was an absolute honour to give you away, Della."

Della's cheeks pinked with affection. "The honour was mine, Uncle John."

My skin prickled with warning as John looked at me. "It's tradition, don't you think, that the father—or at least, pretend father of the bride, gives a gift on their wedding day?"

"John..." I warned. "What did you do?"

"What?" He blinked innocently.

He wasn't innocent.

Smiling, he raised his voice. "Cassie, darlin'? I forgot the file. Do you mind?"

"Not at all." Cassie leapt to her feet, earning a screech from Nina for disrupting the puzzle, then practically skipped into the kitchen where she placed a blue folder in front of her dad, kissed his white hair, then winked at me.

My nervousness blew into all-out alert. "What exactly is going on?"

"You'll see." Cassie blew Della a kiss, then went to sit with her daughter.

"John?" My eyebrow rose as the big man opened the file and smoothed out the papers with a hairy hand.

"Hold your horses, Ren. Give me a moment to find the right words."

"What words?"

"The words to tell you what I did and make you somehow accept it, without getting all high and mighty."

"Oh, for God's sake." I crossed my arms. "If this gift is more than just a bottle of wine then I'm not accepting it."

"Wind your neck in, Ren." John pointed a finger in my face. "Just 'cause you're sick—" He cut himself off with a terrified wince. "God, I'm sorry. I didn't mean to—"

"It's fine." I forced myself to relax and take the blame. "My fault. I'm winding you up."

Della scooted forward, placing a dainty hand on John's massive wrist. "He's the one being an ass. Take all the time you want and don't worry about his reaction." Her blue eyes met mine with a sharp glare. "I'll deal with him."

"You'll *deal* with me?"

"Yep." She stuck her chin in the air.

"Just because I married you doesn't mean I obey you, *Mrs* Wild."

"Oh, yeah?" She tried to stop a smile. "Well, I'll just have to beat you until you do."

"I'd like to see you try."

Lust sprung hotly.

Della averted her eyes, cheeks pinked and skin flushed.

John groaned. "Ever since that phone call from your oncologist yesterday, you've been incorrigible, Ren."

I shrugged, no longer caring what he was about to do. "What can I say? I'm the happiest guy alive."

No one mentioned the part of that sentence that lingered in the dark.

I'm the happiest guy alive...for now.

I could joke and laugh and be truly happy that I'd bought myself more time, but I also couldn't deny that the awful word still existed.

Incurable.

"Right, well, before you two disappear into the forest to do God knows what, I've done something." He laid his hand firmly on the folder like a judge would a gavel. "I've told you that I love you as much as I love my own kids. You *are* my kids. There is no difference. And because of that...I couldn't not do what I've done, if that makes sense."

"Your cryptic reply is not helping my ability to stay calm, John," I muttered, doing my best to read the papers his hand obscured. "What exactly is going on?"

"Having you guys back here, knowing the farm will be taken care of and that you're both happy and safe…that's a gift for me, do you understand? It's a gift because I saw where you guys came from, and I feel as if I played some small part in getting you this far."

"You did," I said fiercely. "Without you, I would've died of pneumonia."

"Without you, we wouldn't have trusted anyone or been fit to be around society," Della murmured.

"Well, I'm glad. But you're both stronger and braver than you give yourselves credit for, so I won't take all the praise." He looked down at the table, refusing to meet my eyes. "What I will do, though, is take your word that you'll accept this."

"Accept what?" My back stiffened, muscles locking.

"Give me your word." He narrowed his eyes. "Before I tell you."

"Not going to happen." I crossed my arms.

"Della?" John turned to her. "Give me your word, sweetie, seeing as that stubborn husband of yours won't."

"I won't risk his temper." She laughed. "Best spit it out. Otherwise, Ren will just snatch what you're hiding and find out anyway."

She's right.

I was seconds away from stopping this charade.

John chuckled. "You're probably right. Look at the man."

They both looked at me, twin expressions of affection and exasperation.

I scowled harder. "Ganging up on me won't make me take this any easier."

John laughed again, before slipping back into seriousness. "I changed my Will and Testament."

My heart stopped beating. The ruckus in the lounge quietened as the adults tuned in to listen. "Excuse me?" I leaned forward, ever so slowly. As methodical as a viper. "*What* did you say?"

John puffed out his barrel chest. "I asked Adam, Liam, and Cassie before I did it, and they're all on board. Don't think for a moment there is any bad blood about this, or that it can be taken away from you in the future. Because it can't."

"You're terrifying me." I swallowed hard. "What. Did. You. Do. John?" My teeth chopped every word.

His chin cocked, daring me to challenge him. "I split the farm five ways."

"*What?*" I shot to my feet. "What does that mean?"

"It means, Cassie has a fifth for her horse business, Adam has a fifth to do what he wants, Liam has a fifth for his interests, Della has a fifth, and you…well, you, Ren, you have a fifth, too. Just because Patty and I only gave birth to three kids doesn't mean we don't have five in our hearts. Our Will didn't include you guys, and now, it does. You each have fifty acres. It's a decision I needed to make. And it's a decision you have to accept because I'm not changing it."

Della started to cry beside me. "Y-you can't do that. It's too much."

"No, sweetheart." John reached across and wiped away a tear, his large hand almost smothering her entire cheek. "It's not nearly enough. I know you and Ren will protect this farm and work it the way it's meant to. If Adam and Liam want to sell out at some point, buy their shares and claim it for your own." He flicked a glance at Cassie. "I know my daughter won't be going anywhere, not now there's help on hand with her horses, and I love that Chip has entered the family business by running the books. I have no doubt between all of you, you'll make this land earn its keep ten times over."

I'd gone silent.

Words had vanished.

Anger twisted with guilt and fired into rage.

Della shook her head. "But it's not fair Ren and I get a piece each. Just give us one."

"No. You were two people before you became one. It's already drawn up." Sliding a stapled together document, he smiled. "See? You're listed as my inheritors, but the farm is officially yours now. I want to retire and enjoy my grandbabies. I don't want to be up at dawn anymore, but I also don't want to leave this place. You're allowing me to stay while doing all the hard yards for me."

I still hadn't said anything.

Didn't know how.

Didn't know if I wanted to yell, kill him, or burst into goddamn tears.

He'd not only given me land but a future I'd been desperate to give to Della. He'd provided for us when that was *my* job.

It felt like charity.

It felt like a slap in the fucking face.

Did he do this because I was dying?

Did he do this because he thought I couldn't give Della what she deserved?

My temper steadily grew until John looked up and made eye contact with me.

And he knew.

He knew what I struggled with because despite not being my true father, we were more alike than we thought.

"I'm not stupid, Ren. I know what you're thinking. You think I did this because of your diagnosis—"

"You don't know a thing about me—"

"Wrong." He stood, squaring off with me. "I know what it's like to love someone so much your only wish is to keep them safe. I know what it's like to fear their future if you're not in it. I know what it's like—" His voice broke, and his fists balled before he growled. "I know what it's like to face a future without the person you love, and it's so hard, Ren."

I vibrated with the urge to hit him.

He made me feel weak and wanting. Made me feel selfish for dying before I'd provided for Della—that I wouldn't be able to pave her future the best I could so she could walk safely ahead without me.

I was sad for him for losing Patricia.

Of *course*, I was.

But our situations were entirely different.

"I don't need your charity, John," I hissed. "I don't need you putting words in my mouth—"

"No, you need to accept that this isn't about you. It has nothing to do with you and has *everything* to do with love. I love you, Ren. And knowing what you're going through, it cuts me up inside. Out of anyone, you did not deserve this. You didn't deserve *any* of it. Not when you were a kid and not now."

My nostrils flared; my teeth grated together. "I'll survive. I always do."

"I know that. But I also know that love can be as much of a destroyer as it can be a gift. I didn't do this out of charity. I did it because you deserve it. You *and* Della. And I did it for me because I want you here. I don't want you to leave again. I want my farm looked after for years to come.

"But I'm also realistic that eventually, you won't be able to work the fields anymore. Your energy levels will mean you'll have to hire people. It's a responsibility and one that will be yours until your dying day. That isn't charity, Ren. That's reality, and I'm giving it to you, knowing you can cope with it."

His gaze fell on Della, who stood taut and stressed, watching us scream at each other. "I'll be beside you every step of this, Della. Ren has the hard part of battling this disease, but you have the hardest part by being left behind. I miss Patty every day. And I would never put that on anyone, especially someone so young."

Della broke into tears, running into his arms.

I couldn't move.

Glued to the floor.

Confused and lost and *howling*.

I would never be prepared to say goodbye to Della and leave her alone like Patty had left John. I wished I could take back my wish to die before her and man up and take that agony on her behalf.

She had the worst part of this.

Her pain wouldn't stop like mine on my dying day.

Her pain would continue, year after year, forever.

Fucking hell.

The urge to vomit prickled my skin with heat.

The diabolical, unchangeable, grief-stricken knowledge that I couldn't change any of this.

I couldn't stop it.

I couldn't refuse it.

None of this was new.

But, somehow, John had made it all so much more *real*.

I was trapped inside a body that had condemned me, and as much as I raged and begged for a solution—*any* solution—I wouldn't get free of my fate.

I clenched my jaw as caustic tears stung my eyes.

Yesterday, I'd married Della and felt as if my world was complete. Today, I wished she'd never met me so I could protect her—like I was born to protect her—and *never* break her heart this way.

I could call every specialist. I could research every study. I could try every drug, treatment, and experiment, hoping, always hoping, praying, threatening, bribing, selling my soul for a chance...*one chance*...but eventually...

Eventually, Della would be on her own.

And I'd be screaming in the void, yelling in perpetuity, pounding on the veil of this world and the next, desperate for Della to hear me. For her to know I might have gone, but I would *never* leave her. I would haunt her. I would be beside her when she slept and next to her when she moved on.

I would be there always because I couldn't accept anything less.

John looked over Della's head, his arms tight around her.

He followed where my thoughts had spiralled and gave me the saddest smile. A smile that said he understood. That he'd hold my wife when I was gone. That he would protect her when I couldn't.

He nodded. He vowed. He made me grateful as well as furious.

Then John's face slipped from understanding into the authoritative I-don't-take-any-shit farmer I knew. His voice was harsh and hard and almost cold in its delivery. "You *will* accept this, Ren. You will be happy about this."

I didn't know if he spoke about his oath to protect what was mine, the inevitability of my death, or the land he tried to stuff into my hands.

"This is merely a gift from one man to his son and daughter." John's temper simmered. "I'm not stepping on your toes or doubting that you can make a fortune for yourself. I'm not stopping you from living the life you want. If you don't want it? Fine, sell it. I don't care. Because it's *yours*. You earned it fair and square every day you broke sweat toiling in those meadows. You earned it the day you proved what a great kid you are. So don't you *dare* argue with me on this. Don't you motherfucking dare."

His voice broke again before he let Della go and grabbed another piece of paper. With a huff, he threw the document across the table to me. "Oh, and before you say anything, this is also for you."

I caught the fluttering piece of paper mid-air. My hands shook as I scanned the form and the rage, despair, and absolute dread at facing a future I didn't want disappeared.

My temper exploded in a bomb of gratitude.

Gratitude I didn't know how to stop, show, or share.

"Fuck," I grunted as I stroked the headline from the local building authority, approving a residential dwelling to be erected on the newly subdivided land of Cherry River Farm.

A home with planning permission on the two sections belonging to Mr. and Mrs Wild.

I could hate John.

I could hate myself.

But I couldn't hate true goodness and generosity.

Lurching around the table, I stood before his large bulk.

A cough fell from my lips.

A cough followed by another, thanks to the stress in my blood and the harsh breathing in my lungs.

And John let me cough.

He didn't flinch or look away as if I were a walking corpse already.

He merely waited.

Father Time himself, giving me every second I needed.

And once I finished coughing, his eyes widened in surprise as I pulled him into a hug. A hug full of violence and fists and curses. But a hug, nevertheless. "Goddamn you, John," I muttered into his ear. "Goddamn you for everything."

He merely patted my back and said, "You're welcome."

Chapter Fifty-Eight

DELLA

2022

THE NIGHT REN told me he was sick, my world fell apart. But…I also fell into something else too.

They said love had the power to make you become someone better than you were, but adversity and hardship revealed the truth about who you were at heart.

Nothing was truer than that.

I learned I had the power to say no to my tears whenever Ren coughed. I had the ability to laugh and stay light, even knowing my husband was on borrowed time.

Sadness was a part of everything we did, but we didn't let it consume us.

We lived life like we had before—throwing ourselves into work and play and tackling everything we could.

And…there was something else.

Something I'd tripped into, thanks to Ren.

Something I didn't figure out for an embarrassingly long time. Something that could be classed as unbelievable or just pure coincidental.

I liked to think it was the first one.

A marvel, a wonder, a phenomenon.

The fact that before Ren destroyed me, he'd made love to me, growling at the gods to impregnate me if they felt a shred of guilt for what they'd done to him.

I'd been off the pill for a week.

We'd had sex once before the forest and then multiple times afterward—thanks to getting married and ensuring we consummated the hell out of our union.

But…it didn't change facts.

My world had fallen apart...

And, I'd fallen pregnant.

I was *pregnant*.

And for months, I didn't know.

My body was used to not bleeding—thanks to being on a mini-pill which shut my cycle down. And Ren was the single most important thing on my mind; nothing else mattered.

If I wasn't with him during the day, I was reading about trials and diet supplements at night.

If we weren't working every hour the sun gave us in the fields, we were making love or sleeping under the stars.

I felt the same as always. I had no morning sickness, no nausea, stomach pains, breast tenderness, or food cravings.

There were no signs from before.

No hint that I was pregnant—ectopic or otherwise.

And then, John went ahead and gifted us a future that was solid and unbelievably safe, and we had even more on our minds.

One hundred acres of land.

Land with our names on it.

Land that Ren would turn into a fortune.

When I'd stood watching them argue about such a gift, I'd been pregnant.

When Ren took me to bed that night and made love to me roughly, dominantly, I'd been pregnant.

When I went with him to his next treatment and check-up with his oncologist, I'd been pregnant.

Son or daughter?

Boy or girl?

I didn't know.

Because I didn't even know I was knocked-up.

The news stayed secret for three and a half months.

There were no missing periods to count. No calendar days to circle. No nudges to perhaps take a test.

As the months went on, Ren and I carved out an hour here and there during the busy season to visit the bank.

The novelty of having drivers licenses—after sitting the tests— and marriage certificates never failed to bring a smile to our faces.

We weren't illegal or unknown.

We were hard working, trust-worthy, and had assets, thanks to John.

The bank approved us for a loan to build a modest three bed, two bath house on the land John had so kindly given us.

Signing the documents—agreeing to a debt named 'mortgage'

which literally translated to death pledge in French—we didn't waste any time. We'd gone from forest children to mortgaged adults, and somehow, we were no longer afraid of ties or roots. We'd found our corner of the world and were perfectly content.

A week later, we'd signed with a building company that promised a full house finished and delivered in six months and broke ground a few days later.

Life sped ahead as if in apology.

The winds blew in our favour, sailing us through smooth waters after being in a storm for so long.

Even Ren's health wasn't as terrifying as before. Another three treatments of Keytruda, and Rick Mackenzie decided he'd reached stable condition.

Ren was taken off the three weekly appointments but kept regular check-ups.

He no longer coughed as badly, and his slight rattle was quieter at night. His body was strong and toned, his appetite big and demanding, his smile bright and pain-free.

He didn't slow down for a moment—despite the nasty secret squatting in his lungs.

If anything, he became more physical, glowing with life and longevity.

I schooled my heart not to get too hopeful.

I begged my ears not to take the good news from doctors and twist it to believe he was cured.

Ren would *never* be cured.

But we had bought some time.

And we spent every second wisely.

When the diggers churned meadow to mud for the house's foundation, Ren and I kissed with our boots in the freshly tilled dirt beneath the moon.

When we weren't overseeing the builders creating our house, we were helping Cassie with her own construction. She'd taken her land and run with it—designing a larger barn, stables, arena, and round pen for her new equine venture.

As I'd been part of the conception and brain storming phase, Cassie asked if I'd help manage it with her. To become her partner, if I wanted, or an employee, if I preferred.

Her eyes gave another offer, too. An offer that said I'd forever have work and a way to support myself…even when Ren wasn't there with me.

We'd hugged with tears streaming and broke apart when Ren appeared with a heavy sack of horse feed over his shoulder.

He constantly worked.

He never stopped.

He made me nervous.

Yes, his body was stable.

But, surely, he shouldn't over-do it?

By the time I noticed what was cooking inside me, the foundations of our house were poured, the framework was up, and Ren was site foreman as well as farm overseer, cracking the whip every day to ensure things ran smoothly.

Watching him stride across pastures in faded, scuffed jeans and a white t-shirt stained with toil and tractor grease, I'd never been more in love with him. When he showered away sweat and grime from a long day working, I'd never been more in lust with him.

Just because I knew an end was coming, didn't mean I could stop loving him. And I fell even deeper when our first income poured in from a smaller paddock that we'd sold as free-standing hay—not having the time to cut and bale ourselves.

The money was more than enough to pay our mortgage payment for the next four months.

Holding that income, Ren had gone quiet, pensive, his thoughts going to that dark place where I couldn't follow.

The place of urgency to create a world for me before it was too late.

I'd left him to his thoughts, and he'd found me as I finished riding Cassie's warmblood Mighty Mo, then merely took my hand, and guided me to find John dozing on the deck of his farmhouse.

Ren didn't wake him up, just merely tucked an envelope of cash into his plaid shirt pocket and smiled at me.

Ren was a proud man as well as selfless and kind-hearted.

And that pride would always be a little bruised at accepting two-fifths of Cherry River Farm.

Thanks to earning money from that gifted land, his principals meant he had to pay John his dues—a rent, a tax...a thank you.

* * * * *

"We'll put the crib here. And we'll paint the walls a light green, don't you think? So he feels at home in the greenness of the forest before we take him there?" Ren spun to face me. "Good idea?"

His health.

His happiness.

His wonderment.

I laughed gently. "*Great* idea."

His gaze fell on my belly that had finally shown what was camping inside it.

Six months pregnant and everything was perfect.

Finally, after seventeen weeks of being utterly oblivious to what we'd created together, I'd stood naked before Ren after a shared shower, and he'd frowned at my lower belly. Dripping wet with a towel wrapped around narrow hips, he'd prodded me gently, his eyebrows knitting together at the firmness.

I'd winced as something sharp responded. Something that didn't feel like me.

I shifted backward from his touch, only for him to fall to his knees. He ran his hands over the area of my stomach that had hardened almost overnight. "Della, a-are you pregnant?"

Funny that he was the one to question first.

We'd made an appointment to see a family doctor the next day, and—thanks to identification and insurance—it was the easiest thing in the world to be seen, have an ultra sound, and be checked over.

According to the doctor, it wasn't unusual for first time mothers not to show for a while. I was physically active with strong stomach muscles and good posture. I already ate healthy and had a vivacious appetite.

I'd been giving my body exactly what it needed with no need for any natural nudges for better.

That had been two and a half months ago. My stomach had stayed flat for as long as it could, but now, it could no longer contain the steadily growing baby bump.

Ren came toward me, running his fingertips around my belly button. "How is he today?"

"Active." I rolled my eyes. "Your son thinks he's a footballer."

He chuckled. "I've never played sport in my life."

"Yes, but you do have a habit of kicking things."

"I also have a habit of loving you. For the past two decades."

"And you better not stop anytime soon, seeing as it's your spawn I'm carrying."

"Never, Ribbon. It's physically impossible to stop loving you." His lips spread into a smile as he bent to kiss me.

I leaned in to him, allowing his tongue to enter my mouth and flatten against mine in a sensual dance of hello and welcome.

I loved this man with every part of my heart.

He was my luck.

My wishing star.

My ever after.

I was pregnant with his child.

His son.

We'd blended ourselves.

We'd beat time at its own game, and instead of death, we'd claimed life.

And we'd keep claiming it.

Again.

And again.

For as long as possible.

* * * * *

Amazing how fast time could skip ahead.

Incredible how easy routine became when you were doing something you loved with the person you belonged to.

My life before—with its stress of loving Ren in secret, going to school, and pretending student friendships—was no longer on my radar.

At eight and a half months pregnant, life had never been so good.

Ren pampered me every night—even though he still worked every hour of sunlight and beyond. He rubbed my back, kissed my belly, brushed my hair, and slipped on my boots, seeing as I could no longer see past my fat stomach.

Jacob wasn't even in the world yet, but his father absolutely adored him.

Ren read articles online on how babies could hear in the womb, and often stayed up late talking to him.

On those nights, when Ren fell asleep whispering stories and telling tales, I'd listen to him in the dark.

For as long as I could remember, Ren was a bad sleeper. He'd toss and turn, pace in the night, and get up before dawn, just to avoid struggling with sleep that wouldn't come.

I was used to it.

It had always been that way.

Yet now, Ren had overtaken me in the sleep awards.

When his head hit the pillow, he was out.

His eyes flickering with dreams, his breath rattling with memory of what lived inside him, his body overly warm with circulation that ran just a little too hot.

Normally, I'd believe it was thanks to his long day at work.

But...I'd read up on his condition, and I knew the symptoms in and out.

Night sweats and fatigue.

Those were the ones I and only I knew that Ren had.

In everyday life, he was the poster boy of good health.

But when it was just us in bed, a scary little beast would sit on my pillow and whisper falsities about what Ren projected.

I didn't trust that he wasn't hiding how he truly felt.

I didn't believe he was as pain free as he made us think.

Instead of suffering silently, I should have spoken up—and I did, *of course I did*; it wasn't a matter to brush aside. I told Rick Mackenzie at Ren's last check-up, even as Ren glared at me as if I'd betrayed his confidence.

But the oncologist had just smiled and nodded and, in a bedside manner that I didn't appreciate—either stress or pregnancy snappiness—said unfortunately, it was to be expected.

Ren was stable, but he was still sick.

His body was fighting the good fight, so of course, he would sleep soundly.

His system was hoarding rest like a starving man hoarded food.

And I got that…but it didn't make it any easier.

The past eight and a bit months had made me believe in a fairy-tale.

The knowledge of what existed in our future was muted somehow beneath summer sun and lazy Sundays around the pond.

I'd stupidly allowed time to fuzz the urgency inside me, and I cursed myself to the depths of hell when, a few days later, my worries were vindicated in the worst possible way.

I stood in our kitchen in our new house.

It wasn't entirely finished—the walls were yet to be painted, curtains put up, and fireplace installed, but we'd moved in a week ago to a night of seduction in a bare bedroom with just a king mattress that we'd bought.

We kissed in every room to christen the place. And eventually, we would have sex in every room, but for now, I was too heavily pregnant for Ren to touch in any other manner than with tenderness.

I'd burst into tears as Ren carried me over the threshold the first time and paraded me around the first home we'd ever owned.

Our home.

No one else's.

Ours.

It wasn't overly large but had a cosy reading nook, cute living room, and country kitchen. Our bedroom was a simple square with large glass doors that led to a wraparound deck that welcomed the outside in.

The whole design was like a large tent with the main dwellings in the middle and sleeping quarters on either side.

We were twenty-three and thirty-three, both so young, so happy, so blessed.

And as I looked up from where I stood in the kitchen, the view of rolling meadows and untouched perfection better than any dream—I melted at how incredible it all was.

I rubbed my bulging belly, poking at the tiny foot making itself known in my side.

I sighed contentedly as I kept one eye on the view and one on cutting the crusts off Ren's turkey and mayo sandwiches.

Height of summer and he was working late.

The field had been cut three days ago and allowed to air dry in the heat. He'd turned it this morning and raked it into long rows, and now, as the sun hung low in the sky teasing with dusk, he was about to bale.

No rest for the farmer in summer.

Packing the sandwich into a bag with an apple, bottle of water, and a couple of Hershey's Kisses, I left the sun-drenched house we'd built and waddled my way down the garden with its flagstone pavers, through the yet-to-be-painted gate, and to the meadow beyond.

The sound of the tractor churned and coughed, the motor of the baler whirring in rhythm and clunking with age as loose grass went in one end and spat out the other as a rectangle bound by string.

Halfway across the large field, the crunch of metal and the abrupt sound of an engine ceasing wrenched my head up.

Oh, dear.

The first cut of the season was always the thickest, and the old equipment sometimes didn't cope.

Peering into the setting sun, I caught sight of Ren as he leapt from the tractor and went to investigate the attached baler.

He staggered a little from jumping from a height.

He stumbled forward as if gathering his momentum.

I thought nothing of it.

I'd seen him trip from the tractor a thousand times.

He might not be the most agile, but he was springy.

My eyes stayed on him, expecting him to solve the puzzle of his legs and stay upright.

Only…this time, he didn't find his feet.

His arms didn't spread out for balance. His body didn't twist for purchase. His spine rolled, his head flopped, and he tumbled forward, vanishing into the rowed grass.

For a second, I couldn't compute what had happened.

My retinas still burned with a picture of him standing.

But he was gone.

Disappeared.

No, no, no, no.

"*Ren!*" My screech sent a cloud of sparrows and starlings feeding on bugs in the grass into the skies. "Ren!" I dropped his dinner and forgot I was pregnant.

I broke into an ungainly sprint. *"Ren!"*

He didn't get up.

He didn't appear.

Please, please, please.

I ran and ran.

Waddled and waddled.

Galloped and galloped.

The field was big, and I was slow.

It took an eternity to reach him, and by the time I did, my belly sliced with an agonising blade.

Grimacing, I ignored it, skidding to my knees beside Ren.

"Come on. You're okay," I gasped, telling Ren he was okay, but maybe telling myself more. "Wake up." Face first in the grass, I brushed aside his sun-bronzed hair and found a closed eye.

Slack lips.

Smooth forehead.

Shallow breath.

Another slice cut right around my middle, wrenching a grunt and groan-scream from my lips.

Once again, I ignored it, and with all my strength, pushed Ren's shoulder until he rolled and flopped onto his back.

His hands stayed unmoving.

His arms bent.

Legs crossed over each other from being rolled.

Grass stuck to his hair and face, and my hands shook as I tried to brush it aside.

He didn't move.

Didn't flinch.

Didn't speak.

Another lacerating pain rippled through my abdomen as I bent over him, tapping his cheeks. "Ren." Tapping turned to slapping the more unresponsive he became. "Ren! Don't you dare do this to me, Ren."

Tears cascaded.

More pain pulverised my belly.

No one was around to help.

Pulling his head close, I had no lap to cradle him, thanks to my pregnant belly. I had to settle with an awkward hug.

I rocked him.

I cried for him.

I did the only thing I could.

I screamed.

And something answered that scream, deep in my belly, twisting and tearing, desperate to get out.

Once again, I ignored it.

"No, no, *no*." I hugged Ren, another blood-curdling cry tumbling from my lips.

I didn't know what I screamed, only that I did.

I screamed again and again.

And still, he didn't wake up.

And then, in a flash of sunset, something winging caught my eye.

Cassie.

Thank God, Cassie.

She bolted fast on Mighty Mo. Bare back and just a halter, as if she'd snatched the horse from his stable and kicked him into a run. His hooves ploughed through grass rows, jumping others. "Della!"

I groaned, tipping forward into the grass as my own pain overcame me. Planting a hand over the worst pressure I'd ever felt, my palm nudged the small hardness of my pocket-stored cell-phone.

Stupid.

So stupid.

Wrenching it out, I shook and grunted as yet another knife punctured my insides. Crawling closer to Ren, I blinked back tears and punched the numbers for help.

The call connected quickly.

An operator urgent and brisk. "What's your emergency?"

My breath tore and laced with misery and woe. Another vicious band of agony worked through my belly, my hips naturally spreading, my thighs growing warm.

"A man. He's unconscious. He has stage one mesothelioma. *Please*—" Pain cut me off. "Send an ambulance. Cherry River—"

I hissed as yet another wave hit me, this one stronger than the last. I moaned into the phone, buckling over, holding the baby in my belly. The baby who'd chosen this exact moment to arrive. "—Farm. Please hurry."

"Okay, ma'am, we're sending someone right now."

A gush of wetness drenched my underwear, and I laughed.

Laughed with sick disbelief and incredulous timing.

"Oh, *Goooddd*," I groaned, not able to hold my belly and my husband at the same time.

Death had visited.

Life wouldn't be ignored.

Both battled to kill me.

"You okay, Ma'am?" the operator asked.

I shook my head, my lips spread wide.

I couldn't speak.

But I didn't need to.

Cassie arrived in a flurry of horse and hooves, leaping off to slam to her knees beside me. Mighty Mo snorted like a dragon, wired and amped, feeding on stress.

Cassie ignored him, took one look at Ren, then focused entirely on me. "Shit, Della." Snatching my phone, she barked. "Ambulance. Two of the damn things. One for a man with asbestos cancer and another who's just gone into labour."

She nodded to whatever the man said on the other end. "Yes. Back meadow. John Wilson will help you."

I screamed as yet another deeper, demanding fury filled me. A fury tangled with bone and blood and bruises.

"You need to hurry," Cassie snapped.

Throwing my phone into the grass, she gathered me close, placed her hand on Ren's shallow breathing chest, and kissed my cheek. "It's okay, Della. You'll both be fine. You'll see."

I was glad she was there.

Grateful for help.

Only problem was...I didn't believe her.

Chapter Fifty-Nine

REN

2022

FLASH.

The field with grass at optimum dryness to bale.

Flash.

A clunk and crunch as the baler wrapped up in stalks.

Flash.

Red and blue lights around me. Sirens loud inside me.

Flash.

Intruders, questions, the swish and sway of reckless driving.

Flash.

Wheels screeching, oxygen flowing, a sharp prick in my arm.

Flash.

Della's screaming, strangers shouting, a world in utter disarray.

Something dragged me down, something heavy and warm and thick. I wanted to go with it, to give in, but the awful, awful sound of the one person I'd promised to protect every day of my goddamn life wrenched me through the fog.

I clung to her voice, clawing to her, crawling to her, fighting mud and sludge and pain.

My eyes opened.

I was no longer in the field.

I was no longer dressed from the waist up.

I was no longer a farmer but a patient.

"Oh, thank God!" Della grabbed my hand, her fingernails digging in. "Ren. I thought…" She shook her head. "You wouldn't wake up."

The outside world had been replaced with the insides of a hospital.

An emergency room with traffic and trauma and triage.

My throat was raw and lungs seared.

I'd been in pain lately.

The backache.

The chest ache.

But I had things to do.

Life to conquer.

A future to pave.

Della bowed over me, pressing her forehead to my cheek. "Please, please don't scare me like that again."

My arm came up from where I lay on a narrow bed, hugging her head, kissing her hard. "I'm sorry, Ribbon." I coughed, and she flinched.

Her eyes widened, then she buckled over me, digging her face into the crutch of my shoulder, her lips spread in a guttural scream.

My weakness?

My confusion?

None of it fucking mattered.

Jack-knifing upward, I tore at wires stuck to my chest and ripped an oxygen tube from my nose. "Della."

"Hey, Mr. Wild. You need—"

"*Stop!*" I roared, clutching onto Della as she stumbled by my bedside. "What the hell is wrong with my wife?"

"She refused to leave," a skinny nurse with mousy blonde hair snipped. "She's in labour. Apart from physically manhandling her, we couldn't do anything about it."

"Goddammit." I swung my legs off the narrow bed, dislodging yet more medical equipment. My lungs burned. Chest throbbed. Heart palpitated in an uneven rhythm.

But I didn't care about any of it.

"Get back into bed, sir," someone commanded.

I grimaced as my world flipped upside down. My feet found a ground that rocked. My mind found a world that sloshed and greyed. I swam in light-headedness, scooping Della into my arms, and laying her pregnant weight on the very same bed I'd just vacated.

"Sir, she needs to be in maternity."

"She's in pain, can't you see? Help her instead of spouting bullshit!"

Della screamed as yet another contraction worked through her. Her legs spread wide and dirty shoes dug into sterilized white. "Oh, *fuucckk*. God, it hurts." Her hand found mine, squeezing me to the point of metacarpals crunching.

"Someone get her something!" I yelled. "What the hell good are you, huh? Do your goddamn jobs and *help* her!"

My lungs wheezed, and a ribcage-splintering cough found me,

bending me in half.

"Sir, you need to calm down."

Coughing, coughing, always fucking coughing, my anger spilled like magma. When I could breathe, I roared, "And you need to fucking help her! *Now!*"

Della groaned, adding another layer to the mayhem.

"Sir—"

"What the *hell* is going on here?!" A doctor with a shaved head and goatee marched forward, waving his arms as if he could part the sea of medical staff like the messiah.

Grabbing a clipboard that hung on the end of the bed, he scanned the notes, then pointed in my face. "You. Seeing as you're awake. Oncology. Now. You need some tests." Spinning to face the skinny nurse loitering around Della, he ordered, "You, go get the midwife assigned to Mrs Wild."

His eyes fell on another staff member. "You, go tell those people demanding answers that he's woken up and she's about to have a baby. We need silence, not anarchy."

When his bossy gaze met mine again and found I hadn't left Della's side, he bared his teeth. "*Get.* Oncology. Now."

"I'm not leaving." I stepped closer to the bed, partly to touch Della's face and partly because I needed to lean against something. Coughs rattled and wheezed, not appreciating I fought their desire to make me bend over again.

I *refused* to cough.

I wasn't the one in need of treatment, Della was.

"My wife is having a baby. If someone doesn't look after her—"

"Threats now?" The doctor rolled his eyes. "Leave before I have you committed."

"I'm not leaving until I know my wife is okay."

"Oh, for Pete's sake," the doctor grumbled. "If you collapse, you'll be strapped in the psych ward just to teach you a lesson."

"I'm not going to collapse." My needs faded every time in lieu of Della's. I could be on death's door and tell the devil to wait until I knew Della was safe.

My jaw locked together as I fought another wave of coughing. "So, are you going to do something?"

"You're in a hospital, Mr Wild. Of course, we're going to do something."

Della moaned and writhed as another nurse dashed toward us. With efficient jerks, she pulled a curtain around us, cutting us off from the emergency room mania.

Once private, she pushed Della's dress up her legs, pulled her underwear down, and laid a green cloth over her lap. With calm hands, she manhandled Della's feet, placing them as close to the side of the bed as possible.

No one mentioned she wasn't in a hospital gown or tried to remove her shoes.

It was too late for any of that.

"The midwife is on the way," the nurse said. "We don't have anywhere else for you to go on such short notice, and you're too far along to be moved. You'll deliver here and then be transferred to maternity."

Della grimaced, her skin blotchy with pain. "Okay."

It wasn't okay.

None of this was okay.

I'd woken to the worst kind of horror.

The goatee, bald-headed doctor nodded brusquely. "Glad order has been restored. They'll look after you from here. Now, if you'll excuse me." Sweeping out from the curtain-created room, his voice barked more commands outside.

I coughed again, fighting it from turning into a fit. "You all right?" I asked Della, pressing my fist into her pillow for stability.

She bit her lip, nodding in agony. Her face shone with sweat, scrunched and red.

I'd done this to her.

I was the monster responsible for such torture.

"I'm so sorry, Della."

For five months—since we found out she was pregnant—I'd been fucking petrified of losing her.

I wasn't a happy, expectant father.

I was surly and snappy and scared shitless of losing her.

So many things tore me into knots, and as the days marched onward, and she grew fatter and more cumbersome, I'd had nightmares of losing her.

At least she hadn't struggled with this pregnancy as she had with her first.

But that didn't make me worry any less.

And now, my wife had gone into premature labour. Only by a couple of weeks but enough to make her every grunt and groan rip my broken lungs into ribbons.

I was so selfish to want a kid with her.

So self-centred to expect her to go through this purgatory.

I didn't know how much time passed.

I didn't know how long the gates of Hell could stay open.

I felt weak and useless and begged time to hurry.

All I could offer was my hand as she bore down and started to push.

The midwife arrived and spoke soothing and calm.

The noise from outside our curtain faded.

The fear that Della would die in childbirth continued to terrorize me.

On and on Della struggled, until finally, she gave one last scream, and something tiny with the wail of something huge arrived.

He sounded pissed off, insulted, and angry.

Once again, my breath rattled and lungs struggled to convert air into oxygen.

My vision danced with greyness as a flurry of activity happened between Della's legs, and something bloody and raisin-like was burrito-wrapped and placed on her heaving chest.

For a second, I hated it.

I despised it for hurting the creature I loved most in the world.

But then, its ugly, pinched face turned to me, and my knees almost gave out.

Because what I'd told Della was true.

My love for her would never change.

It would never diminish.

Never fade or struggle to choose.

Staring into that bloody, new-born face, love grew.

And grew.

And *grew*.

It grew until it spilled into every nook and cranny inside me, a sticky syrup there to stay.

The heart was a miraculous thing—I'd always known it was. And now, it fabricated a new chamber, building a home for Jacob inside the castle where Della had always lived.

My heart was no longer just an organ…it was a city ruled by my wife and son.

My son…Jacob.

The tiny noisy human.

The baby that carried my blood, my breath, my bone.

The child who would protect my wife long after I had gone.

Chapter Sixty

DELLA

2032

THE FOURTH INCIDENT.

Ren's collapse and Jacob's birth.

A date that would forever herald happy and horrified memories.

When they put my baby in my arms and Ren kissed my brow with a look of utter awe and besotted wonderment, I knew it had all been worth it.

The stress of his collapse.

The pain of Jacob's delivery.

I would do it all over again because we held life in our arms.

However, I must warn you.

I must advise you that you have a choice from here, dear reader.

A choice that I never had, but a choice, regardless.

Up until now, life was perfect.

And it can remain perfect…for you.

You've read a story that pens as a fairy-tale with its troubled beginning, love conquering all, happy marriage, and perfect baby.

After all, I did start this book with the words 'Once Upon A Time…' which requisites a happily ever after.

And I can give you that.

You can stop here and bask in our marriage, new home, good fortune, and baby in his baby carriage.

But if you don't…be brave.

Be brave, just like I am, because our tale is based on fact, not fantasy.

It is based on life. A life that everyone must endure.

Life that some would rather not read about because it's too close to the truth.

Why cry for a story when there are so many hardships in your own world?

And I get that.

I really do.

So…I tell you again.
You can stop.
I won't think any less of you.
I won't be sad you didn't stay with me until the end.
But, please know, from here on out, I can't lie to you.
I will give you happiness.
I will give you hope.
But I will also give you pain.
But you already know that.
You know what's coming.
We all know time is never on our side.
This is your final warning.
Stop.
Close the book.
Move on.
But if you're like me and understand that nothing perfect lasts forever, if you're strong enough to accept what life ultimately gives, it taketh away, then thank you.

Thank you for being there beside me.
Thank you for not leaving me alone.

Chapter Sixty-One

REN

2022

"THE TESTS show your mesothelioma has spread."

Any happy feelings I had from watching my son come into the world popped like a shitty balloon.

I balled my hands. "It's not mine. It's never *been* mine. I didn't fucking want it in the first place."

"Sorry. Bad phrasing." Rick had the decency to look apologetic, his white lab coat bright on my over-stretched senses. "But it doesn't change facts. The tumours have increased. You're no longer stage one."

Shit.

Shit.

Shit.

The entire time I'd been subjected to yet more tests, I'd refused to sit down, but now, I tumbled into a chair in front of Rick Mackenzie's desk. He'd come in especially to oversee my results, seeking an answer to why I'd fallen unconscious in the pasture.

All I could remember was struggling to breathe.

And then…nothing.

"Did you hear me, Ren?" he asked gently.

I nodded, leaning forward and wedging my elbows on my knees. "Yes, I heard you." My voice was barely audible, not prepared to accept such things.

How could a single day hold the highest of highs and lowest of lows?

After Della had given birth and Jacob had been cleaned, weighed, and returned, the hospital staff had ensured Della was comfortable, helped dress her in a clean gown, and wheeled her to maternity where she'd earned a much-needed rest.

I'd ignored the annoyingly persistent doctors about heading to oncology while Jacob underwent his own tests—seeing as he was premature. He was carefully checked, just to make sure he was in working order.

And thank God, everything functioned as it should.

He was a robust little thing.

Only once Jacob and Della were asleep, and wouldn't know any better, did I take the lift to the level where permanent sickness slinked down the corridors and death slithered on the air, trawling the wards for its next victim.

I *despised* this place.

I despised it even more after coming from maternity where the flapping of cranes could still be heard from dropping off new-borns, bringing new life to every corner.

My chest ached as I coughed.

Rick's forehead furrowed. "Cough up any blood lately?"

"No." I sat taller, straightening my torso for a better breath. "Not since that first time. Think I'd just irritated my throat."

Rick nodded, studying my file that had grown rather comprehensive. He slouched, running a hand through his salt and pepper hair. "As a doctor, I know these things happen and this was an inevitability, but as your friend, I can't help feeling like I let you down."

I narrowed my eyes. "Why do you say that?"

"You were responding so well to Keytruda. We should've just kept you on it."

"Yeah, but I'd gone stable." I didn't know why I was arguing or trying to make him feel better. I guessed I didn't want him feeling as wretched about this as I did.

How the hell would I tell Della?

How would I admit that the past year—running full tilt into our future with houses and businesses and babies might be one of our last? I'd worked my damnedest to get things sorted. I'd arranged my funeral and paid for it behind Della's back. I'd taken out life insurance on myself in Della's name to cover the cost of our mortgage with enough left to send Jacob to school. The fine print had been exhausting with my diagnosis but as long as I lived seven years, they'd pay out. If I didn't...I'd have to look at alternatives.

I'd covered my bases the best I could.

I'd crossed my t's and dotted my i's or whatever that saying was.

I had the worst parts of my death covered.

But just because we'd finally earned everything we wanted, and I'd protected Della as much as I could, it didn't mean I was ready to fucking die.

We had so much to look forward to, yet I might be leaving her with a brand-new baby and a broken heart.

"Christ." I clamped a hand over my mouth as a rush of horror filled me. My fingers dug into my cheeks as my heart slammed.

Rick looked up. "You okay?"

Dropping my hand, I groaned, "No, I'm not fucking okay. Della just had our child. How the hell can I leave her with that on her own?"

"You're not dying straight away, Ren."

My vision greyed as my heart turned arrhythmic. "How long?"

He shrugged. "There's still plenty of time. You're stage two. Yes, it sucks, but it's better than stage four. We'll put you back on Keytruda and supplement immunotherapy with a few sessions of chemo."

I froze. "Chemo?"

"We'll give you drugs to combat the side effects. They've proven to help with nausea and hair loss. We won't keep you on it long. Just enough to zap those bastards."

I looked away, my eyes dancing over the room, desperate to find something that wasn't a medical sketch or graphic image. I wanted trees and grass and sunlight. I needed to get out of this godforsaken place.

"We should discuss what happened in the field," Rick said. "What made you pass out? Pain? Breathlessness?"

I shrugged, dropping my gaze to the floor. At least that was boringly safe with its grey-yellow linoleum. "I couldn't breathe. I don't remember, really. Just...air that refused to come."

"Okay. Have you been overdoing it?"

I chuckled under my breath. "Define overdoing it."

"Working from sun-up to sun-down, not resting, not stopping to eat a decent meal?"

"Ah." I grinned morosely. "Based on that, then yes. I might have been overdoing it."

Rick scowled, his Scottish accent thickening. "This isn't a joking matter."

"Don't you think I don't know that?"

"I know you're trying to get your life in order...before you can't. But you also have to give yourself the best possible chance—"

"No. I have to give *her* the best possible chance. My pain ends when I die. Hers doesn't."

Rick stilled. "*Are* you in pain?"

I clenched my jaw. I hadn't meant to reveal that. I'd done a good job of hiding that even from Della. It wasn't often. It wasn't all the time. But the discomfort was starting to weigh on me.

"If you need painkillers—"

"I can handle it."

Rick clicked his pen with sharp stabs. "It's not about handling it, Ren. It's about taking that uncomfortableness away, so your body can focus on other things."

"So your answer is yet more drugs? Drugs on top of drugs." I rolled my eyes. "I'm surprised I don't bleed chemicals at this point."

Rick sighed, frustrated. "What other option do you have? Be a walking infusion of pharmaceuticals or die sooner? It's not really something that can be debated."

My hands curled. None of this was fair.

I knew I was being a prick. I knew my surly temper wasn't helping. And I knew that I'd deliberately done this to myself because I shouldn't have worked so damn hard.

I *knew* all of that.

And yet...Della.

I couldn't leave her in a one bedroom stable at the generosity of the Wilsons. Of course, they'd never turn her out, but it wasn't just her anymore.

My allegiance had grown to incorporate my wife *and* my son.

And they both needed protecting the best way I could.

John had overstepped and given us land that we could never afford, and that ate away at me every goddamn day. But at least, by working the fields and making it earn its keep, I had an income to pay him back. A little at a time, a dollar here, a hundred there, until I'd repaid him at market value of what the hundred acres were worth.

I wouldn't finish that duty before my dying day, but I could whittle out a large chunk. Then the land would *truly* belong to Della and Jacob because I'd bought it for them with blood, sweat, and the occasional tear in the dark.

A tear for everything I would miss.

A tear for everything I loved.

"Wh-what about surgery?" My voice was small, hunching in on itself.

I didn't want to be cut open, but I would if it gave me more time.

I would do anything for another year, another day, another hour.

Rick inhaled. "Surgery is an option. However, as with everything, it comes with risks."

"What sort of risks?"

"Well, there are a few procedures. EPP, Extra Pleural

Pneumonectomy, is the most radical as it removes an entire lung, the lining around the lung, and the diaphragm. Needless to say, recovery after surgery can be long, and you'd have to change your lifestyle to accommodate living with a single lung, as well as be prepared for other complications down the line." He clasped his hands together, discarding the clicking of his pen. "I have thought about it, I won't lie. But with your tumours being so small and in both your lungs, it's not something I'd recommend."

I swallowed hard. "And the other options?"

"Pleurectomy/Decortication, also known as lung-sparing surgery. It's more detailed than EPP but leaves the lung intact and only removes the pleura lining. Again, I wouldn't recommend it. The only one I might consider is Thoracentesis, which can be done under local anaesthetic where a long, thin needle is used to drain fluid in the pleural space, or Pleurodesis, where talc is injected into the layers of the pleura and then suctioned out."

I winced. "Sounds painful."

"It's actually a fairly straightforward procedure that requires minimal healing, and ninety percent of patients claim it gives them relief from pain and breathlessness. The lungs create scar tissue, effectively sealing the pleura and preventing any more fluid build-up."

I nodded, doing my best to drink in long words and scary explanations.

Rick picked up his infernal pen again, clicking. "With multimodal treatment, you can still have years left, Ren. Don't give up just because you've progressed. We all knew that would happen. Don't let it get you down, okay?"

I forced a smile. "I'm not giving up, if that's what you're thinking."

"I wouldn't dare think that. Out of any case I've seen, you have something unique tying you here that will prove to be better than any surgery or drug."

"Oh?" I raised my eyebrow, coughing softly. "What's that?"

"Love." He smiled. "True love has its claws in you, and I doubt it will ever let go. Fight for that. *Live* for that. And we'll make sure to buy you enough time to watch your son grow."

Chapter Sixty-Two

DELLA

2023

THAT FIRST YEAR with a new-born and a husband fighting the worst kind of unfairness, I couldn't lie...it was the hardest year I'd ever endured.

After the initial wash of endorphins in the hospital with Ren and me kissing, watching baby Jacob as if he was the most fascinating thing we'd ever seen, and living in a cocoon of delight, life interrupted and sped up far too fast.

There was no time to tell Ren how shit-terrified I'd been when he'd collapsed.

No space to yell at him and tell him to take it slow.

He already knew he'd screwed up, and I didn't need to drag yet more sadness into our tentative world.

So, we buckled down and fought.

God, we fought.

We fought so hard I don't remember anything else.

All I remembered was the exhaustion from a baby thrust into a world of sad instability and eyes that were permanently swollen from all the tears I refused to shed.

While I nursed a grizzly baby, Ren had treatments every other week. One week, he'd be subjected to Keytruda—a drug I was fond of as it had helped him before. And one with chemo—a drug I was not fond of as it made him sick.

Even with the pills that Rick Mackenzie gave him to counteract the side effects, Ren had a rash where the chemicals entered his skin and complained of bone aches so bad, he submitted to taking painkillers on top of all the rest.

By the fourth session of chemo, his cheekbones were more defined and his body more sinew than muscle. He hadn't lost weight exactly but tightened, somehow. The parts of him that made him so dependable and capable sucking deep within to fight.

By the second month of Jacob being home and the builders kindly racing to finish our house, even while we lived there, Ren became allergic to sunlight.

His eyes couldn't handle the brightness, even with sunglasses. His skin burned instantly, even with sun cream. Whatever the doctors had injected into him had done something to his biological makeup, and it was hard not to smash apart everything in our newly finished house.

It was hard to stay strong for him when I was so helpless.

It was hard to keep Jacob happy when I didn't know the meaning of the word myself anymore.

It was in those moments—those life-sucking, abyssal moments—that I carried my child to the willow grotto and sat amongst their fronds.

I'd allow myself to be sad, only for a moment.

I'd allow myself to talk to Jacob about things no baby should know about their terminally-ill father, piecing myself back together again to be brave.

Even dealing with so much, Ren never let me down.

We took turns bathing Jacob and putting him to bed. We'd tell stories together, finding laughter amongst so many heartaches when we relived our own tales of childhood.

John hired an out of town contractor to finish the baling and, on the days when the chemo hit Ren bad, Cassie became a godsend by babysitting Jacob while I held Ren on the bathroom floor as he shivered and vomited and apologised for ever letting me see him that way.

Like I said, that first year was the hardest I'd ever endured.

But even though our life was a sequence of tough and tougher moments, I never regretted for a moment having Jacob.

As he grew from toothless babe to inquisitive bright-eyed creature, I could see why Ren had both hated and loved me when I was young.

I hated not knowing what I was doing. Hated the lack of rest, the loud crying, the struggle to learn a language I didn't know. But I loved, *loved* watching him develop a personality. I loved being responsible for his learning, growth, and the fact that he blossomed in weight, happiness, and joy even while his parents lost those things.

We'd been given the gift of life with our son, and the payment seemed to be the cost of his father's soul. And as much as I loved Jacob, I honestly didn't know if I could afford the price.

My heart broke on a minutely basis.

That was until Jacob's fourth month and Ren's oncologist

announced he was happy with his results and took him off chemo.

The tumours hadn't shrunk like last time, but they had stabilised, and he was given a positive outlook again.

It was all agreed that Ren would stay on Keytruda...for the rest of his life. And slowly, as the chemo side effects left his body, he put back the weight he'd lost and ventured outside again where the sun was no longer his enemy.

We'd walk together over the meadows with Jacob in his arms, and we'd soak in the beauty of a sunset, imprinting the memory, clutching it tight for the day when they'd be no more.

Luckily, by the time Christmas arrived, no one would guess Ren was sick.

His smile was broad, strength impressive, and attitude toward life still as vicious and possessive as before.

When summer returned, there was no argument about who would work the fields, and Ren took his place on his beloved tractor, sucking hay, tipping his hat, his skin tanned and glowing.

On our son's first birthday, he made love to me with such passion and power, he convinced me what we'd lived through was just a nightmare.

A nightmare we'd woken from.

A nightmare we wouldn't have again.

As his body thrust into mine and his lips cast a spell over my mind and heart, I threw myself into a better dream.

One where Ren would be around to watch his son have his own sons and daughters.

A dream where we grew old together.

And for a while...it came true.

* * * * *

2024

Jacob turned two, and we spent the day with the Wilsons in the old farmhouse.

Cassie helped me bake a cake with two *Spiderman* candles, and John bounced his honorary grandson on his knee while Ren shared a drink with Liam and Chip on the couch.

So far, 2024 had been the opposite of 2023.

Ren was healthy—in relative terms—and happy.

Jacob was walking and into everything.

And Cassie's horse business—that she'd named Cherry Equestrian—had been running for six months. So far, she'd broken in three horses and entered one local show-jumping contest where she came second. The prize money was enough to buy more tack and a new saddle.

After an afternoon of birthday presents and eating cake, Jacob passed out as Ren carried him across the field to our house.

Occasionally, he'd cough, but thanks to Keytruda and painkillers, Ren was almost as content as the year when I'd been pregnant and he'd made the impossible possible by building a house, marrying me, and becoming a true Wild.

"By the way, I did what Rick suggested."

Ren's voice settled around our feet as the moon cast him in quicksilver shadows.

I looked up, my heart skipping a beat at the sharp lines of his jaw, slight stubble, and perfect lips. His brow was drawn and eyes dark, but his hair danced to its own beat with the slight breeze over the paddock.

"Oh?" I reached out and squeezed Jacob's tiny foot. It was too irresistible, dangling from his father's embrace, encased in a miniature sneaker. It constantly amazed me that manufacturers could make adult apparel in toddler sizes.

"About the lawsuit."

"Ah, right." I nodded.

Rick had mentioned it to me, too. He'd told me alone, actually. Mentioning the god-awful subject of *after*.

After Ren was gone.

After.

I hated, *hated* that word.

Apparently, due to having his life cut short by unnatural means, Ren was fully within his right to claim compensation. There were claimants and lawsuits toward the asbestos company numbering in the thousands, but the successful pay outs were either while the victim was still alive or the person left behind filed within one to two years.

After that, it was too late.

Letting Jacob's foot go, I shuddered. "I don't like the thought of benefiting from your…" I swallowed, cursing the familiar sting in my eyes.

Ren shuffled Jacob to one arm, then reached for my hand. His grip was warm and dry and strong. "If it wasn't for them, I wouldn't be going anywhere for a very long time." His voice hardened. "You know I hate charity, but this…it isn't like that. This is *justice*. They killed me when I was ten years old, Della. The least they can do is compensate you and Jacob."

"I'm not taking money from those monsters."

"But I will." He squeezed my fingers. "I'd do anything for you. Rick's already filed my case with a lawyer who has a few active claimants. He said there's better success in numbers, so he'll wait for a couple more to come forward and then take it to trial."

I sighed heavily, kicking at weeds and pulling up the roots out of habit. "When will you know if you win a settlement?"

"Not sure." He kissed Jacob's downy blond head. "But hopefully not too long."

He didn't say it, but he didn't need to.

These days, there were conversations flying around all the time that weren't said.

Hopefully not too long.

Hopefully before I'm dead.

* * * * *

2025

Christmas was whiter than usual with a blizzard that meant the tractor was used as a plough, fashioning a pathway between our house and the Wilsons.

Ice laced window frames, and trees were sacrificed to burn to keep the chill at bay.

This year, with Jacob three and Nina eleven, we opted to have Christmas at our place where the sparse amount of furniture meant opening presents and reaping season carnage wasn't nearly as destructive as in John's house with its over-packed bookcases and rooms that held more than just mementoes; it held entire lifetimes.

Ren and I had yet to create that amount of clutter, and the main point of decoration was a small pine tree Ren had cut down, potted, and taken me shopping to buy as many gaudy baubles as I wanted.

I had to admit, I'd gone a bit overboard with the tinsel.

But watching our son laugh and rip into brightly printed paper, revealing a remote-control car, books that could be read in the bath, and a set of miniature diggers to play in the dirt, it was worth it.

"I still remember our first Christmas," Ren murmured, slotting himself beside me as I leaned against the kitchen bench after serving warm apple and cinnamon muffins. We'd had a big lunch of roasted veggies, turkey, and all the trimmings, so appetites weren't all that hungry.

I wrapped my arms around his waist. "I remember it, too."

I remembered how Cassie had come into our room and made fun of me for sleeping in the same bed as Ren. How her tone had been weird, and I didn't like it whenever she looked at the boy who was mine.

"You kissed me under the mistletoe." He chuckled as Jacob fell over the plush rug by the fireplace, chasing his remote-control car as Nina careened it into things, kamikaze style. "Remember?"

I didn't actually.

My five-year-old brain had been obsessing about Cassie and the strangers I didn't like, rather than the comforting presence of my beloved brother. I scrunched up my nose, pretending I did. "I think it was *you* who kissed *me*, not the other way around."

He pursed his lips, his excellent memory that would've made him worthy of any scholar or doctor or any profession he chose whisking through time to a different Christmas and snowy night.

"You know…you're right." He turned me to face him, planting possessive hands on my hips. "I scooped you up and asked you to kiss me." His face glowed with fondness. "I gave you my cheek, but you smacked my lips instead."

"Like this?" I stood on tiptoes, pressing my mouth to his.

But this time, I didn't smack like a child.

I kissed like a wife.

And there was nothing innocent about it.

He groaned, his body tensing for more. "*Exactly* like that."

We laughed together, enjoying our inside joke of five-year-olds kissing fifteen-year-olds—both totally unaware what existed in their future.

Our lips parted, tongues touched, and later, once everyone had left and Jacob was asleep in his bed, Ren took me in all the ways he could.

It was the best Christmas present even though he'd bought me a new laptop and I'd bought him a new oil skin jacket.

Every touch was precious.

Every thrust was infinite.

Every year more treasured than the last.

* * * * *

2026

We hadn't celebrated our shared birthday in a while, thanks to parenthood, hospital visits, farm running, horse businesses, and all the other things that made up a hectic life, but on 27th of June—our official date of creation (even if Ren had borrowed it from me)—we asked Cassie to babysit our monster four-year-old and headed to a local diner for our tradition.

The meal of greasy food and naughty but oh-so-delicious burgers was a flashback to a lifetime of togetherness.

Halfway through the meal, Ren tugged at the ribbon holding my braid together, unravelling it with a look of intensity.

I gulped, burning up in the coffee fire of his gaze, then tears welled as he pulled a fresh string of blue from his pocket. "I'm afraid I've been rather slack on replacing your ribbon the past few years. This one is looking a little faded." With swift fingers—used to tying bows from my childhood—he retied my braid with new, bright cobalt, then went back to eating as if nothing had happened.

I'd wanted to pounce on him there and then, but it was almost a game to him. A game to see how much he could seduce me by not even touching me.

By the time we'd polished off a chocolate brownie for dessert, I was ready to fool around in the back of the second-hand pick-up truck we'd bought two years ago.

However, Ren took my hand and guided me down Main Street.

My skin itched for his touch. My lips watered for his kiss. My patience was stretched with need.

"Are we ambling aimlessly, or do we have a plan?" I asked. "Because I need you and a bed and alone time, stat."

He chuckled. "Stat, huh?"

"Immediately."

"Well, you'll have to be patient. I'm looking for something." Ren smiled, the street lights casting his handsome face in shadows and illumination. I was seriously the luckiest woman in the world to love someone so beautiful inside and out.

I wanted to leap into his arms and force him to take me, but I ordered myself to be a grown-up. "Looking for what?"

He grinned wider, tugging me down a side street with a single glowing sign still on at this time of night. "That."

"Jill's Quill?"

"Yup." He nodded. "For your seventeenth birthday present, I bought you ink that teases me every day you slide out of bed and every moment you walk barefoot toward me. I don't think I ever told you how much that ribboned R means to me. Didn't really know how. So...I figured, why bother telling you when I could show you?"

Coughing once, he dragged me toward the tattoo parlour and through the glass door.

"Ah, you must be my nine o'clock." A spritely woman looked up with colourful tatted sleeves and a stretched hoop in her ear. "Sit. Let's get started."

Ren didn't give me time to ask what the hell was going on before he pushed me toward the black pleather couch and took a seat on the plastic wrapped recliner in front of the artist. "You got the design I emailed?"

"Yup." The artist, who I assumed was Jill, snapped on a pair of gloves and grabbed a stencil already printed and ready to go from the table beside her. "Where do you want it?"

Ren pointed to his forearm. "There."

"Alrighty."

I had no idea what it was or how this had happened so suddenly.

Nerves bubbled in my belly the entire time the tattoo gun buzzed.

Afterward, Ren ordered, "Pay the woman, Della Ribbon. This is, after all, your birthday present to me."

Laughing under my breath, I rolled my eyes at the craziness of my husband. I slipped cash from my purse, waited until Jill rung me up, then turned to face him with a hand on my hip. "Okay, enough of the secrets. Show me."

With a soul-stealing look, he came toward me, holding out his arm. "It's not a secret that I love you."

My eyes locked on his fresh ink.

Blue, the same colour as mine.

A ribbon wrapping around his arm instead of my foot.

A ribbon that looped into a J before finishing in a D, just like mine finished in an R.

He was right.

Telling me how much my tattoo meant to him would've been useless.

Because nothing could describe the tidal wave of lust, love, and loss that filled me.

He'd marked himself forever.

He'd take me and Jacob wherever he went.

He was mine, not death's or pain's or time's.

Mine.

The permanent ink said so.

* * * * *

2027

"I can't believe you're making me do this." Ren laughed, hoisting five-year-old Jacob onto his hip.

The past few years had been a whirlwind of Ren teaching his son everything he could. From camping trips in summer, to tractor snow ploughing in winter, and even sitting with him and doing 'homework' like I'd done even though Jacob only attended preschool.

Ren was besotted with his son, just like I knew he would be.

And I was besotted with both of them, often drifting into a dreamy trance while watching Ren interact with Jacob—laughing with him, joking, arguing, and even scolding.

Each day, I fell helplessly in love with him.

Which only added another layer to my hurt.

And each month I hoped I'd fall pregnant again, desperate to give Ren the daughter he wanted.

But each year, it never came true.

"Don't blame me. Blame Cassie." I stuck out my tongue as Jacob squirmed in Ren's arms.

"Down. Down." Jacob pointed at the ground. "Nina has chocolate. I want some."

"After." Kissing my unruly child on the nose, I made sure his string tie was neat, his black shirt was buttoned, and tiny Wranglers were hay free. Once he was presentable, I tackled my husband, rubbing at a dirt smudge on his cheek, lamenting over the soil beneath his nails, and tucking his matching black shirt into his waistband to reveal the silver belt buckle I'd bought him last Christmas.

He'd rolled his sleeves up to reveal his ribbon tattoo with our initials in it, his hair obscured by a cowboy hat.

He was a quintessential country boy and had some god-like power that made me find him ever more handsome as the years went by.

However, nothing could hide the fact he was lankier than filled out these days.

That was the reason for the photo-shoot.

To permanently etch us in place, where time and sickness couldn't touch us. It'd been Cassie's idea when I'd had a weak moment and sobbed in her arms.

It wasn't often I buckled beneath the always impending knowledge of our future, but when I broke, I broke big.

Luckily, she was always there to pick up my pieces, drown me with wine, and send me back to my family with a patched up heart and paper bravery.

The past few months had been hard.

Ren had gone downhill again.

At the start of the year, his coughing came back with a vengeance, and, whenever he lay down or bent over, he struggled to stop. His throat became raw, his energy levels depleted.

The more he tried to hide his discomfort, the worse it got, and

Jacob flinched just as much as I did when he had a coughing fit.

Rick said Ren's tumours hadn't spread, but he was suffering pleural effusion and suggested surgery. If he didn't, Ren would continue to drown in his own lungs, thanks to fluid constantly building.

For a week, Ren and I tossed up the pros and cons.

Pros—if the surgery went well with no hiccups, it would mean he'd have a better quality of life, wouldn't cough or be out of breath so badly, and be back to being active and strong. If the Keytruda kept his immune system supported and attacking his mesothelioma, there was no reason he couldn't have many more years.

Cons—if the surgery ran into complications, he might be hospitalised for a while, running the risk of becoming ill with pneumonia or worse...putting his body under such strain it suffered respiratory distress or cardiovascular problems.

In the end, it was Jacob who helped us decide.

He ran into our bedroom one morning and slammed to a stop as Ren came out of the bathroom, dripping wet and wrapped in a towel.

His adorable little face scrunched up as he pointed across the room. "You're skinny." Running over to his father, he poked Ren in the side—or as high as he could reach—saying, "One, two, three ribs, Daddy. Eat more, 'kay?"

Ren had looked at me, another awful cough tumbling from his lips.

He just nodded, and I knew.

The next week, Rick organised the Pleurodesis surgery, and Ren had a night in the hospital after the procedure, just to make sure there were no issues. Rick told us to be kind to ourselves and not panic about the results for a few days. However, by the fourth day at home, Ren's colour was already better, his appetite improved, and his coughing nowhere near as wracking.

It had been a gamble, but it'd paid off, and yet again, we had a future with sunshine rather than shadows.

For so long now, we'd existed in the middle of a seesaw. Sometimes sliding one way, only to scramble back to the middle before slamming to the ground.

Ren never missed a treatment of Keytruda, and for now, he remained stable with no side effects. We were optimistic but also realistic.

Hence the photo-shoot to capture Ren fit and smiley...just in case.

"Okay? You ready?" The purple-haired photographer popped her bubble-gum, smiling. "Arrange yourself on the hay bale. The light is good against the barn, so we'll start there, then make our way around the farm and any other places you want, okay?"

I nodded. "Sounds great."

Cassie stood to the side with Chip and Nina, ready for her own photo-shoot once ours was done. John lingered, overseeing with encouragement and wisecracks, occasionally agreeing to photo bomb and be forever immortalized.

As Ren gathered me in his arms, smoothing my white dress, and Jacob stood obediently in front of us with my hand on his shoulder, my heart fluttered for more.

More of this.

More of everything.

Just *more.*

Chapter Sixty-Three

REN

2028

"YOU TRULY ARE a miracle, Ren Wild."

I smirked at my oncologist who'd become a firm friend over the years.

Rick Mackenzie was a rare type of human who I didn't just tolerate but genuinely liked his company. He was calming, encouraging, and made me fight just that little bit harder because to let him down was unthinkable.

"I have too much to live for." I put my t-shirt back on after yet another chest X-ray. If my lungs didn't kill me, the radiation from all the X-rays would.

"I told you love would turn out to be your biggest ally."

I glanced at my tattoo, familiar crests of affection rising in my heart. "Love is worth fighting for."

"I think you just stole that from a Hallmark card." Rick chuckled, typing into his computer the results of today's check-up. I let him finish before he suddenly said, "Oh, almost forgot!" Wrenching open his desk drawer, he pulled out a folder with a flourish. "After waiting so long, the trial went well."

"Oh, yeah?" I sat down, recalling the affidavit I had to give, the tests I'd submitted to from doctors trying to prove I was lying, right through to agreeing to be shadowed for a few weeks seeing as I was one of the younger patients but also one who'd survived the longest.

Lawyers had taken every bill and invoice I'd incurred in the years, along with tallying up the free healthcare I'd received, thanks to the off-label trial.

The asbestos trust did not want to pay out.

But my evidence was conclusive.

"They were found guilty on six counts of negligence and undue personal injury. The trust fund will pay out in three months."

My jaw fell open. "A-are you serious?"

"Deadly."

I flinched. I'd become rather sensitive to that word.

"Sorry." He laughed. "But this is good news, Ren. *Really* good news."

"How good?" I leaned forward.

When Rick suggested suing the asbestos manufacturer, I hadn't held out hope. Pay outs ranged from nothing to mega bucks, but I'd never done this for the money.

It had been my only avenue of revenge—to hurt them in their pocket while they stole my life. In a way, I still didn't feel right about it. I'd gotten sick while at Mclary's. In my mind, I blamed him. It had been a struggle separating the two.

"Two and a half million good." Rick grinned, clicking his pen like an addict.

"Wait. *What?*" My ears rang. "I must have heard you wrong."

"You didn't."

"*What* did you say?" My skin slicked with cold sweat. "*How* much?"

"Two and a half *million* dollars. You've done what you wanted."

My life slowed, saying no to death and thank you to all my wishes coming true.

I couldn't believe it, even as the fears I'd always carried fell away.

Never again would we be destitute or homeless.

Della is safe.

"I've protected her," I breathed, still in shock.

With or without me.

Della and Jacob would always be safe.

It didn't make any of this easier, but the shackles of panic fell away.

I'd beaten the clock at its own game.

"You have." Rick smiled. "In sickness and in health."

"For richer and for poorer." I met his eyes.

My hands shook as I curled them into fists.

Yet another small victory over death.

I smiled, grateful, vindicated, hopeful. "She and Jacob will want for nothing."

* * * * *

2029

"Dad! *Daaad!*"

"In here, kiddo." I tossed back a painkiller, chasing it with orange juice. Morning sunshine streamed into the kitchen, painting everything in summer softness.

Jacob appeared at breakneck speed, his cargo shorts full to the brim with Legos. His blond hair was shaggy and in need of a cut. His eyes mischievous and far too smart for his seven-year age. "I need your help building the tower on my castle."

Reaching down, I grabbed him from the floor and plopped up onto the kitchen bench just as Della padded barefoot from the bedroom wing.

She caught my eye, smiling sexily.

I'd had her this morning. I'd had her on her stomach with my hand fisted in her hair. But that didn't stop my body from reacting.

"Hi." She kissed me, pouring herself a glass of juice before kissing Jacob. "Hey, Wild One."

Jacob wrinkled his nose. "Ugh, kissing is for girls."

"Oh, really?" Della attacked his face with kisses while I held him prisoner.

He squirmed and squealed while I laughed and Della blew raspberries on his neck. "Wrong, mister. Kisses are for little boys who I love."

Wiping his face on my shirt, he stuck out his tongue. "Eww, you suck." A smile twisted his lips, though, reminding me so much of Della that age. The defiance, the independence, the urge to grow up too fast.

God, I loved this family.

Scooting Jacob off the bench, I put him back on his feet. "I'll come help you in a minute, okay? Just need to talk to Mom real quick."

Jacob gave me a stern look. "You better. I'm timing you." He took off, and I let loose the cough that had been tickling my chest, turning away from Della and clamping a hand over my mouth.

She rested her palm on my back, rubbing gently as I rode out the worst of it. Once I could breathe again, I turned to face her. "Had some news today."

"More news like last year when you came home and told me we were millionaires?"

I chuckled. "No, not quite."

The asbestos trust fund had paid out, depositing an unbelievable sum into our bank account. We'd paid off the mortgage, given some to John for the remaining balance of the land—which led to an explosive argument—and set up the rest into an account that would earn good interest while being a safety net for Della and Jacob.

My life insurance was just a cherry on top now, and the relief that gave me—to know they would always have a home—was indescribable.

"Our lawyer contacted us. The bank finally managed to sell the Mclary place." Not once did I ever tie Della to those monsters. It was never *her* parents' farm. It was purely a nightmare where we'd both lived for a time.

"Oh?" Her eyebrow rose. "What does that mean?"

"It means, after the debt was paid, there wasn't much left. Fifty thousand, give or take."

Della wrinkled her nose, looking all the more beautiful. "I don't want it. I won't take anything from them."

Smoothing the tiny wrinkle by her eye, I kissed her softly.

At least I'd earned my final wish—I'd lived long enough to see age change her, just a little—a wrinkle that only appeared when she smiled or scowled.

"Thought you might say that." Letting her go, I placed our empty glasses in the sink. "That's why I asked him to set up a charity for any of the kids found who the Mclary's hurt."

Della froze. "You did?"

"You'll need to sign the forms, seeing as you're the main trustee, but I knew you wouldn't want their money, and at least, this way, it can be put to righting some of their wrongs."

Over the years, the police had found one or two children who'd been sold. The man who'd purchased has-been workers still hadn't been captured, but newspapers had kept track of the story, spreading composite sketches and even a photo that one of the kids—now in his thirties—had of him.

No one mentioned if my mother had been found—just as I requested. And the case was only shared when good news could be given.

Their evil might never be fully erased, but at least some souls had been saved.

"You're the best, husband of mine."

"I'm only what you made me, wife of mine."

"Wrong. You're Ren Wild. The boy who survived and is still surviving."

Kissing her, I murmured, "And I'll keep surviving…for as long as I can."

* * * * *

2030

"Jacob, come here. I found a clue."

My voice vibrated with love as the lanky eight-year-old charged over the field toward me, his face alight and blond hair glowing.

He was the perfect blend of Della and me. Slightly wary of people but entirely fearless in nature. Blond hair from her and dark eyes from me. Quiet seriousness mixed with effortless charm.

Della had turned thirty, and I'd knocked on forty—time extending the dream I didn't think I'd have, watching my son change from kid to boy, and my wife grow in wisdom and kindness every day.

The blue overalls Jacob had dressed in—that were usually reserved for helping me grease and oil the tractor—had paint splashes down the front and a bunny sticker stuck to his chest. His nose had a green spot, and his hands had red and yellow streaks from decorating Easter eggs earlier today.

The entire Wilson crew had come together to enjoy a holiday we hadn't celebrated before.

It had been Della's idea.

Our kitchen had become a warzone of glitter, stickers, and gemstones as the kids decorated eggs in whatever fashion they chose.

Once the novelty of covering themselves and everything else in paint faded, Della and I ushered everyone outside and gave each group of kids a clue to start a chocolate treasure hunt, then set them loose on Cherry River, searching barns, stables, tack rooms, rivers, and grottos.

"Where's the clue?" Jacob asked, his wicker basket knocking against his legs as he slammed to a stop.

I pointed at the chicken coop ahead. Chocolate eggs were mixed with real eggs and the key to collecting them was to scatter a handful of feed for the protective mother hens. "In there. Better go fast; otherwise, Nina is gonna pinch all the good stuff."

"Oh, no she won't." He took off with a whoosh of wildflowers, tripping a little in his haste.

Della laughed softly. "You really know how to wind him up."

"Only because I remember how easy it was to wind you up when you were that age."

She took my hand, linking our fingers. "I was never that competitive."

"Bah!" I laughed, cursing my lungs when it turned into a coughing fit. "I just had to mention something you shouldn't do, and you just had to do it."

Sunshine dappled her beside me. Her hair was longer—almost

down to her ass. Her jeans scuffed and weathered. Her grey jacket torn on the wrist and grass-stained on the elbow.

A typical wardrobe for us.

A normal acceptance that we were part of the wilderness, and a little dirt never hurt anybody.

Seeing her so simple and innocent and gorgeous, I no longer cared about trailing after the chocolate hunting kids.

I wanted to stand still for a moment with the girl of my heart.

Tugging her hand, I waited until she faced me, then looped my arms around her hips. "Hi." I nuzzled her, inhaling her scent and growing instantly hard.

There was something about this woman that I would never get sick of.

No matter how many years we spent together.

No matter how many miracles I burned through to stay by her side.

I would never stop wanting her, loving her, needing her.

Della tipped her head up, her blue eyes begging for a kiss.

I obliged, lowering my mouth to hers, granting a soft hello before slipping into a sinful command. Pressing her against me, I swayed with her in the meadow, allowing the breeze to shift us this way and that, tuning out the world until it was just us again.

Us as children.

Us as newlyweds.

Us with our entire world spread at our feet.

When we broke apart, we both breathed heavier, and my eyes lingered on our house in the distance, wondering if it would be rude to drag her back to bed.

"Don't even think about it." She grinned, clutching my hand and tugging me toward the kids. They fought with high-pitched voices, arguing over who deserved the most chocolate and who would read the next clue.

"What? I wasn't doing anything."

"You were thinking it." She brought our linked hands up and kissed my knuckles. "I love you, Ren Wild."

I smiled softly, my eyes tracking the blue satin in her hair that was always nearby. Last year, the ribbon wheel had run out, and I couldn't replace the fading piece of blue anymore.

I'd ensured her favourite possession never tore since I was fourteen. I had no intention of letting her down now, and had it on my list to find another cardboard circle that would last for the rest of her lifetime.

I might not be there in the future to cut it for her, but at least she'd never go without.

As we walked side by side, like any other happily married couple, I winced at the ever-growing pain in my chest. I'd been hiding it rather well. I'd been lying rather successfully.

I didn't need to hurt her anymore by telling her my stage two had become stage three, and the Keytruda was slowly failing.

My body still fought a hard battle.

And I wasn't going anywhere just yet.

But...I had to be honest.

I was getting...tired.

My body no longer felt as healthy, and there would come a time that the meat on my bones would be sacrificed to keep me alive just a little longer.

I already feared that day.

I already mourned the inevitable.

I already struggled with how to say goodbye.

Chapter Sixty-Four

REN

2032

"YOU CAN'T GIVE him a knife for his birthday, Ren."

I looked up from wrapping the Swiss Army tool that I'd bought from the local hunting and fishing store. I'd also bought a kid's size backpack, collapsible pots, mugs, water containers, a cosy sleeping bag, and everything else I wished I'd had when I was Jacob's age.

"He's ten, Little Ribbon. He's not a kid."

"Ten is *exactly* a kid." Della sat beside me, snapping the scissors I'd used to cut the sticky tape to keep the *Star Wars* wrapping paper in place. "I love you, you know this. And I love that you never let having nine fingers slow you down, but, Ren, I rather like our son with ten."

She laughed quietly as I dragged her chair closer to mine, obscuring my face as I coughed. Once I had my breath back, I smirked. "He's not going to cut a finger off."

"How do you know? He's a menace to himself. He needed stitches last year from falling off Cassie's pony. He broke his wrist a few weeks after that from back flipping into the pond and hitting dirt instead." She clucked her tongue. "I worry about him."

"Don't. He's only testing his boundaries and capabilities."

Just like I'd tested mine and knew the god-awful conclusion.

My battle was slowly coming to an end.

Della knew.

I knew.

John, Cassie, Liam, and Jacob knew.

I'd had a check-up and treatment last week, and the look Rick Mackenzie gave me was as grave as the image in the mirror. Keytruda had been hailed as the miracle drug. It had given me an extra eight years than the normal prognosis.

But sometimes, it just stopped working.

No one knew why, and no doctor could explain it.

And as much as I would never admit it, my body didn't feel right anymore.

There was no denying that I had a cancerous passenger inside me and it was finally winning. My hair no longer shone; my eyes no longer sparkled. My skin was stretched over bones that ached more by the day, and the breathlessness that had been cured for so long, thanks to surgery, was back in full force.

I was a ticking clock, and Della hadn't left my side for longer than an hour or two, both of us so terribly aware that we didn't have many hours left to waste.

We'd done our best to protect my disease from Jacob, but he was just as smart as Della, and the kids at school had done their best to tell him what was wrong with me—just like they'd tried to explain to Della about sex when she was young.

Their explanations did more harm than good with terminology that was terrifying. They'd given Jacob nightmares of me being buried and eaten alive by worms because that's what their dad said happened to great-grandma. Another had promised I'd die but would come back as a zombie and eat him in his sleep.

Turned out, keeping facts from loved ones—no matter how young they were—was never a good idea.

It'd taken a few dinners with Della holding his hand and me talking to him, man to man, for him to calm down and not flinch when I hugged him.

He knew that I wouldn't be around for as long as other dads.

He knew he couldn't beg or argue to make that change.

And he also knew he could be angry with me but never at Della because none of this was her fault.

It'd been a depressing week, but finally, either his brain numbed him to the reality of our future, or his upcoming birthday had pushed his worries aside because he was the same happy kid as before.

He had the choice of a party with all his friends for his birthday or a camping trip just him, me, and Della. He'd chosen camping, and that was exactly what I was going to do. Regardless if the thought of hiking miles into the forest no longer filled me with excitement but worry on how I'd do it without passing out.

Della watched my nine fingers as I finished wrapping the boxed knife and smoothed the neat package.

"He doesn't even realise that that will be his greatest treasure when he's older." Tears glossed her eyes, overflowing as she kept staring at my hands. "His first knife from his dad. A dad I hope to

God he remembers."

"Hey…" Pulling her into my arms, I kissed her hair. "Don't do that. Please. I can't stand it."

She clutched me tight, her arms squeezing until I coughed again. She allowed a couple of sobs before shutting the hatch and smiling with salt-wet cheeks. "Sorry. Moment of weakness, that's all."

I kept holding her, not letting go.

She thought I didn't know, but a few times a year, she'd unload her broken heart to Cassie, talk about me, miss me, then bottle it all back up again to be strong for me.

I never asked what Cassie said to her.

I never pried and begged to know what fears Della shared.

I knew enough not to need to.

Living with a dying man was not easy.

Especially when that dying man had loved you since you were born.

I hated that making love to my wife made me pant as if I'd run two lengths of the paddock at full tilt.

I hated that I couldn't stop the light-headedness and abhorrent sensation of having no control over my body.

I hated everything about this.

Letting Della go, I kissed the soft skin beside her mouth. "It's important he knows I don't think of him as a kid. I was eight when I first used tools and farming equipment—"

"I know he idolizes you, but he's not you, Ren. He hasn't been thrust into survival mode and forced to grow up far before his time. He doesn't know hardship like you do." Her fingers landed on my cheek, tracing the sharper cheekbone and stroking a more angled jaw. "You were never ten years old when you ran with me. You were fifty in a kid's body. You were never a typical child."

"And Jacob is not a typical son."

She grinned sadly. "You're right. He's your son."

"No. He's *our* son." I coughed again, cursing the ever-tightening curse in my chest. "And our son is smart and brave and wise, and he *will* remember me. Just like you will. You'll both remember how much I love you and that I'll never be truly gone."

Della nodded, unable to speak.

For a moment, I let us sit in the puddle of sadness, then I stood, coughed, and tapped her on the butt. "Go get the backpack and the child. It's time to camp."

Chapter Sixty-Five

DELLA

2032

WE SET UP camp as a family.

Erecting the tent, we put our sleeping bags in one wing and Jacob's in the other.

Our journey hadn't been as easy as previous excursions. We hadn't gone as far, but it had taken twice as long. I'd carried the backpack—against Ren's wishes—but I couldn't allow him to lug more weight when he already struggled with his own.

Ren's cough crucified him, bending him over a few times, spitting up blood toward the end.

I'd told Jacob to run ahead as Ren clutched my hand through one attack, stumbling for breath, his hand on his heart as it palpitated to an uneven rhythm.

I'd murmured calm nothings, rubbed his back, cursing the noticeable nodules of his spine.

I'd been strong for him and kept my panic hidden.

But it didn't mean it didn't grow with every little reminder that things were coming to an end. That our life together was almost over.

My heart was held together with sticky tape and bandages.

My eyes were made of tears and terror.

I couldn't explain the toll loving Ren took on me when he faded day by day from this world to the next.

Some days, I wished I could stop loving him.

I wished I could pack up my feelings in neatly labelled boxes, and store them in the attic of my mind for a time when dust and time had made them less painful.

But that only made me feel like a weak, wicked woman, and I'd throw myself into loving him even more.

Here, take my heart. Take my soul. Take every second I have left because I don't want them without you.

By the time we made it to the camp, I was sick with loathing at life and love, utterly unable to talk.

My heart was in knots; my stomach tied up with rotten string.

I missed the man who used to run wild amongst the trees.

I missed the boy who made me believe in fairy-tales.

As we finished the tent, Ren's coughing couldn't be ignored and, after a while, he gave me a tear-invoking smile and went to sit by the log we'd chosen as a bench.

He understood that he wasn't the only one struggling with this.

Jacob hated hearing him cough.

And my nerves were frayed and burning.

As I pottered about doing final tasks, I couldn't keep my eyes off Ren as he sat whittling a stick with his ever-trusty knife. His face pensive and calm.

My heart swelled with injustice and rage. My motions jerky and harsh.

The backpack was my worst enemy.

The twigs and wilderness my greatest foe.

I wanted everything to hurt as much as I did and stomped around, snapping things and kicking others.

Ren caught me as I moved around him, pulling out the small cooler box with our meat for breakfast and dinner, placing it where the fire would go.

"Ribbon." He smiled kindly, his face still so damn handsome but so much more defined than before. A definition that came from sickness. A definition that no one could agree was right.

I tried to pull away, biting my lip from saying hurtful things, painful things, things that I never normally let spill.

I was so *angry*.

So furious.

So *hurt*.

When I didn't bow to his touch like normal, Ren's eyes narrowed. "I know this is hard. But please…don't be angry with me."

For a second, I wanted to slap him.

I wanted to pummel his broken chest and kick him in the shins.

It made no sense.

My violence was confused and smarting.

I *hated* seeing him so skinny.

I despised hugging his once solid, comforting frame only to find bone instead of muscle.

I hated my tears and fears and the fact that as the final day crept closer, my strength grew non-existent.

I didn't like the seething mass inside my belly.

I didn't enjoy having to control my temper toward my husband and son because it wasn't them who made me angry.

God made me angry.

Life made me angry.

Love made me so *fucking* angry.

And I needed to shout at someone, fight something, attack anything to get rid of the tight fury inside me.

My nostrils flared as I continued to look down at him.

He looked so gorgeous and regal. So wise and perceptive and everlasting.

And I wanted to hit him and hit him and *hit him* because he'd achieved the impossible. He'd run from evil, endured horrors, saved me, guided me, loved me, married me, and now...now he was leaving me.

He didn't have that right.

He didn't have that luxury.

He *owed* me.

He owed me to stay because why else had we been given this life together?

"Ah, Della." Ren stood, smothering a cough. With hands that still had strength and dominance, he squeezed my biceps. "Yell at me. Scream at me. Tell me what you're feeling."

I shook my head, short and jerky. "You know I can't."

"Why not?"

"Because Jacob is somewhere close by, and...and it's not your fault."

"None of this is anyone's fault, but I'm just as angry as you. I'm fucking furious that I can't hold you forever and be beside you as you grow old." His voice darkened. "Don't you think I've punched things, kicked things? Tried to somehow relieve that filthy pressure inside?"

"I know you have. I've patched up your bruised knuckles." I smiled, doing my best to make a tense moment into a light-hearted one, but Ren didn't let it go.

"You have to let it out, Della. You can't allow it to fester." His eyes cast into the twilight-shrouded forest, a bird trill whistling from his lips.

A call he'd taught Jacob to recognise and repeat—a way of keeping tabs on him when he tarried off without us.

An answering tune came from the distance, faint but close enough not to panic.

"He's out of hearing distance—for the most part." Ren cupped my cheek. "Tell me. Hit me if you need."

For a second, I considered it.

I honestly contemplated hitting the love of my life.

The love who was dying.

But then, my rage vanished as quickly as it had built, and I melted into his embrace. "I'm just so afraid, Ren. So afraid I won't be able to do this. That nothing will make sense or be worthwhile anymore. How can I look after Jacob when you're not here to look after me? How am I supposed to care about anything when the only thing I've ever cared about is gone?"

Even though tears didn't fall, sadness vibrated in my voice, cloying as smoke.

"I don't know. I honestly don't know." He hugged me tight, the rattle in his lungs a constant song. "All I know is, out of the two of us, you're the bravest one. You'll get through it. Somehow."

Tearing myself out of his arms, I glowered at him. "Don't call me brave, Ren. You know nothing of bravery."

He scowled. "Know nothing? Are you sure?"

"Yes, because for decades *you've* been the braver one, but you've never seen it. You've never once blamed me for what happened to you. You've never once cried for what life has given you. You've never broken down or—"

"Only because I have you."

"Yes, and soon, I won't have you at all."

Jacob came bounding from the trees, his arms chock-a-block with twigs and kindling. "Found some." He pranced to the cleared circle to make a blaze, utterly oblivious to the sort-of-fight he'd interrupted.

And I was glad.

Because I honestly didn't have the strength.

The way I was feeling, I was weak enough to consider a Romeo and Juliet ending and bequeath Jacob to Cassie.

I would be that terrible.

I would be that monstrous to leave my child an orphan because I didn't have the courage to be a widow.

"Who's hungry?" I asked brightly. Too brightly. Tearing myself from Ren's hold, I grabbed the grill plate from the backpack. Ducking to my haunches, I helped Jacob build a fire.

"Me! I'm starving." Jacob rubbed his tummy. "And then, after dinner, please tell me there's cake."

Ren chuckled, sitting back down, forever watching us. "In a diner, a long time ago, a waitress once told me there was always time for cake." His dark coffee eyes met mine. "Your mom was five and blew spit all over the cupcakes instead of blowing out a single flame."

Jacob laughed. "Eww. I'll take care of the blowing. Thanks, Mom."

I couldn't move, entranced by Ren's gaze, enchanted by him.

He whispered, "You made a wish that night, Della Ribbon. A wish I've always tried to honour. Please understand, I'll still be keeping that promise even after I'm—"

"Enough." Tearing my eyes from his, I snatched a lighter from the backpack and let fire chew its way through the carefully stacked sticks.

Ren stayed quiet as the fire grew and, once the blaze was big enough, I placed the grill plate on top—balanced by a few rocks— and slapped three juicy steaks into the flames. I'd made a potato salad back at home with mayo, along with some spinach wrapped rice rolls.

The birthday cake for Jacob's tenth celebration was carefully tucked in Tupperware—a vanilla sponge in the shape of the little white pony, Binky, that he'd been learning to ride.

Organising this trip had given my mind something to hook onto, and I'd slipped back into my role as mother.

Once the steaks were cooked, I divided up the potato salad and rice rolls onto the collapsible plates Ren had bought for Jacob's birthday and did my best to act normal with conversation.

Partway through the meal, I subtly handed Ren a high-strength painkiller as his skin flushed with sweat and his forehead never smoothed.

I'd long since become acquainted with his tolerance levels and pain.

He gave me a look before sighing and holding out his palm.

I dropped the pill into it before Jacob noticed, nodding like a satisfied nurse as he swallowed.

Afterward, I headed to the river, taking a torch to wash up quickly, leaving my two beloved boys to talk about whatever boys do.

And there, in the ether of silence and starlight, I fell to my knees and drove my fists into the leaf-littered dirt.

I let my rage break free.

I punched the earth. I kicked the sky. I ripped time itself apart.

"Why?" I screamed quietly.

"How could you?" I asked painfully.

"Not yet," I begged brokenly.

But no one answered.

No owl hooted.

No shooting star offered salvation.

And yet, howling at the moon and spreading my fears in the dark was cathartic enough to piece myself back together again, wipe away my tears, pick up the clean plates, and head back to the fire and my boys.

* * * * *

"Wow, Dad. Thanks!" Jacob hurled himself into Ren's arms.

Star Wars wrapping paper scattered on the forest floor, forgotten as the Swiss Army knife became his prized possession.

"Don't hurt yourself with that, you hear?" I laughed as he kissed Ren's cheek.

Ren patted his back. "You're welcome. I can show you what each thing does if you want?"

"Nah, it's okay. I've played with one of yours before."

"Oh, you have, have you?" Ren raised an eyebrow in my direction, smirking. "Told you, Della. Our son isn't a kid anymore."

I stood, brushing leaves off my ass. A few floated into the fire with a quick whoosh of fuel. I laughed again, forcing happiness. "Fine. What do I know? Ten seems to be the new adult these days."

Ren chuckled.

"Don't move. I'll be right back." Leaving them to discuss blade points and miniature saw skills, I secretly pulled the Tupperware container out of the backpack and went to hide by the tent to stab ten candles into the poor vanilla pony.

With my pocketed lighter, I lit them all then headed back carrying the birthday dessert singing, "Happy birthday to you. Happy birthday to you. Happy birthday to, Jacob! Happy birthday to you."

Jacob groaned, burying his head in his hands. "Ugh, no singing, Mom. That's just embarrassing."

Ren ruffled his blond head, tugging his son's small ear. "Never take these moments for granted, Wild One. It's these that you'll remember forever." His dark eyes met mine and once again, the fracturing brokenness inside threatened to overwhelm me.

Tearing my gaze away, I cleared my throat and dropped to my haunches, delivering the cake to Jacob. "Make a wish and blow them out."

Squeezing his eyes tight, Jacob paused for a moment, then, as serious as if he sat an exam, he blew all ten out in one breath.

Ren grabbed the knife that was forever wedged in his boot, placed the blade in the fire for a few seconds to sterilize it, then cut off the pony's head and gave it to Jacob. "Birthday boy gets first bite."

"Thanks." Jacob shoved it in his face, icing going everywhere.

Ren and I laughed, sharing another heart-warming, heart-breaking look as he passed me a leg and he had the tail.

We ate quietly for a bit, enjoying the sugar, remembering our first birthday together where cupcakes had been our first taste of refined goodness instead of the fructose found in fruit.

So much had happened since then, yet it felt as if nothing had happened at all.

Ren was still a forest dweller, and I was still madly in love with him.

I'd been in love with him for thirty-two years, and it wasn't enough.

It would *never* be enough.

Sucking in a shaky breath, I scooted closer to Ren. He smiled sadly, coughing a little before putting his arm around me.

I kissed his throat, inhaling the heady wild flavour of the man who'd raised me and the man I'd married.

I'd loved him in every way someone could love another—platonically, sisterly, wifely. And now, I loved him in a way that couldn't be explained. A way that transcended everything. A way that had no name because the way we loved existed past language and law. An astral kind of love that made its home in the stars and vacationed on Jupiter.

"You know..." Jacob looked up, his boyish, beautiful face softening with affection rather than acting annoyed at seeing us cuddle. "I made my wish for you guys." His dark eyes, so similar to Ren's, welled up. "I wished that you were better, Dad. I wished you weren't gonna have to go someplace."

Instantly, Ren reached across and dragged Jacob into a three-way hug. Jacob on his knees between us, his tiny frame so slight but so strong.

Tears trickled down my face as Ren shuddered with emotion.

When we could talk without sobbing, Ren said softly, "I wish that too, Wild One, but you have to understand. A wish is something that you want to come true, no matter how impossible it is. Some do come true. And some...don't. But it doesn't mean I'm not still here. Not still inside you. You'll hear me if you listen hard enough because I have no intention of missing you grow into a man."

Jacob grinned, bucking up and proving just how brave he was. Braver than me by far. "Fine. Just don't yell at me when I screw up, 'kay?"

Ren chuckled. "No promises. Depends how badly you screw up." Letting us both go, Ren placed a hand over his mouth and coughed. Once he'd gotten his breath again, he said, "Now, I know you're old, and it's not cool anymore, but how about a story? I can do a horror, so you won't sleep. I can do a romance, so you gag. I have a lot of stories these days tucked inside this skull." He tapped his temple.

"What's it gonna be?"

Jacob pursed his lips, thinking. "Is the horror about why you have that brand on your hip?"

I stiffened, but Ren merely nodded, sagely, calmly. "Yeah, but you've already heard that story before."

"Meh, tell it again. But do the voices of that nasty farmer and everything."

Ren glanced at me, his head cocked in question.

I smiled and nodded.

We had no secrets from our son. We'd been honest about everything once the kids at school terrified him about Ren's illness. If he had a question, we did our best to answer it. Better our tale came from us than a township who still sometimes thought our last name Wild was brother and sister and looked at Jacob in disgust.

It wasn't many.

But enough to ensure Jacob should be forearmed about our unusual love story.

Throwing more sticks onto the fire, I passed Ren a water from the cooler beside me.

"Thanks, Ribbon." He smiled, sharing a galaxy of things in his stare.

"Always." Dropping off the log, I settled myself between his legs and rested my head on his thigh. *"Always."*

His hand landed in my hair, playing with the strands as his deep, provocative voice filled the forest. "Once upon a time, there was a boy whose mother didn't want him…"

Chapter Sixty-Six

REN

2032

MAKING LOVE TO Della was still my favourite thing to do.

It didn't matter that I had to stay sitting upright so I didn't have a coughing fit.

It didn't matter that my breath came short and my heart went wild.

Nothing else mattered when I slid into my wife and felt that epic sensation of connection. Her heat, her body, her welcome.

She was better than any painkiller and more potent than any cure.

Sex with Della always reminded me to keep fighting, no matter how bad some days became.

With our lips locked, we stayed as quiet as we could.

The tent was large enough to give us privacy from Jacob—with us zipped behind our partition and Jacob zipped behind his—but we had to be careful.

Had to be secret.

We touched in the dark, hands trailing over naked skin that was as familiar to each other as our own. Her fingers found me, squeezing hard. My fingers found her, sinking deep.

We kissed slow and passionate and hungry.

Our bodies quickened for more, thirsty.

I wanted her, but I also wanted to delay and enjoy every moment because there was no denying now, no pretending that we'd have forever.

I was tired.

Exhausted.

It wasn't just about the constant pain or struggle to breathe; it was the agony in my wife's and son's eyes. The hidden tears and smothered flinches as they saw me skinny and coughing.

I didn't want them to remember me like that.

I wanted them to remember me as a man who could protect them from everything, including death itself.

Clutching my last few bursts of energy, I dragged Della up my lap until she straddled me.

She gasped into our kiss as I knocked her hand from my erection, and my fingers slid from her. She positioned herself over me, and I groaned as she slid ever so slowly down.

She took me, claimed me, made me hers all over again until her thighs touched mine and my body fully seated within hers.

Once sheathed, we didn't move.

The darkness was absolute and I couldn't see her face, but we stared at each other as if we could. Because, really, we could see every glitter and glimmer of emotion. We could read each other's breaths, feel each other's souls, understand how bittersweet every day had been.

And when we moved, we did it together. Della arching on my lap before sinking back down. Me rocking upward and filling her.

I held her close with one hand on her hip and one arm around her back.

Her breasts warmed my aching chest as we clutched each other so damn hard.

There was no space between us.

No air.

No crack for sadness to wriggle in.

We were plastered together, concreted, mortared, riding slowly, sensually, ignoring everything but this.

There was no her or me, just us.

An us who rode faster, deeper, stronger.

An us who would never be separated because nothing could ever wedge us apart.

As we moved quicker, chasing pleasure and satisfaction, we didn't speak a word.

We kissed, we licked, we bit and groaned, but we didn't speak.

Speaking would ruin this.

Would ruin the rawness between us.

Because in that tent, we forgot we were human. We didn't communicate in letters and sentences, we communicated in the forgotten tongue amongst soulmates.

We sat in nothingness and made promises webbed from everything.

We re-married in the power of so much more than this world. We pledged and vowed in the eyes of the cosmos that recognised we weren't whole unless we were together.

It accepted our promise that we would wait.

We would be patient.

We would find each other again and be given the gift of ever after once we'd shed mortal shells and accepted that holding onto physical creation was never the answer.

That letting go was.

That threading yourself together with a cord that transcended time and space was the only way to be happy.

To be free.

Goosebumps scattered down my arms as our kisses and thrusts became tangled with the strings we'd just knotted, growing tighter and tighter, never to break apart.

And when we came together, our bliss was also silent. A mere echo of heartbeats as we shared mirroring, quaking pleasure.

It would forever be a regret that I wasn't able to have a daughter with Della. That no matter how many times we went to bed together, we never got pregnant again.

I would never know if it was the drugs that made me infertile or if the universe decided I'd had my happily ever after with my son.

Either way, I would be leaving soon, and Della would have to lean on Jacob.

A ten-year-old boy.

A twisted full circle of life.

I hadn't meant to hold on until Jacob's tenth birthday.

I'd meant to hold on until his twentieth, thirtieth, but ten?

It was almost too cruel.

I'd been his age when I'd first taken Della.

His age when my life changed, and I'd fought to keep us alive and happy.

And through all odds and obstacles, I'd done it.

A runty kid with an abusive past had somehow created a world anyone would envy.

I needed Della to see that—to trust our son wasn't just a kid but had a man inside him. He would be there for her, just like I'd been there for her. He would be brave, just like I'd been brave. He would cope, and together, they would survive.

Della's hands cupped my cheeks tenderly, kissing me in the dark.

I submitted to her, stroking her tongue with mine, tilting my head to deepen.

When my heart was once again skipping and kicking out of sync, she disengaged from me then fell to her side, waiting for me to spoon her.

I knew what would happen if I lay down.

I knew how bad the coughing would get.

My lungs were on borrowed time, and I had no intention of dying tonight.

Reclining just a little, I rolled her over until her head landed on my belly and her arm slung over my hips.

We stayed that way for an eternity. A sleeping bag thrown over us to stay warm, the night crickets and scurrying creatures our symphony.

And then, in the infinite dark, Della started to cry.

Her tears ran over my skin.

Her grief bathed me in salt.

I clutched her close, shuddering against helplessness, my own tears spilling over.

I hadn't fully let myself grieve.

I'd shared a tear or two but never let the torrent go.

But now, where no one could see me, with the dark blinding us, hiding us, I allowed the silent sobs to break me.

My sorrow only made Della's worse, and she cried harder.

I didn't try to comfort her.

I didn't seek comfort for myself.

This was a purging.

This was necessary.

This was goodbye.

We clung to each other as we spent every tear.

We didn't worry about clocks or dawns, only about trying to find peace to our pain.

And when my eyes dried and my heart settled, I stroked her hair softly. "I've loved you every second of my life."

Her body flinched against mine, her head burrowing into my belly. "Don't. Don't do this."

"You're the reason I've been blessed with so much."

"Stop, please stop."

"You've been more than just a wife to me; you've been my entire reason of existence."

"God...Ren." Her tears came fresh. Her hold bound tight.

I knew I was hurting her, but she had to know.

Had to hear me repeat all the things she already knew, so she'd understand that *none* of it would change. My love for her would go on and on. She had to accept that. Had to accept that my physical love was almost done, but my spiritual love would never end.

"Without you, I would've died many years ago, and for that, I want to thank you. Thank you for giving me you, Della. Thank you for giving me a son. Thank you for giving me *us*."

Her fingernails dug deep as if she could latch onto me forever.

"I love you." I coughed quietly. "But those words aren't enough. They don't do justice to how much I care."

A sob broke free. "I love you, Ren. I love you more than I can bear." Her nails turned to lips, kissing my stomach with desperation. "Please, you're still here. Don't talk as if you're not."

I ignored her, telling her a story like I used to when she was a little girl and couldn't sleep. "The moment you took your first breath in that monster's den, you stole mine and have held it in your palm ever since.

"On the days I'd see you with your mother, I'd curse you. On the evenings where I'd slink past, I'd study you. I was forever aware of you, wishing I could share your food, your innocence, your touch.

"My thoughts were that of a starving kid but now, as a man, I look back on those fuzzy childhood memories and wish I could live it all over again. I wish I could go back with the wisdom I have now and understand what you'd mean to me.

"I'd never get angry with you. Never yell or leave. I wish I could relive every touch, every smile, first word, and first kiss. I wish you could feel how grateful I was every time you kissed me, laughed with me, gave me the honour of calling you mine.

"I'm grateful, Della. For all of it.

"Without your selflessness and the unconditional way you made me fall for you, I doubt I'd be whole now. I wouldn't be able to lie here with you in my arms, knowing what is about to happen, and be calm enough to love you until that last fucking second."

"Stop." Her sobs drenched my naked skin, but I didn't stop.

I couldn't.

The story wasn't over.

"I know it wasn't easy for you, waiting until I opened my eyes. Hiding the fact you were in love with me when I was so stupidly blind. But you need to know I was in love with you for far longer than I ever let on. I'd wanted you for years.

"You truly are my other half, Della." My voice broke, cracked, shattered. "And now…now I'm leaving you again. But this time, it's not by choice."

My arm latched her closer, smothering her against me. "It's not fair. I know I should say I'm okay with it, but, Ribbon…I'm fucking terrified." A cough exploded from my lips.

"Ren." Della crawled up my body, curling into me with her knees bent and face tucked in the crook of my shoulder, her tears loud in my ear.

I hugged her closer as my own tears came again, and honesty that I'd promised myself would stay trapped inside overflowed. "For the first time, you won't be there. I won't have you by my side. I don't want to go anywhere without you. I can't do it. I-I—" I coughed again, working myself up, causing my lungs to falter.

"Ren...stop."

"No, I-I have to get this out. I'm so sorry, Della. So eternally sorry that I'm leaving against our wishes. I wish I never got sick. I wish I could continue holding you—"

"I know. Me too."

"I don't want to leave you. I don't want to hurt you. I can't believe I have the audacity to complain about dying while you...you have the harder path. I never wanted to do this to you, Della. Never wanted to cause you so much pain."

"I know you didn't."

"And I'm sorry for being weak now. For ruining this even more."

"You're not—"

"You were my biggest joy, and now, you're my greatest sadness." I swiped my face free from tears, glowering at the blackness. "Fuck, I'm not being fair. I'm being so selfish. So cruel. I should tell you I'm not afraid. That I'm okay saying goodbye—"

A cough ripped my voice apart, tearing through the night.

It took a while before I could breathe well enough to continue. "I should accept that this is just life. But I *don't* accept it. I rage against it. Because fate's plan was *you*. You and me. *Together.* And now..."

I coughed again, shaking both of us.

"Shush, Ren. I know. I know more than you think." Her touch feathered over my wet cheeks, her hand shaking. "I'm just as angry as you. Just as twisted with hate at how unfair all of this is. I'm not ready to say goodbye, either." She kissed me, her sadness mixing with mine. "I never will be."

I held her close, kissing her violently, wanting to drink her soul and take her with me. "Without you, what am I? *Who* am I?" My teeth nipped at her lip. "Almost every memory I have, you're in. Almost every recollection, you're there. And I know I'm the same for you. Our lives are so entwined, there is no *before*. No time where we were separate. Therefore, there can be no ending. Right?"

I kissed her again and again. "We're tied together for life a-and we'll just have to hold onto that. This isn't the end. It can't be. It just can't."

Della nodded, kissing me as furiously as I kissed her. "I'm tied to you just as surely as you're tied to me, Ren Wild. We'll never lose each other. *Ever.*"

Our breathing was haggard as our foreheads pressed together, and Della climbed back onto my lap.

Somehow, I was hard even though I was distraught, and she slid me inside her, connecting us even while we said our goodbyes.

As we rocked together, I allowed myself to be spiteful. To speak the truth. To ease some of the burden I'd been carrying. "You'll have a lifetime without me. I'm fucking heartbroken that it won't be us anymore."

Her sobs came hard. "Me too."

"I'm jealous of your future, Little Ribbon."

"Don't be. I will always belong to you."

"I'm livid at my inability to stop this. I want to bargain with the devil for one more year. I'd sell my soul for just one more day with you."

"I'd sell mine, too."

We grinded against each other, roughly, meanly. My hands guided her hips, clamping her down harder, forcing her to take all of me.

Talking ceased as we fought each other and our grief.

My coughing mixed with our groans, and hands slapped over our mouths to stay silent and not wake Jacob.

Before, we'd made love.

Now, we fucked.

And it was messy, wet, and nasty.

It was our version of the war inside our hearts, the physical need to hurt each other when none of this was our fault.

Finally, when my thrusts went deep and Della came around me, and my body released the sick cocktail of rage and relief, we clung to each other, sweaty and sad, our tempers no longer as hot.

My lungs were in agony.

My heart no longer rhythmical but failing hour by hour.

Kissing her cheek, I breathed, "I need you to move on, Della. I want you to be happy. I need you to live even when I'm no longer here."

She shook her head. "No."

"Yes. Live for Jacob. Live for me."

"I can't."

"You can." Hugging her close, I promised, "You can. Because this isn't the end. We will never end because that isn't what true love is. True love is constant. It has no beginning, middle, or end. Life might end, but love…that's immortal."

"I love you so much, Ren."

"I know."

"I'll always be yours."

I nodded, accepting her vow even when I shouldn't. "I'll wait for you, Della. I'll watch you and Jacob...somehow."

"Promise me you'll always be near."

"I promise."

She kissed me sweet, a single word on her breath. "Good."

And I knew what I needed to say in return.

A phrase that meant so much.

Four little letters that held such history and hope.

Tangling my fingers in her hair, I touched my lips to hers.

And all I whispered was, "Fine."

Chapter Sixty-Seven

DELLA

2032

REN DIED ONE week after Jacob turned ten.

It was as if he'd been holding on until that special age.

Clinging to life to see his son turn the same age he'd been when he'd saved me.

The symbolism in that tore out my heart, injecting exquisite sorrow that I'd never overcome.

I'd been rescued from a life of murder and hell by a ten-year-old boy who'd fallen in love with me. And I'd been left in the hands of another ten-year-old boy who was just as destroyed as I was now that his father was gone.

The fifth and final incident.

The one I'd hoped so badly wouldn't come true.

My tears hadn't stopped since I'd woken in the night, six days ago, and knew.

I *knew*.

I couldn't explain it.

After we'd returned from Jacob's birthday in the forest, neither of us mentioned our goodbyes in the tented dark. We continued as normal, with Ren slowly fading, and his refusals about going to the hospital coming often.

Rick Mackenzie had taken to visiting us, instead of Ren going to him, and the last house call...we'd all known would be the final one.

He'd wanted Ren to be admitted. To be put on Fentanyl and a steady dose of whatever drugs could extend his final moments.

But Ren refused.

His life belonged to the land and sky, and his death wouldn't be spent in a building with concrete and glass.

I honoured that choice even if I hated watching him dim before me. How his body slowly gave up, piece by piece. How his energy levels diminished, breath by breath.

To start with, I trawled the internet for a last-minute miracle. I studied the use of goji berries and apricot kernels and every supposed super food out there.

But in the end, Ren stole my phone.

He turned off the internet, returning us to a world where it was just us and no one else, and we lived in our memories because that was all that was left.

The Wilsons visited often, all of us tasting what lingered in the air.

Liam and Chip and John shared a drink with Ren while they watched some nonsense on TV. Cassie and Nina curled up against him, saying their own goodbyes. And Jacob and me...we were his constant shadow. Part of him. Part of us. So damn aware that he'd be gone soon, and the house would be so empty without him.

And then six days ago, that terrible night arrived.

Ren coughed, but no more than often.

He had a fever, but not hotter than before.

We cleaned our teeth together, read a bit before turning out the light, and kissed each other goodnight like we did every evening.

A simple, domestic night.

The epitome of intimacy and marriage.

I lay beside him, listening to that god-awful wheeze—the wheeze that I hated for stealing what was mine.

And I kissed him again. And again. Never fully satisfied.

Finally, he drifted off with our hands touching and bodies moulded into one.

I had dreams about boys and backpacks and kisses.

Midnight ticked onward, creeping us into a new tomorrow.

But somewhere between two and three, while the moon seduced the stars, I woke up.

Something prickled my awareness.

Something triggered the trip line of my instincts.

I sat up in bed and looked around.

There was something there.

Something unseen.

My breath turned shaky as something cool rippled over my skin.

And I knew.

Just *knew*.

Tears flowed before I even turned to Ren.

He lay on his back instead of propped up, but he wasn't coughing.

He looked more at peace than he had in years—no pain, no torment, no struggle.

Lying down, I pressed against his side, looped my arm around his waist, and hooked my leg over his.

He smiled in his sleep, his nose nuzzling my hair.

I squeezed him hard. So hard.

And then, the rattle and wheeze that had become so familiar hitched and halted.

And tears streamed unbidden down my face.

There was no time to call for help. No seconds to waste screaming for him to wake up or begging him to fight for just one more day.

He'd protected me.

Provided for me.

Given me everything he had to give.

And in that darkness between the hours of two and three, the boy who would forever hold my heart took his last breath.

His body was still beside me…but his spirit…

It'd gone.

And I'd felt him.

I'd woken to his kiss; I'd shivered in his goodbye.

Swallowing silent sobs, I laid a hand on his chest, begging for a heartbeat.

His skin was still warm.

But there was no heartbeat.

For a second, I was repulsed.

The animalistic part of me blaring with warning to stay away from the dead.

But this was Ren.

This was the other piece of my soul.

I was not afraid of him.

And so, I hugged my husband, telling him he was not alone.

And even though it ripped my heart apart, I told him to go and be happy.

To be free.

For the first time in my entire life, I was no longer part of a pair.

He'd gone to a place I could not go.

And as dawn crested and his skin grew steadily colder, life intruded on our bedroom tomb.

Jacob.

He'd be awake soon.

He couldn't see.

And so, I'd done what any mother would do.

I left my dead soulmate and climbed out of bed to lock the door. I picked up the phone and ordered an ambulance. I called Cassie and John and told them.

I dressed in a fugue and went to my son's bedroom to hold him, tell him, break him.

And we cried together.

God, we cried so much.

We cried when Ren was taken away.

We cried when he didn't come back.

We cried when two days passed, then three and four and five.

Without Cassie and John, my son and I would've starved that week.

It was nothing but a blur of black, perpetual despair.

Ren's body was cremated as per his wishes, the funeral already arranged, his Will and Testament activated seamlessly as everything was choreographed from the grave.

I didn't remember sleeping or eating or even living...just existing...just *surviving*.

I'd died with Ren, but on the outside, I still played my part.

I consoled our—*my*—son.

I held him close as he sobbed.

I whispered stories when he couldn't sleep.

I did my best to do what Ren would have done and that was to protect him from the pain.

But now...I couldn't protect him, because today, it was the last time we'd hold Ren in our arms.

The silver urn was heavy and gleamed in the sun.

The trees around us swaying and sad.

The funeral had been announced in the local paper, and I'd expected a quiet affair of the Wilsons and the doctor Ren had grown close to over the years.

I wasn't prepared for the entire town to attend.

Deep in the heart of the forest with no strict address or location, teachers and parents, friends and policemen had all gathered to say farewell.

There were no chairs or service.

No priest or hymns.

Just me holding Ren's ashes.

Standing at the altar of his church.

I didn't think I could speak.

I knew I couldn't do Ren justice, but as Jacob came to stand beside me, a breeze whisked through the trees, kicking up leaves in a wind-devil.

And once again that prickle, that *knowledge* overwhelmed me, and the tears that were in constant supply erupted.

I cried in front of strangers.

I sobbed in front of family.

And when I'd finished hugging Ren for the last time, I stood taller, braver, older, and opened the single printed page from the manuscript I'd been writing on and off for years. When Ren had bought me a new laptop, and I'd tasted the first signs of him leaving me, I'd turned to the salvation of the keys.

I'd done my best to write all the happy moments and try to forget the sad.

I focused on our fairy-tale, never knowing the words I'd chosen for my prologue would be part of the eulogy at Ren's goodbye.

He was forty-two and gone.

A life cut far too short.

Jacob nudged me, holding out his arms for his father. "I'll hold him, Mom. While you—" Tears strangled his boyish voice, but beneath the childhood pitch lurked the rasp of a man.

He'd aged overnight, and I finally understood why it was so important to Ren to never treat him as a kid. To forever nurture that wisdom that was already ingrained in his soul.

Ren needed Jacob to accept his place before he was no longer there to guide him, giving him knives and truths and chores normally withheld for a more mature age.

And he'd known he could handle it.

Because he'd handled it himself.

My vision blurred with yet more tears as I ducked to Jacob's height and held out my arms. Without a word, I transferred my loved one into his son's arms and brushed the skirts of my simple black dress.

Today, I wore no ribbon.

No usual flair of blue.

Today, that ribbon fluttered around the lid of the silver urn, hugging Ren one last time.

Jacob squeezed the urn, pressing his cheek to the coolness, breaking my heart all over again. "I love you, Dad. No matter that you're just ash now."

A sob grabbled with my voice as I forced myself to turn from the touching, breaking moment and face the tear-streaked members of our town.

John cried silently. Cassie hugged Nina while Chip hugged her. Liam hugged his wife and son while Adam and his family hovered close by. Behind them, the town stood poised and waiting for whatever words I could deliver that might stop the pain.

But I didn't have that power. No one did.

And even if such a magic existed, I wouldn't want it.

I wouldn't want my smarting, bleeding grief to be erased because that was the price of love, and I'd loved dearly.

Reading from my printed page, even though the words were typed on my heart, I took lines from the prologue and shared them, all while keeping others just for me.

"First, I want to say thank you. Thank you for falling in love with Ren just as much as me. Thank you for understanding that love spans decades, infects souls, and turns you immortal because, when you love that deeply, nothing can ever die."

I looked up, meeting the eyes of John.

He nodded, biting his trembling lip, his mind awash with Patricia and Ren.

I spoke for me and for everyone with lost loved ones.

I hoped they'd see what Ren and I had seen…that love truly was mystical and miraculous.

My voice threaded tears with truth.

"Love transcends time, space, distance, universes.

"Love can't be confined to pages or photos or memories—it's forever alive and wild and free. Romance comes and goes, lust flickers and smoulders, trials appear and test, life gets in the way and educates, pain can derail happiness, joy can delete sadness, togetherness is more than just a fairy-tale…it's a choice.

"A choice to love and cherish and honour and trust and adore.

"A choice to choose love, all the while knowing it has the power to break you.

"A choice, dear friends, to give someone your entire heart.

"But in the end, love is what life is about.

"And love is the purpose of everything."

John broke from the ranks, striding in leaf-crunching boots to bear hug me. Cassie joined him, her subtle perfume clouding around us.

"We're here. You and Jakey are not alone." John let me go, blowing his nose on a handkerchief.

"I love you, Della." Cassie kissed my cheek and squeezed my arm before guiding her father back to their places.

With their kind support, I stood braver in the face of heartbreak and tucked my page away.

I smiled at the crowd, wobbly and watery. "Ren died knowing how loved he was. And we're still here, knowing he'll always love us in return. Some might say our romance is over. That his death ruins our story. And I'd agree, but only because romance can be killed, but love…it can't. It lives on, and I'm patient enough to wait for our happily ever after."

Townsfolk nodded, some sharing looks, others glassy-eyed with their own memories.

But I'd said what I needed to.

I'd done what was expected for a grieving widow to honour her dead lover.

Now, we had something else much more important to do.

Turning to Jacob, I held out my hand. "Ready?"

He hugged the silver urn tighter. "No."

I kissed his soft hair. "He'll always love you, Jacob."

"I don't want to say goodbye."

"But we're not."

"I don't want to let him go."

Bending closer, I whispered, "We're not letting him go. We're setting him free. The wind will guide him to visit us; the forest will keep him safe. He'll be all around us, Wild One."

His face shone with tears. "But who will I talk to?" He stroked the urn. "At least he's still here."

A tear rolled down my cheek. "He's not in there, Jacob. His spirit is already listening. He hears you when you talk to him, even without his ashes."

"You sure?" He hiccupped. "Promise?"

I opened my arms.

Jacob launched into them, wedging the urn between us. "I promise. He's watching us right now, and he'd want us to be brave, okay?"

Pulling back, he wiped his cheeks with his black-suited forearm. "Okay. I'll be brave. For him."

Standing, I didn't look back at the crowd, merely waited for my son to take my hand.

When he did, we moved farther away, deeper into the green-shrouded forest.

Once we found a perfect sun-lit spot, we stopped.

"Ready?"

"'kay."

Together, with shaking hands and slippery grip, we unscrewed the lid.

Another flute of a breeze found its way through the boughs and leaves to lick around us.

My skin prickled. My heart answered. I felt him near.

I love you, Ren.

As we started to tip, I whispered, "Don't say farewell, Wild One.

Don't say the words goodbye because it isn't. If you must say something, say I love you. Because he'll hear it and know he's not forgotten."

"I'll never forget him," Jacob vowed.

"Neither will I."

Together, we tipped the silver jar and let my husband and his father free.

The grey of Ren's mortal body swirled and clouded, giving wings to his immortal soul, becoming one with the trees and skies he loved so much.

Even though I knew this wasn't goodbye.

Even though I knew I'd see him again, it was the hardest thing I'd ever done to watch him vanish before us.

The faraway murmur of people leaving hinted we should probably head back, but Jacob stalked toward a tree, holding the Swiss Army knife Ren had given him.

Studiously, firmly, he scratched something into the bark, stabbing and carving.

I let him.

I didn't try to stop him or interfere.

And once he'd finished and his face was once again wet with tears, I moved closer to see what he'd done.

And just like the father had wounded me, so did the son.

My heart was no longer intact but a lake of mourning.

"Do you like it, Mom?" He sniffed back sadness.

I shook my head as my fingers traced the wonky lines of Ren's tattoo.

A swirl of ribbon with the initials J and D with an extra kick in its tail with an R.

All three of us.

Always together as the tree grew higher and our family soared closer toward the heavens.

"I don't like it. I love it."

A small smile tilted his lips. "Good."

My eyes shot wide as I spun to study him. The phrase Ren and I had used. The one word that meant so much.

I had to finish it.

To acknowledge that there would always be so much of Ren in this child. That every day he would surprise me, remind me, heal and hurt me.

On a shaky breath, I said, "Fine."

And together, we walked out of the forest, toward the house Ren and I had built together, and crossed the threshold alone.

Ren wasn't in the fields, or on the tractor, or in the barn.

He wasn't in the forest, or baling hay, or dozing in the meadow.

He was gone...*gone*.

And I had to put one foot in front of the other and accept it.

But I also accepted that this new reality was only temporary.

Life had so many paths and different journeys, but eventually, we all ended up in the same place.

I'd been lucky to share my life with Ren.

I was still lucky to share the rest of it with Jacob.

I wouldn't give up, even on the blackest of days.

I wouldn't stop living, even on the saddest of moments.

I would keep trying, learning, surviving, because I owed Ren that.

I owed him my life.

Jacob grabbed my hand, bringing me back from my thoughts and into our living room where we stood.

"You okay?" his innocent voice asked.

I smiled sadly. "Are you?"

"Not yet." He sniffed. "But we will be...right?"

His dark eyes, so similar to Ren's, blazed for an answer—a promise of healing.

Ducking to my knee, I hugged him tight, pressing his lanky body into mine, asking for healing for both of us. He kneeled with me, and I kissed his hair, inhaling deep, smelling the scents of my son mixed with the smells of my husband. A familiar wild intoxication that no soap or time could steal.

Hay and hope and happiness.

"We'll be okay, Wild One. I promise."

And we would be.

Because there was no expiration on love.

Ren was still mine.

Forever.

* * * * *

That night, I went to bed in sheets I hadn't washed and still smelled of Ren.

I crawled from my side into the middle and grabbed his pillow for mine.

And there, hidden beneath the place where Ren rested his head—glaring up as if impatient for me to find it—was a gift from beyond.

With air trapped in my lungs, I sat up and snatched it from where it had been hiding. My fingers shook as I unwrapped the blue paper, revealing something that made tears explode in a flurry.

A new ribbon wheel.

Full to the brim of cobalt satin, tucked in place with a pin.

The cardboard was pristine and untouched, ready to cut off lengths of ribbon to replace the faded old.

I stroked the wheel, feeling Ren all around me as a note fell from the package.

A note that would break me all over again.

Biting my lip to stem my sobs, I unfolded it and read.

Dear Della Ribbon,
I miss you already.
I miss your voice and touch and kisses.
But please, don't miss me.
Because I'm right there beside you. I feel your sadness. I hear your tears.
I know it will take time, but eventually, I need you to be happy because I'm always there.
When you cut off a piece of this ribbon, my hand is enveloping yours.
When you replace old with new, my fingers are on yours tying it in your hair.
Everything you do, I'm there with you.
And hopefully, this cardboard wheel will last until you come find me.
And there, I'll be able to touch you once more.
Until that day.
I love you.
Forever and ever.
For always.
Ren.

Epilogue

DELLA

2033

ANNIVERSARIES CAME IN so many different forms.

Happy and hard and horribly sad.

Today was an anniversary.

The day I lost the air in my lungs and the life in my heart.

The day I lost my Ren.

Three-hundred-and-sixty-five days without him.

Three-hundred-and-sixty-five days of soul-deep sorrow.

But I wasn't a girl left behind with the luxury of grief. I was mother to the best son in the world, and for him, I woke in the morning even when the darkness was acute. I kept living even while my sadness was constant. I helped Cassie with her horse business. I rode often for mental and spiritual health. I learned how to run our acreage and hire help when required.

And John was true to his vow to Ren, always there for me when the loneliness of missing a soulmate became too much.

Life had been gentle even after being so cruel.

And through it all, I had a contract with love.

A contract I did my best to uphold.

I never dared pity myself or begrudge my grief.

I was never angry that I'd loved the best man in the world and lost him.

Ren had given me his legacy, and together, me and Jacob would be okay.

Every day, I spoke to Ren as if he were there beside me.

He was in the sun, the sky, the meadow, the forest.

He was in everything. Waiting. Loving. Watching. And I lived every day for him because I knew a time would come when we would find each other again, and I'd have the honour of regaling a lifetime of tales.

I accepted each new sunrise without Ren. I endured each new sunset without Ren.

I chose to continue because that was what he wanted and that was what I owed.

After a lifetime of sacrifice, it was now my turn.

My turn to keep moving, keep fighting, keep living.

And I did.

I accepted I'd had my epic love story.

I was one of the lucky ones.

And I didn't want another.

My heart was Ren's—no matter where he was—and it would stay his until we met again.

At least, my family understood that.

No one dared murmur I would get over him.

No one dared encourage me to put my past behind me and open my heart for another.

No one dared because they knew the truth.

The truth that a love like Ren and I had…it was once in a lifetime.

And it wasn't over yet.

The five stages of grief didn't matter.

There were no five stages for me.

And I didn't want there to be.

I didn't want the wound to heal because I never wanted to be anything less than Ren's. I still touched him in my dreams, kissed him in my thoughts, and accepted that I might endure in a world without him, but I *would* see him again.

I knew that.

And I could be patient.

"Mom!" Jacob's voice rang through the sun-dappled house. *"Moomm!"*

"What is it?" I pressed a hand to my forehead, pushing aside my melancholy thoughts, tucking them into the pocket of my heart where yearning was a regular friend.

"Package for you. Need you to sign!"

Abandoning my laundry folding, I cut through the living room to the front door where a deliveryman stood on the veranda and held out an e-tablet. "You Mrs Wild?"

I'd long stopped scolding myself at the sharp intake of breath whenever anyone called me that. I both loved and despised that name. "Yes. I am."

"Sign here, please."

I took his tablet, scribbled on the scratched screen, and passed it back to him. "What is it?"

"Dunno, but it's heavy. Need help carting it inside?" He raised an eyebrow beneath his red cap.

Jacob ducked to his haunches, testing the large box. "She doesn't need help. She has me."

I chuckled under my breath, running my fingertips over his dirty-blond head as he stood and huffed. "Ugh, it's too heavy."

"We'll do it together," I said.

"Leave you guys to it." The delivery guy tapped his cap in farewell and bounded off the veranda. My eyes tracked him as the sun glinted off the windscreen of his van, obscuring him just enough to show a tall man running through the garden, giving me a millisecond fantasy that it was Ren.

Tears welled.

Pain manifested.

And I closed the door on the illusion.

"Wait. The package." Jacob rolled his dark chocolate eyes at me, so much like Ren's I sometimes forgot he was part of me and merely saw the boy who'd saved my life.

In a way, he *had* saved my life...just like his father.

Without him, I wouldn't have continued trying.

Ren had saved me when I was a baby.

And his son had saved me when I was a woman.

Two boys of ten years old.

Two boys of my heart.

Charging toward the kitchen, he came skidding back with a pair of scissors.

My hands clamped on my hips. "What have I told you, Jacob Wild? No running with sharp implements." Just like his father, he always had a knife on his person for slicing through ropes and other farm necessities. I was surprised he'd chosen scissors instead of the Swiss Army blade in his pocket.

The blade I was constantly fishing out before washing.

"Yeah, yeah." He rolled his eyes again before falling to his knees and cutting the tape on the box.

Uncle John sometimes did this—delivered boxes of goodies from things he'd ordered online for Jacob and me.

Care packages, I called them.

Love reminders, he called them.

Either way, this wasn't one of those as Jacob tore out brown paper packaging and yanked out a book nestled with countless other books.

A book that my eyes skimmed, discarded, then shot back to with a cry.

A book that took the strength in my legs and crashed me to the floor.

"I-I don't understand." Tears streamed down my face, obscuring the blue cover with a lonely boy walking in a blizzard. A boy almost hidden by the title and wrapped up in a blue satin ribbon.

"*The Boy and His Ribbon by Della and Ren Wild*," Jacob muttered, reading eloquently and smoothly. His eyes flashed to mine. "Mom? Did you and Dad write this?"

My head shook blindly as I held out my hand.

Hardback.

Freshly printed.

Heavy as a gravestone.

It tingled in my hands, warm and alive and filled with ghosts.

What has he done?

"Mom?" Jacob asked again, but for once, I couldn't put him first. I couldn't assure him. I couldn't push aside my own selfish pain. Jacob missed his father as much as I did…but he'd had Ren for ten years. I'd had him for thirty-two.

In this…my heart was cruel.

Standing on shaking legs, I couldn't tear my eyes off the cover, desperate to open it, petrified to read it.

"I…I'm going for a walk, Wild One. Okay?" My voice broke and patched together, thicker and rougher than before. "I…I won't go far."

"Mom?" His voice rose with worry. "Are you all right?"

"I'm fine." I drifted forward as if my legs were no longer made of sinew and bone but air and storm cloud. "I-I'm fine." I repeated, desperate to believe it.

I left my son.

I was a bad mother.

I abandoned my role and slipped back into a girl who missed her boy with every frisson of her soul.

I didn't know how long I walked, but finally, when the shadow strings of willow leaves enveloped me and the grotto where so many things had happened whispered it would keep me safe, I sank to the earth and opened the book.

The first page was copyright jargon.

The second, print information.

The third, the title.

The fourth…the dedication.

For Della and Jacob.

I keeled over, rocking the book to my chest, sobs wrenched from my very toes.

No.

I hadn't cried this badly...well, since the funeral.

I never let myself go.

Never could.

Never allowed.

I had to be strong for Jacob.

But that strength was now shattered and in pieces on the ground.

Four simple words.

Four words that broke me.

They *broke* me.

Ren.

His voice danced on the breeze as if he'd never gone. His wild scent of smoke and freedom swirled in my lungs. And the gentle, delicious pressure of his hand on my cheek forced me to look down at the pages, tear smudged and turning translucent.

Read, the breeze murmured.

Listen, the willow whispered.

Heal, the forest begged.

With another sob, I flipped the page.

A letter to the reader.

A letter from beyond.

Dear Reader,

First, let me explain the nature of this book before I can explain it to my wife.

Once upon a time, a wonderful girl fell in love with an unworthy boy, and she decided to write their tale.

Her tale opened that stupid boy's eyes.

It made true love leap over rules and boundaries.

It survived years wrapped in plastic and protected at all costs in a well-travelled backpack.

It was the best tale the boy had ever read.

But it was also missing something.

It was missing the side of the story from the boy who fell in love with the girl, but he wasn't as eloquent as she.

So he had to improvise.

He enlisted the help of a ghost writer to turn messy dictated thoughts into words worthy of being beside hers, and he didn't have a lot of time to do it.

It was my hardest secret.

And even now, I'm unsure I did the right thing.

But it's too late to change my mind. Too late to approve or deny the finished

copy.
I just have to hope our story is enjoyed.
And I have to trust that every word I chose proves the same thing her words
do.
That I loved her.
Painfully so.

The words danced and bounced as my hands shook and shook.

Sobs and heaving quakes took hold of me as I turned the page and found yet another letter.

I wasn't ready.

I wasn't prepared.

I would never be ready to say goodbye because that was what this was.

A goodbye.

A final farewell organised in secrecy.

My Dear Beloved Ribbon,
I hope you can forgive me for taking our privacy and making it public.
I hope you can understand why I had to do it and why it had to be this way.
And I hope you can still love me for not being there to hold you.
For not being able to stop the pain.
This wasn't an easy thing to do—I almost stopped countless times.
But after years of watching over your shoulder as you typed, reading the
paragraphs you chose, and feeling the love you had for me, it was finally my turn.
My turn to write you a love story.
And, God, what a love story it is.
You were the air I breathed and the life in my heart, Della.
You are the sole reason I existed and always will be.
Without you, I would never have been a father, brother, or husband.
Without you, I would never have known exquisite joy and utter heartbreak.
Without you, I would have been nothing.
And because of you…I am something.
I am loved.
I am missed.
I am wanted.
I was sold to the Mclary's for one purpose and one purpose only.
To find you.
And I'll find you again…soon.
This isn't the end…we both know that.
I'll be waiting…somewhere.
I'll be watching…somehow.
And when the time comes for you to join me, I'll gather you in my arms and

hold you tight.
Come find me.
Come find me on the meadow where the sun always shines, the river always
flows, and the forest always welcomes.
Come find me, Little Ribbon, and there we'll live for eternity.
And now, because I can't stand to leave this tale so unfinished, please read the
end.
The end I wrote for you.
Until we meet again…
I love you.

I closed the book.

Unable to read more.

Not prepared to endure more pain.

One day, I would read it.

But not today.

Today, I needed to grieve…*truly* grieve.

To weep and wail and admit that there would always be a piece of me forever broken. A piece of me that would always be lost until my dying breath delivered me back to my loved one.

But even in my grief, I had responsibilities. I had a son who missed his father, and I had a world that needed to continue.

So, as I clawed my way to my feet, hugged Ren's book to my chest, and stepped from the willow's comforting fronds, I made a promise to keep going.

To do what Ren had said.

To let go…if only for a second.

My eyes fell on Jacob.

He sat in the middle of the hay field, golden all around him, gold sun above him, gold future ahead of him, and my heart did what it hadn't been able to do. What I never believed I was capable of.

It healed…just a little.

It accepted…just a little.

Our love story wasn't over.

It was just…paused.

With my white dress fluttering around my legs, I strode into the sunlight, carrying truth and heartache and everlasting love.

I was lucky.

Eternally lucky to have loved and cherished and adored.

And when that day came when this life was over, I would find that love again.

I would go home to him.

Because our story had never been about a fleeting romance or fairy-tale. It had always been about life.

It was about love.

It was about the journey from nothing to something.

The travels from individual to pair.

The adventure from empty to whole.

And that was what transformed mortal into magic.

It was what songs were made of.

What hearts were formed of.

What humans were born to become.

The sun shone brighter, drenching buttery light everywhere it touched.

The paddock was almost ready for baling.

The land providing routine and clockwork timing.

And as my son looked up from feeling my eyes upon him, he waved just like Ren used to. His hand switched into a come-hither, and I went.

I held my head tall. I let my tears fall. I allowed myself the freedom to love in all its painful, exquisite heartache.

And when I reached him, I sat in the wildflowers and hugged him.

He hugged me back, fiercely, healingly. "Did you read the end like he said?"

I shook my head. "I can't."

"You should." He kissed my cheek as we pulled apart, so wise, so brave, so pure. "If he told you to, you should."

I laughed gently. "Just like I did everything he told me, huh?"

"Yep." He smirked, growing serious again. "There's a whole box of books there. You should at least read one of them."

"Maybe."

"But what if it's good?"

"Then it will be good when I'm ready."

"But what if it makes you happy?"

I swallowed another wash of tears. "*You* make me happy. I don't need anything else."

He looked down, running his small hand through the blades of grass. "I miss him."

"Yeah, me too."

He picked a purple flower and held it to me. "Would you read me the story? If Dad wrote it, and you haven't read it either, it's kinda like him coming back, right?"

My chest squeezed as I took his gift and twirled the pretty petals. "Just because there are pages with his words on them doesn't mean he's alive, Wild One."

"I know. But…" He looked up earnest and imploring and

hopeful. "I think he would want you to read it."

"I know."

"Can I read it?"

"Not until I know what he's written." I tapped his nose, so similar to mine. "Not sure if it's suitable for eleven-year-old nosy parkers."

He grinned. "I think he'd let me read it."

"I think you're getting too bossy."

"I think you're afraid."

I sucked in a breath, jerking back a little.

He noticed, crawling closer and hugging me tight. "I'm sorry, Mom."

It took a moment for me to swallow my sobs. "You're right, Jacob. I *am* afraid."

We sat huddled together for a while, letting the sun warm us even when the hollowness in my heart was always cold.

Finally, Jacob pulled away. "Read it, 'kay? Don't leave him in the box."

A tear escaped. "Okay."

"You will?"

"I will. I'll be brave. I owe him that much."

He nodded. "Yep and then you can read it to me."

I smiled, doing my best not to let my mind run away with questions. What had Ren done? What ending had he written? "We'll see."

Standing, I took his hand in mine and headed toward the house.

Jacob squeezed my fingers with yet another question. "Even though he's gone...he would want us to be happy, right, Mom?"

I nodded. "Yes."

"Do you think he's watching us right now?"

"Undoubtedly."

"Do you think he's happy watching us?"

I pictured Ren somewhere free in the forest, peering through leaves and fantasy to protect us from afar. "Yes, I do."

"Well, that settles it then." His hand slipped from mine as he ran toward the house shouting, "Read it tonight. And maybe you'll be happy, too."

Epilogue Cont

DELLA

2033

THAT NIGHT, ONCE I'd cooked for Jacob and we'd watched some movie of his choosing, I curled up in bed and reached for the book.

I didn't want to.

I wasn't ready.

But I'd made a promise to my son, and I couldn't let my husband down.

The thought of Ren's voice locked in a cardboard box, ready to share his secrets, prepared to shed light on shared circumstances was too sad to refuse.

It would be the hardest thing I'd done since scattering his ashes, but I owed him this.

I owed him my strength to listen.

Tears fell again as I cracked open the pages and re-read Ren's letters.

I cried.

And cried.

And when my tears finally slowed, I sucked in a wobbly breath, gathered my courage, and pushed the heavy, sweet-smelling papers to the end.

One day, I would read the entire thing.

I would break my heart all over again all while being privileged enough to read the innermost thoughts of my husband. But for now, this book would sleep on his pillow beside me, something to hug when it all got too painful, something to stroke when I whispered to him in the dark.

One day, I would be ready.

But not today.

Today, I was barely clinging to sanity, shoved into the awkward admittance of wishing time away so I could find Ren sooner, all while begging the minutes to slow so I could have longer with Jacob.

Ren was a natural storyteller—his skills honed from years of telling me bedtime tales and indulging my every whim.

And tonight, just like old times, he was about to tell me a story.

Our story.

The only one I ever cared about.

The pages fell to the final chapter and I stroked the letters as I breathed, "Chapter Fifty-Nine. Ren, 2018."

My mind skipped back to that time.

A time when emotions were daggers and youth diesel on the fiery burn of desire. Everything was sharper then, more urgent then, more desperate.

Countless memories unravelled, reminding me of what I'd done.

How I'd been so hurt I'd lost my virginity to another.

How I'd been so tangled in my unrequited agony that I'd broken Ren and myself.

Only…as my eyes skimmed Ren's side of the tale, learning how much he loved me, how distraught he was as he left me that note and walked out the door, a strange smile twisted my tear-glossed lips.

The book didn't end there.

It didn't stop in a standalone of tragedy but led into a heart-happy duet.

And I understood what my brilliant husband had done.

And I was braver.

And I was thankful.

And my fractured heart glued a tiny piece back into place.

My fingers itched for my keyboard to finish the magic he'd begun.

A final letter was waiting for me.

This is where you come in, Della Ribbon.
You'll get another box soon.
A box of chapters from the moment I admitted I was in love with you and kissed you for the first time to the second we got married, held our son, and grew as a family.
I've been honest. I've shared everything.
Now, it's your turn.
Finish our story, Della.
But this one, blend fact with a tiny piece of fiction.
Call the book The Girl and Her Ren—*because that is what I am.*
I am yours.
But fashion our story where we found that miracle.
A story where I was healed, grew old, and lived.

And at the end, insert this final paragraph:

"And there, as the sun set on the summer meadow, Della Ribbon turned to her Ren, and said, 'I'm pregnant with your daughter. I suppose you get to choose a girl's name now.'
Her husband turned to her, happy, overjoyed, madly in love and kissed her.
They kissed for days because they knew no time could stop them.
And when they broke apart, he said, "I love you, Della, forever and for always."
And they had that daughter.
They had a family.
They were forever bound through marriage and true love. Together."

And then, if our story is ever made into a film, the credits will roll.
And the music will play.
And the audience will know…
That Della Ribbon and her Ren lived
happily
ever
after.

The End

Thank you for trusting me and coming on this journey.
I hope you enjoyed Ren and Della's tale...despite the pain.

Note to the Reader

WHY DID YOU KILL OFF THE MAIN HERO?

Ever since the moment Ren and Della popped into my head, I knew how it would end. Ren was rather adamant that his tale would be based firmly in reality. And, unfortunately, reality isn't kind.

It was honestly the hardest thing I've ever had to write. On a daily basis, I worried if I was doing the right thing. I'd wake up with panic attacks wondering if I'd upset my readers, wondering if I was strong enough, and if it would be career suicide to do such an ending. But, each time I tried to prevent Ren from dying, he'd just throw it back in my face, and I knew I had to be **BRAVE**. That I had to accept this book wouldn't be for everyone. And hope that, despite its bittersweet ending, the story of Ren and Della Wild would find the audience it's meant to find.

I hope, regardless of the tears, you were able to see the story for what it was.

Brutal, heart-breaking, but somehow uplifting, knowing love never dies.

I'm extremely grateful you read to this point and accepted that this story is firmly based in *life*. We all have different versions of happily ever after. Some last forever, some last for a while, and some don't last at all. But in the end, true love carries on and I am a *firm* believer that once bound together, we will find each other again. Either through reincarnation, heaven, or some other divine intervention.

WHY DIDN'T REN AND DELLA HAVE ANY MORE CHILDREN?

The Ribbon Duet is the first story I've told where I've taken no liberties or added some 'slightly fantastical' element that perhaps wouldn't happen in real life. I didn't want to do that with this. I needed it to be fully realistic, and the reality is, by the time Della had Jacob, Ren was severely ill again, and then submitted to an extensive course of Chemo. I didn't feel it would be realistic for him to be able to make her pregnant a second time.

Obviously, miracles happen, but he'd already been given a miracle by far outlasting the usual prognosis for his disease.

WHY ARE THERE ENGLISH PHRASES & SPELLING

IN A BOOK BASED IN THE USA?

First, I am fully aware that there is English Spelling and English Terminology in this book (because I'm English and also live in an English spelling country). It wasn't a typo or laziness on my part. I wrote it that way because those are the phrases I use and with *The Boy & His Ribbon* and *The Girl & Her Ren*, I turned off all thoughts and just WROTE.

Once the stories were on paper, I went over and changed all the spelling to US, started to remove phrases and words that aren't common in the USA and began 'Americanising it.'

However, a friend suggested that instead of trying to set it in America, why not leave it as a story that is transient of time and place. Not once did I ever mention a town name or city or country. Partly because Ren himself wouldn't know or care as child, but also because I wanted the reader to place Ren and Della wherever they were or even imagine a fictional world of their choosing.

It could be set in Canada, England, Scotland, USA or New Zealand. It could fit anywhere and I liked that.

However, the amazing Will Watt and Hayden Bishop (fully within their creative license) decided—when they started narration for *The Boy & His Ribbon*—that the characters could possibly be from South USA and gave them accents to match. As we hadn't discussed my concept of it being a very 'country neutral' book, once I heard the audio, I realised I'd have to explain why there are some English Phrases spoken in an American accent.

As the Audio was already recorded for *The Boy & His Ribbon*, it's not possible to go back and edit certain English colloquialisms without disrupting the Whispersync capability.

So, I decided to leave *The Girl & Her Ren* in the same manner so the 'voice' doesn't sound different.

I hope you can excuse the blend of two worlds and enjoy the story regardless.

WHAT RESEARCH DID YOU DO FOR THIS STORY?

A lot on Asbestos related illnesses and forced child labour.

For anyone dealing with mesothelioma or know someone who is, I did my best to research and include realistic treatment options and terminology. As all things, there is only so much information available and I apologise if I incorrectly quoted facts.

A few links that were used are:

https://www.asbestos.com/cancer/

https://www.asbestos.com/treatment/
https://www.pleuralmesothelioma.com/cancer/prognosis/
https://www.keytruda.com/
https://www.rxwiki.com/keytruda

Ren's purchase to work a farm isn't that far-fetched and there have been many documented issues of child labour around the globe, in both first world and third world countries.

These are just a few:

http://www.fao.org/childlabouragriculture/en/
https://www.hrw.org/news/2011/11/17/child-farmworkers-united-states-worst-form-child-labor
https://www.huffingtonpost.ca/craig-and-marc-kielburger/child-labour-is-canadas-i_b_1087892.html

Upcoming Books

The Son & His Hope
(a standalone spin-off from **The Ribbon Duet. Jacob Wild's
story that can be read with or separately**).
The Body Painter
The Argument

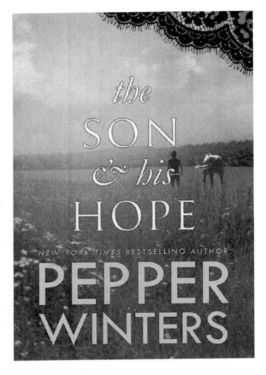

*"Things you should know about me from the very beginning:
I was born to true love, witnessed the destruction it causes, and vowed never to
let such agony happen to me. I am not a story-teller like my father. I am not a
writer like my mother. I am just a son—their son.
I am happy being alone.
And that is all I ever want to be."*

JACOB

The day he was born, Jacob learned his hardest and longest lesson.
It wasn't a lesson a boy should learn so young, but from his
earliest memories he knew where happiness lives, so does tragedy.
Where love exists, so does heartbreak. And where hope resides, so
does sorrow.
That lesson carved him from the kid to the teen to the man.
And nothing and no one could change his mind.

HOPE

I first met him when he was fourteen at a movie premiere of all
places. A movie based on his parent's life.
He was stoic, strong, suspicious, and secretive.
I was only ten, but I felt something for him. A strange kind of
sorrow that made me want to hug and heal him.
I was the daughter of the actor hired to play his father.
We shared similarities.
I recognised parts of him because they were parts of me.
But no matter how many times we met. No matter how many
times I tried.
He stayed true to his vow to never fall.

Add to Goodreads

**For more up to date announcements and releases please
visit:**
www.pepperwinters.com

Playlist

John Legend – Love Me Now
Selena Gomez & Marshmello – Wolves
Pink – What About Us
Selena Gomez - Back To You
Imagine Dragons - Nothing Left To Say
Imagine Dragons - Not Today
All of the Stars - Ed Sheeran
Charlie Puth - Kiss Me
Lana Del Rey – I still love him
Nothing Like Us - Justin Beiber
Calum Scott - If Our Love Is Wrong
Tom Odell - Grow Old with Me
I Found You - Kina Grannis & Imaginary Future
Calum Scott, Leona Lewis - You Are The Reason
Behind Blue Eyes – Limp Bizkit
Photograph – Ed Sheeran

Acknowledgements

The Boy & His Ribbon was the easiest book I've ever written. *The Girl & Her Ren* was the hardest.

As mentioned in the 'Note to the Reader,' I always knew Ren's fate the moment he popped into my head and first told me his story, but it didn't mean I was comfortable with it, or brave enough to go through with it.

Almost daily, I'd message beta readers asking if I was doing the right thing. And every night, I'd wake in a panic wondering how this duet would be received.

However, I had no choice to do the ending Ren intended.

This was never a romance.

It was a life story, and with life comes death—just like Della said.

Saying that, I leaned on beta readers very heavily in this book. I think I wrote close to 210,000 words and ended up deleting 55,000 of them.

Entire scenes were axed. Entire plot points erased. It wasn't easy, but I hope it's made a better book for being ruthless.

I want to thank my husband for allowing me to sit on my butt for twelve hours a day to finish this—it's been two months of relying on him to feed the horses, cook, and clean. He's a rock star.

I want to thank Heather Pollock for being invaluable with her advice and being online at all hours of the day to read chapters and keep me from jumping off the cliff.

I want to thank Melissa Crump for being so diligent, kind, and helpful and incredibly fast in her feedback.

I want to thank Tamicka Birch for giving me her honest opinion when I ruined the book and told her the ending and made her read the epilogue first.

I want to thank Melissa Staley, Vickie Leaf, Rochelle Kroesen, Yaya, Julie Lis, Heather Peiffer, Nicole Hartney, and Chanpreet Singh for their invaluable, kind critique.

I want to thank Jenny Sims and Tiffany Landers for their editing / proofreading, and for turning it around so fast.

I want to thank Will Watt and Hayden Bishop for narrating such excellent audio and making me fall in love with my characters even more.

I want to thank Nina Grinstead and the girls at Social Butterfly for helping with promo.

And finally, but most importantly, I want to thank you, the reader, for allowing me to hurt you with this story.

I hope you enjoyed it, despite the pain.

Xx00xx

Pepper

Made in the USA
Middletown, DE
16 February 2023

25015339R00455